Lords in Love

A Regency Romance Collection

The Viscount's Vow
A Kiss for a Rogue
A Diamond for a Duke
The Earl and the Spinster
Triumph and Treasure

COLLETTE CAMERON

Blue Rose Romance®
Portland, Oregon

Sweet-to-Spicy Timeless Romance®

LORDS IN LOVE
A Regency Romance Collection

The Viscount's Vow (Second Edition)

A Kiss for a Rogue

A Diamond for a Duke

The Earl and the Spinster

Triumph and Treasure (Second Edition)

Cover Design by Jaycee DeLorenzo
Artwork by Teresa Spreckelmeyer

Attn: Permissions Coordinator
Blue Rose Romance®
8420 N Ivanhoe # 83054
Portland, Oregon 97203

eBook ISBN: 978-1-950387-81-6
Print Book ISBN: 978-1-950387-82-3
www.collettecameron.com

Contents

The Viscount's Vow

CASTLE BRIDES, BOOK ONE

1

London, England
Late April, 1814

Vengeance isn't sweet.

Ian Warrick tipped his champagne flute and took a lengthy swallow. He'd far prefer whisky or brandy. He eyed the pale amber liquid in his still half-full glass. The insipid wine masquerading as champagne did little to wash away the bitterness lingering in his soul.

A young woman partnered by a fusty old lord whirled by, and Ian's gaze followed her.

Evangeline Caruthers.

After seeking her the better part of an hour, he'd finally found the chit. Or more on accurately, she'd been pointed out to him. A half-smile tugged his lips upward as he watched the aged poger attempt to steer her into a secluded alcove behind a wall of potted greenery. Even across the ballroom, he couldn't miss her tromping on the ancient fellow's foot.

That had been no accident.

For a fleeting moment, his smile stretched into a grin of genuine amusement. It vanished just as quickly. He wasn't here to be amused. Especially by *her*.

Lounging against the intricately-carved doorframe, he glanced around the opulent ballroom. Candlelight glistened off the crystal chandeliers and framed mirrors gilding the room's far side. The glass reflected the dancers in a blur of pulsing colors.

This was the first social event he'd attended since resigning his commission in His Majesty's army. The first since he'd assumed the duties of the seventh Viscount Warrick. The first since his father had succumbed to heart failure brought on by Geoff's death.

Ian sought Miss Caruthers again, and his gaze lingered. His younger brother was dead. Because of *her*. Like a rapier between his ribs, pain stabbed him sharp and fierce, hitching the air in his lungs. He exhaled—a slow, deliberate breath. Narrowing his eyes, he lifted the flute to his lips.

A lieutenant reeking of strong spirits staggered from the ballroom and plowed into him. Ian choked on the wine trickling down his throat. "Good—God—man," he said between strangled coughs.

"'Scuse me, milord. Don' feel well. Too hot."

Swallowing against the stinging in his throat, Ian beckoned to a liveried servant. "Help that chap, please."

He indicated the lieutenant weaving his way through the doorway and careening into any guest unfortunate enough to be in his path. The crimson-uniformed soldier traveled but a dozen more steps before casting up his accounts on the glossy marble floor. Gentlemen raised their voices in protest as ladies squawked their outrage and yanked their skirts aside.

Ian curved his lips again. *Poor sot.* He'd done it up brown—literally. The ballroom was much too warm; the crush of guests intolerable. He inhaled, and his nostrils twitched. The place stank of sweat, unwashed bodies, and an abundance of cloying perfume. He smirked. No doubt the ball would be touted a *haut ton* success despite the lieutenant's messy mishap.

He cared little. Everything about this falderal left him cold. If the circumstances weren't pressing, he wouldn't be here. He *shouldn't* be here with his brother dead and buried less than a month, his father scarcely a fortnight. Ian's breech of mourning protocol bordered on ruinous—not that he gave a damn.

Miss Caruthers' retribution could not wait.

Nor could the explanation Prinny demanded for Geoff's role in the Duke of Paneswort's death. Ian twisted his lips into a grimace. Paneswort, a royal pain in the arse, had been a particular favorite of the Prince Regent's.

Lecherous cohorts.

At any rate, Prinny was irate. So, Ian had cast off propriety, abandoned the peace and quiet of Somersfield, his country house, and ventured into this fray despite the *ton's* disapproval of his presence. He'd deal with Miss Caruthers, pacify His Majesty, and then return home.

He rested his shoulder against the wall, the deep saffron-colored wallpaper, a similar shade to the mess on the floor in the process of being cleared away by two footmen. With a jaundiced eye, he scrutinized the room once more. Lord, how he despised these garish affairs. The pretentiousness. The fake smiles. The gossip. The social climbing. All of it added to the bad taste in his mouth.

As he'd snooped around to determine who Miss Caruthers was, he'd felt an absolute fool. *My God*, he'd actually stooped to eavesdropping on the spinsterish misses gossiping along the dance floor's periphery. When they'd turned their eager, expectant faces to him, he'd fled like a frightened dog with its tail between its legs.

He was the worst sort of knave, raising their pitiful hopes then dashing off without so much as a, "*How do you do*?" Had the toxic mixture of grief and ire addled him? His tightened his grip around the etched flute's stem.

The idea wasn't that far-fetched.

He'd resorted—without success until now—to asking acquaintances to identify Miss Caruthers. At his less than subtle probing, more than one male mouth had stretched into a rakish grin.

"Want a taste of that, eh, Warrick?"

"Prime mort, she is."

Ian raised his glass to take a sip. *Empty*. The devil take it.

Searching the room for a servant bearing more spirits, he tried to ignore the tittering debutantes and their match-making mamas vying for his attention. He supposed he was ripe for the Marriage Mart now—rather like a piece of prime horseflesh at Tattersalls. Everyone present knew he recently came into his title.

More than one affronted dame glared at him. He'd bet his favorite hunting hound they were more vexed with him for ignoring their transparent attempts to parade their calf-eyed daughters before him than his blatant disregard for mourning customs.

He cared not. Not tonight, leastways.

This evening, Miss Caruthers commandeered his attention. Drawing his eyebrows together and flattening his lips, Ian considered her. Adorned in a shimmering white gown, with some sort of filmy silvery overskirt, she was—he grudgingly admitted—exquisite. A tiara entwined with a filigree circlet adorned her raven hair piled atop her head. The gems twinkled mischievously each time she moved.

She appeared angelic.

He knew better.

Her alluring eyes and seductive smile couldn't gull him. Miss Caruthers might be a diamond of the first water, but he knew the truth concerning her. *He* was immune to her charms. His gaze sharp, he cocked his head. She appeared regal, poised, accepting dance request after dance request. A demure, almost shy, smile curved her rosy lips.

Did she rouge them?

He curled his lip in derision. Likely.

Arms folded, languidly holding his glass, he relaxed against the wall. The young bloods buzzing 'round her like bees to golden honey only confirmed what he'd been told.

His sister, Charlotte, eyes red-rimmed from crying, had wailed, "Miss Caruthers collects men like souvenirs."

Ian grimaced again, his attention never straying from Miss Caruthers as she stepped and dipped to the music. Oh, yes, he *knew* her kind.

She epitomized the type of women he disdained. Fast women, who bewitched unsuspecting swains, like Geoff, and who stole beaus from innocents like Charlotte. Sirens who cast their admirers off with the same regard as a soiled serviette or used tea leaves. Seductresses ever intent on pursuing their new conquests, uncaring of the hearts they crushed or lives they left in ruins as a consequence of their Jezebel triumphs.

Jezebel triumphs.

A familiar twinge stung his heart—or mayhap it was only his pride. Amelia was such a woman, though he hadn't known it until she'd tossed him aside for a bigger prize. Why settle for him, the heir to a mere viscountcy, when there was a duke to be seduced? Ironically, the same duke who now lay dead from the lead ball Geoff had planted in his chest.

Exchanging his empty glass for a full one offered by a passing servant, Ian suppressed a sigh. He didn't want to be here—loathed being here. He'd only come on his brother's and sister's behalf, to set things to right. In one quaff, he polished off the weak wine, barely suppressing a shudder.

Vile stuff, that.

Scowling as Miss Caruthers maneuvered the steps of the lively country-dance, he clamped his lips so hard, a muscle spasmed in his jaw. He trailed her movements, ever closer, across the sanded parquet floor. The dance steps brought her within a few feet of where he stood. Skipping past him, she laughed at something her partner said.

A jolt slammed into Ian's gut.

God's blood! She was laughing, as if she hadn't a care in the world.

His breath hissed from between clenched teeth. Under his breath he vowed, "By all that is holy, by evening's end, I'll put a stop to your dalliances—once and for all."

Precisely how he would go about curbing her, he hadn't yet determined.

Someone jabbed his shoulder.

"Nephew?"

He stiffened at the familiar feminine voice.

"Heard tell you were here. Didn't believe it at first." His aunt poked him again, harder this time. "If I didn't know you better, I'd think you were avoiding me."

Dash it all, he had been.

He sucked in a calming breath before turning around and smiling down into the face of his maternal aunt, Lady Fitzgibbons. Barely reaching his shoulder, Aunt Edith was a formidable dowager in her own right. Tonight, she was attired in a vivid crimson dress. A colorful ostrich feather waved flirtatiously in her silver-streaked hair. Her familiar, cloying violet perfume wafted upward, tickling his nostrils.

Ian bowed over her outstretched hand. "Aunt Edith, you know I always delight in your company."

"Pshaw. Don't try your charming tricks on me, young scamp." She cast a quick look around the room. "Gads, Ian, you're in mourning. Whatever are you thinking, putting in an appearance here?"

He arched a brow, but remained silent.

"None of my business, eh?" She surveyed him with shrewd eyes. "How are you faring?" Then, only out of polite necessity he was sure, she inquired, "Lucinda and Charlotte?"

With a quirk of his lips, Ian said, "You don't care a whit how my stepmother is doing. Or Charlotte either, for that matter."

Aunt Edith inclined her noble head slightly and poked him with the tortoiseshell fan. Again. He was sorely tempted to snatch the accessory from her and toss it behind the greenery—after snapping it in half.

"You haven't answered me. I know how much you cared for Geoff." Worry shadowed her unique gray eyes. His mother's eyes had been the same unusual shade.

His gaze lingered on her. She was a saucy old bird, but a dear through and through. "I'm fine, Aunt."

As if compelled by an unseen force, his gaze was drawn to Miss Caruthers once more. A callow-faced youth escorted her to her seat where a line of eager pups stood ready to claim her for the next set.

What's this?

He stood straighter. Had he imagined it, or had her steps faltered and her shoulders slumped, just the merest bit? Was her smile a little strained? Ian stared, searching her face.

No, she smiled as brightly as ever.

He'd imbibed too much wine—that was all. His faculties were affected, which was why he generally steered clear of the stuff. He fingered the cut crystal glass in his hand. How many had he downed since arriving? He shook his head. More than he ought. He would regret it come the morn. Tonight though, the liquor dulled his senses, his pain, his grief…his rage.

An observant servant offered him another full glass. Ian waved away the offer and handed over the empty flute.

"Ah, I see Miss Caruthers has caught your eye. She's a delightful girl, has exceptional manners, and is quite an accomplished artist."

He shot his aunt an astounded look. Thank God, she didn't see it. She was too busy jabbering on about Miss Caruthers many charms.

"Soft spoken, intelligent, excellent dancer, decorous behavior..."

Ian smothered a contemptuous snort. Miss Caruthers was an accomplished actress, indeed, if Aunt Edith was unaware of her soiled feathers. No doubt she emulated chastity and virtue under the *ton's* watchful eye while tossing up her skirts in the shrubberies after nightfall.

A flamboyantly-attired dandy elbowed his way to her side, and she snapped open her fan and began waving it before her face.

Aunt Edith chuckled, elbowing him in the side. "Gads, would you look at Pickering's togs?" Her shoulders shook with mirth. "La, what a nincompoop. Whatever can he be thinking?"

Ian went rigid, darting his flabbergasted gaze to his aunt then flicking it to the man hovering near Miss Caruthers. "*He's* the Earl of Pickering?" He blinked twice.

Charlotte's beloved Reggie? The man whose affections Miss Caruthers stole?

Ian rolled his eyes at the absurdity. It was laughable. He quirked is mouth into a wry smile at the irony until the memory of Geoff's grinning face intruded. Charlotte's affection for Pickering might be ludicrous. Geoff's and his father's deaths were anything but. Miss Caruthers had much to atone for.

Crinkling her nose, Aunt Edith whispered, "He doesn't favor bathing." She paused, "I take it you've not been introduced to the earl?"

Ian sensed his aunt's perusal. She knew him too well; precisely why he'd avoided her. Mindful of her probing stare, he schooled his features and shook his head. "I've not had the...ah...pleasure."

"He just came into his title. Only because his unfortunate cousin expired without issue." She cast Pickering a censored look. "He's an obnoxious coxcomb."

Ian silently agreed. The ridiculous ensemble Pickering wore pained the eye, clear down to his outdated cherry-red, high-heeled shoes. The shoes pitched his body forward when he walked causing his neck to bobble like the vibrant parrot he resembled.

A moment later Pickering guffawed. The whistling squawks passing for laughter confirmed Ian's initial assessment of the fop. Miss Caruthers' fan swished faster, and her eyes—*were they blue*?—searched the room. Did anxiety crease her otherwise smooth brow? The toes of one foot tapped nonstop. In vexation?

An idea took hold.

"Introduce me, Aunt Edith, won't you?" Ian would've asked Prinny himself to do the honors if it meant making Miss Caruthers' acquaintance. Only for the purpose of delivering her just dues, of course.

Aunt Edith cocked her head. "I seem to recall you prefer more, shall we say, *practiced* damsels. Miss Caruthers is far more gentle-bred than your usual choice of companion." She retreated an arm's length, assessing him with her too-astute gaze. "What are you really about?"

He couldn't very well tell her Miss Caruthers was a promiscuous tart—that she was responsible for his father's and Geoff's deaths. Instead, forcing a smile, he winked. "Perchance, I'm in the market for a wife." He couldn't keep the heavy mockery from his tone.

His aunt snorted. "Rubbish and balderdash. You may be the last in your line, but you're not *that* anxious to produce an heir."

"You wound me, Aunt." Crossing a hand over his heart, he released an exaggerated sigh.

"Tish tosh." She wiggled her damned fan two inches under his nose. "Miss Caruthers is an orphan with barely two farthings to rub together, nephew."

"She doesn't appear destitute," he said dryly.

"Lud, Ian, you of all people should know things aren't always as they appear." Aunt Edith angled her blasted fan in Miss Caruthers' direction. "Her uncle, Gideon Stapleton, paid for her gown. Do you suppose he'll also provide her a marriage settlement?"

"I'm sure I don't know." An neither did he care a jot.

No settlement, not a sixpence to scratch with, and Miss Caruthers dispensed her favors like flour to a baker. If Stapleton didn't dower the chit, her fate was certain: demimondaine or courtesan.

"She's part Roma, you know." One eyebrow lifted in speculation, Aunt Edith sent him a side-eyed glance.

"I was unaware," Ian murmured extending his elbow in a broad hint.

That explained Miss Caruthers' exotic appearance. He regarded her through hooded eyes. He'd heard Romani women were remarkably creative and responsive between the sheets. His groin tightened.

Damnation.

Aunt Edith slipped her hand into the crook of his arm. "It's said gypsy women can cast love spells. Think she knows any? Not that I believe any of that flim flam, mind you." She leaned closer to him and lowered her voice to a covert whisper. "Ian?"

He bent his neck, and the blasted ostrich feather tickled his cheek.

"Perhaps that's why you cannot take your eyes off her? She's enchanted you?"

Now Aunt Edith was making a May game of him. He straightened, drawing his eyebrows together in an irritated scowl. *Damn it.* She thought him enamored of the chit. "I assure you, Aunt Edith, I am not under the influence of any incantation."

She tilted her head upward, a mischievous glimmer in the center of her silver eyes. "Course with her looks and figure, she mightn't need it. A marriage settlement, I mean."

Ian's gaze roamed over Miss Caruthers, then her bevy of suitors. Devil a bit, Aunt Edith might very well be right. Why that irritated him all the more, he couldn't say.

She rapped his arm with her fan. "No, I don't believe she'll have need of a magic charm or a marriage settlement at all. No, indeed." Nodding her head in Miss Caruthers' direction, a devilish smile on her lips, she murmured, "Her kind marries for love."

2

From her seat against the wall, Vangie risked a peek at the tall, striking man relaxing against the ballroom's doorframe. He spoke to Lady Fitz... Fitz... She squeezed her eyes shut in concentration. Popping them open, she grinned. *Fitzwilly.* That was her name, Lady Fitzwilly.

Even from across the room, he oozed power—and something else; something difficult to define. What, precisely, was it? *Danger?* No, that wasn't right.

Waving her ivory fan, Vangie peered over its silver lace edge.

Arrogance? Mmm, perhaps a mite.

Confidence? Oh, most assuredly.

But that still wasn't quite accurate. She scrunched her eyebrows together.

What was it?

His gaze prowled the room, and Vangie's breath caught. Her fan fluttered to a stop.

Anger. He exuded rigidly controlled fury.

She'd noticed him almost the moment he entered. Her partner was leading her to the other assembled dancers, and something compelled her to glance over her shoulder. There he loomed like a panther against the door: Sinewy body tense. Piercing eyes alert. Poised, ready to spring on his unsuspecting victim.

She'd shaken her head, and scolded herself. *Stop your fanciful imaginations Evangeline Caruthers.*

Boredom carved across the planes of his somber face, the panther had stood there several minutes now, burnished brown hair curled lazily over his ears and cravat. Except for his pristine white shirt and neckcloth, he was attired in black without a jot of adornment. One might think he was in mourning. Still she decided with the merest angling of her head, the starkness suited him.

She didn't recognize the man. However, she'd not been in London two full months yet. Though nearly twenty, this was her first—her only—Season. Her social circle wasn't as extensive as other young women's, and it wasn't likely to increase. The simple truth was, she hadn't taken during her Coming Out. The knowledge no longer caused her the twinge it had a few weeks ago.

She glanced at her gown, fingering the delicate overskirt embroidered with pearls and silver rosettes. Uncle Gideon, her step-aunt Adélaid, and dear younger cousin Yvette, had been most generous. Except for their benevolence, she'd have had no appropriate clothing or acceptable company to attend such extravagant gatherings.

Not that she cared overly much about such twaddle. Large crowds unnerved her, although she'd become adept at concealing her unease—much like she'd hidden her naive hope of acquiring a loving husband this Season. That dream had been soundly dashed. Though a Romani princess, the Beau Monde deemed her an undesirable.

No, I'll not think of it.

Pressing her lips together, she straightened her spine. Romani were resourceful and resilient. She'd find a position as a governess; away from London, of course. She could always escape to her Roma relatives too. She rather preferred that idea.

Anything was better than returning to Great Uncle Percival and Great Aunt Eugenia's household. Though they weren't her legal guardians, the stipulations of her father's will had required she live with them for the past thirteen intolerable years.

Vangie could endure their oppression no longer.

She swept her gaze over the teeming room then faltered. *Oh, blast and bother*. Snapping the fan shut, she clasped and unclasped her hands around its elaborately-carved handle. Disquiet tripped across her nerves. A gaudily-attired lord plodded in her direction, and she'd no doubt he intended to request the next dance.

She shuddered in revulsion. Last time they'd danced, she'd resorted to holding her breath and sucking in slight puffs of air. His stench rivaled a beggar's. That gentleman—*who was he again?*—Lord Pickles something or other, was too bold by far in his attentions. When he wasn't making suggestive innuendos or appalling propositions, he took advantage of the waltzes to slyly grope her.

Once more, Vangie drew her eyebrows together. At least Lord Pickles hadn't been as forward as that awful duke. Who was he again? Lord Farnswort? No, his name started with a P. *Didn't it*?

Parlington? Passenberry? Pippleworth?

Dash it all. Ever since she'd begun having headaches as a child, remembering names had challenged her. And in recent weeks, she'd been introduced to a multitude of new people. She couldn't begin to recall even a fraction of their names. Meeting so many pretentious members of Society overwhelmed her, to say the least.

She might've forgotten the duke's name, but she couldn't forget his deplorable behavior. He'd pinned her against the terrace balustrade, planting disgusting, slobbery kisses over her face and neck, while pawing at her breasts. Why, if that young gentleman hadn't come upon them, and demanded the duke release her, she'd have been forced to defend herself with the dagger she kept sheathed on her leg.

What a bumblebroth that would've caused. She slanted her lips upward at the thought then thinned them into a serious line when reality pricked her. Had she dared to use the blade on the duke, the outcome from such a coil was far from certain. Though the daughter of a baronet, her Romani blood would trump any blueblood running through her veins.

That *flaw* weighed heavily against her, and no doubt the scale would've tilted in the duke's favor. How fortuitous for them both that his assault had been interrupted. Vangie had darted inside the moment she was freed, not even pausing to thank her rescuer.

Who was he? Had they ever been introduced?

Her gaze traveled around the crowded room once more. Neither he nor the duke appeared to be in attendance this evening. Come to think of it, she'd not seen either since that awful night, weeks ago. Blowing out a gusty sigh, she wished she dared to out the lecherous lords. *Oafish pigs.* As if she'd ever enter into an illicit arrangement, Roma blood or not.

Fear of social retribution prevented her from informing her hostesses of the boorish behavior of several gentlemen, including Lord Pickles and the nameless duke. Already more than one lady of quality had given her the cut-indirect, a few the cut-sublime. No doubt that, too, was a consequence of her heritage.

She gripped the fan tighter, pressing her fingers against its scalloped edges. She dreaded further snubbing, though her concern was not for herself. From the corner of her eye, she considered the noxious lord mincing his way to her. No, she cared not a groat what these people thought of her. But if Vangie exposed the powerful peers, the scandal would surely spoil Yvette's first Season.

Unclenching her hands, Vangie smoothed the fragile fabric of her gown. She laid her fingers on the rigid length of the blade beneath her skirts. Since a girl of twelve, she'd worn the dagger tied to her thigh. Yvette thought it daring and romantic, and though at first, Aunt Adélaid had been thoroughly shocked, she had grown to understand Vangie's need to wear the concealed weapon.

Truth be told, the fickleness of Polite Society troubled her. If these were London's finest, she could do without them, their affected superiority, and their snobbery.

They'd made it perfectly clear how they felt about her. She'd also heard the spiteful whispers about Uncle Gideon acquiring his fortune through *trade*, and of the Stapleton's *smelling of the shop*. The aristocrats spat the words as if they were offal. No, she quite preferred the sincerity of the gypsy travelers and the simplicity of country life. Though even there, her people were persecuted.

Lord Pickles slithered nearer, waving his podgy fingers at her. She pretended not to see him and snapped her fan open, wrinkling her nose behind it. Gracious, did the man never bathe? Glancing past the other preening lords, she spied Yvette—a flaxen-haired, sapphire-eyed vision, floating in a cloud of pink and white silk—headed her way.

Vangie smiled in relief. *Thank goodness.*

Though supper had yet to be served, she prayed Uncle Gideon was ready to leave. If they hurried, they could escape before the musicians resumed playing.

Lord Pickles sidled near her chair and reached for her hand, snuffling, "My dear Miss Caruthers."

Angling her fan, Vangie fluttered it before her like an infuriated rooster flapping its wings. Lord Pickles was forced to retreat a step, else he find himself thwacked on his prominent nose. He started to make a leg, but she suddenly stood. Without looking at him, she continued waving her fan about as if warding off a pesky insect.

A large, annoying, smelly insect.

Lord Pickles stumbled backward.

"Please excuse me, my lord." She moved past him to embrace Yvette. While they were entwined, Vangie murmured, "Are we leaving?"

Yvette chuckled and shook her head. "Not yet, dear cousin. It's not yet half-past ten, and Father and Belle-mere are engaged in a game of loo. I fear it will not be ending anytime soon. Aren't you enjoying yourself?" She peered around the small crowd encircling them.

Vangie hugged Yvette to her again and took several deliberate steps away from Lord Pickles, drawing Yvette with her. "Of course I am. I have a touch of a headache. That's all."

Her cousin must not know how much these affairs distressed her. Yvette had been so hopeful Vangie would make a match this Season, and she'd be horrified at the lewd propositions her cousin received almost nightly.

Yvette searched her face, before sweeping her gaze around the assembled beaus. Upon spying Lord Pickles, her eyes flexed wide in apparent comprehension. Looping her arm through Vangie's, Yvette said, "Perhaps some ratafia and fresh air will help. Come along. Let's find the refreshments."

They turned as one. However, Vangie stopped short as the object of her prior musings approached with the dignified Lady Fitzwilly on his arm.

Faith, he's even handsomer up close.

Startled at her thoughts, she bit her lip, a hot flush of awareness burning from her soles to the tiara atop her hair. She glimpsed his serious face before ducking her head. What a goosecap. Now she was blushing like a bumpkin.

Yvette sank into a curtsy. "Good evening, Lady Fitzgibbons, my lord."

Fitzgibbons? Drat it all. Vangie had forgotten yet another name.

Momentarily incapable of speech, she kept her head lowered, hiding her rosy face. She sank into a reasonable semblance of a curtsy. At least she hoped it was reasonable. She hadn't wobbled again, had she?

Be mindful of the solemn one, tikna.

Her Romani grandmother's words intruded into her already muddled thoughts. Vangie had thought it odd advice at the time. Now, staring at the panther lord's shiny black shoes while he towered over her, *Puri Daj's* warning almost made sense.

Smiling, Lady Fitzgibbons lifted her hand from his arm. "Ian, may I present Miss Yvette Stapleton, and her cousin, Miss Evangeline Caruthers? Miss Stapleton, Miss Caruthers, please allow me to present my nephew, Ian, the Viscount Warrick."

Yvette dimpled, offering her gloved hand. Lord Warrick bowed over it, a rakish grin on his lips. "Delighted, Miss Stapleton."

He turned his gaze on Vangie. His full lips curved into a slow enigmatic smile, revealing a row of strong white teeth against his tanned face.

She inhaled sharply, the air lodging peculiarly in her lungs.

His eyes glinted silver-gray, the color of honed steel. There was no other way to describe them. Raising her hand to his mouth, she swore she felt his lips brush her fingertips. *Twice.* It was most inappropriate. Why wasn't she shocked or annoyed? Perhaps because the warmth vibrating the length of her arm, when his firm mouth grazed her, still tingled.

"Enchanted, Miss Caruthers."

The way he said her name, the timbre of his voice lowering to a rumbling purr, caused another prickle across her flesh.

She was wrong. He most definitely *was* dangerous.

"I so desired an introduction, I cajoled my dear aunt into doing the honors. I was *determined* to make your acquaintance," he murmured, the sincerity in his melodic baritone not quite reaching his quicksilver eyes.

Determined? She gawked, open-mouthed, only shutting it with a snap when Yvette nudged her none too gently in the ribs.

The musicians struck a few discordant notes. An elderly lord, smelling of camphor and hair tonic, bowed before Yvette. "I believe you promised me this dance, my dear."

Yvette smiled. "Indeed, I did, Uncle Gabriel." She looked to Vangie. "Your headache?"

"Is all but gone," Vangie assured her. It wasn't the truth. The pounding in her skull had increased steadily.

With a smile and a little wave, Yvette placed her other hand on her uncle's arm and allowed him to lead her away.

Vangie flinched as Lord Pickles rudely shoved his way past her cousin. She was certain he thought to partner her for the next dance. For a number of weeks now, the loathsome bore had been trying to persuade her to venture into another, much less respectable, sort of liaison.

With practiced efficiency, a pinched look about her nose and mouth, Lady Fitzgibbons introduced the viscount and earl. Breathing between her slightly parted lips, Vangie only half listened, the whole while silently rehearsing her excuse for declining to dance with Lord Pickles.

Wait. Did her ladyship say his name is Pickering?

Bold as brass, Lord Warrick tucked her gloved hand into the bend of his arm.

Surprised and startled, she glanced upward.

His mouth curved into a confident smile. "Miss Caruthers, do say you'll do me the honor of partnering me for this dance."

She ought to object to his forwardness. Instead, she returned his smile, grateful to have been rescued from the awkwardness of refusing Lord Pickering. Now, perhaps he would scurry away and leave her be.

"I say, Warrick, Miss Caruthers was to be my partner for this waltz," Pickering whined.

Arching an arrogant eyebrow, Lord Warrick smiled possessively, offering what sounded like a half-sincere apology. "Sorry, Pickering, old chap. Miss Caruthers has graciously accepted my request."

Persistent to the point of boorishness, Lord Pickering insisted, "I heard no acceptance." He turned his watery gaze on Vangie, releasing a waft of stale body odor with his movement. "Do you wish to dance with the viscount or myself, Evangeline?"

The way he puffed out his padded chest indicated he'd every confidence she would favor an earl over a minor lord. Most impressionable misses would have done. She, however, wasn't one of them. And *Evangeline?* Did the man have no sense of propriety? Faith, whatever was he thinking addressing her by her Christian name? She'd never given him permission to do so. His cock-sureness and indecorous behavior was embarrassing, not to mention off-putting.

Lady Fitz—*gibbles?*—rounded on him, outraged. "Lord Pickering, you overstep the bounds! How dare you address Miss Caruthers in such a manner?"

"Indeed, bad *ton*, Pickering," Lord Warrick said, "taking liberties with *a lady*."

Vangie cast him a swift, puzzled glance. Did sarcasm tinge his voice?

He returned her regard with an innocent smile.

She must have imagined the mockery.

"Miss Caruthers?" Scratching his bum, Lord Pickering looked at her expectantly.

Gads, but he was gauche. Grateful to be spared his lascivious attention and malodorous company, she answered, "Lord Warrick did ask first, Lord Pickle—er, Pickering."

Sputtering in indignation, the fop stomped off, his face a mottled shade of red; an exact match to his garish, clattering footwear.

"Needs his ears boxed, boorish jackanape." Lady Fitzgibbons jabbed her fan in the direction of his retreating form. Nose wrinkled, she gave the air a delicate sniff. "And a bath, by God!"

Vangie suppressed a smile. *My sentiments exactly.*

Half-turning toward the card room, her ladyship spoke over her shoulder. "Enjoy your dance, dears. I'm off to challenge Lady

Higgenbottom to a game of faro. She's such a poor loser." With a wink, and a naughty chuckle, she made for the exit.

Lord Warrick tilted his dark head, indicating the other dancers. "Shall we?"

3

Aware of the numerous pairs of eyes observing him escort Miss Caruthers onto the polished floor, a wry smile touched Ian's lips. "I haven't danced this evening. No doubt the rumormongers are hissing envious conjectures as to why I've asked you."

She shot him a startled look before glancing around the crowded ballroom. "Why did you?"

"To see if what I'd heard about you was true." He watched for her reaction to his provocative statement.

She opened her pretty mouth then closed it, dropping her focus to his cravat. They waltzed around the dance floor for a few moments in silence. The string quartet was quite satisfactory, and Ian allowed the lilting strains to soothe his troubled spirit.

"What…What did you hear?" Miss Caruthers' hesitant question reminded him of his purpose.

"That you are an excellent dancer."

It was true. She moved with a natural grace, following his lead, all the while holding herself in a most proper stance. He had to acknowledge she was a superb actress. Her gaze remained fixated on a spot above his left shoulder, except for one brief instance when she'd flicked her cobalt-blue gaze upward and unintentionally met his eyes.

"Is that all?" she softly asked.

He'd never seen eyes such a dark, arresting blue before. "All?"

"You've heard nothing else about me?" Her eyes held the perfect combination of trust and innocent curiosity. So convincing was she, that when their gazes fused, a peculiar jolt stabbed the center of his being.

What was that feeling?

Something foreign, tantalizing, rousing from dormancy and flickering to awareness.

Startled by his train of thought, Ian stiffened. *Good God*, now he waxed sentimental claptrap. Even so, he continued to stare into her seemingly guileless eyes. How could someone as jaded as she, appear so innocent? He couldn't very well tell her what he knew, now could he?

He searched her expressive eyes. "Is there something else you'd have me know?"

"No. Why should there be?" Furrowing her smooth brow, she peered at him. Was that confusion in her gaze? She looked away first.

That irked him.

Man, control yourself. She's not even flirting with you.

He could better understand Geoff's fascination now. Miss Caruthers was skilled in her art. Most skilled. Ian would have to guard himself well. He sensed her siren's allure; the tentacles of desire winding their way about his reasoning, holding him in an imperceptible, yet impenetrable grip. It was almost as if she'd cast a spell, bewitching him.

What utter drivel.

Nonetheless, concentrating proved difficult. He was too aware of the voluptuous woman in his arms, their bodies moving as one to the music. No wonder the young blades lined up, waiting for the smallest morsel of attention from her. He could almost believe she was as diffident and unsure of herself as she pretended. Both qualities were designed and employed to stir the primitive male.

He resolutely suppressed the protective response she roused in him with her seductress' wiles. "You truly are an exceptionally graceful dancer," he murmured near her ear.

"Thank you...my lord," she said, her voice a mere thread.

He flared his nostrils at her intoxicating perfume. Tilting his head a bit closer, he drew in a deep breath, savoring her scent. Something citrusy. Maybe orange blossom? And lightly floral. Lily of the Valley. He recognized the aroma. A myriad of the graceful, nodding white flowers blanketed the grounds near Somersfield's pond.

Ian ignored good sense and drew Miss Caruthers' lush form closer. Her décolletage and his height advantage gave him an excellent view of her ample cleavage where a diamond pendant nestled in the valley between her creamy breasts. It gently caressed the flawless, sloping mounds as she swayed in time to the music.

He imagined his fingers doing the same. Blood rushed to his loins, and he cursed inwardly. He'd been too long without a woman. Not since Amelia...Damn, had it really been eight months? Aye, too long without the exquisite pleasure of a woman's body. With his thumb, he caressed Miss Caruthers' spine. One slow, provocative stroke.

She shuddered. Was that a gasp? Perhaps she wasn't as poised as she affected.

Excellent.

Much better to catch her off guard if he was to succeed with his plan. Why then, didn't his vengeful scheme fill him with the same sense of satisfaction it had before meeting her?

Vangie flicked a glance upward, her gaze colliding with Lord Warrick's again. What unusual eyes he possessed. Light blue flecks colored the gray, and those dark eyelashes… She'd never seen eyelashes so thick on a man. Her focus dipped to his mouth, and his well-formed lips curved into a smile. She stumbled, though he didn't seem to notice.

"I've not seen you at other assemblies, my lord," she blurted, as heat skimmed her face at her ineptitude.

His lips slanted again. "I've just returned to London. My father and brother died recently."

Her breath caught. "My condolences."

"Thank you."

Shouldn't he be home, in the comforting presence of his family? Perhaps he didn't have anyone else. At least she had Uncle Gideon, Aunt Adélaid, and Yvette. Had he anyone? "Have you any remaining family?" Faith, now she was blurting her thoughts and prying.

"My stepmother and a sister, Charlotte." Warmth infused his voice when he spoke of his sister.

What possesses a man in mourning to leave his family and attend a ball? She barely finished the thought. That little niggling headache she'd mentioned earlier throbbed full on now, viciously and unmercifully. Lightheaded, her stomach churning, it took every bit of effort not to trip during the dancing.

Why now?

Her last megrim episode had been many months ago. It must be the excitement—and the corsets of course. She only wore short stays at home. Oh, why had she let Yvette talk her into trying one of her new back-laced French corsets? The garment didn't fit properly and pressed against Vangie's ribs, constricting her breathing.

She sucked a meager puff of air into her cramped lungs. She could scarcely inhale, though whether from her ailment or the corset she couldn't say for certain. She didn't care what Yvette and Aunt Adélaid said. The blasted corded stays *did* interfere with her breathing. She detested the thing.

"My lord?" Vangie swallowed against the waves of nausea assailing her as tiny black spots flashed before her eyes. She must leave the dance floor before she disgraced herself in front of everyone. "My lord, I..." Her steps faltered. She swayed, clutching at his hand and shoulder to keep her balance.

Panic scuttled up her spine, and her vision narrowed, the familiar blackness closing in. As the pain throbbing in her temples crescendoed to an excruciating climax, the fuzzy ringing in her ears amplified. She struggled to remain standing, and as if sensing her battle, his lordship tightened his sturdy arm around her.

"Miss Caruthers?" Concerned deepened his voice. "Are you quite well?"

"No." Not daring to shake her head, she swayed and gulped. "I fear...I need some air. Now."

Miss Caruther's faint whisper and sudden pallor alarmed Ian.

The terrace and the fresh air she needed were at the ballroom's other end. After maneuvering her across the crowded floor, he assisted her through the open French windows then onto the veranda. She started to sag, and he slipped an arm around her slender waist.

Turning her head, her hazy gaze met his. "Forgive me," she whispered before slumping in his arms.

This wasn't a fit of the vapors. He'd seen his sister perform that stunt far too many times to be taken in by play-acting. No, Miss Caruthers was truly insensate. Scooping her into his embrace, Ian winced and swore beneath his breath as pain lanced through his shoulder. Should he carry her into the ballroom? Glancing downward, he stood undecided for a moment. A sliver of moonlight illuminated her ashen face.

Her bout of faintness proved most convenient, providential even. She'd played straight into his hands. Only now, holding her slight form, he had second thoughts. *Blast and damn*, he didn't want to feel compassion for her. She didn't deserve any tender emotions, but a weeping or swooning woman had always stirred his protective nature.

Guilt squeezed his chest as he turned in a wide arc. The garden? No doubt there was a bench… No, that wouldn't do.

A dim light glowed beyond the panes of another French window farther along the veranda. Decision made, Ian strode to the entrance. He discreetly peeked through the glass, glimpsing a retiring room set aside for the ladies.

Empty.

He heaved a frustrated sigh. The room held no primping peeresses to which he could transfer Miss Caruthers' care. Ah, but luck was on his side. The doors were open, ever-so-slightly.

His injured shoulder objected to her weight, and flinching, he shifted the bundle in his arms. He toed the door farther open then slipped into the deserted room. Lamps burned low on a carved fireplace mantle under which a fire cavorted brightly. A trio of divans formed a cozy u-shape, and across from the center couch sat two plush armchairs, a table between them. Another lamp glowed upon its surface.

"I say, is anyone here?" he said in a low tone.

Where was the servant who ought to be attending the chamber? Hopefully she wasn't seeing to *her* personal needs behind one of the elaborately painted screens. *Gads*, he didn't even want to think on that. Just in case, he called a bit louder, "Halloo?"

No one answered. It would've been most helpful to have a female presence to assist him. His attention sank to her. Even indisposed and unconscious, Miss Caruthers was exquisite, her dark lashes a stark contrast against her porcelain cheeks.

His left shoulder ached bloody awful from cradling her to his chest, and in four long strides, he made the closest divan. Once he'd laid her down, he shoved a tasseled pillow beneath her head and patted her cheek.

Several of her beaded hairpins had slipped loose, and a few lay scattered upon the floor. Ian gathered the pins and, unsure where to put them, stuffed them into his pocket. Studying her, he shook his head and bent his lips into a wry smile. When had he gone from a ruthless rogue, prepared to give her the dressing-down she deserved, to caring for her welfare?

Despite the cracked doorway, the room was stifling hot. He swiftly unbuttoned his coat before yanking off his gloves and wiping the moisture from his brow with the back of his hand. On another long table laden with needles, threads, hair pins, and other toiletries he discovered a stack of soft linen cloths. After dampening one, he bathed Miss

Caruthers' face.

Still no response.

He cast an exasperated glance around the chamber, fully aware his presence here was beyond acceptable boundaries. There'd be the devil to pay if he were discovered. Vengeance was one thing, but he stood the risk of irreparably not only ruining Miss Caruthers' good standing but also his as well. That certainly had never been his intention.

Tossing the cloth onto the marble-topped table behind the divan, he heaved a frustrated breath. She hadn't stirred a jot but lay still-as-death and every bit as ashen. No, not quite. Her lips were blue-edged and her breathing labored.

Where was the confounded servant?

He needed help.

Miss Caruthers needed help.

God's blood. What had he been thinking, toting her in here? Pushing a hand through his hair, he cocked his head and firmed his mouth. He dropped to one knee before tugging off her gloves and feeling for a pulse. The rise and fall of her well-endowed chest gave him pause.

What kind of a base lecher was he, ogling an unconscious woman?

His gaze traveled to the door. Should he seek assistance? It would be better for their reputations, but dare he leave her alone in her current condition?

"Miss Caruthers? Can you hear me? Wake up." He patted her hand then gently shook her shoulders. She remained limp and unresponsive. Shutting his eyes, Ian tried to recall what Lucinda or the servants did when Charlotte keeled over.

Smelling salts.

Searching the tables for a smelling bottle, he found no trace of the salts. He glowered in disbelief as he strode back to her. *All these damned fallalls, fripperies, and female whatnots, and not a single vial of smelling salts amongst them?*

"Blast it all," he muttered under his breath. "Come on, man, think. Charlotte's flopping around like a loose fish half the time. What else is done to help her?"

He raked his fingers through his hair again, pushing it on end. Miss Caruthers' chest barely rose now, her breaths even shallower. Would her breathing ease if he loosened her stays?

Loosen her stays?

His gaze ricocheted to the door and just as rapidly returned her.

Were her lips the merest bit bluer? Did she struggle to breathe?

"Why do women insist on wearing those blasted contraptions?"

There was nothing for it.

His jaw set against the heady scent of her perfume wafting upward, Ian slid her gauzy gown off one shoulder then the other. Bent over, his face inches from her tempting breasts, he shoved the gown to her waist. Behind her, the fabric caught and held. He gave a little jerk, and swearing again, gave a harder yank. The material didn't budge, and he made an annoyed noise. It was bloody more difficult to undress an insensate woman than one eager to have her clothes removed.

"Of all the damned predicaments." Not more than a couple of minutes had passed since she'd swooned, but each crept by interminably.

Raising her pliant form partway, he peered over her shoulder. A hook had caught on her stays. Sweat broke out across his brow and beaded his upper lip. *It's the heat of the room—nothing more.* Her bountiful breasts crushed to his chest most certainly weren't the cause.

Her head lolling against his shoulder, Ian shifted Miss Caruthers upright a bit, and with a might more force than was necessary, he jerked the gown again. It finally popped loose, leaving a shred of lace stuck to the stays.

He darted another worried look to the door. All he needed was a dame to enter the retiring room and catch him undressing Miss Caruthers. That unwelcome thought spurred him on. Turning her onto her stomach, he made quick work of unlacing her stays. The moment they loosened, she sucked in a shuddering breath. At once, he rotated her onto her back and seized the gaping bodice, pulling the fabric over her breasts.

In his haste his fingers brushed the smooth mounds. At the involuntary tightening in his breeches, he swore. "Hellfire."

Head cocked, he surveyed his handwork. She appeared to have been ravished. He attempted to slide her arms back into their sleeves, but the gown, pulled nearly to her neck now, was too tight. Ian unceremoniously hauled the bodice down, slid her arms into the sleeves, and then once again, covered her breasts. He hadn't accomplished the task with a great deal of finesse, but at least her breathing had eased somewhat.

He wiped his upper lip before standing then grimacing. Her rumpled gown sagged off her shoulders. He adjusted the fabric into some semblance of decency and smoothed her skirts. She still did not rouse, and his concern increased ten-fold. Charlotte *never* remained unaware for this long.

Miss Caruthers needed a physician.

Now.

Striding to the room's entrance, he breathed a grateful sigh that he'd not been interrupted in his ministrations. *Christ.* He could well imagine what the gossipmongers would make of it. Glancing at Miss Caruthers, he smoothed his hair. He'd reached to button his coat once more when a gaggle of twittering women piled into the room. Eyes wide and mouths agape, they pulled up short, stumbling pell-mell into one-another.

Bloody, maggoty hell.

4

Ian finished securing his coat, addressing the lady's maid who'd finally made an appearance. "Miss Caruthers is seriously ill." The servant skittered around the edge of the ladies to gape at Miss Caruthers splayed on the divan. He gritted his teeth to smother the stream of oaths throttling up his throat. "Please find her cousin, Miss Stapleton, and request she come at once."

"Yes, milord." Bobbing a hasty curtsy, the pudgy girl tore from the room as if the hounds of hell nipped her heels. More likely, she was already planning the juicy details she would use to embellish her rendition of what she'd seen.

A warning pealed in his head, and he cursed Fate for playing this cruel trick.

Sputtering in indignation, the rotund Duchess of Beacock drew herself up. "Viscount Warrick, whatever are *you* doing in here?" Upon peering past his shoulders, her bulgy eyes narrowed suspiciously. "And *why* is Miss Caruthers unconscious and *half-clothed*?"

"Half-clothed indeed, sir," Lady Pendelbury—a skinny pinched-faced widow—parroted. "Surely, you've a plausible explanation." Her voice rang with self-righteousness, clearly insinuating the improbability of any such thing.

A few women sidled near the divan, ogling Miss Caruthers and whispering in what was obviously feline satisfaction at her appearance. One of the cackling harpies referred to her as a *heathen, gypsy trollop.*

Rage, hot and furious roiled in his gut, and he swallowed another vulgar curse.

Sharp-clawed, envious hellcats, all. And *these* were the *créme-de-la-créme* of the *ton* from which he was expected to select his viscountess. Not bloody, sodding likely. Cocking up his toes was preferable to becoming leg-shackled to one of these mean-spirited banshees.

Drawing a steading breath, he rocked back onto his heels and clasped his hands behind his back. What maggot had crawled into his head and possessed him to stay and help Miss Caruthers?

She couldn't breathe, dolt.

Sweeping the aristocratic snobs a contemptuous glance, Ian observed a conglomeration of emotions on their faces. More than a few averted yearning gazes from him, their attraction obvious as they blushed self-consciously. Others' expressions reflected embarrassment, sympathy, accusation, condemnation—and yes—even malicious glee. Before the night ended, those biddies' vicious tongues would be flapping all over town.

If Ian had planned this debacle, it couldn't have served his original purpose any better. Now however, he attempted to preserve Miss Caruthers' reputation by assuring these rabid flibbertigibbets he hadn't ravished her. "Miss Caruthers felt faint whilst we danced and asked for fresh air. She swooned on the terrace, so I brought her here to recover." The story sounded preposterous to his ears even if every word was the absolute truth.

A flurry of activity echoed outside the room.

What now? More histrionics?

The ladies turned eager faces to the door, and he eyed them, barely keeping his mouth from curling into a disgusted sneer. As if they needed more juicy tidbits to bandy about.

Miss Stapleton charged into the room, bolting at once to her cousin's side. A striking couple followed her. The aunt and uncle, he presumed.

Their host and hostess, Lord and Lady Armstrong, rushed in behind the pair. Ian couldn't but admire Lady Armstrong's astuteness. With a quick, assessing glance, she comprehended the delicacy of the situation and took matters in hand.

"Ladies, let us remove ourselves to one of the other sitting rooms." Despite their protests, she firmly shepherded the titillated oglers out the door.

Ian disregarded their furtive looks and snide whispers, more concerned that Miss Caruthers had yet to stir despite the ongoing commotion. He turned a carefully bland expression upon her uncle. Was he a hot-tempered sort? The type to jump to conclusions? The devil take it, would he demand satisfaction? By all that was holy, it mustn't come to that.

Firming his lips into a harsh, disapproving line, fire flared in Stapleton's light blue eyes, but he remained silent.

Good. A sensible man.

Ian breathed a trifle—only a trifle—easier.

Mrs. Stapleton joined their daughter, the women intent on reviving Miss Caruthers. After several moments, during which the men watched in tense silence, her eyelids fluttered open.

"Dearest, are you all right?" Miss Stapleton cast an apprehensive glance in Ian's direction. "What happened?"

Furrowing her brow, Miss Caruthers lifted a shaky hand to her forehead. "I had one of my unfortunate episodes. I must've fainted."

For the longest duration any woman on earth ever had.

Closing her eyes, she swallowed.

Ian exhaled bit-by-bit, daring to feel the tiniest smidgen of relief. She had *episodes.* Surely her family would understand this was one of them, and he'd done the gentlemanly thing by assisting her.

The aunt *tsked* comfortingly. "I'd so hoped you'd outgrow your headaches. The physician said you might. You've suffered from them so many years now—ever since your parents' deaths..."

Mrs. Stapleton stopped, her smile forced and strained. "Never mind that. Let's see to your attire, shall we?"

Discreetly positioning herself, she blocked his view as Miss Stapleton made quick work of securing Miss Caruthers' stays and gown. After propping her cousin into a sitting position, Miss Stapleton lifted the dangling tiara and circlet from atop Miss Caruthers' head. She attempted to straighten the mass of midnight curls cascading well-past her cousin's shoulders.

The chit did look like she'd engaged in a rousing romp. Despite the irregular circumstances, the notion fascinated. Far more than it ought to, in fact. His loins contracted again. *Eight months is far too long.*

Mrs. Stapleton handed her niece a glass of water, receiving a weak smile in return.

Miss Caruthers took a sip, her bewildered gaze searching the room over the rim.

"How did you come to be here, *chéri,* and partially *déshabillé*?" Mrs. Stapleton asked.

"She isn't partially disrobed," Ian disputed with calm irritation. She was, but not for the reason everyone likely assumed. "I but loosened her stays, so she could breathe."

Mrs. Stapleton's fair eyebrows rose in twin arcs of disbelief. "And you thought such a thing was appropriate?"

"Her lips were turning blue."

The eyebrows rose higher.

They were as likely to believe that excuse as pigs were to fly. Feeling a noose slip around his neck, Ian released an exasperated huff. "As I—"

"I suggest you not speak at present, my lord," Stapleton said spearing him with a scowl. He turned his intense gaze on his niece, his expression softening. "Vangie, what happened?"

Miss Caruthers' confused gaze swung to Ian. Voice husky, she murmured, "I…I don't know, Uncle Gideon. I often cannot remember anything happening before or after I faint." She clasped and unclasped her hands in her lap.

Ian fisted his hands. "Bloody hell," he ground out between his teeth. This situation was becoming devilishly thorny. The noose tightened a fraction.

"I say, Warrick, bad *ton*. There are ladies present." Lord Armstrong delivered this admonition, cutting his baggy-eyed gaze toward the women.

Ian angled his head. "Please, forgive—"

Aunt Edith burst into the room, alarm etched across her refined features.

"Lud, Ian, whatever has occurred? Everyone's speaking of it. That chinwag Lady Pendelbury's proclaiming you and Miss Caruthers were caught—" She caught herself, and cast a guarded glance toward Miss Caruthers. "Er…that is, in an unseemly situation."

The Stapleton women gasped, exchanging horrified glances. The rope tugged taut, and Ian ran a finger around his neckcloth.

Miss Caruthers lounged on the divan, a bemused, nonplussed look in her beautiful blue eyes. Did she understand any of what was transpiring?

"Armstrong, do you have a private study nearby?" Stapleton asked.

"Yes, yes, o' course." Lord Armstrong nodded, one hand holding his lapel. "Just down the corridor." He moved toward the door. "Gentlemen, let's make our way there and allow the ladies to care for Miss Caruthers."

"I'll join you as well," Aunt Edith announced starchily, a fierce no-nonsense glint in her intelligent eyes.

None dared deny her. She sailed to Ian's side. Giving him a tense smile, she smoothed several errant strands of hair. "Lawks, Ian, you've made a merry mess of it. You should never have been here tonight. None of this would've occurred if you'd observed protocol."

He tugged at his cravat again, the imaginary rope burning his flesh.

"Armstrong," Stapleton said, "would you arrange for our landau to be brought around to the side entrance, please? I presume there's a way to leave the premises through those doors." He indicated the French windows with a slight inclination of his dark head.

Lord Armstrong nodded, his bewhiskered jowls jiggling. "Course, o' course."

"Adélaid, I'll have your wraps brought here," Stapleton said. "I'm confident Lady Armstrong will ensure you're not disturbed. You and Yvette escort Vangie home. Leave by the side entrance, and speak to no one."

Meeting her husband's eyes, Mrs. Stapleton inclined her head whilst draping an arm across Miss Caruthers' shoulders.

Ian observed the exchange with practiced detachment, something he'd learned to do as a child and then perfected while in the army. A nasty premonition niggled. One he wouldn't allow himself to fully explore, or his temper would give way entirely.

From a thick haze, Vangie listened to conversations around her. Without thinking, she answered the questions posed. Something untoward had occurred. Something scandalous. She could see it in Lord Armstrong's embarrassed fidgeting, the troubled looks Aunt Adélaid and Yvette gave her, and the anger Uncle Gideon strictly controlled.

But what, precisely, had happened?

Searching her memory, she pulled her eyebrows together, trying to concentrate. Her head was muddled, and she felt disoriented. Oh, to be able to go home, crawl into her soft bed, and go to sleep. Slouching against the divan, she lifted her gaze to Lord Warrick then quickly averted it.

He was in high dudgeon as well. Though he appeared self-possessed and unruffled, except for a few strands of dark chestnut hair sticking up at odd angles, he simmered with restrained fury. The hooded eyes he leveled on her revealed his rage was, at least in part, directed at her.

But why?

Somehow, she'd caused his anger. For the life of her, she couldn't recall what she'd done; unless swooning while dancing aggravated him so. Vangie trembled, clasping her hands once more. Was he like Uncle Percival, given to fits of irrational rage without provocation? More than once she'd been on the receiving end of a vicious slap from her uncle.

From beneath her lashes, she dared a peek at Lord Warrick. He looked every bit the untamed cat she'd likened him to earlier, right down to the wild, dangerous glint in his eyes. If he had a tail, it would be lashing back-and-forth in agitation.

"Lady Fitzgibbons, gentlemen?" Lord Armstrong waited beside the closed door.

Her ladyship and the men moved to quit the chamber. Viscount Warrick turned to give Vangie an indecipherable look, a steely stare, peering into her soul. His predatory panther gaze captured hers.

Time stopped, held immobile for the scantest of moments. Even in her muddled state, she knew her world had been turned upside-down, irrevocably altered, for better or worse.

5

Bloody, holy hell.

Someone followed Ian, and he blamed his own carelessness. Could this confounded evening possibly worsen? Too furious to take the carriage home, he opted to walk instead, hoping the exercise would alleviate a degree of his ire.

The effort had proved futile.

He'd been ambushed once already this tonight, though the methods used by Stapleton and his entourage of powerful cronies were much more refined than this pair of grimy brutes. A dim streetlamp's light cut a narrow path across the pavement. He quickly scanned the lane for other riffraff. Deserted, as well it should be this time of night.

Lucky for these miscreants his dark thoughts had consumed him, and he hadn't been as attentive as was typical. Unfortunately for them, however, they lacked good sense and selected him to spice. Eyeing the footpads creeping toward him from two different directions, Ian permitted a satisfied smile. Yes, indeed, a chance to expend his wrath might prove just the thing.

Unbridled rage yet throttled through him, and these spawns of Satan would be on the receiving end of a month's worth of ire magnified to the point of violence over the course of the past two hours. Two hours in which Stapleton effectively cornered and entrapped him.

As he took a defensive stance, the smaller of the thieves swallowed. His Adam's apple bobbed up and down his scrawny neck like a chicken pecking corn. Slanting a sidelong glance to his bulgier crony, he licked his lips. "Give us yer purse an' we won't 'urt ye."

The ugly-looking knife he wielded belied his words. Laughing uneasily, he revealed several missing teeth, his rancid breath wafting to Ian on the cool evening breeze. A cloud blew past revealing a quarter moon, but its meager light did little to illuminate the gloomy street corner.

Ian smirked at the thief's false bravado before switching his gaze to assess the larger man. The brute outweighed him by a good three or four stone, though Ian was several inches taller.

"Aye, guvna." He nodded his oafish head, his many chins disappearing in the sweaty folds of fat around his neck. "We only be after yer blunt." His sly gaze danced to his partner's, and he sniggered as if privy to a private joke.

Shifting his blade menacingly from hand to hand, the short fellow cackled.

"Gentlemen—and I do use the term loosely—I welcome the opportunity to have a bit of sport with you." He unhurriedly removed his hat from his head and just as nonchalantly tossed the expensive top hat to the ground. Casually twirling the silver tipped cane he carried in his left hand, he unbuttoned his coat with the other. "It's been far too long since I've had an opportunity to practice my sparring."

The ruffians traded a fleeting, bewildered glance.

Ian grinned at their growing alarm. As he'd anticipated, they both lunged for him at once. In one swift, fluid motion, he slammed his cane into the wrist of the scrounger brandishing the knife. The blade flew through the air, clattering onto the cobblestones and clanking along until it slid to a stop several feet away.

He simultaneously plowed his foot into the other ruffian's pudgy midsection. The kick knocked the bigger man onto his ample bum, and with a loud, pained grunt, he skidded backward on his arse.

Clutching his damaged arm, the smaller robber swore. "Ye broke me wrist, ye bloody bug—"

Discarding the cane, Ian let fly with an uppercut. The blow landed square on the man's pockmarked jaw. The cur spun halfway around, wobbled unsteadily, and then toppled to the ground, bum upward and out cold.

"That's one." Ian grinned, only a bit winded as he faced the other fellow. He beckoned with his hand, wiggling his fingers tauntingly. "Come on then. Let's be about it, blubber guts."

The other blackguard lumbered to his feet, and bellowing his fury, charged forward like an inebriated bull.

Ian ducked the first, ham-fisted punch. "Surely a great lummox like you can do better than that," he mocked.

The thief's second swing connected soundly with his cheek. *Damn.* Too much wine tonight had slowed his reflexes.

"'Ows 'bout that?" the brute puffed, sucking in great gulps of air. "I don' see ye laughin' now."

Taking a couple dancing steps beyond his opponent's reach, Ian touched his face. "Ah, it seems I've underestimated your skills. I do apologize. It shan't happen again."

"Come on, ye dandified twiddle poop." The robber's mouth curled sideways into a sneer.

Ian laughed, swiping the hair off his forehead. He'd never been called a twiddle poop before. An image of Lord Pickering's garish attire sprang to mind. He chuckled once more. Now *there* was a twiddle poop.

The filthy man confronting Ian crouched low, his oversized hands circling about, beating the air. Thick rivulets of sweat trickled down his blotchy face, and his stubby tongue repeatedly darted out to lick the moisture off his thick upper lip.

Best to make short work of it.

"Do forgive me for ending our match swiftly, but I've important matters to attend to." Lunging forward, Ian planted a facer upside his surprised assailant's crooked nose.

His guttural groan muffled the crunch of breaking bones as blood spurted from his broken nose.

Another well-placed punch to his opponent's flabby stomach bent the man over, and Ian kicked the rotter on his broad rear, sending him face-first to the ground.

He rolled onto his back, his hands lifted upward. "No more, guvna," he pleaded, pressing a grubby sleeve to his bloody face.

"Go!" Breathing heavily, fists still raised in defense, Ian stepped backward. He jerked his head toward the unlit street. Wheezing and gasping, the hefty villain lumbered to his feet. Cupping his streaming nose, he tore off without a backward glance, deserting his insensate accomplice.

Bending over to retrieve his hat and cane, Ian winced. His shoulder complained no small amount at the exertion. Scarce a week had passed since his stallion threw him toe over top. Only agile reflexes and quick thinking prevented him from cracking his skull. His aching shoulder had taken the brunt of the fall. He rubbed the bruised muscles with his spare hand.

Pericles had never thrown him before, but Ian blamed himself. He'd been riding the horse, neck or nothing, and when he shifted his weight to leap a hedgerow, he'd been unceremoniously tossed to the ground. At the time, he attributed the fall to Pericles' refusal to take the hedge. But in truth, his foul temper could be blamed for the horse's balking. Incensed and grief-stricken over his brother's and father's recent deaths, Ian had been too enthusiastic with his boot-spurs to Pericles' sides.

Geoff, my beloved brother.

Sorrow pierced his chest, fierce and unrelenting, and he closed his eyes against the pain. Covering his heart with his hand, Ian recalled the last time he and Geoff had raced their horses across that very meadow. The lavender dots of heather now speckling the field and lending their subtle fragrance to the crisp morning air hadn't been blooming that day.

Ian remained motionless until the spasm of grief passed. His cheerful, gullible brother would laugh no more, and Miss Caruthers was to blame. That in itself was a crime far greater than the deplorable state his father had left Somerfield's ledgers and tenants.

Miss Caruthers.

A wave of fresh anger rolling over him, Ian clenched his fist. Pain ripped through his hand. If he wasn't mistaken, he'd broken a knuckle or two. He flexed his fingers and grimaced. The answering twinge confirmed his assessment. Running his uninjured hand over his cheek and jaw, he gingerly opened and closed his mouth. His face throbbed where he'd taken the blow from the ham-handed lout.

He'd have a colorful bruise come morning.

Settling his hat atop his head, he twisted his mouth into a cynical smile. A black-and-blue face paired with his battered pride. Somehow, it seemed fitting and, truth be known, a far more brilliant match than the union proposed to him an hour ago.

"Wake up!"

Why was Yvette trying to wake her so early?

"Please, no." Vangie groaned and pressed her face into the downy softness of her pillow. Sleep curled around her consciousness again.

Yvette gently shook her shoulder, repeating urgently, "Wake up, Vangie."

"*Chérie*, you must rise and dress at once," Aunt Adélaid said, her voice muffled.

Vangie drowsily opened her eyes.

Her aunt poked about inside the wardrobe, rifling through Vangie's borrowed gowns.

She frowned and covered a yawn.

Yvette lifted a fresh chemise and stockings from the bureau. She brought the garments to the bed, dangling them from her fingertips. "Here, I'll help you. You must make haste." Her expression troubled, her voice trembled the merest bit.

Why were her aunt and cousin here to assist her instead of her abigail? Most peculiar. Vangie studied Yvette's pale face. "Where's Mary?"

"She's..." Yvette sent her stepmother a helpless glance.

"Occupied, at present," Aunt Adélaid finished.

Sitting up, Vangie brushed hair away from her face. It hung loose, in heavy waves around her shoulders and back. "Whatever is going on? Is someone ill?"

"Lord Warrick has..." Yvette sent another quick, uncertain glance to Aunt Adélaid. "That is, he...uhm...he's come to call."

"At this ungodly hour?" Vangie looked to the French windows opening onto a private balcony. Muted, early morning light shimmered through the panes, crisscrossing the hand-hooked, blue and pink cabbage rose rug. Taking a sideways peek at her bedside table clock, she widened her eyes. "It isn't even eight straight-up!"

Far too early for a social visit. Downright rude, in fact.

She plucked at the satin coverlet. "Can't Uncle Gideon address any urgent matters with Lord Warrick?"

Her aunt shook her head, lines of worry creasing her face. "No, dear. His lordship specifically asked for you, and your uncle asked us to make haste with your toilette." She sighed, her gaze swinging between the two gowns she held in either hand. She selected the yellow and flung the green across the back of a chair. "Mary may not have been the best choice of a lady's maid for you. She's a dear, but she dawdles terribly."

"I don't understand the rush for me to dress, or why Uncle Gideon has accepted a caller so unfashionably early." Bewildered, Vangie idly twirled a curl, her gaze shifting from Yvette to Aunt Adélaid. Tension radiated sharp and severe across their attractive features.

She stopped twisting her hair. "Is something wrong?"

They exchanged anxious glances, and unease quickened through her again.

"Darling..." Aunt Adélaid drew in a deep breath, "I think it best to let Gideon explain. Now come, we must hurry. Your uncle is impatient this morning."

Vangie slipped from the bed, and with another wide yawn, pulled off her nightgown. "Did something happen last evening?" She slipped her arms into the filmy chemise Yvette held for her. Her question met with pained silence. "I remember feeling unwell, and Lord Warrick assisting me from the ballroom."

A pair of embroidered stockings came next. "I cannot recall most of what happened after I swooned." When Aunt Adélaid made to assist her into the French stays, she shook her head. "Not after last night, Aunt. I cannot breathe properly in that contraption. I'll wear my short stays."

Her aunt shrugged, tossing the offending undergarment on the rumpled bed. She retrieved Vangie's well-worn stays and quickly laced them.

Vangie raised her arms above her, and Yvette's yellow chintz gown was lowered over her head. "I have a vague memory of a conversation about a *tete-a-tete,* but I don't recall the details or individuals involved," she admitted.

The gown settled around her ankles, and Aunt Adélaid smoothed the mussed ruffles bordering the collar and sleeves.

"Was it someone we know?" After twisting her hair into a simple knot, Vangie tied a sunny ribbon across the crown of her head. She scrunched her brow, deep in thought. She tried to remember the ride home. It was a muddled memory. As were her preparations for bed. "Dash it to ribbons, it's no use. I cannot remember—not a single thing."

There was nothing for it then, but to go below and set things straight. How she was to do so with only minimal memory of last evening, she had no idea. What if she'd seen something illicit, and she and Lord Warrick were to be called as witnesses?

Had someone's honor been sullied?

Had there been a duel?

Good God. Had someone been killed?

6

Flanked on either side by Yvette and Aunt Adélaid, Vangie entered the study and stopped just inside the doorway. Yvette's spaniels trotted over to greet her, and she idly petted their mottled heads.

His back to the room, Lord Warrick stared out the bay window. Uncle Gideon sat at his mammoth mahogany desk, drumming his fingers atop a short stack of papers. *He* stared at his lordship. The stern expression marring his usually pleasant features gave her pause.

Something unpleasant was afoot. Her heart skipped then fluttered uncomfortably. Uncle Gideon was rarely out of sorts and never with her. Skirting the dogs and a table displaying carved jade figurines, she approached his desk.

Hands clasped before her, she said softly, "You wished to see me, Uncle Gideon?"

She cast a nervous glance in Lord Warrick's direction. When she'd spoken, he'd stiffened visibly, his shoulders going rigid. He didn't turn around but remained obsessed with the scene beyond the beveled window, seemingly ignoring her.

Fitted out in the first stare of fashion, he was undeniably a handsome spectacle. His hunter-green cutaway stretched across his broad shoulders, and those coffee-colored curls she noticed last evening teased the starched edge of his neckcloth once more. Buff-colored pantaloons, emphasizing his long legs and narrow hips, disappeared into gleaming Hessian boots.

He was a startling attractive man.

His fingers, knuckles newly bruised, curled around the rim of the hat he held. He tapped it against his muscular thigh every now and again, as if he'd a great need to release restrained energy.

"Please have a seat, Vangie." With a casual wave of his hand, Uncle Gideon indicated the striped maroon settee before the fireplace.

Her gaze never leaving her uncle's much too serious countenance, she did so. Only after sitting and arranging her skirts did she turn to look at Yvette and Aunt Adélaid, still hovering near the entrance. Why hadn't they taken a seat too? Apprehension gripped her. Were they waiting for permission to stay? "Aunt Adélaid, Yvette?"

Their gazes remained fixed on Uncle Gideon. She flicked a quick glance at her uncle. A nearly imperceptible shaking of his head denied her aunt's and cousin's silent request.

Giving Vangie a reassuring smile, Aunt Adélaid stepped forward and patted her on the shoulder. "All will be well, *chérie*. Trust your uncle."

Uneasiness pummeled her. If only she could remember what happened last night.

"Come along, dearest." Aunt Adélaid slipped an arm around Yvette's waist and led her from the room, the dogs following at their mistress' heels.

Vangie's sense of foreboding increased, and she shivered, despite the warmth of the cheery fire. She fisted her hands in her gown, taking slow, deep breaths. She thought she heard Lord Warrick heave a gusty huff, but after darting him another fleeting look, decided she'd imagined it. He still faced the window, although he now rested a shoulder against the sill.

Was he to never turn around, the boorish lout? *Thwap* went the hat against his leg.

Waiting for her uncle to speak, she shifted her gaze between Uncle Gideon and Lord Warrick. Her uncle's dark eyebrows were drawn together into a severe line as he studied the viscount. This was not good, no indeed, not good at all. Within the folds of her skirts, she clenched her hands until the tips of her fingers grew numb.

A frown flitted across Uncle Gideon's face before he stood and gave her a kind smile. He spoke plainly. "Vangie, you and Lord Warrick will wed in three days."

"Pardon?" Rounding her eyes in shock, she choked on a gasp. Her attention flew to the viscount.

He'd turned and now lounged against the window sill, his ankles and arms casually crossed. However, he was anything but relaxed. He stared at her, his eyes hooded, his striking features blank. His hat remained in his hand, only now it rested on his folded arm. A shadowy discoloration marred his lordship's cheek, near his eye.

That hadn't been there last night.

The sunlight behind him speared his shadow the length of the room. The distorted silhouette was oddly disturbing. Almost ominous.

She shuddered and rubbed her hands the length of her arms wishing she'd donned her cashmere shawl. Her gaze meshed with his, and she recognized an answering spark of anguish. And anger. That *had* been there last night.

His tail's lashing.

She suppressed the hysterical laugh bubbling from her throat at the absurd thought. Her mind refused to believe what she heard. "I'm sorry, Uncle Gideon. I must have misheard you. Would you please repeat what you said?"

"You heard me, Vangie" he gently said.

He cannot be serious. She peered at him, seeking even a nuance of humor. "Surely you jest, although I don't find this the least amusing, I assure you."

When his expression remained unchanged, a shrieking alarm sounded in Vangie's brain. Throwing caution and manners aside, she cried, "Lord Warrick couldn't have agreed to such a match. We only met yester eve. We're complete strangers."

Lord Warrick spoke then. "It's no jest. We shall wed—two days after the morrow." His modulated tone couldn't conceal his scorching fury.

She swung her head around to gape at him.

No. No. This is a cruel joke.

He'd lowered his arms and slapped his hat against his thigh again.

Vangie's focus dipped to his hand. His white-knuckled fist crushed the hat's brim. He must have noticed her gawking. He tossed the ruined accessory onto a nearby armchair and curled his lips into a mocking sneer.

Faith, but he was in a foul temper today. Or was that his typical attitude? Had last night's courteous behavior been the anomaly? Dragging her gaze from Lord Warrick, she sought Uncle Gideon's eyes. Did sympathy shimmer there? And mayhap compassion? To be sure, but she also glimpsed something more foreboding in their depths.

"Uncle Gideon?" She heard the panic in her shaky voice. Hated herself for sounding weak, but the truth was, she was utterly terrified.

He frowned and rubbed his chin with his thumb and forefinger. "What do you remember of last evening. After you became ill?" He rested his hip on the polished front of his desk.

She licked dry lips before sneaking a peek at Lord Warrick. He remained statue-like, his face devoid of emotion, except for his hostile pewter eyes. "Not much, I fear. I felt unwell, and Lord Warrick assisted me from the ballroom. I fainted then awoke in the lady's retiring room."

Blowing out a lengthy sigh, Uncle Gideon eyed Lord Warrick. "You're quite sure you won't have a seat?"

"Quite."

Abrupt. Cold. Final.

Uncle Gideon crossed the carpet to sit beside her. Holding himself stiffly erect, he cleared his throat. "Vangie, you and the viscount were discovered in, ah…an indiscrete circumstance." His contemplative gaze swept his lordship once more. "Though after questioning him, I am inclined to believe the entire incident was most innocent."

Lord Warrick raised his chestnut eyebrows, his mouth slanting into a jeering grin. "I'm grateful for your confidence, sir, I'm sure."

Uncle Gideon ignored him. Vangie could not. Her heart quickened in a peculiar mixture of consternation and relief. Consternation caused by Lord Warrick's dark temper, and relief that the situation wasn't dire after all.

"That's what this is about? My fainting and Lord Warrick helping me?" A heavy yoke lifted from her shoulders. "Faith, it's all a simple misunderstanding, thank goodness." Laughter bubbled to the surface again, but she only allowed her lips to tilt upward a smidgeon. It wouldn't do to skip around the room in celebration, grinning like a jingle-brained ninny. "Surely, there's no need for matrimony if we," she met each of their gazes in turn, "agree nothing unseemly occurred."

"I concur," the viscount said frostily, a scowl pulling his mouth downward.

Vangie's smile broadened.

Thank God. Thank God. Thank God.

"No indeed. No need at all." Her relief was heady, and not even Lord Warrick's dour expression could wipe the smile from her lips. Gracious, but the man was Friday-faced most of the time. She'd nothing but pity for the unfortunate woman who did eventually find herself his viscountess, poor wretch.

"Nonetheless," Uncle Gideon said, his voice oddly strangled, as if he couldn't bear to say the words. "I'm afraid several peeresses saw you in a partially unclothed state, and as deplorable as it is, my dear, they are spreading the most contemptible tales."

Lifting her chin, she shrugged. "Let them gossip. I know the truth."

He gave her hand a small squeeze. "Vangie, I promised your mother

I'd protect you should anything happen to her."

"Yes, but—"

He raised his hand, cutting off her objection. "To salvage your reputation, I must insist this wedding take place." He slid a cursory glance over Lord Warrick. "By God, if there was *any* other way, I vow I'd take it."

At Uncle Gideon's words, her smile waned, and her head swam dizzily. Lord Warrick's face blurred as a short, sharp pain speared her temple. Raising her hand, she rubbed the spot. *Oh dear, not another one.* For a moment dread gripped her.

No, no buzzing in her ears or zig zagging aura plagued her. It had only been a nasty pang.

"But *nothing* happened." Her gaze riveted on Uncle Gideon, she blindly reached over to grope the carved arm of the settee. "I'm sure Lord Warrick in no way acted inappropriately. He didn't do anything. He wouldn't." She dared a sidelong peep at his lordship. One dark eyebrow hied upward, mocking and condemning, and she quickly averted her eyes at his stony, unsettling stare. "He's not the type of gentleman who'd…" She trailed off in embarrassment.

Uncle Gideon shook his head, kindness and regret crinkling the corners of his eyes. "It matters not. The damage is already done."

"Lord Warrick did not molest me while I was unconscious." Vangie twisted to look fully at the viscount. She knew beyond a doubt what she said was absolute truth.

His eyes warmed the merest bit. "Thank you, for that."

Ignoring the heat sweeping across her face, she pointed a trembling finger at him while looking at her uncle. "He is as outraged and opposed to this union as I am."

The viscount was as much a victim as she was. The knowledge brought her no respite, however.

Sighing, Uncle Gideon pinched the bridge of his nose. "He has agreed—"

"Is that what you're calling it?" Lord Warrick gave a sarcastic snort. "I'd prefer coercion. Extortion. Blackmail."

"Why?" Vangie interrupted. "Why are we to be forced into a union neither of us wants—marriage to a complete stranger?" Her throat clogged, and the tears she struggled to contain rendered her voice a rasping whisper. "This is unjust. Nothing—absolutely nothing—untoward occurred." She fisted her hands in her lap in frustrated agitation. "Lord Warrick committed no offense. He acted the perfect gentleman."

Compassion simmered in Uncle Gideon's eyes. "Be that as it may, dear, you shall wed."

Vangie stiffened. "And, what if I refuse?" She drew herself upward and squared her shoulders. She was no spiritless ninny. Unflinching, she met his gaze straight on and jutted her chin out in defiance. "I refuse to marry him."

Ian almost smiled, and he pressed his lips together, mashing his tongue against the back of his teeth to keep them from curving upward. Despite himself, he admired Miss Caruthers' fiery spirit. Her eyes had narrowed and blue sparks had flown from them when she'd defied her uncle.

Ludicrous though it was, her adamant refusal chafed. Not that he wanted to wed the uppity chit. He most assuredly did not. But did she think her prospects so great, she could reject a viscount? With her breeding, she wasn't likely to receive a better offer.

Why do I care?

He didn't of course. Odd too, that she'd not once mentioned her innocence, but had repeatedly declared his. He shifted to better view her, the movement causing another blinding explosion of pain in his head.

Bloody hell.

He closed his eyes until the agony passed. He really oughtn't to have imbibed so freely last night. The consequences of his indulging only worsened his already disagreeable mood this morning. Or mayhap, it was last night's facer causing the unrelenting pounding in his skull.

Half opening his eyes, he considered Miss Caruthers. Even upset, she was inarguably stunning. He allowed his gaze to travel from her face to her heaving breasts. The flowery yellow frock with its rows of flounces became her. So did the ribbon tied at her nape.

What would that ebony mass look like draped around her shoulders? Her rounded hips? What would it feel like to slip his hands through the silky midnight tresses?

His attention drifted to her pale face, registering the rebellion and distress she made no attempt to conceal. With focused determination, Ian repressed his sensual musings and hardened his heart. Why wasn't she screaming her innocence? Screeching about her virtue?

Because she doesn't have any to claim, that's why.

Miss Caruther's innocent beauty concealed a wanton's heart. Most likely, she was unwilling to curb her promiscuous ways quite so soon. Wasn't prepared to settle for the confines of marriage yet, to limit her favors to her husband's bed. Perhaps she was one of those women whose carnal appetites couldn't be satisfied by one man.

The notion brought an angry scowl to Ian's face and a sickening jolt to his gut.

Well, she'd best prepare herself. He'd have no strumpet to wife. He could do nothing about her immoral behavior before their marriage, but devil take it, he'd curtail her fast ways afterward. She'd not cuckold him. The moment they were wed, it was off to Somersfield with her—under lock and key if need be.

At his frown, Miss Caruthers renewed her efforts. She shifted on the settee to face Stapleton. "I shan't be forced into marriage. I truly shall refuse, Uncle."

"No, you shan't," Stapleton said firmly. "Already your name is being cast around—"

"Oh, posh." She waved a hand back and forth as if clearing cigar smoke from the air. "The gossips always have someone's name on their poisonous tongues. *Puri Daj* says, an evildoer listens to wicked lips, and a liar gives ear to a mischievous tongue."

Who or what, in God's holy name, was a Puri Daj?

"Miss Caruthers…?" Ian wished to speedily put an end to further discourse.

She sent him a surprised glance. Did the tiniest bit of curiosity shimmer in her sapphire-eyed gaze?

"Though apt, that truth is of little help to us." He strode to stand before her, forcing her to tilt her head to look at him. She shook her head and opened her mouth, no doubt to argue her point, but he hurried on, done with the niceties. Far past time she heard the vile truth her uncle hedged speaking. "The scandalmongers are spreading appalling falsehoods, grossly exaggerating the incident in the retiring room."

She pulled a face. "I'm not surprised, but neither do I care."

Flexing his injured hand, he ran the fingers of his other across the bruised knuckles before raising his eyes to meet hers. "Depending on whom you hear the account from, we've either been discovered in a licentious embrace, or caught naked-as-robins, openly copulating on one of the divans in full view of all."

Her jaw dropped open, and she slapped a palm across her mouth. Her eyes growing wide as saucers, the last vestige of color drained from her face.

"I'm portrayed as a scoundrel, an unconscionable knave." He wasn't through, however. Rage and frustration propelled him onward. "While you, Miss Caruthers, have been relegated to the ranks of a lady-bird, a light o' love." His calculated finish was cruel and crude, "A common strumpet."

"That's outside of enough, Warrick!" Stapleton thundered. "Stubble it, else I decide to withdraw my offer and my niece's hand. I *can* find her a more suitable match."

For a fortune—to an ancient, lecherous podger.

Ian had ruined her, albeit not intentionally. He'd only meant to curb her fast behavior, not destroy her reputation beyond repair.

She'd likely never marry if he didn't make things right—unless her uncle bought her a husband. Someone either desperate or decrepit, for no decent man would have her now. Sucking in a gusty breath, he fisted his hands until the nails cut into his palms. He met Stapleton's furious glare far calmer than he felt. Ian wouldn't escape the parson's mousetrap, and they both knew it.

His damnable sense of honor—even for a Cyprian as unworthy as Miss Caruthers— demanded he wed her. That, and the threats posed by Stapleton and his peers. They were a formidable lot. One he couldn't, one he daren't, oppose. Not if he didn't want to face financial and social ruin.

He couldn't do that to Charlotte.

Hell, with Prinny's disapproval and retribution looming overhead, he was already halfway to ostracism. Stapleton could—*would*—destroy him if he didn't make an honest woman of the chit. Her uncle had been brutally clear about that.

Head canted, Ian considered his soon-to-be bride.

Miss Caruthers struggled to retain her composure. Her eyes drifted closed, her thick lashes fanning the tops of her ivory cheeks. A plump tear slipped from the corner of her eye, trailing over her smooth face as she bit her trembling bottom lip.

His chest tightened involuntarily. He hated it when women cried, loathed how helpless it made him feel. He much preferred they rail at him, most especially this woman. He didn't want to pity her. He shot a sidelong glance at Stapleton.

Her uncle glared daggers at him.

Releasing a breath of air, Ian strove for gentleness he was far from feeling. "You understand why we *must* wed, Vangie? Why we're permitted no other option?"

Wounded sapphire eyes, framed by spiky lashes and pooled with tears, met his. He kept his expression carefully bland. If she even suspected he suffered as much as she, she'd use the knowledge against him the first opportunity she was given. Her kind always did.

His wrath was another matter. It created a barrier few men, let alone women, dared cross. Even so, self-recrimination gnawed at him. He'd allowed his fury to rule his tongue. His rashness changed nothing, succeeding only in further lowering Stapleton's estimation of him—something he could ill-afford at present.

Gripping his coat lapels, Ian resisted the urge to check his pocket for the ring he'd soon slip on Miss Caruthers' hand. The vows were as good as spoken and spewing his frustration in a verbal tirade served no purpose. It mattered not that she acted like a flirtatious, loose-moraled *demi-rep.* He daren't voice his contempt in front of her uncle. Even he had limits.

Needing to put distance between them, he crossing to the hearth and kicked a stray coal into the glowing fire. Resting an arm atop the cherrywood mantel, he stared into the flames. They merrily chased one another, over and around the crackling wood, like impish pixies, as if they hadn't any cares in the world.

"It does no good to protest, to proclaim our innocence," he said, his voice taking on a harsh edge. "In the eyes of the *ton*, you're ruined. Disgraced. And only I can rescue you from a life of degradation."

"No!" Devastation etched her beautiful face. She mouthed, "No" again, shaking her head in denial. A raven curl slid free of the sunny ribbon confining it.

Laying the blame solely on her was unfair. Yet being coerced into a loveless marriage, something he vowed he'd never do, galled bitterly. Unlike his father, he'd intended to have a degree of fondness for his viscountess. To support his debauched lifestyle, his sire had married three times with deliberate intent; to increase his coffers and expand his holdings. And he chose wealthy, evermore dowdy and desperate women well past the first bloom of youth, to meet that end.

Two of his wives, including Ian's mother, had died in childbirth as

Roger strove to produce more heirs for the family lineage. Lucinda, his third wife, escaped that fate by barring his father permanently from her bed the instant she became pregnant. Only three—no it was but two now—of the eight offspring his father had sired yet lived. With Geoff's death, Ian became the last remaining male in his line. The very last.

Confound it all to hell.

He leveled Miss Caruthers a fuming glare. He'd have to beget an heir on her. A woman he could barely conceal his disdain for. The physical act wasn't what he objected to. No, she was a tempting morsel and even as furious as he was, he could appreciate her many attributes. He sank his gaze to her full bosom. *A very tempting morsel.* He'd no complaints there—none at all.

Nonetheless, he held her responsible for his father's and brother's deaths, to say nothing of the *on dit* concerning her previous indecorous behavior. If even partially true, she might as well be a member of the muslin company, particularly given her Romani heritage. Lest he curl his lip into a snarl, he forced his attention to the crackling fire and stifled his emotions.

He was a trained soldier, by God. This marriage was simply another battle—another campaign he would win with strategy and logic.

A log fell, sending a flurry of sparks spiraling up the chimney in wild disarray. A few struggled, sputtering out before being sucked up the flue. Their end was predetermined, as was his.

Bit by bit, he released a pent-up breath. He hadn't expected love in his marriage, but mutual respect and admiration would've been sufficient. He doubted he was capable of truly loving. That emotion left one too vulnerable. He'd never experienced anything beyond a warm regard for a feminine companion, even Amelia. Mayhap, he was incapable of feeling the much-touted sentiment.

Just as well. He'd seen what love did to sensible men. It turned them into sentimental chuckle-heads with more hair than wit. He supposed the same could be said of honor. Men did any number of ridiculous things in the name of honor. *Geoff had.* And Ian, more the fool, was no exception.

Turning away from the frolicking flames, he faced her. Linking his hands behind him, he welcomed the piercing heat of the blaze. It matched the fire searing his soul. He repeated, "Miss Caruthers, we've no choice but to wed."

The bitterness weighting Lord Warrick's voice caused Vangie's breath to hitch, his raw pain ripping at her heart. Her mind numb with shocked dismay and justified anger, she stopped protesting. An unholy ache gnawed in her stomach, and with each in-drawn breath, a fresh stab of pain lanced her heart. Clutching her middle, she swallowed against the nausea tickling her throat.

Was she never to be allowed any happiness? Never permitted her own choices? Would she always have to submit to the will and whims of others?

Sighing a trembling breath, she fixed her gaze on her slipper toe, avoiding Lord Warrick's withering glare. He was right of course. She'd known what the outcome would be, must be, but she'd hoped—no prayed—otherwise.

"This is grossly unfair," she whispered, more to herself than the men in the room. How could she bear this?

Toying with the soft fringe edging the silk pillow scrunched beside her, Vangie stifled a ragged sob. Her throat ached from the effort. She swallowed hard against the sting, then swallowed again as a cry of protest welled up, trying to force its way past her compressed lips. She clasped her hands together in a silent prayer. Surely God wouldn't allow this injustice to take place.

Lord Warrick could walk away from the alleged indiscretion, couldn't he? Rakehells who cared nothing for their honor did so quite often, in fact. Her reputation, however, was tarnished beyond repair. To all intents and purposes, she'd been despoiled, at least verbally. Without an immediate marriage, she'd no hope for anything but a lifetime of condemnation and malevolent gossip.

If she were a woman of means, she'd refuse the match. She'd travel, paint, do…do whatever she wished. *Be free at last.* But as things stood, she was a penniless orphan. Hands gripped tight, she closed her eyes against the anguish tearing at her heart and mind.

Lord Warrick sacrificed himself for her; a woman he didn't know. It spoke of his character, of his decency and honor. She should feel gratitude—supposed somewhere in the recesses of her heart she did. Nevertheless, the only emotions she could summon at present were desolation and despair, tempered with a good deal of horror. She sucked in an unsteady breath. He would never forgive her for being forced into marriage. Not like this. How could he?

Would she be able to forgive Uncle Gideon? Perhaps, but not anytime soon.

Marriage without love. *There are worse fates.* Not for a woman with Romani blood running through their veins. A woman who, from girlhood, prayed she would make a love-match.

Uncle Gideon stood, offering a smile somewhere between sorrow and encouragement. "I hope someday you'll understand why I insist on this course, Vangie, and be able to forgive me." He shifted his attention to Lord Warrick, including him in the request as well.

The viscount met her uncle's gaze squarely, though no answering warmth lit his eyes. Instead, his mouth curved into a contemptuous arc. Despite the roaring fire, she shivered and sank deeper into the settee's cushions.

Uncle Gideon strode to the door. He grasped the brass handle before he turned around. His solemn gaze shifted between her and his lordship for a disquieting moment. "Lord Warrick, please, do proceed with the proposal. Vangie, *you will* accept his offer." He opened the door. "I'll allow you privacy." He slipped from the room, closing the door behind him with a firm, final-sounding *thunk.*

Vangie sat stunned. *Run*, everything in her cried. *Escape. Flee.* Why then did she remain inexplicably fixed and mute as her uncle exited the room, leaving her to the viscount's mercy. Or lack thereof?

Except for the purple finches' muted scolding in the lilac bush beside the sunlit window, the room remained tomb-silent. Death had indeed visited today. With the decree she must marry Lord Warrick, her dreams had died. The demise of her heart's desire left a bitter stench in her nostrils, and she twitched her nose, mashing her lips together.

She refused to lift her gaze from her clenched hands. A single unkind look or word from him and the last vestige of her self-control would crumble. She felt his gaze upon her, and it unnerved her to no end. The man truly should acquire some decorum. Holding her breath to calm her stampeding heart, she listened to the viscount's steady breathing.

He rustled about, and she started when he sat beside her on the settee. His cologne, crisp and woodsy, wafted past her nostrils. Without a word, he reached over and pried her icy, clenched hands apart. He slid a heavy ring onto her third finger. He must've had it in his pocket.

She stared at the jeweled band. The sign of his ownership. Smaller and prettier than iron shackles, nevertheless, the circle signified imprisonment. "It's warm," she muttered. So was his hand cradling hers.

His fingers, the nails neatly trimmed, were sun-darkened, and a bit calloused too. Her regard lingered on his injured hand. From beneath her lashes, she stole a covert glance at the door. No, Uncle Gideon wasn't unscrupulous. He wouldn't have hired thugs— "Those cuts and bruises weren't there last night. Whatever occurred after we parted company?"

Eyes downcast and a muscle ticking in his jaw, he didn't answer.

"Have you engaged in fisticuffs?" Vangie winced inwardly. She sounded like a harping wife already.

He remained silent, though he retained his hold on her hand.

Vangie raised her eyes until she met his disquieting gaze. She tried to read his mind. Did he attempt to read hers as well?

He abruptly released her hand and stood. He spun on his heels and left the room without uttering a word.

She remained immobile a long while after he'd gone, gazing blankly through the beveled window panes framed by heavy scarlet and ivory pleated coverings. The morning sun's golden rays illuminated tiny dust bits floating about the room.

In a small courtyard beyond the window, a spot of vivid emerald grass celebrated spring. The lush blossoms of pink and peach peonies burst forth in glorious color. Beneath them, jeweled-colored petunias and geraniums teased and tickled their neighbor's leggy stems.

She appreciated none of it. Her mind reeled, silently protesting in disbelief and wounded rebellion. "I'm to be married—in three days." She spoke the words aloud, trying to convince herself of the awful reality.

Clenching and unclenching her hands in her lap, the awkward weight of the foreign object on her third finger reminded her of her fate. Vangie swung her attention to the closed door. Odd, she'd almost expected his lordship to be there, staring at her with his penetrating, unfathomable quick-silver gaze.

It was as if he could see straight into her thoughts, her soul, yet he kept his emotions shuttered, barring her from viewing any portion of his true self. Clasping her hands again, Vangie felt the ring he'd placed on her finger less than a half hour past. She stared at the emerald-cut sapphire framed by a double row of diamonds. It was a brilliant ring, its fit a trifle loose. She turned it round her finger.

She laughed, a sad hiccupping rasp, saturated with unshed tears. "I should've heeded *Puri Daj's* warning. Should've run as fast as my feet would carry me when I saw him, *the black panther*," she murmured in self-castigation.

Yet, how was she to know her life would irreversibly change because of one innocent dance? A solitary tear slipped down her cheek.

After slowly pushing to her feet, she wandered to the window. A hummingbird moth flitted from flower to flower, greedy for the sweet nectar hidden in the blooms. Resting her head against the warm glass, she frowned then shuddered.

She stood precisely where *he'd* stood as both their lives were shattered. Lifting her face, she allowed a thin sunbeam to bathe her in its warmth. The golden ray gave her strength and hope.

A clock chiming in another part of the house brought Vangie from her reverie. Her stomach growled, reminding her she'd not broken her fast. She angled to stare at the door once more. She wasn't wed yet and, by God, she wasn't marrying *anyone* against her will.

8

Climbing from the curricle, Ian surveyed the weathered two-story brick building. A black-lettered sign, hanging from two hooks, *Joseph Dehring, Solicitor*, swayed and rattled in the damp breeze. He lifted his pocket watch from his waistcoat and flicked it open.

Four minutes to three. He wasn't late. *Hell and blast.* This once he cursed his punctuality. He rather liked the idea of Stapleton stewing a bit at his tardiness, fretting whether he would call at the appointed time. Or, appear at all.

Ian had been sorely tempted not to, truth to tell. Damn his insufferable honor. And damn Stapleton's threats. Tucking the timepiece away, he climbed the steps to the entrance. Although the appointment's purpose was to sign the marriage agreement, he intended to try one final time to extract himself from the compulsory nuptials.

He made no effort to hide his scowl as he was ushered into a large office. The skinny clerk was so nervous, he didn't announce Ian's arrival, but shuffled backward out the door the moment he crossed the threshold. No doubt his glower contributed to the fellow's ineptness.

Ian quickly surveyed the room as he removed his topper and tucked it beneath his arm.

Overflowing shelves filled one entire wall. The pleasant odor of old leather-bound books scented the air. A long since abandoned cobweb dangled from the topmost corner of one of the high shelves. A fern, sorely in need of water, drooped before a tall window.

Stapleton, and a man Ian presumed was Mr. Dehring, spoke quietly whilst examining a pile of papers atop a mammoth double desk. At his entrance, they stopped speaking and lifted their gazes.

He strode to the desk. "Please tell me you don't mean to see this farce through, Stapleton? You, yourself acknowledge no impropriety occurred."

"Ahem." Mr. Dehring cleared his throat. "Why don't I give you gentlemen a moment?"

He slid a handful of official-looking documents to Stapleton before making a hasty retreat.

After the door closed, Stapleton waved a hand at the papers before him. "If you'll examine these, my lord, you shall find I've bestowed upon Evangeline a generous settlement, and—"

"I don't want your niece's marriage settlement any more than I want this damned marriage." Ian couldn't even bring himself to say her name. He'd been furious for the past pair of days and was the first to admit he wasn't the least interested in being agreeable or civil.

Stapleton leaned forward resting his elbows on the desk and formed a steeple with his fingertips. Leveling him a lengthy stare, he tapped his fingers together several times.

Ian supposed the keen perusal might unnerve a lesser man, but Stapleton's attempt at intimidation only irritated him more. He didn't cow easily. Precisely why Stapleton resorted to the tactics he had two nights ago. Arching a mocking eyebrow, he returned the bold perusal.

At once, Stapleton's fierce gaze became unyielding. "You cannot be absolved from responsibility regarding *this farce*." He pointed a well-manicured finger. "You ought to have gone for help at once and not taken it upon yourself to loosen Vangie's stays."

Guilt prodded Ian, none too gently.

Relaxing against the high-backed leather chair, Stapleton folded his arms across his chest, and continued, acid permeating his tone. "Had you done so, her reputation would've remained intact. The gossipmongers wouldn't be bandying her name about with malicious glee and," he lowered his hands to grip the chair arms, disgust written across his face, "taking undue pleasure in her humiliation."

Fiend seize it, he made valid points.

But she couldn't breathe.

Ian blew out a frustrated sigh, though he remained mulishly silent. He'd argue that truth no more. The difficult task proved keeping his lips sealed regarding the damage Miss Caruthers had done to her *own* good standing prior to his making her unfortunate acquaintance.

He forced himself to stubble it. Stapleton would deny such offensive allegations and most likely call him out for voicing them. The result of such a duel was predictable. Ian was a crack shot. He'd no intention of killing a decent man over an immoral tart.

Too bad the same couldn't be said of Geoff. The devil seize it, why did he have to think of Geoff at this moment? His mood was black enough.

Straightening, Stapleton nudged the documents across the scratched and stained desk. "Please, Warrick, do take a seat, and see if the terms meet with your approval."

Ian dropped his hat atop the desk when what he wanted to do was throw it in Stapleton's face. Teeth clamped, he yanked off his gloves and tossed them beside the hat. Sinking into a chair, he eyed the papers before lifting them with the same enthusiasm he would a fresh horse turd.

Perusing the settlement, he barely concealed his astonishment. *Fifty thousand pounds; a stable full of prime horseflesh; numerous pieces of jewelry; and the Sheffleton Cottage.* He shook his head. Cottage, his arse. Sheffleton was a thriving two-hundred-acre estate. He should've been thrilled at the generous dowry Stapleton bestowed upon his niece, but Ian wanted no part of it.

It amounted to bribery, pure and simple.

He felt like a fancy man, being paid to take Evangeline Caruthers to wife. A wife he didn't want. A wife not of his choosing and one he'd *never* have selected for himself. A wife he could never like, much less love.

He sighed, swallowing a vulgar oath. He was as good as hung, and what was more, Stapleton damn well knew it. At least the wench was pleasing to the eye. He'd no doubt she'd also be a pleasure to bed. *If* he could move beyond the men who'd sampled her before him.

The door opened after a quick rap. Mr. Dehring poked his balding head—and only his head—inside the room. His gaze—eyes magnified behind wire-rimmed glasses—darted between Stapleton and Ian. He curled his lips into a thin smile. The diminutive man didn't know if it was safe to come in.

Ian quirked an eyebrow at Stapleton. *Well*, he silently challenged.

Stapleton angled his dark head and gestured with two fingers. "Come in, Joseph. You need to witness Warrick's signature."

Mr. Dehring hurried into the room, another pile of papers beneath his arm.

Waving the foolscap he held, Ian shook his head. He tossed the document onto the desk, mindful of the affronted glance Mr. Dehring shot him for his irreverence. "I want nothing to do with your money, Stapleton. Transfer the entire settlement to your niece as her irrevocable property."

"Come now, Warrick. Don't be hasty," Stapleton said, though he couldn't quite disguise his astonishment. "Somersfield is in disrepair, and the new Arabian bloodline you've invested in would set back a man with pockets much deeper than yours."

Ian glared, again stifling the stream of obscenities thrumming in his throat. "Bloody hell, does your interference know no bounds? What other business of mine have you been prying into?"

Stapleton crossed his legs, lounging against his chair, completely at ease once more. "There's the rather stiff penalty Prinny's assessed."

Ian curled his toes in his boots until they protested in pain. What he truly wanted to do was slam his fist atop the desk—or into Stapleton's much too smug face. "That amercement," he said with a calm deliberation, though fury tunneled through his veins, "is *none* of your concern."

"There you're wrong, Warrick." Stapleton's menacing mien had returned. "Anything affecting Vangie is my concern. A portion of her marriage settlement would certainly soothe the Prince Regent, don't you think?"

God help him from launching himself across the desk and grabbing his throat. "You know nothing of it."

"I know your brother killed one of Prinny's favorites."

Smug arse.

"Geoff was…" How could Ian explain the duel?

By-the-by, Stapleton, my brother found your niece engaging in a ribald dalliance with the Duke of Paneswort on the veranda. Poor gullible, infatuated pup that Geoff was, it appeared to him she was being set upon against her will. Naturally, he was honor-bound to call out the duke.

Or so Lucinda had ranted to Ian when she'd told him the cause of the duel.

Against Miss Caruthers' will? And geese lay golden eggs.

He'd heard men at Armstrongs' ball boasting about sampling her charms, even if her uncle hadn't.

Staring past the sooty-paned window behind Stapleton, Ian rested his gaze on the scarcely-visible ship masts lining London's harbor. Geoff had wanted to join His Majesty's Navy.

Father had soundly forbidden it. With one son already in His Majesty's service, the risk to the viscountcy was too great. Despite his sire's strenuous objections, Ian had used his inheritance from his maternal grandmother to buy a captain's commission.

If he hadn't joined the army to escape his father's control, his brother would be off safely sailing on a ship somewhere. Geoff wouldn't have attended that fateful ball or defended the unworthy Miss Caruthers' reputation. Guilt, a putrefied black knot, settled in Ian's gut.

He couldn't even explain Geoff's role in the duel without besmirching Miss Caruthers to her uncle. Was the man truly completely ignorant of her fast behavior?

Ian sent Stapleton a quick glance. It wasn't entirely impossible. Half the peerage was indebted to the man in one way or another. None dared risk his wrath. He possessed the ability to single-handedly ruin titled lords. So flush were his pockets, Stapleton had even extended several thousand pounds to the Prince Regent.

Stapleton Shipping and Supplies had amassed a colossal fortune. The third son of a viscount himself, Stapleton was the envy of the *ton*: well-heeled, full of juice to be exact, and well-bred. He was nearly untouchable. Only a disastrous scandal could shake his position.

A scandal such as the one Ian was party to.

He forced down a snarl. No doubt great care had been taken to keep the whispers about his coquette of a niece from reaching Stapleton's ears.

He looked up, catching Ian's scrutiny. Something unreadable flickered in his eyes. "Have we an agreement then?" Stapleton paused then inched the ink and quill across the desk. "I'll pay the amercement too. Consider it a wedding gift."

Fury ripped through Ian, and he planted both hands on the desk's worn edge. He bent forward, rigid with rage. "Hear me, Stapleton, and hear me well. I take care of my own. I don't want a single groat from you!"

Stapleton cocked his head to the side. His eyes held that odd glint again. A slow smile curved the corners of his mouth. "So be it." He waved his hand at the solicitor, before sweeping it across the documents. "Joseph, make whatever changes Warrick deems fit."

Ian fought the urge to sneer his thanks. What was Stapleton grinning about, the pompous twit? Ian sank his teeth into the inside of his cheek. Damn but he wanted to tell the ass to go bugger himself.

At Ian's insistence, Mr. Dehring amended several clauses of the contract. As the solicitor—his spindly fingers permanently ink-stained—made the meticulous changes he insisted upon, Ian curled his lips in contempt. Ridiculous practice that—paying a man to take a woman to wife. He didn't care if it was what society did. He wanted no part of it. He'd be no better than his father if he accepted Miss Caruthers' marriage settlement.

And by all the saints, I am not my father.

He picked up the quill, fingering the goose feather's stiff tip. "Tell me, why bestow such an enormous settlement?"

The bequeathment made no sense. Was it because of her gypsy blood? Stapleton had already offered him her hand, and Ian had been forced to accept it—had given his word he'd marry the wench unless Stapleton terminated the agreement. The man didn't have to endow his niece at all.

"She's not even your daughter," Ian murmured, gauging Stapleton's reaction.

The older man paused, papers in hand. His eyes narrowed, his nostrils flaring.

Ian almost grinned. Oh, that had riled him. Interesting. Yes, very interesting indeed.

"Perhaps not in name, but Vangie is every bit as much my daughter as Yvette. I'd have taken her into my home in an instant, but an unfortunate stipulation in her father's will prohibited my doing so."

What kind of a stipulation could thwart a man of Stapleton's means and power? Ian eyed him a moment longer then dropped his gaze to the papers before him. Best to see it finished. He dipped the quill in the bottle of ink. *Blister it.* He was done over. The noose was knotted, the rope stretched tight. There was no escape. The gallows had him.

With bold, angry strokes, he signed the contract. Afterward, he tossed the quill onto the desk, leaving the solicitor to sprinkle sand across the wet ink.

Mr. Dehring frowned his disapproval and *tsked* as he rushed to wipe the ink droplets off the desktop before they left a permanent stain.

Ian rose, and yanking on his gloves, met Stapleton's irritated gaze. Pointing at the drying paper, he said, "You know this compulsory marriage won't restore your niece's reputation any more than it will halt the chatterboxes' tongues."

Stapleton smiled then, a self-satisfied grin that crinkled the corners of his blue eyes. "Perhaps not, but I've recruited several powerful, influential peers and their wives to spread their own *on dit.* Even as we speak, they're busy repairing the damage you caused." Levering to his feet, his expression hardened to steel. "No doubt you're aware how far my hand reaches when necessary."

The merest hint of a threat laced his words.

"Indeed," Ian snapped, slapping his topper on his head before turning on his boot-heels and striding from the room. Another minute and he'd have been tempted to plant Stapleton a facer. Or shake his hand. Even in his anger, Ian could appreciate a great strategist. The man was shrewd. Diabolically shrewd.

Running down the stairs, Ian breathed in London's stagnant air. God, he couldn't wait to leave the putrid city for the countryside. He leapt into the curricle. Balanced on the buttoned, black leatherette seat, he tooled the horse the length of Red Croft Street. Another grudging smile curved his mouth at the colossal fallacy Stapleton likely spread to preserve his niece's character.

Why, there's nothing gossip-worthy at all.

Surely you're aware Miss Caruthers and Lord Warrick are practically neighbors in Northumberland. They've known each other for a number of years and are secretly betrothed. Naturally, that's why he only asked her to dance at the ball.

The wedding was planned for late summer, but due to the recent tragic loss of his father and brother, all the details have yet to be finalized. Yes indeed, it's a simple matter to procure a special license and move the wedding date forward.

What balderdash. Was there a ninnyhammer gullible enough to believe that claptrap? Ian's face split into a grin. Indeed. Most of *le bon ton*.

Turning the equipage down another cobblestone street, he made for Berkley Square. He'd yet to inform his staff that on the morrow they'd have a new mistress. His pulse quickened despite himself. Most likely, his staff had already heard tattle of the marriage. What else might they have heard? A January plunge in the Thames couldn't have cooled his ardor any faster.

He supposed it was acceptable, even expected, for one's betrothed to see to their intended's personal needs when an ill-fated situation presented itself. While some would argue he shouldn't have been in the ladies' retiring room no matter the cause, others could make an equally sound argument it was his duty, as Miss Caruthers' intended, to see to her well-being.

Stapleton was ensuring that particular tidbit was planted in the right ears. As the tale circulated among elite circles, eyebrows would be raised of course, and Ian knew those hoping for a juicy scandal would be compelled to settle for something a mite less succulent.

What utter rot. The *ton* believed what was convenient to believe.

Now he was in a devil's own scrape, soon to be leg-shackled to a flirtatious jade.

He snorted his contempt and maneuvered the curricle around a stable cart buzzing with flies and piled high with filthy straw and horse manure. The crack of the curricle's wheel giving way rent the air. *Bloody hell. What next?* The horse stumbled, and Ian was hurled from his seat, crashing headlong into the manure cart.

9

On the eve of her wedding, Vangie lingered before the closed door to Uncle Gideon's study. She had a plan. Sucking in a calming breath, she rapped sharply upon the heavy panel.

"Enter."

Her shoulders squared, she marched into the room prepared to do battle. Halting before his desk, she scanned her uncle's face. A lone lamp sitting atop his desk lit the room. In the muted light, his expression appeared guarded, though warmth shown in his eyes. Encouraged, she relaxed her shoulders.

"You've need of something, Vangie?" He put the quill aside.

Wasting no time, she came directly to the point. "Uncle Gideon, please reconsider this union." She couldn't bring herself to say, *my* marriage. Searching his compassionate eyes, she played her trump card. "I want love in my marriage, Uncle. Love like my father and mother shared. Love like you and Aunt Adélaid feel for each other."

He sighed, his mouth thinning the merest bit.

Filling her lungs, she challenged him. "Would you deny me that happiness?"

His lips curved in a poignant smile. "My dear, I'd like nothing better than for you to marry for love, but after the affair at the Armstrongs', if you don't marry Lord Warrick, it's unlikely you'll wed at all." He looked away and straightened a short stack of papers. The shadows obscured his face, but he seemed tense. "The *ton* has a long arm, and a far longer reaching memory."

"I don't care about the *haut ton.* I can stay in the country. I'll never venture to London again." She gestured wildly. "I'll…I'll go away, perhaps live with the Roma. Or…or perhaps I'll go to the colonies."

He set the papers aside before meeting her gaze. Torment darkened his eyes and etched deep grooves into his forehead. He extended a hand, palm upward. "Vangie—"

"I've no desire to marry someone of a high station." She heard the desperation in her voice, but she must make him understand. His next words doused the remnant of hope in her heart.

"Dear, the scandal combined with your heritage—"

Vangie's jaw sagged. If he'd slapped her, she'd wouldn't have been more hurt or taken aback. An icy blanket of shock engulfed her, and she grasped the edge of the desk to steady herself. "*My heritage*?" she whispered hoarsely.

Uncle Gideon closed his eyes, rubbing a hand across his forehead. He inhaled a deep breath as if struggling for control. "Forgive me. I oughtn't to have said that."

"But that's the real issue isn't it, Uncle Gideon?" She clung to the desk as the truth of his words hit home. "Because of my Romani blood, I've been labeled a *lóoverni*, a…a loose woman." She searched his remorseful gaze with her own, reading the truth mirrored in their depths. Lord Warrick was right.

Uncle Gideon came around the desk and grasped one of her cold hands in his. "As your guardian, I must protect you. And while an arranged marriage isn't ideal, many couples who enter into such unions have been happy."

And many miserable their entire lives.

"Lord Warrick is a decent man, though at present, he's angry at having his hand forced. Give him time, dear. He'll come around."

"Please. I…" Vangie swallowed the lump of anguish clogging her throat. "I don't want to marry him," she whispered.

"Vangie," Uncle Gideon sighed, compassion and exasperation warring in his eyes. "It's not only your honor at stake."

Her breath caught as she stared at him, aghast. Even in the dim light the lines of strain on his face stood out starkly.

Faith, *that* was the true crux of the matter.

Who else's then? His? Aunt Adélaid's? Would her disgrace adversely affect his and Aunt Adélaid's position in society as well as his business dealings?

Undoubtedly.

Yvette's? Could the gossip destroy her chances of a brilliant match? Any match at all?

Possibly.

She couldn't let that happen. Not after everything Yvette, Aunt Adélaid, and Uncle Gideon had done for her. Then there was Lord

Warrick. What would her refusal do to his honor? Was he the type of man who valued honor above all else? She lowered her trembling chin to her chest, struggling for control. Dash it all, he was, of course.

Uncle Gideon squeezed her hand and smiled reassuringly. "It's a most suitable match for you, my dear."

Scalding tears burned her eyes, but she nodded. "It's a better match than I dared hope for," she managed through the tightness constricting her throat. Yet, she'd settle for a haberdasher if he held some degree of affection for her. Instead, she was to wed a man whose only sentiment for her was scornful contempt. How could she bear it?

Her last encounter with Lord Warrick still stung. He hadn't even bothered with the proposal Uncle Gideon expected. Without a proposal and acceptance, could there even be a betrothal? She'd not spoken of his rudeness to her uncle. The humiliation was crushing enough. If others were aware—well, she had endured all the pitying looks and *tsking* a body could tolerate.

Uncle Gideon grasped both her shoulders, bathing her in a loving look. "You've much of my sister in you, Vangie." He kissed her on the forehead, then admonished gently, "The wedding will take place tomorrow. I'll hear no more talk of it."

Pouting and complaining would change nothing. She had her pride. She would not beg. Head bowed, lips compressed, she nodded again. If it were only her reputation at stake, she would refuse the match. The Roma would take her in. But her aunt, uncle, and Yvette had much to lose too. She could not—would not—bring censure upon them.

"That's my girl." Uncle Gideon folded her into a warm, what should've been comforting, hug. Instead, it felt like imprisonment.

Unshed tears blocked Vangie's throat, and she couldn't speak. On a sob, she jerked from his grasp and bolted to her bedchamber. Throwing herself across the bed, she gave way to her heartache and wept until sleep's forgetfulness claimed her.

A bird's chirps woke Vangie the next morning. She opened her eyes, curving her lips at the cheerful streams of sunshine slanting across the bedchamber's rugs and wooden floor. What a glorious day. Stretching her arms overhead, she froze as an unpleasant memory shattered her happiness.

Today she'd wed.

She let her arms fall to her sides with a thump. The smile eased from her face, replaced by a frown of despair. She sat up and hugged her knees to her chest. Her unbound hair circled about her shoulders. Resting her chin on her knees, she considered the pandemonium of the past couple of days. Everyone had been in a dither, rushing around, preparing for the nuptials.

Such silliness. Why bother with the falderal when neither party wanted to wed at all? Vangie had observed the fanfare with numb detachment, uttering short, monosyllabic replies when her aunt asked for her opinion.

"Peonies or roses?"

"Peonies."

"The peach silk or the white muslin for Yvette?"

"Peach."

"Bonnet or wreath?"

"Wreath."

"Tongue or ham?"

Tongue or ham?

At last, she could take no more. Yesterday, she'd slipped into the wingback chair before her balcony window and rested her aching head against the smooth, silk back. "Aunt Adélaid," she'd said, her voice barely above a whisper, "you and Yvette do what you think best." She'd raised a hand to her brow and closed her eyes against the nagging twinge. "I'll leave the arrangements to you."

"But, Vangie, don't you want…?" Yvette began.

Vangie had lowered her hand and turned her head, resting her cheek against the soft, smooth fabric. She'd met Yvette's, round, worried eyes. "I truly don't care a whit what you decide."

She'd known without being told the sparkle was gone from her eyes. She could have no more summoned a smile than she could have conjured a spell to prevent the travesty of a marriage to Lord Warrick. Turning her head to gaze out the window once more, she had breathed a small, silent, and altogether hopeless sigh.

Now, the dreaded day was upon her.

Vangie shoved off the heavy coverings and sat on the edge of the bed for a moment before sliding to the floor. Her gown was a wrinkled mess from having been slept in. Grabbing her shawl from a chair, she draped it around her shoulders and padded to the French windows on bare feet.

Throwing them open—*for the last time*—she stepped onto the balcony, disturbing a jay grooming itself on the rail. It scolded her soundly while flying away. A pinkish-brown feather floated slowly from the sky, swirling round and round to settle on the landing beside her foot. She retrieved the fallen feather, brushing her fingers along the crisp edge.

Lucky creature. It can fly away from its troubles.

For a fanciful moment after leaving Uncle Gideon's study the day the marriage was announced, she too had contemplated flight—had actually intended to flee to her Romani relatives. He must have considered she might try to run away. For she hadn't been alone, except when she slept, since. She suspected her uncle had her room watched at night too.

A cool breeze wafted by, and she wrapped the shawl tighter around her shoulders. The silk-fringed edge fluttered, and a stray curl caressed her cheek and tickled her nose until she tucked it behind her ear. She bent over the rail, breathing in the tangy air. Even though it had rained last night, the dank, noxious smells of the city lingered heavily this morning.

She missed the fresh, clean air of the country, and she missed her Romani clan. Heart heavy with yearning, she turned her focus toward home. A rainbow struggled to show itself amongst the myriad of ashen clouds gliding across the distant horizon. When the clouds finally passed by, the colorful arc would be free from its gloomy confines. At least the rainbow had some hope of reprieve.

She harbored none.

For a moment when she'd awoke, she'd forgotten the wretchedness she faced today. How she wished last night, the awful conversation with Uncle Gideon, had been a horrible dream. She'd cried herself to sleep hoping—praying—Lord Warrick would jilt her.

She peered at the sun-drenched courtyard below. Two robins hopped in the grass, tugging fat worms from the damp ground. There was yet time. A few hours remained before the wedding took place. Maybe he would cry off.

He is a man of honor.

With a longing so strong it rivaled physical pain, she wished her grandmother was here. Vangie adored Yvette; they were as close as sisters. But she needed her grandmother right now. *Puri Daj* would know what to do about this calamity.

She fingered the shawl's fringe and permitted herself a skeptical twisting of her lips. *Puri Daj* must have known something of this nature was going to occur, hence the mystifying warning.

Grandmother had been mysterious during her last visit. More than once Vangie caught her grandmother studying her with an unnerving glint in her eye. Though a devout Christian, *Puri Daj* wouldn't disavow her gypsy heritage. Or the inexplicable gifts she possessed because of her birthright.

"God made the Roma too," the elder gypsy princess often said with a shrug of her shoulders.

Vangie felt herself fortunate to be as close to her unconventional Romani relatives as she was. Aunt Eugenia and Uncle Percival tolerating the twice-yearly visits was nothing short of astonishing, considering their low opinion of the Roma. They'd never once argued against the visitations, although their noses turned up and their eyes narrowed when *Puri Daj* came to call.

It was most convenient the Travelers always journeyed near Brunswick, typically for a short stay in early winter and an extended duration in the late spring or early summer. Vangie cherished the close relationship she shared with her father's Roma family. Each year, she stayed in their encampment for a few weeks before they moved on.

Puri Daj had agreed to allow Vangie to live with the current baronet and his wife, as long as her visitations were honored. The arrangement was part of the complicated terms of Vangie's father's will. She had long suspected Uncle Gideon padded Uncle Percival and Aunt Eugenia's pockets handsomely to ensure that particular stipulation was honored.

Vangie cocked her head. What was that commotion in the hallway? She ventured to the French windows.

Yvette, Aunt Adélaid, and a pair of lady's maids bustled into the room, their arms overflowing. Yvette laid aside the flowers she carried, then embraced her. "We've brought you breakfast, dearest, and after you bathe, we'll help you dress for your wedding."

Despite her doldrums, Vangie gawked in slack-jawed astonishment as she stood in the grand entry of Lady...*Fitsribbon's*? opulent mansion. At the dame's insistence, the wedding ceremony was to commence at an unfashionable four o'clock in the afternoon in her ladyship's drawing room.

Vangie would've rather it took place in Uncle Gideon's study, *or a prison*, with none present but the cleric, her uncle, and the reluctant groom. She didn't even want Aunt Adélaid or Yvette in attendance. In her mind, this wasn't a joyous occasion in the least, but rather a sentencing. A life-long, irreversible imposition of punishment for two convicted of a crime they'd not committed.

The resplendent foyer, and what she could see of the rest of the manor, teemed with enormous bouquets of flowers and floral swags in every imaginable color. She half expected to hear bees buzzing as butterflies and birds fluttered from flower to flower.

She closed her eyes and breathed in the sweet, perfumed air. Every hothouse in London must've relinquished its blooms for the occasion.

"There you are, my dears."

Vangie turned to see Lady—blast, why couldn't she remember the woman's name?— emerging from an adjoining room.

"Do come along. Ian and the others are already assembled in the drawing room." The matron gestured toward a room at the end of the magnificent hall.

Others? What others?

No one mentioned anyone else being present. Vangie sent a panicked glance to Aunt Adélaide who offered a wan smile but shrugged her shoulders.

She doesn't know either?

"Thank you, Lady Fitzgibbons," Uncle Gideon said. He took her arm and escorted her through the double doors. Was he afraid she might yet bolt?

Too late for that now.

She would do this. She must do this. She squeezed the spray of flowers she held so tightly, the stems nearly snapped. *Lord, how can I do this?*

From across the room, Vangie met Lord Warrick's gaze. Had he been watching the door? She trembled when his cool assessment slowly traveled over her. A tingling followed the route of his eyes, settling in her bosom when his focus lingered there before rising to meet hers once more.

With a sardonic twist of his firm mouth, he turned to speak to the cleric.

She glanced at her gown. She wore the same silver confection she'd worn to that inauspicious ball. She'd refused to purchase a new gown.

"It would be a sorry waste of funds," she'd told Aunt Adélaid.

A lovely bridal bouquet and hair wreath of peach-tinted roses, orange blossoms, and ivy, had been created from the pile of flowers Yvette had toted into her room this morning. One of the lady's maids—Dora? Cora? Flora? Vangie had no idea what her name was—had spent an entire hour arranging her hair into an elaborate Grecian coiffure, the wreath carefully pinned atop.

A pearl and diamond pendant graced her neck and matching drop earrings hung from her ears. The lovely set was her wedding gift from Uncle Gideon and Aunt Adélaid. As her aunt draped the necklace around her neck Vangie asked, "Don't pearls signify tears?"

"Ah, yes, but it's good luck for a bride to cry on her wedding day and," Aunt Adélaid dangled one of the earrings to catch the sunlight, "diamonds mean affection."

Vangie fingered the large pearl resting against her chest. She'd wager there were far more tears than affection as a result of this union.

Uncle Gideon guided her to Lord Warrick's side. Her traitorous feet obeyed his gentle urging, but the whole while her mind screamed for her to turn and run.

Standing before the reverend, a squat, sallow fellow, smelling of garlic and brandy, Vangie almost smiled at the irony. It was somehow fitting this offensive cleric, whose dour countenance suggested that anything remotely resembling joy or happiness should be considered blasphemous, presided over the ceremony.

From the corner of her eye, she peeked at Yvette standing beside her, resplendent in a pale apricot gown. The false smile pasted on her lovely face didn't diminish the unhappiness reflected in her eyes. Vangie looked away lest she give into the despair simmering beneath the surface of her own carefully-constructed poise.

A striking man she didn't know stood next to Lord Warrick. His turquoise eyes—she'd never seen eyes that unique shade before—were riveted on Yvette, though her cousin didn't seem to notice. Vangie cast a hesitant glance to Lord Warrick. His stern profile was marred by another large scrape on his jaw.

Whatever had he been about this time?

She presumed the other guests in attendance, no more than a score total, consisted of the powerful nobility who'd been called upon to dispel the gossip surrounding the hasty wedding.

Her gaze downcast, Vangie quietly recited her vows. The icy contempt in her future-husband's eyes earlier had turned her blood cold.

To the assembled guests, she supposed, her lowered eyes bespoke modesty. But for her, a most reluctant bride, it was the means to stop the burgeoning tears from spilling onto her cheeks. Once they started, she'd become a blubbering fool. She bit the inside of her cheek prevent her lips from trembling. Sniveling females exasperated her, though she greatly feared she was becoming one herself.

Only once during the ceremony did she raise her gaze to meet Lord Warrick's, as the rector intoned, "To love, honor, and cherish, until death do you part?"

The cleric's monotone rendering of the vows mirrored the desolation in her heart and most likely, the black fury in the viscount's. Would he say, "*I do*," or would he spare them both from this catastrophe? Albeit, the humiliation should he do so, would be insufferable.

Which was worse, a forced marriage or being jilted? *Or bearing the label of a demi-rep?*

Lord Warrick's silver-eyed gaze, brimming with cynicism, held hers captive. "I do."

Even as he uttered the words, his piercing eyes shifted ever-so-subtly. Possessiveness reflected in their arresting depths. A slight tremor shook her. His lips twitched and slanted, inching upward, promising something she didn't recognize—didn't understand.

Surely, it wasn't relief she felt that he'd uttered the vow. That and some other peculiar emotion she couldn't identify tumbled around her middle, muddling her thoughts. They left her feeling strange and woozy, as if she'd not eaten in days.

Would casting up her accounts save her from the marriage bed?

10

"You didn't eat much, *wife*."

Ian deftly twirled Vangie around his aunt's smallish ballroom, mindful of the interested gazes watching them. They, alone danced. Stealing a glance at the smiling and nodding onlookers, he suppressed a frown. He felt like a curiosity on display at Bullock's Museum. He wished others would take to the floor, so he could dispense with the devoted bridegroom facade.

The twelve-course dinner had been torturous. His bride hadn't taken more than a dozen bites or said as many words. He'd tried to eat the succulent foods Aunt Edith had gone to such efforts to have prepared, but his anger made everything dry as chalk and every bit as tasteless.

"I hadn't much appetite, my lord."

He chuckled. "Don't you think you might address me by my given name, *wife*?"

"Why?" she asked pertly. "I've known you but four days, certainly not long enough to be so familiar with you."

He lowered his head, breathing in her ear, very aware every eye in the room was trained on them. He'd give them something to gossip about. "Because I want you to, *wife*, and you did promise to obey." He nipped her ear.

She jumped and a tiny yelp of surprise escaped before she clamped her lips together. Her eyes shot sparks again; only this time she directed them at him.

"What's my name, *wife*?"

"Please, don't call me that. I, too, have a name, as you well know."

Drawing her closer, her breasts pressing against the breadth of his chest and cresting the edge of her bodice, he murmured, "Indeed, but Evangeline sounds…angelic, and we both know you're no such thing."

"Pardon?" She stiffened, trying to shove away from him. "I don't under—"

His head descended again. "Say it, or I'll trace your ear with my tongue." He grinned as her breath hissed from between clenched teeth.

She stumbled, her fingers digging into his shoulder and hand. A very becoming flush swept across her face. "Will you cease?" Her worried gaze careened around the room. "We're being watched."

Voice husky, he said, "Say my name, sweeting." Giving her a gentle squeeze, he started to dip his head, caressing her elegant neck with his hot breath.

"Ian. Your name is Ian," she gasped breathlessly, twisting her head away.

Did she know how sultry her voice sounded?

A chuckle rumbled through his chest. He'd no doubt his smile reflected his satisfaction.

"*Bostaris*," she mumbled beneath her breath as she tried to wrench away again.

Bostaris? For certain that wasn't a compliment. His smile widened. He splayed his hand across the gentle slope of her spine, holding her firmly against him. His wife was a sensual thing. He'd but breathed in her ear, and she'd nearly melted onto the floor.

Vangie tilted her head upward. "Please, you're holding me too tight. I cannot breathe."

He immediately relaxed his embrace.

Her gaze fixed on his jaw, a silent question in her eyes.

"My equipage lost a wheel yesterday," he offered shortly.

She met his gaze for a moment before hers skittered away. "You're unharmed?"

"Except for this scratch." He angled his scraped jawbone at her. And a nasty bruise on his thigh where he'd slammed into the side of the livery wagon. He never thought he'd be grateful for a pile of manure and straw. Convenient too, to drop a wheel in front of the livery. The owner tended to his horse, while the blacksmith next door repaired the wheel.

The music ended, and Stapleton claimed Vangie for the next set. Ewan McTavish, the Viscount Sethwick, and Ian's closest friend, made his bow to Yvette. They too made their way onto the floor. Soon the room was full of happy couples, stepping and turning to the lilting music.

Leaning against a marble fireplace mantle, Ian regarded his bride. No gay smile graced her pink lips while she danced tonight. His skewed his mouth into a humorless smirk. He'd kept his vow all right, to make sure she dallied no longer. He shook his head at the incongruity of it.

He'd not tolerate fast behavior from his wife. God only knew how many others had enjoyed her favors, but he'd make it perfectly clear where her affections better lie from this point forward. He'd be claiming no by-blow as his. His gaze never straying from her, Ian permitted himself a moment of cynical musing. It was outside of enough. He'd been shackled with that Jezebel, because he'd suffered a lapse in judgment and allowed a moment's tenderheartedness.

When had he become such a cod's head?

But her lips were blue.

Yes, and look at where that concern had landed him. Forced to marry the chit whose undoing he'd intended. Was God laughing? For the devil certainly was.

Fortunate for him, not only was she pleasing to look upon—quite exquisite if he were wholly forthright—her figure rounded nicely in the appropriate places. His new wife was a passionate woman too. He sensed it, though it galled him to think how many men had already explored her luscious curves.

After that tantalizing dance, Ian keenly anticipated their wedding night. Theirs would not be a marriage of convenience. It would be consummated. He required an heir. Why the continuation of his family line was suddenly of such importance to him remained a puzzle. One he didn't want to explore, let alone solve at present.

How to keep his bride from sharing her favors was easy to remedy. Closet her at Somersfield with strict directives as to her mobility and the company she'd be permitted to keep. Once she'd produced two or three heirs, *his heirs,* he didn't give a fig what she did.

He cast a glance to the mantle clock. *Not yet.*

From half-closed eyes, he studied her as she floated by in her uncle's arms. He rescinded that last thought about giving a fig. He might very well be inclined to indulge himself and sample her charms for an extended duration. She did quicken his blood, though he attributed his arousal to lust. He'd long been without a woman. What other explanation was there for the nagging ache in his innards?

Aunt Edith approached, a knowing smile teasing her lips. "Can't keep your eyes off your beautiful bride, I see."

He had no intention of discussing his wife and pointedly changed the subject. Surveying the decorated room, he angled his head. "Thank you, for this."

She smiled and nodded. "I did it as much for her as you. She needed a pretty wedding. Her life's not been easy."

Unlike her virtue.

Laying a bejeweled hand on his arm, Aunt Edith searched his face. "I'm pleased you decided to give her your mother's ring. Does she know?"

"No."

She stared at him for an intense, lengthy, and ever increasingly uncomfortable moment. "I've always admired your commitment to honor and justice, Ian. The least you can do is to extend the same courtesy to your new wife." Her gaze shifted to Vangie before she admonished. "Give her a chance. She deserves that much from you."

"My *wife* has received precisely what she deserves."

"Balderdash!" Aunt Edith jerked her eyebrows together in disapproval. "You're not the only one who was forced into marriage, nephew," she snapped. "It's much more difficult for a woman than a man. Believe me—*I know*." She slapped him on the arm with her damnable fan. "Stop being such an aristocratic, arrogant cork-brain."

With that declaration, she proudly lifted her head and swept from his side, nodding as she passed Sethwick making his way to Ian.

Feeling like a chastised schoolboy, he shifted his attention to his friend.

"Warrick, I'm afraid I'm off. I've been delivered a communiqué. Night Hawk left an urgent missive at the Home Office." He smiled and shook Ian's hand heartily. "Congratulations, old chap."

"Thank you."

"Didn't think you'd be leg-shackled at twenty and seven." Sethwick angled to look at Vangie, though his aqua gaze lingered far longer on her cousin. He grinned. "Your bride's a beauty."

Ian's roamed his gaze over Vangie, the familiar quickening he'd come to expect tunneling through his veins whenever he allowed himself the luxury. "Indeed."

Vangie covertly observed her new husband while she danced. Lord War—Ian looked anything but happy while conversing with Lady Fitzgibbons and Lord what-ever-his-name was. She didn't blame him. She couldn't understand why he'd gone through with it. The marriage benefited her far more than he.

She mentally ticked off his attributes.

He was handsome, a Corinthian, titled, and fairly well-heeled. And, she'd gleaned from the accounts everyone eagerly filled her ears with, a decent man, though known for his temper, dark moods, and obstinacy. He was fond of horseflesh—a top sawyer in fact—and his pugilistic and firearm skills were renowned.

She turned and dipped, stepped forward and backward in time to the music. Rumor had it he was somewhat of an intellectual as well. He didn't gamble, womanize, or drink overly much. Or so she'd been assured by Aunt Adélaid who'd attempted to placate her into believing the match wasn't a complete tragedy.

Her dear aunt had failed in her effort to comfort Vangie. Indulging in another sulk tempted. *No*. Roma were made of sterner stuff. As if lifted upright by an invisible hand, she raised her chin and straightened her spine.

There *must* be something advantageous about this union.

Another turn, a hop and skip.

I can paint until my heart is content. One.

There would be darling children—eventually. Two.

Poverty and deprivation won't be my constant companions. I will no longer be treated as a servant. And perhaps as a titled lady, I can help the Roma. Three, four and five.

There she'd done it. Found something positive from the union.

There were a goodly number of things this marriage brought her, besides a most reticent groom. Puffing out a little breath, Vangie forced her lips upward and nodded at something Uncle Gideon asked. To be honest, she'd not a clue what it was. He could've been speaking about flying monkeys or singing kidney pie, and she have been none the wiser.

But what could Ian find positive pertaining to their marriage? She supposed there was a marriage settlement involved. Uncle Gideon would've insisted upon it, despite her adamant protests. It was mortifying to be bartered into marriage. Any man could be purchased if the inducement was large enough.

Skipping the length of the line of dancers, she cast a glance at her glowering groom. Mayhap the marriage settlement influenced his decision to proceed with the marriage. Or, perchance he was as chivalrous as she hoped, and his selfless act was indeed to protect her honor.

And pigs ride camels.

Peering at him over her uncle's shoulder, she saw a shadow flicker across his harsh features. No, Ian wasn't pleased to be wed. *Why* had he gone through with it then?

Ma-sha-llah. As God wills, *Puri Daj* would say. Could it be as simple as that? Not likely.

Vangie suppressed a sigh. Would this falderal never end? The pretense of portraying an ecstatic bride bordered on torturous. The day had been a whirlwind of activity, and she was done over, emotionally and physically. After eating but a few mouthfuls of flavorless breakfast, and enjoying a long soak in lily of the valley-scented bathwater, she'd been preened and groomed for hours.

Then there had been a most embarrassing discussion with Aunt Adélaid regarding wifely duties. "Vangie, the union of a man and woman is a beautiful thing. There's pain the first time of course, but a considerate husband will do his best to lessen it and introduce you to pleasure."

She'd wanted to die of chagrin. Worrisome thoughts she'd shoved to a remote corner of her mind consumed her. Surely Ian wouldn't want to consummate their wedding tonight. They scarcely knew each other. Perhaps he could be persuaded to postpone the event for a few weeks. *Or months—*

He was staring at her with those brooding, slate eyes. She felt his gaze on her as surely as if he reached and trailed a finger over her cheek. He wanted her to look at him. She sensed it.

She wouldn't.

He'd not find her easy to manipulate. Her attention flitted about the room, landing here and there, hovering like a bee over a flower before darting on.

She would not look at him. Drat the man. *Stop staring.*

Her attention strayed in Ian's direction. She caught herself and pointedly turned her head pretending absorption in the floor-to-ceiling tapestry depicting a Grecian garden. It was as futile to resist his silent command as it had been to refuse to say his name earlier. *Or refuse to marry him.* He was a man accustomed to getting what he wanted.

Vangie raised her reluctant gaze to his. Their glances meshed and held. She felt like prey caught in a snare, unable to look away. He was dangerous, like the panther she'd likened him to that first fateful night. Every inkling of self-preservation shouted for her to flee.

Angling himself upright, he smiled his disturbing smile. Never breaking his entrancing stare, he crossed to her. She stood rooted and mesmerized in the middle of the room, unable to tear her gaze from his.

Sweeping her into his arms, he guided her around the floor once more. His thighs brushed hers, and her breasts pushed against his coat, the silver buttons cutting into her tender flesh. He was holding her much too close for propriety.

Why didn't she mind too terribly much?

Her new husband's arms were bands of steel, wrapping her in an impenetrable vise. His unusual eyes peered into hers, probing, seeking—what she knew not. They roamed across her face, lingering for a disquieting moment on her parted lips before lowering to the mounds swelling from her bodice.

Vangie felt the heat of his smoldering gaze as surely as if he'd caressed her. It was as if they were alone, no one else in the room, their bodies speaking an ancient language only lovers knew. His breathing quickened, and a low, sensual sound escaped him as he caressed her bare shoulder.

She released a slight hiccupping gasp. Her breath caught and hitched in her lungs.

"I think it's time we gave our excuses and made for *home*, sweeting." His voice was a husky, suggestive rumble.

Oh, dear.

Shaken from the unnerving exchange, Vangie allowed him to lead her from the floor, though the dance had not yet ended. With her on his arm, he circled the room, accepting congratulations and thanking the guests for attending.

Faith, were they truly to leave? She sent a panicked look at Uncle Gideon. He was frowning again, his eyes trained on Ian.

His aunt offered her cheek for a compulsory kiss, then chided him. "Leaving so soon, Ian?" Turning to Vangie, the dame embraced her. "I'm most pleased you deemed to marry this pup, my dear."

The sincerity and playfulness of her tone did wonders to ease Vangie's brittle nerves. "Thank you, Lady Fitz..."

"Pshaw, none of that. Please call me Aunt Edith, Evangeline."

Vangie smiled with sincere warmth. "And you must call me Vangie."

More farewells and good wishes were exchanged before she was finally whisked into Ian's waiting carriage. Her trunk wasn't anywhere to be seen, not that she had too terribly much to take with her. All the clothes she'd worn while in London had been borrowed.

The carriage started to pull away from the mansion, and she blurted, "My trunk?"

"Was sent over during the ceremony."

"Oh." How thoughtful of him. "Thank you."

He flicked his fingers dismissively. "Don't thank me. I had nothing to do with it. Your aunt did."

11

After Ian's clipped retort, Vangie fell silent. With those few words he'd made his feelings all too clear.

He sat across from her, his sheer male essence permeating the coach. The sun had bid the day *adieu*, but dusk lent a faint glow to the plush interior of the comfortable conveyance. She knew without looking, he stared at her with a steady, assessing gaze. He did indeed remind her of a large cat, and she was his quarry.

Despite the mild evening and the light shawl over her shoulders, a shiver stole through her. She daren't look at him but kept her gaze firmly riveted on the dim, unimpressive view beyond the carriage window. He seemed as disinclined to converse as she. Considering his last rude remark, she was most grateful for the small consideration.

Clasping her hands in her lap, Vangie nibbled her lower lip. She was determined to ask Lord Warrick to wait to claim his conjugal rights. At least until they grew to know one another a mite more. Or better yet, a great deal more. Surely that wasn't too much to ask, was it? She'd every intention of consummating the marriage, just not quite yet.

Wouldn't his lordship be uncomfortable with such extreme intimacies with a stranger? Uncomfortable didn't begin to express her feelings on the matter. It was preposterous. People simply didn't engage in *that* with someone they didn't know.

She fidgeted with her reticule strings, twisting the crocheted strands round, and round her fingers. Aunt Adélaid hadn't been altogether specific about what *that* was, and Vangie had tried very hard not to listen by reciting Romani phrases in her head the whole while her aunt was speaking.

"I must be honest. It is a smidgen embarrassing the first time."

The droppings of the flying bird never fall twice on the same spot.

"Or he might prefer you completely unclothed."

It is easier to milk a cow that stands still.

"Don't be alarmed. A spot of blood is quite normal."

You cannot walk straight when the road is bent.

"Joining can be wondrous."

Beauty cannot be eaten with a spoon.

Vangie had still heard more than she wanted. The act had something to do with being naked and joining. She wasn't completely ignorant for pity's sake. She'd seen the chickens and geese mating in the enclosure behind her cottage, and once as a child, she'd seen a mare being bred while in the Romani encampment.

She shuddered. What was the pecking and biting about? And the noises? The squawking and grunting? It appeared rather violent, and it seemed to her, the females found the whole of it rather trying. Faith, she couldn't imagine people engaged in that sort of behavior. She furrowed her brow. Truth to tell, she expected it must be wholly different for men and women when they coupled.

She cast a surreptitious glance at her husband. As if alerted, he turned his gaze from perusing the passing scenery and caught her peeking at him.

His firm lips quirked at the corners. Sensual. Mocking.

Heat swept up her cheeks. *Dash it all*, she was blushing again.

His smile widened. He knew it too, wretched man. Did he just wink?

Fresh warmth skimmed to the roots of her hair. She'd blushed more in the past week than in her entire life. It was most annoying. *And revealing.*

Clenching her hands once more, she squeezed the ring Lord Warrick slipped onto her finger during the ceremony. The band felt foreign. Everything was strange now. This man who was her husband. Where she'd live. The people she'd share a home with. The company she'd now keep.

Exhausted as she was, the gentle rocking of the carriage lulled Vangie into drowsiness. She rested her head against the seat and closed her eyes. A sudden disturbing thought trickled into her mind. Would Ian allow visits with her Romani relatives? Would he be among those who treated the Roma shabbily, as if they were an inferior people?

Did he know her heritage? Would he care?

The carriage rumbled to a stop. Her eyes flew open, and her stomach cavorted as a thousand dragonflies zipped around her ribs. The carriage door opened, revealing a royal blue liveried footman and a modish townhouse in an opulent section of town.

Ian descended first. "Thank you, Lowell." He swiveled back to the carriage then reached into the darkened vehicle. He grasped Vangie's hand, assisting her to the ground.

Could he feel her trembling?

Propelling her along by the elbow, he escorted her into the brightly-lit townhouse. In the foyer, the staff stood in a straight line, ready to greet their new mistress.

Vangie smiled and nodded, at least she thought she did, though she couldn't remember any of their names except perhaps the butler, Flinch, and the housekeeper, Mrs. Porker.

Oh dear, that cannot be right. Mayhap it's Mrs. Perky.

The heat from Ian's hand scorched her through the light fabric of her shawl. It was difficult to concentrate on anything except his disturbing touch.

"Mrs. Parker will show you to your chamber, Lady Warrick."

She glanced at him. It was the first time he'd addressed by her new title. She risked sending him a hesitant smile. It quickly faded when he turned away from her and disappeared through a carved door across the entry.

"Yes, indeed, everything's been made ready for your arrival," the vivacious housekeeper declared, a smile on her jovial face. "Wait 'till you see." Her smile widened until her plump cheeks resembled miniature candied apples. "We've quite outdone ourselves, we have."

Appreciation surged through Vangie at the friendly welcome. Mrs. Parker's chatelaine tinkled as she bustled across the entry. "If you'll please follow me, my lady."

Vangie lifted her gown and followed the housekeeper up the stairs. She paused on the landing to peer at the door Ian had vanished through. A dim light glowed through the crack beneath it.

Would he come to her tonight?

She sincerely hoped not.

Two hours later, she sat at the dressing table in the sumptuous chamber appointed to her. Everything was pink roses, from the silk rose-laced wallpaper to the draperies and bed curtains—even the rugs on the floor. Numerous vases of roses had been placed throughout the room, their bold scent perfuming the air.

There had even been rose petals floating in her bathwater, and more petals lay sprinkled atop the silken sheets. Why would anyone put rose petals on the bed? She'd scooped the petals from the copper tub before picking the others off the sheets. Standing in the middle of the chamber, she'd bitten her lip.

Where to put them? A chamber pot peeked from beneath the bed. She'd pulled it out and grinned. Pink roses smiled back at her. Someone, Mrs. Parker likely, had a fondness for pink roses.

She'd dismissed, Emma, the girl assigned to act as her lady's maid, after the girl helped Vangie from her gown. It was awkward enough having a stranger assist in her undressing. She'd refused help bathing as well. She'd no personal servants in Brunswick and was accustomed to seeing to her own needs.

Now brushing her hair with long, slow strokes, her emotions whirled. Ian hadn't made an appearance, and profound relief filled her. Then why the queer, uncomfortable feeling inside? She mentally shook her head. Tosh, that other sentiment was *not* disappointment. It was embarrassment at being rejected on one's wedding night—that was all. But that was what she'd wanted, wasn't it?

Vangie perused the connecting door once more.

She fingered the diaphanous nightgown and robe she wore—pink as well, except for the embroidered blue roses gracing the neckline and sleeves. Thank goodness for something other than pink. Hopefully, Ian wasn't the one overly fond of the color. Personally, she didn't much care for it.

When she'd entered the bedchamber, the set had been lying across the gargantuan bed dominating the room. She'd no doubt they were meant for her to wear tonight, and so, owning nothing half as lovely, she dutifully donned them.

A smile tugged the corners of her mouth. She would like to see his lordship's reaction if he ever saw her in her plain, serviceable nightdress. Patched in numerous places, the hem and sleeves ragged and frayed, it boasted several tea and paint stains. She adored its well-used comfort, and would've preferred to don it tonight.

Tilting her head, Vangie caught sight of the bed in the mirror. The sheer size of it gave her pause. How many people were meant to sleep in that monstrosity? Her hand froze mid-stroke.

Leaning forward, she peered into the mirror, seeing the shock on her face, before dropping her focus to gape at her chest. The material of her night rail was much too fine, revealing far more than it concealed, including the shadows of her nipples.

"Faith, this will never do." Dropping the brush on the table, she jumped from the bench. Her mouth fell open. The dark shadow of her womanhood showed through the sheer fabric as well. "What could the *modiste* have been thinking, fashioning a gown of such transparent material? Why, it's positively wicked."

She darted to the wardrobe intent on donning her thick, well-worn night robe. Lord Warrick mightn't make an appearance tonight, but should he, Vangie wanted to be prepared. Standing before him in an embroidered, lace covered ensemble, that left *nothing* to the imagination, wouldn't lend itself to the purpose she'd set her mind to.

Yanking the wardrobe open, she removed the familiar garment. She lifted her arm to slip it into the comfortable, woolen arm.

Lord Warrick's deep voice halted her. "Nay, sweeting, lay it aside."

She stood transfixed, one hand clutching the robe, the other her throat. Her pulse beat a rapid cadence beneath her fingertips. She'd not heard him enter through the adjoining door. *Panther feet.*

Draping the garment across a nearby armchair, Vangie gazed longingly at the robe's modest folds before she faced Lord Warrick. His mahogany hair was damp, though neatly combed. He wore a midnight blue banyan, open to the waist. What she could see of his chest was matted in fine, curling hair. Silk frogs secured the remainder of the banyan, which fell to the middle of his calves. The lower part of his muscled legs was covered in crisp, coal-black hair.

Gads, even his toes have hair on them.

Of course they do. Hair probably covers his entire body.

She forced herself to meet his disconcerting eyes, not daring to look anywhere else on his form. Was he naked beneath the banyan? She gulped against an absurd desire to giggle. Clearing her throat, she swallowed against a bothersome lump lodged there then plastered a fake smile on her face. "My lord?"

He shook his head, waving a finger at her. "Not 'my lord,' sweeting. I prefer, Ian, or darling, or dearest, or my love."

There was a bantering tone to his voice, or was that mockery? Puzzled, Vangie's smile faded. "My, uh, Ian, I thought perhaps we might wait to—"

"Wait?" He crooked a hawkish eyebrow, a bland smile on his lips, though the humor failed to reach his eyes. His gaze shifted to her breasts.

Her nipples puckered against the gossamer fabric. *Curse it.* She reached to pull the filmy cloth away from her traitorous breasts.

A slow smile tilted the corners of his mouth.

Rotten knave.

Instead she angled her chin, straightened her shoulders, and folding her arms across her chest, plowed onward. "Well, yes, to become better acquainted before we—" She swallowed again as he purposefully spanned the distance separating them with measured steps. She stood her ground, though every instinct screamed for her to run.

Drawing a thick lock of hair across her shoulder, he idly toyed with the strand. With his other hand, he tilted her chin upward until her eyes grudgingly met his.

His were endless pools, and Vangie struggled to find a nuance of mercy or compassion within their fathomless depths. The look simmering there wasn't reassuring or comforting in the least. He looked about to pounce and gobble her up.

Panther.

Sliding the hand cupping her chin to the back of her head, Ian held her immobile. His gaze sank to her parted mouth. Lowering his head, he brushed her lips, a feather-light wisp of a touch, with his. She stiffened but didn't pull away.

He played with her mouth, gently caressing her lips with his warm, velvety ones. The sensation was unlike anything she'd dreamed. She relaxed, leaning into his solid chest and cautiously moved her lips against his. He tasted of brandy and mint. She breathed in his subtle scent.

"You'd deny your husband what you've freely given others, *wife*?" he whispered against her mouth. Though softly spoken, the bitterness in his tone belied any true tenderness.

Jolted back to awareness, Vangie stood mute. He hadn't just said… No, she must be mistaken. She angled away from him, searching his cold eyes. "Pardon?"

"Come now, no need to be coy or to pretend false chastity." He cupped her buttocks, holding her to his solid length and grinding his hips suggestively. "We both know you've none."

Making an inarticulate sound in her throat, Vangie went rigid, as rage unlike any she'd ever experienced engulfed her. Incredulous, horror streaking through her, she shoved him away. She took a faltering step backward, her arms extended as if to ward off a demonic spirit. Stunned, voice shaking, she said, "Are you implying I've been intimate with another?"

"No, sweeting, no such thing," he taunted coolly. "You've not limited yourself to one man. I'm not pleased, but as long as you're as generous with me…"

The injustice infuriated her. She'd been forced into marriage with a man who thought her a harlot. Hands fisted, Vangie ground between clenched teeth, "You *bostaris*! How dare you?"

"Come now." His hot gaze took in the shadows her gown didn't hide. "Why the false affront? Everyone knows what a tart you are."

The loud smack of her fist connecting with Ian's injured cheek echoed ominously in the room.

12

Jaw slack, Vangie gaped at her husband. *Good Lord*, she'd punched Ian. He was known for his vile temper. What would he do? Where was her dagger? She darted a frantic look at the nightstand.

Not there. *Think.* Where had she laid it?

She wasn't given to violence. Why had she hit him so hard? A welt, red and raw like a fresh branding, was clearly visible on his angled face. The intense, provocative glimmer in his eyes sent a fresh dash of heat across her cheeks.

"Ian…" No, she would not apologize. *He deserved it, the brute.*

Why was he grinning? Was her new husband dicked in the nob? She frowned, inching her way backward. Perhaps he was mad. Mayhap it wasn't bad temperament plaguing the man at all, but lunacy. She sent a sidelong glance to the open wardrobe.

Where is my blasted dagger?

Clasping her hands before her, she warily regarded him. A muscle flexed in his jaw, and he gasped as he stole closer, his gait purely predatory. She sucked in another wheezing lungful of air. It was most difficult to breathe or think when one was stalked.

Ian crept onward, step-by-step.

For every step he advanced, Vangie retreated until she was brought up short by the small bench she'd just vacated. She tried to skirt around it, not daring to take her eyes from him. Her hip grazed the dressing table, rattling the contents on top. Reaching beside her, her gaze fixated on him, she grasped wildly. Her hand closed on the handle of the silver hairbrush.

She sent it sailing at his head.

He ducked then laughed, a deep resounding echo in his chest. He was enjoying this, the cretin.

She tossed objects at him as fast as she could grab them. A crystal perfume bottle. Engraved hand mirror. Jar of face cream. Jewel-encrusted comb. Her wedding wreath. All careened past him.

He dodged each item, stealthy edging nearer.

Broken glass, petals and leaves, globs of cream, and a puddle of perfume, which bathed the room with its citrusy scent, littered the floor.

In desperation, she tossed the last item, a filmy lace-edged handkerchief.

A feral grin on his lips, he followed its fluttering descent onto the rug then raised mocking eyes.

The damned cur. He still laughed at her.

She frantically sought something else to throw at him. Ah, there it was. Her jeweled dagger had been beneath the handkerchief the entire time. She snatched the blade, wielding it before her.

He'd gloat no more.

Ian's focus dipped to the knife, and his mirth lines shifted into irritation. "Put down the blade."

"No."

"Vangie, give me the knife."

She shook her head, daring to take a step forward, the blade tilted at a dangerous angle. The metal glinted in the candlelight. She knew how to use it. *Puri Daj* had insisted upon it.

He retreated a cautious step, his dark gaze narrowed and trained on the blade.

This certainly was not how she envisioned her wedding night.

"I shall not be called a *lóoverni.*" Emboldened, she took another step his direction. No man, not even her husband, had the right to call her a whore.

"Give it to me." His eyes slowly rose to meet hers, his expression unreadable. His lips thinned, and he extended his hand, palm upward. "I shan't ask you again."

A shaky laugh escaped her. "Not likely, my lord." She angled the dagger in the direction of the adjoining door. "Now leave."

It happened in an instant. With his foot, he gave a vicious yank to the rug she stood upon.

Vangie cried out, her arms flailing, desperately trying to stay upright.

He lunged and, seizing her wrist, wrenched the knife from her hand. He flung it across the room. After bouncing against the wall, it thudded to the floor then skidded several feet before disappearing beneath the armoire.

She tottered and would've fallen had Ian not caught her in his strong embrace, pinning her arms to her sides. Without preamble, he scooped her up, then strode to the bed, holding her gaze and arms captive.

Now she'd done it. She'd threatened her husband with a knife on their wedding night. Panic, mixed with a good portion of rage engulfed her. "Let me go, you filthy *bostaris*!"

He smiled, a slow, taunting curling of his lips. "Not likely."

Ian stared at Vangie, taking in her high color, her heaving breasts, the breathtaking body her nightclothes did little to hide. And he grinned. A grin of pure delight. He rather liked this side of his wife. She possessed a feisty spirit, and at this moment, her eyes snapped blue fire.

His attention rested on the subtle shadows her gown hinted at. They were his to explore.

"I'll scream, Ian."

He laughed in genuine amusement. "No, you won't. You would've done so by now."

"I shall too." She wiggled, attempting to free herself, but only succeeded in loosening his banyan and causing her gown to slide off one creamy shoulder. "I'll screech like a banshee from hell."

"The servants will only think me a skilled lover, sweeting." He dropped a swift kiss to the silky flesh at the juncture of her throat and shoulder. "And that I have successfully introduced you to the pleasures of the flesh."

Cheeks blooming with high color, she broke eye contact. She bent her head and pleaded, her voice quivering. "Do not do this, Ian, I beg you."

She pressed her head into his chest, her warm breath caressing his naked flesh. The intuitive gesture roused Ian's protective instinct. She'd not meant to seek comfort from him, had done so unawares, he'd bet Somersfield.

"Sweeting, look at me."

Vangie shook her dark head, her silky hair swinging across his arms as he held her trembling form.

Shaking her gently, his voice a low rumble, he insisted, "Vangie, look at me."

She lifted tormented eyes, the luminous sapphire pools shimmered with uncertainty and fear.

A man could drown in the depth of her eyes. "Have you been ill-treated by the men you've taken to your bed thus far?"

Her eyes grew huge, and her mouth fell open before snapping closed. Twice. Yet she said nothing. Perhaps that's why she discarded men like used tea leaves. She'd become bitter—cynical. What a shame for one so young, and one who possessed such a passionate nature.

"I'll never intentionally hurt you. I swear." He gave her a reassuring smile and feathered his finger across the swell of her breasts. "What's come before us matters naught. I forgive you."

Even as he uttered the words, Ian recognized them as truth. He should be furious that she'd threatened him. Instead, she intrigued him all the more. Confound it all, when had she crept beneath his skin? How had she managed to in such a short period of time?

He forgives me? Is he serious? For what?

Like a dimwit, Vangie gawked at Ian dumbfounded.

He who covers and forgives an offense seeks love.

This was not the time for *Puri Daj's* misplaced wisdom. Vangie was quite sure she was about to be ravished by her husband, and she was equally as certain, that while she feared the unknown, she was also very curious and not a little tantalized.

His caressing voice brought her hurtling back to the present. "We'll consummate this marriage tonight. I promise to be gentle." Eyeing her tenderly, Ian asked, his concern apparent, "Were your other lovers rough and selfish? Is that why you're so skittish?"

Did he think he was being noble, voicing concern over her past unpleasant experiences— *nonexistent experiences*. Incapable of speech, she gaped. This was outside of enough. It was simply too much to bear. He was mad. Cork-brained. He truly was. She was married to a man who believed her a sexually-frustrated wanton.

In a move so swift, she'd no time to protest, Ian set her on her feet then adroitly tugged her nightclothes off over her head. Mortified, eyes squeezed shut, she stood before him naked, desperately trying to cover her womanly places. Any thought of reprieve flitted away. Her protests had been for naught. He would have his way with her, as was his husbandly right. She could only pray he'd be as gentle as he'd promised.

Her body had responded to him since their first encounter, and she was honest enough to admit she wanted to explore the sensations he aroused further. She'd just hoped for more time.

He swept her into his arms, laying her on the bed's silky sheets. Lying nude on the turned-down, rose-scented bed, Vangie's thoughts tripped over one another. Shouldn't she be screaming for all she was worth, doing everything within her power to escape?

Wasn't that what she'd vowed? Wasn't that what she wanted?

But resisting was futile. As futile as the tide resisting the draw of the moon. There was no help for it; the end was inevitable. She was Ian's wife, and he set her pulse to pattering in a way only he was capable of.

There was no sin in this, no shame, except the degradation she felt at having been called a strumpet by her new husband. That hurt intolerably. The stinging words coiled around her heart, opening a deep, painful wound that wouldn't soon heal. A flush of humiliation stole over her. She'd no doubt she was as pink as the rose petals that had recently lain upon these same sheets.

Hearing a slight rustle, she popped her eyes open only to squeeze them shut again. Another blush warmed her entire body. He'd untied his banyan, letting it slip to the floor. Faith, she was no authority on the male form, but she was certain, the lean, well-muscled, naked man standing beside the bed was near perfection, except for…*it*.

The large member boldly protruding from his crisp dark loin hairs was what would join with her. Vangie knew it beyond a doubt. She opened her eyes a slit, peeping between her eyelashes. Surely his great size was an abnormality. She didn't want to stare at his disfigurement, but Lord Almighty—

The breath slowly hissed from between Ian's clenched teeth as he stood transfixed, unable to tear his gaze from the beauty of Vangie's form. If eternity stood still, he'd not have time enough, nor have words eloquent enough, to describe what God had fashioned in such wondrous perfection. Was there anything as marvelous, as splendidly exquisite as the female body?

Her hair, a silky raven curtain, spilled across her sloping ivory shoulders to gently rounded hips. The blushing tips of her firm, round breasts peeked between the silky obsidian strands. Eyes pinched shut, she attempted to shield the tempting curly triangle cradled between silky thighs which tapered to delicate calves, well-turned ankles, and finally, to shapely feet.

He slid his gaze over the turn of her derrière, her narrow waist and flat stomach before traveling back and lingering on the luscious mounds flirting behind her hair. Unable to help himself, he parted the sheltering locks, sucking in another great gulp of air, as her perfect breasts lay exposed. He trailed a finger across one satiny breast, watching in fascinated wonder as the rosy nipple puckered.

Vangie shivered, though whether from trepidation or passion, Ian couldn't be certain. He did know, he didn't want her afraid. It had suddenly become very important that she want him as much as he desired her.

She opened her eyes, the merest trace of cautious curiosity in their beautiful depths. Delicate color lined her cheekbones, but she didn't look away. She would experience pleasure with him like she had with no other. He'd brand her as his for all time. Sweeping his gaze over the length of his wife, an unfamiliar, fierce possessiveness seized his vitals.

She was his. No others—ever again.

Easing onto the bed, he drew her into his arms, letting her become accustomed to his touch. "Relax, sweeting," he urged, his voice a husky rasp. He stroked her smooth skin with skilled fingers. A smile of smug satisfaction curved his mouth as he heard her sigh and the tension eased from her. "That's it, love. Just enjoy this. I promise, I'll stop whenever you say so."

And he meant it. This was no longer about obedience or submission, but about pleasuring his new wife. Every woman should be cherished and adored on her wedding night.

He nibbled her neck and shoulders, his hands cupping and soothing a sensuous path over her full curves. Watching Vangie's face, he trailed a finger across her cheek, then over her slender neck to the fullness of one breast. She arched into his hand. Though timid, she enjoyed his touch. Male pride surged through him. Leaning over her, he kissed her, running his tongue along the sweet seam of her lips.

She sighed again, unconsciously turning her head to allow him better access to her honeyed mouth. Ian wasted no time. He angled his head and deepened the kiss, until at his insistence her mouth opened to receive his tongue. He plunged into her inviting depths, reveling in her hesitant response.

Her tongue tentatively dueled with his.

Had no man taken the time to introduce her to the art of kissing? A growl rumbled deep in his chest. *Selfish bastards*. He'd remedy that tonight.

What in the world was Ian doing to her? Vangie felt as if the world tilted, and the oddest sensations centered in her most secret place. She ached to push her swollen breasts into his rough palm. When his tongue nudged its way inside her mouth, she thought she'd died and gone to heaven so exquisite was the sensation.

His fingers caressing her body ignited desire she'd not known she possessed. She felt alive in a sensuous, urgent way she didn't understand. His experienced hands demanded a response, she realized with a start, she was only too eager to give.

She might've been reluctant initially, but she wanted this. Wanted to experience passion with Ian. Wanted to be his wife in every way.

Turning to her side, she slipped an arm around Ian's torso, needing him closer, rejoicing in the bunching of his muscles at her inexperienced touch. She ran her fingertips across his firm flesh, delighting in the ridges beneath her tentative, exploring fingers. Nuzzling her nose into his neck, she inhaled his masculine scent.

"You smell good."

Ian's ministrations became bolder, and he lowered his head, teasing one nipple, encircling it with his tongue. Moaning, Vangie arched into him, hungry for his touch. The sensation of his lips and tongue on her breast created a frenzy of pulsating need only he could satisfy.

"More," she groaned.

He chuckled, apparently happy to oblige her. He sucked the swollen flesh deep into his hot mouth.

Gripping his arms, she moaned her pleasure aloud, too far gone to be shocked at the noises she made. Her cries of pleasure seemed to fuel his desire.

Angling himself so he lay across her, his elbows bearing his weight, Ian sought her mouth once more. His fingers played across her ripe, ravenous body. She wriggled her hips beneath him, unmindfully asking him to complete the act. He groaned, deep and ragged, low in his throat.

The primitive sound accelerated her pulse, and she opened her eyes.

He rolled her nipple between his thumb and forefinger.

"Yes, oh, yes, Ian."

A smile of pure male dominance crept across his angular face. She shifted restlessly beneath him, and her bent knee brushed his engorged manhood. A strangled gasp escaped him. Gritting his teeth, the corded muscles of his neck straining, he buried his face against her shoulder.

"I had no idea it could be like this," she whispered shyly.

He lifted his head, and his molten, passion-filled gaze ensnared her. Laughing in self-depreciation, he apologized. "I'm afraid I've been without a woman far too long to take this as slowly as I intended, sweeting. You're such a temptress, I cannot wait any longer." He slid a hand between her legs, fondling her most private place, and unexpected bliss engulfed her. He gave a satisfied grunt. "You're ready, sweeting."

She was? Is that what the pulsating ache meant?

He captured her mouth in a plundering kiss, and cupping her buttocks, parted her legs. Plunging his tongue into her mouth, he surged into her with one fierce thrust.

A cry caught in Vangie's throat. She went rigid beneath him, wrenching her mouth from his. *Dear God.* He was buried deep within her. Scrunching her face against the pain, she fisted her hands in the sheets, as hot, salty tears slipped from the corners of her eyes.

"Shh, love. I'm so sorry, sweeting." Deep regret laced Ian's voice. "I didn't know. I thought…" He remained perfectly still, allowing her to become accustomed to him. The pain gradually ebbed, replaced by a vague, fluttery tingle that spread slowly outward. She arched her hips tentatively, and he smiled. "Better?"

She managed a nod, as he moved in and out of her with growing intensity. A new feeling blossomed deep inside of her, undefinable and elusive. She wanted more…just more.

A few moments later, Ian stiffened, a low guttural moan issuing from the depths of his throat. He collapsed atop her, his heavy breathing rasping against her shoulder. Something sticky trickled onto her thighs as she lay beneath.

Where was the pleasure Aunt Adélaid spoke of—that Ian had promised?

Ian withdrew from Vangie and cursing silently rolled to his side, facing her. She promptly turned away, presenting her back and wept

In that moment, he hated himself. He traced a visual path from her shoulders to her thighs. A butterfly-shaped birthmark adorned her right buttock. He reached to touch it, but hesitated. He didn't have the right to caress her—not now.

Not after the cruel things he'd said to her. He'd made a grave miscalculation. She was, *had been*, an innocent. *God's blood*, what had he done?

When he'd felt her tight barrier tearing away, her strangled cry stabbed him to his core. Even then, he couldn't stop. In her innocence, she'd taken him past the point of no return; a first for him. Never in his life had Ian felt as helpless or as much self-condemnation and self-loathing as he did at this moment. His actions had been untenable.

He could still hear her pleas to wait to consummate their vows. She wasn't being coy or denying him her bed. She was an innocent maid, frightened to bed a man she didn't know. She sobbed silently, each shuddering sigh of her slender form, tore into his gut like a knife twisting his vitals. He needed to console her every bit as much as she needed consoling.

Tenderly wrapping his arms around her, he tucked Vangie against his chest. She didn't resist even though he'd treated her poorly. She hadn't deserved the appalling things he'd said to her. Guilt shafted through him once more.

She should've been introduced to passion with care and tenderness, not untamed lust while his cruel, hateful words echoed in her ears. He was a blind fool, a rogue of the worst sort. *Yes, an arrogant, ignorant ass.* He should be rejoicing over Vangie's innocence. Instead, he felt like a man who had stolen someone's sole, most treasured possession.

In truth, he had.

Running a soothing hand along her neck and arm, then over her delicate shoulder, Ian attempted to comfort her. "I'm sorry, sweeting. I was told you—"

She went rigid against him.

Yielding to the scant degree of wisdom and good sense he yet possessed, he changed tactics. Brushing aside the tendrils of hair enveloping her shoulder, he kissed the delicate flesh. "Sleep now, love. All will be better in the morn."

How, he didn't know.

He nuzzled Vangie's neck. "Forgive me."

One thing was for certain, they'd leave for Somersfield first thing. He'd a need to sift fallacy from fact. Something was too smoky by far.

13

Clamoring and banging woke Vangie. Through half-open eyes, she saw Emmy—no, the maid was named Irma—attempting to light the coals in the grate. She rolled onto her side, and resting her cheek on one hand, stared at the pillow beside hers. Though the indentation from Ian's head remained, he was gone. She'd known he would be.

Her gaze shifted to the canopied top. A smile tempted the corners of her mouth. Garlands of pink roses hung from bedpost to bedpost. How could she have missed them last night?

Because I was otherwise engaged.

She'd heard his plea for forgiveness. She lay awake long after he'd fallen asleep, still cradling her in his arms. He'd not heard her whispered, "*Te aves yertime mander tai te yertil tut o Del*. I forgive you, and may God forgive you as I do."

She was no weak-willed, milk and water miss. Roma made the best of whatever lot was cast their way. They found happiness where they could. She sat upright and scooted against the fluffy pillows, tugging the bedcovering higher to hide her nakedness. Yawning behind her hand, she froze.

The mess on the floor.

Her gaze flew to the other side of the room. No trace of last night's debacle remained. Had Ian cleaned it up to prevent gossip? From the corner of her eye, she searched the dressing table. The ill-fated brush and comb sat neatly atop it. Everything else had disappeared.

Irma handed Vangie her faded green robe, behaving like it was the most ordinary thing in the world to wake a naked woman in the morn. Mayhap it wasn't an uncommon occurrence. The notion settled sickeningly in her belly.

"Your bath water is heating, my lady, and I've brought you breakfast." Irma drew the linen and lace curtains open, permitting the morning light to spill unheeded into the room.

Vangie blinked against the sudden brilliance.

"You're to leave for Somersfield as soon as you've dressed, and I've packed your belongings." She indicated the trunk near the door with a slight bobble of her head.

Vangie slipped off the bed, uncomfortably self-conscious about her nudity. She wrapped the robe more firmly about as she padded to the table where Irma had arranged her breakfast. Securing the garment's tie at her waist, she gingerly took a seat. "Somersfield?" She took a sip of savory tea before nibbling a hot, buttered muffin.

"His lordship's country estate in Northumberland."

"Irma, mightn't I bathe straightaway?"

"It's Emma, my lady."

Oh bother, of course it was.

Intent on the rumpled bed, she sent Vangie a quizzical glance. "Before you eat, your ladyship?"

Was that so preposterous? Ducking her head, she nodded, her hair swirling around her hips. *Please, don't ask why.*

Emma tossed back the bedding. "Of course, my—" She stopped short, unsuccessfully stifling a gasp. She spun around and scurried to the door. "I'll see to it at once."

Teacup raised to her lips, Vangie's attention strayed to the bed. A crimson stain marred the surface. Her maidenhead. Was that much blood normal? Ian was very well-endowed, and his great size had torn her.

What would the servants think? For she was certain, even now, Emma filled their ears.

Tea sloshed over the cup's rim, and the china rattled noisily when Vangie clanked the cup onto the saucer with more force than intended. She shoved to her feet then crossed to stare at the indisputable proof of her virginity. To her immense mortification, she'd not completely ceased bleeding. Snatching the bedcoverings over the stain, a hot flush stole across her face.

A few minutes later, a knock rattled the chamber door. "My lady, it's Mrs. Parker and the staff with your bath water," came the housekeeper's muffled voice through the thick wood.

Vangie wrapped the robe tighter around her, clutching the neckline together with one hand. Hurrying to stand near the window, as far from the door as she could, she called, "Come in."

Mrs. Parker and Emma, carrying an armful of towels, bustled into the room. They were followed by three under-footmen, all toting large pails of water. The housekeeper directed the men to fill the copper tub in the corner, watching their every move with a practiced eye. Shooing the footman from the room the moment they'd completed their task, her gaze settled on the nearly untouched breakfast tray. "Have you finished with your meal, my lady?"

"Yes, thank you. I'm afraid I've not much of an appetite this morning."

"Humph, it's no wonder," harrumphed the housekeeper, her gaze meeting Emma's across the room.

Did they know about her quarrel with Ian? Vangie wanted to melt into the floor such was her mortification.

Mrs. Parker accepted the towels from the maid. "Emma, please remove her ladyship's tray, and retrieve the items I prepared below."

Dipping a curtsy, the freckled-face servant hastily gathered the remnants of Vangie's breakfast before exiting the room. Not, however, before she cast her a pity-filled glance.

Beside the tub, Mrs. Parker removed a bottle from her starched apron pocket an after removing the cap, poured a liquid into the water. She recapped the bottle and slipped it into the pocket from whence it had come. She bent and swished the water with her fingers. Drying her hand on her pristine apron she said, "My lady, your bath awaits."

Smiling her appreciation, Vangie slipped off her robe, past the point of caring whether a complete stranger saw her unclothed. She settled into the warm, soothing water, sighing in pleasure. An aroma wafted past her nostrils. *Roses, naturally*. She strongly suspected Mrs. Parker held the penchant for both the color pink and roses.

The housekeeper made herself busy, tidying the room, *tsking* and clucking the whole while. Her movements stopped when she too spied the tell-tale mark upon the bedding while removing the linens. Vangie's face burned with chagrin. Wasn't it normal to bleed? Aunt Adélaid had mentioned it. The pitying look Mrs. Parker sent her had her sinking deeper into the bath water.

Several minutes later, Emma returned with a basket.

All brusque business, the housekeeper assisted Vangie from the tub, then wrapped her in an enormous linen towel. She handed Vangie a jar. "It's an ointment. It will aid in the healing."

Vangie removed the lid, sniffing the aromatic mixture. It reminded her of one of *Puri Daj's* herbal concoctions. Mrs. Parker lifted some soft cloths from the basket. She hesitated, casting a glance in Emma's direction. The maid busily tended the hearth. Lowering her voice, Mrs.

Parker said, "To catch the remnants of your torn maidenhead."

Vangie averted her eyes. This was really beyond the pale. Did all the servants know? She clutched the towel tighter, like an enormous shield against the embarrassment oozing from every pore. Truly grateful, yet equally humiliated, she thanked the housekeeper. "You're most kind."

Mrs. Parker tutted comfortingly again. "You'll be mended in a day or two. Right as rain."

She passed Vangie her threadbare shift and darned stockings. Shooting another look toward Emma, Mrs. Parker muttered for Vangie's ears alone, "So long as your rutting husband leaves you be."

After taking his usual chair at the breakfast table, Ian opened the news sheet folded neatly before him. He stared blindly at the headline. His body was replete—his mind anything but.

He'd fallen asleep with Vangie nestled securely in his arms. Dawn's glow woke him this morning, prompting him to edge from the bed. The coals burned low in the grate. They offered little in the way of warmth, yet emitted enough frail light that he could appreciate the vision of his slumbering wife.

She lay on her side, one hand tucked beneath her cheek, and her ebony hair fanned across her pillow. Several silky curls curved over her ivory shoulder and back. The dark arc of her lashes created a startling contrast to the porcelain cheeks they caressed. Her lips, still rosy-red from his fervent kisses, were parted as she breathed softly in her sleep.

The sheet had slipped halfway to her waist when he'd risen, revealing the sumptuous curve of a breast. She shifted, and the sheet dropped lower.

Ian had sucked in a hissing breath. A slight bruise marred the loveliness of her breast. Had he done that? Blister it all, he was a brute. Tenderly draping the bedclothes over her, he'd silently vowed he'd make it up to her.

By God, his stepmother and sister had better have a good explanation for defaming her character. And for sending him on a wild goose chase to snare a siren-turned-angel.

The clattering of china as Lynch prepared Ian's tea interrupted his reverie. He glanced through the open door. Was Vangie awake yet? Two maids and a footman huddled together beyond the doorway, whispering. Catching Ian's perusal, they ceased talking and scattered.

Returning his attention to the breakfast room, he frowned. What was afoot with the staff? He'd been met with a series of dark scowls and looks of reproach from his usually amiable servants the entire morning.

Lynch finished pouring Ian's tea. He placed the cup and a plate of food before his master. He half-turned to the sideboard muttering, "I forgot the sugar—"

Ian studied him. Something *was* awry. It wasn't his imagination. The man never forgot anything. *Ever*. And where was Mrs. Parker? Ian hadn't seen her all morning. If anything was amiss, Lynch would be the first to know.

"Lynch?"

The butler faced him. "Sir?"

Did he detect the minutest bit of frost tingeing the single word? Crooking an eyebrow, Ian met the butler's indecipherable gaze. He took a bite of sausage. "Is something afoot?"

Lynch pursed his lips and looked down his rather long, hooked nose. Disapproval was etched across his haughty countenance. "Perhaps, my lord," he sniffed disdainfully, "you should make that inquiry of the new Lady Warrick."

Ian paused, his kipper-laden fork almost to his mouth. Frosty, to be sure, and no small measure of censure as well. "Lady Warrick?"

"Indeed," Lynch intoned, his imperious voice ringing with disapproval.

Lynch turned to the sideboard, muttering beneath his breath. Lynch did not mutter. *Ever.* It seemed it was a morning for firsts.

Ian distinctly heard, "Inconsiderate…poor innocent…lout," before the butler snatched up the teapot, and with another loud, disapproving sniff, quit the room.

Ian placed his fork on his plate and wiped his mouth before tossing the serviette onto his full plate. He shoved from the table and strode from the breakfast room. Taking the stairs two at a time, he made straightaway to Vangie's chamber, entering without knocking.

Mrs. Parker and Emma both fussed over his bride. Upon spying him, Vangie dipped her head, lowering her gaze to the floor. The maid continued to twist and pin his wife's raven hair.

Patting Vangie on the shoulder, Mrs. Parker gathered the bed and bath linens before heading for the door. Ian heard her mutter, "Ought to be ashamed of yourself, you great oaf," as she flounced from the room.

Lynch *and* Mrs. Parker muttering?

As if compelled by some unseen force, the unmade bed drew his attention. There in the center, like an unholy beacon, a blemish marred the mattress.

Blast and damn.

Regret swirled in his gut. He swung his gaze to Vangie.

She continued to study the carpet.

He looked to Emma, and she glared at him, accusation and condemnation in her eyes. Pursing her lips, she dipped her gaze to her mistress' hair once more.

The unfamiliar heat of a flush stole across Ian's face. It would seem the whole staff thought he was a monstrous beast. An ugly thought intruded.

Did they think he'd forced himself on Vangie? He couldn't very well assemble the staff and explain otherwise. Humiliated at the notion, he ran a finger around the front of his neckcloth. He'd cleaned up the mess on the floor to still any gossip, but he hadn't considered *that*. His gaze flicked to the bed. There was nothing for it then. Let them think what they would.

He caressed Vangie with his gaze. It was what she thought that mattered. "Emma, please go below, and ask Mrs. Plumperbuns to prepare a basket for our journey."

"Yes, my lord. Just one more curl to pin." Securing the last strand, Emma met Vangie's eyes in the mirror. "You look lovely, my lady."

"Thank you."

Emma dipped a quick curtsy, mumbling a belligerent, "My lord," before hurrying from the room.

Feeling as awkward as a lad in short pants, instead of an experienced man of the world, Ian approached his wife. "Are you? Did I?" Finally, heaving a frustrated sigh, he grasped her hands and drew her to her feet. "I'm sorry, sweeting. I tried to be gentle. If I'd known you were an innocent…"

Raising her head, Vangie met his eyes. Undisguised melancholy lingered in hers. She attempted a smile, though her lower lip quivered the merest bit. "I'm fine. Please, don't concern yourself. It's the way of nature, as God intended."

Guilt and remorse battered Ian's ribs. His sweet bride was reassuring him, *again*, when she was the injured party. He was only now beginning to realize how blessed, rather than cursed, he was at having taken her to wife.

So why had Lucinda and Charlotte done their utmost to tarnish Vangie's character to him? Why had they been eager to see him depart for London to defend the family's honor?

He clamped his teeth until they threatened to crack. What an ironic twist of fate. Vangie wasn't the villain in this marriage. He was.

14

Three days later, Vangie thumped the inn's lumpy pillow for the umpteenth time. Giving up on sleep, she flopped onto her back. As usual, slumber eluded her. She reached under the pillow, seeking her dagger. She closed her hand on the familiar silver handle, her wedding ring clinking against the metal. Though physically fatigued, her mind refused to stop ruminating, replaying the past trio of days.

They stopped only long enough to switch the team and see to their personal needs. Ian even insisted they eat while on the move. He'd set a punishing, exhausting pace. More than once, she'd fallen asleep, and he'd woken her as the coach rolled into a lodging house's dark and dusty courtyard. Tonight, as she had every other night, Vangie sought her lonely bed immediately after supping.

She shifted on the mattress, trying in vain to find a comfortable position. Her backside ached from the hours and hours of sitting and bouncing along in the couch-and-four. However, her heart ached far more. After their wedding night, Ian hadn't come to her bed again. Each night, he dashed her hopes once again when he procured separate rooms for them at the posting houses along their route.

Staring at the fingers of moonlight dancing across the ceiling's beams, she played with an escaped curl. Except to hand her in and out of the coach, he touched her not at all. Neither did he keep her company within the conveyance's boring and stuffy confines. He rode his stallion during the day, only joining her after sunset.

His demeanor remained coolly polite, but a few times she thought she might've glimpsed remorse in his quick-silver eyes. Did he already regret marrying her? Had she so dissatisfied him on their wedding night that he was now averse to touching her?

A nasty twinge gripped the region near her heart, and she absently wrapped the strand of hair around her finger several times. She'd tried to show him she'd been willing, and his eagerness hadn't disgusted her. The things Ian had done to her...

A wistful sigh escaped past her lips as she blinked into the darkness, reliving the sensations. The way he'd made her feel had been utterly exquisite, beyond anything she'd ever imagined. Those delicious little quivers still fluttered along her senses when he looked at her.

One touch from him, and she was willing to throw herself into his arms once more. She wasn't immune to her husband. In fact, he intrigued her. At least that's what she called her growing fascination.

Forgiving by nature, she'd hoped to bear a child from their marriage, someone to love, and who'd love her unconditionally in return. A difficult task, to be sure, when one's husband declined to share one's bed. Even if the initial experience had been something short of ideal. Mortifying heat swept her face. It was beyond demeaning to be spurned so early on.

If Ian would let her, Vangie intended to be a good wife to him. Yes, he was angry and disappointed at being forced into marriage, but hadn't the settlement tempered his disenchantment even a little? She grimaced, pulling her mouth into a taut line. And she wasn't wholly repugnant, else why would those gentlemen in London have been so attentive? Albeit, usually inappropriately so.

Rolling onto her side, she dangled a foot off the mattress.

She'd attempted to talk with him their first evening of traveling. He'd climbed into the coach, settling across from her, his legs stretched before him.

"It's cooling rapidly this evening." *Oh, bother*, she'd scolded herself. Couldn't she contrive something cleverer than that drivel? Talk of the temperature? Every featherheaded ninnyhammer in London babbled on about the temperature or the weather or their latest bonnet.

"Indeed," he'd replied. Polite. Cool. Reserved.

"Have we far to travel yet?" In the darkened carriage, she had rolled her eyes in self-disgust. *Simkin. Naturally, we do. We've but started the journey.* Vangie had floundered a bit more, "Today, er, tonight, I mean."

"A bit."

"Your stallion, he's Arabian, is he not?"

"Yes."

"Do you travel this route often?"

"Yes."

That was it. She'd given up.

He'd obviously not wanted to converse with her, and she'd retreated into confused silence. Moments later, she'd heard the striking of flint as Ian lit the oil lamp. The revealing light wasn't welcome.

Through lowered lashes, she'd watched him settle into his corner of the carriage—without uttering a sound. The man certainly was a miser with his words.

Idly twisting a loose button on her emerald-green jacket, she'd frowned and looked downward. Best to stop before it came off. She brought no other jacket. Yvette had pressed Vangie to take some of her clothes, but she'd refused. Her kind-hearted cousin didn't understand how demoralizing it was to always accept charity. Besides, her aunt, uncle, and cousin had already been too generous by far.

Rather than face Ian's indifference, Vangie had peered out the window into the passing darkness. The painful truth was, she was far more likely to see a shooting star than receive a morsel of kindness from her husband. A wistful sigh escaped, but she swiftly suppressed it lest he hear. She wouldn't wallow in self-pity.

She'd fingered her spencer's worn, faded cuffs. She hadn't many clothes, and those she owned were castoffs, showing signs of constant wear. Tucking her scuffed half-boots beneath her skirt, she'd removed the plain straw bonnet atop her head. Undoubtedly, she'd doze off again and wouldn't chance crushing the humble accessory. She only owned one other bonnet, and the hat was too warm for springtime wear.

The clothing Uncle Gideon and Aunt Adélaid had purchased for her always remained with them when she departed. She'd taken to borrowing Yvette's rather than have them go to the unnecessary expense of purchasing garments she'd only leave behind. The first few times she'd returned home with new clothing, Uncle Percival and Aunt Eugenia had confiscated them. They'd sold the garments for her keep, as was their right, they claimed. They'd also made it clear she'd been a tiresome, unwanted burden these many years.

Greedy buggers.

Vangie had earned her way, and she suspected Uncle Gideon continued to send them monies regularly. She wouldn't be at all surprised if *Puri Daj* hadn't compensated them too.

Despite begrudging her every meal, Aunt Eugenia and Uncle Percival would not be pleased she'd wed. They quite liked the monies her presence afforded them. Placing the hat atop the reticule she'd crocheted herself, Vangie had turned her attention to the inglorious night once more.

She'd awoken to the coach bouncing as Ian hopped to the ground.

After eating a quick meal, she'd bathed and gratefully crawled into bed. And lain there for hours, wide awake, her mind churning. Just like tonight.

Now, eyes gritty with fatigue, she stared at the dancing moonbeams cavorting across the rustic ceiling and walls. The moonlight, bright as day, taunted her, daring her to seek slumber's peace and its welcoming forgetfulness. But she didn't want to forget.

Three nights ago, Ian had bedded her.

In her mind she replayed his tenderness, the regret and undisguised shame, the genuine remorse he'd expressed after discovering his error. Absorbed in her own unhappiness, it had only now occurred to her that he must be suffering too. Every instinct told her he was a *bari* man—a good man—at heart, and *Puri Daj* always said, "God looks at the heart."

Yawning, Vangie turned over. She smiled into the bumpy pillow knowing she could sleep now. She had a plan.

15

Ian idly regarded the raindrops scampering after one another on the foggy carriage window. Only one more night of posting houses remained before they reached his home. Late this afternoon, the weather had turned beastly, reflecting his dismal mood. A passing storm drenched the roads, forcing him to forsake the saddle he preferred, and seek the dry, lamp-lit interior of the luxurious coach.

He'd climbed in, dripping wet. Sitting, he lifted off his hat and removed his gloves before unfastening his greatcoat. Once his sodden garments lay beside him, he relaxed against the seat, arms folded.

Vangie's bewilderment fairly radiated off her. He recognized her confusion in her soulful eyes and sad smile. He called himself a hundred kinds of fool. She'd not complained an iota, but instead, had been amiable and sweet-tempered the entire journey.

He'd neglected her miserably, leaving her alone every day in the coach-and-four. Truth to tell, he wanted her desperately and didn't trust himself to be in such close proximity. One kind word, one soft touch or yearning look, and he'd be undone, no doubt lifting her skirts and taking her right there in the coach.

On the floor. On the seat. In his lap—

Blast it all, cease man.

Thoughts of claiming her once more heated his pulse and caused a predictable reaction in his nether regions. Shifting on the buttoned leather, he rearranged his legs, carefully keeping his face concealed in the shadows the lamp's meager glow didn't reach. He didn't want her to notice him studying her, afraid she'd see the desire he couldn't conceal.

Or insistently bulging in my pantaloons.

Ian had hurt her once. He'd not do so again; not intentionally leastways. Retreating into the controlled, impersonal shell he'd adopted as a child, where he didn't permit himself to feel anything, served his purpose well.

Only he *did* feel. Something elusive, mystifying, and consuming. *Drivel.*

Something that haunted his increasingly distracted waking moments and his evermore restless nights.

Rubbish and balderdash.

His heart skipped a beat and turned over in an unfamiliar manner.

Dunderheaded dolt.

From across the coach, a muffled sigh sounded, and he cursed inwardly. Through half-lowered lids he watched Vangie. The lamp's dim light cast moving patterns across her delicate, downcast features, and he berated himself. His guilt had created a great, gaping chasm between them.

He roamed his gaze over her, taking in each refined feature, each supple curve. He permitted his eyes what he denied his hands and mouth and body.

As if sensing his perusal, she shifted her worn boots a bit further beneath her faded skirt. Her humble attire embarrassed her and also made no sense. He'd seen her in quality clothing; the yellow frock and the filmy silvery gown. Eyebrows scrunched together, he frowned. Why she now wore scarcely more than rags when Stapleton's pockets overflowed remained an enigma.

She removed her bonnet—if the sad thing could be called a bonnet—and patting her hair, placed it on the seat beside her. After wedging it into the corner, she folded the ribbons into a neat pile.

"You'll need a new wardrobe, of course," he blurted.

Vangie stopped fussing with the satin strips and stared at him, her expression unreadable. What went on in that keen mind of hers?

Feeling uncharacteristically gauche, he picked a piece of imaginary lint off his sleeve. "My housekeeper, Mrs. Tannsen, can take your measurements. She used to be a seamstress." Decades ago, but Vangie didn't have a lady's maid. *Yet.* Still, he wasn't asking Lucinda or Charlotte for any favors. Unfortunately, Charlotte was becoming more like her spiteful mother every day.

Vangie remained mute, and to fill the awkward silence, he said, "You may order whatever you like. Gowns, under things, bonnets, boots, slippers, fallalls, fripperies—" He waved his hand in a circle. "And whatever other whatnots you women find necessary."

A vision of her in that revealing pink confection sprang to mind, and a smile tugged the corners of his mouth upward. *Several more of those tempting, filmy nightgowns too.*

That idea cheered him enormously. More than it ought, given the current circumstances. If he'd buffered himself behind his battlements of indifference, why did tantalizing visions of his wife in scanty nightclothes keep bumping around in his mind? He shifted on the seat once more, cursing the rain and his ardor.

Vangie remained silent as he pressed into the dim corner.

He sent her what he intended as an encouraging smile. Although in his current uncomfortably aroused state, it may have been a lecherous grimace. "I'll arrange to have the order sent straightaway to London. New garments should begin to arrive within a fortnight."

"I have clothing, Ian."

"Not befitting your new station."

She flinched and shrinking against the squab, averted her gaze. Smoothing her skirt, she lifted a shoulder. "As you wish." Even in the subdued light, he couldn't miss the rosy color blooming across her cheeks.

Curse his loose tongue, he'd embarrassed her.

Had he not been in such a hurry to uncover the truth about Lucinda and Charlotte's blatant deception, he would've delayed his departure to Northumberland and purchased a new wardrobe for Vangie in London. With her aunt's and cousin's assistance, she would've enjoyed the venture, no doubt. Instead, he'd unintentionally reminded her of her prior status and humiliated her.

So much for his vow not to hurt her again.

Vangie repositioned herself on the seat, and although almost undetectable, a wince pinched her face.

Other than offering Ian a half-smile, Vangie hadn't bothered attempting to engage him when he'd first clamored into the carriage. When she'd exited the inn this morning, a smile of excitement and anticipation on her face, he'd been atop Pericles already. Last night's well-laid plans evaporated with the dawn's dew, and she fought foolish tears as, Malcolm, the driver, assisted her into the coach.

One could only take so much rejection, and after her husband had rebuffed her yet again this morning, she'd determined to protect herself from further despair and humiliation. The fragile wall she'd carefully erected since climbing in the coach would crack and disintegrate if he rejected her once more. With each saturated mile they traveled, her heart grew heavier, and her ire rose a bit higher as well.

How could she bear a lifetime of this?

There's always the Roma.

Stealing a glance at her husband lounging across from her, Vangie had no doubts that Ian was none too pleased the weather had forced him to share the coach hours before he typically did.

Arms folded, he sighed and shifted slightly, his face only partially visible in the half light. "Vangie, I truly meant no offense. I…" He faltered to a stop as she met his eyes for an instant before aiming her attention to her frayed gloves. "Do you have any personal belongings you'd like to retrieve in Brunswick before we continue on to Somersfield?" he asked considerately.

Uncertain what to make of his solicitousness, she lifted her gaze to his and nodded. "If it wouldn't be too much trouble. I do have a few things I'd like to collect."

"No trouble at all. We'll stop on the morrow as we pass through." He bestowed a warm smile upon her.

Taken aback by his change in demeanor, she searched his face for a long moment. "Thank—"

The coach lurched violently before bumping to a sudden, rough stop, practically tossing her onto the floor. Only clutching the seat prevented her from plummeting onto Ian's booted feet. Her reticule and hat weren't as fortunate. She bent over to recover them. Whatever caused them to stop so abruptly?

Shouts echoed outside.

Stifling the worry skittering across her shoulders, she inhaled sharply as he pulled a mahogany gun case from a compartment beneath his seat. Her alarm ratcheted upward once more when he removed one of the flintlock officer's pistols from its royal blue velvet bed. His mouth pressed into a grim line, he loaded the gun with practiced efficiency.

"Ian?" Vangie managed to sound poised though her pulse beat an uneven staccato, and her breath refused to leave her lungs in a normal fashion.

He smiled reassuringly before returning his attention to loading the other pistol. "Most likely nothing to be concerned about, sweeting. I'm only being cautious."

More shouting commenced, and the coach rocked as a driver

climbed down.

Her stomach caught and quivered. *Stay calm.* Coachmen disembarked for any number of reasons.

Ian raised a finger to his lips, mouthing, "Don't move." He quickly extinguished the lamp. From the edge of the window, he peered outside.

Was he serious? Vangie had no intention of sitting demurely by while God only knew what occurred outdoors. She bent forward determined to take a look herself.

The murky twilight hindered visibility, and only indiscriminate shapes and shadows met her scrutiny. Trying to see anything out there was like peering into a deep, dark pond. One knew something lurked beneath the surface, moving about, but one had no idea what *it* was—or whether it might be dangerous.

Ian opened the door, scarcely wide enough to squeeze through.

She barely swallowed the cry rising to her lips. Heavens, he wasn't going out there?

Slipping through the narrow opening, pistols in hand, he whispered, "Stay here."

The door closed with a soft *snick.*

Trepidation coiling in her stomach, she scooted to the edge of the seat. Balancing awkwardly, her backside hanging halfway off, she poked her nose around the sash just in time to see him disappear behind the rear of the coach.

A shot echoed, immediately followed by a profusion of cursing.

Dear God, please keep Ian safe.

An eerie silence descended, and she strained her ears, clenching and unclenching her hands. Only her uneven breathing punctuated the ominous stillness. Another gun's report disturbed the dusk's tranquility, and she jumped, her thoughts ricocheting around in her head. *Whatever is happening? Where is Ian? Is he injured? Where are the drivers? Who is swearing such foul oaths? How many highwaymen are there?* Then ludicrously—*has the rain stopped*?

She stuffed her gloved fist in her mouth, muffling the hysterical giggle gurgling forth.

Chin up, old girl. Gypsy blood. Sterner stuff and all that.

Rot and rubbish. She was utterly terrified.

Suddenly, the door wrenched open with such force, it cracked against the coach's side.

Hitching in a great gulp of air, Vangie jumped backward, hitting the squab with a solid clunk and banging her head on the carriage wall. The air whooshed from her lungs with the impact. Clutching the seat with one hand, she managed to right herself while keeping her other hand hidden beneath her skirts. Her head throbbed where it had connected with the carriage.

A surprisingly well-dressed man, a red handkerchief tied over the lower portion of his face, lurked in the opening. He waved the pistol he held menacingly. "Where's the gent?"

Vangie searched beyond him. Nominal daylight remained. Where *was* Ian? She shifted her attention to the highwayman and inched backward on the seat. Lifting her chin in the arrogant manner of the aristocratic dames in London, she answered icily. "You, sir, are mistaken. As you can plainly see," she angled her head haughtily, "I am alone."

He chuckled, a malevolent, alarming rumble that sent a frisson of fear creeping across her skin. His cold eyes narrowed. "Ye be a clacky wench. Mighty pleasin' to me eyes too."

Scots.

As Vangie edged a hand farther under her skirt, she swallowed against the alarm clawing at her chest

"Och, tanight willna be a total loss." A lewd gleam entered his eyes. He licked his thin lips and his black eyes dipped to her bosom. "I bet ye'd be a wild lassie to bed."

Her focus locked on his leering face, she stealthy crept her fingers closer to her dagger. His gun trained on her, the robber advanced, intent on stepping into the carriage.

Where is Ian? Why hadn't he stopped this lecher? Oh God, was he hurt or—?

A deafening blast shook the coach, and the thief lurched to an abrupt halt. Eyes widened in astonished disbelief, he toppled face-first onto the coach floor. Dead. His lower body dangled awkwardly in the opening, a bloodied hole in his back.

Behind him, clothing dirty and torn and lip bleeding, Ian brandished a smoking pistol.

Vangie slapped a hand across her slack mouth, smothering her terrified screech. *Dear God.* Gaze riveted on the dead man, she gulped against a wave of nausea then gulped again. *Dead. He's really dead.* She'd never seen anyone killed before. Injured, yes—gruesomely at times in the Romani encampment—but not dead.

As silently and as lethal as the panther Vangie likened him to, Ian had disposed of his prey. "You'll never know, you hell's spawn," Ian snarled, rage sparking in his baleful glare. He looked like the very devil himself.

A chill washing over her, she swallowed again.

Blood thundering in his head, Ian searched his wife's face. "Vangie, are you—?"

She yanked a dagger from the folds of her shabby skirt. She had the strangest expression on her face—a curious blend of resolution and dread—and her lips trembled.

Like a loadstone, his heart dropped to his boots. He'd die by his wife's hand this day, and she could blame his demise on the highwaymen. How she must hate him.

Her mouth moved, but no sound emerged. The subtle shifting of her gaze past his left shoulder alerted him.

Fiend seize it!

Twice now he'd been caught unawares, because his thoughts had been consumed with her. He ducked and spun around simultaneously, just in time to catch a glint of steel from the corner of his eye. Jerking his head to the side, he seized the thief's wrist. Ian slowed the plunging blade, but couldn't stop the descent entirely. The knife's finely-honed tip scraped the length of his neck, leaving a stinging trail. Caught unawares, even with both hands gripping his opponent's wrist, he was at a disadvantage.

His adversary suddenly stiffened, issuing a guttural grunt.

Ian's focus flew to fixate on Vangie's ashen, horror-stricken face. She appeared as if she were going to swoon or be sick or both. Her stunned indigo gaze never wavered from the man he been grappling with.

Straightening to his full height, Ian released the robber and retreated a pace

The man swayed from side to side. His eyes glassed over, rolling back in his head. He slowly tipped backward, bouncing against the edge of the carriage opening before landing on the soggy ground with a loud, heavy thud.

Ian gaped, his jaw hanging slack. He flashed hot then cold then hot again, scarcely believing his eyes.

Impaled to the hilt, Vangie's jeweled dagger protruded from the robber's back.

"God, forgive me. Oh, God, forgive me."

Her hoarse whisper jolted him from his stupefied trance. Grasping the coat of the other dead robber, he yanked him from the carriage entrance then dumped the man in an undignified heap on the ground beside his deceased cohort.

His mind still whirling in flabbergasted amazement, Ian bounded into the carriage and without hesitation, drew his quaking wife into his arms.

She buried her face in his shoulder, shaking and mumbling incoherently against his coat. "I had to, Ian. I had to."

He patted her back soothingly, brushing his lips across her hair. "Shh, sweeting. It's all right."

She sucked in a ragged breath. "He'd have killed you." Raw regret laced her voice. Head angled, her haunted gaze sought his. "I couldn't let him hurt you. I had to kill him. Don't you see?" Her tears flowing freely and fingers trembling, she clasped his lapel and pleaded for him to understand. "I didn't want to, but I'd no choice. I wouldn't let him take you from me." Weeping softly, she closed her eyes and pressed her face into his chest, her tears saturating his coat.

Take him from her? Did she possess some minuscule degree of affection for him after all? Hope flickered to life. Vangie's confession staggered far more than the knife tip pressed to his neck mere moments before.

Hugging her to his chest, he soothed, "Shh, it's over now." He ran a calming hand down her trembling spine. "The drivers and I kept the first four from the coach, but the other two must've been hiding."

Six highwaymen.

Truthfully, they were lucky to have survived. He wouldn't have done if it hadn't been for Vangie. How could he have believed she'd hurt him? She was everything good and decent and gentle. And, she killed tonight—killed to protect him.

Despite his stinging lip, he kissed the crown of her head and tightened his arms around her slim form. Something wondrous sprang free in his chest, liberating him. Initially painful, the sensation resolutely exploded forth with a life and vigor of its own. It was marvelous, implausible, and consuming.

And this time, he didn't call it rot and rubbish.

Disheveled and holding his right arm, Malcolm appeared in the coach doorway. "M' lord, milady. Are ye unharmed?"

"Shaken, but unharmed," Ian assured him.

Malcolm's gaze meshed with his. "They was waitin' fer us, sir."

16

Vangie opened her tear-blurred eyes upon hearing the humble coachman, injured though he was, inquiring after her well-being. Gifford, the junior coachman, his face battered and bloody, hovered nearby. Lurching to an upright position, she began issuing orders while tearing at the hem of her petticoat.

"Ian, have we any water? Mr. Gifford, I need light, please, and my small box tied with the purple ribbon. Mr. Malcolm, do climb in the carriage, so I can attend to your wound." She edged Ian's cravat away from his neck. "It's little more than a shallow cut, thank God. Best to clean it though."

After she removed her gloves, she gathered the torn petticoat. The three men remained motionless, gawking at her open-mouthed. In the act of ripping her petticoat into strips, she paused, quirking an eyebrow at the dumbstruck trio.

"Faith, gentlemen. Don't dawdle. Let's be about it then!"

Gifford and Ian obediently scrambled to do her bidding. Minutes later, she squatted beside Malcolm, dabbing at his injured arm. She'd blanched at the blood when cutting away his shirt, but made quick work of dressing the wound.

"Vangie, might I use a strip of your petticoat?"

At Ian's question, she glanced across the coach, and her heart pinged painfully.

His neckcloth stained scarlet, Ian was a sight. Bruised, his left eye was horribly swollen as was his puffy lower lip.

Her scrutiny dipped to her spencer. A wonder she wasn't covered with blood too. She wrinkled her nose. The coach reeked of blood, sweat, mud and manure. She eyed the smears on the Malcolm's boot only inches from her skirts.

Ian pointed at his cut neck. "I'll wash away the worst of this while you look after Malcolm."

"Of course. Here's one for Gifford too." She handed him two strips. "See to your lip first, Ian." From the corner of her eye she watched him divest his coat and his bloodstained neckcloth, which he tossed through the open door. Using a portion of the water, he cleansed his lip and neck.

She kept up a constant diatribe as she worked. Chatting had always calmed her nerves. "My *puri daj,* that's grandmother in Romanese, taught me how to tend wounds." She shifted, fully facing Malcolm to take advantage of the lamp's light. "I'm not as accomplished as she is, but your injury is not terribly serious." She curved her mouth reassuringly. "Though, I'm certain it hurts like the very devil, Mr. Malcolm." She swabbed his injury with a damp cloth.

"Just Malcolm will do, milady." His features a mask of confusion, he stared across the coach. He clearly didn't know what to make of a lady tending him.

She twisted to glance at her husband too. A wide grin split his face. Whatever was he so jovial about? Heaven's above, six dead men lay outside. She darted a glance to the open door, and giving herself a mental shake, forced her attention back inside. Never mind. Best to return to the task at hand and not dwell on that ugliness and the part she'd played.

"Very well, Malcolm. The ball passed clear through, nice and clean. It's fortunate I always carry my medicines and my dagger with me. *Puri Daj* taught me the art of healing with plants and herbs. She taught me to use a dagger too."

"Too?" Ian threw the stained piece of petticoat he'd washed with onto the ground. "Your *grandmother* taught you to use a dagger?" Astonishment tinged his voice. "Obviously, you were an apt pupil."

Vangie stopped her ministrations, staring at the upholstery wistfully. "The Romani should be arriving any day now." She cut her gaze to Malcolm for a moment before gravitating her attention to Ian. Despite the heaviness in her heart, she attempted a smile. "It will be the first time in my memory I'll not stay with the travelers for a few weeks." She fidgeted with the cloth in her hands. "They are an honorable people but suffer much persecution because their ways are different."

Crouched as she was, her legs' cramping drew her attention to the present. She slid onto the seat beside Malcolm. Returning her focus to his wound, Vangie declared defiantly, "If I'd the means, I'd help them. They deserve to be treated with dignity."

"I agree," Ian said, sincerity and warmth ringing in his voice.

She wrapped a length of petticoat around Malcom's arm. "Were you aware I'm part Roma—that gypsy *ratti* runs in my veins?"

She regarded Ian guardedly, daring him to object to her heritage. How would he respond to her revelation? How would *she* react if he rejected her again?

"I know, sweeting." He leaned over and kissed her soundly on the mouth, despite the flabbergasted coachman's twitching nose but inches from their meshed lips.

"Ahem." Malcom cleared his throat, his ears crimson.

Vangie promptly shifted away, no doubt her cheeks as red as his glowing ears.

Ian regarded her as if besotted.

Another discreet cough brought a flurry of heat to her face and another fool's grin to Ian's. Was he daft, kissing her mere inches from the coachman? Pleased and confused, Vangie bent to her task once more, efficiently tying off the last bandage. "There you are, Malcolm."

"Thank ye, milady." He nodded as he fingered the bandage.

She rested against the plush seat, her hands clasped tightly. Now that the crisis had passed, she'd become self-conscious, unsure of her skills. "You'll need to see a physician of course—to be sure it has been properly treated. I've not dressed a firearm wound before, only knife cuts and gashes."

"Knife cuts and gashes?" One sable eyebrow arched, Ian's expression held admiration and surprise.

"Mmm." She nodded. "Sometimes, the brethren are involved in fights with each other, but more commonly with *gadjo,* non-Roma. Knives are the Roma's weapon of choice."

Ian reached over, tugged her knotted hands loose, then raised one to his lips. "You were absolutely marvelous." He kissed the back of her hand before turning it over to place a hot, lingering kiss on her palm. He caressed the inside of her wrist with his thumb, causing her pulse to frolic alarmingly. Or mayhap, the smoldering glint in his eyes caused her heart's cavorting.

"Uh hum!" Malcolm noisily cleared his throat once more, this time sounding as if he gargled glass.

"Aye, milady. I ain't ne'er seen a lady o' quality willin' to dirty 'er 'ands afore." Gifford offered this compliment from the open doorway, bobbing his head all the while. He gingerly placed her clean dagger on the seat. All evidence of the knife's recent resting place had been erased.

"Me either, yer ladyship. Thank ye. It's grateful I be." Malcolm made this pronouncement while gingerly exiting the coach.

Vangie beamed, delighted with their approval, and more importantly, their acceptance of her Romani heritage. "Thank you, gentlemen." Noting the coachman's sudden pallor, concern gripped her. "Malcolm, you don't mean to drive?"

"Nay, milady." He jogged his chin toward Gifford. "I jus' needs to be next to this goosecap. He'd 'ave us lost inside of five minutes."

"Wouldna," Gifford objected indignantly.

"Aye, lad, ye would," Malcom said, closing the door behind him.

Still arguing, the two climbed aboard the outer seat, and with a yell and the crack of a whip, the coach lurched forward and continued on its way.

"Ian, what about…those men?" Vangie sliced a glance at the shadows outside and shuddered, gooseflesh prickling her neck and shoulders.

He followed the direction of her gaze. "Gifford pulled their bodies to the side of the road. I'll send for a magistrate when we stop for the night a few miles farther along. He will deal with them."

She gave a reluctant nod. "I suppose that will have to do."

"Sweeting…?" Ian hesitated, looking like a confused schoolboy rather than a commanding lord. "Did your grandmother truly teach you to use a knife?"

She curved her lips at the corners. She'd wager her pin money, if she had any that was, he'd been burning to ask the question since she'd disposed of the robber. Guilt and remorse washed over her once more stealing her smile with it.

Declaring the opposite seat required the blood cleansed before it was usable again, Ian had claimed a spot beside her when they'd resumed their journey. Coatless, he'd rolled his sleeves to the elbow and unfastened the shirt's top buttons. A dark claret-colored stain marred the collar.

Thoroughly unnerved by his close proximity and his state of undress, Vangie was unable to concentrate on anything but the muscular leg pressing intimately against her thigh. Or the hand and forearm smattered with fine dark hair, which rested inches from her leg.

"Vangie?"

She raised her eyes to his.

He regarded her expectantly.

"Hmm? Did you say something, Ian?"

"Grandmother? Knife?" He held her dagger and dipped it up and down.

"Ah, yes." She accepted it from him, turning it over in her palm. "I'm quite skilled with blades. *Puri Daj* was adamant I be, so she and Yoska taught me the art."

"Yoska?"

"The *bandolier*. The leader of our clan." She slid her dagger into the medicine basket. "It isn't unusual to have unfriendly or unwelcome visitors at the encampment. Assault is not common, but it does happen on occasion. Roma women do what we must to protect ourselves."

"I had no idea," he murmured.

Vangie scrutinized his face. Her disclosure didn't appear to have disturbed him. This might though. She grinned. "Uncle Gideon insisted Yvette and I be trained in weaponry. Whenever I visited, he'd give me lessons. I'm proficient with firearms too."

Ian's brows climbed to his hairline.

An unwelcome thought snaked its way into her mind where it coiled menacingly. The robber had known she didn't travel alone. "Ian, why did the highwayman ask where you were? How did he know there was a gentleman traveling with me?"

Though Ian was loath to admit it to Vangie, the same thought troubled him. If he counted the vagrant attempting to waylay him on his journey to London, this was the third time in as many weeks he'd been set upon by ruffians. Plus, there'd also been the incident with the curricle's wheel.

He finally settled on the most plausible and least alarming explanation. "It would be most unusual for a female to travel alone," he reassured her. "Naturally, since you'd no companion, he assumed a male accompanied you."

Ian didn't believe a word of that flim flam. A persistent notion niggled in the recesses of his mind, as if he had overlooked something. He turned his mouth downward, but only for a moment. He'd not fret on it. The answer would come to him. It always did. His mind had a way of sifting and sorting information subconsciously, forming a logical explanation from a conglomeration of facts, nuances, and details. The ability was really quite extraordinary.

Not as extraordinary as his new bride, however.

Blades and pistols. Would wonders never cease?

He wasn't altogether certain whether to be reassured or concerned about this newly acquired knowledge regarding his wife. Vangie was turning out to be a deucedly fascinating catch after all. His face split with what he was positive was an imbecile's grin, and he chuckled inwardly. He quite liked the idea of having taken a gypsy to wife. For certain, life would never be dull.

A few inches separated their hands, and Ian gathered hers in his. She'd not donned her gloves after tending to Malcolm. He rubbed a finger against her wedding ring. "It was my mother's."

An unspoken question shone in her pretty eyes. He smiled an answer, chagrined to see a hopeful light flicker in his wife's gorgeous gaze. She so wanted his acceptance, his approval. She deserved it after proving her loyalty to him. No, she deserved it before then, when she'd gone willingly to his bed, an untried maid, trusting him, her stranger-of-a-husband.

A spark of anger flared, burning hot behind his breastbone. He'd not be as forgiving with his stepmother and sister as his bride had been with him. They'd caused incalculable harm to her, though his conscience whispered he was to blame for listening to their gossip and reacting with anger instead of self-control and logic.

These past days had tried him to the limits of his endurance. He wanted her in is bed. Wanted to taste her sweet lips once more. His attention strayed to Vangie's mouth. Slowly, giving her plenty of opportunity to turn away, he lowered his head. When his mouth met hers, a wistful sigh escaped her plump lips, and she tentatively returned his kiss.

Gently, reverently, he caressed her mouth with his. Not a kiss of passion or lust, but a tender, heartfelt apology. He explored, yearning, seeking, hoping he'd find what he desperately sought within the honeyed cavern—*forgiveness*—though unwarranted.

With a final press of his lips against her beautiful mouth, he leaned away, smiling contentedly. She hadn't rebuffed him, and he now knew what he must do to win his wife over.

He'd woo her.

There'd been no courtship before their nuptials, but he vowed, he'd charm his bride. He'd dazzle her with everything a young damsel's heart desired. She'd willingly given herself to him, and not only her luscious body, but her heart as well.

What an incredible and wholly unpredictable turnabout.

Barely a week ago, he'd cursed fate for her role in forcing him to wed Vangie. And today, he rejoiced at his good fortune. He caressed his wife with his gaze, and as if sensing his perusal, she gifted him with an exquisite smile. More optimistic than he'd been the whole of the previous week, he returned her smile, gently squeezing her hand.

Perhaps he'd found favor with God at last. Why the recent streak of misfortunes then? If only the feeling he'd missed something obvious didn't persist annoyingly like a sliver in his finger.

17

Ian jolted awake, confused and disoriented. The coach no longer rocked and swayed. Bending forward, careful not to disturb Vangie nestled against his side, he peered through the window. He breathed a sigh of relief upon spying The White Stag Inn. It was well into the late-night hours; a dangerous time to be on the road, which was why a loaded pistol lay on the seat beside him.

He nudged her. "Sweeting, wake up."

The gut-wrenching terror pummeling him when he'd seen her cornered at gun-point whipped him anew. He well-knew the salacious intentions of the blackguard he'd consigned to the grave, courtesy of the lead ball he planted in him. Reflexively, he tightened his arms around her. God help anyone intending to harm this woman. His woman. His wife.

"Vangie." He kissed her forehead.

"Hmm?" Shivering, she snuggled further into his side.

"We've arrived at the inn." Ian's gaze roamed her face, relaxed and unbelievably beautiful in repose.

He hoped she felt something for him too. Mayhap, she didn't understand the feeling, but perhaps it had compelled her to take a life to protect him. The elusive emotion was foreign to him, and only now did he recognize the sentiment. The understanding left him desperate and vulnerable. And utterly terrified.

Were he and Vangie predestined for one another? Had God ordained from the beginning of time that they should find each other and through freewill, or otherwise, bound them together? A week ago, he'd have scoffed at these fanciful notions, calling them fustian nonsense, balderdash and claptrap, but now?

She stirred sleepily, her eyes fluttering half-open, a shy smile teasing her mouth.

He placed another feathery kiss upon her tempting lips. Her smile widened beneath his mouth. Elation sluiced him, and he settled her closer, never breaking contact with her lips. This was not a kiss borne of desire but one of tender, awe-inspiring emotion. A tantalizing kiss which wordlessly offered his heart to her.

Somehow, he knew she perceived the gift. She reached between them, laying her palm against his heart. He raised his head, dropping a reverent kiss upon her forehead before edging away.

"I'll see to our rooms." With his forefinger, he flicked the sable curls tumbled to her shoulders. "You might want to restore your appearance." He winked wickedly. "People might talk."

A tiny squeak escaped Vangie, and she immediately reached to straighten her hair.

A roguish chuckle reverberated in Ian's chest. He teased her, and she grinned. The ramparts he'd erected around himself had disappeared, and even in the coach's dim light, an unmistakable glimmer shone in his eyes. She drew in a calming breath. His doting attention excited her, causing her heart to beat a pace or two quicker.

"I'll be but a few minutes," he said. "Stay here."

Once he stepped from the equipage, she smoothed her skirt, donned her hat and gloves, and waited for him to return. She deliberately avoided looking at the dark stains on the opposite seat.

A wave of nausea assailed her, accompanied by a burst of pain behind her eyes. The discomfort spread, becoming an incessant throbbing, spanning her forehead and temples. Searing pulsations radiated from her temple to her jaw.

Another headache? So soon?

Would she never be free of them? For thirteen long years she'd suffered these horrid megrims. *Better now than when I needed my wits about me to save Ian's life.*

She could yet see the face of the man she'd stabbed, and a shudder rippled through her. Surely God would forgive her for taking his life. His wasn't innocent blood, but that of a devious, black-hearted scoundrel. Besides, she'd killed to protect her husband.

She drew in a raggedy, shallow breath. She'd do it again too.

The drumming in her head increased ferociously, pounding and thrumming like the leather-topped *djembe's* played during Romani celebrations. She raised a shaky hand to cup her forehead. *Dear, God.*

Through the buzzing in her ears, Vangie was vaguely aware of Ian speaking to Malcolm and Gifford. No doubt giving them instructions for the night and departure on the morrow. The door opened, and smiling, he poked his head inside.

She detected a smidgeon of worry when his perceptive gaze lit on her face.

"Have you a headache, sweeting?"

She didn't dare nod. "Yes."

"Come, I'll help you alight." Ian lifted her from the carriage then set her on her wobbly legs.

Grateful for the bracing arm he slipped around her waist, she attempted a weak smile.

"The White Stag Inn is a farmhouse turned public lodgings," he said, escorting her inside.

As long as there's a bed.

Vangie was beyond caring. She needed to lie down. Through the fog numbing her senses, she worked a labored glance over the common room and the blazing fire in the hearth. Spots floating before her eyes, she clutched at Ian's arm with one hand to steady herself whilst pressing the other to her gyrating stomach. She'd never cast up her accounts before but feared she might this time.

A rotund woman with rosy red cheeks and a smile to match her substantial girth trundled to them. Her wiry gray hair constrained into a semblance of a knot, she dropped an awkward curtsey. "Yer room's been made ready, m'lord, and I'll 'ave yer food—" She lunged forward and grasped Vangie's elbow, steadying her. "Yer ladyship, ye be ready to keel over!"

Vangie swallowed, fuzziness encapsulating her. Lord, how she hated this. "Ian?" Panic riddled her voice.

Without preamble, he scooped her into his arms. "Our room?"

"This way, yer lordship." The proprietress beckoned him to follow as she waddled to the stairs.

Vangie daren't close her eyes. Blackness would engulf her. Instead, she pressed her head into Ian's chest and counted to five with each inhalation and exhalation. Squinting against the sparkling zigzags rotating before her eyes, she concentrated on the proprietress' ample backside as she labored up the staircase.

Wheezing, the woman opened a door at the far end of the corridor.

She shuffled to the bed, and tossing back a quilt said, "I'll 'ave Peg bring ye water and yer supper." Her chuffy face crinkled with concern, she asked, "Do her ladyship be needin' anythin'?"

Ian laid Vangie on the bed. The room swirled, gyrating around and around, as the black, spiraling tunnel tried to suck her into obscurity. He touched her forehead and traced a gentle path over her cheek. She locked her attention on his calm, reassuring gaze.

He glanced at the woman. "Have you any smelling salts?"

Vangie tried to focus on Ian's voice, but it echoed so far away.

The innkeeper shook her head, her loose chins flapping with her vehemence. "Nay, sir. Not much call fer salts."

It's too late—

Vangie awoke slowly. Snuggled beneath layers of blankets, she felt more refreshed than she had in weeks. She sighed contentedly, burying her face in the pillow in an attempt to avoid a persistent ray of sun angling across her face. A few moments passed before Vangie realized she wasn't alone in the bed.

"Good morning, my lady," Ian purred close to her ear.

She cracked open her eyelids.

He lay in his pantaloons and shirt atop the bedding, his dark head but inches from hers.

Feeling shy, she softly replied, "Good morning."

His gaze held hers, and she couldn't look away, didn't want to. He said not a word, but something deep in his eyes spoke to her spirit. He angled his head and lightly kissed her.

A firm knock rattled the chamber's door, shattering the moment.

Ian bounded from the bed. "Breakfast, at last. I'm ravenous."

Vangie scooted to a sitting position. She wore her threadbare nightgown. *How?* Ah, her ill-fated episode last evening. Heaven above, Ian must've undressed her. The flush sweeping her wasn't entirely due to embarrassment.

Out of habit, she skimmed her thigh with her fingertips. Her dagger wasn't there. She quickly scanned the room, searching for the knife. Except for when she bathed, she always wore it.

His back to the closed door, and holding a laden tray, Ian observed her. "Your blade is on the nightstand. Do you typically tie it to your leg?" His attention slid pointedly to her thigh.

Vangie nodded. "Almost always. Many Roma women do."

She shifted her attention to the pillow beside her. A couple of strands of wavy chestnut hair lay atop it. She smiled. Had he slept here, in this room with her all night? She followed him with her gaze as he carried their breakfast to a small table. A jar filled with wildflowers stood atop its scratched surface. Nonetheless, the chamber possessed a rustic charm. Last night, she'd taken scant notice of it or anything else, for that matter.

Simple gingham curtains hung from the lone window, and braided rag rugs lay on either side of the bed. The table and two chairs occupied one corner of the chamber, a washstand and mirror the other. A nightstand, an oil lamp in its center, was the only other piece of furniture in the room.

Leaning closer, Vangie examined the hand-painted porcelain lampshade. An intricate bouquet of blue and white roses graced the surface. She curved her mouth in appreciation. Self-taught, she adored painting. She was quite good at it too, though the opportunities to indulge the pastime solely for pleasure were few.

"Are you hungry?" Ian placed the tray on the table. He peeked under the serviette and grinned.

"Yes. Very." She nodded again as she slipped from the bed. Her night rail swished around her bare feet as she approached the table. "I haven't eaten since breakfast yesterday. I'm famished." As if to confirm her claim, her stomach rumbled loudly.

"So I can hear," he quipped.

She put her hand on her middle. "Goodness."

Glancing at her rail, Vangie hesitated. She couldn't eat wearing nothing but her thin nightgown. Ian must have sensed her concern. He crossed to her open valise, and after digging around, removed her robe.

He settled the familiar folds over her shoulders, and Vangie smiled her gratitude. "Thank you."

Lifting a warm scone, she bit into it with relish. "Mmm, scrumptious."

Closing her eyes, she took another blissful bite. Several crumbs from the pastry stuck to her mouth. She traced her lips with her tongue, licking them clean. Hearing a strange sound, she opened her eyes. Had Ian groaned?

Looking abashed, he patted his stomach and said, "My stomach's protesting in hunger too."

His was the oddest hunger pang she'd ever heard. He took the chair opposite hers, then filled his plate. "We'll reach Somersfield this afternoon."

Something in his tone gave Vangie pause, and she searched his face. Wasn't he pleased to be returning home? Or perhaps, explaining her presence to his family had caused the coolness in his voice.

Three hours later, Vangie's childhood home loomed before the coach. She'd pressed her lips into a thin line the moment the house appeared on the horizon. Biddlethorpe Hall's familiar golden-honey facade stirred complex emotions she'd rather leave unexamined.

An oversized stone cottage boasting five bedrooms, four chimneys crowned with terra-cotta stacks stood at attention atop the roof. An uneven ivy hedge blanketed a stone fence framing the lawn she'd seldom been permitted to play on. A curving flagstone footpath led the way through an open gate to a charming, arched wooden entrance.

She'd adored this house, the Caruthers' ancestral home and grounds when her father was the baronet. Since his death and Great Uncle Percival had assumed the baronetcy, the place held little happiness for her and had ceased to truly be home. Drawing in a slow, deep breath, she carefully schooled her features into blandness.

Dragging her gaze from Biddlethorpe, she briefly met Ian's eyes, before shifting hers away. She clutched her hands in her lap, bunching her washed-out skirt. "I've but a few items to collect, Ian. You needn't trouble yourself with alighting. I'm sure my aunt and uncle won't object if you remain in the coach." *Please, don't ask me why.* She didn't want him to know the reason. Aunt Eugenia and Uncle Percival were so miserly, they begrudged guests a spot of tea and a biscuit.

"Are you certain?" Three lines puckered his brow, the movement emphasizing the sharp angles of his striking face as his gaze poured over her. Did he see through her ruse?

Nodding, Vangie reassured him, a mite more enthusiastically than necessary, "Oh, yes, I'm quite sure." She breathed a silent sigh of relief, having feared he'd object to remaining in the conveyance. She didn't want anything to disrupt the amiable disposition he'd adopted, for she quite liked this charming rogue.

Studying him from beneath her lashes, she concluded he was

relaxed, not the least disgruntled by her ill-mannered suggestion. Noticing her perusal, Ian's lips tilted slowly, sensually upward, a clear invitation in his gray eyes.

Vangie's stomach flip-flopped, at having been caught staring at him and from his seductive roguery. Blushing, she swiftly averted her gaze. He was the only person capable of causing her to turn cherry-cheeked with such regularity. A simple smile or an innocent look from him and she was aquiver.

He'd been all polite concern and solicitousness since last night. It seemed their misadventure with the highwaymen yester eve had wrought some benefits. Mayhap he harbored a morsel of tenderness for her after all.

Please, let it be so.

The carriage rolled to a stop, and anxiety gripped her. She purposefully relaxed her tense muscles and cast a glance at Ian. He smiled again, a gleam in his quick-silver eyes she couldn't identify but which caused a whorl of emotions.

Yes, last night and this morning did indeed give her cause for optimism. Now, to brave the ordeal of informing Aunt Eugenia and Uncle Percival of her marriage, gathering her sparse belongings, and leaving her childhood home. She'd be in and out of Biddlethorpe in ten—mayhap fifteen minutes—at most. Knowing Ian waited in the coach gave her courage.

He opened the trap door in the roof. "Gifford, please assist her ladyship from the coach."

"Yes, m'lord."

"I'll be but a few minutes, no more than fifteen." She laid her hand on his arm, searching his eyes. "You don't mind waiting?"

Ian covered Vangie's hand with his. She was reluctant to introduce him to her relatives. Why? Was she ashamed of him, their forced marriage, and the necessity of having to explain the hasty nuptials? Or was it something else?

He lowered his attention to her hands. Earlier she had clasped them together so tightly he could see the white tips of her fingers. Though married less than a week, he knew her well enough to know she clenched her hands when distraught.

Curious, and not a little intrigued, Ian angled his head. She was obviously apprehensive. Again, he asked himself why? He peered past her, taking in the attractive house and grounds. Not ostentatiously affluent but still well-kept, and certainly not poverty stricken as he'd been led to believe.

"Your aunt and uncle won't be offended if I don't come in and introduce myself?"

"Oh, no. Not at all." Vangie shook her head. "They aren't expecting me home just yet, and…" Her shoulders slumped, and she looked uncomfortable. "Ian," she paused. "I'm not sure how to say this except plainly. They don't like unexpected guests."

His curiosity piqued further. "They shan't be curious whose coach this is?"

"No." Her faint smile barely tilted her lips and didn't wipe the unease from her face. "They'll assume it belongs to Uncle Gideon. He has several."

Something was definitely amiss. Squeezing her hand, Ian gave a nod toward the house. "Go along then. I don't mind."

She sent him a grateful smile, which only increased his determination to know exactly what was afoot.

Gifford opened the door and assisted her down the small step. As she made her way to the cottage, a black-haired bantling called to her. A brilliant smile illuminated her face. She obviously knew the child and held him in great affection. She bent and embraced the boy, wrapping her arms around his thin body and hugging him tight to her.

She likes children.

The realization pleased Ian enormously. His pulse quickened when he considered precisely what was necessary to impregnate her. He allowed himself the luxury of a moment of erotic daydreaming to further explore that particular pleasant musing.

Vangie and the urchin spoke briefly. The child withdrew something from his vest pocket and passed it to her. With a wave, the boy trotted off, his bare feet kicking up small poufs of dust in his wake.

She watched him for a few moments. Was that sadness shadowing her face? Did her shoulders droop slightly? Ian scooted forward, his regard traveling between her and the child. It settled on the slip of paper she held.

A note? From whom? A man?

Stop it, old chap.

Vangie flipped the smallish rectangle over, studying it for a second before opening her reticule and tucking it inside. After cinching the strings tight, she looped the bag around her wrist and turned in the direction of the cottage.

Shoulders squared and chin up, as if preparing to enter a battle rather than her home, she marched through the open gate. However, instead of entering through the front door, she skirted the house and disappeared around the corner.

To use the rear entrance? Uneasiness skittered down his spine.

There was only one way to find out.

Follow her.

18

Before trailing his wife inside, Ian gave his drivers instructions. His soldier's instincts pealed in alarm. Without a qualm or a hint of repentance, he opened the back door, letting himself into a deserted kitchen. Fresh-baked bread and pies cooled on a long table, and something savory simmered atop the iron cookstove. He sniffed in appreciation as he pushed the door closed behind him.

Head tilted, listening for voices, he strode the length of one corridor then turned down another. Taking care to tread silently, he glanced into the rooms he passed. High quality, if somewhat older, furnishings graced each of them. This was far from a pauper's residence.

A scowl pulled his eyebrows tight.

Then why did his wife wear little more than rags?

"What, did they send you packing?" A woman's haughty, strident voice demanded.

Ah, here they were. He edged along the wall until just outside the room's entrance. The door stood open, giving him an almost unobstructed view of the interior.

Dressed in the latest fashion, ruby earrings sparkling in her earlobes, a hatchet-faced woman reclined in an armchair and berated Vangie.

"I must say, I expected you'd be banished from Polite Society sooner. I told you, the *haute ton* wouldn't tolerate a *gypsy* tainting their fancy drawing rooms and elitist assemblies." A sneer distorting her face, she waved a beringed hand as if she shooed a smelly beggar from her presence. "Well, change your clothes, and be swift about it. You've weeks' worth of chores to catch up on."

The shrew pointed to a glistening window. "You can start with the windows, inside and out, and then polish the silver. Frieda hasn't had the time, poor dear. Your gadding about London left her to complete your chores too. It was most inconsiderate of you."

"But, Aunt Eugenia—"

"You'll give us none of your jaw, Evangeline." A reedy masculine voice interjected. *The uncle?* "I suppose you've returned empty-handed once more. No clothes, fallalls, jewels…*coin*?"

Greedy scrounger.

Ian crept a few inches closer. The rail-thin hog grubber lounged on the settee, picking at a pasty of some sort.

"I've brought nothing of value back with me, Uncle Percival."

Ian smirked. *Except a well-heeled, titled husband.*

Glaring daggers at her, the aunt curled her mouth into a pout. "Surely you could've solicited Gideon for funds. After all, *he's* your legal guardian and has such well-padded pockets, while we must make do with the bare necessities. It's most unfair."

Ian examined the well-appointed drawing room again. *Bare necessities?* Hardly.

The aunt huffed out an exaggerated sigh before continuing with her fustian monologue. "For over thirteen years, we've been burdened with your care." Tapping her long nails on the chair arm, Lady Caruthers continued her harping. "The pittance your parents left in trust for you is long gone—"

"Wait! There was a trust? For me?" Vangie stared at her aunt in astonished outrage.

The harpy ignored her question. "The dolts made no provision for your care, and the meager work you do around here barely compensates for your food."

"Some days I eat but one meal," Vangie protested. "And there have been days, I've not eaten at all, except for fruits or vegetables I've scavenged from the garden."

Her aunt sent Vangie another thinly-veiled hostile look. "What of your painting and crochet work? Have you any ready to sell? The funds for your time-wasting hobbies don't appear out of thin air, gel."

The pained expression on his wife's face deepened. "The Stapletons' gifted me with those supplies, as you well know."

Gritting his teeth to keep silent, Ian glowered. *Bloody harridan.* Was the woman completely void of decency? My God, to think Vangie had endured this—*them*—for over a decade?

Standing, Lady Caruthers sliced a self-important glance to her fusty husband, gingerly licking a blob of clotted cream off his bony finger. He grimaced in distaste. "Percival, do pay attention," she snapped, her piercing voice scraping like pointed claws along Ian's nerves.

Ducking his head, Sir Percival whined, "Of course, my dove," before daring one last, defiant slurp of his finger.

Henpecked.

Ian twisted his mouth, then eyes narrowed, scowled again, outrage bumping around in his chest. Behind his wife's back, the bloody lecher ogled Vangie. She was his niece, for God's sake, the perverse old podger.

Was Vangie aware? Poised, her face wan and fraught with tension, she sliced her uncle a swift, wary glance. She shuddered and promptly averted her gaze. Hell yes, she knew. Had the reprobate dared touch her?

Ian clenched his hands against the urge to throttle Caruthers.

She met her aunt's glare straight on. "I'm sorry to have been an encumbrance to you for so many years, Aunt Eugenia."

Ian detected a sharp shred of sarcasm lacing her words.

Vangie heaved what he determined to be a resigned sigh. "I do have several pieces of crocheted work completed and some cups and plates painted as well."

"You do?" Greed lit her ladyship's face. "Where are they?"

"In my room. I'll fetch them." Vangie turned halfway, but her aunt's words froze her in place.

"Oh, well, as for those, er…" Lady Caruthers hedged before plowing on. "They've already been sold."

Vangie whirled around to face her fully, disbelief etched on her beautiful face. "You went into my chamber, took my belongings, and sold them—*again*?"

Again? They'd done this before? Indignation rose in Ian, simmering dangerously near the surface, testing his self-control.

Rage contorting his face, Sir Percival lurched to his feet. "You don't have any belongings except for those our Christian charity permits you." He advanced until he was but inches from her.

Though quaking, Vangie stood her ground. Unflinching, she looked him straight in the eye. "Did you sell my mother's china?"

Silence greeted her question.

Sucking in a great draught of air, she whispered. "How could you? Those four cups were all I'd left of her." She tilted her chin proudly. "You had no right."

"Hold your tongue, you insolent chit." Eyes enraged slits, he raised his hand, and she threw her arm upward to ward off his blow.

So, this wasn't the first time the bloody sod had struck her. By God, it *would* be the last.

Ian stormed into the room. "Don't you dare!" he roared.

Sir Percival froze. His pig eyes grew huge, and crimson dashed his gaunt face. No sound emerged from his flapping mouth.

Lady Caruthers seemed petrified too, rooted to the floor, staring bug-eyed at Ian.

His eyes skewered Sir Percival and dared her ladyship to utter so much as a peep. "If you lay a hand on my *wife,* it will be the last thing you ever do. I promise you."

"Your *wife*?" Lady Caruthers said in a strangled voice. Her attention darted between Vangie and him, astonishment causing her beady rodent eyes to bulge.

"Wife?" squawked Sir Percival before a sly glint entered his calculating gaze.

Lowering her arm, Vangie retreated until she bumped into Ian. He wrapped an arm around her and spoke quietly into her ear. "Vangie, go gather whatever you need. You shan't be returning here—*ever*."

After one sharp nod, she edged past him. Then lifting her skirt, she tore from the room.

Vangie glanced up from packing as Ian bent to enter the tiny attic chamber that had served as her bedroom for thirteen years. It didn't surprise her he'd found his way here. She raised her chin, refusing to be ashamed of her modest room. The roof slanted downward on both sides, and only in the middle could one stand upright. A single-paned, curtainless window at one end allowed a trickle of light inside.

"Aunt and Uncle?"

"Are *graciously* keeping Gifford and Malcolm entertained."

She raised her eyebrows. "Meaning?"

Ian's gaze roamed the chamber before meeting hers. "Meaning, I've bought them off and threatened them with legal action if they so much as mention your name again." He shook his head. "What was your father thinking, appointing them to be your guardians? They spent your trust fund."

"Pardon?" She snapped up her head. "They aren't my guardians. Uncle Gideon and my father's Romani mother are…were."

Married now, she no longer had guardians.

Ian's smile turned apologetic. "Then they altered the documents to gain access to your funds."

Anger surged through her, hot and sharp. She would be well rid of them. "I'm not surprised. Their perfidy knows no bounds."

Sucking in a calming breath, she went about her room, gathering her possessions, scarce though they were. From the corner of her eye, she watched Ian explore the rustic chamber. She cast a loving gaze around the small space. She'd miss this attic room, despite its austerity.

Nestled under one eve stretched a hard, narrow cot covered with a faded quilt her mother had made. That treasure she wouldn't leave behind. A sideways wooden crate formed a makeshift nightstand, a neat pile of books stacked within. Pegs protruding from the opposite wall held no more than a half dozen garments.

One was her brightly colored, multi-layered *padma*. The full skirt swirled around her ankles like a vibrant, pulsating rainbow when she danced. Beside the *padma* was an embroidered, full-sleeved blue blouse with an extraordinary embellished vest draped atop it. *Puri Daj* had sewn the garments.

"Vangie, did you draw these?"

Tucking a book into one of the crates, she glanced up. Ian examined one of her sketches of Roma children tacked to the rafters.

"Yes. I do draw a bit, but I much prefer to paint. Aunt Eugenia insisted I sell anything I painted, though."

He gestured at the sketches. "These are good, very good. Have you nothing you've painted?"

Vangie smiled, a sad half-smile. "Only this."

She handed him a wooden picture frame. A miniature portrait of a man and woman smiled at him. "My parents." She'd painted the frame with delicate vines, flowers, and birds. "I but painted the frame. The portrait was done before I was born. Aunt Eugenia was going to toss it in the rubbish."

He returned the portrait to her, and the compassion in his eyes caused hot tears to spring to hers, blurring her vision. She blinked rapidly several times. Ian pointed to the portrait. "She allowed you to keep it?"

Vangie nodded. "Wood is of minimal value. Otherwise, they'd have sold it too. If you look closely, you can see the frame is cracked, though I tried to conceal the crevices by painting vines over them."

"It's still exquisite."

"Thank you."

Her soft reply didn't reflect the joy she felt at his praise. While his attention appeared focused on the frame, she could tell he was thinking. His brows formed a vee whenever he was deep in thought. His gaze whisked about the room once more.

"Vangie," Ian's tone was gentle, yet probing. "How is it you wear little more than rags while your aunt and uncle wear expensive, new clothing?"

She ducked her head, heat sweeping her face. He needn't voice what was obvious.

"You've been treated worse than a servant, living in this attic room with bare essentials." He waved a hand in an arc. "But the rest of the cottage is furnished rich enough."

"Ian—"

He stood with his hands on his hips and peered around her room in disapproval. "The grounds are well-cared for, and based on the delectably tray of pastries your uncle sampled, food is not in short supply."

"They are not impoverished." She tucked the portrait in her valise.

He crossed the narrow room in two long strides and gathered her into his comforting embrace. "Sweeting, does Stapleton know how you've lived?"

She shook her head against his chest. No one knew of her misery, but Uncle Gideon must've suspected, hence the monthly packets. In addition to monies for her care, she was certain the parcels contained other fanciful whatnots. Aunt and Uncle never spoke of it, and Vangie never saw any improvement in her position.

Ian placed his finger beneath her chin, tilting her face upward until their eyes met. "You will *never* go without again. I promise you."

She curved her lips into a smile. "Ian, I don't require much to be happy." *Only someone to love me.* "That's what I've been trying to tell you." Breaking eye contact, she released a short breath, "To be honest…" Hesitating, she peeked at him, unsure if she dared voice the truth.

He arched a hawkish eyebrow at her.

"I don't much care for grand parties and extravagant entertaining," she blurted. "Fancy clothing makes me feel artificial, and I've absolutely no use for dozens of pairs of slippers or silly bonnets. And," in a rush she finished, "I don't care if I *ever* attend another assembly or Season in London." There, she'd said it. He could make what he would of those truths.

Ian laughed, a genuine laugh of pure delight. It transformed his features, and an answering giddiness flitted behind her breastbone.

"By God, I've been blessed," he said. "I, too, cannot abide the trappings and antics of the *le bon ton*."

"You don't like London either?" Vangie grinned, delighted at the revelation.

"Cannot stomach it." He grasped her valise and extended his elbow. "I'll have the drivers collect the rest of your belongings. Let's go home, my lady."

Home. Oh, that sounded lovely indeed.

Vangie slipped her hand into the crook of his elbow. She hesitated, searching his gray eyes. "Ian, are your stepmother and sister aware we're coming? That *I'm* coming?"

A shadow whisked across his face. "Ah, as to that—no. I thought to surprise them."

19

Eyes wide and jaw slack, Vangie stared speechless and awestruck at her first glimpse of Somersfield. A majestic stone archway proclaimed their entrance to Warrick lands. Truly having no idea of Ian's wealth or the size of his estate, she could only gawk, stunned. Stately yew trees standing at attention on either side of the neglected drive allowed glimpses of once manicured lawns, overgrown formal gardens, and untrimmed mazes.

At one time, Somersfield had been spectacular, and she made a mental note to tell *Puri Daj* about the yews. The trees had many medicinal uses. The coach lumbered down the half-mile long, convoluted lane. Her breath caught again when the grandiose Baroque-style manor house materialized on the horizon.

"Faith, Ian, it's enormous. A veritable castle. Are those turrets?" She gaped, entranced.

"Indeed," he murmured, his gaze riveted on the horizon and his mouth bent upward. Unrestrained pride glimmered in his eyes as he gazed at his ancestral home.

He loves Somersfield.

Vangie smiled again and directed her attention out the carriage window once more. At least a hundred beveled windows caught the afternoon sun, brilliantly refracting the golden rays. The building glowed as if it were alive, a living breathing entity. She was overcome with the splendor of the magnificent manor and grounds.

How was she to be mistress of such a grand estate? She didn't have the skills or training to manage such a vast household. Worrying her lower lip between her teeth, she clasped her reticule, pressing her fingers into the woven threads. Her gaze never left the mansion.

Did Ian have any notion how ill-prepared she was for such an overwhelming task? Would he be disillusioned with her yet again?

Before the equipage rolled to a stop, two liveried servants descended the manor's granite steps. After alighting, Ian handed Vangie down and gave her an encouraging smile, probably to ease the discomfort caused by the footmen's openly curious glances.

Two yapping white and tan harriers, their white-tipped tails wagging fiercely, lopped across the drive, eager to greet him. Whining, the dogs bounced about his feet. "Halloo, chaps." He patted each of their heads before the hounds turned their attention to her. The larger of the dogs nuzzled her hand.

"That's Horace," Ian said. "He's a terrible flirt."

Vangie obediently scratched the hound's ears. The other dog circled her twice, sniffing her skirts before he sat on his haunches and raised one paw, gazing at her with woeful hazel eyes.

She giggled, and shook it. "How do you do?"

"Ah, Blake, ever the gentleman." Ian took her by the elbow. "Come along. I have someone I want you to meet." He guided her to the top of the stairs, a wide grin on his handsome face.

A diminutive, rigidly proper butler, attired in cobalt blue livery manned the doorway. "Welcome home, Lord Warrick."

"Thank you, Jasper. May I introduce you to Lady Warrick?"

Except for a singular twitch of Jasper's beetle eyebrows, the butler's face remained expressionless, though his warm brown eyes twinkled merrily. "Indeed, my lord."

"My lady, this is Somersfield's majordomo, and my dear friend, Francis Jasper-Faulkenbury. I've called him Jasper since I was in short pants. I couldn't pronounce Faulkenbury and my toddler attempts sounded like profanity." Ian winked and grinned at the butler. "You don't mind, do you, Jasper?

"Not at all, my lord." Humor danced in the butler's eyes, but his face remained impassive. Bowing formally, Jasper intoned, "Welcome to Somersfield, my lady."

Vangie smiled. She liked him already. "Thank you, Jasper."

She tried not to stare at his head. Given he was nearly her height, and he'd just bowed, providing her with a clear view of his oddly-styled hair, it was rather difficult not to, so she focused on the immense, opulent entry.

At the far end of the foyer a grand staircase split halfway up. Likely each side led to a separate wing. Four carved doors, two on either side, graced the entrance. From one of these rushed a distraught woman, garbed in full mourning attire, a piece of paper clutched in one hand.

The Dowager Viscountess Warrick?

Vangie cast a quick glance to Ian.

He spoke with Jasper, his back to her. "Please send for Dr. Farnsworthy. A gunshot wound needs tending."

"Thank God, you've returned, Ian. Charlotte—" Upon hearing his request, the matron stuttered to a halt. "You…you're wounded? Shot?" Her gaze flew over his form, seeking any sign of injury.

Facing her, he shook his head, a lock of russet hair falling over his forehead. "No, Lucinda. We were set upon by highwaymen yester eve, and Malcolm suffered a gunshot wound, Not I."

A peculiar expression crossed her thin face. Not relief exactly. For the first time, she glanced directly at Vangie, and the dowager stiffened, her eyes narrowed with unconcealed antagonism. "What is *she* doing here?"

The contempt in her voice and expression took Vangie aback. For once, she was certain she'd have no problem remembering a name. Lucinda. *Lucifer*.

The footmen entered, each encumbered with armfuls of luggage, further adding to the commotion in the entryway.

Ian reached for Vangie's elbow, drawing her to his side. "Lucinda, it's my immense pleasure to introduce my wife to you."

"Your *what*?" The dowager sucked in a sharp breath, her hand flying to cover her heart. She impaled Vangie with a hostile glare. "Surely you're not serious," she exclaimed, enunciating each word with haughty anger.

This wasn't going well. Had Ian's stepmother hoped he'd marry someone else? The thought didn't settle well with Vangie, and a sickening knot twisted in her belly. She hadn't considered the possibility. Were Ian's affections engaged elsewhere?

A sly look crept across the dowager's plain features. "Ah, is this part of the *plan*?" She laughed then, a markedly humorless snicker.

Plan? Vangie searched Ian's face. He didn't reply but glared at his stepmother, his face a mask of cold fury. Was there a challenge in his eyes?

She eyed her ladyship.

A conglomeration of emotions skittered across the dowager's face before settling into a pinched scowl. "There's no time for this now. We can discuss your travesty of a *marriage* later."

Sensing an undercurrent that didn't bode well, Vangie swung her gaze between Ian and his stepmother. Obviously, she emphatically objected to the marriage. Very much wishing she could disappear, she cast a quick glance at Jasper.

He nodded, one sharp movement then winked.

Despite the tense atmosphere, her lips twitched. Yes, she most certainly did like Jasper.

Dismissing her, the dowager faced Ian. "I must speak with you now. *Alone*." She cut a rude glower toward Vangie. Thrusting the scrunched paper beneath his nose, she cried, "Charlotte's run off to Gretna Green with that penniless squire, Trevor Monroe!"

"Monroe?" Ian scrunched his brow. "But I thought she was in love with Lord Pickering?"

"As did I." Lucinda shoved the paper at him. "Until I found this."

He took the note and quickly scanned it, his jaw muscle twitching. "Jasper, please escort her ladyship," Ian's focus flicked to his stepmother for an instant, "to the drawing room. Then send for the leech. Lucinda, wait for me in the study."

She speared Vangie with another animosity-laden glare. "But, Ian—"

"In the study, Lucinda. I'll be with you shortly."

Huffing her outrage, the petulant woman scowled. Spinning on her heels, her spine ramrod straight, she marched from the foyer. The crape of her stiff skirts crackled with each resolute stride.

Wrapping her arms around her torso, Vangie watched her go. She shivered and rubbed her arms as she stared at the doorway for several seconds after the dowager disappeared through it. Had she traded one hostile home for another?

Ian addressed the butler one more. "Please, fetch Tanny to my wife. She'll need to prepare a temporary chamber for Lady Warrick until the Dowager Viscountess Warrick removes herself to the dower house." He leveled a contemplative glance to the study door. "Jasper, I'd be most grateful if you'd oversee Lucinda's packing. I'd like her to take up residence there tomorrow. See that she doesn't help herself to the silver, will you?"

Vangie breathed easier. Thank goodness. She'd not have to reside under the same roof with Lucifer—Lucinda. *Would she really take the silver?*

"At once, your lordship," Jasper offered enthusiastically.

Taking her hand in his, Ian gazed into her eyes. "Sweeting, wait for me in the drawing room. I'll explain everything after I've spoken with her." Before she could respond, he swiveled and strode to the doorway the dowager had entered.

"The drawing room is along this corridor, Lady Warrick." Arm extended, Jasper looked at her expectantly. "If you will please follow me, Lady Warrick."

Vangie started. He meant her. She trailed behind the butler, feeling terribly alone and unsure of herself. This wasn't the reception she'd expected, though truth to tell, she'd not known precisely what to expect.

"Ah, here we are, Lady Warrick." Opening the double doors, Jasper stood at their entrance waiting for her to enter. "Lady Warrick, would you care for some refreshment?"

Each time he called her Lady Warrick, she had to mentally remind herself, he spoke to her. "Yes, thank you. Tea would be wonderful, if it's not too much trouble."

Dipping his head, he replied, "No trouble at all, Lady Warrick. Please make yourself comfortable, Lady Warrick. I'll return momentarily, Lady Warrick."

The man seemed delighted to address her by her formal title. How long would it be before she grew accustomed to the title herself?

She wandered over to the fireplace dominating one wall. A woman's portrait hung above the gleaming white marble. Peering at her, Vangie recognized the silver eyes and high cheek bones. The artist had captured a lingering unhappiness in the woman's expression, and though her hair was lighter than Ian's, the painting was unmistakably a likeness of his mother.

"I'll try to make him happy," she whispered. "If he'll let me."

With a sigh, she turned away and surveyed the rest of the room. Intricate scrollwork detailed the plaster border along the ceiling's edge, whilst a filmy yellow shade of paint covered the walls. Floor to ceiling leaded glass windows graced the opposite side of the chamber, their sun-faded silk draperies wide open.

Brilliant streams of sunshine cascaded into the chamber, casting a myriad of rainbows throughout the room. A tall, marble-topped table stood between a pair of worn saffron brocade-covered settees, and a variety of threadbare oriental rugs covered the scratched parquet floor here and there.

Tucked beneath a window on the west end of the room sat a small writing desk where the mistress of the manor might enjoy the garden view while attending to her correspondence. An elaborate Taj Mahal-shaped birdcage graced another wall. Two silent canaries watched her from within.

Vangie perched on the edge of one of settees, twisting her hands. She scrutinized the room once more. Though the furnishings were of the highest quality, they were generations old and well-worn. Not that she minded. It gave the room a homey, comfortable ambiance.

Jasper arrived with the tea service, followed by a stern-faced woman in a crisp black dress. A jangle of keys was secured on a chatelaine at her waist.

A trilling whistle rent the air.

"Ah, Leopold is attempting to woo Lily again." Jasper jutted his chin toward the birds.

Vangie turned to peer at the pair. The male, a gorgeous cinnamon canary, puffed his chest out. He dipped and twisted in a courtship dance for the timid lemon-colored female sitting in their food dish.

She smiled at his antics, glad for the momentary distraction from her dour thoughts. She directed her attention to the tea tray and poured a steaming cup. Adding a bit of milk, she murmured, "Thank you, Jasper. You're most kind."

His, "Not at all, Lady Warrick," was interrupted by Leopold chirping excitedly. The bird halted instantly when Jasper ordered, "Cease your infernal chittering, you lovesick fowl."

Vangie curled her lips in amusement, though she hid the smile by taking a sip of tea. It wouldn't do to have him think she laughed at him. She needed an ally here.

A harrumph startled her. *Oh, dear.* She'd almost forgotten about the dour housekeeper. The woman had been silent up to this point.

"So, it's true then? Master Ian has taken you to wife?"

"Yes." Vangie sent a hesitant glance to Jasper.

"My lady, Mrs. Tanssen is Somersfield's most *cordial* housekeeper." A hint of sarcasm shaded Jasper's words. He duly ignored the glower the intimidating woman sent him.

Her lips pursed, Mrs. Tanssen considered her new mistress. "Well, what to do? One cannot evict her ladyship without notice from the room she's occupied for over twenty years, though you certainly have the right to claim the chamber."

"His lordship wants her moved to the dower house tomorrow," Jasper offered helpfully.

"Yes, but there's tonight to consider." The housekeeper tapped her chin with her forefinger.

Vangie ventured a hesitant response, "Mrs. Tanssen, is it?"

Piercing hazel-green eyes met hers, accompanied by a curt nod.

She nearly danced a jig. She'd recalled a name correctly the first time. "I'm content to leave the arrangements as they are. Please, use your discretion, and place me in whatever chamber you deem most appropriate. Lord Warrick already suggested a temporary chamber for me, and he may have other preferences he's yet to make known."

A flicker of approval entered the housekeeper's eyes. She angled her head, though Vangie wasn't certain if the movement indicated her concurrence or irritation that she'd voiced an opinion. "I'll prepare a chamber for you at once, my lady." With that, the formidable woman departed the room, hauling the reluctant butler with her. She claimed she required his assistance in directing the footman.

Vangie sincerely doubted the capable Mrs. Tanssen needed anyone's assistance with anything—ever.

20

No sooner had Vangie finished the thought than Ian entered the drawing room. *Silent panther feet.* She was fast becoming accustomed to them—to him.

"Vangie, I must be off at once."

Her heart plummeted to her feet. He was leaving her here. Amongst strangers.

"Charlotte has eloped," he said grimly. "She's underage, and I must try to stop them. I know little of Trevor Monroe, other than he's the nephew of our neighbors, the Landthrops."

What a caring brother. "Of course you must go. I shall be fine."

She would be. Jasper liked her. That was a good start.

"I may be gone for a fortnight or more." Ian shoved one hand into a glove. "Gretna Green is several days' ride from here, and they may not travel directly there."

Two or more weeks? Dismay wrenched her, though she hid it from him. She knew no one in this vicinity—in this house—for that matter. She'd yet to meet all the servants, and her new mother-in-law had made her antagonistic feelings regarding Vangie abundantly clear.

Nevertheless, she attempted a brave smile. "It will provide me an opportunity to become acquainted with the staff and to learn how to manage an estate of this magnitude."

"I wanted to introduce you to Somersfield myself, but Charlotte is impetuous and not altogether logical. Even when at her best." Ian paused in pulling on his second glove. "I'd never forgive myself if she marries Monroe on a whim, making a mistake she'll live to regret for the rest of her life." Brusqueness tempered each clipped word.

Awkward silence greeted his vehement declaration. How did one respond to that? Marriage… *A mistake one lived to regret for the rest of one's life*? Was he speaking of his sister or himself?

"Ian, I thought you'd left already. Do you care nothing for your sister?" The Dowager Viscountess Warrick's grating voice disturbed her musings. She glared at Vangie, making no attempt to hide her dislike. "Dear Charlotte's the *only* family you have left."

"I'm just going." He stepped nearer to Vangie.

The obstinate woman refused to leave, allowing her a moment's privacy with her husband. The dowager stood impatiently tapping her toe, her vexation tangible.

Ian cast a shuttered glance in his stepmother's direction. His baritone voice hushed, he said, "If you have need of anything, you've only to ask Jasper or Tanny—Mrs. Tanssen."

"Yes, I shall." Vangie roved her gaze over his face, memorizing each angle and plane. She wanted to trace the almost healed scratch on his jaw, but he'd donned the cold, unemotional façade once more. Perhaps worry about his sister had brought about the change. She daren't contemplate on what else may have caused his sudden coolness. "You'll be careful?"

The encounter with the bandits last night continued to plague her.

"Always."

Searching his eyes, Vangie whispered a Romani blessing. "*Zhan le Devlesa tai sastimasa.* Go with God and in good health."

Ian half bowed. "Thank you." He strode toward the door and stopped before his stepmother standing in the door frame. "See that my viscountess is treated as she deserves. And please, do make the arrangements we discussed at once."

An unspoken message passed between them before the dowager turned her hooded gaze to Vangie.

What arrangements, and why was his stepmother looking at her like that? Like a cat that had a canary? The dowager's wintery eyes sent the hairs rising along Vangie's skin. She wrapped her arms protectively about herself and shivered. Faith and good Lord. That woman's eyes could freeze hell's scorching flames with one glance.

The dowager answered smoothly, "Of course, Ian." She drifted into the room, trailing a finger across a table. Her compliant gaze met his once more. "Rest assured, your *wife* will be treated with the respect and consideration a woman of her station deserves."

Jasper entered. "Pericles is saddled and waiting, sir."

"Thank you, Jasper." Ian gave Vangie one last, lingering look then passed through the doorway. He met Mrs. Tanssen just outside. Pausing, he spoke to her quietly.

She darted a fierce glower at the dowager before answering him.

Vangie couldn't hear the exchange, nor could his stepmother if her annoyed scowl was any indication. When she again glanced in his direction, he was gone. The ache his leaving caused took her by surprise. She'd known him barely a week. How could she be so affected by him or his absence?

With a sigh, Mrs. Tanssen's prickly mask descended once more. All brisk business, she marched into the drawing room. "Lady Warrick—"

Vangie and Lucinda both turned to her.

Oh, dear. This was discomfiting. The dowager wasn't ready to relinquish the position of Viscountess Warrick.

Mrs. Tannsen pulled her rigid spine straighter and looked directly at Vangie. "*My lady*, your chamber is readied."

"Put her in the south tower."

At the crash of a teacup shattering, Vangie's gaze flew to Jasper. He remained stooped over the service, slack-jawed, gawking at the Dowager Viscountess Warrick in utter disbelief.

"I beg your pardon?" Mrs. Tanssen croaked, her eyes dinner plate wide.

A shiver stole over her. Something was too smoky by far. Was there something wrong with the south tower?

"You heard me. Lock her in the south tower." Though softly spoken, the dowager's tone was jubilant.

Lock me in the tower? Vangie mentally shook her head. She'd heard wrong. Surely she must have. Lucinda couldn't mean to imprison her.

Jasper drew himself up, indignation written across his noble face. "Madam, you overstep your bounds."

"Do I?" she mocked. "Who's here to say otherwise? You heard Warrick yourself. Did he not ask me to make the arrangements we'd discussed at once?"

Ian told her to lock me in the tower?

Confident of her position and authority, her mien smug, she arched an eyebrow expectantly.

Jasper straightened, outrage emanating from every pore.

With an arrogant angle of her graying head, she said, "Just what do you think he was referring to?"

"I'm sure I wouldn't know," he said, his flared nostrils a sign of his contempt. He adjusted his waistcoat, leveling her a lethal glare. "But I doubt it had anything to do with relegating his bride to the tower as a prisoner."

Vangie felt the glimmer of hope she'd foolishly nourished, sputter and die.

"She's the lady of the manor now, not you." Mrs. Tanssen turned down her mouth into a mutinous frown. "I shan't do it." She folded her arms, challenging the dowager.

"Won't you?" The Dowager Viscountess Warrick inspected the black lace on her sleeve and shrugged nonchalantly. "Fine. You're terminated then." She raised her gloating gaze, an unpleasant smile distorting her thin lips.

Mrs. Tanssen exhaled sharply. "I've been in residence at Somersfield far longer than you, my lady." She pointed at the dowager. "You don't have the authority to dismiss me without a character. Only Lord Warrick can give me my *congé*."

"Mrs. Tanssen is correct, and I answer to Lord Warrick, and only his lordship as well," Jasper said, a challenge in his eyes too.

"Shall I send for the magistrate? I'm sure he'd be willing to escort two trespassers from the premises." Her eyes frigid, yet eerily hollow, the dowager's attention vacillated between the majordomo and housekeeper.

Vangie's stomach roiled at the vengeance in the Lucinda's eyes. "I'll go," she said, with a great deal more calm composure than felt.

Everyone's attention whipped to her.

She almost smiled at the disappointed expression that flashed across the dowager viscountess' face. Likely, she'd hadn't expected her to acquiesce easily. In fact, she suspected Lucinda had hoped she would have to be hauled, bound and gagged, to the tower.

With poise Vangie was far from feeling, she started for the drawing room's doors. She paused after a few steps, sweeping Mrs. Tannsen and Jasper with her gaze. "I'll not have you lose your positions or permit your forcible removal on my account."

She was quite sure the dowager didn't have the authority to dismiss the housekeeper or butler, but she could have them barred from the premises until Ian returned. "It's only for a fortnight," she stoically reminded them. Meeting the dowager's wintry eyes, she angled her chin. "When Ian returns, things will be put aright."

Though, if the dowager spoke the truth, how she would overcome this latest wounding to her soul, she knew not. Turning her back on her mother-in-law, Vangie closed her eyes, fighting the urge to burst into tears. She willed herself to be strong.

Please God, let her be lying.

A lying tongue lasts only a moment, tikna, but truthful lips endure forever.

Again, *Puri Daj's* wise words brought a degree of solace to her. The prospect of at least two weeks locked within a chamber caused her no small amount of trepidation. Uncle Percival had locked her in her room for two days once. The inactivity and boredom had been nearly intolerable.

She looked over her shoulder, scrutinizing her ladyship, trying to gauge the truthfulness of her words. Did she expect her to bolt from the premises without so much as a glance behind her? Did she think to frighten her off by threatening weeks of confinement?

A spark of defiance flickered in her core then surged forth. She squared her shoulders and tilted her chin. She'd not cower and beg. Nor would she flee. She would hear the words from Ian's mouth before she passed judgment, though the scales didn't weigh in his favor at present.

Mrs. Tannsen came alongside her and slipped an arm through the curve of Vangie's elbow. Her voice low, she murmured, "We've been brought to *point non plus*, my lady. We've no other recourse but to do her bidding." With the merest movement of her head, Mrs. Tanssen indicated the dowager. "She can have us removed, though Master Ian would promptly reinstate us upon his return."

In two weeks.

"We need to be here, though." She gave Vangie's arm a small, reassuring squeeze. "It's the best way to protect you."

Jasper moved to her other side. "We cannot shield you from her if we're banned from the premises."

"Stop your twattling, and remove the chit from my sight, or I *shall* dismiss you."

The butler turned and bestowed a withering glare on the crow in black. He started to speak, but Vangie gripped his arm.

Shaking her head, she said beneath her breath, "Please, don't anger her further. I need you." She turned her gaze on Mrs. Tannsen. "Both of you." Even as she spoke the words, Vangie realized they were true. Her mother-in-law wasn't just being spiteful. She was evil and, Vangie feared, dangerous if crossed.

And what of Ian? She earnestly wanted to believe he'd not subject her to such humiliation. But whatever was the dowager referring to when she'd mentioned the arrangements he insisted upon? She grudgingly acknowledged she'd already seen her husband's darker side.

"Oh, and Mrs. Tanssen?" Lucinda said silkily.

The housekeeper turned hostile eyes to the dowager.

"Do bring me the tower key upon securing our *guest*." A gloating smile on her lips, her ladyship finished with sarcastic triumph.

"Dicked in the nob witch." Jasper's breath hissed through his clenched teeth

Wordlessly, Mrs. Tanssen turned on her heel, her mouth firmed into a grim line of indignation. The trio swept from the room.

Once out of earshot Vangie asked, "Would she really have sent for the magistrate?"

Jasper's gaze meshed with Mrs. Tanssen's. The housekeeper looked over her shoulder and taking Vangie by the elbow, hustled her first down one corridor and then another. Jasper puffed along beside them.

Finally slowing her pace, and with a hasty glance over her shoulder, Mrs. Tannsen answered Vangie's question. "Undoubtedly, my lady."

"Sir Doyle, he's the magistrate, is deep into the dowager's pockets." Jasper swung his head this way and that, as if afraid of being overheard.

Vangie glanced at the portraits in their ornate frames balanced on the wall. She could only imagine what Ian's ancestors had seen and heard over the decades.

"Gossip has it, not that Mrs. Tanssen or I ever indulge in such prattle…" Jasper peered around a corner and beckoned the women to follow. "Sir Doyle was her, ah…" His face grew bright red.

"*Amour*. Before she married the previous Lord Warrick," Mrs. Tannsen finished for him. She nodded knowingly. "And their current association is somewhat less than proper."

"A great deal less," Jasper agreed, still claret-colored about his ears.

Mrs. Tannsen, clicked her tongue. "I fear they're a dangerous pair."

21

It took over a week for Ian to track his sister to Gretna Green, only to find the giddy twosome had never been there. Charlotte and Monroe had sent decoys in their places. Ten days later—after inquiring at every parish, village, township, and hamlet on the way—he finally caught up with the newlyweds. Merry as grigs, they were ensconced in a quaint inn in Edinburgh.

He cursed himself for a fool. He should've known his sister would send him on a false trail. Edinburgh was just across the border from Northumberland. It was only logical Charlotte and Monroe would fly there, not Gretna Green. She'd made a May game of him, yet she was miffed with him for thinking she was genuinely interested in Pickering.

"Really, Ian, Lord Pickering is such a clod-pate. You, of all people, should've found it unfathomable I would have any interest in that buffle-headed coxcomb." She formed her mouth into a moue. "For pity's sake, he has more hair than wit, and that's saying something since he's bald." Frowning, she declared puckishly, "I'm offended, truly I am. That you'd think I'd make a cake of myself over the likes of stinky Pickering—" She huffed and folded her arms. "Well, it's beyond the pale."

Infuriated and incredulous, Ian clenched his hands and clamped his teeth to keep from telling her what a spoiled, inconsiderate, scheming chit she was. By God, the gammon she'd pitched him and her mother. And they'd believed her. Lips pinched tight, he remained obstinately silent, lost in his own recriminations.

I am an idiot.

After harrumphing a bit more, she dimpled and clasped her new husband's hand. "I'm so very happy. I simply cannot stay annoyed with you, dear brother, and I suppose I do owe you an apology."

"Indeed, you do. And not only me, but Miss Caruthers." He

narrowed his eyes and made no attempt to keep the anger from his voice. "You intentionally tarnished her good name, all as part of a hoax? I never would've thought you capable of such calculated cruelty."

He'd always hoped she'd be more honorable and kinder than her mother.

Charlotte blinked at him, opening and closing her mouth like a gasping trout. Finally, she sputtered, "I was but play acting."

Recalling her most convincing histrionics and her hourly flood of tears, Ian said dryly, "Even your mother believed you enamored with the earl."

Looking taken aback, a shadow flitted across Charlotte's features. Casting an adoring glance at her husband, she conceded Ian's point. "Well, yes, but it was necessary lest Mother suspect my true affections lay elsewhere. And she was acting so odd of late."

Ian allowed there was some substance to that; a great deal of substance, truth to tell.

"She was always talking to herself, wandering about the woods in the wee hours, gathering all sorts of weeds and such." Two neat rows wrinkled her usually smooth brow. "Ian, she really was most peculiar, especially after Papa's and Geoff's deaths. It…frightened me."

"It was still wrong, Charlotte. You could've spoken to me." He was her guardian after all.

"After Papa and Geoff died, I couldn't bear to lose Trevor too." Charlotte's doe-like brown eyes filled with tears. She snuffled into her handkerchief. "I simply couldn't."

"Why did you drag Miss Caruthers into your Cheltenham tragedy?" Genuinely curiosity promoted Ian to ask. Why had she involved Vangie in her theatrics?

"Well, as to that, brother dearest, one has only to meet Miss Caruthers to know she's not any of those horrid things Mother and I alluded to." Now it was Ian's turn to gape as Charlotte rattled on. "You're so perceptive. I knew I could rely on you to fudge out the truth regarding her moral character straightaway." Angling her head, Charlotte studied him. "You didn't seriously attempt to ruin the sweet girl, did you?" For the first time, she appeared truly chagrined, concerned for someone other than herself.

"I married her."

Charlotte's reaction wasn't at all what he expected. Squealing, she clapped her hands before launching herself at him and covering his face with kisses. "It's so perfectly romantic. I knew you'd see what a darling she is. You two are simply ideal for each other."

Vangie mightn't agree.

She descended on her husband, wrapping her arms around him and sighing. "Is it not wonderful, Trevor? Ian's found love too."

Judging by the hungry look smoldering in Monroe's eyes, Ian concluded his new brother-in-law had much more pressing matters on his mind than offering his congratulations. Namely how to courteously suggest Ian push off so he could entice his wife into a satisfying afternoon tussle on the feather tick dominating the small rented room.

Obligingly, Ian bid them farewell, eager to return home to his own wife. And if fate smiled kindly on him, mayhap he'd have his own honeymoon.

Twenty-two days after leaving Somersfield, Ian trotted Pericles into the paddock outside the extensive stables. Past midnight, a cocoon of tranquility swathed the night. A dove cooed sleepily, perched aloft in one of the massive oak trees looming over the main barn.

He had envisioned breeding the finest horseflesh in the north of England here. Now, with the acquisition of the Arabian-blooded stock, he pursued that dream.

Gerard, the stable master, approached lantern in hand. His slow, shuffling gait gave Ian plenty of time to dismount. Another form plodded unhurriedly from the barn. Gerard waved the sleepy groom away. "Go on with ye, Ben. I'll see to the beasty."

Mumbling an unintelligible answer, the young stable hand ambled back into the dark building. Soft welcoming nickers accompanied his return.

"Pleased to have ye home, Lord Warrick." Gerard yawned sleepily, patting the lathered animal on his glistening neck. "Ye rode him hard, ye did." He crooned softly to the stallion, his hands never breaking their soothing contact with the horse.

"Aye, I did at that." Ian smiled and patted the horse's rump. "I've a bride waiting for me." Slapping the dust from his thighs, he made for the manor, calling over his shoulder, "Rub him down well, won't you, Gerard? And an extra portion of grain for him too. He earned it."

Entering the silent manor, Ian went directly to his bedchamber. Though he ached to see Vangie, he didn't want to waken her this late.

Besides—he sniffed, crinkling his nose in distaste—he sorely needed a bath. But he'd not wake his valet or disturb the other servants and demand bathwater at this ungodly hour. He'd have to wait until morning to greet his wife.

My wife.

He'd missed her more than he ought after such a short acquaintance. How had she fared in his absence? And more on point, were her thoughts as consumed with him as his were of her?

Exhaling a deep breath, Ian toed off his boots before stripping his garments with swift efficiency. Padding to the bathing chamber, he poured water into the basin then washed off the worst of the travel grime.

He smiled to himself. He hoped Vangie was an early riser, for Lucinda assuredly was. She'd be demanding his attention straightaway once she learned of his return. His smile faltered, and a scowl took its place.

She had better have removed herself to the dower house as he'd directed. He'd no intention of residing under the same roof with that termagant now that Charlotte wasn't in residence. He'd have preferred to have been present for the transition, especially to ease the adjustment for Vangie. Instead he'd hied off in needless pursuit of his sister. Shaking his head in self-reproach, he splashed his hair and his unshaven face with the tepid water.

Charlotte was blissfully happy. She obviously adored the man she'd married, and Monroe was completely agog over her as well. As a wedding present, Ian, despite being thoroughly piqued with her, had offered the newlyweds a generous purse and sent them on a well-deserved wedding journey.

Well-deserved because he had never given Charlotte credit for any degree of intelligence—or thought her the least bit capable of standing up to her mother. That lamentable business with Pickering? All a wretched ruse Charlotte concocted to keep Lucinda off Monroe's scent. She'd been successful, if he didn't count his own forced marriage.

Charlotte hadn't done poorly for herself, by half, Ian concluded, toweling his dripping hair. He quickly wiped his face then finished drying off. Lucinda wouldn't be pleased he'd returned empty-handed. He'd deal with that difficulty on the morrow, *after* becoming reacquainted with his bride.

Slipping between the cool sheets, he lay back with his elbows bent, hands beneath his damp head. He'd send a message to the dower house in the morning, requesting an appointment with Lucinda in the afternoon. Staring at the canopied bed, his eyes drifted closed, his thoughts shifting to Vangie.

Morning couldn't come soon enough.

Vangie tore to the chamber pot, casting up the contents of her stomach for the third time in the past week. She tottered to the makeshift washstand and rinsed the foul taste from her mouth before running a damp cloth over her face. Hunched over the cracked basin, she drew in a deep breath. Another wave of queasiness assailed her.

Her stomach was empty, hollow to her backbone. The bland breakfast of watery porridge, tea, and dry toast she'd eaten moments ago now resided in the slop bucket. Dinner wasn't much better. It usually consisted of a weak soup, a hunk of dry bread, and if she was lucky, a slice of cheese or a piece of fruit.

How much longer could she tolerate this unappetizing food? It often tasted peculiar, not unlike some of the medicinal herbs *Puri Daj* used to treat respiratory afflictions. No doubt Lucinda fed her half-spoiled leftovers which accounted for Vangie's roiling stomach. She'd little appetite and as the days passed, ate less and less of the unappealing fare.

She wandered to the dilapidated armchair she'd tugged near the window and releasing a weary sigh, flopped into it.

Jasper and Mrs. Tanssen had been absolute dears. They'd smuggled candles, books, including Vangie's Bible, her paints and crocheting, as well as more tempting, palatable foods into her whenever they could. It wasn't often enough. According to Jasper, the dowager inspected every tray and bucket and made the servants turn out their pockets before entering the tower.

The first night, Mrs. Tanssen had sneaked into the tower, and when the door creaked open, Vangie, huddled in a corner under a filthy blanket, had been terrified. Recognizing the housekeeper illuminated in the doorway, she'd gasped, "Mrs. Tanssen? What are you doing here? How did you enter?"

Holding a candle in one hand, Mrs. Tanssen dangled a key in the other. "I provided that she-dog the key to this turret." She smiled and shrugged her shoulders. "But I don't feel the least bit obligated to tell her I have a master key. I can open every door in the manor."

She dropped the key inside her pocket and bent to retrieve something outside the door. “Here, my lady. It’s only a blanket, a candle, and a bit of bread. I couldn’t hide anymore beneath my skirts this trip.”

Vangie hugged her. “Thank you.”

“I’d best be going. I have several more things stashed in a closet at the bottom of the stairs. I want to bring them to you while Jasper keeps watch outside the dowager’s chamber.”

Two days later, Jasper had crept into the tower. “The dowager is like a rabid watchdog. She monitors our every move.” He withdrew a book from his pocket along with some biscuits wrapped in a cloth. “We have outwitted her though. One of us distracts her, and the other high-tails it here.”

The sweet-faced maid who brought Vangie her food, often stayed to visit, even though she was under strict orders not to. With her sandy-blonde hair and sky-blue eyes, Ailsa reminded Vangie of an unrefined version of Yvette. She was the same age as her cousin, too, ten and seven.

“I don’t want you getting punished for defying the dowager, Ailsa,” Vangie told her.

“Her ladyship can blow biscuits out her bony arse,” Ailsa snorted. “You’re the lady of the manor now, not that witch.”

Despite herself, Vangie’s lips had twitched. Though her face was angelic, Ailsa’s speech was anything but. She had no qualms about speaking her mind and doing so quite crudely.

Wrapping a blanket around her shoulders and across her lap, Vangie gazed at the early morning scene beyond the window. Not even eight of the clock yet, she guessed.

She was lonely, cold, hungry, and desperate for Ian to return. Each day that passed without his appearance, sent her further into the doldrums. A multitude of misgivings worked their wiles, whispering discouragement and filling her with hopelessness.

His continued absence gave credence to his stepmother’s claim he’d ordered her locked away. The thought wrenched her heart. Despair squeezed her wounded spirit like an unrelenting vice. A tear trickled from her eye. She brusquely rubbed it away. No more tears.

She surveyed the travesty of a room the dowager had incarcerated her in. The window panes tossed thin shadows across the dusty floor. The cruelty behind her ladyship’s actions was beyond Vangie’s understanding. What drove someone to be so altogether vindictive?

The room's disarray and disrepair proved it was never used, except by a pair of bats that made their way inside each night. Vangie had sneezed for a quarter hour straight the first day, such was the dust. Her bed originally consisted of a few moth-eaten blankets tossed on a lumpy, mildew-laden straw pallet on the floor.

Mrs. Tanssen smuggled clean blankets and a fresh tick over the course of the first few days, though how she managed without the dowager's knowledge baffled her. Except for the chair she currently sat in, and a rickety three-legged pedestal table, the chamber was devoid of furnishings.

Gazing out the window, a half-smile tilted the corners of her mouth. She was certain the dowager had no idea how splendid the view was from the tower. It was a perfect setting for drawing and painting—if Vangie had the desire.

She didn't.

Scanning the formal gardens and mazes below, she settled on her favorite scene—a pond on the other side of a large expanse of grass glistened happily in the morning sun. Black and white swans swam leisurely across the blue-green surface. A listing footbridge hugged the east side of the pond where it joined a meandering path to a glorious wisteria covered arbor. Everything was overgrown and neglected, but the underlying beauty of Somersfield's grounds remained undeniable.

Nestled in a glen on the other side of the pond, barely visible through the trees, sat a stately stone cottage. The dower house, she presumed.

Somewhere beyond her view lay the Romani camp. She hadn't remembered the note Milosh handed her in Brunswick until her eighth day of imprisonment. Retrieving her reticule, Vangie had dumped the contents on the table. Unfolding the note, she recognized her grandmother's familiar writing. The Roma were encamped in a meadow under a maple grove near the Ouseburn River.

Oh, how she missed Grandmother.

A week ago, Jasper had brazenly dared to seek a few moments with Vangie after her grandmother had called at Somersfield. *Puri Daj* had visited the Caruthers and learned of her marriage.

The dowager had refused to receive *Puri Daj*, going as far as to instruct him to forbid her access to Somersfield lands. The dowager had even threatened Grandmother with arrest for trespassing if she dared to attempt to contact Vangie again.

Jasper, bless his heart, had endeavored to reassure her. "I promised

Madam Caruthers I would personally see to your well-being as much as I am able to." He withdrew an apple and a scone from inside his coat. Standing a mite taller he'd said, "I would consider it an honor to carry missives between the two of you."

Vangie sighed, closing weary eyes, gritty from lack of sleep. How she wished to explore Somersfield's lovely acreage and to visit her Romani relatives. Grandmother anxiously waited for word from her, and Besnik, a dear Romani friend, covertly watched the estate, lest Vangie attempt to communicate with her Roma *vitsa*, her kin.

How long did Ian and his stepmother plan to keep her imprisoned?

22

Feeling unusually optimistic, Ian descended the stairs. The long-case clock hadn't chimed half-past seven yet, but he'd a small, if somewhat unrealistic hope, Vangie might've risen early herself. No sooner had he settled into his customary chair, teacup at his lips, than his stepmother strutted into the sun-streaked breakfast room.

Her steps faltered, and the self-satisfied look dropped off her face.

Damn and blast. Why was she still here? It wasn't bloody-well likely she just popped over for breakfast.

From beneath hooded eyelids he scrutinized her. What had his father seen in her? *Blunt.* Father would do most anything for money. *But lie with that?* No wonder his father had been perpetually in his cups, though how he got his pizzle stiff when he was foxed and laying atop that squeeze crab was beyond Ian's ken.

"I wasn't aware you had returned, Ian."

An obvious understatement if ever there was one. Cocking a hawkish eyebrow, he said, "I arrived late last night, or rather, early this morning. No doubt you were abed."

Helping herself to several hot cross buns and tea from the sideboard, Lucinda made her way to the table. She avoided his eyes, making a show of buttering a roll then adding two lumps of sugar to her tea.

"Lucinda, I presume your presence indicates you didn't do as I requested and remove yourself to the dower house?" He made no effort to conceal his displeasure.

In the act of stuffing a large piece of warm bun into her mouth, she gulped it down. She took a hurried sip of tea and from her grimace, she'd burnt her mouth. He was positive she'd have spewed the mouthful onto the table if it wasn't for his presence. Instead, she swallowed, her face pinched with pain. Composing herself, she heaved dramatic sigh as if greatly put upon.

He tapped the side of his mouth. "You've—"

"You're correct." Meeting his eyes, she scowled, pursed her lips, and blew a large breath out her nostrils. All signs she was about to work herself into a state. "It was most impractical…"

"Lucinda, there's…" Ian tried again, looking pointedly at her chin.

"Ian, you asked me a question. Do let me speak!"

"You've a dab of butter about to—"

The blob rolled over her chin, then plopped onto her chest. "Hell and damn," she grumbled, wiping at the oily stain. "Now look what you've done. It's ruined." She tossed her serviette on the table and slumped in her chair. Folding her arms across her bosom, she shot daggers at him with her eyes.

Ian ignored her, long accustomed to her blaming others—usually him—for everything. "You were saying?"

"Yes, well, it was most impractical for me to remove myself with the disruptions that half-breed gypsy caused in your absence." She drummed the fingers of her right hand on her bent arm. "I needed to remain here to maintain some degree of order."

Ian leveled her a thunderous glower. "You dare to call my wife a half-breed gypsy to my face?" Incipient anger crackled beneath the surface of his calm composure. "You go too far, Lucinda!"

She paled beneath her sallow complexion.

"Her name is Evangeline Hamilton. The Viscountess Warrick." He stabbed her with his gaze while stressing each word, "You had best *never* call her anything else again."

Jasper plowed into the dining room, his movements so uncharacteristically hasty, he skidded three feet across the floor before coming to an unsteady stop.

Ian quirked an eyebrow in askance. Whatever was the man about? Jasper never moved faster than a rigidly-measured gait.

A long wisp of hair flopped over his high forehead and dangled atop his nose. He calmly shoved the strands back onto his head then smoothed them from one side of his balding head to the other. *Ah, that explains that.* For years Ian had wondered about the odd, waxy strand across the butler's nearly bald pate.

"My bride has been troublesome, Jasper?"

"Really, Ian," Lucinda objected, her thin face registering annoyance. "Surely you're aware how those belowstairs are given to tittle-tattle."

Those abovestairs too.

With an air of patronizing superiority, she tilted her head and attempted to look down her pointed nose at the majordomo. The affect was comical, and Ian fought to control the grin tugging at his lips. She looked rather like one of his hounds. Nose in the air, Lucinda sniffed haughtily, "One simply cannot rely on candor from the likes of *them*."

With great dignity, Jasper lifted his chin and cast a contemptuous glance at the woman. "Indeed, my lord. My lady's imprisonment in the south—"

"That's outside of enough. You may go," Lucinda hissed, bolting upright in her chair.

"Her imprisonment in the south tower these three weeks past, has been severely troublesome to be sure," the butler finished in a rush.

Ian froze, his fork half-raised to his mouth. He better had heard wrong. With deadly calm he asked, "What did you say?"

"Her ladyship has been locked in the south turret with barely enough food to survive on. No fire, no candles, no comforts whatsoever. Except those which Mrs. Tanssen, Ailsa, and I have smuggled to her whenever *she,*" Jasper sent Lucinda another fleeting look, this one indisputably defiant, "wasn't watching."

Ian fisted his hands under the table. The urge to wrap them around his stepmother's neck and strangle the life from her was overwhelming. Never had he felt such burning hatred toward another human.

At Jasper's triumphant revelation, her face paled with shock. She swiftly masked her astonishment and attempted a light-hearted laugh. The smile faded from her lips when Ian shoved to his feet, regarding her with unmitigated fury.

She speared Jasper with a deadly glower. Had it been a sword, Ian had no doubt the butler would've been skewered or eviscerated. Face twisted with hatred, she demanded, "You dared to defy me?"

"I did and would do so again." Jasper met her glare straight on, regarding her with such open revulsion, she might have been dung on his shoe. He pointedly turned his back to her and faced Ian.

"My wife is locked in the tower?" Each carefully enunciated word dripped with rancor.

"Indeed, my lord."

"Come, Ian, surely you're not going to listen to a hireling." Waving a hand dismissively at Jasper, Lucinda tittered again. The sound emerged half-strangled, and her skin assumed a grayish pallor which couldn't be attributed to her black dress.

Head pounding, ire throttling through his veins, Ian scowled too furious to speak.

She changed tactics. "That uncivilized gypsy was causing all manner of problems." Her black-eyed gaze darted between him and Jasper. "I…I had to do something to keep the household in order."

"She lies, sir." Jasper didn't spare her a glance.

Ian curled his lips in derision. "I've no doubt she does."

She shot Jasper another deadly glare. "I was afraid. That uncivilized chit, she threatened me." Lucinda raised a hand to her throat and contrived to appear frightened.

"Not bloody-well likely." *My God.* What must Vangie think? How could she trust him after this?

"What else was I to do?" the dowager whined.

"What else? Are you utterly addled?" Ian banged a fist on the table rattling the china and silverware. "Nothing, and I do mean nothing, justifies you imprisoning my wife!" Fire blazed in his blood and cold fury in his mind. "You have no idea how close I am to doing you harm, Lucinda. You've gone too far. I should have charges brought against you," he gritted between clenched teeth.

"You…you wouldn't." She gasped and clutched at her throat with her spindly fingers.

Satisfaction surged through him. *Good, now she's truly frightened.* "The only thing preventing me from doing so is my affection for Charlotte. However, since she saw fit to deceive you in order to run off and marry Monroe, I doubt she'll fret overly much about you."

A whimpering noise escaped her.

He turned to Jasper. "Have the dowager's possessions and person moved to the dower house within the hour by whatever means necessary. Hog tie and gag her if needed."

"It will be my utmost pleasure, my lord." A satisfied smile wreathed Jasper's face. "Am I to assume her ladyship is no longer welcome in the manor?"

"You are."

"Excellent, my lord."

Marching to the room's entrance, Ian halted beside the butler. Laying a hand on the man's shoulder he said, "Thank you."

Jasper replied with a slight, regal nod of his head.

"Wait, Ian." Lucinda jumped to her feet, rapidly shoving her chair backward. It tottered before toppling to the floor with a loud bang. "What of Charlotte? She's wed?"

At the double French windows, Ian paused, half-turning to glance over his shoulder. Lucinda's gaze faltered, sinking to her plate. She toyed absently with a piece of bun lying there.

He caught a glimpse of himself in the mirror above the sideboard. The harsh features of the man reflected were nothing compared to the endless ire in his eyes. He looked like a man possessed.

He was. Half-crazed with worry and wrath.

His gaze swooped to Lucinda. "Charlotte is happily married and enjoying a holiday at the shore. You'd do well to bless the union, for she has made her choice and it's irrevocable."

Lucinda's gasp was muffled by his bellow for the housekeeper. "Tanny, I need you at once. Tanny!"

Where was she? Tanny was far more than his housekeeper. She'd taken him under her wing and nurtured him when his mother died. Ian had never ceased calling her Tanny, his childhood name for her, and to this day, she addressed him Master Ian.

Tanny bustled into the corridor, eyes widening at the unmistakable sound of china breaking in the dining room. "Whatever is she up to now?"

"Never mind her." Ian strode purposefully across the foyer.

Tanny scurried to meet him at the bottom of the stairs.

"You've a key?" he asked, not slowing his stride.

"Yes. I have the master key." She cast a glance toward the dining room, wincing as another ill-fated piece of china shattered. "Though *she* doesn't know it."

He made for the tower, the housekeeper hastening up the stairs beside him. Breathless from his brisk pace, she fumbled with the chatelaine at her waist. Ian paused one foot on the step above. Tanny was likely to tumble down the staircase if he didn't give her a moment to remove the key and catch her breath.

He glanced at her. "How is she?"

Tanny shook her head as she finally freed the skeleton key. "I honestly don't know. As well as can be expected, I suppose. We've been sneaking food and other items to her as we've been able. The dowager has an eagle eye, and she threatened to dismiss Jasper and me if we didn't comply with her demands."

They reached the top of the staircase. Turning right, they rushed the length of the portrait gallery paralleling the west wing. "Naturally, we refused to do her bidding, to lock Lady Warrick in the tower."

Ian sent Tanny a sidelong look but didn't slow. "How came she to be in the tower then?"

Puffing along beside him, Tanny said, "The dowager vowed she'd have the magistrate remove us, forcibly if need be, for trespassing."

Sir Doyle, damn frig pig. Ian should've guessed he'd be involved somehow.

He and Tanny turned a corner, before heading down an extended carpeted corridor ending at another flight of stairs. Scrambling to keep up, her breath coming in harsh little huffs, she continued, "That poor dear went voluntarily so Jasper and I wouldn't be forced from the manor. It was plain to us, the best way to protect her ladyship was to remain here."

"A wise decision, and one I'm most grateful for." He wasn't the least surprised Vangie had willingly made the sacrifice to protect Jasper and Tanny. His gut knotted tighter.

"Ailsa helped too," Mrs. Tannsen said. "She has gumption, she does. More than once that pigeon diverted the dowager, taking a vicious slapping as a consequence, so Jasper or I wouldn't be caught returning from the tower."

At the bottom of the stairs Ian held out his hand. "I'll go from here."

Tanny placed the key in his palm. He closed his hand around the cool metal and had already ascended the first step when she placed her hand on his forearm.

"Master Ian—"

He stopped, peering into her worried eyes.

"Your stepmother implied you told her to put your bride in the tower. Lady Warrick has reason to believe it was your order that placed her there. We've tried to convince her otherwise, but she simply changes the subject."

The fury he previously held in check spewed forth. "Hell and damnation!" Hands fisted, through clenched teeth he said, "Get my stepmother out of this house. Use force if need be. I want that malevolent crone gone by the time I bring my wife belowstairs."

"If I may be so bold, nothing would delight me more. For over two-score years the dowager has wreaked unhappiness and havoc within these walls." Her color high, Tanny fairly spat the words. "It is an honor to rid this mansion of that heartless woman."

With that pronouncement, his usually refined and impeccably behaved housekeeper hoisted her skirts and dashed down the corridor.

Ian climbed the last few stairs to the tower. Each one groaned and grumbled as if in pain, protesting his presence. The heartache in his chest mounted with each successive step. Reaching the turret's vaulted door, he closed his eyes. He was afraid. Afraid to open the door. Afraid of what he would find on the other side.

Afraid of Vangie hating me.

Inserting the key, he quietly turned the lock. Holding his breath, he shoved the heavy door. He was surprised when it silently swung open, given it was not maintained and rarely used.

Vangie sat in a dilapidated chair, her head resting against the torn fabric, her eyes closed. A new wave of fear assailed him. She looked unwell—thinner than he remembered, and so pale. The dark line of her lashes a startling contrast against her ashen cheeks.

Ian crossed to her on soundless feet. He knelt beside the chair. He didn't want to startle her. Gently touching her cheek, he whispered, "Sweeting?"

Her eyelids slowly crept open. She stared at him, her lovely eyes, unfocused and sad. Dark blue-violet shadows beneath them made her eyes appear huge in her wan face. A tremulous smile played around the edges of her mouth. "Ian?" She lifted her hand to touch his face. "Are you real? Am I dreaming?"

"I'm real." Turning his head into her hand, he kissed the palm.

He knew the instant she came fully awake and reality rudely rushed in.

Vangie's drowsiness fled. She dropped her hand and jerked away from him, retreating against the chair. Her pupils shrank to fine points, accusation simmering in her eyes. "Did you…?"

Ian hushed her with a finger to her lips. "Vangie, I give you my word. I did not, nor would I *ever*, instruct Lucinda to lock you in here. She's a bitter, vengeful woman, though I never thought her capable of this kind of maliciousness."

"But she said, the arrangements…?"

He took her cold hand in his. The veins stood out, vivid blue ribbons, against the thin skin. "Her moving to the dower house was the only arrangement we spoke about."

For the first time, Ian surveyed the chamber. To his knowledge, it had been vacant for at least thirty years. The squalor staggered him. Disbelief and anger registered simultaneously. Vangie had lived *here* the past three weeks? My God, he'd promised her she'd not go without again.

He'd failed her. Colossally.

His gaze grazed to her fine-boned face. Wariness lingered in her eyes. Angling to his feet, he extended his hand. "Come, let's be away from here."

She placed her hand in his, and let him draw her upright. She swayed before he put a steadying arm around her shoulders.

A movement outside caught the corner of his eye. Excellent. He smiled in satisfaction. There, along the footpath, making their way to the dower house, trudged Lucinda and numerous servants, each encumbered with parcels and baggage. One of the footmen pushed a hand-cart piled high with possessions.

"See, sweeting." Ian pointed at them.

Vangie turned to peer out the window. She raised her curious, yet relieved gaze to his. "She's gone?"

He smiled tenderly, kissing her on the nose. "Yes, and she'll not be back. She's not welcome in this house any longer. I intend to send her far away." Guiding her to the door, Ian said, "I think a substantial breakfast is in order, my lady, and a lengthy soak as well."

"That sounds nice." Her listlessness worried him. Had Lucinda succeeded in breaking Vangie's spirit?

With one arm around her waist, he led her down the narrow, curving flight of stairs. His hand skimmed her ribs. Already slender, she'd lost weight she could ill afford to lose. *Damn Lucinda.* What maggot had entered her head?

What maggot had crawled into *his*, leaving Vangie at her mercy? He of all people knew his stepmother's penchant for cruelty. Hadn't he endured it while trying to protect Geoff from her almost their entire childhood?

He should've never listened to her lies about Vangie. He typically wouldn't have except Charlotte, for her own selfish reasons, had validated her mother's fabrications. *Good God*, in all likelihood the entire tale Lucinda told of Vangie's role in Geoff's death was an exaggerated falsehood too.

Tanny and Jasper hovered at the bottom of the stairs. Both appeared immensely relieved upon seeing him and Vangie.

She offered them a reassuring smile, quipping, "My handsome prince has rescued me from my tower." She turned a grateful smile on him, and in that moment, she captured Ian's heart forever.

23

Soaking in the deliciously lilac-scented water, frothy bubbles to her neck, Vangie sighed contentedly. The remnants of a delicious meal sat on a table by the window. Never had hot rolls dripping with butter or strawberries smothered in clotted cream tasted so wonderful. The eggs had been light and fluffy, the ham exactly the right crispiness, and the tea steaming hot. Her shrunken stomach couldn't hold much, but she'd sampled everything on the tray at least twice.

Her gaze roved the stately room, taking in the blue, peach, and white rose-themed wallpaper, the damask royal blue silken draperies, and the ornate cherrywood furnishings.

Cabbage rose hand-hooked rugs in the same hues as the walls adorned the floors, and a dozen matching embroidered pillows were strewn in the window seat. It was a lovely room, but it brought her no peace or contentment. Her mind whirled with confused emotions that tumbled chaotically over and around one another.

Her thoughts turned once more to Ian. He'd appeared genuinely contrite. Every instinct told her he was truly an honorable man. The twin demons of doubt and confusion, however, had a way of raising their grotesque heads, causing her no small amount of consternation. She supposed the most practical course was to become acquainted with the man who was now her husband.

Toward that end, she dressed with care, donning her only decent gown. The vibrant green poplin frock trimmed with black lace boasted a filmy translucent overskirt with brilliantly-colored floral embroidery. The garment, a birthday gift from *Puri Daj*, was a unique blend of Romani inspiration and English fashion.

Aunt Eugenia hadn't confiscated and sold the gown, claiming no decent English woman would wear anything so appallingly vulgar. Vangie liked the dress. The bold hues complimented her dark coloring.

She'd had no opportunity to wear the gown, but today, she refused to put on her threadbare rags to celebrate her husband's homecoming.

Making her way below, she ran her damp palms over the fabric, smoothing an imaginary wrinkle. Would Ian find her attractive in the unusual garment? Or would he be repulsed by the obvious Romani influence? She tilted her chin fractionally. If he truly accepted her as his wife, then he would have to embrace her heritage as well.

Brow furrowed, she stood uncertainly at the base of the grand staircase. Should she seek him out? His study was that door, to her right, wasn't it? She hadn't been on this level since the day she arrived. She bit her lip. What if he wasn't in the study? Where was the drawing room again?

As if sensing her presence, Ian exited the study. He stopped short, examining her from her hair to her slippers. The masculine smile of approval tilting his mouth caused Vangie's toes to curl deliciously in her worn footwear.

He lifted her hand to his mouth, his warm lips caressing her knuckles. "You are a vision, sweeting."

When had he moved across the room?

His smoldering gaze traveled her form again, pausing momentarily at the fullness of her bosom. Her nipples puckered under his visual caress. That he was aware of her arousal was obvious. His nostrils flared, and his pupils enlarged before his gaze returned to her eyes. Could he see how flustered she was?

Her pulse beat a neck or nothing cadence, and her stomach churned from nerves.

"Did Tanny take your measurements? I'm sending a courier to London this afternoon and would like your shopping order to be sent along."

"Yes, she did."

Vangie searched his face. Gone were the scratches and bruises he'd come to their marriage with. "I truly don't require an entirely new wardrobe—"

"But sweeting, I want to provide you with one." He turned his lips up into that wholly disarming smile of his. "Would you deny me my pleasure?"

At the carnal glint in her husband's eyes, Vangie swallowed and shook her head. Though precisely what *pleasure* he referred to was a bit obscure.

"Good, it's settled then." He drew her hand through the curve of his elbow. Tucking it near his side, he covered her fingers possessively with his. "Do you feel strong enough to take a stroll in the garden? They're untidy, but still quite charming."

"Oh, yes. I've admired the grounds from the tower window—" She changed the subject abruptly. "I'd love to go outdoors. It's a beautiful day."

He guided her onto the rear terrace.

Vangie gazed at the beauty before her. Weathered, whimsical stone statuary speckled the gardens and pathways, though several were chipped or missing limbs. Apparently, once a gardener had been adept with sheers. Several evergreens had been sculpted into fanciful topiaries, though it was difficult now to determine precisely what some of the shapes were.

"Ian, is that a horse?" She pointed to the four-legged bush.

"Indeed. And over there is what used to be a bear." He indicated a large humped shrub with blobs for ears. "And that one is—"

"Don't tell me. A pig?"

"Madam, you insult me." He lifted his nose loftily. "Pig indeed. That, my dear lady, is a noble hunting hound."

She giggled. "It has no nose or tail, and it's short and fat."

He cocked his head and studied the shrub. A deep chuckle rumbled through his chest. "A pig-hound, then."

"Can we walk the gardens?" Three weeks of staring at them from the tower window made her eager to explore the gardens in person.

Ian flashed a charming smile. "What, and leave these zoological masterpieces?"

Vangie laughed. She'd not felt this carefree in ages. His good humor was contagious. And the sun felt marvelous. Closing her eyes, she turned her face upward, savoring its warm rays. A soft kiss brushed her mouth, and her eyes flew open.

She stared at his finely sculpted lips. They had been warm and tender on hers. Her tongue trailed the seam of her mouth trying to capture the sensation of his lips on hers again.

His knowing chuckle drew her from her reverie. "I thought you wanted to see the estate?"

"I do." Vangie forced her gaze from his gorgeous mouth, then met his humor-filled eyes.

Lord, but she sounded like a breathless goosecap.

"Very well, come along then." He grinned boyishly, his boot heels clicking on the flagstone path as he led the way. "Watch your step.

Some of the stones are cracked or broken."

She and Ian wandered the formal gardens all afternoon, strolling among the various floral rooms. An abundance of ornamental trees—complete with arbor covered stone benches—were strategically placed throughout the terraced gardens. The buzzing of fat honey-burdened bees and the lilting strains of birds filled the air with nature's song.

Vangie craned her neck to peer at the heavily laden dogwood trees drooping overhead. Several fragrant shrubs lent their sweet essence to drift on the warm breeze. "Is that a yellowhammer?" She pointed to a yellow and brown-streaked bird perched on a branch.

Ian's gaze followed her finger, and he nodded. "I believe so."

She stopped, bending to smell a peach-etched rose, its petals just beginning to open. Straightening, she gazed around the unkempt rose garden. It was too early in the season for the roses to be fully in bloom, but hundreds of plump rosebuds dotted the greenery with a profusion of pastel and vivid hues. The garden's neglect was not long-standing. These lands had been well-cared for in recent years.

"What happened?" She swept her hand in an arc to indicate the roses.

Ian reached behind her and pinched off a bud. He handed the rose to her, and then hands on his hips, he scanned his estate.

Raising the coral rose to her nose, Vangie inhaled deeply. However, she only detected a hint of fragrance.

"In recent years, my father deemed it unnecessary to spend monies on Somersfield." A shadow darkened his features when he spoke of his father. "That will change now that I have inherited the viscountcy."

She gently caressed the fragile petals. "He died recently?"

"Just over six weeks ago."

"And your brother?"

Ian turned to stare at her. Grief and something else, regret perhaps, was tangible in his pewter eyes. He opened his mouth as if to say something but shut it.

An unpleasant sensation tingled along her spine. *Dash it all*. Had she offended him? He didn't want to speak of it. She understood his pain. The loss of her parents had left her numb for months. "I'm sorry. I ought not to have mentioned them. Please forgive me."

He closed his eyes and pinched the bridge of his nose. Had he a headache? Or was he struggling to suppress tears? He opened his eyes and peered into hers for a long, unnerving moment.

Vangie couldn't tear her attention away.

Voice husky, he said, "You've done no wrong."

She had the oddest feeling he wasn't referring to her insensitive questions.

Ian rubbed his forehead. Mayhap he did have a headache. "Geoff died two months ago. He was five years younger than me. We had different mothers." He crossed the short distance separating them. Once more he started to speak and stopped.

She searched his tormented eyes. Yes, regret lingered there—and guilt. Did he feel responsible for his brother's death? How awful.

"How did he die?" The words rolled from her mouth before she could corral them. *Drat, my blasted tongue.*

A pained expression flicked across his face, but he swiftly smoothed his countenance into indifference. No, not indifference. There was a harsh edge to his lips, and he clenched his jaw. His chest expanded as he drew in a deep breath. With visible effort, he relaxed his jaw. "A duel with a lord."

"Dear God!" Vangie wished she hadn't asked.

He gazed over her head, as if seeing the scene on a stage. "He was defending the honor of a woman he didn't know but came upon being accosted. Both he and the duke were wounded. The duke died two days afterward."

Tears pricked behind her eyelids.

"Geoff was shot high in the chest, near his shoulder. I was stationed in Portsmouth. Father sent word, insisting I return home even though Geoff's wound was not fatal. In fact, the leech thought he'd make a full recovery."

She would not cry. She would not.

Ian sucked in a ragged breath. "The day I arrived, he took a sudden turn for the worse. Most likely an infection or undetected internal injury, the surgeon said."

Oh, God, why had she asked? Ian was reliving the horrid event. Tears trickled from the corner of one eye. She blinked several times, but the dratted droplets kept falling. She wanted to throw herself into his arms and wail for everything she was worth.

"He died that night. For once, I was grateful my father was such a controlling sot. I was able to say goodbye to my brother."

A sob caught in her throat. "Oh, Ian."

He wiped the tears from her face with his thumbs then caressed her jaw with the back of his hand. "You would've liked him, I think."

If he was anything like you, I would've adored him.

"Enough of this morose talk. We cannot undo what's already done." He smiled, a melancholic half-smile. "Come, I want to show you the pond."

He wrapped his hand around hers, and it fit neatly within his. The calluses on his palms rubbed against her fingers. Unlike the majority of the dandies she'd met in London, he was a man accustomed to hard work. The fops' hands had been softer and whiter than hers.

Walking beside Ian, Vangie considered him. He was a man who loved intensely. The knowledge sparked and simmered deep in her breast. Would he—could he—ever love her that much? A queer flutter disturbed her stomach.

They crossed a large lawn—more of a meadow really—and came to a tree-shaded footbridge. Hundreds of lilies of the valley blanketed the ground beneath the trees. She bent to lean on the rail, watching several swans below the bridge.

"Vangie, don't!" Ian drew her away. "Take care, sweeting. The bridge is in need of repair." He guided her to the other side. "This side is safer." Shaking the rail, he said, "See, this barrier is sturdy. The other is rotted along the planks and won't support any weight. I really should set Olson to repairing it."

Leaning over the support, she exclaimed in delight. "Look."

A female swan passed under the bridge, four cygnets gliding in her wake. Swimming in a circle, the pen waited for her mate. She arched her neck in a caress as he passed by and replaced her at the front of the line.

Ian slipped his arm around her waist and tugged her into the circle of his powerful arms, whispering, "Swans mate for life, sweeting."

His breath tickled her ear, sending errant flickers of sensation across the sensitive flesh. She forced her attention back to the swans. "They are magnificent, especially the black swans. I've never seen any before. Do they stay here year-round?"

"Yes. The pond is really more of a smallish lake. It extends clear into those trees, yonder." He inclined his head in the direction of some evergreens. "It's deep too. As boys, Geoff and I often swam in it." Pointing to the far side of the pond, he asked, "Do you see where the cattails and bull rushes are—that boggish area just this side of the tall vegetation? Two nests are over there, and each pair of black swans has hatched four eggs. The hatchlings are light though, nearly white."

Grasping his muscled forearm, Vangie cried, "Look, there are some of the little ones, near the middle of the pond." She turned to look at him and smiled. "God's creation is exquisite, is it not?"

Ian's eyes darkened as they roamed her face. He was going to kiss her. Her gaze fell to his mouth, and she parted hers in invitation.

Dipping his head, he murmured, "It is indeed."

The softest touch of his lips, the whisper of her sigh, and an onslaught bubbled from within, breaking down each of her reservations. This was right. It was meant to be.

Every doubt fled on the wings of wonder under the velvet softness of his lips. She rejoiced in his firm mouth playing atop hers, invoking tantalizing sensations in the most interesting of places. Tilting her head, she allowed him better access. She parted her mouth, welcoming him, inviting him to explore its depths.

Groaning, Ian trapped Vangie within his arms. Her tentative response vanquished him, shook him, igniting his passion until he was consumed with her. Only her. When her slender arms clasped behind his neck, he was overcome. This kind-hearted, generous woman held no ill will, but forgave freely, giving of herself unreservedly. She felt something too. It was apparent in her fervent, if somewhat untried responses.

Holding her tight, chest-to-chest, hip-to-hip, he yielded to the pent-up emotion he'd buried deep inside. He conveyed his adoration with his mouth.

A distant *thunk* intruded—likely from the stables. With one final kiss, he lifted his head then surveyed the perimeter. Two forms lurked under the trees, one on either end of the pond. The first, a swarthy-complexioned man turned swiftly, and in one deft move, leapt onto his horse. He vanished into the trees bordering Somersfield.

Who was he?

The other, a darkly-clad woman hovered in the shade of the grove. Icy fingers of unease clawed the length of Ian's spine. *Lucinda*. Even at this distance, he sensed her fuming rage.

24

Vangie awoke the next morning to Ailsa warbling a ribald ballad. As she lay watching the maid blundering around the chamber, she couldn't help but suspect the girl was deliberately noisy. She kept slicing covert glances at the bed as she flung the draperies open, banged about in the fire grate, and sang much too loudly for possible further sleep.

Peeking at the servant through half-closed lids, and squinting at the torrent of sunshine now permeating the chamber, Vangie considered feigning sleep just to see her response.

"You're awake at last," Ailsa fairly chirped.

Oh, dear, she was caught. Smiling good naturedly, she sat up. "It was somewhat difficult to continue sleeping with you—"

"Oh, I know," Ailsa interrupted, oblivious to her breach of decorum. "But I couldn't wait to wake you."

Clearly.

"Look." She pointed to a mound of garments piled atop a nearby chair. "Lord Warrick said I was to select some of Miss Charlotte's dresses for you to wear until your new wardrobe arrives." Ailsa snatched a gauzy champagne-colored gown and held it before her. "Isn't it lovely?"

"It is." Almost as lovely as the silver gown she'd borrowed from Yvette the night of the ball.

Ailsa tossed the frock aside and grabbed a filmy white and gold gown next. "Set your peepers on this one, will you? Coo, it shines like the stars, it does."

Intrigued despite herself, Vangie allowed the boisterous maid to persuade her to try on a dozen of the gowns. "I've never owned more than two or three gowns at once," she admitted.

She paused as the maid lifted a green confection over her head. She eyed the garments strewn on the chair and bed. How could she choose which one to wear? They were all beautiful. At last, she selected a pale teal masterpiece trimmed in primrose. Its cheery colors matched her mood.

She was taller than Charlotte, but overall, the gowns fit reasonably well. A trifle loose at the waist and snug at the bodice, but certainly, a vast improvement over the rags she'd arrived in. The slippers, on the other hand, were another matter. While Vangie's feet weren't overly large, Charlotte's were as petite as a child's. It didn't seem right wearing the stunning gowns with her worn slippers, but there was no help for it.

The next ten days passed in idyllic peace. Vangie's appetite improved, and the odd odors previously accompanying her meals disappeared. The dowager truly must have been feeding her food on the verge of spoiling. The knowledge neither surprised nor made her more inclined to feel charitable toward the woman.

Her stomach continued, however, to object on occasion to the delicacies Cook prepared. Truth be told, Vangie wasn't accustomed to rich fare in such abundance. Aunt Eugenia had hoarded the most delectable foodstuffs for herself and Uncle Percival. She twisted her mouth into a droll smile. To gaze upon Uncle's emaciated form caused a person to wonder if the man ever consumed nourishment.

A few neighbors called to pay their respects, and she slipped into the role of lady of the manor with a great deal more ease than she'd anticipated. To her surprise, she'd become cautiously content in her position as Lady Warrick.

With Ian's encouragement, she'd sent word to her Roma relatives that she was well, and arranged for *Puri Daj* to pay a visit Saturday. Vangie wanted to ask her grandmother to concoct the medicine from the yews which would ease the housekeeper's rheumatism pain. Vangie wouldn't attempt the mixture herself. One had to be extremely careful with yew. In the wrong dosage, it could be deadly.

Of the Dowager Viscountess Warrick, Vangie saw nothing, for which she was eternally grateful. She never wanted to encounter that spiteful woman again. Ian hadn't sent her away yet, but as long as Vangie didn't have to ever see her, she could almost forget the woman lived nearby.

Ian proved a doting and attentive spouse. He didn't make any husbandly demands, but he made no qualms regarding his desire for her either. She wasn't sure what to make of it. If he desired her, why didn't he seek her bed?

She made no objections to his overtures, for she quite liked his attentiveness. And he was oh so, charming in his attempts to woo her. A tender, fleeting caress here. A skimming touch of his fingertips there. Multitudes of feather-light kisses dropped on her nape or shoulder while she was bent upon a task. Yes, he pursued her with feline persistence and cat-like patience.

She never thought she'd enjoy being his prey. If only he would snare her.

Had he known how effective his attentions were, she was sure he'd have been wallowing in masculine pride. She often woolgathered, immersed in fanciful musing, of which her handsome husband was the cause. On more than one occasion, her daydreaming brought a bloom of color to her cheeks.

Faith, he had her at sixes and sevens, she admitted to herself after dinner two evenings later. She and Ian sat in the drawing room in companionable silence. He read while she crocheted a fichu.

She tried to concentrate on the stitches and loops, but his close proximity and the sheer maleness he exuded, caused her to tear out missed stitches several times. She paused, eyeing the piece. *Drat*, it was much too long on the end.

That's what comes of trying to crochet while wondering whether one's husband sleeps naked.

Vangie began counting the stitches then stopped abruptly, her jaw sagging.

She hadn't.

Yes, she had.

No, she couldn't have.

She peered at her work. *But I did.*

It was the same length and general shape as his…*disfigurement*. She began frantically unraveling it, wrapping the yarn around and around her hand.

"What are you crocheting, Vangie?"

She froze, scrunching the *thing* in her fist. When had he stopped reading, and how long had he been watching her? Had he seen *it*? She glanced up, forcing a genial smile. At least she thought she did. Her lips were turned upward, weren't they? "Ah, a fichu. Charlotte's gowns are too revealing for my figure."

Well, listen to that. I sound quite normal.

Casually unwinding the yarn from around her hand, she noticed his gaze slide to the material stretched taut across her breasts. The low décolletage exposed a generous portion of her flesh.

Ian murmured throatily, "I quite like the fit."

Startled at the timbre of his voice, her gaze flashed to his. Spying the ravenous look in his eyes, her breath hitched, her mouth rounding into an "O" of surprise. His scorching gaze dropped to the mounds straining against the muslin, and to her chagrin, her nipples hardened.

Dash it all, why must they always do that?

He closed his book and held it up. "I've read the same passage four times and have no greater knowledge now what the page contains than I did when I began reading."

At least he hadn't crocheted a *willy*. That showed where her mind was, for pity's sake.

Ian set his book aside then plucked the crocheting from her hands. He edged closer, his thigh pressing intimately against hers, and wrapped one arm around her shoulders. Tilting her chin upward, his attention lingered on her lips. The slow descent of his head allowed her ample opportunity to resist should she be so inclined.

She wasn't in the least.

Vangie angled closer, one hand resting on his marble-like thigh, a mere inch from his maleness. When their lips met, passion crashed over her in undulating waves. Flooded with unfamiliar sensation, she could only float on the torrent of want Ian masterfully invoked.

His tongue toyed with her lips, licking the crease until she opened to his insistent entreaty. With his mouth, he taught her what she was eager to learn. Her hesitant responses became bolder as consuming desire swept her along.

She moaned low in her throat, protesting when Ian tore his mouth from her lips. He trailed feathery kisses down her neck, edging lower and lower, until they skimmed her breasts swelling above her bodice. She was mindless against the onslaught, of the quivers spreading through her. She ran frantic hands across the muscular ridges and planes of his chest and torso.

He shifted away.

"No, Ian."

Ian smiled wickedly at her mew of protest as he shrugged off his jacket. His waistcoat and cravat swiftly followed. He unbuttoned his shirt, yanked the fabric from his waistband then let it slide off his broad shoulders.

My, but he is a finely built man.

Vangie flattened her palm against the smattering of dark hair covering his chest. The curls tapered to a seductive triangle before disappearing into his unfastened pantaloons. A tell-tale bulge proudly strained against the opening.

He reached for the hem of her gown, scrunched halfway up her thighs. Never breaking eye contact, he edged the material upward, inch by inch. Shimmering with the intensity of dozens of miniature stars, the flecks in his eyes held a promise.

Flicking her tongue out, she moistened her lips.

Brushing his calloused fingers over the flesh of her inner thigh, he continued to raise her gown, swirling his fingertips over her skin.

Reality fled as he worked his magic, smothering her breasts and lips with adoration, urging her on with words of love and passion. His whiskers scraped her sensitized flesh, and every pore, every nerve ending, awakened in anticipation.

Vangie tossed her head on the settee cushion, striving for what she knew not. What was he doing to her? Her hands clutched his rigid forearms and his muscled shoulders. Overcome, she had no inclination to be self-conscious or ashamed of the passion-invoked sounds she breathed.

She gasped, nearly incoherent, "Ian, please—" Sensual fire coursed through her veins, a demanding, aching thrumming at her apex. She groaned, her hips frantically undulating. "I can bear no more."

"Yes, you can, love," he whispered against her mouth. "Let go, sweeting. Let me take you to heaven."

She felt the first quivers of her release and yanked her mouth free. Head thrown back, she keened her pleasure. A kaleidoscope of colors erupted behind her eyes as sensation after pulsating, effervescent sensation rippled through her.

Ian glided into Vangie before she finished climaxing. He remained perfectly still, her muscles constricting rhythmically around his length. He gritted his teeth against the exquisite pull, resisting the urge to pour himself into her.

She raised passion-drugged eyes to his, and the muscles in his neck bunched as he struggled for control sheathed in the midst of her hot depths. She would enjoy the full measure of their union this time, though from the stunned look on her lovely face, she'd not as yet realized he possessed her.

He rocked ever-so-gently.

Her eyes widened in startled wonder. *And now she did.* "You're inside me?"

Ian growled, "Me and no other, ever." He flexed his hips again.

She groaned, arching her back, and pushing her hips flush to his. "It doesn't hurt," she gasped.

Sliding his hands beneath her buttocks, he tilted her hips, relishing in her cries of renewed bliss. He bent to claim her lips once more, promising, "You've had a mere sampling of passion's rapture this night, my love." He withdrew, his distended tip hovering at her womanhood. "Now, you'll experience the wholeness of ecstasy."

Plunging into her, Ian fulfilled his pledge. She crested the pinnacle, her euphoric cry mingling with his moan of ecstasy. One stroke later, he toppled into the abyss of consummate bliss. Several moments passed before he stirred, withdrawing from his satiated wife.

She lay sprawled beneath him, making no attempt to put her gown aright or cover herself. Lifting a hand, she traced the line of his jaw before placing a kiss on his lips. Her voice husky, she whispered, "Thank you."

Overcome, Ian lifted his head and gazed into her sincere eyes. "It's I who should be thanking you. I treated you appallingly—"

"Shh." Vangie placed a finger over his lips. "That's behind us. I much prefer what we just shared." She frowned, the slightest furrowing of her smooth brow and downward tilting of her perfect mouth. "Except…"

He stiffened, uncertainty adding a sharp edge of fear to what she was about to say.

Lifting wanton eyes to his, a siren's invitation curving her lips, she suggested throatily, "I should like to try coupling again, entirely naked in bed."

Before she finished speaking, he'd risen and scooped her into his arms.

25

As Vangie lay fulfilled in the aftermath of their lovemaking, snuggled securely in Ian's arms, she drowsily smiled. Replete and contented, she suspected the sentiment budding within her was indeed love. She smiled against his chest. He'd wasted no time in escorting her upstairs where he demonstrated to her not once, but three times, in as many positions, how delightful lovemaking could be in a magnificent, oversized bed.

She had no further doubts about how wondrous the physical union between husband and wife could be. Her happy sigh earned her a gentle squeeze and a caress on her buttock. Her last conscious thought, before she fell into a blissful sleep was more of *Puri Daj's* wisdom.

Manuš paťal, hoj džanel, aľe oda, ko džanel, hin ča o Del. Man thinks he knows what's best, but really only God knows.

Upon awakening in the unfamiliar bed the next morning, Vangie forgot for a moment where she was. A single yellow rose bud lying in the indentation of the pillow next to hers brought a smile to her lips. Tenderly plucking the blossom from Ian's pillow, she buried her face against the cool silk. She inhaled deeply, breathing in his musky scent.

The silky petals to her nostrils, she rolled onto her back. It would seem he had a fondness for roses after all.

Where was he?

She surveyed his chamber, having never been inside it before. Shades of gold and hunter green enhanced the opulent furnishing. A tidy writing desk stood near the window, and above the desk, a familiar sketch, now framed, caught her attention. She climbed from the bed, and after wrapping the sheet around her like a Grecian robe, wandered to the desk. Lifting the bud to her nose, she tilted her head.

"He took my drawing." The sketch depicted two Romani toddlers and a dog playing beneath a tree. "And had it framed."

Did Ian have a penchant for children too? She curled her lips upward at the notion.

The door burst open and Ailsa bounded into the room, looking entirely too satisfied. Vangie's robe slung across one arm, she carried a breakfast tray.

"My lady, I'm sorry to be late with your breakfast. I went to your usual chamber—" She placed the tray on a table and turned to eye her from toe to top. "Imagine my surprise to find your bed undisturbed," Ailsa said with a cheeky grin and a bold wink while handing Vangie her robe.

Gracious, the girl was an impudent minx.

Smiling despite herself—the maid's gaiety was truly contagious—she, slipped into the familiar green folds. "Did Lord Warrick leave word for me?"

Nodding pertly, Ailsa withdrew a folded piece of paper from her apron pocket. She passed it to her before turning her attention to arranging her breakfast.

Vangie sat at the table an unfolded the crisp foolscap. Ian's bold, slanted strokes slashed across it. He'd signed it, *Lovingly, Ian.*

"Good news, my lady?"

"His lordship wishes to picnic this afternoon."

Vangie nibbled a crumpet topped with clotted cream as she reached for the fresh sliced strawberries. She hesitated, heat creeping across her cheeks. Last night, Ian had whispered he'd like to take her picnicking. He'd gone on to suggest several creative things he'd do with their meal, one of which involved something deliciously naughty with strawberries.

"It's good to see your appetite has returned, my lady."

Vangie was somewhat surprised how hungry she was, and her stomach didn't twitch in the least this morning. She jumped to her feet. She didn't want to wait for Ian to return to the manor. "I'd like to surprise his lordship. After I've dressed, will you show me the way to the stables?"

Grinning, Ailsa nodded her head. "Of course."

Less than an hour later, she and the maid crossed the greens, headed for the barn.

"Hurry, I want to reach the stables before Lord Warrick leaves." After last night, Vangie was feeling emboldened and eager to tell him her feelings.

"I know a shortcut," Ailsa said. "It's a trail the stable hands use. Come, it's this way." She cut through the ankle-high grass intent on an outcrop of trees a few yards farther ahead. "Do you ride, my lady?"

Vangie nodded. "I do, but not often and certainly not well. And not sidesaddle. I didn't have much opportunity to ride in Brunswick. Truthfully, horses make me a bit nervous."

"Gads, your ladyship, his lordship's stalls are crammed full as dairy teats of the sweetest mares. My favorite is Marigold. She's docile as a puppy, and she never kicks up her heels and dumps me on my backside."

"You ride?" Vangie stopped trudging along and stared at the maid, though not because of her indecorous speech.

Ailsa, nodded in excitement. "Oh, aye, his lordship allows it. He says the horses need to be exercised and gentled."

Ian permitted the staff to ride? At every turn, his generosity and thoughtfulness continued to amaze her.

Ailsa skipped several paces ahead before whirling about, her arms wide. "Isn't he grand, letting us ride? I adore the beasties, especially the foals."

Waiting for Vangie to catch-up, she said, "Yesterday, Ben told me a mare is due to foal any day now."

Having taken a wending dirt path through the woods, they emerged from the trees. The trail opened into a clearing a hundred feet from the rear side of the barn. Skirting around a pile of horse manure and used straw, Vangie and Ailsa paralleled the building. At the corner, they both stopped short, covering their mouths to stifle their giggles.

Ian and the stable master circled the paddock examining several horses, each haltered and held steady by a groom. A jet-black stallion followed the stable master like a trained puppy. Attempting to hail his attention, the horse tossed his head, wickered, and nudged the man's bony backside every few steps.

Exasperated, the stable master pivoted to face the stallion. "Cease, ye blasted brute."

The horse nickered in his ear then probed the groom's coat pocket for a treat.

"Gerard, couldn't you come up with a more suitable name for that fawning creature than Thor?" Ian goaded in a syrupy voice, grinning ear to ear. "Mayhap Muffy or Pookie? Does he do any parlor tricks? Beg? Roll-over?"

The other grooms snickered.

Other than raising his grizzled eyebrows, Gerard paid them no heed. Thor snorted and pushed his muzzle into the man's calloused hand, eager for the apple he held. Patting the horse on the neck, Gerard turned his back on the others. "I have me a mare to check on. She's nigh on ripe to foal." Obviously affronted at being the object of everyone's amusement, he stomped across the paddock to the stables, muttering under his breath all the while.

The ever-faithful stallion followed on the stable master's heels. Thor bumped his large head into Gerard from behind every few steps, earning gap-toothed grins from the grooms and another hoot of mocking laughter from Ian, trailing a foot behind Gerard.

Nearly bent double, one hand over her mouth and the other clutching her stomach, Vangie tried to suppress her laughter.

Evidently, the stallion decided he didn't appreciate being ignored. He blew a long, horsey breath on Gerard's neck before extending his large tongue and licking the groom's cheek. Howling with amusement, Ian slapped Gerard on the back.

Laughing so hard he could scarcely speak, Ian entered the stables. "God Almighty…The brute…even licks…like a dog."

"Leave off with the lickin', or ye'll be gelded by nightfall, ye old poger," Gerard groused, his voice barely audible through the wood.

Upon hearing the muffled threat, Vangie and Ailsa erupted into another round of hushed giggles

It seemed the men were bound for the exit on the other end. With the maid in tow, Vangie reversed her direction, and they headed back in the direction they'd come. Nearing the end of the elongated building, she caught sight of Ian leaving the barn. He must've been momentarily blinded by the brilliant morning sunshine, because a few feet beyond the exit, he stopped, shielding his eyes.

Obscured by the trees and the barn's shadow, she carefully picked her way around the putrid pile once more. Glancing up, she pulled up short, and Ailsa plowed into her from behind.

The Dowager Viscountess Warrick stepped from the path the women had used minutes before.

26

An eerie prickling skirted across Vangie's flesh. Shivering, she wrapped the shawl tighter around her shoulders as Ailsa muttered a prayer under her breath.

"Ian, there you are. I apologize for keeping you waiting." The dowager's chilly voice floated across the clearing.

He was meeting with her? Why? He'd said he wanted nothing to do with the vile woman and that he intended to send her far away. Actually, Vangie was somewhat surprised he hadn't done so already.

After throwing a fleeting look behind him into the stables, he faced her. His long legs eating up the distance between them, he strode to where she waited in the oaks' shade. "Lucinda?"

With his back to Vangie and the increased distance between them, it made hearing him difficult.

"It was wise of you to suggest meeting here, Ian. It's unlikely your, ah, *bride* will interrupt us."

At the coldness in her voice, Vangie shuddered again. There was something oddly disconcerting about Lucinda's appearance today as well. Trailing her gaze over the dowager, she couldn't determine precisely what the peculiarity was. Dressed impeccably in mourning weeds, the woman hadn't a hair out of place. Loosely clasping a fringed jacquard shawl against the persistent breeze, she seemed composed. *But...*

Vangie flicked her attention to Ailsa, still muttering prayers beneath her breath. Lips pinched tight, she returned her regard to the dotty dowager. An icy shiver washed over her, and her breath caught. *Oh, my God.* Her ladyship *knew* she stood there.

The woman stared straight at her, her eyes empty, vacant pools; the eyes of a dead person. No soul remained. Another shudder rippled across Vangie, causing the hairs on her arms and nape to stand on end.

Voice quivering, Ailsa shakily whispered, "Lawks. That addled fly-by-night witch is off her broom and abroad in daylight. Gawd save us all!"

"Hush, Ailsa."

Vangie scrunched the shawl in her hands. Should she make her presence known to Ian or retreat and allow him privacy with his stepmother? Another swift glance at the dowager decided the matter for her. She touched Ailsa's arm to turn her about, but her ladyship's words rendered her immobile.

"Your diligence in seeking that gypsy's undoing is truly admirable."

Ailsa's horrified gasp didn't muffle the gloating triumph in the dowager's voice.

Diligence? Undoing? More lies?

"When we plotted your trip to London, after what that slattern did to my poor, dear Charlotte—oh, and Geoff, of course—I thought you only sought to tarnish Miss Caruthers' reputation." Brushing a hand down her arm, she cut another sideways glance to Vangie.

Charlotte? Geoff? Whatever have they to do with me?

Ian answered his stepmother, though it was difficult to hear him clearly. Vangie strained to understand his indistinct words. "Liar…vulgar…Vangie…immoral light skirt."

He didn't believe that of her, did he? Dizziness battered her. No, he couldn't. *Could he*? But if he did, that would explain his loutish inferences during their wedding reception. And what came after too. She trembled, though whether from nerves, anger, or cold she couldn't be certain.

Ailsa laced her fingers with hers. "Your hand is freezing," she whispered. "That witch could turn the devil's blood to ice, she could." She tugged on Vangie's hand. "Let's go, my lady."

Vangie shook her head, shushing the maid with a stern look. She ventured forward several steps. What was Ian saying?

"Bringing her to Somersfield was absolutely brilliant." Looking past Ian's shoulder, Lucinda met Vangie's eyes with her shrewd stare. "When are you going to tell her the marriage is a sham? That the rector was a drunkard? A boosey retained to perform the vows?" She smiled nastily. "I must say, it was a stroke of genius hiring Reverend Tipsyton. He could never resist a bribe or a bottle."

The blood roared in Vangie's ears, and her breath left her lungs in a loud, painful hiss. Was Tipsyton the reverend's name who'd performed the ceremony? Had she even been told his name? She couldn't remember to save her soul. But Lucinda hadn't attended the ceremony and had no way of knowing the cleric's name. *Unless they'd conspired together.*

She stood horror-struck, unable to draw in even a wisp of air.

The marriage was a sham?

The rector *had* reeked of spirits. *Oh dear, God.* The ground wavered, undulating alarmingly. Her pulse slowed to an irregular tempo, and her head began to spin. She shook it fiercely. *Not now.* She couldn't—wouldn't by all that was holy—have a damned episode now.

Her gaze riveted on Ian, she murmured through stiff lips, "Ailsa, have a horse readied for me, not a sidesaddle either."

"But, my lady."

"Now, Ailsa!" The firm resolve in her tone brooked no argument.

"Yes, my lady." Ailsa spun around to do her bidding, murmuring dire threats and uncouth allegations about the dowager's character until out of earshot.

"It would be the *coup de grâce* in our pursuit for vengeance if you knapped her with child before you turned the unworthy *didikko* out." A sneer curled the dowager's thin lips.

Nausea speared Vangie. Ian meant to cast her off? Step-by-step, she slowly retreated, swallowing against another surge of nausea.

The dowager's gaze flicked to the barn's shadows. "Mayhap she already carries your seed?"

Ian ran a hand through his hair before shaking his head. "Not yet. Soon I hope."

That, Vangie heard clearly.

Dear Lord. Devastation ravaged her as something irreplaceable shriveled in her center. Planting a palm against the barn's rough siding, she fought for composure. She'd allowed herself to love Ian, and he'd used her for selfish gains. No, he'd used her in a premeditated scheme of spiteful revenge.

To what end, her heart cried? Why did he detest her so? What had she done to earn such loathing? She sucked in a bracing breath, nearly gagging at the stench of rotting manure. She withdrew several more unsteady steps, her gaze trained on Ian the whole while.

His rancor had something to do with his brother and sister. Had she ever met either? Closing her eyes, she endeavored to conjure Charlotte's or Geoff's face. She'd been introduced to so many people throughout the Season that trying to recall a pair of faces was futile. Surely she'd remember Ian's sister if something untoward had occurred between them, wouldn't she have?

And what of his brother? Did he look like Ian? There'd been no portrait of him on the gallery wall. Had she met a Geoff Hamilton? She simply couldn't remember. A sickening thought slithered into her mind. Mayhap he'd been one of the gentlemen whose advances she'd spurned.

Her tormented mind tripped down another equally horrific path.

A child? Was that why Ian had been intimate with her last night? He wanted to impregnate her before abandoning her? Sucking in a tremulous breath, her eyes filled with tears, and her heart broke, sharp fragment by sharp fragment. The familiar queasiness welled up again, its nauseating waves clawing at her throat. She cupped her belly. Even now, did a poor, innocent babe lie there?

Righteous anger sluiced through Vangie, and she hardened her heart. From the moment she'd met him, Ian had plotted her ruination. Every caress and kind word—all were part of his perverse ploy. He was no better than the dowager. No—he was worse. Pretending anger at being forced to marry her. Making her feel guilty. Feigning affection in order to seduce her with the intent of destroying her.

Unconscionable, despicable knave.

"You'll hurt me no more, Ian. Under Roma law, I divorce you." Resolute, she turned away and barricaded her crushed heart, as well as her newfound love, from the man she once called husband. One could only forgive so much.

No matter what trials life brings, do not harden your heart, Nukkidai.

Vangie shook her head, purposefully turning deaf ears to the voice of wisdom whispering in her mind. *Not this time, Puri Daj*. By God, not this time. One doesn't cast pearls before swine then complain when they are trampled upon.

Barely keeping his tempter in check, Ian studied Lucinda. Why did her attention keep veering beyond him?

Vangie. God damn, bloody hell.

Even before he half-turned and looked over his shoulder, he *knew* she stood there. At her devastated countenance, he sucked in a great gulp of air as if struck by a battering ram. Stuffing a fist to her mouth, she darted around the other side of the barn.

How long had she been standing there? How much had she heard? *What* exactly had she heard? Desolation had ravaged her beautiful face, and her eyes. God help him, the expression in her haunted, betrayed gaze.

"She believed me, Ian. Every calculated lie. Yes, even that you asked me to meet you here." Lucinda laughed, an insane cackle reverberating amongst the early summer greenery. "I could see it in her eyes, stupid gypsy whore," she gasped between her maniacal chortles.

Ian rounded on her, snarling, "Damn you, you evil, possessed bitch." He lunged at her, itching to shake some sense into her. To punish her for what she'd done.

Stumbling backward a pace, she threw one hand to her throat, the other palm out to ward him off.

Breathing heavily, his fists clenched, he halted. "You're not worth it. Confine yourself to the dower house and grounds until I make the arrangements for your banishment."

Intent on pursuing his wife, he swiveled around. He'd taken a single step when Lucinda seized his arm. He tried to shake her off, but her frenzied grip was surprisingly strong. Her long nails bit into his flesh through the fabric of his coat. *Witches talons.*

"I want what's mine," Lucinda hissed, madness reflected in her glassy eyes. "You don't deserve the settlement I brought to my marriage with Roger. Charlotte must have it." Spittle gathered at the corner of her mouth as she clawed his arm. "She's from my loins, not you. *My* monies, *my* lands, *my* holdings must go to *my* offspring, not Roger's spawn."

She's utterly insane.

She scratched frantically at his coat. "They're mine, mine, not yours." Her last words ended on a shriek as he roughly shoved her away.

"You're mad. Father long since sold the properties you brought to the marriage, and he frittered your settlement away decades ago. Every last guinea of it." He didn't have time for this. He must find Vangie.

"No, no. You lie!" She shook her head vehemently, causing several pins to come loose. Her graying hair hanging haphazardly around her head and shoulders gave her an even more demented appearance. "He couldn't have. It's not possible. I've planned for so long…" Head slanted, she peered at him bewildered, her eyes glazed with madness. She muttered to herself, "No one else would have me after…My father paid Roger a fortune to marry me. The settlement was enormous."

"Lucinda, I cannot change what's been done." Ian impatiently shoved a hand through his hair. Every second she delayed him was time his beloved wife believed her lies.

Wringing her hands, Lucinda didn't seem to hear him. "It cannot be gone. He's lying. Of course he is. Charlotte must have my dowry."

"Charlotte is married—"

"To a penniless cork-brain!" she snapped, a glimpse of lucidity shining through. "No, my daughter must have position, wealth, a title." She cut him a side-eyed glance, and an eerie light glimmered in her eye. "Men always take everything."

Enough. His wife was his primary concern. "Lucinda, go to the dower house, and stay there. Or I swear, I'll have you arrested today for imprisoning my wife."

With a final hate-filled glare, she shuffled away, grumbling beneath her breath.

He ran a hand through his hair again, drawing in a calming breath. The woman was unhinged, and needed to be kept under constant surveillance. He'd exile her to his cottage in the northernmost part of Scotland with a couple of brawny Scots to oversee her care. She'd either live out the remainder of her days there or in Bedlam.

A more urgent matter consumed him. He must find Vangie.

Was she still nearby? Had she returned to the house?

He ran back to the stables.

A new stable hand hovered at the entrance, staring at Lucinda's retreating form. He spit on the ground and turned to go inside the barn.

"You there." Ian called. "What's your name?"

The young man paused and flushed. "Ben, sir."

"Have you seen Lady—"

Two riders exploded from the paddock, their stockinged legs exposed as they galloped their horses across the pasture.

Sprinting to the corral fence, Ian jumped onto the lower rail and yelled, "Vangie, stop! Let me explain."

27

The wings of the gentle breeze sweeping across the clearing carried Ian's words away. In frustrated horror, he watched Vangie's horse rear. *Good God*, had his shouting spooked the beast? She slid off the horse's broad rump, tumbling to the ground and lay in a heap, unmoving.

His heart stopped, terror numbing his mind. "Van—gie!" He didn't recognize the tormented voice that ripped from his throat.

Ailsa swung her horse around, evidently intent on rescuing her mistress. But before she reached her, a gypsy on horseback emerged from the trees and pounded to her side.

The man at the pond.

Vangie obviously knew him, for she stumbled to her feet, holding her side. The Roma leaned down, and in one smooth movement, swung her behind him on his sorrel gelding.

She looked over her shoulder, and across the distance, her gaze collided with Ian's. Her shoulders slumped, and she closed her eyes before laying her head on the gypsy's broad back.

With a yip, the unknown man kicked his gelding. He and Ailsa raced their horses over a knoll and out of sight.

Mind numb, Ian roamed his gaze over the stunned audience assembled in the paddock. A couple of stable hands coughed and averted their eyes. In full view of a dozen of his staff, his bride had fled with another man. Humiliation scorched his cheeks.

They didn't know about Lucinda's lies he reminded himself, though it did little to appease his battered pride.

Neither did Vangie.

Her mare dutifully trotted back to the enclosure, and Ben snared the reins. He led the docile horse into the barn, Ian close on his heels. At once he set to saddling Pericles. He was going after his wife and nothing would stop him from bringing her home.

Glancing up, he froze, eyes narrowed in furious disbelief. His focus trained on Ben, he walked around the other side of the stallion, pretending to adjust the saddle.

The groom had loosened the mare's girth strap. Deftly, he edged his fingers beneath the saddle then casually slipped his fist into his pocket.

Lashing out, Ian gripped the groom's smaller hand in his own. "Give it over." he demanded, rage lacing each syllable.

Ben dared bravado. "S…sir?" he gulped, terrified. His eyes, already bulging in fright, widened further when his gaze swept the barn.

Ian glanced over his right shoulder. His men had formed a semicircle behind him. Their loyalty in the wake of Vangie's flight was balm to his wounded pride. He squeezed Ben's hand mercilessly, ignoring the cur's gasp of pain.

"Ye better do as he says, lad. It will go better for ye if ye do," Gerard advised solemnly before spitting.

With a cry of defeat, Ben relaxed his hand.

Blood and hair matted the horseshoe nail Ian snatched from the groom's palm. Seizing Ben's lapels, he jerked the boy eye level with him. "You ought to be thanking God my wife was able to ride away." He gave the groom a teeth-cracking shake. "And you'd better be praying she isn't injured, or so help me God, I'll…"

Ben went ashen beneath the light fuzz smattering his pimply face.

"Hell." Ian shoved him away.

Staggering backward, Ben almost fell. Not a single man offered him a hand.

"The only reason I'm not beating you to within an inch of your miserable life is because I don't have the time to waste." He returned his attention to hastily saddling his horse. Teeth clenched, he grated, "You have exactly fifteen minutes to gather your belongings and leave Somersfield lands."

"Good riddance."

"Rotten scunner."

Seemed he was no favorite with the other grooms. Ian jabbed a finger toward him. "Venture within twenty miles of Somersfield again and I'll have charges brought against you—after you've felt the lash." Ian veered his gaze to Gerard. "You'll see to it, and notify the magistrate?"

Not that informing Sir Doyle amounted to a whole lot. The man was an incompetent, dishonest buffoon.

Nodding, Gerard spit again. "Aye, yer lordship, with pleasure. Never took to the boy. Her ladyship insisted I hire the corn-faced lad. Distant relative, she said." He snorted, giving Ben a hard shove. "Get on with ye then, ye bloody cur."

Tell-tale moisture darkening the front of his trousers, Ben scurried to do Gerard's bidding.

Hours later, after making numerous inquiries, Ian located the Romani encampment. Sitting atop a knoll, he peered down on the deceptively peaceful scene. Except for a dagger concealed in his boot, he'd come unarmed. In his haste to reach his wife, he hadn't thought through with his usual logic. Truth be told, he didn't have a plan of any sort.

Rage and worry had befogged him. Only within the past half hour had his rationale returned. He couldn't very well ride into the encampment and demand they hand over his wife.

Can I?

The Roma were notorious for their hospitality *and* their skill with knives. Scrutinizing the encampment once more, he wiped his brow with his forearm. What had Vangie told them? Would he be received as friend or foe? He released a gusty breath. It mattered not. They had something of his. Something precious he'd not leave without.

He highly doubted the fiercely loyal and occasionally hot-tempered gypsies would see it his way. He oughtn't to have come devoid of reinforcements, but it was too late to remedy the oversight now. Perhaps riding into the camp unaccompanied would be less threatening to the leery travelers, and perchance his unannounced arrival would work in his favor.

Ian sent a silent prayer heavenward that it be so. He'd done more praying since meeting his wife than he had the whole of his life prior. Shaking his head, he grunted. He was becoming soft. No, love was subduing him. He smiled wryly. *Ah, the truth will out.*

Pericles took a couple prancing steps, and Ian patted his neck. He didn't doubt there'd been a short nail or two impaling the horse's back beneath the saddle when he'd tossed him weeks ago. Poor beast.

Standing in the stirrups to stretch his legs, he stiffened.

One broken curricle wheel.

His rump hit the saddle with a sharp thud.

Two thrown riders.

Pericles side-stepped and snorted his displeasure.

Three random robbery attempts.

Job's own luck? Coincidence? Not bloody-well likely.

Dammit. Why hadn't he considered this before? Lucinda had always been obsessed with power and position. Her erratic behavior and even more irrational speech this morning pointed to one thing—she meant him harm. An image of Vangie's pale face in the south tower loomed to the forefront of his mind.

Not only him, but his wife.

"How could I have been so blind?" he muttered aloud.

Because, altogether foreign sentiments had crept into every fiber of his being. They'd muddled his good sense and distorted his sound judgment, making him impervious to everything but winning his beautiful gypsy wife's affections.

Rot and rubbish? Not anymore, the devil take it. Love was indeed hazardous.

Pericles snorted and impatiently shifted his stance as if to say, *Let's get on with it, shall we?*

"Aye, my friend, let's be about it then." Ian clicked his tongue while giving a light twitch of the reins. Pericles lunged forward, eager to run, but Ian held him to a slow canter, still mulling over his epiphany.

The pieces snapped neatly into place now. Lucinda's intent at last became glaringly apparent. His stepmother sought to secure through any means what, in her unhinged mind, she believed rightfully belonged to her. Another nasty niggling taunted the recesses of his conscious, but he dismissed it as the Romani camp loomed before him.

His practiced gaze efficiently scanned the clearing. Vangie wasn't in sight. A score of brightly-painted wooden caravans and several simple tents were neatly arranged beneath the towering trees. An equal number of laughing children and barking dogs played beside the wagons or cavorted throughout the encampment.

Two larger *vardos,* one at either end of the glen, drew Ian's attention. A handsome woman sat within the opening of one of them, watching him with keen, assessing eyes. She tilted her head when their gazes met, almost as if she were greeting him across the distance.

In a roped-off area near the river, two score horses and mules milled about. Several nickered upon catching Pericles' scent. The stallion shook his head and neighed a greeting. Highly impressed, Ian took in the magnificent horseflesh. Tattersalls boasted no finer horses than many of these. Making a mental note to pursue that avenue later, he returned his attention to the encampment.

Several men and women were engaged in various activities along the river's edge. Others gathered in small groups around fires, some smoking pipes, or strumming mandolins or violins. A few Roma, settled against the massive trees, played cards.

Conversations ceased, and even the children stopped their joyful antics, as he rode to the camp's center. As a single entity, the Roma turned their dark, expressive eyes to stare at him.

Four men separated themselves from the others, including the striking gypsy who'd taken Vangie behind him on his horse hours ago. Who the devil was he? A relative? A would-be-lover? Jealousy ripped a jagged course through Ian.

Steady old chap. Keep your head.

A distinguished-looking man, his hair peppered with gray and sporting a neatly-trimmed mustache and beard, approached him. The Roma bowed. "*Sastimos*, Lord Warrick, I am Yoska Bailey."

So, they had been expecting him. No surprise there.

Yoska made a sweeping gesture, "I am *bandolier* to these noble people. Please, won't you dismount, and join us in a cup?"

Ian gave a sharp nod. As he dismounted, he combed the area of any sign of Vangie. He searched in vain. If she was here, and from the greeting he'd just received, he'd wager Somersfield she was, she hid from him.

"I'll see to your horse, your lordship." The lad reaching for Pericles' reins looked vaguely familiar. "Thank you. He would benefit from a drink…"

"Milosh, my lord." The boy gave him a toothy grin before leading the stallion away.

Ah, he *was* the boy Vangie had spoken to in Brunswick. Ian watched him with the horse. The lad knew what he was about. Pericles would be fine. He turned his attention to the man who'd carried Vangie off.

The man elevated an arrogant eyebrow, and returned Ian's bold perusal.

He wanted to punch him. "Where's my wife?"

Smiling, his white teeth a stark contrast to his dark skin, Yoska gently chided, "In good time, your lordship, in good time. Come, sit with us," he cordially invited gesturing in the direction of the other, larger *vardo*. "My nephew, Besnik, brought Zora to us."

Ian met Besnik's hard, unyielding stare. No contrition gleamed in his black eyes, and Ian curled his hands into fists. He really, really wanted to punch him. Scowling, he said, "Zora?"

Still smiling—*did the man perpetually wear a smile*?—Yoska explained, "Evangeline is Zora's *Gadžo* name, her Christian name. All Roma have one." He angled his head toward the other men trailing behind them. "The brothers Zimmar, Nicu and Tobar."

Each man inclined his head though they, like Besnik, remained silent.

At the *vardo*, Yoska indicated a stool with a wave of his hand. "Please, have a seat, my lord." He waited until Ian was seated then claimed another stool. "Eldra, bring *lavina.*"

A stunning young woman leaned from the wagon and smiled seductively. The loose neckline of her canary-colored blouse gaped, exposing her heavy, swinging breasts. One of the gypsies—*Nicu?*—frowned at her blatant display before lifting impassive eyes to Ian.

"*Aue, Dai*, at once," she murmured in a husky, accented voice.

The woman Ian had noticed upon first entering the clearing approached. Though middle-aged, her hair threaded with silver, she was still remarkably beautiful. She greeted him in flawless English. "I am Simone Bašavel Caruthers, my lord. Zora's grandmother."

He rose and swept her a formal bow. "I am pleased to make your acquaintance, Madam Caruthers. Vangie speaks of you often."

Madam Caruthers angled her head, and he met her fathomless, penetrating gaze. Why did he feel like she measured him? Weighing him against something unsaid?

Eldra descended the wagon's steps, balancing a jug and wooden mugs on a tray. She sashayed the few steps to the men and handed each a mug. Tugging the stopper from the jug, she filled the cups, leaving Ian's until the last. Bent over him, she offered another tantalizing view of her full breasts. She smiled a blatant invitation as she poured his dram.

Ian kept his gaze trained on the *vardo* behind her, very aware of the five pairs of eyes assessing him. Eldra's bosom was mere inches from his nose, her heavy, sultry perfume filling his nostrils. He angled away from her and took a healthy quaff of the beer.

Madam Caruthers said something in Romanese, and Eldra straightened abruptly. A pout on her full lips, she glared at the older woman. With a huff and a shrug of her bare shoulders, she strutted away, swinging her curvy hips. She joined a group of giggling women.

They kept sending sidelong glances in Ian's direction.

Surely they knew he was married?

He met Madam Caruthers' gaze. "I assume my wife is in your wagon?"

Ailsa bounded across the clearing. Barely dipping Ian a hasty half-curtsy, she panted, "Madam, my lady asks for you. She's in an awful way. It's not her bruised ribs or one of her megrims either."

"It's as I feared." Madame Caruthers closed her eyes, drawing in a deep breath. "May God be merciful." Opening them once more, she sent Ian an indecipherable look before she hurried to her wagon then nimbly climbed inside.

What was wrong with Vangie?

He directed his attention back to the quartet. They regarded him with hooded eyes. Worry niggled unrelentingly. "Gentlemen, I shan't be kept from my wife any longer." He set his cup aside before striding purposefully in the direction of Madam Caruthers' *vardo*.

No one tried to stop him, and he gave a silent thanks. A brawl wouldn't endear him to Vangie's family and clan, but he would not be deterred again. He slowed his steps as he neared the wagon. Just how did one go about seeking admittance to this miniature home on wheels?

Yoska appeared by his side, and Ian suppressed a start of surprise.

"You bid permission to enter, though they'll not likely grant it just yet," he said.

Could all Roma read minds? Ian was beginning to think so. It was uncanny and unnerving. He traveled the remaining few steps to the *vardo*. He could hear rustling around inside. Was that a woman softly weeping? *Vangie?*

"Madam Caruthers?" He spoke quietly, feeling irrationally uncertain.

Several moments passed before the door finally opened, and Ailsa poked her tousled head out.

"My wife?"

"Um, yer lordship, I'm to bid you—" She slid her gaze over her shoulder, then sucked in a bracing breath before forging on. "You need to cool your heels and rest your arse over yonder 'till the princess bids you come." The maid slanted her head at a grove of trees behind the wagon and shut the door in his face with a firm thud.

Rest my arse?

Princess?

28

Ian wasn't sure which statement shocked him more.

The camp resumed its activities, though an unmistakable aura of heaviness loomed over it now. He wandered to the maple trees situated some distance behind Madam Caruthers' *vardo*. The Roma left him to himself, whether as an act of courtesy or pointed ostracism was unclear.

He relaxed against a trunk, alternating his attention between the camp and the wagon. What was happening inside? Was Vangie seriously injured? Surely Madam Caruthers would've told him if that was the case. Unless his wife had told her Lucinda's lies, and Madam Caruthers believed them.

God's blood. He should've sent for a physician the moment he arrived. He straightened, intending to pound on the wagon door until he had an answer. *Patience,* wisdom whispered in his ear. He slumped against the tree. He'd yet to master that virtue.

Dusk settled over the clearing, the smells of the evening meal permeating the temperate air, and his stomach growled. He hadn't eaten since breaking his fast early this morning. He shifted his stance away from the gypsies and stared blindly at the strip of water meandering along the shallow embankment.

So much had transpired since this morning.

He'd awoken with his arms wrapped around his incredible wife. His heart brimming with unfamiliar happiness, he'd slipped from their tousled bed. Standing nude, he'd been content to stare at her for several minutes.

A slow smile had bent his mouth.

She slept soundly, curled on her side and lips parted. Every few minutes, she made a soft noise in her throat. Did she dream of the vigorous night they'd spent together? Exploring each other's bodies, reaching untold degrees of ecstasy, unlike anything he'd ever experienced before?

He'd tried to introduce her to lovemaking gradually. "Sweeting, I don't want you to be shocked or disgusted."

"Pish, posh, Ian. God created this glorious gift for husband and wives." She said while climbing to lie atop him. "I don't understand why people whisper about it like it's something wicked or sinful." Peering into his eyes, a naughty glimmer in hers, she said, "I expect you to teach me everything you know."

She proved to be a very apt pupil, completely uninhibited and eager to try whatever provocative idea he suggested. He hardened at the sensual memories, a smile hovering on his mouth.

"My lord?"

Ian swiveled to face Madam Caruthers. Engrossed in his musings, he hadn't heard her approach. In the deepening dusk, he searched her countenance. She appeared drained. Defeated. Was that sorrow etched on her face and mirrored in her eyes?

"Vangie? Is she all right? Was she badly injured when the horse tossed her? Should we send for a physician?" He cursed inwardly. Why hadn't he insisted someone go for a leech immediately?

"She suffered some bruised ribs—"

"So it's nothing serious? There's no need for alarm?" Ian released his breath in a whoosh.

"My lord." Madam Caruthers laid her hand on his arm. "Sadly, she lost the babe."

Ian gawked, his mind gone blank, not comprehending her words. He refused to believe what he'd heard. Shaking his head, he tried to dislodge the buzzing in his ears. "The babe? There was a *baby*?" he rasped, barely able to form the words. "She didn't tell me." Agony tore him asunder, stinging tears pooling in his eyes. He whispered hoarsely, "Why didn't she tell me?"

Bright tears shimmered in her sympathy-filled gaze. "Zora didn't know she was with child." She lifted a shoulder and looked heavenward. "It happens sometimes. Especially with the first."

Ian's head reeled. Disbelief, fear, and absolute rage toward Lucinda buffeted him. And then…complete and utter devastation for his beloved wife. "I want to see her."

Vangie's grandmother tilted her head and studied him for a long, disquieting moment. What did she seek? Her lips curved into a sad, half-smile. "I thought you would." Slipping her hand into the crook of his elbow, she led him to her *vardo*. "My lord?"

"Please, call me Ian. After all, we are family now."

"Ian, Zora—Vangie—is desolate. She needs time to heal, physically and emotionally." She peered into his eyes, the evening shadows making it impossible to read her expression. "Please, permit her that. Don't make any decision right now, no matter what she says."

Surprised by her vehemence, he gave a slow nod.

She squeezed his arm. "Promise me, Ian."

In the darkness, she hadn't seen his curt nod. "I promise, Madam Caruthers," he answered solemnly.

"As you said, we're *familia* now, Ian. Please, call me Simone."

"I give you my word, Simone. I'll be patient with my wife." Even if it killed him, he'd be patient and understanding.

"I'll allow you some privacy then." With a graceful angling of her head and a swirl of her colorful skirts, she strolled to a nearby wagon. A fire burned merrily before it, and Ailsa sat near the dancing flames talking animatedly to Besnik.

The gypsy raised his head, glaring at Ian. Across the distance, their gazes clashed, accusation blazing in the gypsy's hostile glower. Now wasn't the time to deal with the Roma.

Turning, Ian climbed the narrow stairs to the wagon's entrance. He opened the door and paused, momentarily taken aback at the caravan's deceptively roomy interior. A lantern hanging from an iron hook on the ceiling to the left of the door cast a soft glow on the still form huddled beneath a vibrant quilt. The bed looked more like a folding shelf, which was practical and efficient given the *vardo's* close confines.

Vangie had her back to him. Was she awake?

Vangie stiffened. Though the door swung shut without a sound, she knew the moment Ian stepped inside. Two short steps, and he stood beside her. The stool scraped the floor as he scooted in near, and he bumped the small bed with his long legs when he sat.

Where was *Puri Daj*? Why had she allowed him in? She'd told her grandmother she didn't want to see him. Ever again.

"Sweeting, are you awake?"

What was he doing here? Hadn't he caused her enough heartache? She whispered, "Leave me alone."

"Your grandmother told me about our baby." He placed a hand on her shoulder. "I'm so very sorry."

Oh, how she needed a comforting touch. But not his. Never again his. She wrenched away and her voice ringing with scathing condemnation said, "Tell me, Lord Warrick. Are you terribly disappointed I'll not have a distended belly proclaiming to the world I carry your seed before you discard me?"

He sucked in a harsh gulp of air. "She lied, Vangie."

She clamped a hand over her mouth to stifle the sobs demanding release.

Did she? Or is Lucinda telling the truth, and Ian is the liar?

When she didn't respond, he pressed, "Lucinda knew you were behind me. She contrived those lies to cause you pain and grief." He laid a hand on her shoulder. "We're legally married. By all that is holy, I swear it."

What did *he* know of holiness?

Vangie struggled to turn over, the weight of the quilt adding to the burden of her grief. She pinned him with a direct look. "Tell me one thing," she rasped, "Did you or did you not venture to London for the express purpose of causing my downfall?"

He paled slightly. "Vangie—"

"Perhaps downfall isn't accurate," she snapped. "Putting me in my place? Giving me my just due? *Ruining me*?"

He remained silent. Had guilt rendered him speechless? She searched his face, once so dear to her. Sorrow etched his handsome features, and his eyes… Was that regret glimmering there? Or, could it be? Were those tears awash in the silvery depths?

Her heart twisted painfully, but she smothered her sympathy. *No. No. No.* She wouldn't feel compassion for him. *She* was the victim in this, and she would offer him no quarter, no mercy. "Well, did you? Is that why you asked me to dance?"

"That was before I…" He pinched his eyes shut for a blink.

Pain, razor-sharp pierced her heart, leaving it shredded and bleeding. She had her answer, but she'd hear it from his mouth. "It's an easy question, Ian. Yes or no?"

"It's not that simple." He tried to take her hand, but she jerked it away.

With a doggedness that even astounded her, she persisted. "Yes or no?"

"Sweeting, I'd been told—"

"Told?" Fury whipped anew within her breast. She bit out, "Yes.

Or. No?"

Absolute, resolute, demanding truth's validation, either to mend her shattered heart or annihilate it completely, Vangie would him admit the truth. No more a corked-brained, beguiled miss, blinded by love. Looking through the twin lenses of betrayal and deceit, she could at last see Ian clearly.

His eyes pleaded with her to understand. His voice low and filled with self-condemnation, he uttered but one syllable. "Yes."

Vangie rolled onto her side, murmuring in a tear-choked voice, "Go away." Her shoulders shook with the sobs she couldn't suppress or hide from him. She needed to find some meager degree of release for the agony destroying her soul.

"Vangie?" He brushed a finger over her hair.

Flinging his hand away, she jerked upright. A torrent of scalding tears flowed from her eyes, and she had no doubt her face mirrored the abject misery in her heart. She angrily swiped at them then pointed to the door. "Leave, you despicable *bostaris*. I've already divorced you," she shouted, not caring the Romani camp could hear every bitter word.

Where was her dagger? Her heart splintering impossibly further, she groped beneath the pillow until her fingers closed on the familiar engraved hilt.

"Divorced" Ian's face paled, and he lifted a hand in supplication "You don't know what you're saying—"

"I'm not addled, just gullible." She revealed her dagger, brandishing it before her. "Now leave!"

The door flung open, banging violently against the *vardo's* side. Ian twisted to see who'd entered. Simone, hovered in the entrance, worry stamped across her face. Sighing, he stood and shoved the stool beneath the bed once more. It scraped loudly in the tiny structure.

Simone scooted by him and gathered Vangie into her arms. "Hush, *bad inderi*, my dear child." Tilting her head, indicating the gaping door, she silently ordered Ian to leave.

With one last glance at his sobbing wife, he turned and took the two short strides to the open door. He bent to step through the narrow entrance and faltered briefly before descending the short flight of stairs. A group of concerned Roma had gathered outside the wagon. From the reproachful looks on their faces, he guessed they'd heard every word of his painful exchange with Vangie.

He scowled and lowered his chin defensively.

Ailsa, her eyes huge and worried, swung her gaze from Ian, to the closed door, and back to him. "Lord Warrick?"

He met her troubled gaze.

Flicking a glance to the door again, she had the audacity to blurt, "How could she divorce you?"

Holy hell. Ian felt a flush steal its way to his neck then in blazing glory, to his face. Thank God, the darkness concealed some degree of his humiliation. Aware of numerous ears straining to hear his every word, he chose them with care. "Ailsa, Lady Warrick is distraught. She hasn't divorced me."

Someone gave a contemptuous snort, and someone else, muttered, "*Dinilo gawdji*. Stupid non-Gypsy."

Ian scanned the shadowed faces. Though not openly hostile, neither were they friendly.

Besnik stepped forward. He met Ian's gaze square on, a challenge in his eyes. "Roma ways are different from the *gawdji*. Zora left you, *aue*?"

Ian clenched his jaw so tight, a muscle throbbed painfully, and his teeth threatened to crack. He wasn't answering this damn interfering man.

The gypsy shrugged, the crimson fabric accenting his muscular shoulders. "Then she has divorced you."

"Gawd a'mighty," Ailsa gasped, before slapping a hand across her mouth.

If the burly, entirely too handsome, Roma had landed a planter square on his jaw, Ian couldn't have been more astounded. "Divorced? Surely you jest. Only the Church can grant a divorce."

"Not so with the Roma. If a *manishni* willingly leaves her *rom*, she's divorced and can marry another." The gypsy's deep voice echoed around the clearing.

Fury, raw and savage pumped through Ian. "And, dare I suppose, *you* intend to be the other?" He growled, reconsidering his earlier decision not to exchange blows. A good fight might be just the thing. It had been the night of the ball.

"Caution, *didkai*, my gypsy friend." Yoska edged near Ian, advising softly, "Besnik is our *kallis*, our king. To fail to show him proper respect would be *most* unwise."

King? *God dammit to hell.* Could things become any more preposterous? He had no choice but to heed Yoska's thinly-veiled threat.

"King? Blast and bugger me eyes," Ailsa breathed.

Her gushing exclamation drew Ian's attention. She stared at Besnik like he was the Prince Regent himself. Except the gypsy wasn't obese or dissipated from years of excess. *More's the pity.*

Besnik crooked an eyebrow at her uncouth declaration, and his mouth firmed into a thin line of reproach.

Ailsa eyed him then pertly asked, "Gawd, don't you *ever* smile?"

"Don't you *ever* control your tongue?" Besnik glowered at her.

"Oh, tosh." She waved a hand at him. "You're so stiff. I bet you've got a stick up your rump."

Good God, whose idea was it to make Ailsa Vangie's abigail? If Vangie returned to Somersfield with him—*no, when she returned*—a new lady's maid would promptly be assigned. One who knew her station, possessed a mild temperament, and had the ability to control her tongue.

Anger or perhaps astonishment whisked across Besnik's face.

Ian couldn't be sure which.

"Be careful, *manishni*," Besnik softly warned.

Ailsa stuck out her tongue, taunting, "Go to the devil," before she skipped away and scooped a toddler into her arms. They both giggled as she twirled them about the fire.

"Gawji woman." Besnik shook his head, and his dark eyes met Ian's. "That one needs a man's firm hand on her *bool*."

Ian refused to agree with him, though he'd been harboring similar thoughts. For all he knew, the gypsy king baited him, to see if he was the type of man who'd hit a woman. His gaze rested on the gypsy before roaming the restless crowd. Already a head taller than most of the men peering at him, he drew himself to his full height.

"I am not leaving without my *wife*."

Yoska offered him a congenial smile.

His perpetual cheerfulness was irksome. He reminded Ian of his friend, Flynn, the Earl of Luxmoore. Always—*always, blood sodding hell*—smiling. Made a man want to plant him a facer just to wipe the unending grin from his face. He didn't dare draw Yoska's cork, however.

"I would be honored if you'd consent to share my table and *selta* for the duration of your visit, my lord," Yoska cordially offered.

Selta? What the hell was that? Ian didn't recall ever feeling so out of step. He knew nothing of these people, their culture, or traditions. Nonetheless, he'd no choice but to accept. "Thank you, for the kind offer."

Eldra made no effort to conceal her delight. Looping her arm through his, she pressed her ripe breasts against him while dragging him to her father's campsite. Ian barely repressed a derisive snort. The woman *he* wanted, wanted nothing to do with him, and the one he wanted nothing to do with, quite obviously, wanted him.

Was it his imagination or was she deliberately rubbing his upper arm against her bosom? He tugged firmly, but she tightened her grip and smiled seductively.

No, he wasn't imagining it.

Bloody hell.

29

Unable to sleep, Vangie rose and swiftly donned her Romani garments. She wanted no part of the English today, not even in her dress. Her shawl lay neatly folded on a shelf above *Puri Daj's* bed. As she grasped it, her gaze fell on her grandmother. She slept on, bundled securely in her narrow bunk. Poor *Puri Daj*. Even in sleep, lines of worry creased her face.

Stealthily, holding her boots, Vangie crept from the wagon. Physically, she felt no different than she had upon wakening yesterday morning. Emotionally, however, she was forever altered. Scarred.

The brisk early morning air sent stiff gooseflesh chasing the length of her arms. Shivering, she perched atop the narrow steps and tugged on her boots. Except for the birds and a sleepy dog that raised his head when she'd stepped from the *vardo,* no one was about yet. Wrapping the embroidered woolen shawl tighter across her shoulders, she set off at a brisk pace for the river.

It wasn't right. She'd experienced more discomfort and bleeding the morning after losing her maidenhead than she did after losing her child. No, it wasn't right. There was nothing the least bit right about any of it. *Nothing will ever be right again.*

At the river's edge, a bevy of jays, magpies, and other hungry birds scolded her for interrupting their breakfasts. She took in the glorious sunrise as her riotous thoughts churned.

What am I to do now?

Ian used me. He cares nothing for me.

How could I not have known I was with child?

The dowager is despicable. So is Ian.

I didn't want to love him.

My poor, sweet, sweet baby.

Desperate to stop the chattering in her mind, she let her eyelids drift shut. On and on prattled the inner voices, until she wanted to cover her ears against the silent onslaught and shriek at them to stop tormenting her.

Her eyes flew open at a particularly loud squawk from a raven overhead. She frowned at the grand display on the horizon. How could God allow the splendid pink, lavender, and coral streaks to splay across dawn's newborn sky? The day should be dark and grim with gloomy shadows and dismal gray clouds to reflect her crushed spirit. Not this jubilant, hopeful new morn.

The joy of her love for Ian had vanished, and Vangie was certain she'd carry her sorrow for the rest of her life. The remnants of her shattered heart she'd bury under the guise of self-preservation. She'd sent him away last night, and despite his unconscionable betrayal, her soul ached at his going. God help her, she loved the knave even now.

Vangie place a hand on her flat stomach. The loss of the babe only magnified Ian's treachery. She hadn't known she cradled a child in her womb. But oh, how she'd wanted it.

Had it been a boy or a girl?

Stop it!

Such thoughts served no purpose.

Vangie didn't have any aspirations about acquiring a title or wealth, or advocating for a cause—other than her Roma kin. Her heart's desire, for as long as she could remember, was to have a child. She needed someone to love unconditionally and who would love her in return.

She wandered to a log, her boots crunching on the riverbank gravel. Sitting, she gazed at the river. A trout jumped, snatching a hovering insect.

What would it have been like to hold her baby? Her heart was full of love, waiting to be poured out on another. Except for the infrequent visits with Uncle Gideon and *Puri Daj*, her life had been void of love and compassion since she was six. She hadn't felt sorry for herself. There'd always been the hope she'd have a child to love. Until now.

She'd even convinced herself Ian felt something for her. He'd been so tender—

Vangie kicked a rock. *Fool. Ninny. Goosecap.* Exhaling slowly, she spoke aloud. It had always helped her sort her thoughts. "Without Ian's love, could I have been content?" She toed another round rock. "Especially surrounded by our children?" Bending over, she selected a smooth, flat greenish stone. "I would've loved him and always hoped he might come to love me."

She sent the stone skimming across the burbling water. Sighing, she stood and stretched. Would that have been enough? Perhaps not for some women, but for her? Yes, it might have been. She turned her lips up. She blamed her Romani blood. Her people were perpetually optimistic.

But now? Things were different now.

Ian had intentionally sought to cause her misery. Why? Trudging through the trees on the way back to the encampment, she pressed her lips together. The unanswered question taunted her, and she shook her head in disgust. She was naive, the intricacies of love far beyond her understanding. It was one thing to harbor hopeful, adolescent fantasies about unrequited love. It was another entirely to have the object of her affection black-heartedly contrive her disgrace.

Soft nickering drew her attention. Sweeping a glance at the horses, she was caught off-guard. Ian, his shirtsleeves rolled to his elbows, stood inside the makeshift corral speaking with Tobar. Their backs were to her, their attention riveted on a magnificent honey-colored mare prancing at the end of a lead rope.

Ian must have sensed her presence. He swiveled, his haunted eyes roaming over her. His hungry gaze lingered on her face, and she felt his visual caress across the distance.

No. She wouldn't think of him like that anymore.

Chin tucked to her chest, she continued on her way. The ruffles of her layered skirts swished through the green blades. She lifted the fabric and carefully picked her way up the slippery slope, casting sideways peeks at the corral the entire time. She couldn't face him. Not yet. She must to make her way to the *vardo*.

She slipped and almost fell. *Dratted, damp grass.*

Ian started toward her but turned his head when Tobar spoke to him, drawing his attention back to the horse. He said something and gestured in her direction before ducking beneath the rope.

Vangie increased her pace, skidding again on the dew-laden grass. Ian reached her as she crested the ridge. She didn't want to talk to him. Couldn't without crying.

"Vangie, please, wait."

Keeping her head bowed, she didn't slow. *Lord, blasted tears again*? What was he still doing here, anyway? She thought he'd left last night.

Ian gently grasped her elbow, forcing her to halt. "How do you fare?"

He sounded genuinely concerned, and she flicked a swift glance at him through her lashes then lowered her gaze. He appeared exhausted. No doubt, she looked a sight herself. Likely dark circles rimmed her eyes from a sleepless night and the many tears she'd spent at his expense.

"Why are *you* here? I thought you left last night." Vangie plucked at the shawl's fringe, refusing to meet his eyes again.

"I shan't leave you, Vangie. You're my wife."

The breath hissed from between her teeth. She hadn't expected that. Tobar came up behind him. Pausing briefly, his black eyes questioned her. He answered the gentle shake of her head with a terse nod and strode past them. She didn't need him to fight her battles.

"Ian—"

"Please, let me explain." He blew out a breath, running his hand through his russet hair. "I've wronged you, terribly, deplorably, and for that I beg your forgiveness."

Vangie stood gazing at a bunch of bluish-purple lupine waving in the early morning breeze. A carpet of bluebells and cowslip blanketed the slope. Her gaze intent on the flowers, she murmured, pain lacing her every word, "Why do you hate me?"

"*Hate you*?" Ian reached across the distance separating them and touched her face. "Sweeting, I do not hate you. I…"

Angling her head away, she broke the contact. She couldn't think straight when he touched her.

Ian dropped his hand to his side. "I love you." he whispered hoarsely.

That was the wrong thing to say. The absolute worst thing he could've said at that moment. Vangie snapped her head up. Disbelief whipped through her turning her grief to ire. Furious, she glowered at him. "Oh, so that sets everything right? Do you expect me to throw my arms around you? Tell you I forgive you and vow my undying devotion and love?"

He blinked, obviously not anticipating this reaction.

She poked him in the chest. "You're sorely mistaken, Ian Hamilton, Viscount Warrick!" Hands on her hips she railed at him. "If I were a man, I'd call you out. You're cruel to jest about something so precious. Something you know naught of, or you'd never have treated me with such calculated contempt and callousness."

Turning, she ran several steps before wheeling around to face him. Her shawl dangled off one shoulder. "You know *nothing* of love."

She tugged the shawl around her back, then across her chest, never stopping her tirade. "Love is patient, kind, considerate. It's what I've tried to show you, day after day." Her voice broke as emotion rendered her nearly incapable of speaking. She pulled in a shaky breath. "Only to have you repeatedly trample my heart underfoot." She wrapped her arms around her middle in an effort to ease the crushing pain in her chest.

Ian lifted his hands in supplication. "I do love you. I wanted to tell you, tried to tell you the day we first explored the gardens together."

Vangie's thoughts skipped to that wonderful morning. Ian had opened his mouth to say something. More than once, in fact. She'd mistakenly believed renewed grief brought on by discussing Geoff's duel with the duke had caused his inability speak.

An unbidden thought flashed into her mind, and she stood stark still. *Lord, no.* Her head whirled, and she clutched a nearby oak to steady herself. She must be wrong. *Oh, God, please, please let me be wrong.* She wasn't though, and she knew it with every fiber of her being.

"Vangie?" He took a step toward her, worry furrowing his forehead. "Are you all right?"

Am I all right? God no, you jackanape. I'm not bloody well all right.

"Lord, how you must be laughing." Her voice shook with the strength of her emotion. "The duke—your brother—the woman whose honor he defended. It was me, wasn't it?"

Ian paled beneath his tan, his slate eyes rounding in guilt. He closed them briefly, as if he couldn't bear to look at her.

Everything made perfect sense now.

She continued, speaking to herself. "That's why I never saw either of them again. Geoff called the duke out. They both died—because of me." She lifted her gaze to Ian, accusing him with her eyes, and he sucked in a ragged breath. "You knew, Ian, and that's why you sought me. You said you were determined to meet me. You planned on leaving me half-naked in the retiring room, didn't you?"

"Vangie, I had a change of heart—"

So, he as much as admitted it. She'd rather he'd denied any such thing.

Grimacing, she shook her head. "I'd be ruined with no hope of atonement. But you didn't leave soon enough and were caught in your own trap." She heard a laugh, a pathetic gut-wrenching, agony filled laugh ending on a sob. Was that her? He'd reduced her to this. "No wonder you were furious."

"Sweeting, I'll admit. I was at first but…"

Tears threatened anew, and Vangie presented her back. *Blasted waterworks.* She scrunched her eyes tight against the stinging. Clenching her hands, she bit her lip to stop the sobs struggling to escape. Ian didn't deserve her tears. She would cry no more for him. She knew what she must do.

"Just leave, Ian. You cannot hurt me anymore. I shan't allow it." Sucking in a shaky break, her voice devoid of any life, Vangie delivered the death blow. "I hate you."

Ian had no idea how long he remained staring at the spot Vangie vacated. She'd revealed her soul to him then crushed his with her tormented words. He'd no one to blame but himself.

Sometime later, Simone found him there. She didn't question him. Instead, she handed him a plate piled high with food. "Eat, Ian. Without wood, the fire would die."

"Forgive me, but I don't understand." His gaze traveled between her and the plate.

She smiled, and a pang kicked his ribs. Vangie had her smile. "You cannot fight for what you most desire when you have an empty stomach."

Lifting his eyes to her calm, sympathetic gaze, he asked, "Is there any reason to fight?"

She inclined her head and laid a hand on his arm. "Love is always a reason to fight. It is *the* reason to fight, to hope, to endure."

"I fear it's too late." Ian shook his head. "I've wronged Vangie. Mightily. She has good cause to distrust and despise me."

"Ah, but is that not the key? Zora doesn't despise you, and for that you should be praising God," Simone sagely advised.

He wiped a hand across his brow. "She said…," his voice caught and grief constricted his throat and burned behind his eyelids. "She hates me."

"At this moment, she may believe she does. But trust me in this Ian, she does not. Now eat." She pointed at the plate. "It is *peržala*, scrambled eggs with meat and herbs."

Leaning against a tree, he obediently lifted the spoon to his mouth.

He took several bites of the tasty concoction. Simone lingered nearby, gathering wildflowers. He was sure she had more to say but wanted to give him a chance to eat first. He was beginning to understand how wise she was.

Eldra sauntered his way, a siren's smile on her lips. Two children pranced near her skirts, one carrying a fat puppy. Her primrose blouse hung low, revealing her creamy shoulders and a generous portion of her ample chest. Upon spying Simone staring at her with her hands full of flowers, Eldra thrust out her chin and glared. Was she daring the older woman to chastise her? Was the chit dimwitted?

She greeted Ian with an invitation. "The morning is lovely, my lord. What say you and I enjoy a walk?" It was perfectly clear no one else was invited. "I know a lovely *secluded* grove some distance upriver."

No surprise there.

"I'm not—" Ian began.

"Acting the part of a *singorus* doesn't become you, Eldra." Leveling the brazen beauty with a steady look, Simone spoke plainly. "Enticing a man from another woman is common and contemptible, and far beneath a Roma."

"Zora's divorced him." Smiling unpleasantly, the girl declared, "He's no longer hers."

Simone slanted a glance in his direction, and he raised an eyebrow, curving his mouth slightly at the corners. She was handling Eldra quite nicely. "Lord Warrick's heart is committed to another. You'd do well to remember that," Simone admonished.

Indeed, it was. Forever and always. He finished his breakfast and set the plate on a nearby stump.

The grubby-faced cherub holding the puppy said, "Look, your lordthip. I goths me a *babbi jakkel.* You wanths to hold her?" Grinning, and exposing her two missing front teeth, the urchin thrust the wiggling pup at Ian.

Eyeing the brown, pudgy ball, he took the pup into his arms and cradled it. The dog licked his face in excitement. A thought niggled its way into his brain. At first, he discarded it, but the notion persisted and wouldn't leave off.

His gaze accidentally met Simone's, and he swore she nodded, before giving him a closed-mouth smile.

She continued descending the sloping path. As she passed Eldra she said, "Your father's looking for you. He's none too pleased."

Eldra glowered at Simone before she hurried off, muttering under her breath.

Ian examined the dog in his arms. “Are there anymore pups in the litter?”

“*Aue*. Two more but I gots the only *chai*,” the child announced proudly, jumping up and down. “Only *chavvi* are left.”

Obviously, the imp believed male puppies inferior to females. Suddenly feeling the smallest smidgen of hope, Ian smiled. “Show me, will you please?

30

Vangie sat cross-legged atop a sloping wildflower-covered hill some distance from the camp. Twelve days had passed since she'd fled Somersfield; days of seeing Ian from afar. She hadn't spoken more than a half dozen words to him since the morning he'd told her he loved her, though he'd tried to talk to her several times since. The man was obstinate and persistent if nothing else.

Being near him was painful and awkward. *And heartbreaking.* So she'd become adept at avoiding him. He was too perceptive, and if she spent any time in his company, he'd uncover her secret. She didn't hate him, though Lord knew she'd tried to. Hating someone for betrayal was natural. Loving them despite their perfidy was excruciating. What would he do with the knowledge? She didn't trust him not to hurt her further.

She scrutinized the encampment, her attention falling on Eldra posed provocatively on a rock by the corral. Vangie didn't trust her either. For nearly a fortnight she'd watched Eldra act a shameless wagtail. The girl touched, leaned on, or draped herself all over Ian at every opportunity. Vangie was loath to admit it, but it infuriated her no end.

It was true she'd left Ian, but Eldra needn't be blatant in her attempts to beguile him. The trull displayed her voluptuous wares so vulgarly, Vangie blushed for her. Today, everything but the tips of Eldra's monstrous breasts bulged above her blouse. If she sneezed, the nipples would pop over the edge and give her two black eyes.

How could she be so forward? Why was Yoska allowing it? He'd never permitted such fast behavior in his daughter before. Had he washed his hands of the wanton girl? Then again, mayhap, he hoped to snare Ian as his son-in-law.

While considered divorced according to *Romaniya*, gypsy law, her Christian upbringing held that she remained, inarguably and forever,

Ian's wife. Unless *he* divorced her.

The notion didn't bring the relief it ought to. She didn't know which culture she wanted to honor, to be a part of anymore. She uncrossed her legs, careful not to wake the pup snoring lightly in her lap—a peace offering from Ian. Releasing a long breath, she ran a hand over his silky black-and-white speckled coat. What did she want? *I don't know.* Nothing was simple anymore. Her feelings were a paradox of mixed emotions.

She returned her regard to the corral where Ian studiously ignored Eldra. He seemed totally put off by her evermore ardent efforts. That pleased Vangie enormously.

Only yesterday, from her perch on *Puri Daj's vardo* steps, she'd watched him spurn the wench. Eldra threw her arms around his neck, pressing against him so tightly, a malnourished flea couldn't have squeezed between them. He'd gripped her arms, prying them off his neck as he stepped from her. The dark scowl on his face revealed his irritation. He'd said something to Eldra and strode away.

Pouting, she'd peered after him, her arms folded across her abundant chest.

Vangie's breath had caught as Nicu stomped to Eldra, hauling her aside and berating her. She'd been infuriated. She'd angled her chin, shook her upraised fist at him, and issuing a sharp retort, had flounced away. Poor Nicu. He and Eldra were expected to wed. It had been arranged between their families when they were children.

Vangie had chewed her lower lip. Nicu hadn't moved after Eldra stormed off. He glared at Ian across the encampment, one hand on the knife tied at his waist. Nicu didn't blame Ian, did he? Ian wasn't the first man Eldra had acted like a *dinli* with. Nicu knew that. Faith, everyone in the encampment knew it. Unlike most Romani women, Eldra was neither chaste nor discreet.

The plump pup in Vangie's lap stirred in its sleep, interrupting her musings. He rolled onto its back, his fat belly upward. She rubbed his smooth tummy, grinning as his hind leg twitched reflexively.

Vangie had slipped into the *vardo* late that first morning in camp. Her encounter with Ian left her physically and emotionally overwhelmed. If she had to smile at one more clan member, she feared she'd scream like a *dinilo manishi*, crazy woman. She wanted nothing more than to climb beneath a quilt, bury her head, and sleep—for a month.

The puppy, a blue ribbon tied around its chubby neck, had been inside when she opened the door. The little darling lay in the middle of her bed, along with a telling puddle. She knew full well how the dog came to be in *Puri Daj's* wagon. A puppy was by no means sufficient to mend the chasm between her and Ian, but her heart was oddly touched by his boyish gesture. And strangely enough, the pup had helped to ease her grief.

Desperate to be rid of the mongrels, the ancient crone, Dika, had been begging the members of the gypsy troupe to take them. The next afternoon when Vangie walked by the old woman's fire with the pup in her arms, Dika had winked. "His lordship paid five pounds for him," she cackled, quite pleased with herself.

"Five pounds? Dika, that was robbery!"

She nodded her *diklos*-covered head and rubbed her gnarled hands together in glee. "I told him, 'Ze *jakkle* is a rum bugher, a blessed dog. He will bring to you *kushti bok*.'" She grinned, exposing a missing front tooth.

"For shame, Dika," Vangie said, chuckling. "He's a common mongrel. No more a good luck dog than you're a duchess."

Gazing at the puppy, Vangie smiled at the memory. Dika was cunning, and apparently, Ian was gullible at times. The puppy awoke and promptly set to chewing on Vangie's fingers. She glanced up as a shadow fell across her lap.

Leading Pericles, Ian climbed the hill.

At his approach she stilled, flicking her gaze to the saddled stallion then to Ian. Was he leaving at last? Her stomach sank and sorrow swathed her. Well, wasn't that what she'd told him to do? Truthfully, he'd stayed much longer than she'd expected. Why didn't the knowledge bring her relief, but instead felt as if a millstone had been tied to her already burdened heart?

"Thank you, for the puppy."

He was leaving, and she was thanking him for the puppy? What was she thinking?

Ian tilted his head. Was he waiting for her to go on? When she didn't, he sighed. "Have you named him?"

Vangie nodded, while attempting to save the end of her scarf from the pup's sharp teeth. "Lancelot." She flushed hot. Would Ian recognize the analogy to a knight in shining armor, or worse yet, Lancelot, both the greatest and worst of knights?

The puppy growled playfully as he tugged at her scarf. *Little beast.*

Ian said nothing, though his mouth twitched upward. Mortified,

Vangie almost groaned aloud. Why had she told him that? Why hadn't she named the dratted dog Herbert, or Archibald, or…or…Zebulon?

"Vangie, I must return to Somersfield."

"I know." Her eyes once again downcast, she clenched her hands.

Lancelot chose that moment to defend her from Pericles. Tumbling off her lap, he bounced on his short, pudgy legs around the stallion's mighty hooves, yipping ferociously.

Pericles' nostrils flared, and his eyes widened and rolled at Ian as if to say, "What an annoying, inferior little rodent. Please do remove him from my noble presence."

Ian scooped up the pup and deposited him wriggling and barking in protest, onto Vangie's lap. She smiled at the brave, if somewhat misguided antics of her new charge.

He swept a calming hand the length of Pericles' neck. "You misunderstand me, sweeting."

She skirted her gaze away from his again. The deep purr of his voice stirred her purposefully buried sentiments. Why couldn't she be done with him? Why did her optimistic heart yet hold a smidgeon of hope?

"I've purchased horseflesh from Tobar and must arrange for their transfer." He tapped his thigh in the same manner he had the day they'd become betrothed. "I also need to update my steward and leave him with my directives for an extensive absence."

"That seems wise." Absence? *He's not staying at Somersfield?* Disappointment wrenched her. London then. She hadn't expected that.

"And truth to tell, Vangie, if I have to wear this clothing one more day, I'll go mad."

"You might have borrowed—"

Ian's elevated eyebrow halted the suggestion. No, she couldn't picture him asking Besnik or any of the others for a change of clothing. Ian was taller and leaner than the Romani men. She suspected pure pride prevented him from asking anything more from them. They'd housed and fed him for nearly two weeks.

Ian tapped his thigh with his hat again. He did that when he was nervous or aggravated. "Vangie?" *Thwap* went the hat. "Lucinda's bizarre behavior has me truly concerned." *Thwap. Thwap*. "I want to assign someone, a trusted servant or perhaps even an agent, to watch her."

Slanting her head, Vangie frowned. "Why?"

"I don't trust her in the least. I think she may have slipped into complete madness. She's always been a bit unhinged." *Thwap.* Ian's gaze meshed with hers. "I fear she may be dangerous."

"Oh." *Oh*? That's it? Ian suspected Lucinda was dicked in the nob, and all she could say was, "*Oh.*"?

Mayhap because all she really cared about was that he was leaving her.

In fact, Ian wished Ewan McTavish was available right now. He excelled at covert operations and spying. Ian should've returned to Somersfield days ago, but he couldn't bear to leave Vangie. This was the first time she'd said more than one or two words to him in over a week.

"I'll return sometime this evening," he promised.

She seemed absorbed with the pup plopped in her lap, but her white-knuckled hands atop the dog revealed otherwise. She still wore his ring on her finger, and relief swept over him. If she looked up, she'd see the love he couldn't hide brimming in his eyes.

Neck bowed, her dejection was tangible. Did her lips tremble?

He considered her for an extended, searching moment.

Ah, it came to him then. She didn't believe he'd return. She thought he was abandoning her. Squatting, Ian gently cupped her chin and tilted it upward. Her gaze, riddled with suspicion and doubt, reluctantly met his.

Staring into her expressive eyes, the blue flecks in the irises as deep and dark as any ocean, Ian reassured her. "Sweeting, I'm not leaving you. I'll stay with you here or travel with you wherever you," his gaze roved the encampment before returning to her, "or they go."

Her eyes widened.

Was she pleased?

"You're my wife. We belong together." He rubbed his finger over her ring. "It matters not to me if it's at Somersfield, London, or the circuit your family travels. I *shall not* forsake you."

Vangie's eyes misted, and the tiniest smattering of hope sputtered in Ian's soul where it flickered dim, but intrepid.

"I love you," he whispered. "I care not where I live, as long as I'm with you. Even if you're never able to forgive me, or can never love me in return."

A tear balancing precariously in the corner of her eye toppled over the edge. It trailed down her cheek where he caught it with his forefinger. A subtle shifting in her eyes gave him courage.

He grazed her lips with a feather-light, butterfly-wisp of a kiss. The corners of his mouth slanting upward, he leaned back. Her eyes remained closed, her mouth parted. Pressing a firmer kiss to her forehead, he patted the playful pup—who had been chewing on the buttons of his coat the whole while. Ian levered to his feet in a swift, fluid motion. "Goodbye, Vangie."

His boot was already in the stirrup when her soft voice crossed the distance between them.

"*Latcho drom*. Goodbye, Ian."

Swinging into the saddle, he brought Pericles around, reining in the prancing horse. The muscles in his thighs bunched as he held his mount with his knees. "I give you my word. I shall return."

Ian sent her a penetrating look. With his gaze he tried to communicate the feelings he knew she wouldn't believe if he spoke them aloud. He kicked his heels into the stallion's sides and, with one hand lifted in farewell, they bolted across the meadow.

The time had come to deal with his stepmother.

31

Vangie glanced to the sun again. Perhaps two minutes had passed since the last time she'd checked. *Stop looking.* It was late afternoon. Ian hadn't returned last evening like he'd promised. Sighing in resignation, she lowered her gaze in disappointment. She shouldn't care. She *didn't* care. *Liar,* her heart taunted.

She'd believed him to be a man of his word before they married. Now, she didn't know what to make of him. The hoofbeats of an approaching horse echoed in the distance, but she was afraid to look. Afraid it wasn't him. *Afraid it was.*

From beneath her lashes she dared a peek. There he sat, straight and tall and handsome, and staring straight at her. He slowed Pericles from a gallop to a canter when he reached the periphery of the Romani camp.

Relief swept over her—only because she'd been concerned for his welfare, of course. Vangie firmly set her other emotions aside. She remained beside *Puri Daj* and the young girl, Lala, *Pur Daj* was treating for a campfire burn.

Ian rode Pericles directly across the clearing, stopping before her. Something delicious skimmed across her senses before she returned her attention to the child. She handed *Puri Daj* a soft linen cloth to wrap Lala's calf in.

He had returned.

She truly hadn't thought he would. Surely the fluttering in her middle wasn't gladness? *After what he did?* She wasn't completely addle-witted. No, she'd not eaten anything since morning. She was hungry—*that was all.*

Nonetheless, from the corner of her eye, she watched him. Holding the reins in his left hand, he grasped the horse's mane and then swung his right leg over the stallion's hindquarters. Giving a powerful shove, he dropped to the ground.

With a smart bow, Ian honored *Puri Daj* by greeting her first. "*Droboy tume Romale*."

A pleased expression flashed across her face. She inclined her head in welcome. "Thank you, Ian. You learn our language. This is good." She smiled her approval.

He was learning Romanese? Vangie squelched the happiness attempting to bubble to the surface. Balderdash and rubbish. It meant nothing. If he thought he could wheedle his way into her affections by learning a bit of Romanese—Drat, now he turned that rakish smile on Lala.

Ian bowed to the child. "*Droboy tume tinka.*"

Lala giggled, burying her face in *Puri Daj's* skirt.

Vangie dipped her head and hid a smile. He could charm a stick into throwing itself into a fire then have it thanking him for the honor of burning to ash.

"Vangie." His deep voice interrupted her musings. "I'm sorry I didn't return last evening." He rubbed Pericles' forehead before patting the horse's sweaty neck. "I was delayed."

Obviously.

"It's of no importance." Vangie placed the stopper on the jar of pungent ointment. She wiped her hands on her apron, and searched his face. Lines of fatigue marred his brow and crinkled the corners of his eyes. Had he slept at all? Unease washed over her. Something was wrong. Picking up the ointment, she tucked the jar into the medicine basket.

"Come *tinka*," *Puri Daj* said, taking Lala by the hand. "Let's see if your mother has finished the *pirogo*. Mayhap she'll give us a taste while it's yet warm. It's my favorite dessert."

"Mine too," the child piped as she limped away.

Vangie watched them go. She couldn't even think of an excuse to ask *Pur Daj* to stay. The silence after her departure hung heavy and awkward with constrained emotion. Ian's gaze kept wandering; first to Yoska's *vardo,* then the river and corral, and finally to the hillside behind the camp.

"All is well here?" He scanned the clearing again before he settled his gaze on her once more. Something indecipherable glimmered in his eyes before he masked it. "You are well?"

"Yes." Vangie tilted her head, scrutinizing him.

Ian appeared reserved and preoccupied. Did he regret his promise to return? His gaze roved around once more. "A letter arrived for you." He withdrew the slightly crumpled paper from inside his coat pocket. "It's from your cousin."

She took the rectangle. "Thank you."

"Forgive me, Vangie, but I must speak with Yoska and Tobar." He bowed and then leading Pericles, he went in search of the men.

Eyebrows pulled together, she stared after him, perplexed. Untying her simple apron, she tossed it across the makeshift table. She didn't know what to make of his peculiar greeting. He'd seemed happy to see her, almost anxious to talk to her. Then he'd retreated into his shell of indifference. She'd not seen him behave that way since the night she shot the highwayman.

Well, there had been those few moments in Somersfield's drawing room too.

Why had he returned if he only meant to keep her at a distance?

Do I really want to know?

No. Yes. No. *Oh, bother and blast.* She'd never been so double-minded in her life.

She turned the letter over. Yvette's dainty writing slanted across the front of the foolscap. Finding a quiet spot behind *Puri Daj's* wagon, and comfortably settled on a blanket, Vangie broke open the wax seal. She quickly scanned the contents.

Papa is expanding his shipping enterprises once more. He is moving us to Boston, Massachusetts for two years. Dearest cousin, how can I bear being away from you so long? We are to leave in September. Papa has said I may come for an extended visit next month...

Yvette was leaving England? For two years?

Vangie fought bitter tears. She should be overjoyed at the prospect of a visit from her beloved cousin, but despair better suited her mood. She worried her lower lip while twisting a strand of hair. What was she to do? She wasn't ready to explain her altered marital status to anyone yet, most especially her family.

Heaven help her, she could already envision the secretive pitying looks. It simply wouldn't do to have Yvette visit if Vangie weren't in residence at Somersfield. But how could she tell Yvette she couldn't come? And she did so want to see her cousin before she sailed.

"*Latchi divvus*, Zora."

Vangie hadn't heard Besnik approach. Smiling a welcome, she patted the blanket. "Good day to you too. Come, sit with me, dear friend."

Besnik's dark gaze searched her face. "You are well, *nukkidai*?

"*Aue*."

"Will you remain with us now?"

Something in Besnik's tone caused her to twist and peer at him intently. "I don't know," she answered honestly.

Angling back onto his elbows, one knee crooked, he smiled, revealing strong, white teeth. He truly was a handsome man, and if her heart weren't already engaged, she might have come to love him.

"You *kam* him?" he asked.

Vangie dipped her chin and closed her eyes in acknowledgement. "*Aue,* I love him."

"I would still gladly make you my *rommadi.*" His dark gaze roved her face.

Yes, if only she hadn't met Ian, hadn't danced with him at that wretched ball. She'd have been blissfully happy as Besnik's wife. But now? It wouldn't be fair to him when her heart, though mangled, belonged to another. Laying her hand on his muscled arm, she offered a nascent smile. "Thank you, but no. My heart is too full of him. You deserve someone who will love you with her whole heart."

He accepted her rejection with the merest inclination of his raven head. "I thought as much, but I wanted to be sure." He looked around. "Where is your *jakkel*?"

"Ailsa is playing with Lancelot."

His gaze followed the fair-haired lass as she darted through the encampment with her usual entourage of children. As if sensing his perusal, she looked up. She smiled and waved cheerily before continuing on her way.

"She'd make a good wife, Besnik." Vangie had seen the yearning looks Ailsa gave him.

"It is easier to milk a cow that stands still," he said frowning. "With that one, I'd not have a moment's peace."

Grinning—her first heartfelt smile in days—she stole a sideways glance at him. The twitching of his lips and the intensity aglow in his eyes were far more revealing than the words of denial he spoke.

He rose then helped her to her feet. "There will be dancing tonight. Will you join us?"

She shook her head. "No. I'm sorry." She couldn't. Not yet.

"In time, *nukkidai.*" After squeezing her shoulder, he turned to go.

"Thank you, Besnik."

He stopped, bending his mouth into an understanding smile. Shrugging his wide shoulders, he said, "*Ma-sha-llah.* As God wills."

Her gaze trailed him as he swiftly made his way to Yoska's *vardo*. He was a good man. Far better than the fops she'd met in London. She relaxed against a tree trunk, observing Ailsa and her playful antics with the children and Lancelot. Yes, indeed. The bubbly maid might be exactly what the gypsy king needed.

A dust cloud on the horizon drew her attention. Numerous riders grew closer. It wasn't unusual for the Roma to have visitors. Truth be told, it was quite common, even expected. Nonetheless, uneasiness gripped her. Guests didn't stampede into the camp. They approached respectfully and waited for an invitation to enter. These visitors didn't bode well. She folded the letter and tucked it into the pocket of her skirt.

Where was Ian? She must find him at once. Her intuition screamed something was wrong. Hurrying to the front of the wagon, she searched the encampment. Lifting her skirt, she ran to the improvised corral. Upon seeing her approach, he excused himself and ducked beneath the rope.

"What is it?" He rested his hands on her shoulders. "What's wrong?"

"Ian, look." She pointed to the approaching riders. "I fear something is afoot."

He followed her worried gaze. A scowl drew his dark eyebrows together, his eyes troubled.

Tobar approached, his focus fixed on the horsemen as well. "We best make our way to the others."

Ian thrust Vangie at him. "Keep her with you," he ordered before running to Yoska's campsite.

By the time she and Tobar reached the center of camp, most of the other Roma were assembled, their unease apparent in their quiet murmurs and the anxious gazes they darted, over and over again, to the approaching horsemen. Even Yoska appeared concerned, his perpetual smile absent and replaced by a grim expression.

Ian, now attired in his hunting coat, joined them as the first riders thundered into the travelers' encampment. The Roma scattered lest they be trampled. Another group trailed the first at a more sedate pace.

Vangie recognized Gerard and another five men from Somersfield stables. Despite the seriousness of the moment, she bit her lip to keep from laughing aloud. Jasper, with a look of fierce concentration on his face, and his tongue between his teeth, clumsily drove an overflowing dog cart into the clearing.

Yoska and a handful of others, including Ian and Besnik, approached the newcomers. The gypsy king's gaze met Ian's, and he gave one curt nod.

Vangie inhaled sharply. Besnik had given his consent. The simple gesture implied much more. He'd proclaimed Ian one of them.

Yoska stepped forward. "Welcome to our humble camp, *didkai*," he said cordially, though hardness edged his voice. "How can we be of service?"

A fleshy man spit, the nasty glob missing Yoska's foot by a mere inch. The darkening of the bandolier's swarthy skin was the only outer indication of his anger.

How dare he, the fiend!

She bit the inside of her cheek to keep from objecting aloud. She sliced a glance toward Ian; the muscles in his jaw rippled. She swung her attention to Besnik. His face was impassive, but fury spewed from his black eyes. As his gaze slowly traveled the semi-circle, Nicu, Tobar, and several others dropped a hand to the knifes they wore at their waists.

She stiffened, fear coursing through her. *No.* They must not fight. The riders were armed. More than one sported a pistol in his hand. As was their custom when danger arose, the Romani women melted into the shadows along with their children.

"I've received several complaints you gypsies have been stealing poultry, livestock, and other goods," the man sneered.

"That seems unlikely, Sir Doyle," Ian countered.

Vangie glanced between the two men.

A droll smile touched Ian's mouth, and his eyes held a dangerous gleam. "I've been here a fortnight and can personally attest that coins or goods have been exchanged for everything the Roma have acquired. Why, I've purchased some fine horseflesh from them myself."

Sir Doyle belched and spit again. "A fortnight?"

His baleful glare flicked around the glen. "Why would you stay with the likes of *them* for that long?" Bending forward, he licked his full lips. "Is it true? The wenches spread their legs for a groat?" He narrowed his eyes before sitting straight again, his saddle creaking in protest. Beads of perspiration dotted his forehead. "Course, I'd be afraid of getting the clap." He grabbed his crotch and shuddered theatrically, his beefy jowls waggling with the movement.

At his vulgar insinuation, rage whipped through her. *Revolting cur.* She leveled him a scathing glare. An offended growl rumbled through the Roma, but Besnik raised his hand, and the furor gradually abated.

"Guard your tongue, Doyle." Ian spoke softly, but the threat in his voice permeated the air.

With a condescending, ill-considered smirk, Sir Doyle dared, "Say, didn't *you* make an honest woman of a gypsy wench?"

Indignation coiling her muscles into tight, tense knots, Vangie went rigid, Oh, how she longed to skewer the hoggish lout. She brushed her fingers over her thigh. Where was her dagger? Had she left it on the table behind the *vardo* when she opened Yvette's letter?

A course laugh erupted from the magistrate, and his cronies cackled their approval. He slapped his thigh and swung his gaze over the crowd. His attention riveted on her, and a lascivious gleam entered his watery eyes as a lewd sneer curled his fat lips.

Utterly repulsed, she glared in defiance.

"I might even consent to spend a few days with these vermin if I'd *that* to sink my wick into." He nodded in her direction, then licked his fat mouth once more.

When Vangie stepped forward, the outraged gasps and furious murmurs ceased abruptly. She angled her head and eyed him from his sweat-rimmed hat to his grimy boots. With icy disdain she said, "Hell would freeze over and the devil would dance in heaven with Christ himself before *that* ever happened." She made no attempt to hide her satisfied smile when red streaked across Sir Doyle's flabby face.

He kicked his horse, advancing on her until he was only inches away. "Why you little—" He raised a foot.

He wouldn't dare kick her. Nevertheless, she stumbled backward, bumping into Ian.

The clicking of a pistol hammer reverberated uncannily loud in the too-still clearing. Ian leveled his gun directly at Sir Doyle's head. "Vangie, step behind me."

She didn't argue but slipped just behind his left side. She'd seen the magistrate's shifty eyes dip to the gun across his stout lap. No doubt he was trying to decide if grabbing it was worth the risk.

"Make another disparaging remark about my wife or her kin, Doyle, and I promise you, it will be the last thing you do," Ian said with eerie calm.

A thrill vibrated through her. He defended her people. She took a step to the side, observing him from the corner of her eye. She wanted to throw her arms around him and rain kisses across his handsome face. He sent her a knowing glance and a half-smile before returning his attention to Sir Doyle.

The color drained from the magistrate's face just as quickly as it appeared. He glowered at Ian, his gaze flitting to the pistol then to her. Malice contorted his features, and she stepped nearer Ian again. "You wouldn't be threatening me, would you, Warrick?"

Ian had yet to lower the pistol. "Threatening you?" He shook his dark head. "No." He regarded the magistrate for a moment longer before aiming the pistol's muzzle at the ground. "Let's call it a warning. One you'd best heed." He released the gun's hammer, and as he tucked the pistol into the waist of his pantaloons, he shot a glance to Gerard. "Pray tell me, why are *you* in their company?" With a wave of his hand, he indicated Sir Doyle and his motley entourage.

Gerard dismounted. Grimacing, he stretched his bowed legs.

With a slight slant of his head, Ian indicated the other Somersfield staff should dismount too. They complied straightaway.

Removing his cap, Gerard scratched his balding head. After shoving the hat back on, he contemplated the magistrate before his attention gravitated back to Ian. "Well, my lord, we was nearly here to fetch the horseflesh like ye bid, when they come on us." He angled his head in the direction of Sir Doyle and his henchmen. "I figured it prudent to arrive together."

Vangie had no doubt the presence of a half-dozen armed Somersfield men gave the magistrate a moment's pause. She smiled at Gerard, and flushing until his ears turned red, he averted his gaze.

Nodding, Ian said, "Excellent decision, Gerard." He turned his steely eyes on Sir Doyle. "Who, exactly, has grumbled about the Roma?"

The magistrate snorted causing his jowls to jiggle. "I don't have to reveal my sources to you."

"No? Well, it will be difficult to bring charges, now won't it? What are you going to do, take tales of a few missing chickens and ducks to London's busy courts?" Ian's mouth curved into a humorless smile. Idly flicking an imaginary speck of dust off his well-tailored coat, he eyed Sir Doyle contemptuously. "Who do you suppose the courts will believe? A magistrate, whose reputation is, shall we say, less than pristine? Or a lord of the realm, whose connections to the Home Office, the peerage, and the Crown are favored?"

Well done, Ian.

He squared his shoulders and met the magistrate's infuriated glare directly. "I shan't hesitate to reveal every illegal and despicable act you are *rumored* to be connected with if you breathe a word of this drivel in London."

Vangie wanted to applaud.

His face bright red, Sir Doyle nearly gnashed his teeth. "It doesn't matter leastways," he said. "They've," his gaze scanned the Roma, scathing contempt written across his face, "been here more than the allotted time. His Majesty's edict says they must move on."

Vangie gasped, clasping a hand to her chest. She'd never been present before when the Roma were evicted. Naturally, she'd heard tell of it, but her visits to the camp typically occurred when the travelers first arrived, not when they were forced to leave. She sought Ian's eyes, then *Puri Daj*'s, who smiled in composed reassurance.

When had she joined the crowd?

Jasper climbed from the cart, and with the dignity and aplomb of a titled lord, marched to Ian. His progress was momentarily impeded when his foot sank into a fresh pile of horse manure. He shook off the offending shoe and continued onward, his gait now lopsided due to his one stockinged foot.

Vangie hid a smile. Did the man never lose his composure?

Once he stood before Ian, Jasper withdrew official-looking documents from beneath his arm.

Ian's brow rose, and his lips twitched.

"You did say to make haste in delivering them, sir," Jasper said with his usual formality.

Ian's gaze strayed to the butler's stained stocking before meeting his austere gaze. "Indeed, I did," he offered drolly.

Vangie tried to imagine the staid Jasper driving the dog cart the entire distance from Somersfield. As if reading her mind, he winked at her. A grin teased her lips, and she winked back. Jasper was an absolute dear.

Perusing the papers, a broad smile widened Ian's mouth.

"Get on with you." Sir Doyle issued orders for the disbandment of the gypsy camp. "I want you vermin gone within the hour."

The Roma scurried about in preparation.

Vangie didn't know what to do. Should she go with *Puri Daj*? Would Ian come too?

"Halt." Ian's firmed voice boomed across the site. Every eye turned to him in expectation.

The magistrate's and his men's gazes contained irritation and something a tinge more malevolent.

She looked at Ian expectantly. What was he about? They needed to make haste.

"Roma friends, you do not have to depart," he announced, triumph resounding in his voice.

Sir Doyle straightened in his saddle. "Here now, Warrick, old chap."

Ian stiffened beside her. Sir Doyle dared to address him so familiarly? He quirked his eyebrows in askance at the magistrate's impudence.

"You don't have authority to make such a declaration, my lord. The law is clear," he reminded Ian. "Gypsies cannot camp on public land beyond the duration the King's law allows." Sir Doyle made a sweeping gesture. "These, *people*," he couldn't keep the scorn from his voice, "were to be gone weeks ago. They're vagrants, thieves, and trespassers, and they must go." The last was spewed in a threatening growl.

A wave of guilt swept Vangie. The Roma had lingered longer than usual in hopes of seeing her. And then, when she'd fled Ian and he'd followed her here, they couldn't very well pack up and leave, could they? She was responsible for their predicament, and she feared for them. If Sir Doyle was as unscrupulous as she suspected, her people were in danger.

Ian gave an amiable nod. "What you say is true."

Her heart sank, and a sickening sensation crept into her vitals. She gazed around the encampment. How could they possibly depart within the hour? They'd have to leave possessions behind, and they'd so little to begin with.

"But these travelers are not trespassers."

What?

Vangie's attention flew to Ian.

He took her elbow and lowered his head. "Trust me, sweeting." His warm breath caressed her ear. "I'll explain all."

Trust him? How she wanted to. But did she dare? He'd just defended her and the Roma. She nodded, cautiously.

"What say you, Lord Warrick?" Sir Doyle exclaimed. "Of course they're trespassers."

Ian shook his head, making no attempt to conceal his glee.

She was thoroughly confused. What was he up to?

"'Fraid not, Doyle, *old chap*." A grin curled Ian's mouth, and a merry glint twinkled in his eyes.

She suppressed a smile at his boyishness. He was thoroughly

enjoying the magistrate's agitation.

"The property on this side of the river is part of Sheffleton Cottage Estate. Though the manor house is some distance away, these grounds are privately owned," he said.

Sir Doyle shrugged his massive shoulders. "What do I care? Gypsies cannot camp on private property either."

Ian scratched his nose. "True, but they can be deeded portions of estates." He lifted the papers in his hand. "I've the paperwork allowing such an act."

Clearly annoyed by the turn of events, Sir Doyle rubbed his chin with a ham-like fist. "If you've acquired Sheffleton, I've not heard of it. I make it my business to be abreast of everything in my jurisdiction." He folded his arms across his massive chest. "You wouldn't be lying to an officer of the Crown now, would you?" A nasty smile skewed his mouth. "Are you *certain* you own Sheffleton Cottage, my lord?"

"No, I do not," Ian offered wholly unperturbed. "But my wife does."

"Pardon?" Vangie's stunned gaze flew to meet his. "What do you mean I own it?"

His tone hushed, Ian swiftly explained. "It was part of the terms of the marriage contract. I had the entire settlement transferred to you before we married." He brushed a stray lock of hair off her face. "*You* can deed a portion of the estate to the Roma if you wish."

"Oh, Ian," she breathed, overcome with emotion. He'd done this wonderful thing, even before they were married. The glint in his gaze caused her heart to skip. It left a giddy pattering in its wake. She stared into his eyes, momentarily forgetting the world around her.

"Shit." Sir Doyle's crude curse yanked her back to the present. He spit again before threatening, "I best not hear another complaint, or I'll arrest the lot of 'em." He jerked a thumb at a group of women and children.

Ian crooked an eyebrow mockingly. "*All* of them, truly? There are at least two score Roma, not including infants and children."

Fury contorting his face, Sir Doyle ignored Ian. "I intend to investigate the legality of deeding gypsy tramps good English soil. I ain't accepting your word for it."

"You do that, Doyle," Ian said, grinning

Tugging on his unfortunate horse's reins, the magistrate spewed foul oaths at the solemn-faced Roma as he thundered from the encampment.

"Good riddance, oversized, flatulent windbag." Jasper's declaration earned him an appreciative smile from Simone.

"Mr. Jasper-Faulkenbury, may I offer you refreshment?" she asked. "After your long journey, I'm certain a spot of tea would be in order."

"Please, call me Jasper. Everyone else does." He sent a tolerant glance in Ian's direction. "I would be delighted to accept your gracious offer, madam. First, however, I have an issue of importance to impart to his lordship."

32

Ian faced his man "What is it, Jasper?"

"The dowager has disappeared," he said without preamble.

Disappeared? *Blast and damn.* This wasn't good.

Lancelot came bounding across the camp.

"There you are." Vangie bent to scoop him into her arms, but before she could, the pup introduced himself to Jasper by wetting on his stockinged foot.

The butler's nostrils flared the tiniest bit as he bowed to Lancelot. "I'm pleased to make your acquaintance, too, sir."

"Naughty dog," she chastised, gathering the pup in her arms. She buried her face in his coat, her shoulders shaking with laughter.

Jasper lifted his dripping foot, eyeing the offensive appendage as if he'd like to sever it from his body. "I fear, my lord, I am in need of a new pair of stockings." He crinkled his nose while casting a sidelong glance at his stuck shoe. "And shoes."

Ian struggled to keep a straight face. He glanced at the overflowing dogcart. "I presume there are both in the cart?"

"Indeed, my lord."

He couldn't suppress his grin as Jasper hobbled to the cart. Gerard held the horse's harness. "Gerard, please assist Jasper with the unloading."

"Aye, my lord." Gerard motioned to a pair of stable hands. "George, Finney, ye untie the cords. Ye others, pull off the tarps and start unpacking the goods." His gaze swept Jasper's soggy foot. "And find somethin' fer his feet."

The men scurried to do his bidding.

Nuzzling Lancelot, Vangie sent Ian a curious glance. "What's in the cart?"

"I told Jasper to collect goods for the Roma." Ian surveyed the crowd gathered around the cart. "There are foodstuffs, clothing, sewing goods, blankets…" He grinned at her sheepishly. "Honestly, I don't know everything he brought."

"Thank you." Vangie's eyes shone. Was it merely gratitude in their depths or dare he hope it was something more? "Please excuse, me. *Puri Daj* beckons, and I need to find my dagger."

His gaze trailed her, lingering on the gentle sway of her hips as she sauntered to her grandmother. Amusement played along the edges of his mouth.

Simone smiled and began a rapid monologue in Romanese. Vangie nodded and squatted. She lowered Lancelot to the ground and patted his head before straightening. Arm in arm, they crossed to a group of chatting women.

Ian's smile faded. Was Doyle's appearance in the Romani camp mere coincidence? Especially in light of Jasper's unwelcome news regarding Lucinda vanishing? Not bloody-well likely. He'd ask his men to wait until morning to return to Somersfield. Having a few extra armed men here this evening seemed prudent.

He glanced around the encampment at the ecstatic Roma. From this point onward, when their travels brought them to this part of Northumberland, they had a haven. A place they could call their own. A place safe from persecution they could remain for as long as they wished.

Yoska's voice boomed across the encampment. "*Patshiv* tonight my friends. To celebrate our good fortune and," he extended a hand to Ian, "thank our new *phral*."

The Roma cheered their approval.

When their cries faded, Yoska said, "See my friends, *so o Del dela, oda ela.* What God gives will be." A wide grin on his face, he lifted his cup overhead. "Come, brother Ian, join me in a cup."

As dusk fell, an enormous bonfire blazed in the center of the encampment. The night was balmy. An unseasonably warm breeze periodically whisked by like a fickle maiden unable to decide if she'd stay with her lover for the night.

Makeshift tables groaned under the weight of an assortment of succulent foods, many of which Ian never tasted before. The Roma brought out their instruments, and the night came alive with music, the singing and dancing unlike anything he'd experienced.

These were an uninhibited people, embracing life vigorously and celebrating with the same carefree abandonment they lived by. He now understood why the Roma, clapping and stomping and swirling around the scampering flames, preferred their unrestrained lifestyle.

How different they were from the sophisticated and artificial denizens of the *haut ton*. The Roma lived free from the confinements and judgmental protocols of society.

Ian suspected they were the better for it.

Eldra whirled by, gyrating her full hips provocatively. She raised her arms overhead, thrusting her breasts upward. She stared at him, a clear invitation in her sultry eyes. With marked deliberateness he averted his gaze and sought his wife.

Where was she? She'd been speaking with Simone a moment ago.

He shoved to his feet intent on finding her. Slipping away from the celebration, he ventured into the neighboring darkness. The night was clear except for an occasional drifting cloud. The muted brightness of the moon and stars illuminated the ambling brook. The water surging over and around the stones, caressing them with its cool touch, was a peaceful melody in the darkness.

Vangie, her head bent, stood beyond the fire's flickering light, apparently watching the river.

"Vangie?"

She looked over her shoulder, the hint of a welcoming smile on her lips.

"Sweeting, are you well? You left the festivities—"

"I'm fine." She faced the river once more.

Ian gently grasped her shoulders, turning her to face him. "Are you?"

Her gaze flicked to his before she lifted her shoulders, breathing out a deep sigh. Attuned to her every mood, he sensed her uncertainty.

"What is it?" His thumbs caressed her shoulders. "Is it the babe?"

She shook her head, her midnight curls swirling around her shoulders. The silky strands stroked his hands. "No, I…" A cloud glided past, permitting the moon's full radiance to shine. She tilted her chin upward and peered at him. "Ian, I don't blame you for the loss of the baby."

Her gaze dipped to his mouth. "I did at first." She shook her head and pursed her lips. "But not anymore."

His breath caught and hitched in his lungs. She didn't blame him? Relief, pure and cleansing, surged through him. His eyes misting, he closed them for a moment and slowly exhaled. Her words didn't alleviate the entire weight of his guilt. He still blamed himself. Always would. His deceit and thirst for vengeance had cost them their child.

"I would've cherished our baby, and its loss pains me greatly." Her voice caught.

He opened his eyes and rapidly blinked. How could he ever make recompense to her? Vangie's attention wandered to the dark row of trees behind him. Tears glistened in her eyes. He'd caused those tears. Those, and countless others.

"But it's unfair to blame you when even I didn't know I carried your child." She tucked her chin to her chest. "Because of our hasty marriage and the numerous changes in my circumstances these past weeks, I paid no heed to…" She trailed off into an embarrassed silence.

Ian bathed her in a love-filled gaze. He understood. She hadn't realized she missed her monthly menses. He braced himself to ask the other question that had been tormenting him for days. Dread kicked him in the ribs, but he knew in his heart what he must do. What he would do, though he didn't know how he'd bear it, if she confirmed his greatest fear.

"Is it Besnik, then? You harbor a *tendresse* for him?"

Vangie gave a watery chuckle, wiping her eyes with her shawl. Faith, was the man addled?

Besnik?

"Why are you laughing?" Ian furrowed his brow, his expression as nonplussed as a schoolboy. He sent a glance in the direction of the merrymakers. "It's obvious he's enamored with you."

Was he jealous? The notion sent a jolt of pleasure skittering through her spine. It was really wicked of her, but she savored the moment.

"Do you?" His question was an agonized whisper. "You can tell me."

Vangie searched his silvery eyes. Were those tears? No, it must be a trick of the moonlight.

"I promise, sweeting." He trailed a finger across her jaw. "I shan't be angry."

The remorse in his voice tore at her heart. She couldn't bear his pain. "I'm convinced Besnik's affections lie elsewhere, though he may not, as yet, be aware."

Ian's strong hands cupped her shoulders more firmly. "You," he hesitated, "you aren't in love with him?"

"Besnik is a dear friend. Nothing more."

"Ah."

Ah? That was it? What did *ah* mean?

He wrapped his arms around her and drew her into his embrace. She didn't resist, but rested her head against the wide planes of his chest and listened to his steady, comforting heartbeat. The circle of his arms offered her solace. He spoke against her hair. "What is it then? Why aren't you celebrating with the others?" He kissed the top of her head and gave her a slight squeeze. "You can trust me."

Vangie remained silent, snuggled against him. Trust again. His actions today had done much to restore her faith in him. She wanted to trust him, but did she dare?

A passing cloud covered the moon once more. He took a step away. With his forefinger, he gently tilted her chin, until her gaze met his. "What is it?"

"I don't belong here—with them." She angled her head in the direction of the boisterous revelers. "I adore visiting my *kinshna*, but their way of life isn't mine. Not any longer."

Surprise flickered in his eyes.

The revelation astonished her as much as Ian. She attempted a smile. "I find I prefer stability. I guess I'm more English than Roma after all."

He had said he'd stay with her and the Roma. She'd eliminated that option. He only had two left. Ian didn't say anything, just stood there solemn-faced peering at her, unblinking and unwavering in the intentness of his stare. He angled his head the merest bit and opened his mouth. He shut it again and sighed. He was trying to decide something.

Would he offer her his love—or her freedom.

Which would she choose?

Which would cause less heartbreak?

"Vangie, Sheffleton Cottage is truly yours. You can live there—"

She stiffened and covered her mouth, barely stifling the cry surging to her lips. She backed away from him, pain wrenching her heart. It was to be her freedom then. She should be overjoyed.

He didn't want her.

"You misunderstand." Ian rushed on, stumbling over his words. "I love you. Love you enough to let you choose." He spread his hands in entreaty. "I want to give you a child—no—a dozen children. I long to see your belly swell with my seed. I beg you, give me a chance to show you the kind of man, the kind of husband, I can be."

The sincerity of his words rang true, touching an answering peal in her heart. She remained stock still, silent and stunned. He wasn't casting her off. He was giving her a choice.

She so wanted to believe him. To trust him. To forgive him. Didn't he deserve another chance? Hadn't he shown her his inherent decency only hours ago?

He stood before her, his head bowed, beaten and defeated. "I'll let you go, if that's what you truly desire. If you cannot forgive me." He raised his head, begging her with his gaze.

Overcome, she shook her head. She didn't want him to let her go. A life without him would be meaningless. Shudders quaked her, and she shoved a fist against her mouth to quiet the sobs she struggled to conceal. Bitter tears of regret cascaded down her cheeks.

Ian's shoulders slumped. "So be it. I'll keep my word."

Vangie wept harder. "No," she gasped between sobs.

Reaching for her, he wrapped her in his arms. "It's all right, darling." He kissed the crown of her head. "I only want you to be happy." Ian ran a soothing hand up and down her spine. "Shh, sweeting. In the morning I'll make the arrangements for your things to be sent to Sheffleton Cottage."

"No, Ian, No!" She threw her arms around his neck, clinging to him as if she was drowning. "Don't cast me off. I couldn't bear it. I know you didn't want to take me to wife, but please let me stay with you. I love you."

"You love me? You forgive me?" he asked in stupefied awe, unable to hide the astonishment from his voice or face. "You want to stay with me?"

"Oh, yes. Please, yes." She clutched at his neck and shoulders, raining kisses across his throat.

Ian enclosed her in a fierce embrace, bending his neck to meet her seeking lips. His hot assault deepened her chaste kisses. It was as if the past fortnight had never been; the memory erased by a hidden hand.

Looping an arm beneath her knees, he swept her into his embrace. Vangie clung to him, pressing her face to his throat. She licked him, smiling when his throat muscles worked against her lips. He strode to the maple trees huddled beside the river. Passing between their massive trunks, he entered a sheltered nook. Lowering her to her feet, he tugged her shawl loose and laid it on the ground. Straightening, he ran his fingers through her hair.

"I love your hair."

Sighing, she closed her eyes. She remained motionless as he tugged her blouse over her head and shoved her *padma* off her hips. She stepped from the many ruffles before kicking off her boots. Clad only in her light shift, she stood before him unashamed.

He gathered her hair, spreading the strands across her shoulders.

Her gaze never left Ian's as he discarded his clothing until only his pantaloons remained. He untied the ribbons of her chemise, and his passionate gaze marked its path as the garment slipped from her shoulders until it puddled at her feet.

He grinned at the sheathed dagger strapped to her thigh. "I see you found your knife." Kneeling, he used his mouth to untie the ribbon holding the blade in place.

She'd become a quivering mass of sensation when the knife finally dropped to the ground, and he stood. Beads of perspiration dotted his forehead, his breathing shallow and harsh. Did she have the same effect on him, as if she was tumbling into sensation, unable to stop?

Hands at his waist, he made to unfasten his buckskins.

Vangie nudged his hands away. "I want to do it." She brushed her fingertips across his abdomen, and the muscles jumped and quivered. "Have you any idea how arousing it is to be undressed?" Pressing against Ian, she nuzzled the crisp hairs on his chest and slid her hands across his contoured ribs. She flicked his nipple with her tongue. His gasping groan further emboldened her.

He grasped her naked derrière and lifted her against him, rotating his hips upward.

She laughed softly. "Not yet."

"Temptress," he growled.

Inch by sinuous inch, she drew the soft doeskin pantaloons downward, across his tightly flexed buttocks and rock-hard marbled thighs. Her fingernails grazed his protruding heaviness. Surly a siren's smile tilted her lips at his harsh expulsion of air through clenched teeth. She cupped his fullness, running her hands along its velvety length as his pantaloons pooled around his ankles.

Fragile moonbeams slanted through the tree's branches casting Ian in ribboned light. Her gaze locked with his. Though they'd joined before, it was as if she were seeing him for the first time. This time when they came together, she could express her love. The anticipation was unbearable.

She stepped into his embrace and was lost. Her mouth fused with his in a kiss frantic with hunger.

When had they sunk to their knees?

His hands were everywhere, caressing, stroking, and igniting. He whispered, "I love you," over and over, like a holy mantra.

She lay on her back and tugged him to her. "Now, Ian. Take me now."

He growled his consent then lifted and parted her thighs. Hovering for a moment, he threw back his head and plunged into her depths. Vangie cried out, clutching him to her and matching his rhythm, stroke for stroke. This joining wasn't gentle, but wild, almost violent. She was desperate to reach the ultimate place he could take her.

Only moments later, she stiffened as glorious sensation pulsed through her core. He slammed his mouth atop hers to muffle her scream of fulfillment then groaning his pleasure aloud, pumped his seed into her.

33

Satiated into drowsiness, Vangie roused to angry shouts and frightened screams. Ian leapt to his feet, cursing. He yanked on his discarded clothing, scarcely enough to be considered decent, and charged from the enclosure.

She followed suit, frantically searching for one misplaced boot in the shadowy shelter. Her hand closed on the cold steel of her dagger, and snatching the blade, she slipped it into her waistband. At last she located the errant boot, and hopping on one foot, tugged it on. She ran to catch up, darting into the clearing behind him.

Ian skidded to a halt, and she bumped into him.

Masked men on horseback stampeded through the campsite, torching tents and wagons. The horsemen brutally kicked aside the Roma that tried to stop them. Mothers scooped terrified children into their arms and ran to escape the willful destruction.

"Vangie, this way." Ian grabbed her hand and plunged toward Yoska's tent, shouting, "Gerard!"

In a flurry, Somersfield's armed staff surged forth joining the enraged gypsies. Reaching Yoska's tent, Ian dove inside. He emerged moments later, face grim and holding a sword and a pistol in his hands. He'd stuffed another pistol into his waistband, and a knife handle protruded from his boot top.

"Vangie, go." He jerked the pistol to the side. "Hide in those trees behind Yoska's *vardo*."

She started to shake her head, but his lips thinned in warning.

"Don't argue with me. I cannot help your people if I'm worrying about you. If I have to choose who to protect, it will be you."

Gulping against the fear clawing at her, Vangie nodded, her loose hair whirling around her hips and shoulders.

Ian pointed to the trees again. "Go. Now." Without waiting for a response, he swiveled toward the chaos, pistol and sword at the ready.

"Ian?"

Pivoting around, he speared her a questioning look.

"Please, be careful." She struggled to smile. "I love you."

His expression softened. "Aye, I love you too, my lady." Grinning wickedly, he added, "And, we've not had our wedding journey yet."

Despite the chaos reigning around the camp, a silent message passed between them. He jerked his head in the direction of the towering trees then spun and ran into the fray.

Vangie scampered to the trees, only staying long enough for him to believe she'd obeyed. If he thought she'd remain docilely hidden in the woods while he put himself in danger, he didn't know her at all. She skirted the edge of the encampment, careful to remain obscured in the darkness beyond the fires' glow.

She tore to Grandmother's *vardo*. *Puri Daj* and Jasper were huddled inside, Lancelot cuddled between them. "Get outside, into the trees. They're torching the wagons! Take your medicines, *Puri Daj*. We'll have need of them this night." Vangie crawled across them, intent on the tiny cupboard above her bed. She yanked the door open, reached inside, and retrieved a leather pouch.

"Zora," Simone breathed, alarmed.

Vangie deftly loaded the small gun. "It's only a precaution." She met Grandmother's worried eyes. "Ian's out there. He might need me." With that, she slipped from the wagon and into the riotous night.

Sidling along the *vardo*, she took stock of the situation. Only four of the assailants remained on their horses. The others had either been killed or were fighting on foot. Nicu dispatched one assailant with his blade while Besnik wrestled violently with another.

Ailsa charged to his aid. "No, you don't," she shrieked, laying a stout branch across his opponent's head. The man toppled over, a nasty gash in his skull. "Besnik." She burst into tears before throwing herself into his sturdy arms.

"Shh, *pirrini*," he soothed, caressing her shoulders and back.

A few feet beyond them, Vangie spied Ian grappling with a scruffy man. The scarf intended to mask the bandit's face had come loose and hung around his neck.

She gasped recognizing one of Sir Doyle's men.

The man outweighed Ian by a good three stone, but Ian's quicker reflexes gave him the advantage. He danced circles around the clumsy oaf, his sharp jabs hitting home each time.

His opponent swung his beefy hand. Ian ducked and planted a solid facer on his foe's ruddy cheek. The man tottered, weaving unsteadily. His legs crumpled beneath him, and he sagged into a heap in the dirt. A rider charged forward with a gun pointing straight at Ian's back.

Please, God, no.

"I-a-n!" Vangie screamed. Aiming the gun, she fired. *Click.* Nothing.

She threw it to the ground, stark terror ripping through her. At a dead run, she yanked the dagger from her waist then hurled it. The blade sliced through the air with lethal accuracy, landing between the man's shoulder blades. He was dead before he toppled to the ground.

The unholy, animalistic fear permeating Vangie's voice raised the hair on Ian's nape. He wheeled around, sidestepping a horse's thrashing hooves. Astonishment etched the rider's face. He pitched from his saddle, so close, his lifeless fingers brushed Ian's chest.

Sunk to the hilt, Vangie's dagger protruded from his back.

Holy Mother of God.

Twice she had killed to protect him. Where was she? He whirled around. She stood tight-lipped and sagging between Ailsa and Besnik. Terror lingered in her sapphire eyes. Her mouth worked, but no sound emerged. She was in shock. The remaining marauders pounded from the clearing like the cowards they were as Ian bolted to her.

He embraced his shaking wife and held her firmly against his chest. "Shh, sweetheart."

His gaze met Yoska's and Besnik's in turn. Both men's mouths were twisted into grim lines, and fury simmered in their guarded gazes. Blood dripped from a gash in Yoska's lip, and bright reddish-blue fingerprints marked Besnik's neck.

"This," Ian's gaze prowled the clearing, "wasn't random, was it?"

"*Niks.*" Yoska shook his shaggy head while wiping at the scarlet dripping down his chin.

The fury faded from Besnik's eyes, replaced by a kind of defeated weariness. "We've not been so blatantly attacked before, though a small *kor* or two is not unusual."

Ian surveyed the ravaged camp. He'd wager Somersfield that Lucinda and Doyle had orchestrated this. The attack reeked of the magistrate's greed and treachery, and it was just like him to send his henchmen to do his dirty work while he kept out of harm's way. "I fear, my friends, I may have brought this upon you," Ian said.

"How so?" Yoska asked.

Vangie trembled in his arms, pressing closer to him. Ian cast a swift glance at her bowed head. He met Yoska's probing gaze and gave a slight negative shake of his head.

The gypsy inclined his.

Good. He understood. Ian wanted to keep his concerns from Vangie, at least for now.

Yoska's dark gaze searched the shadows. "Here are our *tikna's*." He waved at them. "Come, it is safe now."

With trepidation, the Romani women and children hiding in the woods crept into the encampment, grief and bewilderment stamped on their faces.

Simone bustled forward toting a large basket, and Jasper tagged behind her, lugging an equally cumbersome satchel. "Zora, I need your help."

Puri Daj's voice roused Vangie from her fear-laced stupor. Ian held her in a tight embrace, and she tipped her head to look at him. "I must help tend the wounded."

He relaxed his arms, but worry shone in his eyes. "Are you able?"

She nodded, giving him a wobbly smile.

He cupped her face against his chest and rested his cheek on the crown of her head. "Thank you. Once again, you saved me from certain death."

Vangie closed her eyes and breathed his scent. Yes, she'd killed to protect him; her husband, her lover, and God willing, the father of her children. Bitter tears pricked behind her eyelids. No, she'd not think of it. Later, she would grieve and ask God for forgiveness for killing again. But at present she focused on her joy.

Ian is alive.

"You cannot discharge your obligations so easily," she mumbled against his shirt. When he didn't respond, she plastered a pleasant smile on her face and tilted her head upward.

He frowned at her, his bewilderment endearing.

"You promised me a dozen children."

His quick-silver eyes deepened to charcoal. "I did indeed." He kissed her nose as he released her. "You've tear streaks…" He rubbed her cheek with his thumb.

Scrubbing at her damp face, Vangie surveyed the encampment. Eight raiders lay in the dirt. Two were unconscious thanks to Ian's sound right hook and Ailsa's questionable skill with the branch. Were the others dead?

The sobs and cries of Romani women filled the clearing. How many Roma were hurt? Dead? Her stomach churned.

"Zora," *Puri Daj* called. "Come." Grandmother knelt beside Nicu. His arm lay at an odd angle and lacerations marred his face and chest. Weeping loudly Eldra cradled his head in her lap, dabbing at his wounds with her skirt.

Vangie rushed to them. "How is he?"

Puri Daj met her eyes before combing the groups huddled around the other wounded. "He's injured the worst. His ribs are cracked and his arm broken."

"No Roma are dead, truly?" Vangie inhaled an unsteady breath, struggling to contain her tears of relief.

"No, praise God." *Puri Daj* paused, sitting back on her heels. She assessed Vangie with her intelligent eyes. Affection sparkled in their depths. "You are leaving." Covering her hand with her own she said, "That is how it should be." She cast a glance at Ian and smiled. "He loves you."

Warmth infused Vangie. "*Aue*, I know."

An hour later, just as dawn whispered her palette of colors across the sky, she hugged *Puri Daj*. "I'll return with the land deed in a fortnight."

Grandmother brushed an errant curl from her cheek. "Your father and mother would be proud, *tikna*. What you've done for our people…"

Emotion clogged Vangie's throat, and she sent a loving look to Ian sitting patiently atop Pericles. He threw his head back, laughing at something Yoska said. "Ian made it possible, and he is the one who deserves the Roma's gratitude."

Besnik lifted her to sit before Ian, and Yoska handed her Lancelot. Her gaze fell on Jasper, sitting on the dog cart seat. His spine ramrod stiff, he led the caravan from the encampment. The two surviving bandits, had been stuffed into the box of the dog cart, bound and gagged. Gerard and the other stable hands led a string of horses. Pericles brought up the rear of the odd entourage.

Shifting, she peered over Ian's shoulder and smiled at Ailsa standing beside Besnik. Vangie waved gaily. "We'll return for the wedding. Two weeks will pass before you know it."

Besnik stood with his arms folded, a surly scowl on his face.

Ian cocked a slanted eyebrow. "Sweeting, why's he so churlish?"

She giggled. "He wanted the wedding to take place immediately, but Ailsa insisted on waiting two weeks. She said her family would want to attend. She wasn't even going to remain in camp, but Besnik, poor besotted fool, wouldn't hear of her leaving." Tapping her chin, Vangie mused. "Would Charlotte mind overly much if I sent one of her gowns for Ailsa to remake?"

He nuzzled her neck and squeezed Pericles in the sides with his heels. "Send her a dozen of the blasted things."

The stallion ambled forward, and with one last wave to her grandmother, Vangie settled against Ian, peeping at him through her lashes. "I don't understand it." She smiled coyly while trailing a finger across his chest. "Besnik wasn't the least pacified. Even after Ailsa kissed him soundly."

"I doubt he'll have to wait two weeks for what he wants," he muttered as he tugged Vangie against him and cupped her breast beneath her shawl.

"Ian, stop." She pushed at is hand. "Someone will see." She cast a worried glance around them.

Grinning, he wiggled his fingers beneath the covering.

"Lout." She swatted at his hand.

Lancelot latched onto one of Ian's fingers, sinking his needle-like puppy teeth into the soft flesh.

Ian yelped. "Let go, you little bugger."

"He thinks you're playing." Vangie erupted into giggles.

Shaking the off pup, Ian returned to exploring beneath her wrap. He brushed the nipple protruding through the soft fabric of her blouse, and Vangie bit the inside of her cheek to keep from groaning aloud.

"Ian?" She tried to sound scandalized, difficult to do when sultry yearning permeated every syllable. "You're wrong about Ailsa."

He murmured in her ear, "Am I?"

Unconscionable cur, teasing her so. She nearly melted from the delicious sensations his warm breath tickling her ear aroused. Instead, she sagged against him and filled her lungs with a deep gulp of bracing air. "Indeed. I heard her myself. *'I'm no easy wench you can tumble before our vows, Besnik Bailey.'"*

"Ah, my lady, therein lies the difference. We've exchanged our vows."

Vangie tried to hide her blushes for the next several miles as Ian proceeded to explain in great detail, precisely how he intended to tumble her. When Pericles stopped before the mansion at last, she wiggled her numb bottom against Ian's loins.

"Stop it, minx," he ground out. "I'm already hard as stone."

"Fifteen minutes, my lord."

"Fifteen minutes?"

She drew his head downward and whispered in his ear.

34

"Vangie," Ian called.

Vangie smiled and waved at him striding across the meadow, a basket dangling on his arm. Jasper must've told him where she'd gone off to. She eyed the sky doubtfully. Mayhap if they hurried, they could squeeze a picnic in before the clouds burst.

She'd left Lancelot at the house so as to enjoy her romantic picnic.

"Look, Ian." She hurried to the other side of the rickety bridge and pointed to the black swans circling below. She'd been tossing bread crumbs to the ducks and geese for the past half hour. A strong gust of wind blew across the pond creating small frothy peaks. "A baby is riding on its mother's back. Isn't it cute?"

"Careful, sweeting. That rail is still in need of repair." Ian set down the basket. He grasped her elbow as she peered over the edge. "Do you know how to swim? The water is deep at this end."

A nearby oak tree groaned and crackled as it wrestled with the wind. Another flurry ruffled her skirt and teased the curls around her face. She smiled and nodded. "Like a fish. *Puri Daj* insisted I learn after my parents drowned."

She raised her eyes to the churning, pewter sky. It had been a day much like today when a fierce summer storm had orphaned her. Her parents' carriage had been swept downriver after a bridge gave way. A chill washed over her as she scanned the tree tops. Dark gunmetal gray clouds swirled above them, and the trees swayed and dipped, their branches waving wildly. Damp earth, pine, and lily of the valley scented the air.

She tossed another crust of bread to the birds. Apprehension squeezed her ribs, but her head didn't ache. Not yet, anyway. The megrims had started after the death of her parents, and storms—like stress—almost always brought on an episode. She bathed Ian with a loving gaze. Perhaps this time would be different, for she wasn't lonely and afraid anymore.

"You shouldn't come here unaccompanied." Hands on his lean hips, he surveyed the area, obviously looking for the men he'd assigned to guard her. "Where are Beau and Bryce? And your new maid? What's her name?"

Vangie almost giggled. She wasn't the only one who couldn't always remember names. "Ayva. She's helping Mrs. Tanssen with Ailsa's wedding preparations. They *are* twins after all."

"What was the good Lord thinking, molding *two* of them?" He shook his head in disbelief. "What about the men assigned to guard you?"

"Gerard sent a message. He needed them in the stables to help move something." Throwing the last piece of bread in the water, Vangie sent Ian a sideways glance. Worry hardened his features. He had been edgy and troubled since they'd arrived home.

Well, not the *first* day. He'd been quite content that afternoon. She smiled to herself at the fond memory. "I'm sorry, Ian. I thought it would be all right. There's been no sign of your stepmother since Jasper reported her disappearance." She heartily hoped the woman had left for good.

"It's of no consequence, sweeting. I'll speak with Gerard and remind him the two have other duties until further notice." He smiled, the tension easing from his face as the wind whipped through his chestnut hair.

She rather liked the unkempt look. Securing her shawl tighter, she shivered. The weather had turned foul fast, and it appeared as if the promised picnic would have to wait—again. She searched the pond, rather startled to find it deserted and the water now a mass of seething foam. "Where are the birds?"

Ian wrapped his arm around her waist and pointed with his other hand. "Look across the water there. They've taken sanctuary in the marshland." He eyed the turbulent sky. "We'd best return to the mansion ourselves."

Even as he spoke the heavens opened with a torrent of frigid rain. A raging gust of wind pummeled them, and Vangie caught her breath at its intensity. Icy pellets buffeted her, making it difficult to see. He gripped her hand, and they turned for the manor house, only to pull up short.

Sir Doyle and the Dowager Viscountess Warrick blocked the bridge. Each wielded a pistol.

The storm had allowed the pair to sneak up on her and Ian unawares. She squeezed his hand. "I'm sorry. I should've listened to you."

Shouldn't Beau and Bryce have returned by now? Likely they'd assumed she'd already returned to the manor because of the weather.

She peered past the dowager and magistrate to the trail that ended at the stable. A subtle movement caught her eye. Did someone lurk in the woods? She squinted against the driving rain. No, it was only the wind twisting the trees' shadows.

"You've made it so very easy. Out here, away from the manor and your henchmen otherwise engaged." A warped smile contorted the dowager's mouth. "You must be commended, on your dutiful staff, Ian. Why, those two nincompoops arrived at the stables less than ten minutes after your wife gave them the note I sent."

He speared Vangie a rueful glance, a crooked grimace twisting his mouth. "I should've known. Gerard cannot write."

"How could I have been so gullible?" Vangie fumed.

"This storm is most providential." The dowager waved her pistol toward Ian. "Alas a tragic accident might occur." She giggled, an eerie demented cackle. "It's not quite fair, I suppose, as only we have weapons."

That was what she thought. Vangie slipped her hand from Ian's. "*Miri tshurii*," she whispered through stiff lips, sliding her hand to her thigh.

Had he heard her? Did he understand?

Ian turned his sopping head, his acute gaze tangling with hers. "*Scran pushka tshurri*," he murmured.

Thank God above, he understood.

Sir Doyle stepped onto the bridge. It swayed and groaned, protesting beneath his weight. "Speak English, not that filthy gypsy gibberish."

"He was but reassuring me," Vangie said, inching forward a mite, forcing herself to meet the magistrate's lecherous gaze. The picnic basket concealed a knife and a gun Ian had said, but the basket sat between them and Doyle and the dowager.

Rivulets of water streamed into her eyes, and she wiped them away with her soggy shawl.

Ian stepped forward, half in front of her, shielding her from their pistols. "I've already alerted the authorities that you've tried to kill me, Lucinda. If anything happens to me or Vangie, you'll hang."

Her heart lodged in her throat, she spun to face him. Fear, outrage, and disbelief sluiced through her in rapid succession. "She tried to *kill* you?"

His gaze never straying from the dowager or the magistrate, he gave a brief nod. "More than once." He looked pointedly at his stepmother before his focus dipped to her weapon. "You won't get away with it."

"Shan't I?" Her crazed laugh echoed above the howling wind. "Fool. I already have." She crowed again then licked her lips. Insanity glimmered in her wild, unfocused eyes.

"Sir Doyle, why are you doing this?" Vangie gestured at the dowager. "You'll hang right alongside her."

He wiped his bulbous nose on his sleeve, and his bulgy-eyed gaze darted to the woman beside him. Did his lips curl the merest bit? "With both of you out of the way, Charlotte inherits everything. She's a minor, so naturally, her mother will control her estate." He puffed out his flabby chest. "I shall receive half of everything. I'll be a rich man."

"But Charlotte is married." Vangie pulled her eyebrows together. Her husband controlled her monies now.

"Not for long." He chuckled unpleasantly. "She's about to become a widow."

She gaped at the dowager. "You'd kill your daughter's husband?"

"Of course I would," Lucinda sneered. "I killed mine."

Despite the storm's furor raging about them, the air on the bridge became eerily still. Ian fisted his hands, taking another step forward. The basket was almost within his reach. "What, precisely, are you saying?"

"Yew berries, Ian." The dowager waved her hand in a circle by her head. "They're all over this place. Your father didn't have a heart attack, you idiot. I poisoned him."

Ian sucked in sharp breath. "You, heartless bitch!"

Lord, no. Yew berries were deadly.

She lifted her bony shoulders. "Geoff too. He was recovering from his wound. I couldn't have that, could I? Now, you're the only remaining obstacle." She pointed her gun at Vangie, her calm demeanor incongruous with her ravings. "You and that gypsy harlot, that is."

"By, God!" Ian took a menacing step forward but froze when she aimed the gun at Vangie's head.

"Tut, tut. Have you a wish to see your wife's end so soon?" Lucinda sliced Vangie a scornful scowl, irritation lacing her words. "She's stronger than she looks. Three weeks I tainted her food, and yet she survived."

Mother of God. Vangie clamped a hand over her mouth to keep from crying out. The odd taste she'd detected. If she'd eaten more, if she hadn't been smuggled other food, if she hadn't cast up her accounts several times, she might've died.

"You'll pay for what you've done," Ian threatened through tight lips.

Another insight clobbered Vangie, and she reeled. *Yew induces miscarriages.* What if her fall from the horse hadn't caused her to lose the baby? Fury tunneled through her veins, scorching and uncontrollable. How could anyone be so evil? Surely the devil himself possessed the dowager, and a special place had been reserved for her in hell.

"I heard she lost the bratling you sired on her." Her face wreathed in triumph, gloating filled Lucinda's voice.

Ian's breath hissed from between clenched teeth.

Vangie gripped his forearm, restraining him when he surged toward his stepmother. "Don't. That's what she wants." She raised her head permitting the full measure of her scorn and loathing. "You're utterly mad."

"*Mad?* I think not. I've plotted my revenge for years. Geoff's injury was most providential. I eliminated both him and Roger, and no one was the wiser. Not even that quack of a doctor." She snarled at Ian. "That only leaves you to dispose of." The dowager laughed again. "Roger failed, the miserable rotter. He did his best to ensure the Hamilton line wouldn't die out. Today, it will cease to exist."

Ian stiffened, peering at the trees, and Vangie followed his gaze as another sodden figure emerged from the nearby woods.

"Ben? What the devil are you doing here?" Sir Doyle glowered at him. "I told you to wait in the village, you idiot."

The dowager swept Ben a contemptuous glare. "Can't you do *anything* right, imbecile?"

Vangie's regard whisked between the trio before she covertly cut a side-eyed look to Ian. He'd crept forward a scant bit more, and ever so slowly, she gathered the fabric of her skirt in her hand.

Suddenly, Ian lurched for the basket.

Moving amazingly fast for such a rotund man, the magistrate kicked the basket into the frenzied pond. "No, you don't," he wheezed, easing his way backward to stand beside the dowager.

No! Vangie silently cried, a lock of hair whipping across her face. Her pins had long since come out, and she shoved the strands aside, tucking the soaked hair behind her ears. *God, please send help.* She prayed someone at the mansion or stables would come in search of them. With only her dagger to defend them, she and Ian didn't stand a chance against the other three.

Unless… She eyed the pistols. Black powder flintlocks? She swallowed a hysterical giggle. Would the guns fire in this downpour?

Ben reached the bridge, and it dipped and bucked over the churning water. A large branch broke nearby, crashing to the earth and shaking the ground from the impact. He wore a peculiar expression on his thin face. "What about me?" he said, more whine than demand.

"What about you?" Lucinda spat, derisively.

"You promised that if I helped, I'd receive a share of the estate." His gaze flicked to Sir Doyle, and the magistrate averted his rodent eyes.

"Did I?" She curved her mouth into humorless smile. "I don't recall making any such promise."

Ian edged nearer to Vangie.

"You heard her, Pap. You were there." Ben balled his hands, his lips quivering and frustration leaching into his voice. "She vowed because I was her firstborn, I was entitled to a share too."

Ben was the dowager's son? Her firstborn? And Doyle was his father?

Vangie threw Ian a stupefied sideways glance. He appeared as astonished as she. She raised her skirt a few inches higher, but no one noticed.

The dowager turned on Ben, scathing contempt contorting her countenance. "You'll receive nothing. Did you really think I'd give you a single shilling? No, my darling Charlotte shall have everything."

Tears leaked from Ben's eyes, and he blinked several times.

She pointed and laughed. "Sniveling fool."

He staggered backward as if struck, slipping on the muddy ground. "But…but, I'm your son. Your firstborn. I've done everything you asked. *Everything.*" He sent a perplexed glance toward Ian and Vangie. "I put horseshoe nails under their saddles." He gestured toward them. "I've worked in the stables all these months. Sneaked around, doing your bidding—"

"You're a bastard," his mother hissed, her face twisted with rage and hatred.

"No!" Ben screamed, charging at her.

She fired her gun, but nothing happened. Crying out, she hurled it at him.

He easily deflected it and grabbed her by the throat. "I'll kill you. I'll kill you," he said, choking on gut-wrenching sobs. "You never loved me. Why couldn't you love me?"

Eyes bulging, Lucinda clawed at his hands all the while making rattling, gagging noises.

Sir Doyle wrapped his beefy arms around Ben, trying to pry him off the dowager. "Let go, boy." He jerked hard then harder still. "Damn you, let go!"

Vangie never would've believed the scrawny young man could be so strong.

Waves from the pond crashed over the bridge.

Ian clamped a hand around her upper arm and inched them backward. Step by torturous step, they edged away from the grappling forms.

The magistrate slipped on the slick wood, losing his balance. He teetered precariously, his arms churning like a miniature windmill. He stumbled and slid about before plowing into Lucinda and Ben. The trio crashed into the rotten railing, and it gave way with a resounding crack. Shrieking, they toppled into the roiling water.

The bridge jerked and quivered, listing further. It creaked and groaned, as one by one, the supporting posts snapped.

Ian grabbed her hand. "Run, Vangie!"

They raced the few remaining steps toward land. Just as the footbridge tore loose from its piling, he snatched her into his arms and jumped the last foot. The far end shuddered, sinking beneath the frothing waves.

Vangie clutched Ian, straining to see through the curtain of rain. "Where are they?" She swiped at the droplets streaming down her face. They were warm. Tears. "I don't see them, Ian."

"They're gone, sweeting." He pulled her into his embrace.

Jasper's voice rang through the din. "My lord, my lady, where are you?"

She slumped in Ian's arms.

Eyes closed, Vangie swatted at the fly tickling her cheek. It then landed on her nose. Dratted, pesky insect. She rolled onto her side, mashing her face into her pillow. Bother it all. Now it crawled across her ear. She tugged at the bedcovers intent on burying her head beneath them.

They wouldn't budge.

A low, familiar chuckle sounded, and she opened one eye. Ian sat on the edge of the bed, waving a feather and grinning raffishly.

"Rotten knave." Yawning and stretching, she deliberately let her nightgown slide off her arm, exposing all but the tip of one breast. His sharp intake of breath brought a satisfied smile to her lips. He wasn't the only one who knew how to tease.

The feather whisked across her breast.

She yanked the sheet up. "Unfair."

"*Tsk, tsk*, sweeting. Don't start something you don't mean to finish." He bent over and kissed her, his tongue sweeping hers.

Lord, but the man knows how to kiss.

Vangie forgot everything else for several delectable moments, until he tapped her nose with the feather. "Are you going to lie abed all day, my lady?"

His weight shifted from the bed, and she opened her eyes. "Why are you grinning like a buffoon?"

Ian bent over and lifted a basket from the floor.

She raised an eyebrow before sliding a glance at the bedside clock. "It's not yet eight o'clock. Isn't it a bit early for luncheon?"

"Ah, but who says a picnic cannot be breakfast?" He wiggled his eyebrows as he peeked inside the basket. "There's champagne and orange juice and strawberries."

Flashing him a smile, she scooted into a sitting position. "My lord, you promised me something weeks ago."

"Indeed?" Eyebrow quirked, Ian pulled his gaze away from the basket's contents.

She smoothed the bedding over her lap. "Something delicious having to do with strawberries—"

"Ah, indeed, I did." He lifted a plump, red berry from the basket. "Shall I demonstrate now?"

"Please do, my lord."

And he did, most satisfactorily.

Somersfield
July 1817

Vangie gritted her teeth against another wave of pain. Her labor had begun nearly sixteen hours ago, and she wasn't sure how much more she could endure. She tried to return her cousin's encouraging smile but moaned softly instead.

Yvette wiped a cool cloth across her forehead. "You're doing splendidly, darling. Just a little longer."

"Indeed, my lady," Midwife Godfrey said, patting Vangie's knee. "Your wee one is nearly here.

Vangie clasped Yvette's hand. "I'm so glad you are here." She'd arrived a week ago in the company of none other than Ewan, Viscount Sethwick.

Dr. Farnsworthy, his glasses low on his thin nose, puttered about the room, making the final preparations for the grand event.

Closing her eyes, Vangie breathed in, counting slowly as another contraction racked her. She'd been so afraid of losing this child too, but the pregnancy had progressed normally until she'd unexpectedly gone into early labor yesterday.

"Doctor, it's time," Midwife Godfrey informed him.

"Good. Good." He smiled kindly, taking the midwife's place. "Ah, yes. I see the baby's head." He glanced up. "Push, my lady."

Squeezing Yvette's hand, Vangie tucked her chin to her chest and pushed with all of her might.

"Again," he ordered.

She obeyed, desperate to bring her child into this world and make the pain stop.

A moment later, the doctor chuckled and the midwife rushed to his side. Beaming, she met Vangie's worried gaze. "You have a healthy daughter, my lady."

Tears leaked from her eyes. "I have a daughter, Yvette," she said, wonder in her voice.

Her eyes suspiciously moist, Yvette smiled and smoothed the damp hair back from Vangie's forehead. "You do, darling. A beautiful little girl."

Cooing softly, Midwife Godfrey wrapped the screaming bundle in a linen.

Another excruciating pain gripped Vangie, and she clutched her belly, crying out.

"Vangie, what is it?" Yvette cried in alarm as the midwife whirled toward them.

"I suspected twins," she said matter-of-factly, giving the doctor a nod as she went about tending to the infant.

Twins?

"Not much longer now," Dr. Farnsworthy assured Vangie when another pain rippled through her abdomen.

"I need to push," she gasped.

Two minutes later, the second baby slid from her body, and she flopped back onto the pillows panting. "What is it?"

Grinning, the doctor held up the wriggling newborn. "The next Lord Warrick, my lady."

Twins. A boy and a girl. "Ian," she whispered, her heart aching with the need to see him. To have him see and hold their babies. "I want Ian."

He and Lord Sethwick were sequestered in the study.

"I'll send word to him at once." Yvette hurried to the door and whispered something to the maid waiting outside. Mere moments later, a forceful knock rattled the bedchamber door. Grinning, she opened it.

His hair wildly mussed, dark stubble covering his face, a humble and unsure Ian hovered at the entrance, his attention riveted on the bed.

Propped against a pile of pillows, Vangie beamed, cradling a babe in each arm. "Ian, we have a son and a daughter."

His eyes misty, he maneuvered onto the bed beside her. Reclining against the headboard, he took his son into his arms then kissed her. He bent and kissed their daughter's forehead. "Twins," he said, eyes shining with wonder. "Are you all right?" He slid a questioning glance to the doctor and midwife.

Dr. Farnsworthy nodded and smiled. "She and the babes are perfectly fine. Textbook labor and delivery. I do want Lady Warrick to rest, however."

Vangie kissed her daughter's downy head, breathing in her sweet scent. "We're so blessed, Ian. We lost a child, but God gave us two to mend our hearts."

He wrapped an arm around her shoulder, drawing her to his side. Their son made a soft noise, his little eyes peering up at them. "We are blessed indeed, and I shall always be grateful a beautiful gypsy temptress accepted my dance request."

Smiling up at him, she said, "And I'll always be grateful that a certain viscount's vow for revenge has brought me untold happiness and love beyond anything I ever dreamed."

If you've enjoyed reading **The Viscount's Vow**, *Castle Brides Book 1*, then perhaps you'd enjoy the rest of the books in the series:

Highlander's Hope
The Earl's Enticement
Heart of a Highlander (*prequel to Highlander's Hope*)

A Kiss for a Rogue

THE HONRABLE ROGUES®, BOOK ONE

1

A lady must never forget her manners nor lose her composure.
~A Lady's Guide to Proper Comportment

London, England
Late May, 1818

"This is a monumental mistake."

God's toenails. What were you thinking, Olivia Kingsley, agreeing to Auntie Muriel's addlepated scheme?

Why had she ever agreed to this farce?

Fingering the heavy ruby pendant hanging at the hollow of her neck, Olivia peeked out the window as the conveyance rounded the corner onto Berkeley Square. Good God. Carriage upon carriage, like great shiny beetles, lined the street beside an ostentatious manor. Her heart skipped a long beat, and she ducked out of sight.

Braving another glance from the window's corner, her stomach pitched worse than a ship amid a hurricane. The full moon's milky light, along with the mansion's rows of glowing diamond-shaped panes, illuminated the street. Dignified guests in their evening finery swarmed before the grand entrance and on the granite stairs as they waited their turn to enter Viscount and Viscountess Wimpleton's home.

The manor had acquired a new coat of paint since she had seen it last. She didn't care for the pale lead shade, preferring the previous color, a pleasant, welcoming bronze green. Why anyone living in Town would choose to wrap their home in such a chilly color was beyond her. With its enshrouding fog and perpetually overcast skies, London boasted every shade of gray already.

Three years in the tropics, surrounded by vibrant flowers, pristine powdery beaches, a turquoise sea, and balmy temperatures had rather spoiled her against London's grime and stench. How long before she grew accustomed to the dank again? The gloom? The smell?

Never.

Shivering, Olivia pulled her silk wrap snugger. Though late May, she'd been nigh on to freezing since the ship docked last week.

A few curious guests turned to peer in their carriage's direction. A lady swathed in gold silk and dripping diamonds, spoke into her companion's ear and pointed at the gleaming carriage. Did she suspect someone other than Aunt Muriel sat behind the distinctive Daventry crest?

Trepidation dried Olivia's mouth and tightened her chest. Would many of the *ton* remember her?

Stupid question, that. Of course she would be remembered.

Much like ivy—its vines clinging tenaciously to a tree—or a barnacle cemented to a rock, one couldn't easily be pried from the upper ten thousand's memory. But, more on point, would anyone recall her fascination with Allen Wimpleton?

Inevitably.

Coldness didn't cause the new shudder rippling from her shoulder to her waist.

Yes. Attending the ball was a featherbrained solicitation for disaster. No good could come of it. Flattening against the sky-blue and gold-trimmed velvet squab in the corner of her aunt's coach, Olivia vehemently shook her head.

"I cannot do it. I thought I could, but I positively cannot."

A curl came loose, plopping onto her forehead.

Bother.

The dratted, rebellious nuisance that passed for her hair escaped its confines more often than not. She shoved the annoying tendril beneath a pin, having no doubt the tress would work its way free again before evenings end. Patting the circlet of rubies adorning her hair, she assured herself the band remained secure. The treasure had belonged to Aunt Muriel's mother, a Prussian princess, and no harm must come to it.

Olivia's pulse beat an irregular staccato as she searched for a plausible excuse for refusing to attend the ball after all. She wouldn't lie outright, which ruled out her initial impulse to claim a *megrim*.

"I ... we—" She wiggled her white-gloved fingers at her brother, lounging on the opposite seat. "Were not invited."

Contented as their fat cat, Socrates, after lapping a saucer of fresh cream, Bradford settled his laughing gaze on her. "Yes, we mustn't do anything untoward."

Terribly vulgar, that. Arriving at a *haut ton* function, no invitation in hand. She and Bradford mightn't make it past the vigilant majordomo, and then what were they to do? Scuttle away like unwanted pests? Mortifying and prime tinder for the gossips.

"Whatever will people *think*?" Bradford thrived on upending Society. If permitted, he would dance naked as a robin just to see the reactions. He cocked a cinder-black brow, his gray-blue eyes holding a challenge.

Toad.

Olivia yearned to tell him to stop giving her that loftier look. Instead, she bit her tongue to keep from sticking it out at him like she had as a child. Irrationality warred with reason, until her common sense finally prevailed. "I wouldn't want to impose, is all I meant."

"Nonsense, darling. It's perfectly acceptable for you and Bradford to accompany me." The seat creaked as Aunt Muriel, the Duchess of Daventry, bent forward to scrutinize the crowd. She patted Olivia's knee. "Lady Wimpleton is one of my dearest friends. Why, we had our come-out together, and I'm positive had she known that you and Bradford had recently returned to England, she would have extended an invitation herself."

Olivia pursed her lips.

Not if she knew the volatile way her son and I parted company, she wouldn't have.

A powerful peeress, few risked offending Aunt Muriel, and she knew it well. She could haul a haberdasher or a milkmaid to the ball and everyone would paste artificial smiles on their faces and bid the duo a pleasant welcome. Reversely, if someone earned her scorn, they had best pack-up and leave London permanently before doors began slamming in their faces. Her influence rivaled that of the Almack's patronesses.

Bradford shifted, presenting Olivia with his striking profile as he, too, took in the hubbub before the manor. "You will never be at peace—never be able to move on—unless you do this."

That morsel of knowledge hadn't escaped her, which was why she had agreed to the scheme to begin with. Nevertheless, that didn't make seeing Allen Wimpleton again any less nerve-wracking.

"You must go in, Livy," Bradford urged, his countenance now entirely brotherly concern.

She stopped plucking at her mantle and frowned. "Please don't call me that, Brady."

Once, a lifetime ago, Allen had affectionately called her Livy—until she had refused to succumb to his begging and run away to Scotland. Regret momentarily altered her heart rhythm.

Bradford hunched one of his broad shoulders and scratched his eyebrow. "What harm can come of it? We'll only stay as long as you like, and I promise, I shall remain by your side the entire time."

Their aunt's unladylike snort echoed throughout the carriage.

"And the moon only shines in the summer." Her voice dry as desert sand, and skepticism peaking her eyebrows high on her forehead, Aunt Muriel fussed with her gloves. "Nephew, I have never known you to forsake an opportunity to become, er ..."

She slid Olivia a guarded glance. "Shall we say, become better acquainted with the ladies? This Season, there are several tempting beauties and a particularly large assortment of amiable young widows eager for a *distraction*."

Did Aunt Muriel truly believe Olivia don't know about Bradford's reputation with females? She was neither blind nor ignorant.

He turned and flashed their aunt one of his dazzling smiles, his deeply tanned face making it all the more brighter. "All pale in comparison to you two lovelies, no doubt."

Olivia made an impolite noise and, shaking her head, aimed her eyes heavenward in disbelief.

Doing it much too brown. Again.

Bradford was too charming by far—one reason the fairer sex were drawn to him like ants to molasses. She'd been just as doe-eyed and vulnerable when it came to Allen.

"Tish tosh, young scamp. Your compliments are wasted on me." Still, Aunt Muriel slanted her head, a pleased smile hovered on her lightly-painted mouth and pleating the corners of her eyes. "Besides, if you attach yourself to your sister, she won't have an opportunity to find herself alone with young Wimpleton."

Olivia managed to keep her jaw from unhinging as she gaped at her aunt. She snapped her slack mouth shut with an audible click. "Shouldn't you be cautioning me *not* to be alone with a gentleman?"

Aunt Muriel chuckled and patted Olivia's knee again. "That rather defeats the purpose in coming tonight then, doesn't it, dear?" Giving a naughty wink, she nudged Olivia. "I do hope Wimpleton kisses you. He's such a handsome young man. Quite the Corinthian too."

A hearty guffaw escaped Bradford, and he slapped his knee. "Aunt Muriel, I refuse to marry until I find a female as colorful as you. Life would never be dull."

"I should say not. Daventry and I had quite the adventurous life. It's in my blood, you know, and yours too, I suspect. Papa rode his stallion right into a church and actually snatched Mama onto his lap moments before she was forced to marry an abusive lecher. The scandal, they say, was utterly delicious." The duchess sniffed, a put-upon expression on her lined face. "Dull indeed. *Hmph*. Never. Why, I may have to be vexed with you the entire evening for even hinting such a preposterous thing."

"Grandpapa abducted Grandmamma? In church, no less?" Bradford dissolved into another round of hearty laughter, something he did often as evidenced by the lines near his eyes.

Unable to utter a single sensible rebuttal, Olivia swung her gaze between them. Her aunt and brother beamed, rather like two naughty imps, not at all abashed at having been caught with their mouth's full of stolen sweetmeats from the kitchen.

She wrinkled her nose and gave a dismissive flick of her wrist. "Bah. You two are completely hopeless where decorum is concerned."

"Don't mistake decorum for stodginess or pomposity, my dear." Her aunt gave a sage nod. "Neither permits a mite of fun and both make one a cantankerous boor."

Bradford snickered again, his hair, slightly too long for London, brushing his collar. "By God, if only there were more women like you."

Olivia itched to box his ears. Did he take nothing seriously?

No. Not since Philomena had died.

Olivia edged near the window once more and worried the flesh of her lower lip. Carriages continued to line up, two or three abreast. Had the entire *beau monde* turned out for the grand affair?

Botheration. Why must the Wimpletons be so well-received?

She caught site of her tense face reflected in the glass, and hastily turned away.

"And, Aunt Muriel, you're absolutely positive that Allen—that is, Mr. Wimpleton—remains unattached?"

Fiddling with her shawl's silk fringes, Olivia attempted a calming breath. No force on heaven or earth could compel her to enter the manor if Allen were betrothed or married to another. Her fragile heart, though finally mended after three years of painful healing, could bear no more anguish or regret.

If he were pledged to another, she would simply take the carriage back to Aunt Muriel's, pack her belongings, and make for Bromham Hall, Bradford's newly inherited country estate. Olivia would make a fine spinster; perhaps even take on the task of housekeeper in order to be of some use to her brother. She would never set foot in Town again.

She dashed her aunt an impatient, sidelong peek. Why didn't Aunt Muriel answer the question?

Head to the side and eyes brimming with compassion, Aunt Muriel regarded her.

"You're certain he's not courting anyone?" Olivia pressed for the truth. "There's no one he has paid marked attention to? You must tell me, mustn't fear for my sensibilities or that I'll make a scene."

She didn't make scenes.

The *A Lady's Guide to Proper Comportment* was most emphatic in that regard.

Only the most vulgar and lowly bred indulge in histrionics or emotional displays.

Aunt Muriel shook her turbaned head firmly. The bold ostrich feather topping the hair covering jolted violently, and her diamond and emerald cushion-shaped earrings swung with the force of her movement. She adjusted her gaudily-colored shawl.

"No. No one. Not from the lack of enthusiastic mamas, and an audacious papa or two, shoving their simpering daughters beneath his nose, I can tell you. Wimpleton's considered a brilliant catch, quite dashing, and a top-sawyer, to boot." She winked wickedly again. "Why, if I were only a score of years younger ..."

"Yes? What *would* you do, Aunt Muriel?" Rubbing his jaw, Bradford grinned.

Olivia flung him a flinty-eyed glare. "Hush. Do not encourage her."

Worse than children, the two of them.

Lips pursed, Aunt Muriel ceased fussing with her skewed pendant and tapped her fingers upon her plump thigh. "I would wager a year's worth of my favorite pastries that fast Rossington chit has set her cap for him, though. Has her feline claws dug in deep, too, I fear."

2

Displaying envy or jealousy reflects poor breeding; therefore,
a lady must exemplify graciousness at all times.
~A Lady's Guide to Proper Comportment

Duty.

An heir apparent must marry.

Allen snagged a flute of champagne from a passing servant.

Bloody well wish it were a bottle of Sethwick's whisky.

Part Scots, Viscount Sethwick boasted some of the finest whisky Allen had ever sampled. The champagne bubbles tickling his nose, he took a sip of the too sweet, sparkling wine and, over the crystal brim, canvassed the ballroom.

Which one of the ladies should he toss his handkerchief to and march down the aisle with?

A posturing debutante, beautiful and superficial?

A cynical widow, worldly-wise and free with her favors?

A shy chit past her prime but possessing a fat dowry?

Or perhaps a bluestocking or a suffragist who preferred reading books and carrying on discourses about women's oppression rather than marry? At least with the latter he could have intelligent conversation about something other than the weather and a bonnet's latest accoutrements.

He really didn't give a damn—didn't care a wit who he became leg-shackled to or who the next Viscountess Wimpleton would be. The only woman he'd loved had left England three years ago, and he hadn't heard from Olivia since. His gut contracted and shriveled up.

So much for forgiveness and love's enduring qualities.

Livy's gone and not coming back. You drove her away and now must pick another bride.

Familiar regret-laced pain jabbed Allen's ribs, and he clamped his jaw. He had been an immature arse, and the consequence would haunt him the remainder of his miserable, privileged life. Heaving a hefty breath, he forced his white-knuckled grip to relax before he snapped the flute's stem.

Mother, no doubt, was pleased as Punch at the crush attending his parents' annual ball. If too many more guests made an appearance, the house might burst. Devilishly hot, the ballroom teemed with overly-perfumed, sweaty—and the occasional unwashed—bodies.

God, what he wouldn't give for a more robust spirit than this tepid champagne. The weak beverage did little to bolster his patience or goodwill. At this rate, he would be a bitter curmudgeon by thirty. A drunkard, too. Given the brandy he'd imbibed prior to coming down stairs, he was half-way to bosky already.

After finishing the contents in a single gulp, he lifted the empty glass in acknowledgement of his mother's arched brow as she pointedly dipped her regally coiffed head toward Penelope Rossington.

He might not give a parson's prayer who he wed, but his parents did. She must be above reproach, and if Mother thought Miss Rossington suitable ...

Responsibility.

Allen had an heir to beget.

Miss Rossington was pretty enough, exquisite some might say, and generously curved too. Her physical attributes made her quite beddable. She was also dumb as a mushroom and shallow as a snowflake. He'd had more intelligent conversations with barmaids.

He cocked his head as she gave him a coquettish smile before murmuring something to her constant companions, the dowdy and turnip-shaped Dundercroft sisters. They giggled and turned an unbecoming, mottled shade of puce.

A practiced flirt, Miss Rossington had recently become possessive of him and exhibited an unflattering jealous streak. Still, she would do as well as any other, he supposed, since those behaviors seemed universally present in the *ton's* marriageable females.

Allen released a soft snort. He never used to be so judgmental and jaded.

Exchanging his empty flute for another full one—only his third this evening—he caught his mother's troubled expression. She pulled on Father's arm before lifting onto her toes and fervently whispering in his ear.

Father speared him a contemplative glance, and Allen raised his glass once more.

Cheers. Here's to a bloody miserable future.

His parents couldn't fathom his cynicism since theirs had been a love match.

Frowning, Father murmured something and patted Mother's hand resting atop his forearm.

Casting Allen a glance, equally parts contemplative and maternal, she nodded before smiling a welcome to Bretheridge and Faulkenhurst, two of Allen's university chums.

Steering his attention overhead, Allen contemplated the gold plasterwork ceiling and newly painted panels adorned with dancing nymphs and other mythical creatures. Mother had begun massive redecorating shortly after Olivia Kingsley had left. He'd always suspected she had done so to help erase Olivia's memory.

Bloody impossible, that.

Fully aware Olivia had ripped Allen's heart from his chest and hurled it into the irretrievable depths of the deepest ocean, his parents worried for him. They also fretted for the viscountcy's future if he didn't shake off his doldrums and get on with choosing a wife.

Propriety.

He'd always been the model of decorum.

Tedious, dull, snore-worthy respectability.

Except for a single time when he had rashly shoved aside good sense, Allen had always heeded his parents' and society's expectations. Never again would he indulge such an impulse. His position required he attend these damnable functions, dance with the ladies, and ensure the Wimpleton name remained untarnished. Bothersome as attending the assemblies was, pretending to enjoy himself proved Herculean, though, he had become quite adept at the subterfuge.

Copious amounts of spirits helped substantially, but drowning self-recriminations in alcohol fell short of noble behavior, or so his Father had admonished on numerous occasions, most recently, this afternoon.

Finally acquiescing to his parents' gentle, yet persistent prodding, Allen had set his attention to acquiring, what would someday be, the next viscountess. Another blasted obligation. Those not borne into the aristocracy didn't know how fortunate they were, especially only sons.

However, once he had made his choice, he needn't feel obligated to attend as many social functions, and when he did appear, he could spend the evening in the card room, or better yet, escape to the study with a few coves and indulge in a dram or two.

Maybe he and his bride would retire to the country, at least until the title became his—not that he wished his father into an early grave or was overly eager to assume the viscountcy. Since seeing the magnificent horseflesh bred at Sethwick's castle, Craiglocky, Allen had considered entering into a cattle breeding venture of his own. Surely that would keep his mind occupied with something other than melancholy musings.

His wife would want for nothing except his affections. Those weren't his to give. A certain tall, fiery-haired goddess possessing sapphire eyes had laid claim to them, and his love would forever be entangled in her silky chestnut hair. But he would be a kind and faithful husband. He quite looked forward to dangling his children upon his knee, truth to tell.

An image of a chubby-cheeked imp with sea-blue eyes and wild cinnamon curls sprang to mind. On second thought, he did have one stipulation for his future wife. She could not have red hair.

Taking a sip of champagne, he rested a shoulder against a pillar.

Miss Rossington glided his way, a coy smile on her rouged lips, and if he wasn't mistaken, a bold invitation in her slanted eyes. Her dampened gown left little to his imagination, and though she wore virginal colors, he would bet the coat on his back, she'd long ago surrendered her maidenhead.

He quirked his mouth. Perhaps, she wouldn't do after all. Though he must wed, he didn't relish cuckoldom.

Barely suppressing an unladylike curse, Olivia gave her aunt the gimlet eye. Did she say a year's worth of pastries? Hound's teeth, then it was a given. Aunt Muriel took her pastries very seriously, as evidenced by her ample figure.

Olivia scowled then immediately smoothed her face into placid lines.

Ladies do not scowl, frown, or grimace.

Or so Mama had always insisted, quoting *A Lady's Guide to Proper Comportment* as regularly as the sun rose and set from the time Olivia was old enough to hold her own spoon.

She hadn't quite decided how to go about competing for Allen's affections, if any chance remained that he still cared for her. Perhaps she should ask Aunt Muriel for advice.

On second thought, that might prove disastrous. Her aunt had already suggested a clandestine kiss. No telling what scandalous, wholly inappropriate notion Aunt Muriel would recommend. Why, Olivia might find herself on the edge of ruin in a blink if she followed her aunt's advice.

Tonight, she would find out precisely where she stood with Allen, whether she dared still hope or should concede defeat and accept her heartbreak. Just what kind of woman was she up against, though? "No doubt this Rossington miss is excessively lovely."

If only Aunt Muriel would say she's homely as a toad with buggy eyes and rough, warty skin. Oh, and Miss Rossington was missing several teeth and had a perpetual case of offensive breath.

"Hmph. If you consider a heavy hand with cosmetics, dampened gowns, and bodices that nearly expose entire bosoms lovely, I suppose she is." Aunt Muriel resumed her preening.

Bradford's mouth crept into a devilish smile. "I quite like dampened gowns—"

"Brady!" Olivia kicked his shin. Sharp pain radiated from her slippered toe to her knee. *Bloody he—*

Proper ladies do not curse, Olivia Antoinette Cleopatra Kingsley! Mama's strident voice admonished in Olivia's mind.

"—and exposed bosoms." Brady risked finishing, nestled in the carriage's corner with his arms crossed and a mouth-splitting, unrepentant grin upon his face.

He enjoyed quizzing her, the incorrigible jackanape.

"Of course you do." Aunt Muriel lifted her graying eyebrows. The twitch of her lips and the humor lacing her voice belied any true censure. "My poor sister would perform one-handed somersaults in her grave if she knew what a rogue you have become, always up to your ears in devilry. Don't know where you got that bend. Your father was as stiff and exciting as a cold poker, and your mother never did anything remotely untoward, always quoting that annoying comportment rubbish."

Another rogue dominated Olivia's thoughts.

What if Allen dismisses or cuts me?

The possibility was quite real.

She had no reason to believe he might yet hold a *tendre* for her, but she most know for certain, no matter how devastating or humiliating. She feared her rehearsed speech would flit away the moment she opened her mouth, leaving her empty-headed and tongue-tied, and although she had attempted to prepare for a harsh rebuff, practicing imaginary responses couldn't truly ready her for his or the *ton's* rejection and scorn.

As the carriage lurched to a rumbling stop, she sent a silent prayer heavenward. No stars, dim from the new gas streetlamps before the mansion and the coal-laden clouds blanketing London shot across the sky for her to wish upon. It had been on a night very much like this that she'd been a young fool and crushed her and Allen's dreams of a future together. However, in her defense, she had only known him for a blissful fortnight before he proposed.

Already completely taken with Allen, she'd become teary-eyed during a waltz and shared her dismay. In a matter of days, her father intended to move the family to the Caribbean for a year. Father hadn't given them any notice or time to prepare, just announced, in his impulsive, eccentric way, that they were off to Barbados to oversee a sugar plantation. She had been full of girlish hopes and dreams, and Father's plans severed them at the root.

What maggot in his brain had possessed him to buy a plantation? He had known nothing of farming or harvesting, preferring fossils and rocks to humans and their usual activities. Even Olivia's Season could be ascribed to a deathbed vow Father had made to Mama; one he had repeatedly attempted to renege on until Bradford had intervened on Olivia's behalf.

She had long suspected Father never intended for her to marry, but to remain at his side as his companion, housekeeper, and nurse until his days ended.

Closing her eyes, she pictured that romantic dance three years ago.

Allen had held her closer than propriety dictated, but not so much as to be ruinous. After whisking her onto the veranda, he'd captured her hand, and they had sped to a garden alcove. Whether he'd planned to ask her, or had been caught up in the moment and spontaneously decided to, she would never know, but he had hurled convention to the wind, dropped to one knee, and after promising to love her for eternity, asked her to share the rest of his life.

She had loved him almost from the first moment she'd seen him standing across the ballroom, sable head thrown back and laughing unrestrained. Her chest welling with emotion, she had tossed aside her mother's constant harping on proper comportment as carelessly as used tea leaves, and said yes, even though Papa wouldn't have approved.

Olivia hadn't cared.

Especially when Allen had smiled, his countenance full of joy, and then had sealed their troth with a scorching kiss. Her nipples pebbled and a jolt of arousal heated her blood as recollection of their potent embrace produced a familiar response. A quick survey of her wrap assured her that her body's reaction remained a secret, and Aunt Muriel and Bradford hadn't a hint of her sensual musings.

That had been the happiest moment of her life, and the cherished memory elicited a tiny, secretive smile.

Then, Allen had revealed his intention to elope to Gretna Green.

That night.

Taken aback at his impetuous suggestion, uncertainty had niggled, its sharp barbs pricking and stirring her misgivings. Mother had died a year ago, and Father suffered from ill-humors. It might have been too much for his frail health if Olivia had eloped. She had thought to have a few weeks, months perhaps, before wedding Allen. Besides, a fortnight wasn't enough time to truly fall in love—not a deep, abiding, eternal love, was it?

More than enough time when your soul finds its other half.

She breathed out a silent, forlorn sigh. Her silly doubts had fueled her fear of making a hasty, impulsive decision. And so, regretfully, she'd said no to hieing off to Scotland, and instead, asked him to wait a year for her to return to England.

"We could write back and forth, truly get to know one another and plan for our future together. A year isn't so very long." She tried to persuade Allen to wait. "Many couples are betrothed for a lengthy period."

Setting her from his embrace, his answer had been an emphatic, "Like hell I shall. I love you and want to marry you now, not in a year, dammit. That's a bloody eternity."

"But, I cannot elope tonight." She touched his arm, trying to reclaim the happiness of a moment before but, shoulders and face stiff, he had turned away from her. "It's too sudden, Allen, and I'm worried what the shock would do to Papa."

Head bowed, his forearm braced against the arbor entrance, and his other hand resting on his narrow hip, Allen had spoken, his voice so raspy and quiet, she had strained to hear him.

"If you really loved me, you wouldn't want to wait to marry. You would be as eager as I am." Dropping his hands to his sides, he faced her, his voice acquiring a steely edge. "It seems I have misjudged your affection for me. Go to the Caribbean. I won't try to dissuade you again."

He had left her standing, crushed and weeping, in the arbor. Wounded at his callousness, after regaining her composure, she had made her way to the veranda where she'd encountered Allen's sister, Ivonne. Claiming to feel unwell, Olivia had asked her to find Father and Bradford and tell them to meet her at the entrance. Betrayal fueling her anger, she hadn't even bid her hosts farewell.

It wasn't until the ship was well out to sea did she realize, she hadn't ever told Allen she loved him. Not a day had passed since sailing that she hadn't lamented not eloping. Wisdom had arrived too late, and she had destroyed her greatest opportunity for love and happiness.

Maybe my only opportunity.

No doubt the torturous road to Hades was paved with a myriad of regrets, for life without him would surely be—*had been*—hell.

A white-gloved footman in hunter green livery opened the door. He set a low stool before the carriage and smiled. "Good evening, Your Grace."

"Good evening, Royce. My nephew will see us alighted." Aunt Muriel waved her hand at another carriage where a large woman teetered within the doorway. "Go help over there before Lady Tipples topples onto the pavers and cracks them." A grin threatened. "Tipples topples. Didn't plan that. Funny though."

"At once, Your Grace." After bowing, Royce dashed to the other conveyance. He and another footman managed to wrangle the squawking woman, swathed in layers of orange ruffles and bows, onto the pavement.

"Wouldn't mind her absence tonight, truth to tell." Jutting her chin toward the commotion, Aunt Muriel slipped her reticule around her wrist. "She always wants to bore me with the latest clap trap or her current revolting ailment. I heard more about gout and constipation last week than a body ever needs to know."

Chuckling, Bradford descended first then turned to hand Aunt Muriel down.

Hands clasped so tightly, her fingers tingled, Olivia remained rooted to her seat, her attention fixed on the entrance.

Allen is in there.

Bradford stuck his head inside the carriage. All signs of his former joviality gone, he regarded her for a long moment, kindness crinkling the corners of his eyes. He chucked her beneath her chin.

"Come along, Kitten. Put on a brave smile, and let's go meet the dragon. I dare say the past three years have been awful for you, always wondering if Wimpleton still cares. Who knows, mayhap tonight is providential. In any event, you'll have an answer, and you can get on with your life."

Bradford had suffered the loss of his first love, and his facade of a carefree, womanizing rake, hid a deeply injured man. If anyone understood her plight, it was he.

"I suppose that's true." Although her existence would be only a shadow of what life might have been with Allen.

Such a pity hindsight, rather than foresight, birthed wisdom.

Bradford extended his hand. "Let's be about it then."

Sighing, and resigned to whatever providence flung her way, Olivia placed her palm in his. "All right."

"That's my brave girl." He gave her fingers a gentle, encouraging squeeze.

Not brave. Wholly terrified. "So help me, Brady, you step more than two feet away from me, and I shall—"

"Never fear, Kitten. I shall forsake my romantic pursuits and act the part of a diligent protector for the entire evening. I but lack my sword to slay your fears."

Despite her rioting nerves, Olivia grinned. "How gallant of you, dear brother, and a monumental sacrifice, at that."

"Indeed. A selfless martyr." Sarcasm puckered Aunt Muriel's face as if she had sucked a lemon. "For certain he's deemed for sainthood now."

"Anything for you, Liv. You know that." He tucked Olivia's hand into the crook of one elbow while offering the other to their aunt before guiding the women up the wide steps. A few guests smiled and nodded in recognition as the trio entered the manor.

Olivia forced her stiff lips upward and reluctantly passed her wrap to the waiting footman. Had he detected her shaking hands? The scarlet silk mantle provided much more than protection from the spring chill; it shrouded her in security. Her stomach fluttered and leaped about worse than frogs on hot pavement, threatening to make her ill.

She ran her hands across her middle to smooth the champagne-colored gauze overlay of her new crimson ball gown Aunt Muriel had insisted on purchasing. The ruby jewelry she wore was her aunt's as well.

Though Bradford, now the newly titled Viscount Kingsley, had inherited a sizable fortune, Olivia had balked at acquiring a new wardrobe. "My gowns are perfectly fine. I'll simply wear a shawl or mantle until I become accustomed to England's clime once more."

Besides, if she didn't reconcile with Allen, she was leaving London, and a wardrobe bursting with the latest frilly fashions was a senseless waste of money as well as useless for country life.

"Chin up and smile, Livy. You look about to cast up your crumpets." Bradford clasped her elbow, as if lending her his strength.

Casting up her accounts was the least of her worries. Swallowing her panic, she offered him a grateful smile as they stood before the butler.

"Her Grace, the Duchess of Daventry, Lord Kingsley, and Miss Kingsley." The majordomo announced them in the same droning monotone he had the previous guests.

Behind Olivia, someone gasped.

Perfect.

A low murmur of hushed voices circled the room in less time than it took to curtsy as the three of them advanced into the ballroom. Perhaps Bradford's rise in status caused the undue interest. After all, he had been third in line to the viscountcy, and if their curmudgeon of an uncle and two cousins hadn't drowned in a boating accident, Brady would have been spared a title he disdained.

Combing the room from beneath her lashes, her stomach lurched.

Every eye was trained upon them. Her. At least it seemed that way from the brief glimpse she had braved.

This is a mistake.

Head lowered and her attention riveted on the polished marble floor, she prayed for strength. Where was the pluck Papa had praised her for, or the feistiness Bradford often teased her about? Or the spirit Allen had so admired?

She could do this. She must if she were ever to discover the truth. Otherwise, not knowing would badger and pester her, preventing her from ever finding the peace she craved.

Had Allen forgotten her? Did he love another now? That Miss Rossington?

There was only one way to find out.

Olivia forced her eyes upward. Inhaling, she squared her shoulders, commanded her lips to tilt pleasantly, and lifted her head.

Her gaze collided squarely with Allen's flabbergasted one.

3

A lady of gentle-breeding should never appear too eager to engage the attentions or affections of a gentleman.
~A Lady's Guide to Proper Comportment

What the hell is *she* doing here?

Allen damned near dumped his champagne down Miss Rossington's ample bosom upon hearing Olivia's name announced. Unprepared to see the woman he had once loved more than he had thought humanly possible standing in his home again, her presence had blindsided him.

Utterly lovely, staring at him, her eyes startled and huge, Olivia's beauty clobbered him with the same force as a horse's kick to the gut. Those huge, Scottish beasts Sethwick's sister raised with hooves the size of carriage wheels.

Vises clamped his heart and squeezed his lungs as whooshing echoed in his ears, wave after wave, in accompaniment to his frantic heartbeat. Perspiration broke out across his upper lip and beaded his forehead. He didn't need a looking glass to know he had gone white as new-fallen snow.

For one very real moment, he couldn't suck in an ounce of air and feared he would swoon. Wouldn't that give the quartet of chinwags standing by the potted ficus something to bandy about? Especially Lady Clutterbuck, the worst gossipmonger in Town.

Say, did you see Wimpleton? Keeled over like an ape-drunk sot.

That he had taken to imbibing freely for some time now would lend credence to the tattle.

Tiny blackish specks frolicked before his eyes, and the roaring in his ears became deafening.

Breathe, man.

Jaw rigid, he marshaled his composure and dragged in a painful, inadequate breath, then another. The blood thrumming in his ears lessoned a degree.

One more ragged breath and his vision cleared a mite.

Olivia's presence sent him hurtling back to the evening she had announced her father's intention to move her family to Barbados— *in two bloody days*.

Desperate not to lose her, and willing to endure censure and scandal, Allen had thrown his pride aside and implored her to flee to Scotland with him that very night. His one instance of selfish impulsiveness. Look how well that had turned out.

Now, she hovered, hesitant and anxious, at the ballroom's entrance, and a tidal wave of devastation and hurt crashed down upon him, drowning him in remorse. It took every ounce of self–control to regard her impersonally.

One hand pressed to her throat, Olivia looked positively wan—terrified even.

Hell's teeth. She better have a damned good reason for showing up on her aunt's coattails.

When had the Kingsleys returned to England? Why hadn't anyone told him? Warned him?

Likely because he had been absent from London the previous week, overseeing the delivery of some prime horseflesh to Wyndleyford House, their country estate. He'd only returned to London this morning.

The duchess, stately as any queen, perused the ballroom. Her regard lit on Allen for an extended moment, and she dipped her head, her mouth arcing before her scrutiny gravitated onward.

No blatant snub from her grace. Well, at least that was something.

Allen fought dual impulses. One, to turn on his heel, giving Olivia the cut direct, and the other, to charge across the room, sweep her into his embrace, and beg her forgiveness in front of everyone.

Only she had the ability to make him act recklessly, and the last time he'd done so hadn't gone all that well. No. Much wiser to keep his distance, pretend she hadn't once been his reason for living, and focus on his pursuit of an acceptable bride.

Miss Rossington clawed at his arm, her citrine eyes sparking with jealousy, and her ruby-tinted lips tightly pursed. She looked about to fly into one of her starts.

"Who is she? I don't recall seeing that creature before." She squinted, her tightly furrowed brows forming a vee between her eyes. "Egads, she's a longshanks, isn't she? Probably starves herself to stay that slender. And would you look at her hair? Colored, to be sure, just like a lady of the night."

Her almond-shaped eyes tapering to slits, she tittered with feline satisfaction. Haughtiness turned her striking features into an over-indulged, petulant child's.

What did she know of ladies of the night?

He took a half-step back and took her measure, as if finally seeing her for the first time.

Deuce take it.

Allen cupped the back of his neck where a pair of cannon balls seemed to have taken up residence. Was he addled? He had half-heartedly contemplated courting this hellcat. Large bosoms and a beautiful face didn't compensate for a narrow mind and spiteful shallowness.

"Men prefer a woman with curves, or so I've been told." She rubbed her breasts against his arm, fairly purring. This was no innocent miss, but a woman skilled in using her physical charms. Very experienced, or he missed his mark. "She's a bit long in the tooth, isn't she?"

Allen clamped his jaw, his nostrils flaring, as she hurled yet another insult at a woman she had never met. It said much about her character. ... Or lack, thereof.

His too, that he had slid to such depths, that he would have ever considered tainting the Wimpleton name, his family's heritage and exemplary standing, with a trollop like Penelope Rossington just so he could put the distasteful task of marriage behind him.

That had been before Olivia's unexpected return.

Now the notion of making a match with Miss Rossington was as welcome as gargling hot coals. Allen contemplated his half-full champagne flute. More fine bubbles floated to the top and popped. Truthfully, a union with anyone except Olivia held as much appeal.

How could he still want her?

His treacherous eyes searched her out again, a brilliant scarlet bloom in a bouquet of pale pinks, creamy ivories, and chaste whites.

How could he not?

"Do you know who the gentleman with her is?" Miss Rossington practically licked her lips as she ogled Kingsley. "He seems far superior in breeding. Perhaps she's a poor relation—"

"He's her brother. Her name is Olivia Kingsley, and she's ..." He paused and looked at Miss Rossington.

She glared at Olivia, jealousy distorting her face.

My God, such a bratling.

"How old are you?" Odd, he'd never wondered at her age before.

Miss Rossington shifted her focus to him and elevated her chin. Her green eyes flashed with confidence, even as a seductress's smile bent her overly-rouged mouth. "Eighteen. Almost nineteen."

The same age as Livy when we met.

He tipped his lips at the edges. The termagant clutching his arm was about to receive a proper set down. "She only boasts three years on you, and I assure you, that *is* her natural hair color."

From the corner of his eye, he covertly scrutinized the crowd. Most of the guests had made a pretense of resuming their activity prior to the announcement of the Kingsleys' and duchess's arrival.

Olivia had drawn the consideration of nearly everyone present. Beauty such as hers commanded recognition, though she would be the first to decry the attention. Modest, she'd never seen the exquisiteness in her looking glass others did when gazing upon her. Maneuvering her way along the perimeter of the crowded ballroom, her brother and aunt, like alert sentinels, guarded her.

Rather, the Duchess of Daventry, much like a schooner, the wind filling its canvases, sailed forth, parting the seas before them. With furled brows and piercing gazes, she and Kinsley cowed the more brazen or insolent guests who dared to stare at Olivia outright.

Though her face held a placid expression, Olivia's stiff posture and the firm set of her shapely mouth revealed she was well-aware of the murmurs behind fans and hands directed her way. Her vibrant coppery hair and ruby jewelry shone beneath the glowing chandeliers, but Allen detected vulnerability in her sooty-lashed eyes.

His heart pinched painfully at her discomfort. Why he should care a whit about her feelings was beyond him, and that he yearned to comfort and protect her rankled him no end. A man should be able to control his deuced, capricious emotions, yet his disloyal heart—what was left of the mangled organ after she had shattered it to hell and back—ached for her.

Nodding at something Kingsley said, the bronze highlights in Olivia's cinnamon hair glinted like dark honey.

Allen had always adored her glorious hair. "The color of her hair is splendid, is it not?"

Miss Rossington released an irritated huff, her talon-like fingers tightening on his forearm. Clearly, she did not agree. "And how would you know about her dull hair? Rusty nails shine brighter. Assuredly that shade is not God-given." Accusation rang in her petulant voice, and his estimation of her dove lower. "Women of her ilk are quite skilled at artifice."

You ought to know.

Taking Miss Rossington's measure, he gave himself a violent mental shake. God spare him title-hungry viragos with the morals of a bitch in heat. She had become much too possessive of late, and her disparaging Olivia was beyond the mark.

Yes. It was far past time to put Penelope Rossington in her place and disabuse her of any notion she was viscountess-worthy, once and for all. If ever a woman was beneath the privilege, it as she.

Feeling far freer than he had in a long while, Allen took a deep breath and notching his chin, he caught site of his mother poised, statue-still, her focus riveted on Olivia.

Her eyes round as tea saucers, Mother's gaze traveled from Olivia, lingered on Miss Rossington for a fraction then drifted back to Olivia once more. She unfurled her fan, and Allen swore he saw her grin—a face splitting show of white teeth—before she began frenetically waving the fan and bustled toward Father, shoving guests aside in her haste.

"Well, don't you intend to answer me, Allen?" Miss Rossington's voice rose shrilly with all the charm and appeal of someone chewing glass. "How do you know her?"

Allen handed his flute to a passing footman. "It isn't any of your concern, but I shall indulge you anyway."

And quite enjoy your reaction.

He peeled her claws from his arm, finger by finger, and once free, smoothed his wrinkled coat sleeve.

"Olivia Kingsley is the woman I almost married."

4

Other than her gloved hands, at no time should any part of a lady's form touch a gentleman's while dancing.
~A Lady's Guide to Proper Comportment

Allen.

Olivia's heart cried silently across the distance as she ravenously scoured every inch of him from his burnished hair to his gleaming shoes, before returning to his adored face. Their gazes locked, and time hung suspended for an intense, agonizing moment.

"Olivia, stop gawking. People will think you're fast or desperate." Speaking under her breath, Aunt Muriel nudged her. "Come along. Let's find a seat, shall we?"

Olivia dragged her gaze from Allen, and Bradford took her by the elbow. Skirting the guests, they wove their way through the crush toward the black Trafalgar chairs bordering one side of the ballroom.

Allen was exactly as she remembered—ruggedly handsome and wholly irresistible.

With an utterly exquisite young woman on his arm.

Using her brother as a shield, Olivia covertly eyed Allen, drinking him in with her gaze.

Attired in black, except for a scarlet and silver waistcoat, he exuded maleness. High cheekbones framed a nose too strong to be considered aristocratic, but his lips were perfectly sculpted.

She had tasted those delicious lips once. So long ago. She touched her mouth with her gloved fingertips in remembrance.

"Olivia!" Aunt Muriel hissed from the side of her mouth while smiling and inclining her head at acquaintances as she sailed forth, towing Olivia in her wake. She squeezed Olivia's elbow when she didn't respond immediately. "Put your hand down. Compose yourself at once. I'll not have you disparaged for acting the ninny."

Olivia pretended to scratch her upper lip—indelicate, but a far cry better than pressing her fingers to her mouth—then dropped her hand, her attention still locked on Allen. "But, Aunt Muriel, you said you wanted Allen to kiss me. Surely that's scandal-worthy."

"True, but an indiscretion in a secluded nook is a far cry from making a spectacle in full view of the *beau monde*. A lady can do exactly what a strumpet does, the difference being, she doesn't carry on in the street." Exchanging nods with a dour-faced peeress, Aunt Muriel steered Olivia forward and muttered an almost inaudible, "Lady Clutterbuck. A pedantic fussock, and the worst tattlemonger in all London."

Adopting a smile, Olivia spared the dame a glance, nearly recoiling at the disapproval lining the woman's close-set eyes and, pouting fish lips. No ally there.

A group of arrogant, young bucks swaggered toward a cluster of giggling debutants, and Olivia seized the opportunity to sneak another look at Allen. His thick, sable hair swept across a high brow, accented his heavy-lashed malachite eyes. He had the most arresting eyes she had ever seen on a man. An errant lock curled over his tanned forehead, giving him a rakish air. Even across the room, his unusual green eyes glinted with something powerful.

Umbrage? Anger? Outrage?

Her step faltered, and she swallowed, not at all positive that what glistened in the depths of his gaze was hospitable. For certain, the black look his lovely companion glared at Olivia radiated hostility.

Miss Rossington?

"Buck up, Kitten. The *ton* is watching, their pointed teeth bared and ready to attack anyone showing the least weakness." Bradford whispered the warning in her ear as he led her to a trio of empty seats along what had once been a peach and ivory silk-draped wall, now a sunny primrose yellow.

Lady Wimpleton had recently redecorated and refurbished the inside of the mansion too.

Everything was much the same, yet different as well. Rather like Olivia and Allen. She stole another glance at him. His dark visage offered her no quarter, and her legs gone weak, she sank thankfully onto a chair.

Yes, indeed, this was the worst possible idea. Rather like setting sail upon the ocean in a leaky skiff.

During a tempest.

Without provisions.

Naked and blind.

Perhaps she would seek out the ladies' retiring room and spent the next hour or two cloistered there.

"Ah, I see Lady Pinterfield." Aunt Muriel indicated a woman wearing copious layers of puce and black, almost as garishly attired as she. "I need to speak with her. Her chef concocts the most delicious ratafia cakes. I simply must acquire the recipe, though she's been impossibly difficult to persuade to part with it. I haven't given up yet, mind you. I shall invite her to tea to sample her very own recipe. She cannot refuse me then." Pulling a face, Aunt Muriel sighed. "I suppose I can be persuaded to endure her company for an hour in exchange for those delicacies."

With a fluttering wave, she all but bolted toward the unsuspecting woman.

Olivia gave a closed-lip smile as Aunt Muriel swooped in on her startled prey. Heaven help Lady Pinterfield if she still wasn't eager to share the recipe.

True to his word, Bradford, after snaring a flute of champagne from a cheerful footman, took a position beside an enormous, cage-shaped potted ficus to Olivia's left.

Several twittering damsels openly ogled him, lust in their not-so-innocent eyes.

He curved his lips into a knowing smile and gave them a roguish wink.

A chorus of thrilled giggles and blushes followed, and then a quiet buzz hummed as they bent their heads near and a flurry of whispering commenced with an occasional bold peek from below fluttering lashes.

Others—older, more experience ladies—spoke behind their fans to one another or, with a seductive curving of their painted mouths, brazenly stared.

His grin widened as he leaned, ankles crossed, against the wall and perused the assembled female guests from beneath his hooded eyes. He quite enjoyed the reactions he garnered.

Incorrigible scapegrace.

At six and twenty, he ought to stop behaving recklessly, but to do so meant he had put Philomena's memory aside. That wasn't something Olivia was certain he would ever be able to do. He had been just shy of twenty when Philomena had died, but he'd truly loved her. Still did, for that matter.

Olivia and Bradford made quite the pair, both doomed to suffer for their lost loves, although a large portion of Olivia's misery could be attributed to her own making.

A young woman pointed at her and snickered.

Tendrils of heat snaked from Olivia's neck to her cheeks. Edging her chin up a degree, she whipped her fan open. Waving it briskly, she surreptitiously studied Allen and attempted to ignore the not-altogether-kind feminine tittering further along the neat row of chairs. Let them prattle. She didn't count any of them as friends. Groups had gathered in nearly every open space, and from one, several gentlemen scrutinized her, likely trying to decide whether to ask her to dance.

Please don't.

To discourage their attentions, she angled her back toward them. Not that she didn't enjoy dancing—she rather adored the pastime, especially the waltz. It had been three years since she'd attended any event with dancing as part of the entertainment, but tonight, she only cared to partner with one man.

Deliberately turning even farther away from their appraisal, she caught her breath.

No. It cannot be.

A woman bearing a striking resemblance to Philomena disappeared through the French windows.

Impossible. Utter piddle.

Olivia had become so flustered upon seeing Allen, she now imagined things. See what the man did to her?

Allen stood across the ballroom, his stance rigid and his countenance an unreadable mask. He didn't acknowledge Olivia's presence with as much as a blink or a nod.

That stung. More than she cared to admit. She had attempted to brace herself for this response but underestimated how painful the actual rejection would be.

She flapped her fan faster, her grip on the slender handle tight enough to snap the fragile wood. Well, what had she expected? That he had forgiven her and would charge across the ballroom, take her in his arms, and profess his undying love in full view of all?

Yes. Though unrealistic, far-fetched, and idealistic, that is what she'd hoped for.

It would have been wonderful—more than wonderful—an answer to three years' worth of desperate prayers. Instead, it appeared he intended to disregard her. To give her the cut. He had never been cruel before, which proved how much she'd wounded him.

Deeply. Irrevocably. Permanently

A crest of disappointment engulfed her, and a sob rose from her chest to her throat as stinging tears welled in her eyes.

I will not cry. I. Will. Not!

Not here. Not now.

She wouldn't give the gossips the satisfaction. Later, in her bedchamber, when no prying or gloating gazes could witness her heartache and mortification, she would indulge in a good cry. One final time. Then, she would dry her eyes, square her shoulders, and march, head held high, into her lonely future.

Like waves to the shore, Allen drew her perusal once more. He held a champagne glass in one hand, his other arm commandeered by that stunning, petite blonde.

Olivia quirked her lips into a cynical smile. At five feet ten inches, and with a head of unruly auburn hair, she was neither petite nor blonde. Nor nearly as curvaceous as the creature clinging to Allen, gazing at him with adoration, her full breasts crushed against his arm.

Ridiculously huge breasts, truth to tell.

Did she stuff her gown? How did her small frame support those monstrosities? With her nipples poking forth so, it was a wonder she didn't topple forward onto her face and crack the parquet flooring with them.

The blonde shifted away from Allen slightly, bringing Olivia's less than charitable musings to a screeching halt.

She blinked in disbelief.

Were those ...?

No. They couldn't be.

Olivia's jaw loosened, but she managed to prevent it from smacking against her chest.

She squinted at the girl's bosom.

Yes. They were.

Dual earth-toned circular shadows were clearly visible through the gown's light fabric.

Good God. Wasn't she wearing a chemise?

Parading about naked beneath one's gown, displaying one's ware like a Friday night harlot was beyond the pale.

The woman peered up at Allen, her countenance enraptured, and blister it, from where Olivia sat, he appeared as entranced as the young lady. Or maybe it was the blatant display of womanly attributes he found spellbinding.

Her bountiful bosoms certainly held numerous other gentlemen's rapt attention.

Dropping her gaze to her beaded, crimson slippers, jealousy nipped Olivia, sharp and deep. Scorching tears pricked behind her eyelids again, and hiding behind her fan's protection, she shut them.

Too late. I'm too confounded late.

She drew in a shuddery breath, willing her eyes to stop pooling with moisture.

Well, that was that. Bradford could find their aunt while Olivia waited in the carriage. At least she knew Allen's feelings now, but the knowledge brought her no respite.

"Miss Kingsley, may I request the pleasure of a dance?"

Startled, Olivia eyes popped open, and she clutched her throat, her fan tumbling to the floor. Allen had approached, rapid and soundless. And oh, so very welcome.

Where had the female barnacle gotten to? The way she had clung to Allen, Olivia doubted the chit had been pried loose voluntarily and was likely vexed. Offering a poised, albeit timorous smile, she peered past his black-clad muscled form as he straightened from his bow.

Ah, there she was, attached to another attractive gentleman, so scandalously close a starving flea couldn't have squeezed between them if the insect held its breath. Her cat-eyes sparked with irritation as she took Olivia's measure before turning her back in an intentional snub.

Had she some claim to Allen? An informal promise? A secret betrothal?

Olivia's stomach and hope withered.

"Has another requested the next dance?" Allen's melodious baritone drew her ponderings back to him.

Olivia opened her mouth, but her mind went blank—empty as a beggar's purse, just as she had feared.

Then dear Bradford was there, picking up her brisé fan and saving her from her gaucheness. "No. No one has requested a dance with my sister as yet. You are the first."

Bradford!

He avoided looking at Olivia as he stood upright. "Of course she would be delighted to accept your offer."

She chastised him hotly with her gaze.

Just you wait, Brady, you traitorous toad.

After returning the accessory to her, he extended his hand to Allen.

"Good to see you, Wimpleton."

Allen smiled and clasped her brother's palm. He seemed genuinely pleased to see Bradford. They had been good friends before the Kingsley's departure.

"Likewise, Kingsley. Are you finding London's temperature a mite cool after your time in the tropics? No doubt you're eager to return to the milder climate." Green fire burned in the gaze he slid Olivia as he uttered the last slightly clipped words.

His stinging innuendo met its mark, and she flinched inwardly but refused to let him see he had affected her. Rather amazed at her ability to appear composed, she met his cool regard.

"We're not returning, Mr. Wimpleton. After Papa died last year, Bradford sold the plantation."

Allen's forehead creased in momentary surprise, and then he swiftly schooled his expression. "I heard of your loss. Please accept my condolences."

"Thank you." She inclined her head and another bothersome curl flopped free.

Dratted hair.

Allen's lip twitched. He'd forever been tucking stray tendrils behind her ears or helping her re-pin errant strands. More than once, he had expressed the wish to see her hair down.

Bradford grinned, his attention directed across the room. "Olivia, since Wimpleton is partnering you for this dance, I've a mind to reacquaint myself with his sister and ask her to introduce me to that delectable creature standing beside her."

Olivia followed his regard.

A ravishing brunette wearing a stunning lavender-pink gown burst out laughing at something Ivonne said. The raven-haired beauty really ought to be warned, so she could flee before Bradford ensnared her. Poor dear. Once under his spell, women usually stuck fast, like ants in molasses, for a good while.

Until he broke their heart.

He didn't do it intentionally, but when they became too clinging, their sights set on marriage, he gently severed his association. Only, they didn't always willingly go their own way, and then he was forced to brusqueness.

"Behave yourself, Brady."

He chuckled wickedly and wagged his eyebrows. "Always, Kitten."

With a devilish wink and half-bow, he took his leave and sauntered away.

So much for gallant promises.

His expression somber, Allen extended his hand, palm upward. "The waltz is about to begin. Shall we?"

Olivia stared at his outstretched hand.

Did she dare? Wasn't this why she had come?

Now was as good a time as any to test the waters. Sink or swim. Unable to take a decent breath, she did feel she was drowning, especially when she gazed into his eyes. Intense emotion simmered there, and her pulse quickened in response. She inhaled, an inadequate, puny puff of air. Mayhap her new French stays were to blame for her breathlessness.

Fustian rubbish.

Allen was to blame.

The musicians' first strains echoed loudly in the oddly quiet room. Perhaps he commanded all her senses, and everything else had faded into the background.

"Miss Kingsley? The waltz, if you please?" Allen's soft prompt steadied her nerves.

"Yes, of course." Summoning a tremulous smile, Olivia placed her equally shaky fingers in his hand and allowed him to assist her to her feet. His unique scent—crisp, spicy, yet woodsy—smacked her with the force of a cudgel.

She inhaled deeply, savoring his essence as he tucked her hand into the bend of his elbow and led her onto the sanded floor.

A path opened before them. Like the parting of the Red Sea, several other couples moved aside, allowing them to pass, a few speculating openly as she and Allen walked by.

She had anticipated the *ton's* long memory but found it discomfiting, nevertheless.

Prickles along her spine warned her that dozens of guests watched their progress, some not at all pleased with the turn of events. A quick glance over her shoulder confirmed Miss Rossington's pinched face and fuming gaze.

Precisely what was Allen's relationship with the woman?

Please God, don't let them be betrothed.

He bowed, and Olivia curtsied, somehow managing to keep from teetering over from nerves. The floor soon filled with other couples, many of whom craned their necks and rudely gawked in her and Allen's direction. She felt rather like a curiosity at Bullock's Museum; a peculiarity to be stared at and discussed.

Why couldn't they mind their own business? She conceded this public reunion might not have been the wisest course after all, but the bread had been put to rise and there was no unleavening it now.

Allen took her in his arms, his stance too near to be considered wholly respectable. Nonetheless, she melted into his arms, reveling in their familiarity and comfort, much like returning home after a lengthy journey, which ironically, she had just done.

Shoulders stiff and coolly silent, he began circling them about the room.

He's angry.

Olivia peeked up at him through her eyelashes.

He looked straight ahead, his jaw clenched and a scowl pulling his eyebrows together.

No. He's livid.

While she couldn't get enough of him, he barely tolerated touching her. Why had he asked her to dance when he obviously struggled as much with her proximity as she did his, though for entirely different reasons?

For appearances? To prove she meant nothing to him?

She should never have come to the ball.

Such utter foolishness to think something might be salvaged of their love. She would endure this dance with some semblance of dignity, and afterward, she would make short work of finding Bradford and Aunt Muriel. They would bid their hosts a hasty farewell, and Olivia would leave her dreams of happiness and reconciliation behind forever.

Expertly guiding her between two couples, Allen's shoulder muscles stiffened even more when she clutched him during a complicated turn. Relaxing her grip, she tried to ease away, to put a bit of distance between them. He either ignored her effort or was so lost in his thoughts and discomfort, he didn't respond to her subtle attempts.

Like strangers forced to spend time together, silence loomed, awkward and heavy. She and Allen had never had trouble talking before. In fact, their ease at conversing is one of the first things that attracted her to him. Now a cavernous chasm, eroded by years of separation, misunderstanding, and hurt divided them.

Nibbling her lower lip, she strove for something sensible to say, but all coherent thought had vanished the instant he touched her. His hand upon her back branded her with possessive heat, and each time his thighs brushed her gown, her legs responded by going weak in the knees.

Ridiculous things.

Ridiculous her.

For pity's sake. Allen was just a man, not a god with divine powers capable of mesmerizing the fairer sex. True, he was the first man to hold her in his arms in years, and the only one she ever wanted to from now until eternity flashed to an end, but she reacted like a wanton.

She concentrated on counting in time to the waltz's lilting strains—*one, two, three, one, two, three*—in an attempt to keep her mind occupied, but her cluttered thoughts hurtled around, bouncing off each other, dissonant and jarring, like church bells clanging on Sunday morning.

How could she have been so naïve as to think they might put the last three years behind them? While she had remained trapped in the Caribbean, caring for her dying father, Allen had gone on with his life. A tiny sigh escaped Olivia at the injustice, but then fate never claimed to be a mistress of fairness.

The lulling music wound its way around her taut nerves until she became lost in the music and gradually began enjoying the dance. She truly did adore dancing. With him.

She closed her eyes, remembering another waltz, where she and Allen had danced indecently close. Cheeks heated by the recollection, she opened her eyes and searched Allen's dear face. Though tall herself, she had to look up to meet his eyes.

He still stared at some point beyond her, tension ticking in his jaw.

His slightly spicy scent wafted past her nostrils again, flooding her senses. She stifled the impulse to bury her nose in his neck and kiss his throat, but she couldn't help drawing in another deep breath and inhaling his essence, not only into her lungs, but into her spirit.

These last treasured moments, dancing with him, were all she would ever have, and she was determined to savor each one fully.

Did he hold the minutest trace of warm regard for her still, or had his disappointment and anger irrevocably hardened his heart? Did he remember that fateful evening—their dance and kiss too?

His focus lowered, lingering on her lips for a brief moment. His nostrils flared, and his molded mouth tightened.

Yes. He remembered.

His expression closed and unreadable, except for the amber shards sparking in his eyes, he met her gaze. "Why are you here? Did you think to take up where we left off?"

5

Infinite care and consideration should be given when a lady chooses her words and even more so when she elects to speak them.
~A Lady's Guide to Proper Comportment

Allen cursed inwardly for asking Olivia the confounded question. He'd sworn to himself he would ask her to dance, uncover her scheme, and send her on her way. Completely unaffected, he would then go about his life and she about hers

What a colossal, stinking pile of horse manure.

"You humiliated me, Olivia, practically leaving me at the altar."

Holy hell, do stubble it.

She gasped and stumbled, and he tightened his embrace, steadying her.

Her azure gaze, huge and alarmed, flitted about the room, probably seeking a means of escape. The tip of her pink tongue darted out and touched the pillow of her lower lip. "That's not true. We hadn't told anyone of our plans to marry. You had just proposed. No one knew."

He ought to give her that, but his anger wouldn't allow any concession.

The moment he'd seen her standing in the entry, he had sworn he wouldn't acknowledge, let alone speak to her. Olivia was none of his concern. She held no interest any longer. He didn't want anything more to do with her. When she had chosen her father over him and left to go gallivanting off in the tropics, he'd slammed that door closed and drove the bolt home.

Ballocks, you unmitigated liar. You love her every bit as much as you did the night you rejected her.

His tongue, fueled by offended pride, paid his conscience no heed. "There were wagers on White's books, betting we would wed by summer's end. The entire *bon ton* recognized me as a besotted fool."

Maybe not the entire *ton*, but a sizable number had.

Olivia's beautiful eyes widened in wounded shock, and her lower lip quivered the tiniest bit before she dropped her thick-lashed gaze to stare at his shoulder.

The pulse in her throat beat erratically, and she trembled. "I beg your pardon. This dance was a mistake. Please return me to my aunt or brother."

"Like hell I will." He grated the words out beneath his breath, his voice a harsh rasp.

She stiffened and looked about, half panicked.

Dragging in a juddery lungful, he hauled his attention back to his surroundings. At the end of the opulent, overheated ballroom, his parents stood beside the Duchess of Daventry, concern etched upon their countenances.

They feared he would make a scene.

He feared he would make a bloody scene.

Allen had never been this out of control before. Olivia' presence had damned near knocked him head over arse, and he still hadn't completely recovered his composure.

Drawing in another fortifying gulp of air, he forced a smile to his taut lips and nodded at the gawkers stretching their necks to see what transpired between Olivia and him.

Bloody ballroom full of giraffes and ostriches.

Allen would've loved to tell the lot to bugger off.

Instead, he elevated a brow and leveled them a civil, yet quelling look.

Dancing nearby, Miss Rossington jerked her attention away with such abruptness she mashed her partner's foot. Tripping, the man muttered an oath and bumped into another couple. They too, faltered before regaining their balance.

An amusing vision of the dancers tumbling over like stacked cards, one after the other, and ending in a writhing pile of arms and legs upon the floor flashed before Allen. The corner of his lips skewed upward. It would give the guests something to blather about other than him and Olivia.

"Mr. Wimpleton, I demand you release me at once." Her face constrained, Olivia attempted to pull away. She gave his shoulder a small shove. "Let go."

She had tried that earlier, too, but he held her fast, craving her nearness. Desperately, dammit.

"Cease." He bent his neck, his mouth near her small ear. Another inch and he could trace the delicate shell with his tongue. How would she react if he did? He drew in an extended breath. God, she smelled divine. Warm, and flowery with the faintest hint of citrus. The creamy column of her neck beckoned, as did the silky spot just below her ear, and the velvety hollow at the juncture of her throat.

He swallowed, lest he give into the urge to trail his lips from one, to the other, to the other. "We shall finish this waltz, and you shall smile and pretend to enjoy the dance. I'll not intentionally give the gossipmongers a single morsel to toss about at my expense ever again."

Casting the dancers a sidelong glance, she stopped trying to escape. Her lips ribbon thin, she shook her head. A russet tendril sprang loose, toppling onto her ear. "Too late for that, I'm afraid. My being here has stirred that unpleasant pot into a bubbling froth. I never should have come. It was foolish of me."

"Why did you?"

"I ..." Her shoulders slumped, and she tucked her chin to her chest. "I wanted to see you."

He had to strain to hear her whispered words.

Her head sank lower. "Just one more time."

As simple as that. No pretense. No expectations or demands.

Was it possible Olivia had missed him as much as he had missed her? Despite his reservations, his treacherous heart rejoiced. Words were beyond him at the moment, and swallowing, he canvassed the room.

Mother poked Father with her fan and sent the duchess a sly, knowing smile at something her grace said.

The Duchess of Daventry looked much too pleased.

By thunder. Did she just wink at him? Had she orchestrated this?

Given her reputation for being unconventional and high-handed, he shouldn't be the least surprised. Befuddled, he wasn't sure whether to thank or curse her.

Allen edged Olivia even closer, until the crown of her head almost touched his chin. Despite insisting he release her a moment ago, she didn't resist.

Her light perfume tormented him, shooting a blast of sensation to his loins and sending his lust soaring. Hound's teeth, as if his manhood bulging in his breeches wouldn't cause more whispers and titters. And trying to dance with a stiffened rod bumping against one's leg presented an uncomfortable challenge.

Women didn't realize their good fortune in wearing skirts, for their arousal didn't tent their trousers—bloody apparent for the world to see.

Sixty seconds in his arms and Olivia had him at sixes and sevens.

And hard as marble.

Only she had this power over him. Even after an extended absence from her, he responded like a wet-behind-the-ears pup with his first woman.

Well done, old man. Your self-control is pitiable.

He dismissed his musing. All that mattered was this moment and holding her in his arms. Caressing the curve of her rib, Allen guided her through another difficult turn, made more so by the blatant eavesdroppers pressing near.

A slight smile edging her mouth, she unerringly followed his lead.

They had always been superb dance partners, and he hadn't a doubt she would have been unequaled as a bedmate. He'd been eager to introduce her to passion's promises once she became his wife.

His already-stirred member jerked, yanking his attention back to the present. He scrutinized Olivia through half-closed eyes.

She had grown even more beautiful.

Her gorgeous red hair, untamed and wild, like her, was streaked with gold, no doubt from exposure to the tropical sun. A jeweled ruby band peaked between artfully arranged curls—curls every bit as silky as they appeared.

Her eyes, the clearest ocean blue he'd ever seen, stayed riveted on his neckcloth. Her unique gown—cherry-red with an overlay somewhere between ivory and light gold—enhanced her glowing skin, giving her an almost ethereal appearance. Few red-heads dared wear crimson tones, but she managed to look exquisite in the becoming gown. A slight pout marred her pretty lips, slightly damp and pinkened from being nibbled, and vexation creased her usually smooth brow.

She possessed a woman's figure now. Her breasts were fuller, the creamy mounds surging above the neckline of her gown hinting at the treasures hidden beneath the fabric. Treasures he longed to sample. No, was desperate to taste and touch.

Fiend seize it, he had thought himself over her, and truth to tell, feared ever again experiencing the pain her betrayal caused him. He'd drowned himself in drink and staggered about half-foxed for a month after her departure. If he was honest, he taken to drinking too much since, as well.

The waltz's steps brought them near the French window at one end of the ballroom. The terrace doors stood wide open, summoning him.

Before his conscience had a chance to raise an objection or dared to spout good sense, Allen whirled Olivia out the opening, just like he had that fateful night.

She stopped dancing at once and pulled from his embrace, glowering at him.

Not the same as three years ago.

"This is most improper." She attempted to step past him and reenter the house, but he blocked her path. Her color high, she glared at him. "I must return inside immediately or my reputation will be compromised."

"Not until I've spoken my piece." Allen grasped her elbow, preventing her escape. Intent on seeking a private bower, he glanced swiftly around before releasing her elbow only to clasp her hand.

"Allen, let me go." Eyes narrowed, she wriggled her fingers. "You cannot go about dragging ladies here and there willy-nilly at your pleasure."

His pleasure? Not by a long shot.

"Don't kick up a fuss. I simply want to talk without a score of ears listening to my every word." He steered her down the narrow flagstone steps and onto the lawn. Lanterns dotted the landscape, bathing the flowers and shrubberies in a warm glow, and where the lanterns couldn't penetrate the darkness, the moon's silvery beams provided a subtle half-light to all but the remotest recesses.

A woman's giggle echoed from somewhere within the garden. Seemed he wasn't the only one intent on bit of air and privacy. Her laughter sounded again, likely from the arbor further along the curving path that split the lawn as neatly as parted hair. A few stolen kisses might be had there away from the sharp eyes of the dowagers and watchful mamas.

"What are you doing?" Olivia tugged at her hand clamped within his. "Are you trying to ruin me? You just said you didn't want any more gossip. You don't think this," she gave another yank and bobbed her head toward the veranda, "won't signal the rumormongers that something's afoot?"

That halted Allen in his tracks. Standing in the center of the manicured garden, he scanned the area. They were fully visible to the few guests taking the air on the terrace, but far enough away that no one could easily overhear their conversation. Her reputation would remain intact, and he could say what he had burned to say since she stepped into the ballroom.

"I'm sorry I came tonight. It's evident my presence has upset you.

That was never my intent." Olivia released a jerky breath, misery etched upon her lovely face. "Please let me return to the house, and I shall leave at once and not bother you with my presence again."

"Not yet." He shook his head and straightened his waistcoat before slanting her a wry glance. "I must confess, I am grateful I didn't wait the year you asked for, Livy." He leaned closer, holding up three fingers. "Since it has taken three for you to reappear on the London scene."

Gasping, she flinched as if struck. Her gaze faltered, but not before raw pain darkened her eyes, and she took a reflexive step back.

He released her hand. Hell, he was an unmitigated, chuckleheaded ass.

"I didn't think you wanted me to return." She lifted her chin a notch, her incredible blue eyes lancing him with accusation. "I remember your words from that night quite clearly, Allen."

God, he remembered, too, every grating, cold syllable spewing from his lips. Guilt and shame kicked him in the ribs, pulverizing his pride.

She stared at a point beyond his shoulder, her eyes swimming with tears. She blinked several times, and swallowed audibly, obviously attempting to control her emotions. Her voice hoarse, she repeated his hateful words.

"'Don't expect me to wait for you, Olivia. If you choose your father over me, we're finished."

6

A lady of refined breeding will, at all times, avoid raising her voice or engaging in public displays of histrionics.
~A Lady's Guide to Proper Comportment

"Olivia, I ..."

Allen reached for her once more. He mustn't cause her more anguish, must make amends for his cruelty. In that moment, he hated himself, hated what love had turned him into.

Olivia lurched away, hiding her hands behind her back.

Did she fear him? A knife, jagged and rusty, twisted in his bowels.

Poised to flee, distrust lurked in her gaze—her gorgeous eyes that had once sparkled with adoration.

He had done this to her, yet he had suffered equally. "Not one letter in three years. I assumed you had stopped loving me."

"You made no attempt to contact me either, Allen. You're the one who said we were finished. Surely, you knew the Duchess of Daventry had our address. For all I knew, you had married by now." The sorrow in her voice ripped at his gut.

"There's never been anyone else, Livy."

Never would be, either. He cast a swift glance over his shoulder. No one seemed to pay them any heed, unless ... He squinted. Unless that was Mother hiding amongst the draperies beside the French Windows. No. The figure was larger than Mother. Her Grace? He suppressed a chuckle. The woman knew no bounds.

Perhaps he could convince Olivia to join him in the library or Father's study to finish this conversation. Who knew who might be loitering in the shrubberies, eavesdropping on their every word? This discussion was too private to have bandied about by a loose-tongued tattlemonger.

"What about Miss Rossington?" Lips pursed, Olivia darted a telling glance toward the manor. "She seemed quite attached to you. I didn't imagine the darkling glowers she showered upon me."

He shook his head again, noting Olivia's high color. Was she jealous? The notion gave him a jot of hope. A disinterested woman didn't harbor envy.

"Her father and mine attended Oxford together. She's a guest of my parents, that's all, no more important than the bevy of other woman they have invited tonight."

Close enough to the truth, for Allen had never entertained any serious intentions regarding the chit. A drunkard's ale lasted longer than his brief foray into insanity when he had fleetingly considered courting her. She had proved an amusing diversion—a way to keep his parents content that he dutifully searched for a wife—that is, until Miss Rossington's true nature emerged. She'd fully exposed herself this evening, and her revelation had relegated her to an unsuitable.

"Oh." Olivia fiddled with the elaborate pendant nestled above her décolletage.

Envy seized him. He would like to take the pendant's hallowed place.

The matching ruby bracelet on her wrist sparkled in the muted light when she waved her hand. "And I suppose, as their son, you must do your *duty*?"

He hid a delighted smile.

Yes. Jealousy most definitely tinged her husky voice, though she attempted to disguise it with sarcasm. He quite enjoyed the notion she was jealous. It meant she still cared.

Rolling his head, he nodded once and grinned. "I like to think I'm a very dutiful son."

Actually, except for a couple years before meeting Olivia when he had sowed his wild oats, he had been the epitome of propriety. Not only did his parents insist upon it, he'd found he wasn't cut out to be a man about town. The drinking, whoring, gambling—all favorite pastimes of many of the *ton's* privileged—held little appeal for him. Though hopelessly unpopular with the elite set, he rather favored a quiet life with one woman in his bed. Olivia.

She cocked her head, one earring swinging with the action. "Ah, yet you expected me to forsake my duty as an obedient daughter and leave my father?"

Her words ripped apart Allen's attempt at lightheartedness. Damn, this wasn't the path he'd intended their conversation to take. Olivia had neatly turned the tables on him.

"Did it ever occur to you that demanding we elope at once scared and unnerved me?" She pressed her palm to her chest, her features taut. "Every bit as much as Father announcing we were off to the Caribbean in two days' time? Both situations frightened the living daylights out of me."

Her revelation rendered Allen mute. Her situation had been wholly impossible, made worse by his juvenile ultimatum.

"Papa's health had deteriorated since Mama died." Tucking a loose tendril behind her ear, Olivia inhaled deeply, as if struggling for control. She sent a furtive look to the terrace, no doubt worried about her reputation. "Defying Papa might have killed him. How could I have lived with myself then?"

Her eyes glistened suspiciously once more.

Whirling away, she wandered to a row of rosebushes edging another neat path. "You hadn't even asked Papa for my hand yet. He knew nothing of your intentions."

"We had only known each other a fortnight, Livy." Allen rubbed his nape before folding his arms. "I doubt your father would have received my request with any enthusiasm."

You could have made the effort, dolt.

"I'm not sure it would have made a difference in any event." She shrugged and offered a rueful tilt of her plump lips as she removed one glove. "My father was impetuous and disinclined to think about how his impromptu decisions might affect others. I've always suspected he didn't want me to ever wed."

Allen canted his head again. "And you truly knew nothing of his intentions? To pack you off to the Caribbean with no warning?" He gestured in the air. "I'm sure you can understand why I might find that hard to believe."

"Allen, you come from a stable home. You know nothing of living with a parent who acted on the slightest whim. It wasn't unusual for Papa to pack us up and cart the family off to some absurd location when he became obsessed with another peculiar notion. Bradford was spared somewhat when he went off to university. I've often wondered if the only reason he came back home when he finished was to act as a buffer and protect me."

Olivia bent and sniffed a creamy rose then released a small cry of pain. Thrusting her finger into her mouth, she sucked the scarlet droplet from the tip where a thorn had scratched her.

At the sensual sight, Allen's throat went dry as a more erotic image leaped to mind.

Egads, she's hurt, and I'm envisioning lewd acts.

After a moment, Olivia regained her composure. After tugging on her glove once more, she continued her hesitant exploration of the flowers.

"Why Papa kept the news of our departure a secret is anyone's guess. He was always been a bit eccentric and reclusive. After Mama's death, he became more so. And at times—I'm ashamed to admit—quite addlebrained, especially as he aged."

Another wave of guilt hammered Allen. Her father was ailing and, apparently, dicked in the nob, to boot. "I had no idea."

Stroking a velvety petal, she lifted a shoulder. "No one did. One doesn't discuss such delicate matters. It wasn't until after we'd arrived in Barbados that Papa confessed his physician had recommended a change of climate in order to extend his life. The milder tropical weather was supposed to improve both his health and his doldrums."

Remorse crushed Allen's chest. He hadn't known any of this, though it didn't excuse his brash behavior. He'd wager his inheritance that after his harsh ultimatum, Olivia's had pride kept her from telling him. Tarring and feathering was too merciful for him. His handling of the whole affair bordered on—no, *was* completely—despicable.

Striving for control, Allen tilted his head skyward and sucked in a steadying breath. "How long have you been in England?"

He lowered his eyes, unable to keep his gaze from feasting on her in the soft light. He needed to soothe her pain, to make amends for the hurt he'd caused. He yearned to hold her in his arms, as he had ached to do every day while she had been away.

"Just over a week." Head bowed, she folded her hands before her. "Bradford and I are staying with the duchess until other arrangements can be made. Our uncle let the Mayfair house and Bradford's never been fond of it so we're seeking accommodations elsewhere."

She's been back a week and made no effort to contact me?

"Three years, Olivia. You asked me to wait one, but you've been gone three years." Allen winced at the pain he heard in his voice.

Her gaze collided with his. Regret and something else flashed in the azure depths.

"I intended to return after a year. We all did, but Papa had apoplexy four months after we arrived. He never fully recovered, and the physician advised us travel was out of the question." Her eyes shone glassy with tears. “He said it would kill Papa.”

“You never wrote.” Allen wandered to the flower beds to stand beside her. She was so close, only a handbreadth away, yet a yawning abyss of unbridgeable misunderstanding lay between them.

Olivia touched another rose. “And what would I have said? You made your position very clear. You also said you wouldn’t wait for me.”

Each bitter truth impaled him. “You might have told me of your father’s ill health.”

“To what purpose?” She cast him a sidelong look.

He snapped a rose’s stem then offered it to her.

“I would have known why you didn’t return.” *To me,* he ached to add.

“I thought you had come to hate me, Allen.”

7

Intelligence, wit, and a polite smile are a lady's greatest weapons.
~A Lady's Guide to Proper Comportment

Accepting the scarlet rose, Olivia solemnly faced Allen. Even in the dim light, with only moonbeams and the glow from the house's windows, she glimpsed a trace of vulnerability in his turned down mouth and hooded gaze.

She had never been able to hide her emotions from him. What did she have to lose by being completely candid now? Not a blasted thing. After tonight, she would likely never see him again. She lifted the flower to her nose. Shutting her eyes, she sniffed deeply.

He'd given her a red rose. Did he know they symbolized love? Likely not. Purely chance he had selected that color of bloom. Foolish of her to wish the gesture meant more.

"I was so young—having just seen my eighteenth birthday the month before—and when you suggested we run away to marry that night, I panicked." She waved her hand back and forth. "Everything happened so fast between us."

He scowled, kicking at a stone lying on the grass. "Our love was real. Don't tell me it wasn't."

Olivia nodded, and another curl slid free to tease her ear. Why bother to put her hair up at all?

"Yes, I know it is ... was." She stumbled over her words, but recovered, her voice softening. "I've never doubted it for a moment."

He fingered a fragile petal. "Then why did you leave?"

"Why did you let me go?" She peered into his unfathomable eyes.

If he had only made some sort of effort, had come to her house or the ship, done anything to prevent her from leaving, her resolve would have melted as rapidly as sugar in hot tea.

The Lady's Guide to Proper Comportment says a lady never

complains or criticizes—

Do hush, Mama.

Rubbing his thumb and forefinger together, Allen gazed off into space for an extended moment. The quiet hum of the guests on the terrace, the faint strains of the orchestra, and an occasional cricket's rasping song interrupted his weighty silence.

"My devilish pride," he finally murmured, splaying his fingers through his hair, leaving several tufts standing straight up. If his valet saw his destroyed handiwork, he would gnaw Allen's hairbrush to a nub. "I've always been too prideful. Arrogant some might say. Definitely privileged, and I seldom don't get what I want."

Allen's honest confession startled her, and Olivia dared to harbor the tiniest bit of optimism.

Grinning sheepishly, he rolled a shoulder. "I couldn't credit that you would leave me, that you expected me to wait a year for your return. I desired you then, and I acted the part of an intractable bratling."

"You broke my heart." Utterly shattered it was more apt.

He hadn't indicated he still cared for her, only that he had been as hurt as she. A breeze wafted past, and she crossed her arms, suddenly chilled. She must return inside soon, else Aunt Muriel and Bradford would become worried, not to mention the gossip Olivia and Allen's extended stay outdoors would ignite. "Fearing your scorn, I didn't dare reach out to you afterward. I have my pride too."

"I know, and I'm remorseful beyond words."

Stepping nearer, he took her hand in his. With his other, he lifted her chin until their eyes met. "Can you forgive me? Please? Might we begin again and take our time this go round?" He playfully tugged on of the escaped curls then caressed her cheek with his forefinger. "I promise not to be demanding and to always consider your feelings and needs. I beg you, give me another chance."

Blinking back tears of joy, Olivia swallowed the lump of emotion choking her. Even when the carriage had rattled to a stop before the mansion, she couldn't have imagined this most welcome turn of events. She nodded as one tear spilled from the corner of her eye.

Allen caught it with his forefinger. "I never want to make you cry again, Livy. A least not from sorrow I caused. Happiness or passion, yes, but never ... never tears of unhappiness again."

He kissed her forehead before resting his against hers.

They were probably being observed, and the tattlemongers would be flapping their tongues until next Season, but she didn't care. In fact,

Olivia wouldn't be surprised if Aunt Muriel—silently cheering, and clapping, and congratulating herself soundly for contriving this whole wonderful evening—wasn't lurking somewhere nearby, perhaps in those bushes just there, watching everything that transpired between Allen and her.

"I never stopped loving you." He kissed Olivia's nose. "Not for a single moment. When you left, the light went out of my life. I never wanted to smile again, and I cursed the sun for rising each day. I knew my selfishness and inconsideration had cost me the one thing that mattered most. You."

"Oh, Allen." She traced his jaw with her fingertips. "If only we had talked this through, this misunderstanding wouldn't have kept us apart all this time. Promise me we'll always be able to tell the other anything, and that we'll listen before ever jumping to conclusions or acting rashly again."

"Always." He grasped her hand and pressed a hot kiss into her palm. The heat of his lips burned through the fabric of her glove, sending delicious frissons spiraling outward. "Tell me you love me still, Livy. That there's a morsel of hope for us."

"Yes." She grinned and nodded. More curls sprang free. She didn't care. "I do love you."

He released a long breath, as if he had been afraid of her response. "Will you marry me? Not right away. We can wait if you wish. I won't rush you. I know I asked you before, but I want to go about it properly this time."

"Of course I will." She toyed with his jacket's lapel, giving him a coy smile. "Then you'll ask Bradford—?"

"Ask Bradford what?"

She whipped around to see her brother standing behind them. So caught up in the magical moment with Allen, she hadn't heard him approach. From the nonplussed expression on Allen's face, he hadn't either.

"Ask me what?" Bradford repeated, curiosity glinting in his eyes as he came nearer.

Allen stood taller and met his gaze straight on. "For your sister's hand in marriage."

Bradford's face broke into an immense grin, and he clapped his hands.

"Thank God. I had no idea what I was going to do with her if you two didn't reconcile." He planted his hands on his hips. "She has been in the doldrums for months and months, a regular Friday face, I tell you, scarcely cracking a smile during her fit of the blue devils and—"

Olivia whacked his arm with her fan. "That's enough, Brady. Say another word, and I shall not invite you to the wedding."

Revealing his perfect white teeth, Allen returned Bradford's silly grin. "Then we have your approval?"

"I'll say." Bradford chuckled heartily while pumping Allen's hand "My approval, consent, permission, blessing—"

"Bradford," Olivia warned. Must he carry on so? She hadn't been so awful, had she?

His eyes widened. "By George, I'll even pay for a special license, and we can have the deed done tomorrow."

"Not so fast, brother dear, else I may take offense at your eagerness to be rid of me." Olivia swung her amused gaze to Allen. "I should like a short courtship, but I would also like a wedding. Aunt Muriel will insist upon it, in any case."

Allen raised her hand to his lips. "Whatever you wish, sweetheart. I'm eager to make you my bride, but won't rush you. I'm just as certain my mother will want an elaborate showing too." He winked. "I think it may be dangerous to allow the duchess and my mother to put their heads together. We might very well end up with the wedding of the decade."

Olivia laughed. "Yes, Aunt Muriel is a force to contend with."

"There you are, Allen, my dear." Miss Rossington glided across the lawn.

Allen?

Only intimate acquaintances addressed one another by their first names, and unless betrothed to a gentleman, a young lady never did so in public. And she most certainly did not call him her dear.

A Lady's Guide to Proper Comportment, page thirty-six.

Her fine brow puckered in puzzlement, Miss Rossington looked between Allen and Olivia then turned her attention to Bradford, eyeing him like a delicious pastry she would like to savor. Or gobble up, rather. She batted her eyelashes and licked her lips provocatively.

Brazen as an east end bit of muslin.

"Whatever is going on?" She lowered her voice to a sultry whisper, her wanton wiles in full play.

Wasted on Bradford. He might like dampened gowns and appreciate a beautiful face and form, but he couldn't abide fast women, and Miss Rossington would make it round the racetrack swifter than The Derby's prime blood.

Olivia couldn't suppress her pleased smile as Allen wrapped a muscled arm about her waist and tucked her to his side, even if his actions were outside of acceptable.

"Miss Kingsley has just done me the greatest honor by consenting to become my wife."

"What?" Miss Rossington, sounding is if she had gargled gravel, blanched and clutched her throat. "Your ... your *wife*?"

"Indeed. I told you she was the woman I almost married." He gave Olivia's waist a squeeze. "Well, now I'm beyond blessed to say that dream will at last come to pass."

Miss Rossington stomped toward Allen, her countenance contorted in rage. "You damned churl, toying with my affections. Do you know how many men's address I refused?"

Allen lifted a brow. "We both know that's utter gammon. An alley cat has more discretion."

The blonde sputtered and choked, daggers shooting from her eyes. She whipped her arm back as if to strike Allen. "Why you—"

Bradford swiftly stepped forward and snared her hand.

"I wouldn't. Do you truly want those denizens witnessing you acting the part of a shrew?" He thrust his chin toward the terrace. "I assure you, a dead codfish, green and rotting, has a greater chance of finding a husband amongst the *haute ton* than you do if you strike the son of a peer."

Yanking her hand from his, Miss Rossington turned on Allen. "You bloody bastard."

The curl of his lips simultaneously expressed his scorn and amusement.

Teeth clenched and seething with rage, she glared at Bradford then Olivia. "Damn you all to the ninth circle of hell."

Hiking her gown to mid-calf, Miss Rossington spun on her satin slippered heel. She proceeded to stomp her way back to the house, muttering additional foul oaths a woman of gentle breeding should never have let pass her lips.

Page nineteen, paragraph two.

A form separated from the shadows on one side of the French windows.

Olivia blinked in disbelief as Aunt Muriel emerged from behind the drapes. Olivia would wager the Prussian jewels she wore, her aunt had been watching the whole while.

Aunt Muriel lifted her nose and pulled her skirts aside as Miss

Rossington tramped into the house. Then with a little wave at Olivia, Aunt Muriel bolted out of sight. Likely to apprise the Wimpletons of what she had witnessed.

The adorable sneak.

"It seems we've drawn a crowd." Chagrin heated Olivia's cheeks as she canted her head slightly in the terrace's direction. At least a score of guests mingled about the porch, their rapt attention focused on the trio left standing on the grass.

Dash it all. Allen hadn't wanted additional fodder for le bon ton's gossipmongers.

A roguish glint entered his eyes. "Let's make it worth their while, shall we, darling?"

A lady never participates in public shows of affection.

Olivia cast a glance heavenward.

Then I guess I'm not a lady, Mama.

She didn't resist when Allen drew her into his embrace, although she cast her brother a hesitant look.

Bradford winked. "Please do, Wimpleton. Give the chinwags something to babble about. Make it something quite spectacular, will you? Something scandalous to keep their forked tongues flapping for a good long while."

With a smart salute, he turned his back on them and, whistling a jaunty tune, strolled along the path wending into the garden's depths.

Bradford was proving to be every bit as indecorous as their aunt.

Olivia inclined her head and eyed Allen. "Well? What outrageousness do you have in mind?"

"A kiss, perhaps?" He ran his thumb across her lower lip.

Olivia quite liked this rakish side of him. "Oh, yes."

Allen took another step closer, and his thighs pressed against hers, their chests colliding.

Winding her arms around his neck, she raised her mouth in invitation.

A scandalized voice carried across the expanse. "Do you see that? They're kissing. Right there on the lawn. In full view of all."

"Yes. It's utterly lovely, isn't it?" Aunt Muriel's delighted laugh filled the night air.

Allen dipped his dark head until their lips were a hair's breadth apart. "A kiss for Miss Kingsley?"

"Perfect." Olivia smiled as his mouth claimed hers.

Wyndleyford House
September 1818

"Do finish up, Olivia darling. We'll be late."

Allen lounged against the bedpost, looking irresistibly dashing as he watched Olivia's last-minute fussing. His pristine cravat was tied in another new, complicated knot, and his waistcoat matched his green eyes to perfection. However, it was the gleam of male satisfaction in his jungle gaze that sent her pulse cavorting again.

"It's not my fault you decided to exercise your husbandly rights just as I exited my bath."

Olivia gave him a playful pout as she deliberately applied perfume to her cleavage. That quite drove him mad. She touched the emeralds at her throat. He had placed them there just before they'd spent a blissful half an hour abed. "My *toilette* would have been completed long ago."

"I didn't hear you complaining overly much." Allen straightened and after adjusting his jacket sleeves, crossed the room, his long-legged strides covering the distance in short order. He bent and kissed her bare shoulder. "I knew the Wimpleton emeralds would look exquisite on you."

"They are stunning. Thank you." She turned her head up for a kiss. The scorching meeting of their mouths had her considering an even tardier arrival to her new in-laws' anniversary celebration. "I'm honored to wear them to the festivities tonight."

"It's our anniversary too, love. One month today, Mrs. Wimpleton. Slowest three months of my life, waiting to make you my bride."

She grinned. "I told you it was dangerous to let my aunt and your mother help plan our wedding. I about tripped over my dress when I saw Prinny sitting in a front pew."

"You and I both. I'd never seen a man attired completely in that shade of pink before. Looked rather like an enormous, glittery salmon." Allen withdrew a bracelet from his pocket then lifted her hand.

"More?" Olivia shook her head. "It's magnificent but, you know, I'm not a woman who requires jewels. I have all I ever wanted."

He settled it around her wrist and set the clasp. "Would you deny me my pleasure?"

Quirking her brow, she gave him an impish smile. "When have I *ever* denied you your pleasure?"

With a mock growl, he pulled her to her feet. Swinging her into his embrace, he plundered her mouth.

A scratching at the door interrupted the kiss. "Sir, madam, everyone has arrived."

"I suppose we must put in an appearance." Allen sighed and leaned away, acting put-upon.

Giggling, Olivia collected her shawl and fan. "Of course we must. Your sister and my brother are below with their spouses. Your parents must host more balls. Three weddings came about as a result of that one in May."

"I do believe that rout set a record." He chuckled and scratched his nose. At the door he caught her arm. "Have I told you that I love you today, Mrs. Wimpleton?"

She touched his face. "Yes, but I shall never tire of hearing it."

He dropped a kiss onto her forehead. "And I promise I shall never tire of saying it."

If you've enjoyed reading **A Kiss for a Rogue**, *The Honorable Rogues® Book 1*, then perhaps you'd enjoy the rest of the books in the series:

A Bride for a Rogue
A Rogue's Scandalous Wish
To Capture a Rogue's Heart
The Rogue and the Wallflower
A Rose for a Rogue

A Diamond for a Duke

Seductive Scoundrels, Book One

Introduction

“A Diamond for a Duke” is loosely based on Charles Perrault’s 1697 French fairytale, “Les Fées" or “The Fairies,” also known as “Toads and Diamonds” or “Diamonds and Toads.” I’d never heard of this tale until I began research for an unusual fable to base a Regency novella upon.

As in Perrault’s tale, there are two sisters, Adelinda Dament, the eldest—contentious, self-centered, rude, and who values all things related to the socially elite. Metaphorically speaking, because of her inner ugliness, her words manifest as vipers and toads. The sisters’ mother, Belinda, blatantly favors Adelinda, who resembles her in looks, attitude, and behavior.

Jemmah, the younger sister, is portrayed as gentler, kinder, and as someone who cares more about people than their status. She possesses a beautiful soul, and when she speaks, her words spill forth as jewels and flowers. She, too, is banished from her home, as is the younger daughter in “Diamonds and Toads.”

The fairy takes the form of two feisty characters, Faye, the Dowager Viscountess Lockhart, and the Viscountess Theodora Lockhart. Theodora is Adelinda and Jemmah’s aunt, and godmother to Jules, the sixth Duke of Dandridge. He plays the role of the hero and has his own nemesis to contend with in the form of Phryne Milbourne.

My quirky humor worked overtime when I selected the characters’ names. Several of them were chosen specifically for their meanings:

Adelinda - noble snake
Belinda - beautiful snake
Charmont - charming
Dament - diamond
Jasper - bringer of treasure
Jemmah - gem
Jules - well, it sounds like jewels!
Faye - Fairy
Phryne - toad

A final thought about “A Diamond for a Duke”...

In today's culture, Belinda would be considered an abusive parent—unfortunately, a common and often accepted motif threaded throughout fairytales of old, as was parental partiality. The authenticity of my tale required both of these unpleasant themes.

I want to encourage everyone who has experienced or is experiencing abuse that, as in the fairytale and my novella, there is hope for you.

Help is available in many forms.

Please ... please, don't wait another day to seek it.

1

April 1809
London, England

A pox on duty.
A plague on the pesky dukedom too.

Not the tiniest speck of remorse troubled Jules, Duke of Dandridge as he bolted from the crush of his godmother, Theodora, Viscountess Lockhart's fiftieth birthday ball—without bidding the dear lady a proper farewell, at that.

She'd forgive his discourtesy; his early departure too.

Unlike his mother, his uncles, and the majority of *le beau monde*, Theo understood him.

To honor her, he'd put in a rare social appearance and even stood up for the obligatory dances expected of someone of his station. Through sheer doggedness, he'd also forced his mouth to curve upward—good God, his face ached from the effort—and suffered the toady posturing of husband-stalking mamas and their bevy of pretty, wide-eyed offspring eager to snare an unattached duke.

Noteworthy, considering not so very long ago, Jules scarcely merited a passing glance from the same *tonnish* females now so keen to garner his favor. His perpetual scowl might be attributed to their disinterest.

Tonight's worst offender?

Theo's irksome sister-in-law, Mrs. Dament.

The tenacious woman had neatly maneuvered her admittedly stunning elder daughter, Adelinda, to his side multiple times, and only the Daments' intimate connection to Theo had kept him from turning on his heel at the fourth instance instead of graciously fetching mother and daughter the ratafia they'd requested.

A rather uncouth mental dialogue accompanied his march to the refreshment table, nonetheless.

Where was the other daughter—the sweet-tempered one, Miss Jemmah Dament?

Twiddling her thumbs at home again? Poor, kind, neglected sparrow of a thing.

As children and adolescents, he and Jemmah had been comfortable friends, made so by their similar distressing circumstances. But as must be, they'd grown up, and destiny or fate had placed multiple obstacles between them. He trotted off to university—shortly afterward becoming betrothed to Annabel—and for a time, the Daments simply faded from his and society's notice.

Oh, on occasion, Jules had spied Jemmah in passing. But she'd ducked her shiny honey-colored head and averted her acute sky-blue gaze. Almost as if she was discomfited or he'd somehow offended her.

Yet, after wracking his brain, he couldn't deduce what his transgression might've been.

At those times, recalling their prior relaxed companionship, his ability to talk to her about anything—or simply remain in compatible silence, an odd twinge pinged behind his ribs. Not regret exactly, though he hardly knew what to label the disquieting sensation.

Quite simply, he missed her friendship and company.

Since Theo's brother, Jasper, died two years ago, Jules had seen little of the Daments.

According to tattle, their circumstances had been drastically reduced. But even so, Jemmah's absence at routs, soirees, and other *ton* gatherings, which her mother and sister often attended, raised questions and eyebrows.

At least arced Jules's brow and stirred his curiosity.

If Jemmah were present at more assemblies, perhaps he'd make more of an effort to put in an appearance.

Or perhaps not.

He held no illusions about his lack of social acumen. A deficiency he had no desire to remedy.

Ever.

A trio of ladies rounded the corner, and he dove into a niche beside a vase-topped table.

The Chinese urn tottered, and he clamped the blue and white china between both hands, lest it crash to the floor and expose him.

He needn't have worried.

So engrossed in their titillating gossip about whether Lord Bacon wore stays, none of the women was the least aware of his presence as they sailed past.

Mentally patting himself on the back for his exceptionally civil behavior for the past pair of vexing hours, Jules permitted a self-satisfied smirk and stepped back into the corridor. He nearly collided with Theo's aged mother-in-law, the Dowager Viscountess Lockhart, come to town for her daughter-in-law's birthday.

A tuft of glossy black ostrich feathers adorned her hair, the tallest of which poked him in the eye.

Hell's bells.

"I beg your pardon, my lady."

Eye watering, Jules grasped her frail elbow, steadying her before she toppled over, such did she sway.

She chuckled, a soft crackle like delicate old lace, and squinted up at him, her faded eyes, the color of weak tea, snapping with mirth.

"Bolting, are you, Dandridge?"

Saucy, astute old bird.

Nothing much escaped Faye, Dowager Viscountess Lockhart's notice.

"I prefer to call it making a prudently-timed departure."

Which he'd be forced to abandon in order to assist the tottering dame back to her preferred throne—*er, seat*—in the ballroom.

He'd congratulated himself prematurely, blast it.

"Allow me to escort you, Lady Lockhart."

He daren't imply she needed his help, or she'd turn her tart tongue, and likely her china-handled cane, on him too.

"Flim flam. Don't be an utter nincompoop. You mightn't have another opportunity to flee. Go on with you now." She pointed her cane down the deserted passageway. "I'll contrive some drivel to explain your disappearance."

"I don't need a justification."

Beyond that he was bored to his polished shoes, he'd rather munch fresh horse manure than carry on anymore inane conversation, and crowds made him nervous as hell.

Always had.

Hence his infrequent appearances.

Pure naughtiness sparked in the dowager's eyes as she put a bony finger to her chin as if seriously contemplating what shocking tale she'd spin.

"What excuse should I use? Perhaps an abduction? *Hmph.* Not believable." She shook her head, and the ostrich feather danced in agreement. "An elopement? No, no. Won't do at all. Too dull and predictable."

She jutted her finger skyward, nearly poking his other eye.

"Ah, ha! I have just the thing. A scandalous assignation. With a secret love. Oh, yes, that'll do nicely."

A decidedly teasing smile tipped her thin lips.

Jules vacillated.

She was right, of course.

If he didn't make good his escape now, he mightn't be able to for hours. Still, his conscience chafed at leaving her to hobble her way to the ballroom alone. For all of his darkling countenance and brusque comportment, he was still a gentleman first.

Lady Lockhart extracted her arm, and then poked him in the bicep with her pointy nail.

Hard.

"Go, I said, young scamp." Only she would dare call a duke a scamp. "I assure you, I'm not so infirm that I'm incapable of walking the distance without tumbling onto my face."

Maybe not her face, but what about the rest of her feeble form?

Her crepey features softened, and the beauty she'd once been peeked through the ravages of age. "It was good of you to come, Dandridge, and I know it meant the world to Theodora." The imp returned full on, and she bumped her cane's tip against his instep. "Now git yourself gone."

"Thank you, my lady." Jules lifted her hand, and after kissing the back, waited a few moments to assess her progress. If she struggled the least, he'd lay aside his plans and disregard her command.

A few feet along the corridor, she paused, half-turning toward him. Starchy silvery eyebrow raised, she mouthed, "Move your arse."

With a sharp salute, Jules complied and continued to reflect on his most successful venture into society in a great while.

Somehow—multiple glasses of superb champagne might be attributed to helping—he'd even managed to converse—perhaps a little less courteously than the majority of attendees, but certainly not as tersely as he was generally wont to—with the young bucks, dandies, and past-their-prime decrepitudes whose trivial interests consisted of horseflesh, the preposterous wagers on Whites's books, and the next bit of feminine fluff they might sample.

Or, in the older, less virile coves' cases, the unfortunate woman subjected to their lusty ogling since the aged chaps' softer parts were wont to stay that way.

Only the welcome presence of the two men whom Jules might truly call 'friend,' Maxwell, Duke of Pennington, and Victor, Duke of Sutcliffe, had made the evening, if not pleasant, undoubtedly more interesting with their barbed humor and ongoing litany of drolly murmured sarcastic observations.

Compared to that acerbic pair, Jules, renowned for his acute intellect and grave mien, seemed quite the epitome of frivolous jollity.

But, by spitting camels, when his uncles, Leopold and Darius—from whom his middle names had been derived—had cornered him in the card room and demanded to know for the third time this month when he intended to do his *ducal duty*?

Marry and produce an heir...

Damn their interfering eyes!

Jules's rigidly controlled temper had slipped loose of its moorings, and he'd told them—ever so calmly, but also enunciating each syllable most carefully lest the mulish, bacon-brained pair misunderstand a single word—"go bugger yourselves and leave me be!"

He'd been officially betrothed once and nearly so a second time in his five-and-twenty years. Never again.

Never?

Fine, maybe someday. But not to a Society damsel and not for many, *many* years or before *he* had concluded the parson's mousetrap was both necessary and convenient. Should that fateful day never come to pass, well, best his Charmont uncles get busy producing male heirs themselves instead of dallying with actresses and opera singers.

Marching along the corridor, Jules tipped his mouth into his first genuine smile since alighting from his coach, other than the one he'd bestowed upon Theo when he arrived. Since his affianced, Annabel's death five years ago, Theo was one of the few people he felt any degree of true affection for.

Must be a character flaw—an inadequacy in his emotional reservoir, this inability to feel earnest emotions. In any event, he wanted to return home early enough to bid his niece and ward, Lady Sabrina Remington, good-night as he'd promised.

They'd celebrated her tenth birthday earlier today, too.

Jules truly enjoyed Sabrina's company.

Possibly because he could simply be himself, not Duke of

Dandridge, or a peer, or a member of the House of Lords. Not quarry for eager-to-wed chits, a tolerant listener of friends' ribald jokes, or a wise counselor to troubled acquaintances. Not even a dutiful nephew, a less-favored son, a preferred godson, or at one time, a loving brother and wholly-devoted intended.

Anticipation of fleeing the crowd lengthening his strides, he cut a swift glance behind him, and his gut plummeted, arse over chin, to his shiny shoes.

Blisters and ballocks.

Who the devil invited *her*?

2

Jules's brusque sound of annoyance echoed in the corridor.

Miss Phryne Milbourne, the only other woman he'd considered marrying—for all of a few brief hours—had espied him. Given the determined look on her lovely face, she again intended to broach his crying off.

London's perpetually foggy and sooty skies would rain jewels and flowers before he ever took up with the likes of that vixen again, no matter how beautiful, blue-blooded, or perfectly suited to the position of duchess others—namely, Mother and The Uncles—believed she might be.

Within mere hours of his uncles and his mother taking it upon themselves to broach a *possible* match between Miss Milbourne and him, which she'd bandied about with the recklessness of a farmwife tossing chickens table scraps—Jules had observed her true character, quite by chance.

And thank God, he had, or she might well be his duchess by now.

The notion curdled the two servings of *crème brûlée* he'd indulged in at luncheon.

Truth to tell, he would've been hard put to decide which rankled more: Miss Milbourne's callousness or her promiscuousness. Or perhaps, her ceaseless, nigh on to obsessive, pursuit of him was what abraded worse than boots three sizes too small. In any event, he had neither the time nor the inclination to discuss the issue with her tonight.

Or ever, for that matter.

Familiar with the manor's architecture, he ducked into the nearest doorway and sidled into an elegant, unlit parlor situated between dual sets of ornate double doors. Doors which provided him with another, less obvious, route from the house through an adjacent passageway.

Unaccustomed to the room's darkness, he blindly groped until he found what he searched for. With the merest scrape of metal, he turned the key, and chuckled softly, if perhaps a might wickedly, to himself.

He truly was a social misfit, and that he rather liked the peculiarity made him more so.

Staid, abrupt, off-putting, somber, reticent, taciturn, reserved...

He knew full well what others thought of him and, for the most part, their descriptions were accurate. What they didn't know was why.

Jemmah Dament knew.

As timid, overlooked children, they'd sought refuge in each other's company and whispered their secret fears to one another, too.

Peculiar that twice in a matter of minutes Jemmah had popped to mind. Must've been encountering her bothersome family that caused the dual intrusions.

Feminine footsteps accompanied by a heavier, uneven tread echoed on the corridor's Arenberg parquet floor as Miss Milbourne neared.

"I'm positive I saw Dandridge a moment ago, Papa." A hint of petulance flavored her words. "He's still avoiding me, though I've repeatedly explained that he misunderstood what he thought he saw and heard."

The devil I did.

Keaton's arm had been elbow deep inside her bodice, and his tongue halfway that distance down her throat too.

Far worse, in Jules estimation, was Miss Milbourne's treatment of sweet, crippled Sabrina. Whorish behavior was repugnant, but cruelty to an unfortunate, doubly so.

Intolerable and unforgivable in his view.

There and then, he'd told Miss Milbourne as much and that she'd best cease entertaining notions of a match between them. His ire raised, he may have suggested he'd welcome starved chartreuse tigers at the dining table with more enthusiasm than continuing their acquaintance.

"Why, the stubborn man dared return the perfumed note I sent him last week, Papa. Unopened too, the obstinate wretch," she fumed, her footsteps taking on a distinct stomping rhythm. "How many times must I apologize before Dandridge forgives me?"

"Tut, m'dear. I wish you'd let me sue the knave for breaking the betrothal," Milbourne wheezed, great gasping rattles that threatened to dislodge the artwork displayed above the passage's mahogany raised panel wainscoting.

If wishes were food, beggars would eat cake, old chap.

There'd have to have been an actual proposal and a formal

agreement, including a signed contract.

Not a mere wishful suggestion in passing, which Miss Milbourne latched onto like a barnacle to rock.

She'd led her father on a deuced merry chase the past two years, setting her cap for, and then tossing aside, one peer after another, each ranking higher and with fuller coffers than the last. Served him and the late Mrs. Milbourne right for naming her Phryne after a Greek courtesan.

Dotty business, that.

Whatever could they have been thinking?

Breathing heavily, Milbourne grumbled from what must be directly outside the door, "Would do the arrogant whelp good to be taken down a peg. He'd be lucky to have you, my pet, he would. I can pull some strings—"

"No, Papa! That would only anger Dandridge further. He must be made to see reason. I'm confident he'll come 'round in time. His uncles and her grace are easily enough manipulated, and they want me at his side. I shan't be denied my duchy because of a prudish misunderstanding. I'd remain faithful to him until an heir was produced. Perhaps even a spare. Surely, he must know that."

How very obliging.

The door handle rattled, kicking Jules's pulse into a gallop.

An unladylike snort carried through the walnut.

"Locked. I suppose Lady Lockhart, the pretentious tabby, is afraid the guests will make off with her vulgar oddities."

Jules drew in a prolonged, grateful breath. By discovering Miss Milbourne's vices early on, he'd been spared a lifetime of misery.

"Papa, did you see her expression when we entered with the Wakefields tonight? Looked like she'd swallowed newly-sharpened needles." Miss Milbourne's scornful laugh faded as she and her father explored the rest of the passageway.

Jules remained still, listening as doors swished open and clicked close as they snooped in room after room in their search for him.

And here he cowered, like an errant child, his temper growing blacker by the minute. However, an ugly confrontation was the last thing Theo warranted at her birthday celebration. Hence her decision, no doubt, not to send the Milbournes packing when they showed up uninvited on the Wakefields' coat strings.

Zounds, Jules loathed manipulators.

A stunning beauty—a diamond of the first water according to the *haut ton*'s standards— Miss Milbourne was intelligent, accomplished, versed in politics, a gracious hostess, and popular among the social set. In short, she possessed all the trivial qualifications Mother and The Uncles deemed necessary for the next Duchess of Dandridge, and of as much value and importance to Jules as a hangnail or pernicious boil on his bum.

Naturally, his mother would approve of Miss Milbourne.

She was cut from the same calculating, mercenary fabric, after all.

Plato had it right, by Jove. Like does indeed attract like.

Jules didn't much care one way or the other who the next duchess was. Or, for that matter, if there was another while he lived. Young and smitten, he'd dared gamble on love once, and when Annabel—always petite and frail—died from influenza a mere month prior to their wedding, his ability to love must've been buried with her. For no sentiment stronger than warm regard or affection ever stirred him again.

Except for where Sabrina was concerned.

And long, long ago, Miss Jemmah Dament too.

Contemplating a match with Miss Milbourne had nothing to do with affection and everything to do with benefiting the dukedom. More fool he for not having listened to Theo's blunt warnings against such a hair-brained notion.

Jules was capable of finding a diamond of his own choosing, thank you very much.

One whose multi-faceted inner beauty glowed far more brilliantly than Miss Milbourne's exquisite outward countenance.

Shaking his head, he rubbed his brow against the slight twinge tapping there and glanced around the lavish parlor. The undrawn draperies permitted moonlight to stream through the emerald-and-gold brocade-festooned windows and cast a silvery, iridescent glow over the gilded, carved furnishings. Muted music filtered into the peaceful chamber even as the Sevres mantel clock lazily chimed ten o'clock.

He'd best hurry or Sabrina would think he'd decided to remain at the ball longer and she'd retire for the night. She'd only been permitted to stay up so late because she'd obediently taken an afternoon nap. To disappoint the child after she'd already endured so much tragedy in her short life was unthinkable.

Jules didn't make promises he didn't mean to keep.

Should he unlock the door before taking his leave through the other pair?

No. Theo's servants would see to the matter.

She really ought to consider securing unused rooms when she entertained, especially with the likes of Miss Milbourne prowling about.

He'd mention the subject when next he saw his godmother.

Wending between the numerous pieces of furniture in the moon's half-light, he smacked his shin into the settee. Pain spiraling from calf to knee, he softly cursed and bent to rub the offended limb.

"Dammit. Must Theo constantly rearrange the furniture? Two hell-fired times since December."

A startled gasp, swiftly stifled, had him jerking upright, whacking his shoulder this time.

Bloody hell.

"Who's there?"

Silence met his inquiry. Had he stumbled upon a lover's tryst? A thief? A wayward servant or inquisitive guest? He fingered his throbbing shoulder, pressing the pads against the pain.

"Reveal yourself at once."

Silence.

Running his fingers along the settee's back, he located the pedestal sofa table.

Other than shallow breathing, the culprit kept quiet.

Squinting, he made out a light-colored form reclining on the dark blue-and-silver striped cushions. A woman, and by all the stampeding elephants in Africa, he bet his silver buttons, and the two new bruises he surely sported, he knew who lay there.

Like a slowly uncoiling rope, the tension eased from his taut muscles.

He fumbled a bit until he found the engraved silver tinderbox beside the candelabra, and moments later, a wax taper flared to life.

"Hello, Your Grace."

Miss Jemmah Dament, her rosy lips curved upward in a small closed-mouth smile and her face still sleep-softened, blinked groggily.

Hello, indeed. Adorable, sleepy kitten.

He lifted the candle higher, taking in her svelte figure, her delectable backside pressed to the sofa, one hand still cradling her cheek. Surprise and carnal awareness, pleasant and unexpected, tingled a rippling path from one shoulder to the other.

The plain, awkward little mudlark had transformed into a graceful dove. One who rivaled—no, by far exceeded—her sister's allure.

"Well, hello to you as well, Miss Jemmah Dament."

As if it were the most natural thing in the world to be found napping during a ball at her aunt's house, and then awoken by a man crashing into her makeshift bed, she sat up and brushed a wayward curl off her forehead.

Jules set about lighting the other three tapers. Their glow revealed striking pale blue, wide-set almond-shaped eyes, fringed by dark lashes, and tousled hair somewhere between rich caramel and light toffee.

He hadn't seen her up close in...?

How long had it been?

Cocking his head, he searched his mind's archives.

At least since last summer.

Yes, that afternoon in August, in Hyde Park, when she'd walked past wearing a travesty of a walking ensemble. A sort of greenish-gray color somewhere between rotten fish and bread mold.

Yawning delicately behind one slender hand, she smoothed her plain ivory gown with the other.

Except for a yellowish-tan sash below her breasts, the garment lacked any adornment. The ribbon didn't suit her coloring, and although he couldn't claim to be an expert on feminine apparel, the frock seemed rather lackluster for such a grand affair.

Another of Adelinda's cast-offs?

Jules canted his head as he closed the tinder box.

He couldn't recall ever seeing Jemmah wearing anything new. And yet her sister always appeared perfumed and bejeweled, attired in the first stare of fashion. Such blatant favoritism wasn't uncommon amongst the elite, nor did it shock nearly as much as appall.

He, too, was his mother's least-favorite child, but by all the candle nubs in England, *if* he ever had children—in the very distant future—they'd not know the kind of rejection and pain he and Jemmah had experienced because of their parents' partiality.

He'd love and treat his offspring equally as any good and decent parent should.

"Ah, Your Grace, you're surprised to see me, I think."

Rather than coy or seductive, her smile and winged brows indicated genuine amusement. Her vivacious eyes sparkling with secret knowledge, she ran her gaze over him, the full radiance of her smile causing something prickly to take root in his chest and purr through his veins.

"I am, but pleasantly so. Your appearance at these farces is even rarer than my own, Miss Dament."

His by choice, but what about Jemmah?

Did she want to attend and was prohibited?

"I'm here at Aunt Theo's insistence. Mama couldn't put her off this time. But I'm afraid even I have too much pride to be seen in a morning gown from three seasons ago. Besides," she lifted a milky-white, sloping shoulder as she fiddled with a pillow's tassel, "I don't know how to dance, and this is a ball after all."

No self-pity or resentment weighted her words, just honest revelation.

Jules had forgotten how refreshingly forthright she was.

Still, how had such an important part of her education been overlooked?

Did Theo know?

Probably, since she'd mentioned trying to intervene on Jemmah's behalf many times. Much to Theo's dismay, Mrs. Dament refused all offers benefiting Jemmah, but when it came to Adelinda...

That was an entirely different matter. For that greedy puss, nothing was spared.

Pity for Jemmah engulfed him.

She unfolded—for there was no other way to describe the smooth, catlike elegance as she angled to her feet—and after sliding her obviously-mended stockinged toes into plain black slippers a trifle too large, and gathering her gloves, dipped a nimble curtsy.

"Please excuse me, Your Grace."

"Wait, Jem." Too forward, that. Addressing her by her given name, but she'd been Jem and he Jules for over a decade before their paths separated.

She hesitated, her pretty blue-eyed gaze probing his.

A swift glance to the mantel confirmed he might spare a minute or two more. He'd told Sabrina he'd be home no later than half past ten. Odd that he should be this happy to see Jemmah. But they were old friends, and as such, once together again, it was as if they'd never been apart.

After all, he'd known her since, as a pixyish imp with eyes too big for her thin face and wild straw-colored hair, she'd tried to hide beneath the same table as he when Lord Lockhart, his godfather had passed.

They'd seen each other intermittently over the years, but seldom traveled in the same social circles. Her father had died—heart attack in his mistress's arms if the dark rumors were true—a year before Jules's elder brother and sister-in-law were killed in the carriage accident that disabled Sabrina.

Jules and Jemmah had much in common.

Both had known grief and loss, endured the disdain of an uncaring mother, and lived in the shadow of an adored older child. But discovering her sequestered here, self-conscious about her unfashionable gown with salty dried tear trails upon her creamy cheeks, roused the same protective instincts he had for his niece.

What you feel for Jemmah isn't the least paternal.

Sensation and sentiments long since dormant—so long in fact, he thought they'd died— slowly, and ever so cautiously raised their bowed heads to peek about.

Jules stepped 'round to the settee's front and offered her a sympathetic smile.

She must've noticed his speculation, because she turned away and swiped at her face, erasing the evidence of her unhappiness.

"I must go. I'll be missed."

No. She wouldn't.

Other than, perhaps, by Theo.

He doubted her mother or sister had given her a single thought the entire evening. Probably forgot she'd accompanied them altogether, so insignificant was she to them.

That weird spasm behind his breastbone pinged again.

Jemmah's pale azure gaze—he couldn't quite find anything to compare the delicate, yet arresting shade to—caught his, and she captured her plump lower lip between her teeth before shifting her focus to the frilly settee pillows.

Her shoulders lifted as she pulled in a substantial breath and notched her pert chin higher, while something akin to defiance emphasized the delicate angles and curves of her face. The earlier light he'd glimpsed in her eyes faded to a resigned melancholy. When she spoke, a kind of weary, beleaguered desperation shadowed her gentle words.

"No one, Your Grace, appreciates being the object of another's pity."

3

At Jemmah's frank pronouncement, Dandridge's deep set amber eyes widened a fraction, immediately followed by a contemplative glint. He probably wasn't accustomed to such candor, but in her limited experience, artifice seldom ended well.

"Say what you mean and mean what you say," Papa had always advocated. "Speak honestly, my precious Jem. But temper your words with kindness and gentleness so they're diamonds, not toads. One is welcomed, even appreciated. The other detested and often feared."

Lord, how she missed her father's jovial smile, perpetually rumpled hair and clothing, and his tender kisses upon her crown. Missed the fairytales he used to tell her as she sat upon his knee. "Toads and Diamonds," "The Sleeping Beauty," "Little Red Riding Hood," and so many more.

Tears stung behind her eyelids, but she resolutely blinked them away. She must continue to be strong. But at times—times like these when humiliation and shame sluiced her—it was so very hard. And she was so very weary and discouraged despite the cheerful mien she presented.

A whisper of a sigh escaped her.

Pshaw.

Enough wallowing in self-pity. Imprudent and pointless.

Perhaps recalling Papa's counsel hadn't been the best example for bolstering her courage, especially since he had died in his lover's bed.

Most mothers would've kept that tawdry detail from their children, but Mama used the ugliness to regularly and viciously besmirch Papa's character to her daughters.

Jemmah in particular.

One didn't have to think overly long and hard to understand why he'd sought another woman's comfort. Not that Jemmah excused his infidelity, but neither could she deny he'd been miserable for most of her life.

So had she, and she longed for the day she might finally, somehow, escape and know joy and peace, not constant ridicule and criticism.

Her emotions once more under control, she returned Dandridge's acute assessment, determined to show her lack of cowardice, and that she wasn't a weak, pathetic creature deserving of his—or anyone else's—pity or sympathy.

Well? Have you nothing to say?

The laurel wreath diamond cravat pin gracing his snowy waterfall of a neckcloth cheekily winked at her, and as if he'd heard her silent challenge, and with an unidentifiable gleam crinkling his eyes' outer corners, the edges of his strong mouth twitched upward.

She'd risked voicing her innermost thoughts, and the handsome knave laughed at her?

Chagrin trotted a spiky path from her chest to her hairline, no doubt leaving a ribbon of ugly, ruddy blotches. No soft flare of flattering, pinkish color accompanied her blushes, but rather ugly splotches mottled her skin, very much resembling an angry sunburn or severe rash.

Papa had attributed the tendency to their Irish heritage.

If that were true, then why didn't Adelinda with her coppery hair suffer the affliction?

Jemmah knew full well why.

Because in that, as was true of everything else, Adelinda took after Mama.

Jemmah's looking glass revealed daily, and objectively, that her light coloring and unremarkable features paled in comparison to her mother's and sister's flamboyant looks with their rich ginger hair and dark exotic eyes. Neither did she possess their high-strung temperaments nor delicate constitutions. All of which Mama contended a lady must possess in order to become a *haut ton* favorite.

As if Jemmah cared a whit about any of that fiddle-faddle.

People mattered far more than titles or positions.

Her rather ordinary appearance, robust health, and kindly nature were more suited for docile cattle or sheep, and as such, frequently served to vex and disappoint her mother.

Indeed, how many times since Papa's death had Mama admonished—her voice arctic and condemning—"You look and behave just like your father, Jemmah. I can scarcely bear to look upon you.

You'll disgrace us one day, too. Just you wait and see."

I shall not.

If anyone brought more shame on the Daments, it would be Adelinda. She'd become so bold in her clandestine rendezvous, someone was sure to come upon her and one of her numerous unsuitable beaux.

Naturally, Mama knew nothing of Adelinda's fast behavior.

After attempting to broach the subject once, Mama had accused Jemmah of envying her sister. She then confined Jemmah to her room with only gruel and broth for two days, and thereafter Jemmah resolved to keep her own counsel on the matter.

Adelinda could suffer the consequences of her rash choices, which likely as rain in England would bring shame and censure down upon all their heads.

Jemmah eyed Jules from beneath her lashes. A partial smile yet curved his mouth.

She knew full well how pathetic she appeared to others. Yet to see fellow feeling engraved on the noble planes of his face and glistening in his warm treacle eyes... Well, by cold, lumpy porridge, the injustice of it burgeoned up her tight throat, choking her.

And her dratted tongue—blast the ignoble organ—saw fit to ignore even a scrap of common sense. Her mouth had opened of its own accord, spewing forth her innermost thoughts. Thoughts she took great care to keep buried in the remotest niches of her mind, even from herself at times.

Still, pity was the last thing Jemmah wanted from anyone, most especially from The Sixth Duke of Dandridge, and for him to also find her an object of amusement, pricked hot and ferocious.

Wealthy and powerful, much sought after, and too absurdly handsome for his own good—*hers too*—made her one-time friend's mockery all the more unbearable.

He slanted his head, the paler hues ribboning his rich honey-blond hair catching the candles' light. Cupping his nape, his gaze traveled from her rumpled hair to her too-large slippers, and she wanted to melt into the floor or crawl beneath the side table and hide as she'd done so often as a child.

"You needn't stare. I'm perfectly aware of my deficiencies, Your Grace."

Hadn't they been drilled into her almost daily for years?

When he didn't answer but continued to regard her with that

amused, curious, yet confused expression, her seldom-riled temper chose to snap to attention.

"You, Your Grace, are being rude."

Brow knitted into three distinct furrows, he finally veered his astute gaze away to contemplate the moon through the window and his familiar reserved bearing descended.

The devil take her loose tongue. She'd offended him.

Why, for all the tea in England, had she'd just insulted a duke?

And not just any duke, but Aunt Theo's beloved godson, a man more of a son to her than he was to his own mother. Her aunt, the only person in Jemmah's memory, besides Papa, to show her any compassion or kindness, would not be pleased.

Don't forget how kind Jules—his grace—used to be to you, as well.

Aunt Theo had always admired Jemmah's pleasant disposition, and Jemmah would've been hard pressed to explain why he'd riled her to the point of insolence.

It must've been humiliation-induced anger brought about because he'd felt sorry for her.

Dandridge, the devilishly handsome, wonderful smelling, garbed in the first crack of fashion peer, regarded her with those darkened, hooded eyes and his lips tweaked downward as if she were a pathetic charity case or a poorhouse worker.

He, for whom she'd harbored a secret *tendre* since the first time he'd joined her beneath a lace-edged tablecloth's security almost fifteen years ago, when she'd been a five-year-old imp, and he a brawny, mature lad of ten.

More fool she. But her dreams, no matter how trivial or silly or unattainable, were hers to entertain and treasure, and no one could take them from her. If one didn't have dreams, something to look forward to, then life's everyday tedium and drudgery, Mama's harsh criticisms and fault-finding, might steal all vestiges of her joy.

Jemmah mightn't have much in the way of appearances or possessions, but she had a remnant of pride and a handful of wonderful memories. Still, the realization that Jules pitied her...

Well, her very soul panged with indignation as well as mortification—each as unwelcome as vermin droppings in seedcake or oozing pox sores upon her face.

At least he'd been forced to acknowledge her this time, unlike the half dozen other encounters over the past two years.

In each of those instances, he'd looked straight through her as if she didn't exist or was something as inconspicuous as tree bark, a pewter cloud in an armor-gray sky, or a fingerprint smudged upon a window.

Present, but invisible to all.

An accurate depiction of Jemmah's life, truth to tell.

That rather smarted too, for whenever he entered a room, passed her on the street, trotted his magnificent ebony mount down Rotten Row, she'd noticed him straightaway—discretely observing him through lowered lashes, her countenance carefully bland.

She knew her place. Knew she was beneath his touch.

But to gaze upon his somber handsomeness, and recall how infinitely thoughtful he'd always been to her.

What possible harm was there in that?

They were much like a diamond and a lump of coal.

He the former; she the latter.

The gem's polished radiance and brilliance, its innate and intricate beauty, drew attention without trying, while the grubby fuel was only noticed and needed if a room or stove grew cool.

Speaking of cool, the parlor had grown quite nippy, and Jemmah rubbed her bare arms.

How long had she slept anyway?

She examined the mantel clock.

Only two hours?

Surely it has been longer.

She'd needed the rest after staying awake until a quarter past four this morning finishing Adelinda's gown. But now, she truly must go. Even if Mama and Adelinda hadn't wondered where she'd got off to, Aunt Theo might.

"Please forgive my churlishness, Your Grace. I assure you, it's not typical. I didn't sleep much last night, and I find these sorts of assemblies trying, even under the best of circumstances."

Dressed in castoffs, unqualified to dance with any degree of skill, and aware she sorely lacked her sister's grace and beauty, social events proved excruciating.

Dandridge didn't respond, and to cover the awkward silence, Jemmah bent and tidied the pillows she'd mussed. Satisfied the room appeared as it had when she entered, and that she'd done whatever she could to apologize for her peevish behavior, she swiveled toward the door.

Eager to escape, she hoped to find another cranny to lurk in until Mama deemed it time to depart.

Likely hours from now.

"Would you like to dance?"

His soft request halted her mid-step, and jaw slack, she flung an are-you-serious-or-mocking-me-glance over her shoulder.

He extended his hand, the movement pulling his black tailcoat taut over enticingly broad shoulders and a rounded bicep. The gold signet ring upon his little finger gleamed, as did the jeweled lion's head cuff link at his wrist.

His unbearably tender smile caused Jemmah's blood to sidle through her veins rather like honey-sweetened tea—rich and warm and strong—even as another sensation embedded behind her ribs, slowly burrowing its way deeper—and dangerously deeper, yet.

Dandridge was dangerous for her peace of mind.

Dangerous for the life she'd resigned herself to.

Staring hard into his eyes' unfathomable depths, Jemmah tried to gauge his sincerity and motives.

"One dance, Miss Jemmah. I've never had the honor of partnering you."

More pity directed her way, or a genuinely kind, if somewhat irregular gift?

She might be able to manage an English country dance with reasonable finesse, but a cotillion or quadrille?

Utterly impossible.

"Your Grace, I told you, I don't know how."

More shame scorched her cheeks—probably red as crushed cherries—but she wouldn't break eye contact.

There hadn't been funds for both her and Adelinda to learn. Though Jemmah had begged to be permitted to watch her sister's instruction, Mama refused her even that. She'd taken to peeking through the drawing room window until her mother caught her one day.

Ever after, Jemmah had been confined to her room during dance lessons, rather like in the tale of Cendrillon, except in her situation, there was no evil stepmother.

No fairy godmother to rescue her or a prince to sweep her away, either.

Merely Jemmah's own haughty and proud mother, who hadn't a qualm about voicing her partiality for Adelinda. And why shouldn't she prefer the daughter who was practically a mirror image of herself, rather than the offspring resembling her detested, unfaithful spouse?

"I'll teach you." Dandridge stepped forward and lightly grasped her hand.

She'd forgotten to don her gloves, but he didn't appear to notice her work-worn fingers, and Jemmah refused to be self-conscious about them. Not now anyway. Later she might examine the dry, reddened skin, the roughened cuticles, the overly-short nails, and her face would flame with renewed chagrin.

"I really shouldn't. I'll tromp your toes."

But she would dance, for being in Jules's arms, even for a few stolen minutes was worth Mama's assured disapproval and Adelinda's certain jealousy, as well as the resulting unpleasantness should they find out. The experience, committed to memory, was even worth the risk of scandal.

Never mind all that.

Jemmah melted into his embrace and placed her hand upon his firm shoulder, the muscles rippling beneath her fingertips.

His smile, broad and delighted, exposed straight, white teeth and ignited every plane of his rugged face with joy. Rarely had she seen him smile from sincere happiness, and the transformation in his visage, temporarily robbed Jemmah of her breath.

She managed to restart her lungs and ask, "What will we dance to?"

"Listen." Jules tilted his tawny head, his hair the color of ripe wheat at sunset.

Lilting strains from the string quartet floated from the ballroom. The glorious music, enchanting and irresistible, almost fairy-tale like, nudged her few remaining, crumbling barriers aside.

"It's a waltz." Jules planted a broad palm on her spine—*Oh, crumb cakes, what utter deliciousness*—and cupped her hand in his other.

"Just follow my lead, Jem."

A waltz was most risqué and hardly acceptable in proper circles, which was probably why Aunt Theo permitted the dance. She, too, liked to push acceptability's limitations, one of the things Jemmah adored about her audacious aunt.

Jules proved an adroit partner, and in a few moments, Jemmah had caught on to the simple steps and the one-two-three rhythm.

Much too aware of the broad chest mere inches from her face, she rummaged around for something to say. "I had the privilege of meeting your charming niece, Lady Sabrina, in Green Park last month."

"Out for her daily constitutional with her governess, no doubt. Sabrina likes to sketch the landscape. She's asked to take lessons." His palm pressed into Jemmah's spine, sending her nerves jockeying. "I've been meaning to ask Theo if she could recommend someone."

"I'm fond of drawing myself. Papa taught me."

His thumb brushed the swell of her ribs, and a shiver—at least that was what she thought the melting, buttery feeling was—capered across her hips. Mentally schooling herself, she summoned her composure.

"I'm not gifted by any means, but I am fairly accomplished and would be happy to teach her what I know."

"I think she'd like that."

Jules edged Jemmah closer until his thighs brushed hers, and his hand upon her back induced the most tantalizing frisson down her spinal column—tiny tremors which sent delicious, warm sparks that slowly swirled outward, until her entire body came alive with the tingling sensation.

"I've missed our friendship—missed you—Jemmah. I didn't realize how very much until just now."

"I've missed you too."

And she had.

Unbearably.

Particularly since Papa died and she hadn't anyone to act as a buffer between Mama's harshness and Adelinda's cruelty.

Small wonder Jemmah hadn't become bitter or hadn't come to hate and resent her mother and sister. More than anything, their conduct saddened her.

How could they treat anyone, but most especially a family member, so spitefully?

Jules's scent, crisp, slightly musky, perhaps even a suggestion of cloves, surrounded her.

She stood so near him, that even in the subdued candlelight, she could see the faintest shadow of his whiskers along his jaw, and when her gaze met his, slightly bewildered, simmering topaz eyes regarded her.

His regard sank to her mouth, and the peculiar stirrings of earlier burgeoned once more.

Only stronger, more insistent.

The faint music faded into the background as he dipped his head lower, then lower still, until his mouth—oh, his lovely, warm, soft, yet firm mouth—brushed hers.

In that instant, Jemmah was lost, utterly, irreversibly, and unreservedly.

She rose up on her toes, entwined her arms around Jules's sturdy neck, and kissed him with the abandon of a desperate woman seizing her one and only chance to kiss the man she'd loved for years.

He groaned deep in his throat, the sound primitive and animalistic, and all the more arousing because of its baseness. Using his tongue, he trailed the seam between her lips, teasing her mouth open, and the headiest of sensations spiraled through every fiber of her being.

Their tongues danced together, mating in an age-old cadence, while thousands of moonbeams ignited behind her eyes.

"Jemmah, my sweet, precious Jem," he murmured against her neck, his voice thick and husky, the sound sending delicious tremors to her toes. "Tell me I may call upon you, tomorrow."

"Dandridge!"

Insistent scratching on the locked door had Jemmah springing away from him.

"I know you're in there," a feminine voice all but hissed. "We must talk. This is no way to treat the next Duchess of Dandridge."

4

The next duchess?

But how could that be?

Jemmah touched her fingertips to her throbbing mouth and backed away from Jules.

She could still taste him on her tongue, feel his powerful arms encircling her, smell his manly scent yet in her nostrils. How glorious his kisses had been. And more fool she, for having allowed it, for now she craved more.

Intuition told her, she'd never, ever have enough of him.

"Dandridge. Answer me."

Scrape. Scrape.

"I saw that Dament chit batting her stubby eyelashes at you. The duchess and your uncles won't approve. I don't know how the Daments are even permitted in respectable circles. They smell of the shop."

The scorching glower Jules hurled at the voice behind the door would've ignited wet wood.

"Insufferable, long-winded baggage," he muttered, hardly above a whisper.

Sacred sausages, Mama would fly into a dudgeon if she ever learned Jules had kissed Jemmah. And she'd kissed him back. And it had been the most wonderful of things. And she'd do it again without compunction or remorse.

And by horse feathers, she *would* let him call on her.

She would.

Well, she'd suggest he meet her here for tea. She daren't risk no more.

But, if he was truly to marry Miss Milbourne...

No, something smelled to high heaven, even if she didn't know exactly what it was, like the time a creature of some sort had died in her attic bedchamber wall.

No man who'd shown such honor, even as a reserved child, grew into an unscrupulous lout. Jules was loyal to his impressive backbone.

She'd bet on it. *If* she had anything of worth to wager.

The least she could do was to hear his explanation, especially since Aunt Theo had happily shared—actually clapped her hands and tittered, and Aunt Theo did not titter—that he had refused the match with Miss Milbourne, despite the furor it caused within his family.

Truly, his availability was the only reason Mama agreed to come tonight, and had kept Jemmah up to the wee hours sewing—to thrust Adelinda beneath Jules's nose in hopes of garnering his attention.

And how could he not notice Adelinda's outward loveliness?

However, her beauty masked an entirely different woman inwardly, and Jemmah ought to know. More often than not, she was the recipient of her sister's calculated unkindness.

Nothing, nevertheless, would deter Mama from assuring Adelinda make a brilliant match before Season's end, and dear Jules had a giant target on his broad back they'd set their conniving sights on.

Jemmah ought to warn him, but surely a man of his station was aware the Marriage Mart considered him prime cattle. A somewhat degrading analogy, but accurate in its crudeness, nonetheless.

With his aristocratic profile yet angled toward the creature scratching at the door, Jemmah permitted herself a leisurely perusal. From his gleaming shoes to his neatly trimmed side whiskers, several shades darker than his hair, he emanated pure masculine beauty.

True, his nose might be slightly too prominent and his forehead and chin a trifle too bold to be considered classically handsome, but his was a strong face—an honorable, trustworthy countenance.

All the more reason she couldn't allow Mama or Adelinda to sink their talons into him.

Jemmah just couldn't.

He deserved someone as kind and thoughtful as he.

Not a selfish, vain girl who cared nothing for him, and who would—Jemmah didn't harbor the slightest doubt—make him wretchedly miserable.

As unpleasant a miss as she was, Miss Milbourne was preferable to Adelinda.

Jemmah's stomach flopped sickeningly, and she swallowed. What a nauseating notion, rather like eating moldy, maggoty pudding.

Adelinda and Miss Milbourne didn't merit him, and somehow,

instinct perhaps, or because Jemmah had loved Jules so long—couldn't remember when she hadn't, truth to tell—she simply knew, neither woman would make him happy.

His Annabel Bright might have, for she seemed gentle and kind the one time Jemmah met her.

That awful, unforgettable day her heart had splintered into pieces like stomped upon eggshells when Jemmah learned Jules was to marry the doll-like in her perfection, dainty, and altogether exquisite young lady.

And when Annabel had died, Jemmah had wept, great gasping sobs into her pillow at night—cried for Jules's devastation and heartache.

She couldn't fathom weeping like that if Miss Milbourne, or even Adelinda had been the one to die, and Jemmah winced inwardly at her uncharacteristic spite.

Thank goodness, to her knowledge, Aunt Theo's invitation to tea didn't include Miss Milbourne, and because Mama barely tolerated her sister-in-law, more often than not, she turned down the invitations as well.

Adelinda seldom rose before noon and had no more interest in taking tea with their aunt than cleaning grates or chamber pots.

Neither of which she'd ever done, unlike Jemmah.

She couldn't help but observe that her aunt's feelings toward Mama seemed quite mutual. In fact, Jemmah had suspected for years, but most especially since Papa's death, that her Aunt Theo's cordial mien and continued hospitable offers were for Jemmah's benefit.

That, and also so Mama wouldn't put an end to Jemmah's visits.

Which was as unlikely as Mama suddenly favoring Jemmah.

She also knew full well that Aunt Theo paid Mama a monthly allowance intended to assist with the girls' needs.

Jemmah never saw any of it, not a shilling.

In fact, when she'd asked for new stockings for tonight, she'd received a resounding slap for her impertinence. The nubby, mended stockings rubbing against her toes, as well her tender cheek were other reasons she'd sought sanctuary in Aunt Theo's parlor.

For certain, Jemmah's toes would sport blisters by morning.

Some weeks, tea with Aunt Theo's and hearing her aunt's encouragements were all that kept Jemmah from wallowing in self-pity or having a fit of the blue devils.

Treated scarcely better at home than the Daments' maid-of-all work, Mary Pimble, Jemmah treasured the time at Aunt Theo's. They were the only hours free from insults or demands that she perform some chore or task for Mama or Adelinda.

"Dandridge." The voice rose to an irritated screech on the last syllable.

Tap, tap, tappety-tap.

"Open this door!"

TAP

"I must insist."

Miss Milbourne might be admired for her persistence.

If it didn't border on unhinged.

Jemmah dipped her head in the entrance's direction, and her voice, a mere vestige of sound, asked, "*Have* you an arrangement with her?"

No need to ask who *her* was, since Miss Milbourne continued to hiss and scratch like a feral cat sealed in a whisky barrel.

"I most emphatically do not. Miss Milbourne has convinced herself that I shall concede to my mother's and uncles' preference, but she's gravely mistaken." Jules grasped Jemmah's hand, gently yet firmly enough she couldn't pull away without some effort. With the forefinger of his other hand, he traced her jaw. "I mean what I said, dear one. Please allow me to call upon you tomorrow. I've missed you more than I can say."

"Your Grace—"

"Might you address me as Jules, or Dandridge if you prefer, when we are alone? Please?"

He quirked his mouth boyishly, and she couldn't resist an answering bend of her lips.

It had always been so. She was clay, soft and malleable, in his hands.

"Precious, Jemmah, perhaps you'd prefer a ride in Hyde Park tomorrow?"

Heaven and hiccups, no.

It would never do for Jules to pay his address to her at home, and a ride would likely be reported as well. Mama wasn't above locking Jemmah in her chamber to assure Adelinda received his undivided attention.

Good thing he wasn't as besotted as most men by her sister's exquisiteness.

When Adelinda did finally marry—for certain her beauty would snare some unfortunate fellow—how long would it be before her sulks and vile tongue obscured her bewitching beauty and the poor sot regretted his choice?

Still, Jemmah could no more deny Jules's tempting request than she could ignore the impossibility of his calling on her.

The scraping and frenetic whispering at the door had finally ceased, but her alarm increased.

She mustn't be found, here alone with him.

No telling what Mama would do.

Jemmah speared an anxious glance to the other doors.

"It's impossible. Mama won't allow you to call upon me. She had hoped Adelinda would attract your notice, and she'll be furious if you show any interest in me."

"Yes, so I became acutely aware, earlier this evening. However, Adelinda isn't the Dament sister who fascinates me. I've always preferred the one with gold and amber streaks glinting in her hair and eyes so pale blue, I lose myself in their color each time I look into them." He grazed his thumb across her lower lip. "And she has the most tempting mouth, soft, honey sweet, with lips I cannot wait to sample again."

He swept his mouth across hers.

Tender, fleeting, a silent promise.

Joy, and perhaps the minutest amount of triumph that he preferred her—plain and unremarkable Jemmah—over Adelinda's exquisiteness, sang through her veins. A jaunty celebratory tune. And for the first time in the veriest of times, a spark of hope ignited deep in her spirit.

For once, she believed Papa's assurances that she was lovely in her own way, and that someday she'd find the man who gazed at her through love-filled eyes and found her beautiful.

"Do you know what the Dandridge motto is, Jemmah?"

She shook her head. "No."

"In adversity, the faith." Jules's touched his lips to hers again. "I shall find a way, if you want me to."

Her stomach flopped over again, and the air left her lungs on a fluttering breath.

Thundering hogs' hoof beats when he looked at her like that—like she was the most precious of jewels, his gaze reverent, yet also slightly hooded—although logic screeched "No," her desperate heart whispered, "Yes."

Yes. Yes. Yes.

If this was her chance for happiness, no matter how brief or implausible, she damn well—*yes, damn well!*—had every intention of grasping it.

"My aunt invited me for tea tomorrow."

Comprehension dawned on Jules's face, and she entertained another, small victorious smile.

"Ah, I do believe Theo mentioned something of that nature to me as well. I find I am quite available at that hour."

He lifted Jemmah's hand, and rather than brush his lips across her bare knuckles, he turned it over and grazed her wrist.

A jolt shot to her shoulder while her knees, ridiculous, worthless things, decided to turn to mush.

"I shall look forward to it. Now if you'll excuse me," he blew out all but one taper, "I promised Sabrina I'd be home to tuck her in tonight. It's her birthday too. The second since her parents died, but at the first one, we didn't know if she'd recover from the carriage accident. I don't want her to fall asleep without bidding her good-night."

Such a flood of emotion bubbled up in Jemmah's chest that tears blurred her vision as she pulled her gloves on, trying to ignore the frayed spots on the fingertips.

"She's lucky to have such a devoted uncle. Would you wish her happy day for me too?

"I would indeed, and if I may be so bold, might I tell her you'll give her drawing lessons?" He turned her toward the other set of doors. "Naturally, I'll approach your mother and explain I'd like to retain you."

Mama would take any earnings, thinking they were her due, and she'd still expect Jemmah to do all of her regular chores.

"Honestly, Dandridge, I think it would be better if I were to give Sabrina lessons when I come to tea. And please allow it to be my gift to her. I have a standing invitation with Aunt Theo on Mondays and Thursdays. I could use one day for lessons so Mama's suspicions won't be aroused."

His head slightly angled, he considered her. "Very well."

"Aunt Theo usually only sends the carriage 'round for me when the weather is foul, but I'll explain our plan tonight and ask her to send it every tea day. That way, I'll have more time to instruct Lady Sabrina."

"We can discuss those details tomorrow. Until then, my precious Jem." He cupped her shoulders with both hands, and leaning down, kissed her forehead with such reverence, she almost could believe he cared for her as much as she did for him. "Go along. I'll wait a respectable amount of time, and then take another route to the manor's entrance."

She nodded. “All right.”

“And Jemmah?”

“Yes?”

A strand of hair had fallen across his brow, and with the warmth radiating from his brandy-colored eyes, he very much resembled the young man she’d fallen in love with.

“Your mother can fuss all she wants, but once I set my mind to something, I am seldom dissuaded. I mean to court you.”

5

Incapable of speech, her heart teeming with happiness, Jemmah nodded again and quit the parlor. She could yet taste and feel Jules's mouth on hers, and an odd heat throbbed at her wrist as if branded by his lips.

Glancing down, she half expected to see his mouth's imprint there.

A few moments later, having brought her exuberant smile under control, she edged into the ballroom, as unnoticed as a fly upon the corniced ceiling. No one paid her any mind as she wove between guests, headed toward the empty seat beside the Dowager Lady Lockhart.

Jemmah's silly legs still hadn't returned to their normal strength after Jules's bone-melting kisses, and feeling slightly off-balance, she gratefully claimed the seat.

Her ladyship bestowed a beaming smile on her. "Where've you been, child? I saw you arrive and hoped to have a coze with you. It's been some time since we chatted, and you always brighten this old woman's day with your wit and intelligence."

"How kind of you to say so, my lady. I enjoy your company as well. Aunt tells me you have a cat now."

From the corner of her eye, Jemmah caught site of Miss Milbourne prowling the dance floor's perimeter, a half-pout upon her lips while her miffed gaze roved the ballroom. They narrowed for an instant upon sighting Adelinda dancing with the exceedingly tall, raven-haired Duke of Sutcliffe.

Miss Milbourne wouldn't find what she sought.

He'd already left.

"I do indeed," Lady Lockhart agreed. "A darling little calico I named Callie. I thought the name quite clever."

Miss Milbourne's attention swept over Jemmah without pause, the way one dismissed a potted plant or a piece of furniture.

After all, who'd suspect the nondescript Miss Jemmah Dament had just spent the most wonderful twenty minutes in the embrace of the distinguished and oh, so alluring Duke of Dandridge—the very man the Milbourne beauty wanted for herself?

Unaccustomed confidence squared Jemmah's shoulders and notched her chin higher. She'd never felt more attractive or worthy than she did at this moment, and she had Jules to thank for the new self-assurance.

The dowager gently tapped Jemmah's forearm with her fan. "You're pale as a lily, but your cheeks are berry bright. Are you feeling quite the thing?"

"Yes, my lady. I'm quite well." Very well, indeed. Better than she had been in a great while. "I confess to falling asleep in the parlor, which may contribute to my flushed appearance."

Not nearly as much a duke's ravishing kisses had.

"Your mother has paraded past here thrice searching for you. A ripped hem or some such twaddle. Doesn't she know how to mend a simple tear? Don't know why she or your sister can't see to the task."

Disapproval pinched the dowager's mouth for an instant.

Jemmah was used to urgent summons at all hours of the day and night for whatever trifling needs Mama or Adelinda might have.

Two months ago, she'd walked four miles in the pouring rain to purchase barbel blue embroidery thread for Mama—not azure or cerulean, her mother had insisted, but barbel.

"This is mazurine blue, Jemmah," Mama had scolded when Jemmah returned home sopping wet and shivering. "Fortunate for you, I decided lavender better suited, else you'd turn yourself around and fetch me the color I need."

Never mind the prodigious cold Jemmah contracted as a result of her soggy trek, which left her sneezing and with a reddened nose and eyes for a full week.

On another occasion, she'd been awoken in the wee morning hours when her sister couldn't sleep and deemed a cup of hot chocolate the perfect insomnia cure.

Jemmah had dutifully gone through the time-consuming task of making the beverage only to find Adelinda slumbering soundly when she brought her the required pot and cup.

Snuggled on her window seat, a tattered quilt about her shoulders while she gazed at the stars flickering between moonlit clouds over the rooftops, Jemmah had drunk every last drop herself.

A rare treat indeed.

Oh, and she couldn't possibly forget last month when the family had been invited to the Silverton's soirée.

Jemmah couldn't attend, of course.

After all, since Papa died, they'd been required to economize and naturally there were only funds for one remade gown.

For the eldest daughter.

Always the confounded eldest daughter.

That was the excuse for most everything Jemmah was deprived of.

Nonetheless, she'd dutifully dressed and coiffed Adelinda, even allowing her—Mama's orders to stop being such a selfish sister—to borrow Jemmah's best gloves and the delicate pearl earrings Papa had given her for her sixteenth birthday.

Adelinda had misplaced the gloves and lost an earring.

As Jemmah fought bitter tears, Adelinda had pouted. "You know better than to lend me your things. I always lose them, Germ."

Germ, the hated knick-name Adelinda insisted upon calling Jemmah.

Mama thought it quaint and amusing, a show of sisterly affection.

Balderdash and codswallop. Crafty and mean-spirited better described the moniker.

However, the one time Jemmah dared call Adelinda "Adder"—a fitting moniker since Adelinda meant noble snake, Mama had berated Jemmah for a full thirty minutes before sending her to bed without supper.

Small comfort knowing Jemmah meant precious gem while her sister's name meant a cold, slithery, vile creature.

Mama's given name, Belinda, meant beautiful snake, which was probably why she became so peeved at Jemmah calling Adelinda Adder.

A raspy chuckle filled the air.

"You actually fell asleep, my dear? While all these other young women are trying to snare a husband, you're napping in Theo's parlor. By all the crumpets in Canterbury, I admire you. Indeed, I do."

"No need for admiration, I assure you. I simply didn't find my bed until almost five this morning." Jemmah licked her lower lip and searched for a footman. "Truth to tell I am quite thirsty."

The dowager tutted kindly. "Five, you say? *Hmph.*"

She made a brusque sound of disapproval.

"I'll wager staying up all night wasn't of your own choosing." She opened her mouth then snapped it shut. "I could use a glass of punch myself, my dear. Would you oblige an old woman and fetch me a cup?"

"*Punch*?"

Jemmah tried to hide her shock. Ladies didn't drink the spirit-heavy libation. "Are you sure you wouldn't prefer a ratafia?"

"Too syrupy." Eyes flashing with mischief, the dowager shook her head, and the ostrich feathers tucked into her stylish coif bobbed in agreement.

"Lemonade? Or perhaps an iced champagne?" Jemmah offered hopefully. Rather frantically, truth be told.

"I think not. Too insipid. Like men, I prefer something with a bit—actually, a great deal—more vigor and potency."

Not quite believing her ears, and trying to subdue the heat crawling up her cheeks, Jemmah tried one last time.

"Tea? Wine?"

Lord, she couldn't just stride up to the table and snatch a glass of punch. Tongues would flap faster than flags in a hurricane.

Cocking her head, humor sparring with patience in her gaze, the dowager chuckled. "My dear Miss Dament, do you truly believe none of the ladies present tonight ever imbibes in alcohol?"

Not publically.

"Look there, beside Lord Beetle Brows." With her cane, the Dowager Lady Lockhart gestured at a proud dame.

Lord Dunston does have rather grizzled eyebrows.

"See Lady Clutterbuck?"

How could I miss her in that primrose gown?

"She trundles her thick backside off regularly and takes a nip from the flask she has hidden in her reticule."

Jemmah bit the inside of her cheek to keep from giggling.

"Over there," the dowager swung her cane toward a regal dame, epitomizing *haut ton* elegance. "Lady Dreary—

"I believe that's Lady Drury—"

"*Hmph*. She's as dreary and cold as frozen fog on a grave. But that was beside the point. Her ladyship is most clever—keeps whisky stashed in her vinaigrette instead of ammonia or smelling salts."

How, for all the salt in the sea could Jemmah have forgotten the ... erm ... *unique* labels the clever dowager attributed to others? Sometimes she explained a name's genuine meaning, but others, as she'd just demonstrated, a droll play on words.

A speculative glint entered her ladyship's watered-down-topaz-colored eyes. "Even Lady Wimpleton, whom I admire very much indeed, is wont to take a nip on occasion."

Jemmah laughed and threw her hands up in defeat. "You win, my lady. I shall return shortly. Pray my mother doesn't espy me."

Though how she would manage the task without Mama hearing of it or some other nosy dame deciding it was her duty to chastise Jemmah, she hadn't yet conceived.

"I can deal with Belinda well enough, my dear. You're kind to humor an old woman's idiosyncrasies."

As Jemmah neared the table, a footman loading a tray with filled punch glasses smiled a polite greeting. "Good evening, Miss Jemmah. Mary said you were attending your aunt's ball."

"Frazer Pimble, isn't it?"

Here was Jemmah's answer to her dilemma. Most providential to come upon her maid's brother.

"Aye." He nodded once, a kindly smile emphasizing the swath of freckles across his nose and cheeks.

"May I impose upon you?" When he nodded, Jemmah angled toward the ballroom's west side. "See that lovely lady in the gold and black, with the spray of black ostrich feathers in her hair. The one holding a cane and peering in our direction?"

"I do, miss."

"She desires a glass of punch, and I don't dare take it to her." Jemmah bent a tiny bit nearer and murmured, "Can you imagine the gossip? Would you be so kind as to put a serving in a teacup for her?"

Frazer gave a quick glance around. "Leave it to me, miss. Do you need a beverage as well? If I may be so bold, you look a bit flushed."

"I would love lemonade, if it wouldn't be too much trouble."

He nodded and gave a small wink. "Return to your seat, and I shall be along straightaway."

Jemmah resumed her seat and had just turned to explain the plan to the dowager when, true to his word, Frazer approached, carrying a tray with a glass of lemonade in addition to a teacup and saucer.

He presented the china cup to the elderly dame, and Lady Lockhart's eyebrows crept up the creases of her forehead to hang there suspended.

"Tea?" fussed the dowager, giving Jemmah the gimlet eye. "I most definitely declined tea."

"Oh, but this is a *very s*pecial brew, my lady. I'm sure you'll quite like it." Frazer inclined his head, and the dowager's eyes rounded.

She took a dainty sip, then smiled in pure delight. "Indeed. An exceptionally fine brew. Thank you."

Frazer left them, and her ladyship turned an approving eye on Jemmah.

"That was well done of you, Miss Dament. Clever too." Her watery gaze bored into Jemmah for a long moment before she nodded slowly, as if coming to a conclusion. "I've been of a mind to sponsor a worthy young woman this Season, someone to act as my companion too. I would be honored if you'd consider the proposition."

Jemmah choked on her lemonade.

Eyes watering and swallowing against the burning at the back of her throat, she gaped.

Smack her with a cod.

A way out?

A way to escape Mama and Adelinda?

She wiggled her toes and gave a tiny glee-filled bounce upon her seat.

Aunt Theo had tried for years to persuade Mama to let Jemmah live with her, but truth be told, Mama was reluctant to lose Jemmah as a servant.

But turn down the dowager's sponsorship?

That Mama wouldn't do.

The only thing she valued more than Adelinda was money, something the Daments were perpetually short of.

Jemmah laid her hand atop the dowager's. "I would consider it the greatest honor to be your companion, your ladyship, and there's no need to sponsor me. I'm not meant for routs and balls and such."

"Oh, posh. What rot. Of course you are, my dear," Lady Lockhart assured Jemmah. "But if it makes you more comfortable, you may begin as my companion straightaway. We'll take the Season sponsorship a jot slower."

"Companion...?" Mama sidled up to them, a ribbon-thin, forced smile tweaking her mouth's corners. "If anyone is granted a sponsorship and the privilege of being her ladyship's companion, it must, quite naturally, be Adelinda. I'm sure you understand, my lady. She's the elder daughter, after all."

All hail the elder daughter.

Bah!

"Are you entirely daft, Mama?" Adelinda hissed near Mama's ear, her usual artificial smile making her seem the mild-tempered innocent to the casual onlooker. The fury in her coffee-colored eyes told an entirely different tale.

Lady Lockhart slid Jemmah an I-knew-she'd-pitch-a-tantrum look.

Adelinda grumbled on, a pout upon her rouged mouth.

"You expect *me* to wait upon another? An *old* woman? At her beck and call?" She huffed her outrage, flinging a hand toward the dowager while thrusting her dainty chin upward in haughty arrogance. "*I* am not companion material. Most especially not to a deaf, demented, aged crone."

Her chin descended an inch as if granting a royal favor. "Jemmah may act as the companion, and as the eldest, I shall accept the sponsorship."

La de dah.

The last she uttered with the austerity and entitled expectation of a crown princess.

Jemmah lifted her cup whilst eyeing the dowager.

Lady Lockhart planted both gnarled hands upon her cane's floral handle and cut Adelinda a glare of such scathing incredulity, only the dame's irises remained visible.

This ought to be very entertaining.

Her ladyship was precisely the person to knock Adelinda and her pretentious superiority off her self-appointed pedestal and onto her well-rounded arse.

"An old crone, most certainly, but not at all deaf, Miss Dament."

Jemmah bit the inside of her cheek.

Most diverting, indeed.

The dowager's gaze raked over Adelinda who didn't have the refinement to look abashed, but rather contentious.

"I'd have to be demented to consider *you* for the position. But since it's already been filled by your utterly charming sister, we needn't worry on that account, need we?" She graced Jemmah with a wide—yes, distinctly smug—closed-mouth smile. "Oh, and the two go hand in hand—the sponsorship and the position, lest there be any confusion."

Adelinda's smile slipped a fraction and displeasure pursed her mouth. However, accomplished in artifice, she quickly masked her true feelings and pressed her point.

"My lady, surely you cannot mean to waste expense and time on my plain, wholly unexceptional sister, when both would be so much better spent on the more attractive of the pair of us. The little toad is hardly worth the effort, and I fear you'll find the outcome most unsatisfactory."

Adelinda tilted her head and summoned her syrupiest, most

beguiling fake-as-a-purple-wig-on-donkey expression. The calculated one that inevitably ensured she acquired whatever the pampered darling coveted at the moment.

"Thank you for your kind words, *sister*." Jemmah couldn't attribute the acidic taste on her tongue to the lemonade she'd just choked on.

How could Adelinda be such a cruel, insensitive bacon-brain?

Adelinda laughed, the often practiced before her looking glass tinkle ringing hollow and shrill rather than light and musical. Snapping her fan open, she fiddled with the spines, expectation still arcing her winged brows.

Dense as black bread.

"*Hmph.*"

A sound very much like a stifled snort or oath escaped Lady Lockhart. She fumbled in her reticule for a moment then glanced up in triumph as she withdrew a pair of wire-rimmed spectacles. "Aha, here they are."

She extended them to Adelinda.

"I believe you are in more need of these than I am, if you think your sister is inferior to you in any way, but most especially in comeliness."

In a soundless challenge, the dowager's eyebrows crept upward as well.

They glared at each other, brows elevated and eyes shooting daggers in a silent battle.

At the imagery of Lady Lockhart's and Adelinda's eyebrows jousting, Jemmah muffled a giggle.

"I simply cannot believe this treachery." Adelinda averted her gaze first, and in her typical harrying fashion, turned an accusatory scowl on Jemmah. "How long have you been scheming behind my back, Germ? Worming your way into her ladyship's good graces so you could steal this opportunity from me?"

"You know as well as I, Adelinda, that I rarely am permitted to attend these functions, and I haven't had the pleasure of Lady Lockhart's company in months. And—"

"One year, two months, and ... ah ..." Lady Lockhart scrunched her eyes as she examined the ceiling, her mouth working silently. "...twelve days. Valentine's Day last year, it was."

She veered her knowing gaze at Jemmah. "You spent most of the afternoon hiding in the library."

How on earth had she remembered that?

Mama seemed to rouse herself from her gawking stupor and

touched Adelinda's forearm. "We'll discuss this later, darling."

After taking a long pull from her teacup, God knew she needed it after a confrontation with Adelinda and Mama, the dowager bestowed a satisfied smile on Jemmah. "After tea tomorrow, we'll need to see to acquiring you a wardrobe suitable for a young woman of your new station."

"But... but..." Jealousy contorting her face, and seemingly oblivious to the small crowd that had gathered, hanging onto each recklessly-spoken word, Adelinda planted her hands on her hips and confronted their mother.

"Mama, tell Germ she can't. You won't allow it."

Jemmah straightened.

No. No. No.

They would not steal this opportunity from her.

Mama opened her mouth, but before she could affirm Adelinda, Aunt Theo's voice cut the air, firm and unrelenting.

"Oh, she'll allow it, all right."

They swung their attention to Aunt Theo, her approach having gone unnoticed due to Adelinda's unbecoming show of temper and the semi-circle of intrigued spectators blocking their view.

Smiling at her guests, Aunt Theo angled her head before suggesting, "I'm sure you'll allow me a moment for a private family conversation."

As Aunt Theo cordially looped her arms in Mama's and Adelinda's elbows, the onlookers scattered like roaches in sunlight. Drawing her mother and sister nearer, Aunt Theo dipped her head, her face granite hard.

"You've overstepped the bounds, Theodora. I shall determine which of my daughters is most suited for the position." Mama slid Adelinda a smug, sideway glance.

"As I said, Belinda, you will allow Jemmah this honor. Because if you refuse," Aunt Theo directed her wrath squarely at Adelinda, "this selfish, spoiled bratling will feel the full effects of my displeasure, and I assure you, after I'm done, a haberdasher won't consider Adelinda for his wife."

6

Sighing, feeling more content than he had in—well, in months, perhaps years—Jules untied his cravat, and after tossing it atop the French baroque table behind the sofa, sank onto the charcoal damask-covered cushions.

He'd bid a sleepy-eyed Sabrina goodnight, then retreated to his study to contemplate the evening's remarkable events.

One specific incident, that was.

Stumbling upon Miss Jemmah Dament, and in an instant his life had changed.

He touched two fingertips to his lips, not surprised to find a cock-eyed smile bending his mouth. In the last two hours, he'd smiled more than in the past two years, and his providential encounter with Jemmah had set him on a new course.

By all the chirping crickets playing a grand symphony beyond the study's French window, a path he eagerly anticipated.

He'd found his diamond in the rough.

Perhaps not so rough, except for her humble attire.

Jemmah would polish up brilliantly, and then those who'd ignored her, overlooked her loveliness, would grind their teeth in vexation.

She'd blossomed into a remarkable and sensuous young woman. Tall, lithe, and boasting delightful, rounded womanly curves, two of which had taunted him unmercifully above her bodice, her features and form had embedded themselves in his memory.

A self-depreciatory, yet joy-filled chuckle, burgeoned in his chest then rumbled forth, filling the silent, fire-lit room.

Mere hours ago, he'd avowed himself indifferent to marriage, and now, he calculated just how soon he might take the charming, witty, a trifle shy and awkward, but wholly delectable and precious Jemmah Dament to wife.

If someone asked him how he could be so absolutely positive he should do so, he couldn't have answered them with logic and reason, for neither had anything whatsoever to do with the giddiness—yes, by all the cigars at Whites's, *giddiness*—humming through him.

He just knew.

Simple as that.

Not a damned lucid thing about it.

Like wild creatures recognize their offspring, a river discerns what course its waters must flow, wildfowls' instincts urge them to fly south for the winter, or even the sun understanding that it must rise every morning and then slowly descend each eve—

He knew.

Drowsy, content, and resolute, Jules shut his eyes and daydreamed about when he'd see his precious, sky-eyed Jemmah again.

Was tomorrow too soon to propose?

"Miss Jemmah. You needs wake up. Now. The mistress wants you to run an errand."

At the frantic whisper and Mary Pimble's small hand insistently shaking her shoulder, Jemmah cracked an eye open. A bit of drool leaking from her mouth's corner and her head resting on her forearms, she surveyed the assortment of papers, pens, and drawings scattered mere inches before her line of vision.

She must've fallen asleep over her sketches while trying to decide which to take with her to show Jules at tea today.

After wiping her mouth, she yawned and blinked sleepily.

By all the brandy in Britain, no one could fault her for her for dozing off.

After all, the clock had struck two before she'd managed to undress Mama and Adelinda, see their sheets warmed, and their chamber fires stoked, the whole while subjected to their rancorous litanies of why Adelinda ought to have reaped the dowager's favor, not Jemmah.

Their mutual fury over Aunt Theo's blunt threat to cease all monetary support had nearly sent Mama into apoplexy, and for the first time ever, Adelinda's face had mottled bright red as she sobbed and ranted into her abused pillow.

Jemmah arched her stiff back and stretched her arms overhead, almost touching the slanting ceiling's rough boards with her fingertips.

"A missive arrived for you, too. I hid it in my pocket." Her eyes wide and curious, Pimble whispered, "It's from a *duke*."

A thrill fluttered Jemmah's tummy.

Pimble fished the hunter green-beribboned rectangle from her apron and pitched a worried gaze toward the door as Jemmah stood and stretched again while glancing to the busy street.

Bless Pimble.

It wouldn't be the first time Mama or Adelinda intercepted a missive meant for Jemmah.

"Thank you, Pimble."

Jemmah accepted the note, stamped with Dandridge's seal.

Mama definitely would've confiscated the letter. She had Dandridge earmarked for Adelinda.

Jemmah flipped it over to examine the bold, slashing strokes across the face.

Too bad the duke had other plans.

The smile quirking Jemmah's mouth as she traced his writing with her fingertip might've been a teeny bit jubilant.

Or a lot.

For someone who seldom prevailed, this triumph was far more profound. Something to be cherished and kept private, away from prying eyes. Formerly servants' quarters, perched three stories above the street, her tiny bedchamber allowed her that luxury.

Mama and Adelinda loathed climbing the stairs, especially the last narrow, steep risers, and the room was generally either arctic frigid or blistering hot. But the chamber had served as Jemmah's private haven for over a decade, and she was content here even if it lacked creature comforts.

She cracked the seal and using the window for light, perused the unfamiliar writing.

My Dearest Miss Dament,

I eagerly look forward to renewing our friendship and would consider it the greatest privilege if you would permit me to escort you to the theater tonight.

Theo is attending as well, so we'll be well chaperoned.

I anticipate the hours until I next see you today,
Dandridge

Pleasure, secretive and acute, bent Jemmah's mouth again as she refolded the letter.

Amazing, how in less than twenty-four hours, her prospects had changed so dramatically. Attending the theater was out of the question, of course. She quite literally hadn't a single gown appropriate for such a lavish affair; not that she was complaining.

Last night, she'd had scant to look forward to, and today...

Well, for one thing, Jules would be at tea and perhaps Lady Sabrina also. So, too, would her soon-to-be employer, the Dowager Lady Lockhart.

God love that dear, feisty woman.

Last night, unperturbed and fully aware of her position and power, she'd regally looked directly at Mama.

"You best teach that one to retract her claws." The dowager bounced her gray head toward Adelinda, the ostrich feathers atop the dowager's head pummeling one another with the motion. "Envy turns even the comeliest of young ladies into ugly, spiteful creatures no one wants about. Not at all becoming, I assure you. And if you both wish to continue to be welcome in Society, as Theo has implied, you'll behave as is expected of someone awarded the privilege."

Jemmah had barely refrained from clapping.

She would've permitted a triumphant smile, except, blast her worn-out slippers, she'd felt pity for Mama and Adelinda. More so that neither had showed the least chagrin or remorse, and the censure leveled at them from those eavesdropping on their conversation had Jemmah's face flaming in embarrassment for her family.

It had always been so.

She might think uncharitable thoughts and on occasion grumble beneath her breath, and for good reason too. But in the end, a deep-rooted hope that Mama and Adelinda would change —or perhaps it was naught more than fanciful wishing—stirred the remnants of her compassion.

A moment later, Aunt Theo's carriage trundled to a stop before their humble cottage, earning curious stares from passersby. Only this time, Jemmah's anticipation of leaving for a few hours meant even more than it usually did.

Today might be the last she'd return to this house as a resident.

Hereafter, she'd only be a visitor; if Mama deemed to invite her, that was.

Jemmah had best not hold her breath waiting for that invitation any time soon.

Unlike Jemmah, Mama did not possess a forgiving nature.

"Good news, miss?"

Pimble puttered about, not doing much of anything, but every moment the maid spent here was far more pleasant than returning below.

"Of a sorts, yes."

Better not to divulge too much to Pimble, yet. Jemmah slipped the letter into her reticule, afraid to leave it in her room.

"Mama's up earlier than I expected."

The servant offered a lopsided, apologetic smile. "And if I may be so bold, in as a foul a mood this morning as I've ever seen her."

A wonder Mama had roused herself before noon; a guarantee she'd be crotchety the rest of the day. Far worse for poor Pimble when Mama or Adelinda felt peevish. Both were as prickly and hard to handle as an infuriated hedgehog.

"Jemmah, are you going to dawdle the day away?"

Breathing heavily, her skirts swishing about her ankles, Mama trudged into Jemmah's chamber. Her pretty, plump, slightly rosy face puckered in displeasure when her gaze lit on the many sketches pinned to the rafters, depicting drawings from new fashions to birds perched upon flowering tree branches.

"I sent Pimble to fetch you a full half hour ago. Whatever is keeping you both?"

Jemmah brushed the wrinkles from her simple Pomona green day gown, or at least tried to, before going to stand before the small, slightly blurry, rectangular looking glass hanging from a support beam.

She smoothed her hair and repinned a few loose strands as she watched her mother in the reflection.

Pimble ducked from the chamber, making good her escape.

Smart girl.

If only Jemmah might do the same.

"It's only been ten minutes, Mama, and I'm afraid the errand will have to wait until after I call upon Aunt Theo and the dowager takes me shopping this afternoon." She flicked her fingers toward the arched, four-paned window, the lower right divided by a long crack. "The carriage already awaits outside."

Scrutinizing her reflection, she frowned.

Dark circles ringed her eyes, and the dress, a brilliant shade on Adelinda, made Jemmah's skin appear sallow. She did quite look forward to acquiring a gown or two in hues which flattered her coloring, rather than wearing more castoffs from Adelinda, as Jemmah had for as long as she could recall.

Did that make her shallow, or simply a typical woman who enjoyed looking her best?

Especially now that she had a reason to care about her appearance?

Drat, if only she had a fichu to drape about her neck to diminish the gown's ill effects on her appearance. Perhaps she could leave her redingote on?

"Tell me what it is that you need, Mama, and I shall be happy to take care of it before I return home. Or perhaps, if the matter is terribly urgent, Pimble or Adelinda might attend to it for you."

Not the least mollified, her mother angled away from the table where she'd been poking about, occasionally scowling or grimacing at something she saw.

"Don't get impertinent with me, young lady. You know full well Pimble has more than enough to do, and whilst you reside here, you're expected to do your share."

As Adelinda does?

"You're not Lady Lockhart's pampered pet just yet," Mama snapped, as she tossed the drawings she'd been examining onto the scarred, uneven table top.

By King Solomon's treasure, if Adelinda's wasn't still fast asleep—*snoring*—Jemmah would skip her breakfast. Her gaze fell to the unappetizing glob plopped in the wooden bowl atop her desk.

Oh, that was right. She'd eschewed her plain porridge breakfast earlier.

Mama cut Jemmah a disdainful look and crossed her arms. "You know full well, as the eldest, it ought to have been your sister receiving Lady Lockhart's benevolence."

Ah, here came the true reason Mama dared the strenuous climb.

"A dutiful daughter and affectionate sister would've insisted upon it. I cannot quite conceive your selfishness, Jemmah. I truly cannot. Excepting," she notched her chin higher and gave a contemptuous sniff, "you are your father's daughter."

A jab to Jemmah's ribs with a short sword would've hurt less.

She pivoted, incredulity and injustice spiking her temper to a heretofore new height.

From their hook on the post's other side she snatched her unadorned straw hat and seven-year-old faded blue redingote, more appropriate for an adolescent than a woman grown.

"I've never been deliberately selfish, nor treated you or Adelinda with a margin of the unkindness you've both regularly bestowed upon me." She blinked away the stinging tears blurring her vision and fastened the garment's frogs at her throat. "I have an opportunity to leave this household. And by truffle-hunting pigs, I'm seizing it!"

"Just like that." Mama snapped her fingers, anger crackling in her slit-eyed gaze and strident voice. "You'd desert your family with no care of how we'll manage?"

"If you'd shown me even a jot of kindness or consideration. Ever asked what I desired. Ever set aside your self-centeredness, and your…" Jemmah inhaled a raggedy, tear-logged breath, "…*hatred* of me, I might've urged her ladyship to consider Adelinda too."

Eagerness, or perhaps desperation, gave the planes of Mama's face a softer, more vulnerable mien.

Almost like the mother of long ago, before she'd found everything about Jemmah objectionable and ridicule worthy.

Mama wrung her hands and licked her lips. "Think of your sister. And me. We're not as accustomed to hardship and want as you are."

Holy hypocrisy. Did Mama hear herself?

Jemmah jerked her head up and clamped her jaw against the hot retorts tickling her tongue. Hell's teeth, even now Mama attempted to use guilt to sway her. Not out of concern or thoughtfulness.

Oh, no.

Always—*always, dammit!*—to benefit her and Adelinda.

Not this time.

She must have seen the denial in Jemmah's rigid form and compressed lips, because Mama rushed across the room, and clutching at Jemmah's arm stuttered, "I'll … I'll permit you to attend more functions. And ... and even order material so you can stitch yourself a couple of new gowns. If funds permit, of course. However, surely you must know, I can't possibly manage the house without your help."

She procured what was no doubt meant to be a heartening smile. But the calculated glint in her eye and the rigidity of her barely-upturned lips revealed her true sentiment.

Jemmah was far past politesse.

Years of injustice and ill-treatment had taken their toll, and she feared—dreaded—becoming rancorous like her mother. So full of hatred and resentment, her presence was toxic to everyone who encountered her.

"Tell me, Mama. Will Adelinda attend fewer functions then? And start contributing to the upkeep of our home rather than act the spoiled puss and lie abed till afternoon while I wait upon her?"

Mama blinked at Jemmah as if she'd asked her to waltz naked covered in peacock feathers through Hyde Park.

"I thought not."

Jemmah jerked on her gloves, putting her forefinger through the threadbare tip of the right one.

Hounds' teeth!

Something very near a growl bubbled up the back of her throat. "The carriage awaits. I must go."

Before she vented every wounded, ugly, and pent-up thought now careening about in her head.

"It's not too late, Jemmah," Mama pleaded. "You still can refuse the position. Insist that Adelinda have it instead. I'm certain Theodora and the dowager will yield to your wishes if you stand firm and tell them that's what you want."

"But it's not what I want. It's what *you* want. And as always, it's what benefits you and my sister without a care of how I'll be affected."

Jemmah bit her tongue to stop the rest of her infuriated thoughts from spewing forth. After stuffing her hat on her head and tying the ribbon, she grabbed her reticule and the stack of sketches she'd set aside for today, then marched to the doorway.

"I'm going now, lest I say something I'll regret."

"Well, I most assuredly have no such misgivings." Mama stabbed a finger toward Jemmah, all the malice and animosity she'd held partially in check until now, etched onto her harsh features. Undeniable, glaring, and meant to draw blood.

To wound.

"I regret the day you were born, Jemmah Violet Emeline. I shall be well rid of you, and the constant reminder of your blackguard of a father staring at me through your countenance. Go, and do not return. You are no longer welcome beneath this roof!"

7

Jules whistled as he strode the several blocks to Theo's house, his boots clacking in a comfortable rhythm upon the damp pavement.

Given the cannon-gray clouds suspended across the horizon, perhaps not the wisest choice. A more sensible man might've ridden or taken his curricle, but not only did he enjoy the exercise, he had an ulterior motive for choosing to walk.

Theo had sent her carriage for Jemmah, which meant she'd return home the same way.

His conscience chastised him.

Conniving wretch.

Righto, indeed, I am, Jules agreed cheerily.

He intended to accompany her and ask her mother for permission to pay his addresses. The idea had taken root last night, and by this morning was firmly entrenched.

Most likely, in fact, he'd wager on it, Mrs. Dament would initially object. However, no caring parent would deny their daughter a duchy, for that was Jules's eventual intent. And that he believed, was fairly certain, truth be told, he was halfway—*all the way*?— to being in love with Jemmah already, well ... that was just a tremendous bonus.

On the ride, he might very well hold Jemmah's hand or even pinch another savory kiss or two. Or a dozen.

At the provocative notion, his nether regions twitched. Again.

Worse than a frog on August-heated pavement, by Jove.

Since last night, he'd been hard as the cast iron statues gracing the corner pillars of Theo's grand house too. He hadn't slept more than fifteen uninterrupted minutes without his aroused, disgruntled body pulling him from slumber, demanding release.

Touching his hat's brim, he acknowledged acquaintances he encountered along the route, earning him several wide-eyed, stupefied expressions.

London was unaccustomed to the Duke of Dandridge sporting a Cheshire's broad smile or tipping his hat in a cordial manner. The spring in his step and the idiotic grin carved on his face took even him by surprise.

Jemmah had done this.

In a twinkling, his childhood friend, now turned into a gloriously lovely woman, had unlocked his dormant heart. Had him casting off his melancholic shroud and regarding the world with a newfound, optimistic view.

Seeing her again last night...

Everything had become as clear to him as newly-polished crystal.

Jemmah was what he desired. She always had been.

That was why he'd been so drawn to Annabel. Blonde and blue-eyed, she'd resembled Jemmah, even boasting a similar temperament.

His spirit, his intuition, whatever part of him that acknowledged Jemmah had been branded upon his soul, had tried to tell him that very thing.

Only he'd been stupidly deaf and blind to the promptings—hadn't recognized them, hadn't even known what he craved until she'd drowsily smiled up at him, the full radiance of her smile tilting his world topsy-turvy.

Then as if the narrow crack in the doorway he'd been peering through with one eye suddenly sprang wide open, he could see everything, down to each perfect, minute detail.

And yes, by God, he savored the implausibility, relished the paradox, laughed out loud at the glorious coincidence that drove him to slip into the very room she slept within.

"You're looking especially chipper today, Dandridge," drawled a familiar bored voice. "Did you enjoy the ball after all?"

Pennington, blast his bunions.

Jules met Pennington's and Sutcliffe's amused gazes.

"I'm surprised to see either of you about. Thought you were off to the gaming hells after leaving Lady Lockhart's last night."

"We did." Sutcliffe cocked his head, regarding Jules for a lengthy moment. "Pennington, did my eyes deceive me or was Dandridge smiling? You know that queer thing where his mouth twitches upward occasionally?"

He veered Pennington a falsely-confused glance. "The phenomenon occurs so rarely, I cannot be sure."

"No, Sutcliffe, I saw it too. Thought I might be still feeling the effects of our late night." Pennington made a pretense of examining Jules's face with his quizzing glass.

"You're both utter twiddlepoops."

Jules stepped around them and continued on his way. He wasn't ready to explain his happiness, nor was he prepared to endure their sarcasm and mockery. Not when it came to his feelings regarding Jemmah.

"Twiddlepoops? *Twiddlepoops*?" Sutcliffe repeated, affronted. "Damn. Dandridge, are you getting soft? Dandies, fops, and moon-eyed bucks are twiddlepoops." He thumped his chest. "Pennington and I are knaves, scoundrels, jackanapes, blackguards, rakehells, reprobates. But never anything as tepid and asinine as a twiddlepoop."

"I should say not," Pennington agreed with a sharp jerk of his head. "I'm truly offended."

Sutcliffe fell in step beside Jules, his expression contemplative.

Pennington came alongside Jules as well, and eyes narrowed, rubbed his chin. "Does this have anything to do with the chit you kissed at Lady Lockhart's last night?"

Jules stalled mid-stride.

"You saw?"

How, in bloody hell?

"Old chap, the draperies were wide open." Pennington slapped Jules on the shoulder. "Not to worry. Sutcliffe and I were having a smoke. No one else ventured to the house's rear. Only we witnessed the pathetic peck you gave the pretty thing before she tore from the room. You really need to work on that, old boy. I was almost embarrassed for you."

Ah, so they'd only seen the last kiss.

"Who is she?" This from Sutcliffe, wearing a sly grin.

"None of your business."

Jules resumed his walk and lengthened his stride.

He couldn't compromise Jemmah.

"Devil it," Pennington said as he replaced his quizzing glass. "He's protecting her. Must be serious then. I didn't recognize the gel. Did you?"

He leaned around Jules to poke Sutcliffe's shoulder.

Sutcliffe shook his dark head. "No. But she did look familiar. We could ask Lady Lockhart, I suppose."

"Oh, for God's sake. She's someone I knew a long time ago. Someone I shall do anything to protect from gossip and speculation."

Hands on his hips, Jules glared back and forth, prepared to wipe the smirks off their faces.

Instead, both regarded him with calm, keen interest, but not a hint of ridicule.

Pennington grinned, his one green eye and one blue eye twinkling with suppressed mirth. "Are we to wish you happy?"

Jules sighed and shook his head. "Not yet. But I intend to change that as soon as possible. And you," he jabbed a finger at each of them in turn, "are to keep my confidence in this matter. I'll have your words, gentlemen."

"Of course," they murmured in unison, a trifle too quickly and subdued for Jules's comfort.

Sutcliffe nodded at an acquaintance, and after he'd passed, extended his hand. "We leave you here, but please accept my heartiest best wishes that you are successful. Just be careful, my friend. Such behavior is totally out of character for you, and that's why I'm inclined to believe you actually love Miss Dament."

Thundering hippopotamus's hooves.

How the hell had they learned Jemmah's name?

"Damn it, Sutcliffe. We agreed not to reveal we knew who she was." Pennington scowled darkly. "You never could keep a secret."

"True, but look at him." Pennington gestured toward Jules. "I cannot bring myself to taunt someone so obviously smitten. Can you? 'Twould be cruel, and we do profess to being his closest chums."

"I'm standing right here, and can hear every word." They wouldn't talk. That Jules knew beyond a doubt. "You're sure no one else saw her with me?"

"You can rest easy on that account, Dandridge," Pennington said.

"Well, keep your ears open, just in case. I must be off. I'll be late for tea at Lady Lockhart's." With a wave, Jules continued on his way, ignoring their chorus of guffaws.

Damn them.

They knew he didn't attend tea.

Not until Jemmah turned up in his life again.

He truly wasn't given to rash, impulsive behavior.

Quite the opposite, in fact.

Which was one of the reasons he knew, beyond whimsy or doubt, Jemmah must be his.

Oh, his mother and uncles would pitch conniption fits equal to the Regent's, but in the end, they'd concede.

What choice had they?

He was the Duke of Dandridge.

He controlled the purse strings.

His word was law, and it was far past time they acknowledged his position rather than treating him like a feckless, incompetent booby in need of their constant guidance.

His gratified chuckle earned him a curious glance from a pair of plump matrons dressed in the finest stare of fashion.

How wonderfully free and unencumbered he felt.

But how to persuade Jemmah that he was serious in his intentions after years of scant contact with her?

Such impulsiveness on Jules's part would've send a buzz through the *ton*'s elite parlors if he were a rakehell or knave, but his reputation as a grave, severe sort made the notion preposterous to all but Theo, Sutcliffe, and Pennington, and he anticipated a full-blown cacophony when word leaked out.

And it would.

All it took was two or three visits to the same address, and the upper ten thousand would eagerly check their post daily for a wedding invitation.

How could he expect Jemmah to take him earnestly when what he proposed flew in the face of common sense and contradicted his typical behavior?

True, she'd kissed him like a long-starved woman, but he suspected she had been deprived of affection for years.

Had she responded because she desperately craved acceptance and love, or because she felt something for Jules?

Male pride demanded the latter, but prudence suggested the former.

Mightn't Jemmah's reaction be attributed to both?

Yes.

That seemed most logical.

He stepped to the side, permitting a nurse and her three rambunctious charges to pass.

Jules would use every advantage to win Jemmah and her mother over. He began making a mental list of tactics he intended to use.

A few minutes later, he rounded the corner onto Mayfair, just as Theo's carriage rumbled to a stop before her mansion. He quickened his pace, his pulse keeping time with his hurried stride.

Jemmah alit, wearing a simple blue coat, a trifle too short, and a plain straw bonnet. She reached inside the conveyance, and after withdrawing a battered valise, faced the grand house.

Did her shoulders slump the slightest? The regal column of her neck bend as if she bore a weighty burden?

"Miss Dament."

His regard never left her as his legs ate up the distance between them.

Never had he beheld anything half as lovely as when she turned, and upon spying him, joy blossomed across her face. All these years of being a sensible, logical sort, and now he felt as giddy as a lad in short pants or a foxed-to-his-gills tippler at being gifted a wondrous smile.

"Your Grace."

She dipped into a smooth curtsy as he bowed, but not before he saw her red-rimmed eyes, framed by spiky lashes.

And the telltale salty trail across her cheeks once more.

An ink-stained fingertip poked from the gloved hand clutching the valise. Perhaps the drawings she'd promised were tucked within the dilapidated piece of luggage that was older than she, if it was a day.

She'd known deprivation, and a dull ache settled in his gut at the awareness.

Much had happened to his Jemmah in the years since they'd parted ways, most of it not good.

As the carriage rattled away, he took her valise and her elbow, but rather than escorting her up the front steps, Jules directed her 'round back, toward the mews.

Confusion knitting her brow, she cast a glance behind her.

"Where are we going?"

"Where I can have a word with you in private."

Once hidden from the street, he placed his forefinger beneath her chin and raised her face.

"What has happened, dear one?"

The light faded from her lovely eyes, and the tears pooled there slowly leaked from the corners.

Such anguish of spirit reflected in her soul that he gathered her in his arms.

To hell with decorum and propriety.

She needed comfort.

Simple as that.

Sagging into his chest, she wept softly, brokenheartedly.

Her scent, that light clean smell of soap and lavender and perhaps the tiniest hint of rose water wafted upward as her shoulders shook with her grief.

"My dear, Jemmah. Please tell me. What has caused you such distress?"

Her hat's tattered edge scraped his chin as she struggled to compose herself.

"Mama has turned me out, and I've nowhere to go but to impose upon Aunt Theo's hospitality."

"Why would she do such a thing?"

He veered a swift glance around.

Good.

No one ventured near or detected their presence behind the neatly-trimmed seven-foot shrubs bordering Theo's house.

In a few concise, shuddery sentences, Jemmah explained what happened after he left the ball last night.

"So, because I refused to cede the opportunity to Adelinda, as I have almost everything of import my entire life, my mother put me from our house. I was only permitted to take what I could fit in one bag."

Jules stroked her slender spine, desperate to comfort her. "Well, I can think of two ladies who will be euphoric at this turn of events. Three, if you count Sabrina. She was over the moon with excitement when I told her you'd generously offered to teach her drawing."

He wasn't exactly distressed either.

Her change in circumstances played quite nicely into his intent to woo her.

Jemmah sniffled and dashed her fingers across her face. "May I impose upon you to borrow your handkerchief?"

Great galloping giraffes.

The poor darling didn't even own a scrap of cloth with which to dab her impossibly expressive eyes.

Jules passed her the starched and neatly-folded monogrammed square and waited while she dried her face, then blew her nose. Once she regained her self-control, he collected her bag and tucked her hand into the crook of his elbow.

Gazing down at her, he smiled tenderly. "I'd be a liar if I pretended I'm not thrilled I shall be able to call upon you here now."

An adorable flush swept her face, accompanied by a winsome upward tilt of her mouth.

"Yes, there is that to look forward to. If Aunt Theo agrees to me staying with her."

"She will, of course. And do you look forward to me paying my addresses?"

He hadn't meant to go that far just yet, but the opportunity had presented itself, and he had impulsively told her he meant to court her.

Rather than using the front entrance, he steered her to the open French windows outside the ballroom.

Servants drifted in and out of the room, clearing up the remaining vestiges of last night's celebration.

Theo's poodle, Caesar, trotted through the empty ballroom, ebony nose and tail in the air, his nails clicking on the parquet floor.

Instead of answering straightaway, Jemmah tilted her head and regarded him through those thick, tear-damp lashes, her speculative gaze penetrating, yet reflective.

"The dowager has offered me an opportunity someone in my position isn't likely to have replicated."

"So have I, my precious Jem."

Drawing her to the side of the house, Jules pulled her near. A damp breeze fluttered the cherry blossoms, sending a pink petal shower onto the sandstone pavers they stood upon.

"Why now, when you've scarcely paid me any notice for years?" She fiddled with her reticule strap. "I know I acted… Well, I was awfully glad to see you last night, and I did enjoy the dance. And after too. Very much, in fact. But that was… is a fairytale. I'm not a simpleton. Women like me don't have the Duke of Dandridge paying them court when there are far lovelier, more suitable, and wealthier prospects."

"Then don't think of me as the duke, but as your friend of many, many years. One who has never held another as dear, and one who with all of his heart, wants to be more." He trailed his finger along her jaw. "Much more, if you'll let me."

Jules settled his lips onto hers, tasting once again the sweetness of her mouth. He poured all of his yearning, his love into the kiss, communicating what he so desperately needed to tell her.

Without prompting, Jemmah opened her mouth, and using the skills he'd taught her last night, proceeded to send any vestige of logical thought he retained, spiraling out of control.

Holding her face between his palms, he angled her head to kiss her deeper still, savoring her velvety tongue sparring with his.

A muffled *woof,* followed by snuffling near his ankles reined in his passion.

What was Jules thinking, kissing her in broad daylight?

Evidently, even a pragmatic somber fellow such as himself, once besotted, didn't think at all clearly.

What a splendid realization.

Still, he'd already been seen kissing her once, and even if his intentions were honorable, he'd not bring censure upon Jemmah.

Theo stepped halfway out the door and pulled her bold-colored Norwich shawl more snugly around her shoulders.

"My footman said he heard voices out here. Whatever are the two of you doing?"

"I'm trying to persuade Miss Dament to permit me to court her."

Jules didn't care who knew, and he needed Theo as an ally.

"And I haven't agreed, as yet." The warmth radiating from Jemmah's eyes encouraged him.

She would agree. She must.

A smile wreathed Theo's face, so exuberant, her ruby earbobs trembled.

"Well, if that isn't the most splendid news I've heard in a great while." With a swift glimpse about the courtyard, she beckoned them. "Come inside and tell me all."

Her focus alit on the portmanteau near Jemmah's foot, and her questioning gaze vacillated between Jules and Jemmah.

"Are you eloping?"

Jemmah gave a small, water-logged laugh and shook her head. "Nothing so romantic, I'm afraid, Aunt Theo." She summoned a brave smile. "I'm in need of a place to stay. Indefinitely."

"Ah." Theo looped her arm through Jemmah's leaving Jules to collect the beaten-about-the-edges valise. "You are welcome for as long as you want, my dear. I'm quite thrilled, actually."

"I'm ever so grateful, Auntie." Jemmah hugged her aunt's arm.

Theo tossed a saucy glance over her shoulder.

"Now, tell me, what's this business about Dandridge courting you?"

8

Three glorious weeks later.

Jemmah angled first one way, and then the other before the floor length oval looking glass.

The black-edged cerulean-blue walking ensemble was quite the loveliest thing she'd ever seen. But then again, that was what she thought with each new gown dear Aunt Theo or the Dowager Lady Lockhart bestowed upon her.

And each time, she'd insisted they'd gifted her quite enough and forbade them to purchase her a single thing more.

They'd laughed and pooh-poohed her.

One would think it should be easy to become accustomed to the gorgeous gowns, fallalls, fripperies… scented soaps and lotions… enough sleep for the first time in years. But it wasn't easy, and Jemmah still couldn't as yet reconcile herself to this new way of life.

Each time she approached the dowager about beginning her companionship duties, the dame dismissed her concerns, insisting there was time enough to worry about that later. She wouldn't even permit Jemmah to attend her on their evenings out, claiming Aunt Theo more than capable of the task.

Aunt Theo would then take Lady Lockhart's arm, leaving Jules to offer Jemmah his elbow. She suspected the two of match-making. How could she fault the dears when she desired the same thing?

After supper tonight, they were off to the theater again.

Oh, that first time had been so magical.

In a hastily-altered, borrowed gown of Aunt Theo's, Jemmah had entered on Jules's arm, for once appearing in public confident and proud.

Tucked in Auntie's gallery box, Jemmah had tried to watch the ballet performance, but his hand holding hers, his lips mere inches away as he whispered in her ear, the timbre of his melodic baritone causing delicious little tremors...

Why, she couldn't even recall the name of the ballet they'd watched.

Dabbing a bit of lily of the valley perfume behind each ear and upon each wrist, she grinned at Caesar sprawled before her balcony doors, muzzle on his black forepaws, and his big soulful eyes watching her every move.

He'd taken to her, almost as if he sensed she needed unconditional love, and Aunt Theo didn't seem to mind. Or if she did, she kept the knowledge to herself. But Jemmah's aunt also loved her without restriction, and even that would take time to become accustomed to.

She would, though.

She had every reason to, and he'd be here shortly.

Jemmah's stomach tumbled in that wonderful wobbly way it did whenever her thoughts gravitated toward Jules. A wonder she could hold her food down with all the cavorting taking place in her middle these days.

"Miss Jemmah, that color becomes you. You look like a real lady, you do." Mary's mouth tipped into a cheeky grin as she fluffed the bed's pillows. "Forgive my impertinence, but your sister would gnash her teeth if she saw you now."

Undoubtedly.

"I'm so glad you're here, Mary."

Within a week of Jemmah's leaving, Frazer Pimble had approached Jemmah and revealed Mama had dismissed Mary without reference. And since Aunt Theo insisted Jemmah needed a lady's maid—to do what, for pity's sake?—quite naturally, Jemmah had been determined to see Mary have the position.

Having two Pimbles in the household caused a bit of a conundrum at first, but Aunt Theo, always one to throw convention into the gutters, advised everyone to simply call the maid by her given name.

After tying her bonnet's ribbons, Jemmah gathered her reticule and parasol.

Everywhere one looked, signs of an early spring were evident. Including the bright vivid green fern fronds, sunny jonquils, cheery primroses, and the shining orb in the sky splaying its golden fingers across the heavens.

Her heart glowed with warmth every bit as permeating and

pleasurable.

These had been the happiest weeks of her life, and sometimes when she awoke in the middle of the night and the familiar despondency cloaked her, she had to remind herself she'd left her oppressive life behind.

Goodness, so much had changed in such a short while.

Not the least of which was Jules's actively courting her—

Without permission.

Mama had refused to receive him each time he'd approached her on the matter.

He vowed he wouldn't give up, that she'd eventually come around.

He didn't know Mama.

She held a grudge and was about as malleable as dried mortar.

Sighing, Jemmah booted her unhappy musings aside.

As Jules had done every day since Jemmah had come to live with Aunt Theo, he'd be here momentarily for their daily outing. They'd explored all of the major parks and Covent Garden, visited Astley's Amphitheatre, eaten ices at Gunter's, and shopped along Bond Street several times.

Today's plans included an excursion to Vauxhall Gardens.

She intended to return in the evening sometime too, but for this initial visit, she wanted to see the famed gardens in the daylight.

A soft knock rapped at her bedchamber door.

"Come."

Jemmah drew on one soft kid glove.

"His Grace, the Duke of Dandridge, awaits you in the gold parlor, miss." Pimble winked at his sister. "Let me know if Mary gets sassy. I'll straighten her out, right quick, I shall."

Mary stuck out her tongue and laughing, chucked a pillow at her brother's head.

Observing their antics, Jemmah twisted her mouth into a wistful smile.

She didn't remember ever playing like that with Adelinda.

"Never fear. Your sister attends her duties with conscience and efficiency. Mary, collect your cloak. I don't want to keep the duke waiting."

Ten minutes later saw Jemmah comfortably seated in Dandridge's landau as his driver expertly tooled the conveyance along the busy lane. Mary dutifully sat in the rear groom's seat to allow Jemmah and Jules privacy while still acting the part of chaperone.

As he was wont to do, despite the slight impropriety, Jules promptly tucked Jemmah's gloved hand into his buff-clad one. He bent his head near, his breath tickling her ear.

"I called upon your mother again yesterday."

"And?"

Jemmah searched his face, reading the answer in his compassionate gaze.

Drat Mama's obstinance and pride.

"She refused me once more."

The sun bounced off the diamond in his cravat, and the hunter green of his jacket reflected in the jade flecks in his irises.

Such kind, gentle eyes, yet also intelligent, alert, and assessing.

"I'm not surprised. In her bitterness, Mama blames everyone else for her circumstances. She sees herself as the victim, and that prevents her from hearing reason."

Jemmah returned the mild, reassuring squeeze he gave her fingers.

The comfortable *clip-clopping* of the horses' hooves on the cobblestones, the sun's caressing rays, as well as the vehicle's plush seat had her blinking sleepily and fighting a yawn.

"I'm sure it's been quite difficult for her and Adelinda, now that Mary's left and Aunt Theo has withdrawn her financial support."

Jules made a confirming sound in the back of his throat, causing his Adam's apple to bob. "I've no doubt, but once we are wed, I fully intend to provide her with an allowance as long as she agrees—"

Jemmah clutched his hand, and jaw sagging, she stared in stunned incredulity.

Confusion yanked his brows together, and he patted her hand twice.

"Why do you look at me like that? Don't you want me to give your mother any funds? I thought you'd be pleased, but if not—"

Shaking her head, Jemmah's mouth quivered.

"No, no. It's not that at all. I think it very generous of you, and most forgiving too."

More forgiving than she was capable of so soon.

Mama didn't deserve Jules's magnanimity.

He bent nearer, and brazenly brushed his lip across the top of Jemmah's ear.

"Then what is it?"

Jemmah slid Mary a covert glance.

Completely absorbed in the passing scenery, the maid hadn't heard Jules.

Jemmah scooted a little nearer, brushing her thigh against his in a most provocative way.

Keeping her voice low, so neither the driver nor Mary might overhear, she murmured, "You said... Well, at least I thought you said, 'When we wed.'"

She raised hopeful eyes to Jules's.

How pathetic she must look. How mortified she'd be if she'd misunderstood.

They'd never discussed marriage, but his courting and repeated visits to Mama must mean he'd contemplated the matter at some length. And when the time was right, he'd broach the subject with Jemmah.

Although, as long as Mama refused to let him officially address Jemmah, they'd little choice but to wait for her to come of age or elope to Gretna Green.

Not an entirely awful notion by half.

Actually, a rather grand one. Mayhap she should mention it to him.

If he proposed.

And if he didn't? If she'd misheard?

Well then, when the dowager returned to the country, Jemmah would accompany her.

Thank goodness she had the promised position to fall back upon. The knowledge brought her a great deal of comfort.

Tenderness bent Jules's mouth and pleated the angles of his face, deepening his fascinating eyes to a simmering cognac.

"Indeed, I did say that very thing, my precious Jem. I thought you understood that's always my intention, my sweet, since I found you cozily slumbering in Theo's parlor. To make you my duchess, the keeper of my heart."

She couldn't quite subdue her tiny elated gasp.

Sudden wariness filtered across his face, and he straightened a bit. "Did I assume wrongly? Misjudge your affections?"

"No, not at all, Your Grace."

"Jules," he reminded her.

Jemmah's eyes misted and giving him a tremulous smile, she dragged her handkerchief from her reticule. Chin tucked to her chest, she angled her parasol and discreetly dabbed her eyes. "I didn't dare dream something so wholly marvelous would happen to me."

"Dare I hope your answer is yes? It's not too soon?"

Jemmah gave a jerky nod, afraid she'd weep for joy if she spoke.

The carriage gave an abrupt shudder as the rear wheel sank into a hole, jostling them against each other.

Jules beaver hat smacked her parasol, skewing it to the side.

As he straightened it, he sought her eyes.

"Yes, it's too soon, or your answer is yes?"

"Yes, I'll marry you, darling man," she whispered, perhaps not as quietly as she might since she didn't care who knew this wonderful news.

They'd still Mama to convince, of course, but Jemmah refused to let that obstacle steal a single speck of her elation.

Jules released a long, shuddering breath.

"Thank God. I almost swallowed my heart. I think it's still lodged somewhere in my throat." After patting his neck, he winked and tucked her scandalously closer. "We can discuss the details while we wander Vauxhall, and I promise to propose properly. Too many ears, right now."

He waggled his eyebrows toward Mary.

"But, I must tell you," his voice dropped to a low purr, causing the most remarkable of sensations to sprout in unmentionable areas. "I adore you, Jemmah, love."

A plump tear did escape then. One of pure, unadulterated joy.

"And I love you too, Jules."

Had for years, but she wasn't ready to share that just yet. Not until they were alone, and she could show him just how ecstatic she was.

Knuckle bent, he caught the wayward droplet. "I only want to see tears of happiness in your beautiful blue eyes from now on."

"They will be."

Sparing a glance overhead, Jules closed his eyes. "Doesn't the sun feel glorious?"

"Yes." Though he was far more spectacular.

Trailing her gaze over his refined profile, she put her other hand to her middle to still the odd spasm that always occurred when she gazed upon him thusly. She didn't remember a time she hadn't loved him, and that he felt the same...

Galloping turtles, such glee made her lightheaded.

Gone was the stiff, stern, unapproachable peer others had mocked for his severity. Jules now let the rest of the world see the man she'd always known existed beneath his prickly, protective exterior.

A contented sigh passed between her lips.

A half an hour later saw Mary settled beneath a tree with a book and several gossip rags, while Jemmah and Jules strolled the gardens.

She'd lived in London her entire life and had never been inside Vauxhall.

Father's pockets had always been in dun territory, made worse by the funds he frittered away on his mistresses.

"Have I told you how beautiful you are today, Jemmah?" Jules deep voice rumbled low in his broad chest.

A pleasure-born blush bathed her that he would think her so. "No, but I know a taradiddle when I hear it. But it does my womanly pride wonders to hear the nonsense, nevertheless. You forget, I have a looking glass."

He tweaked her nose. "And you, my dear, are blind to your own loveliness."

"Well, isn't this a coincidence. I was just speaking of you, Jemmah."

Upon hearing Adelinda's spiteful voice, Jemmah spun around.

Boils and bunions.

Attired in a lovely emerald green and peach gown—new and expensive if she wasn't mistaken—Adelinda hung on the arm of an attractive man Jemmah didn't recognize.

Where had Adelinda come by monies to purchase a gown of such high quality?

And who was this newest admirer? Another of Adelinda's unsuitable swains, no doubt.

He might be handsome, but something unnerving, dark and oily, shadowed his soulless eyes.

From the languid way his gaze slid over Jemmah before something more than polite interest sharpened his features, she'd bet all the buttons in France he wasn't a respectable sort. In fact, he made her want to race home, dive beneath the bedcovering, and pull them over her head to block his leering gaze.

Adelinda's perusal of Jemmah was no less thorough, but the look in her eye could never be described as appreciative or cordial.

"Miss Dament. Perkins." Jules still possessively cradled Jemmah's elbow, and he gave the new arrivals a distinctly cool and the briefest possible greeting.

Not friends, then.

"Dandridge." Perkins's equally frosty acknowledgement confirmed her suspicion. The smile Perkins then bestowed on Adelinda didn't quite reach his shrewd eyes. "Aren't you going to introduce me?"

Mouth pinched in displeasure, Adelinda raised an annoyed brow.

"My sister, Jemmah. Jemmah, Mr. Samuel Perkins. He owns a club on Kings Street," she said all smug superiority.

The last was declared as if he maintained a private suite at Buckingham Palace.

"So, Adelinda, this is the younger sister you've told me so much about."

I'll wager she has.

Perkins's lascivious chuckle sent Jemmah's skin scuttling, and unnerved by the predatory glint in his eye, she edged nearer to Jules.

His palm tightened on her arm the merest bit before he looped her hand through his elbow, the movement drawing her closer.

"You misled me, my dear Adelinda," Perkins said with another slippery upward twist of his mouth. "Your sister's a diamond of the first water if I ever saw one."

He dares address Adelinda by her given name?

Appearing like she'd been served amphibians or reptiles for supper, Adelinda managed a sickly smile.

"I've nearly convinced Mama to permit you to return home, Jemmah. If you put off your grand airs. After all, you cannot expect to take advantage of Aunt Theo's benevolence indefinitely."

Still the same spiteful Adelinda, though granted, a trio of weeks was hardly time enough to change one's character.

It was long enough to fall more profoundly, marvelously in love with Jules.

"I won't be returning, Adelinda. Of that you may rest assured."

Jemmah sent Jules a secretive glance, but her sister saw it.

Adelinda stepped closer, her perceptive gaze narrowed. "If you think—"

"Dandridge, darling. I thought I saw you from across the way."

Oh, for all the kippers in Kensington.

Two misses determined to trap Jules in their webs, and this one with the audacity to call him darling in public?

Momentary uncertainty skipped about the tattered edges of Jemmah's composure.

Inhaling a bracing breath, she swung 'round to see Miss Milbourne, accompanied by two men she didn't recognize, but whose unusual topaz eyes and honeyed hair decreed them Jules's relatives.

Jules's forearm stiffened beneath Jemmah's fingers.

"Miss Milbourne. Uncles."

Ah, the famed Charmont uncles who believed Jules incapable of making his own decisions.

Tension thicker than custard settled onto the uncomfortable group, everyone eyeing the other with speculation and suspicion.

Miss Milbourne minced closer, absolute perfection in an exquisite ivory and plum confection, all frothy, feminine lace. And she smelled positively divine.

Drat and dash it all.

Why couldn't she have a flaw or two or three?

Buck teeth?

A hairy mole upon her nose?

Crossed eyes? *Fangs*?

"I've missed you." She ran her white-gloved fingers down Jules's chest, and blinked coyly at him from beneath her preposterously thick eyelashes.

Brazen as an alley cat twitching her tail for a mate.

"I've been otherwise engaged." The steely look he impaled his uncles with had them shuffling their feet and raptly examining the foliage.

Cowards.

Acutely aware of the elegantly coiffed, perfumed, and hostile woman standing but inches away, taking her measure, Jemmah arched a starchy brow. She was newly-betrothed to the Duke of Dandridge, and for all of Miss Milbourne's posturing and attempts to intimidate, the woman was, quite frankly, and most gratifyingly... the loser.

Her condescending gaze flicked to Jemmah, and Miss Milbourne's pupils contracted to pinpricks as she oh-so casually twirled her parasol.

"So I see," she drawled. "I'd heard rumors you were doing the pretty and escorting your godmother's dowdy ward about town. I must say, I never took you, of all men, for a nursemaid, Dandridge. Most decent of you, inconveniencing yourself to oblige Lady Lockhart's unreasonable requests."

Adelinda's giggle, earned her an exasperated glower from Perkins.

"Yes, quite right, Miss Milbourne. No man has ever willingly directed his attention at my frumpy sister."

At her sister's barbed insult, Jemmah stiffened and set her jaw against the oath bucking to escape the narrow barrier of her lips.

A duchess doesn't tell ladies to go bugger themselves.

Miss Milbourne and Adelinda exchanged a gloating glance.

Enough of these two vixens trying to draw her blood with their jealousy. "You can both—"

"Rest assured, ladies, I'm never coerced into doing anything I don't want to." In an intimate, comforting gesture, Jules laid his other hand atop Jemmah's. "And you're woefully incorrect if you presume there is any woman on earth I'd rather spend time with than my betrothed."

9

"Betrothed?" sputtered Miss Milbourne and Miss Dament in horrified unison.

Each appeared to have swallowed wriggling spiders whole.

Jules quashed his laugh, but couldn't contain the slow, satisfied upsweep of his mouth.

He bent his neck and murmured in Jemmah's ear.

"I beg your pardon for announcing it this way."

The Uncles stood slack-jawed and dazed, too.

Zounds, their expressions were priceless.

Jemmah dimpled and lifted a shoulder, whispering back, "I rather enjoyed the results."

Jules did laugh then, a mirth-filled explosion from his middle, which drew the attention of two lads chasing a pug with a ball in its mouth.

God, he loved her unique perspective on things.

But so much for the romantic proposal he'd intended within the arched arbor facing yonder pond. Inside his coat pocket an emerald-cut, rare blue diamond, a shade darker than Jemmah's eyes, lay nestled in its ivory velvet box.

He'd arranged a picnic luncheon complete with champagne in the quaint retreat. Damn his eyes, he'd even hired musicians to play in the background and a boatman to make sure the pond's many swans paddled by in a timely fashion.

His precious Jem warranted such regal treatment.

"You can't marry the duke, Jemmah." The elder Miss Dament pointed a shaky finger at her sister, her voice wavering every bit as much as the wobbly digit extended toward her sister. "You must have Mama's consent. And, she'll never give it. Never."

"Then I'll wait until I'm of age. Or we'll elope." Jemmah's quiet, confident reply sent her sister into high dudgeon.

Face puckered and turning the most spectacular shade of puce, Miss Adelinda fisted her hands and growled. Actually growled, before giving them her back and stomping across the green.

Perkins followed, but not before daring one last lewd appraisal of Jemmah.

He'd bamboozled Adelinda, the imprudent chit.

The club Perkins owned was nothing more than a low-end gaming hell and whorehouse. If the girl had taken up with the likes of him, she was thoroughly ruined. If she wasn't careful, she'd be spreading her legs for his paying customers.

Jules couldn't even buy her respectability now, which only made his case for winning Jemmah stronger. Mrs. Dament couldn't count on her eldest daughter making a suitable match and directing funds her mother's way.

He could, however, pay them a substantial sum to retire to the country.

Permanently.

If they agreed to never bother Jemmah again.

Yes, that was just what he'd do. As soon as he returned home. Mrs. Dament would have no choice but to agree now.

"Elope? Preposterous," blustered Uncle Darius, finally finding his tongue, while Uncle Leopold waggled his head up and down like a marionette on a string.

"Utterly absurd. What would people say?" Leopold managed at last.

"Then I suggest you put your support behind Miss Dament and me, Uncles. And convince Mother to do the same. For I shall have *no* other, and all attempts to dissuade me will be met with swift recourse. Do I make myself clear?"

They nodded, albeit grudgingly. And then, mumbling something about needing to count cigars or some such rot, they departed, their tawny heads bent near. Every few steps, they tossed a befuddled and disgruntled glance at Jules.

He didn't give a fig whether they approved or not.

He smiled down into Jemmah's upturned, amazingly composed face. Lambasted thrice in ten minutes and here she stood, the epitome of grace and poise, beaming with love for him—*for him!*

His heart had chosen well.

Statue still, her countenance pale as the scalloped lace edging her fashionable spencer, Miss Milbourne peered around.

Blinking slowly, as if someone had whacked her upon the head with her frilly parasol, she murmured, "Excuse me. I see an acquaintance I must speak with."

Head held high, she spun about and glided toward the pond, where nothing but a few ducks napped in the sun.

Taken to chatting with ducks, had she?

"Ho, what have we here?" Sutcliffe gave them a jaunty wave from across the green, and ambled their way accompanied by Pennington. Brow furrowed, he turned and watched Miss Milbourne's progress.

Jules shook his head and rolled his eyes toward the greenery overhead.

"My God. Did someone extend invitations unbeknownst to me?"

"Invitations? Is there a special occasion I'm unaware of?" Sutcliffe's attention veered to the departing uncles, Miss Milbourne, and lastly Jules. His grin threatened to split his face in two upon greeting Jemmah.

"Miss Dament." He bent into an exaggerated courtier's bow. "May I say how delighted I am to see you taking the air with Dandridge?"

"As am I." Pennington clasped a hand to his waist and bent low, too.

Jemmah canted her head, and eyes sparkling, offered them a bright smile. "Thank you, your graces. You're exuberance is... refreshing."

"*Is* there any special reason you're visiting the pleasure gardens today?" One hand on his hip, Sutcliffe, as subtle as a nubby toad on a pastry, attempted a nonchalant expression.

"I intended to propose, if you must know, you two interfering tabbies. But they," Jules jabbed his thumb in the direction of his uncles' and Miss Milbourne's departing figures, "ruined the occasion."

"By Jove, that's the best news I've heard in ages!" Pennington pumped Jules hand while Sutcliffe bent over Jemmah's. "Not that they ruined the occasion, but that you've at last declared yourself."

"I wish you the greatest happiness, Miss Dament," Sutcliffe said. "Now, we'll take our leave and let our friend be about this most important business."

Rubbing his thumb across the back of Jemmah's hand, Jules remained silent as the pair strode away. Everything he'd planned to make the day romantic and memorable had been quashed.

"Jules?"

He met Jemmah's slightly disconcerted eyes. "Yes, my dear?"

"Why is everyone staring in our direction?"

Jules raised his head and took a casual glance around.

She was right, though several people hastily looked away, finding either the sky or the ground profoundly fascinating.

Damn, the news of his intentions had travelled faster than the wind in sails, thanks to Jemmah's bitter sister.

Hmm, perhaps not a bad thing at all. With a few dozen witnesses...

He withdrew the ring box from his pocket.

"Jules?" This time Jemmah's voice went all soft and melty, as did her eyes. "Here?"

"Indeed."

Raising the lid, he folded to one knee.

His valet would scold him soundly for getting grass stains on his pantaloons. But this was right in its simple, unpretentiousness.

Just like his precious Jemmah.

With the sun shining upon them, bees busy gathering nectar, a frog or two croaking in the ponds' underbrush, while various birds called to one another, he would ask her to be his duchess.

"Jemmah, you are the jewel I've carried in my heart since I was a wee lad of ten. No one else makes me smile like you do. You consume my thoughts, and I cannot imagine any greater joy than spending the rest of my life with you." He smiled into her shining eyes. "Will you marry me?"

Jemmah squatted and extended her left hand.

Leave it to her to do something wholly unexpected.

"I shall, Jules. I've loved you for so long, I don't remember what life was before I did." She gave a little self-conscious laugh, as he slipped the ring on her finger.

"As a little girl, I imagined myself a princess, wearing a sapphire and diamond tiara, and locked in a tower. And you were the handsome prince who rescued me. On a white steed, of course, and carried me off to his castle to live happily ever after."

"Well, the duchy has a castle, and I believe several tiaras too. I own a white horse or two as well," he said assisting her upright. "And I shall strive every day to make you happy."

"I need nothing but to be with you to be deliriously so."

Then, in typical Jemmah fashion, she levered onto her toes, and kissed him.

On the mouth.

In public.

And it was perfect.

Epilogue

Chalchester Castle, Essex, England
July 1810

"Darling, Teodora giggled again."

Grinning in her excitement, Jemmah, holding her three-month-old daughter, gingerly picked her way between the smooth stones to Chalchester Lake's edge. The afternoon sun's rays reflected off the water as if a thousand brilliant diamonds had been cast across its surface.

She'd believed she couldn't be happier when she married Jules just over a year ago; after Mama had finally agreed to the match, because Adelinda found herself scandalously pregnant.

But Jemmah had been wrong.

Each day as Jules's wife brought her a new measure of joy and contentment she'd only dreamed of.

Oh, there'd been worries in the beginning, but not between her and Jules.

He'd kept his word and settled Mama and Adelinda in a charming cottage in Sussex, with a generous monthly allowance. But after Adelinda lost her babe and ran off with a traveling performer, Mama had fallen gravely ill, dying shortly thereafter.

The rancor and bitterness she'd harbored for so long, combined with a broken heart killed her, the doctor said.

On her death bed, Mama had pleaded for Jemmah's forgiveness, and she'd given it. She refused to harbor malice, for eventually, it would corrupt her soul as it had Mama's and Adelinda's.

Jemmah had no idea where her sister was now, but truly hoped she'd found even a small degree of the peace and joy Jemmah had.

Her bonnet's lavender ribbons stirring in the faint breeze, and the gravel crunching beneath her half-boots, she made her way to her husband.

Jules, standing knee deep in the gently-flowing current, and holding a fishing line, glanced behind him.

Teodora cooed and waved her little fists.

"She's a happy darling. Like her mother."

"Like her father too, although you do your best to convince people otherwise."

"Well, how else can I maintain my dour reputation?"

He chuckled as he stepped from the river, and after laying his pole beside the blanket spread upon the shore, extended his arms.

Jemmah laid Teodora within his sturdy, secure embrace.

The baby promptly smiled at her father, her almond-shaped eyes the same unusual topaz as his, and seized his forefinger in her tiny grasp.

She yawned and blinked sleepily.

Jules adjusted the infant then draped his other arm across Jemmah's shoulders. "We are happy, aren't we?"

Blissfully so.

Her head resting against his brawny shoulder, Jemmah nodded. "I'm so glad we decided to live here after marrying, rather than in London. I never realized how much I didn't like the hubbub. I enjoy visiting once in a while, especially since Aunt Theo won't venture to the country, but honestly, I never want to live in the city again."

"Did you really love me all that time we were apart?" Jules gazed down at her with such adoration, her heart stuttered a bit. "When you never spoke to me or even saw me?"

Jemmah poked his rib. "I've told you so dozens of times. I think it puffs your head to think so."

"It puffs other things too." He looked meaningfully at the bulge in his trousers.

"Well, husband, I believe I might have just the cure for what ails you." Jemmah took their sleeping daughter from him and once she'd tucked Teodora into her basket beneath a tree, extended her hand.

Asleep in the shade, their daughter would be safe. Besides, they were but a few steps away. "There's a lovely little grove yonder."

"Duchess, do you mean to have your way with me in broad daylight?"

The seductive twinkle in Jules's eyes and tugging at his delicious mouth told her he liked the notion every bit as much as she.

Following an animal trail through the grass, she arched him an invitation over her shoulder as she began to disrobe.

"I do, indeed, Your Grace."

If you've enjoyed reading **A Diamond for a Duke**, *Seductive Scoundrels Book 1*, then perhaps you'd enjoy the rest of the books in the series:

A Diamond for a Duke
Only a Duke Would Dare
A December with a Duke
What Would a Duke Do?
Wooed by a Wicked Duke
Duchess of His Heart
Never Dance with a Duke
Earl of Wainthorpe
Earl of Scarborough
Wedding her Christmas Duke
Earl of Keyworth

Coming soon in the series!
The Debutante and the Duke
How to Win A Duke's Heart
Loved by a Dangerous Duke
When a Duke Loves a Lass

The Earl and the Spinster

THE BLUE ROSE REGENCY ROMANCES:
THE CULPEPPER MISSES, BOOK ONE

1

Even when most prudently considered, and with the noblest of intentions, one who wagers with chance oft finds oneself empty-handed.
~*Wisdom and Advice—The Genteel Lady's Guide to Practical Living*

Esherton Green,
Near Acton, Cheshire, England
Early April 1822

Was I born under an evil star or cursed from my first breath?

Brooke Culpepper suppressed the urge to shake her fist at the heavens and berate The Almighty aloud. The devil boasted better luck than she. My God, now two *more* cows struggled to regain their strength?

She slid Richard Mabry, Esherton Green's steward-turned-overseer, a worried glance from beneath her lashes as she chewed her lower lip and paced before the unsatisfactory fire in the study's hearth. The soothing aroma of wood smoke, combined with linseed oil, old leather, and the faintest trace of Papa's pipe tobacco, bathed the room. The scents reminded her of happier times but did little to calm her frayed nerves.

Sensible gray woolen skirts swishing about her ankles, she whirled to make the return trip across the once-bright green and gold Axminster carpet, now so threadbare, the oak floor peeked through in numerous places. Her scuffed half-boots fared little better, and she hid a wince when the scrap of leather she'd used to cover the hole in her left sole this morning slipped loose again.

From his comfortable spot in a worn and faded wingback chair, Freddy, her aged Welsh corgi, observed her progress with soulful brown eyes, his muzzle propped on stubby paws. Two ancient tabbies lay curled so tightly together on the cracked leather sofa that determining where one ended and the other began was difficult.

What was she to do? Brooke clamped her lip harder and winced.

Should she venture to the barn to see the cows herself?

What good would that do? She knew little of doctoring cattle and so left the animals' care in Mr. Mabry's capable hands. Her strength lay in the financial administration of the dairy farm and her ability to stretch a shilling as thin as gossamer.

She cast a glance at the bay window and, despite the fire, rubbed her arms against the chill creeping along her spine. A frenzied wind whipped the lilac branches and scraped the rain-splattered panes. The tempest threatening since dawn had finally unleashed its full fury, and the fierce winds battering the house gave the day a peculiar, eerie feeling—as if portending something ominous.

At least Mabry and the other hands had managed to get the cattle tucked away before the gale hit. The herd of fifty—no, sixty, counting the newborn calves—chewed their cud and weathered the storm inside the old, but sturdy, barns.

As she peered through the blurry pane, a shingle ripped loose from the farthest outbuilding—a retired stone dovecote. After the wind tossed the slat around for a few moments, the wood twirled to the ground, where it flipped end over end before wedging beneath a gangly shrub. Two more shingles hurled to the earth, this time from one of the barns.

Flimflam and goose-butt feathers.

Brooke tamped down a heavy sigh. Each structure on the estate, including the house, needed some sort of repair or replacement: roofs, shutters, stalls, floors, stairs, doors, siding...dozens of items required fixing, and she could seldom muster the funds to go about it properly.

"Another pair of cows struggling, you say, Mr. Mabry?"

Concern etched on his weathered features, Mabry wiped rain droplets from his face as water pooled at his muddy feet.

"Yes, Miss Brooke. The four calves born this mornin' fare well, but two of the cows, one a first-calf heifer, aren't standin' yet. And there's one weak from birthin' her calf yesterday." His troubled gaze strayed to the window. "Two more ladies are in labor. I best return to the barn. They seemed fine when I left, but I'd as soon be nearby."

Brooke nodded once. "Yes, we mustn't take any chances."

The herd had already been reduced to a minimum by disease and sales to make ends meet. She needed every shilling the cows' milk brought. Losing another, let alone two or three good breeders...

No, I won't think of it.

She stopped pacing and forced a cheerful smile. Nonetheless, from the skeptical look Mabry speedily masked, his thoughts ran parallel to hers—one reason she put her trust in the man. Honest and intelligent, he'd worked alongside her to restore the beleaguered herd and farm after Papa died. Their existence, their livelihood, everyone at Esherton's future depended on the estate flourishing once more.

"It's only been a few hours." *Almost nine, truth to tell.* Brooke scratched her temple. "Perhaps the ladies need a little more time to recover." *If they recovered.* "The calves are strong, aren't they?" *Please, God, they must be.* She held her breath, anticipating Mabry's response.

His countenance lightened and the merry sparkle returned to his eyes. "Aye, the mites are fine. Feedin' like they're hollow to their wee hooves."

Tension lessened its ruthless grip, and hope peeked from beneath her vast mound of worries.

Six calves had been guaranteed in trade to her neighbor and fellow dairy farmer, Silas Huffington, for the grain and medicines he'd provided to see Esherton Green's herd through last winter. Brooke didn't have the means to pay him if the calves didn't survive—though the old reprobate had hinted he'd make her a deal of a much less respectable nature if she ran short of cattle with which to barter. Each pence she'd stashed away—groat by miserable groat, these past four years—lay in the hidden drawer of Papa's desk and must go to purchase a bull.

Wisdom had decreed replacing Old Buford two years ago but, short on funds, she'd waited until it was too late. His heart had stopped while he performed the duties expected of a breeding bull. Not the worst way to cock up one's toes...er, hooves, but she'd counted on him siring at least two-score calves this season and wagered everything on the calving this year and next. The poor brute had expired before he'd completed the job.

Her thoughts careened around inside her skull. Without a bull, she would lose everything.

My home, care of my sister and cousins, my reasons for existing.

She squared her shoulders, resolution strengthening her. She still retained the Culpepper sapphire parure set. If all else failed, she would pawn the jewelry. She'd planned on using the money from the gems' sale to bestow small marriage settlements on the girls. Still, pawning the set was a price worth paying to keep her family at Esherton Green, even if it meant that any chance of her sister and three cousins securing a decent match would evaporate faster than a dab of milk on a hot cookstove. Good standing and breeding meant little if one's fortune proved meaner than a churchyard beggar's.

"How's the big bull calf that came breech on Sunday?" Brooke tossed the question over her shoulder as she poked the fire and encouraged the blaze to burn hotter. After setting the tool aside, she faced the overseer.

"Greediest of the lot." Mabry laughed and slapped his thigh. "Quite the appetite he has, and friendly as our Freddy there. Likes his ears scratched too."

Brooke chuckled and ran her hand across Freddy's spine. The dog wiggled in excitement and stuck his rear legs straight out behind him, gazing at her in adoration. In his youth, he'd been an excellent cattle herder. Now he'd gone fat and arthritic, his sweet face gray to his eyebrows. On occasion, he still dashed after the cattle, the instinctive drive to herd deep in the marrow of his bones.

Another shudder shook her. Why was she so blasted cold today? She relented and placed a good-sized log atop the others. The feeble flames hissed and spat before greedily engulfing the new addition. Lord, she prayed she wasn't ailing. She simply couldn't afford to become ill.

A scratching at the door barely preceded the entrance of Duffen bearing a tea service. "Gotten to where a man cannot find a quiet corner to shut his eyes for a blink or two anymore."

Shuffling into the room, he yawned and revealed how few teeth remained in his mouth. One sock sagged around his ankle, his grizzled hair poked every which way, and his shirttail hung askew. Typical Duffen.

"Devil's day, it is." He scowled in the window's direction, his mouth pressed into a grim line. "Mark my words, trouble's afoot."

Not quite a butler, but certainly more than a simple retainer, the man, now hunched from age, had been a fixture at Esherton Green Brooke's entire life. He loved the place as much as, if not more than, she, and she couldn't afford to hire a servant to replace him. A light purse had forced Brooke to let the household staff go when Papa died. The cook, Mrs. Jennings, Duffen, and Flora, a maid-of-all-work, had stayed on. However, they received no salaries—only room and board.

The income from the dairy scarcely permitted Brooke to retain a few milkmaids and stable hands, yet not once had she heard a whispered complaint from anyone.

Everybody, including Brooke, her sister, Brette, and their cousins—

Blythe, and the twins, Blaike and Blaire—did their part to keep the farm operating at a profit. A meager profit, particularly as, for the past five years, Esherton Green's legal heir, Sheridan Gainsborough, had received half the proceeds. In return, he permitted Brooke and the girls to reside there. He'd also been appointed their guardian. But, from his silence and failure to visit the farm, he seemed perfectly content to let her carry on as provider and caretaker.

"Ridiculous law. Only the next male in line can inherit," she muttered.

Especially when he proved a disinterested bore. Papa had thought so too, but the choice hadn't been his to make. If only she could keep the funds she sent to Sheridan each quarter, Brooke could make something of Esherton and secure her sister and cousins' futures too.

If wishes were gold pieces, I'd be rich indeed.

Brooke sneezed then sneezed again. Dash it all. A cold?

The fresh log snapped loudly, and Brooke started. The blaze's heat had failed to warm her opinion of her second cousin. She hadn't met him and lacked a personal notion of his character, but Papa had hinted that Sheridan was a scallywag and possessed unsavory habits.

A greedy sot, too.

The one time her quarterly remittance had been late, because Brooke had taken a tumble and broken her arm, he'd written a disagreeable letter demanding his money.

His money, indeed.

Sheridan had threatened to sell Esherton Green's acreage and turn her and the foursome onto the street if she ever delayed payment again.

A ruckus beyond the entrance announced the girls' arrival. Laughing and chatting, the blond quartet billowed into the room. Their gowns, several seasons out of fashion, in no way detracted from their charm, and pride swelled in Brooke's heart. Lovely, both in countenance and disposition, and the dears worked hard too.

"Duffen says we're to have tea in here today." Attired in a Pomona green gown too short for her tall frame, Blaike plopped on to the sofa. Her twin, Blaire, wearing a similar dress in dark rose and equally inadequate in length, flopped beside her.

Each girl scooped a drowsy cat into her lap. The cats' wiry whiskers twitched, and they blinked their sleepy amber eyes a few times before closing them once more as the low rumble of contented purrs filled the room.

"Yes, I didn't think we needed to light a fire in the drawing room when this one will suffice." As things stood, too little coal and seasoned firewood remained to see them comfortably until summer.

Brette sailed across the study, her slate-blue gingham dress the only one of the quartet's fashionably long enough. Repeated laundering had turned the garment a peculiar greenish color, much like tarnished copper. She looped her arm through Brooke's.

"Look, dearest." Brette pointed to the tray. "I splurged and made a half-batch of shortbread biscuits. It's been so long since we've indulged, and today is your birthday. To celebrate, I insisted on fresh tea leaves as well."

Brooke would have preferred to ignore the day.

Three and twenty.

On the shelf. Past her prime. Long in the tooth. Spinster. *Old maid.*

She'd relinquished her one chance at love. In order to nurse her ailing father and assume the care of her young sister and three orphaned cousins, she'd refused Humphrey Benbridge's proposal. She couldn't have put her happiness before their welfare and deserted them when they needed her most. Who would've cared for them if she hadn't?

No one.

Mr. Benbridge controlled the purse strings, and Humphrey had neither offered nor been in a position to take on their care. Devastated, or so he'd claimed, he'd departed to the continent five years ago.

She'd not seen him since.

Nonetheless, his sister, Josephina, remained a friend and occasionally remarked on Humphrey's travels abroad. Burying the pieces of her broken heart beneath hard work and devotion to her family, Brooke had rolled up her sleeves and plunged into her forced role as breadwinner, determined that sacrificing her love not be in vain.

Yes, it grieved her that she wouldn't experience a man's passion or bear children, but to wallow in doldrums was a waste of energy and emotion. Instead, she focused on building a future for her sister and cousins—so they might have what she never would—and allowed her dreams to fade into obscurity.

"Happy birthday." Brette squeezed her hand.

Brooke offered her sister a rueful half-smile. "Ah, I'd hoped you'd forgotten."

"Don't be silly, Brooke. We couldn't forget your special day." Twenty-year-old Blythe—standing with her hands behind her—grinned and pulled a small, neatly-wrapped gift tied with a cheerful yellow ribbon from behind her. Sweet dear. She'd used the trimming from her gown to adorn the package.

"Hmph. Need seedcake an' champagne to celebrate a birthday properly." The contents of the tray rattled and clanked when Duffen scuffed his way to the table between the sofa and chairs. After depositing the tea service, he lifted a letter from the surface. Tea dripped from one stained corner. "This arrived for you yesterday, Miss Brooke. I forgot where I'd put it until just now."

If I can read it with the ink running to London and back.

He shook the letter, oblivious to the tawny droplets spraying every which way.

Mabry raised a bushy gray eyebrow, and the twins hid giggles by concealing their faces in the cat's striped coats.

Brette set about pouring the tea, although her lips twitched suspiciously.

Freddy sat on his haunches and barked, his button eyes fixed on the paper, evidently mistaking it for a tasty morsel he would've liked to sample. He licked his chops, a testament to his waning eyesight.

"Thank you, Duffen." Brooke took the letter by one soggy corner. Holding it gingerly, she flipped it over. No return address.

"Aren't you going to read it?" Blythe set the gift on the table before settling on the sofa and smoothing her skirt. They didn't get a whole lot of post at Esherton. Truth be known, this was the first letter in months. Blythe's gaze roved to the other girls and the equally eager expressions on their faces. "We're on pins and needles," she quipped, fluttering her hands and winking.

Brooke smiled and cracked the brownish wax seal with her fingernail. Their lives had become rather monotonous, so much so that a simple, *soggy*, correspondence sent the girls into a dither of anticipation.

My Dearest Cousin...

Brooke glanced up. "It's from Sheridan.

2

As is oft the case when wagering, one party is a fool and
the other a thief, although both may bear the title nincompoop.
~*Wisdom and Advice—The Genteel Lady's Guide to Practical Living*

What maggot in Heath's brain had possessed him to set out on the final leg of his journey to Esherton Green on horseback when foul weather threatened? The same corkbrained notion that had compelled him, the Earl of Ravensdale, one of the most eligible lords on the Marriage Mart, to miss the peak of London's Season in exchange for a saddle-sore arse.

He pulled his hat more firmly onto his head. The bloody wind tried its best to blast every last drop of rain either into his face or down the back of his neck, and he hunched deeper into his saddle. Fat lot of good that did.

The sooner I've finished this ugly business with the tenant, the sooner I can return to London and civilization.

The road from the village—if one deigned to grace the rutted and miry track with such distinction—lay along an open stretch of land, not a single sheltering tree in sight. He hadn't spotted another living thing this past hour. Any creature claiming half a wit laid snuggled in its nest, den, or house, waiting out the foulness. He'd seen two manors in the distance, but to detour to either meant extending his time in this Godforsaken spot.

People actually *chose* to live here?

Hound's teeth, he loathed the lack of niceties, abhorred the quiet which stretched for miles. The boredom and isolation. Give him London's or Paris's crowded and noisy paved streets any day; even if all manner of putridity lined them most of the time.

Despite his greatcoat, the torrential, wind-driven rain soaked him to the skin. Heath patted his pocket where the vowel proving his claim to the farm lay nestled in a leather casing and, with luck, still dry. He'd barely spared the marker a glance at White's and hadn't taken a peek since.

Reading wasn't his strong suit.

His sodden cravat chaffed unmercifully, and water seeped—drip by infernal drip—from his saturated buckskins into his Hessians. He eyed one boot and wiggled his toes. Bloody likely ruined, and he'd just had them made too. Stupid to have worn them and not an older pair. Wanton waste and carelessness—the calling cards of sluggards and degenerates.

Ebénè snorted and bowed his head against the hostile weather. The stallion, unused to such harsh treatment, had been pushed to the end of his endurance, despite his mild temperament. The horse increasingly expressed his displeasure with snorts, groans, and an occasional jerking of his head against the reins.

"I'm sorry, old chap. I thought we'd beat the storm." Heath leaned forward and patted the horse's neck. Black as hell at midnight when dry, now drenched, Ebénè's silky coat glistened like wet ink.

The horse quivered beneath Heath and trudged onward through the sheets of rain.

Indeed, they might have outpaced the tempest if Heath hadn't lingered at breakfast and enjoyed a third cup of Turkish coffee at Tristan, the Marquis of Leventhorpe's, home.

Leventhorpe actually enjoyed spending time at his country house, Bristledale Court. Heath couldn't understand that, but as good friends do, he overlooked the oddity.

Reluctance to part company with Leventhorpe hadn't been Heath's only excuse for dawdling. Leventhorpe had proved a superb host, and Bristledale boasted the latest comforts. The manor house's refinement tempted far more than venturing to a rustic dairy farm with the unpleasant tidings Heath bore.

He'd won the unwanted lands in a wager against Sheridan Gainsborough. The milksop had continued to raise the stakes when he didn't have the blunt to honor his bet. And it wasn't the first time the scapegrace had been light in the pocket at the tables. To teach the reckless sot a lesson, Heath had refused Gainsborough's I.O.U. and demanded he make good on his bet.

When the sluggard offered a piece of property as payment instead, Heath had had little choice but to accept, though it chaffed his sore arse. A tenant farmer and his family would be deprived of their livelihood as a consequence. No one—including this dairyman, months behind in his rents—should be put out of his means of income because a foxed dandy had acted rashly.

Now he owned another confounded piece of English countryside he didn't need nor want. He didn't even visit his country estate, Walcotshire Park. With a half dozen irritable servants for company, he'd spent his childhood there until fifteen years ago when, at thirteen, he'd been sent to boarding school. Instead, Walcotshire's steward tootled to Town quarterly, more often if the need arose, to meet with Heath.

A ripple of unease clawed his nerves. He shifted in the saddle. Discomfort inevitably accompanied thoughts of *The Prison*, as he'd come to regard the austere house, a scant thirty miles from the path Ebénè now plodded.

For a fleeting moment—no more than a blink, truthfully—he contemplated permitting the farmer to continue running the dairy. However, that obligated Heath to trot down to the place on occasion, and nothing short of a God-ordained mandate would compel him to venture to this remote section of green perdition on a regular basis. Not even the prospect of Leventhorpe's company. The marquis would be off to London for the remainder of the Season soon enough, in any event.

Heath had experienced enough of country life as a boy. The family mausoleum perched atop a knoll overlooking the cemetery held more warmth and fonder memories than *The Prison* did. The same could be said of his parents buried there. A colder, more uncaring pair of humans he had yet to meet. He wouldn't have been surprised to learn ice-water, rather than blood, flowed through their veins.

Besides, he didn't know a finger's worth about cattle or dairy farming other than both smelled horrid. He swiped rain from his forehead and wrinkled his nose. How could his favorite cheese be a result of such stench? The reek had carried to him on the wind for miles. How did the locals tolerate it? An irony-born grin curved his lips. Much the same way he tolerated London's, he'd wager. People disregarded flaws when they cared deeply about something or when convenient to do so.

Gainsborough hadn't blinked or appeared to have a second thought when he put up his land as collateral for his bet. He'd laughed and shrugged his thin shoulders before signing the estate over, vowing the neighbors adjacent to Esherton Green would jump at the opportunity to purchase the farm. Then, snatching a bottle of whisky in one hand and snaring a harlot years past her prime around the waist with the other, he had staggered from the gaming hell.

Heath hoped to God the man had spoken the truth, otherwise, what would he do with the property? A gusty sigh escaped him as he slogged along to make the arrangements to sell his winnings. He should've been at White's, a glass of brandy in one hand and cards in the other. Or at the theater watching that new actress, a luscious little temptation he had half a mind to enter into an arrangement with—after his physician examined her for disease, of course.

Heath sought a new mistress after Daphne had taken it into her beautiful, but wool-gathering, head that she wanted marriage. To him. When he refused, she'd eloped with another admirer. That left a bitter taste on his tongue; she'd been cuckolding him while beneath his protection.

Thank God he always wore protection before intimate encounters and insisted she underwent weekly examinations. Laughable, Daphne daring to broach matrimony when she'd already proven herself incapable of fidelity. Not that married women were better. His mother hadn't troubled herself to provide Father a spare heir before lifting her skirts for the first of her myriad of lovers.

Both his parents had died of the French disease, six months apart.

Heath snorted, and the horse jerked his head. Now there was a legacy to be proud of.

If and when he finally decided to become leg-shackled—at forty or fifty—he'd choose a mousy virgin who wouldn't draw the interest of another man. A chit painfully shy or somehow marred, she'd never dare seek a lover. Or perhaps a woman past her prime, on the shelf, whose gratitude for saving her from a life of spinsterhood would assure faithfulness.

Not too long on the shelf, however. He needed to get an heir or two on her.

Didn't matter a whit that half of *le beau monde* shared their beds with multiple partners. His marriage bed would remain pure—well, his wife would, in any event.

A gust of wind slammed into Heath, sending his hat spiraling into the air. The gale lifted it, spinning the cap higher.

"Bloody hell."

Ebénè raised his head and rolled his big eyes at the cavorting cap then grunted, as if to say, *I've had quite enough of this nonsense. Do find me a warm comfortable stable and a bucket of oats at once.*

Two more miserable miles passed, made worse by the absence of Heath's head covering. Water trickled down his face and nape, and, with each step, his temper increased in direct proportion to his dwindling patience. The return trip to Bristledale Court would be more wretched, given his sopped state, and dusk would be upon him before he reached the house.

He should have accepted Leventhorpe's suggestion of a carriage, but that would have meant Heath's comfort at the expense of two drivers and four horses. He shivered and drew his collar higher. He anticipated a hot bath, a hearty meal, and a stiff drink or two upon his return to Bristledale. Leventhorpe boasted the best cognac in England.

Heath glanced skyward. The roiling, blackish clouds gave no indication they had any intention of calming their fury soon. He wiped off a large droplet balancing on the end of his nose. Strange, he hadn't paid much mind to storms while in Town. Then again, he wasn't prone to gadding about in the midst of frightful gales when in the city either.

Perhaps he could bribe a cup of tea and a few moments before the fire from the tenant.

What was his name?

Something or other Culpoppers or Clodhopper or some such unusual surname. The bloke wouldn't likely offer him refreshment or a coze before the hearth once he learned the reason for Heath's visit. Guilt raised its thorny head, but Heath stifled the pricks of unease. A business matter, nothing more. He'd won the land fairly. The tenant was in arrears in rents. Heath didn't want another parcel of countryside to tend to. He knew naught of dairy farming.

The place must be sold.

Simple as that.

Keep spouting that drivel, and you might actually come to believe it.

3

Although gambling is an inherent tendency in human nature,
a wise woman refrains from partaking, no matter
how seemingly insignificant the wager.
~Wisdom and Advice—The Genteel Lady's Guide to Practical Living

Brooke scrunched her forehead and tried to decipher the words. Not only did Sheridan possess atrocious penmanship, the tea had ruined much of the writing.

...writing to inform you I have...

A large smudge obliterated the next few words. She smoothed the wrinkled paper and squinted.

Esherton Green...new owner.

Brooke couldn't suppress her gasp of dismay as she involuntarily clenched one hand around the letter and pressed the other to her chest.

New owner? Esherton Green was entailed. Sheridan couldn't sell it.

Yes. He could.

Only the house and the surrounding five acres were entailed. Even the outbuildings, though they sat on those lands, hadn't been part of the original entailment. The rest of the estate had been accumulated over the previous four generations and the barns constructed as the need arose. She'd memorized the details, since she and Papa had done their utmost to finagle a way for her to inherit.

He'd conceived the plan to send Sheridan half the proceeds from the dairy and farm, so she and the others could continue to live in the only home any of them remembered and still make a modest income. They'd gambled that Sheridan would be content to pad his pockets with no effort on his part, and wouldn't be interested in moving to their remote estate and assuming the role of gentleman farmer.

And our risk paid off. Until now.

She needed the acreage to farm and graze the cattle. Their milk was sold to make Cheshire's renowned cheese. Without the land, the means to support the girls and staff was lost.

"What does he have to say?" Blaire exchanged a worried glance with her twin.

Blythe pushed a curl behind her ear and slanted her head, her intelligent lavender gaze shifting between the paper and Brooke. "Is something amiss, Brooke?"

"Shh." Brooke waved her hand to silence their questions. The tea had damaged the writing in several places. She deciphered a few disjointed sentences.

Pay rent...reside elsewhere...at your earliest convenience...new owner takes possession...regret the necessity...unfortunate circumstances...commendable job managing my holdings...might be of service

Brooke's head swam dizzily.

"Pay rent? Reside elsewhere?" she murmured beneath her breath.

She raised her gaze, staring at the now-frolicking fire, and swallowed a wave of nausea. Sheridan had magnanimously offered to let them stay on if they paid him rent, the bloody bounder. How could she find funds for rent when he'd sold their source of income? They already supplemented their income every way possible.

Brette took in sewing and embroidery and often stayed up until the wee morning hours stitching with a single candle as light. The twins managed a large vegetable, herb, and flower garden, selling the blooms and any excess produce at the village market each week during the growing season. Blythe put her musical talents to use and gave Vicar Avery's spoiled daughters weekly voice and harpsichord lessons.

The women picked mushrooms and tended the chickens and geese—feeding them, gathering their eggs, and plucking and saving the feathers from the unfortunate birds that stopped laying and found their way into the soup pot.

The faithful staff—more family than servants—contributed beyond Brooke's expectations too. Mabry and the other two stable hands provided fish, game fowl, and the occasional deer to feed them. Duffen spent hours picking berries and fruit from the neglected orchard so Mrs. Jennings could make her famous tarts, pies, and preserves, which also sold at the market. And dear, dim-witted Flora washed the Huffington's and Benbridge's laundry.

Sheridan remained obligated to care for them, save Brooke, who'd come of age since he gained guardianship of the girls. It would serve him right if she showed up on his doorstep, sister, cousins, pets, and servants—even the herd of cows—in tow, and demanded he do right by them.

Brooke didn't know his age or if he was married. Did he have children? Come to think of it, she didn't have an address for him either. She'd directed her correspondences to his man of business in London. Where did Sheridan live? London?

Was he one of those fellows who preferred the hubbub and glamour of city life, rather than the peace and simplicity of country living? Most likely. She'd never lived anywhere but Esherton. However, the tales Papa told of the crowding, stench, and noise of Town made the notion of living there abhorrent.

Heart whooshing in her ears, she dropped her attention to the letter once more.

Expect your response by...as to your intentions.

Her gaze flew to the letter's date. Tea had smudged all but the year. Moisture blurred her vision, and she blinked furiously. The unfairness galled. She'd worked so blasted hard, as had everybody else, and that pompous twit—

"Brooke?" The hint of alarm edging Brette's voice nearly undid her.

Fresh tears welled in Brooke's eyes, and she pivoted toward the windows to hide her distress. After dragging in a steadying breath, she forced her leaden feet to carry her to the unoccupied chair and gratefully sank onto the cushion. However, flattened by years of constant use, it provided little in the way of padding.

She took another ragged breath, holding the air until her lungs burned and willed her pulse to slow to a somewhat normal rhythm. Though her emotions teetered on the cusp of hysteria, she must present a calm facade. The quartet weren't given to histrionics, but something of this magnitude was guaranteed to cause a few waterworks, her own included. Pressing shaking fingers to her forehead, Brooke closed her eyes for a brief moment.

God help me. Us.

"I fear I have disquieting news." She met each of their wary gazes in turn, her heart so full of dismay and disbelief, she could scarcely speak.

God rot you, Sheridan.

"Sheridan..." Her mouth dry from trepidation—*how can I tell them*?—she cleared her throat then licked her lips. "He has sold the lands not attached to the house."

The study echoed with the girls' gasps and a low oath from Mabry.

Outrage contorted his usually jovial face into a fierce scowl. "The devil you say!"

Freddy wedged his sturdy little body between Blaike and Blaire, his soulful eyes wide with worry.

"Told you the day be cursed." Duffen shook his head. Highly superstitious, he fingered the smooth stone tied to his neck by a thin leather strip. A lucky talisman, he claimed. "Started with me putting on my left shoe first and then spilling salt in me porridge this morning."

"Sheridan cannot do that." Blaike looked at Brooke hopefully. "Can he, Brooke?"

"Yes, dear, he can." Brooke scowled at the illegible scribbles. She took her anger out on the letter, crumpling it into a tight wad before tossing it into the fire. "He's offered to let us stay on if we pay him rent."

The last word caught on a sob. She'd failed the girls. And the servants.

She couldn't even sell the furnishings, horseflesh, or carriages. Everything of value had long since been bartered or sold. The parure set would only bring enough to sustain them for a few months—six at the most.

What then? They had no remaining family. No place to go.

She clenched the cushion and curled her toes in her boots against the urge to scream her frustration. She must find a position immediately. A governess. Or perhaps a teacher. Or maybe she and the girls could open a dressmaker's shop. They would need to move. There were no positions for young ladies available nearby and even less need for seamstresses.

London.

A shudder of dread rippled through her. Nothing for it. They would have to move to Town. They'd never traveled anywhere beyond the village.

Did she have the legal right to sell the cattle and keep the proceeds? She twisted a curl beside her ear. She must investigate that posthaste. But who dare she ask? One of her neighbors might have purchased the lands from beneath her, and she couldn't afford to consult a solicitor. Perhaps she should seek Mr. Benbridge's counsel. She couldn't count the times he'd offered his assistance.

Silas Huffington's sagging face sprang to mind. Oh, he'd help her, she had no doubt. *If* she became his mistress. Hell would burn a jot hotter the day that bugger died.

"Did he say who bought the lands, Miss Brooke?" Duffen peered at her, his wizened face crumpled with grief. Moisture glinted in his faded eyes, and she swore his lower lip trembled. "That churl, Huffington?"

Brooke shook her head. "No, Duffen, I'm afraid Sheridan didn't say."

What would become of Duffen? Mrs. Jennings? Poor simple-minded Flora? Queer in the attic some would call the maid, but they loved her and ignored her difficulties.

How could Sheridan sell the lands from beneath them?

The miserable, selfish wretch.

Never had Brooke felt such rage. If only she were a man, this whole bumblebroth would have been avoided.

"Man ought to be horsewhipped, locked up, an' the key thrown away," Duffen muttered while wringing his gnarled hands. "Knew in my aching joints today heralded a disaster besides this hellish weather."

"Perhaps the new owner will allow us to carry on as we have." Everyone's gaze lurched to Blaire. She shrugged and petted Pudding's back. The cat arched in pleasure, purring louder. "We could at least ask, couldn't we?"

A flicker of hope took root.

Could they?

Brooke tapped her fingers on the chair's arm. The howling wind, the fire's crackle, and the cats' throaty purrs, filled the room. Nonetheless, a tense stillness permeated the air.

Why not at least try?

"Why, yes, darling." Brooke smiled and nodded. "What a brilliant miss you are. That might be just the thing."

Blaire beamed, and smiles wreathed the other girls' faces.

Duffen continued to scowl and mumble threats and nonsense about the evil eye beneath his breath.

A speculative gleam in his eyes, Mabry scratched his nearly bald pate. "Aye, if he's a city cove with no interest in country life, we might convince the bloke."

"Yes, we might, at that." Brooke stood and, after shaking her skirts, paced behind the sofa, her head bowed as she worried the flesh of her lower lip.

Could they convince the new owner to let them stay if she shared her plans for the farm? Would he object to a woman managing the place? Many men took exception to a female in that sort of a position—

the fairer sex weren't supposed to concern themselves with men's work.

Hands on her hips, she faced Mabry. "Ask around, will you? But be discreet. See if our neighbors or anyone at the village has knowledge of the sale. If the buyer isn't local, we stand a much better chance of continuing as we have."

What if the buyer was indeed one of the people she owed money to?

Not likely.

She would have heard a whisper.

Wouldn't I?

Something of that nature wouldn't stay secret in their shire for long. In Acton, rumors made the rounds faster than the blustering wind, especially if the vicar's wife heard the *on dit*. The woman's tongue flapped fast enough to send a schooner round the world in a week.

Brooke turned to Duffen. Often loose of lips himself, he *had* to keep her confidence. "We want this kept quiet as possible. I cannot afford to have our debts called in by those afraid they'll not get their monies."

Duffen angled his head, a strange glint in his rheumy brown eyes. He toyed with his amulet again. "Won't say a word, Miss Brooke. Count on me to protect you an' the other misses."

She smiled, moisture stinging her eyes. "I know I can, Duffen."

Wringing his hands together, he nodded and mumbled as he stared into the fire. "Promised the master, I did. Gots to keep my word. Protect the young misses."

"Brooke?" Blythe's worried voice drew everybody's attention. "What if the owner wants to reside at Esherton? What will we do then?"

4

Only ninnyhammers mistake preparation meeting opportunity as luck.
~Wisdom and Advice—The Genteel Lady's Guide to Practical Living

Lifting his head, Heath squinted into the tumult swirling around him. At the end of a long, tree-lined drive, a stately two-story home rose out of the grayish gloom. A welcoming glint in a lower window promised much-needed warmth.

Deuced rotten day.

The indistinct shapes of several outbuildings, including two immense barns and an unusual round structure, lay to one side of the smallish manor. A cow's bawl floated to him, accompanied by a pungent waft of damp manure.

Ebénè must have seen the house and stables too, for the tired horse quickened his pace to a trot, ignoring Heath's hands on the reins.

"Fine, get on with you then."

He gave the horse his head. Splattering muck in his haste, the beast shot down the rough and holey roadway as if a hoard of demons scratched at his hooves.

The thunderous crack of an oak toppling mere seconds after Heath passed beneath its gnarled branches launched his heart into his throat and earned a terrified squeal from Ebénè. The limbs colliding with the earth launched a shower of mud over them. A thick blob smacked Heath at the base of his skull then slid, like a giant, slimy slug, into his collar. The cold clump wedged between his shoulder blades.

Of all the—

Another horrendous, grinding snap rent the air, and he whipped around to peer behind him. The rcmainder of the tree plummeted, ripping the roots from their protective cover and jarring the ground violently. More miniature dirt cannonballs pelted him and Ebénè.

Could the day possibly get worse?

The horse bucked and kicked his hind legs.

Yes. It could.

Heath lurched forward, just about plummeting headfirst into the muck. Clutching his horse's mane and neck, he held on, dangling from the side of the saddle.

The mud oozed down his spine.

I'm never setting foot outdoors in the rain again.

With considerable effort, he righted himself then turned to look at the mammoth tree blocking the drive. Had the thing landed on him, he'd have been killed.

Another ripple of unease tingled down his spine, and he glanced around warily. Didn't feel right. He couldn't put his finger on what, but disquiet lingered, and he'd always been one to heed his hunches.

He returned his attention to the shattered tree and the ground torn up by the exposed roots. Disease-ravaged. He glanced at the others. Several of them, too. Dangerous that. They ought to come down. He'd best warn the new owners of the hazard.

You are the new owner.

Heath swiped a hand across his face, dislodging several muddy bits. Nothing like arriving saturated and layered in filth to evict a tenant.

He scrutinized the dismembered tree. A man on horseback could traverse the mess, but passage by carriage was impossible. To expedite the sale, it might be worth paying the tenant to remove the downed tree. That meant delaying tours to prospective buyers for at least a day or two. Unless a neighbor familiar with the place was prepared make the purchase at once—a most convenient solution.

Turning his horse to the unremarkable house, he clicked his tongue and kicked his heels.

A few moments later, Heath halted Ebénè before the weathered stone structure. A shutter, the emerald paint chipped and peeling, hung askew on one of the upper windows, and the hedge bordering the circular courtyard hadn't seen a pair of pruning shears in a good while. Jagged cracks marred the front steps and stoop, and a scraggly tendril of silvery smoke spiraled skyward from a chimney missing several bricks. An untidy orchard on the opposite side of the house from the barns also showed signs of neglect.

The manor and grounds had seen better days, a testament either to the tenant's squandering or to having fallen on hard times. No wonder Gainsborough hadn't been reluctant to part with the place. Why, Heath had done the chap a favor by winning. Gainsborough had probably laughed himself sick with relief at having rid himself of the encumbrance.

Ebénè shuddered and shifted beneath Heath.

Poor beast.

Heath scanned the rustic manor then the barns. Should he dismount here or take the miserable horse to the stables? A single ground floor window in the house glowed with light, rather strange given the lateness of the afternoon and the gloom cloaking the day.

The entrance eased open, no more than three inches, and a puckered face surrounded by wild grayish-white hair peeked through the crack. "State your business."

This shabby fellow, the tenant farmer? That explained a lot.

Heath slid from the saddle, his sore bum protesting. The mud in his shirt shifted lower. Shit.

"I'm the Earl of Ravensdale, here to see the master."

A cackle of laughter erupted from the troll-like fellow. The door inched open further, and the man's entire head poked out. He grinned, revealing a missing front tooth.

"Mighty hard to do, stranger, since he's been dead these five years past."

The man snickered again, but then his gaze shifted to Ebénè and widened in admiration. The peculiar chap recognized superior horseflesh.

Ebénè nudged Heath, none too gently.

The remainder of Heath's patience dissolved faster than salt in soup. He jiggled the horse's reins. "My mount needs attention, and I must speak to whoever is in charge. Is that you?"

"Is someone at the door, Duffen? In this weather?"

The door swung open to reveal a striking blonde, wearing a dress as ugly and drab as the dismal day.

Heath's jaw sagged, and he stared mesmerized.

Despite the atrocious grayish gown, the woman's figure stole the air from him. Full breasts strained against the too-small dress, tapering to a waist his hands could span. And from her height, he'd lay odds she possessed long, graceful legs. Legs that could wrap around his waist and...

Though cold to his marrow, his manhood surged with sensual awareness. He shifted his stance, grateful his long overcoat covered him to his ankles. He snapped his mouth shut. Evict this shapely beauty? Surely a monumental mistake had been made. Gainsborough couldn't be so cold-hearted, could he?

Heath snapped his mouth closed and glared at the grinning buffoon peeking around the doorframe. Making a pretense of shaking the mud from his coat, Heath slid a sideways glance to the woman. Probably thought him a half-witted dolt.

She regarded Heath like a curious kitten, interest piqued yet unsure of what to make of him. Her dark blue, almost violet, eyes glowed with humor, and a smile hovered on her plump lips. The wind teased the flaxen curls framing her oval face.

A dog poked its snout from beneath her skirt and issued a muffled warning.

"Hush, Freddy. Go inside. Shoo."

The dog skulked into the house. Just barely. He plopped onto the entrance, his worried brown-eyed gaze fixed on Heath. She neatly stepped over the portly corgi, and the bodice of her gown pulled taught, exposing hardened nipples.

Another surge of desire jolted Heath.

Disturbing. Uncharacteristic, this immediate lust.

Rainwater dribbled from the hair plastered to his forehead and into his eyes. He swiped the strands away to see her better.

"Miss—"

A disturbance sounded behind her. She glanced over her shoulder as four more young women crowded into the entry.

Blister and damn. A bloody throng of goddesses.

Surely God's favor had touched them, for London couldn't claim a single damsel this exquisite, let alone five diamonds of the first water.

Gainsborough had some lengthy explaining to do.

The one attired in gray narrowed her eyes gone midnight blue, all hint of warmth whisked away on the wind buffeting them. She notched her pert chin upward and pointed at him.

"You're him, aren't you? The man who bought Esherton's lands? Are you truly so eager to take possession and ruin us, you ventured out in this weather and risked catching lung fever?"

Bought Esherton's lands? What the hell?

5

A wise woman refrains from laying odds,
well aware that luck never gives, it only lends,
and will inevitably demand payment, no matter the cost.
~Wisdom and Advice—The Genteel Lady's Guide to Practical Living

He's come already.

Brooke's hope, along with her heart, sank to her half-boots at the peeved expression on the man's chiseled face. Much too attractive, even drenched, mud-splattered, and annoyed.

The girls' sharp intakes of breath hadn't gone unnoticed. She hid her own surprise behind a forced half-smile. Her breasts tingled, the nipples pebble hard.

It's the icy wind, nothing more.

She imagined his heavy gaze lingering on her bodice.

Why couldn't he have been ancient and ugly and yellow-toothed and...and balding?

Shock at his arrival had her in a dither. She'd counted on a scrap of luck to allow her time to prepare a convincing argument. To have him here a mere hour after reading Sheridan's letter had her at sixes and sevens. The letter must have been delayed en route, or her cowardly cousin had dawdled in advising her of the change in her circumstances.

She'd lay odds, ten to one, on the latter.

The gentleman still stood in the rain. That would make a positive impression and gain his favor when she broached the possibility of her continuing to operate the dairy and farm.

Come, Brooke. Gather your wits and manners, control yourself, and attempt to undo the damage already done.

"Looks like a half-drowned mongrel, he does." Duffen sniggered, his behavior much ruder than typical.

Brooke quelled his snicker with a sharp look. "See to the horse, please, and tell Mr. Mabry we have a guest. Ask him to join us as soon as he is able."

"Yes, Miss Brooke. I'll get my coat." Duffen bobbed his head and went in search of the garment.

She wanted the overseer present when she explained her proposition to his lordship. After all, although she'd read dozens of books and articles on the subject, Mabry's knowledge of the dairy's day-to-day operation far surpassed hers.

Brooke folded her hands before her. "He'll return momentarily, Mister...?"

The gentleman, with hair as black as the glorious horse standing beside him, crooked a boyish smile and bowed. Yes, too confounded handsome for her comfort. The wind flipped his coat over his bent behind. "Heath, Earl of Ravensdale at your service, Mistress...?"

"Earl?" *He's a confounded earl*?

An earl wouldn't want to run a dairy farm, would he?

She scrutinized him toe to top. Not one dressed like him. His soaked state couldn't disguise the fineness of the garments he wore or the quality of the beautiful stepper he rode. The wind tousled his hair, a trifle longer than fashionable. It gave him a dashing, rakish appearance. She shouldn't have noticed that, nor experienced the odd sparks of pleasure gazing at him caused.

A lock slipped onto his forehead again. The messy style rather suited him. Where was his hat anyway?

She winced as a boney elbow jabbed her side.

"Tell him your name, Brooke."

Ah, Blythe. Always level-headed. And subtle.

"Forgive me, my lord. I am Brooke Culpepper." Brooke gestured to the foursome peering at the earl. "And these are my sister, Miss Brette Culpepper, and our cousins, the Misses Culpeppers, Blythe, Blaire, and Blaike."

His lips bent into an amused smile upon hearing their names, not an uncommon occurrence.

Named Bess, Mama and Aunt Bea had done their daughters an injustice by carrying on the silly B name tradition for Culpepper females. Supposedly, the practice had started so long ago no one could remember the first.

Brooke dipped into a deep curtsy, and the girls followed her lead, each making a pretty show of deference. She wanted to applaud. Not one teetered or stumbled. They'd never had cause to curtsy before, and the dears performed magnificently.

Freddy lowered his shoulders and touched his head to his paws, a trick Brooke had taught him as a puppy.

Lord Ravensdale threw his head back and laughed, a wonderful rumble that echoed deep in his much-too-broad chest. At least, it looked wide beneath his coat. Maybe he wore padding. Silas Huffington did, which, rather than making him look muscular, gave him the appearance of a great, stuffed doll.

A very ugly doll.

"What a splendid trick, Mistress...?" His lordship inquired after her name again.

"It's miss, your lordship." Brette nudged Brooke in the ribs this time. "We're *all* misses, but Brooke's the eldest of the five and—"

Brooke silenced her with a slight shake of her head.

A puzzled expression flitted across the earl's face. He took her measure, examining her just as she'd inspected him, and a predatory glint replaced his bewilderment.

Her gaze held captive by his—titillating and terrifying—the hairs from her forearms to her nape sprang up. Awareness of a man unlike anything she'd ever experienced before, even with Humphrey, gripped her.

A man of the world, and no doubt used to snapping his fingers and getting whatever he desired, including wenches in his bed, Lord Ravensdale now scrutinized her with something other than inquisitiveness. The look couldn't be described as entirely polite either.

He wasn't to be trifled with.

She'd bet the biscuits Brette made today, Brooke had piqued his interest. Why, and whether she should be flattered or alarmed, she hadn't determined. What rot. Of course she was flattered. What woman wouldn't be?

He approached the steps, his attention locked on her. "There's no *Mister* Culpepper?"

Brooke tilted her head, trying to read him. Why didn't she believe the casualness of his tone?

"No, not since Father died five years ago." She pushed a tendril of hair off her cheek, resisting the urge to wrap her arms around her shoulders and step backward. The wind proved wicked for April. Why else did she remain peppered in gooseflesh? "Didn't Cousin Sheridan inform you?"

"Cousin? Gainsborough is your cousin?" Disbelief shattered his lordship's calm mien. His nostrils flared, and his lovely lips pressed into a thin line. His intense gaze flicked to each of the women, one by one. "He is cousin to *all* of you?"

"Yes," Brooke and the others said as one.

The revelation didn't please the earl. He closed his eyes for a long moment, his impossibly thick lashes dark smudges against his swarthy skin. Did he ail? He seemed truly confounded or put upon.

Wearing a floppy hat which almost obliterated his face, Duffen edged by her. He yanked his collar to his ears. "I'll see to your horse, *sir*."

"Duffen, that will do," Brooke warned gently. She wouldn't tolerate impudence, even from a retainer as beloved as him. "Lord Ravensdale is our guest."

Astonishment flitted across Duffen's cragged features before they settled into lines of suspicion once more. Duffen hadn't expected a noble either.

"Beg your pardon, Miss Brooke."

He ducked his head contritely and, after gathering the horse's reins, led the spirited beast toward the stables. Eager to escape the elements, the stallion practically dragged Duffen.

"My lord, please forgive my poor manners. Do come in out of the wretched rain." Brooke stepped over Freddy and turned to Brette. "Will you fetch hot tea and biscuits for his lordship?"

Brooke sent him a sidelong glance. "And a towel so he might dry off?"

"Of course. At once." Brette bobbed a hasty curtsy before hurrying down the shadowy corridor.

Hopefully, she would brew just enough tea for the earl. They were nearly out of tea and sugar, and there would be no replacing the supplies.

Brooke motioned to Blaike. "Please stir the fire in the study and add another log? I don't wish his lordship to become chilled."

Her attention riveted on their visitor, Blaike colored and stuttered, "Ah…yes. Certainly." After another quick peek at him, she pivoted and disappeared into the study a few doorways down.

He'd been here mere minutes and the girls blushed and blathered like nincompoops. Brooke pursed her lips. It wouldn't do, especially not when he might very well be here to put them out of their home. She drew in a tense breath.

Lord Ravensdale stepped across the threshold and hesitated. He wiped his feet on the braided rag rug while his gaze roved the barren entrance. A rivulet of rainwater trailed down his temple. Soaked through. He'd be lucky if he didn't catch his death.

Surely claiming the lands hadn't been so pressing he'd felt the need to endanger his health by venturing into the worst storm in a decade? A greedy sort and anxious to see what he'd purchased, perhaps. Well, he'd have to wait. She wouldn't ask Mr. Mabry or the other hands to show the earl around, not only because the weather was fouler than Mr. Huffington's breath, but Brooke needed the men attending the cows and newborn calves.

Lord Ravensdale exuded power and confidence, and the foyer shrank with his presence. Except for Brette, the Culpepper women were tall, but he towered above Brooke by several inches. He smiled at Brooke, and her stomach gave a queer little somersault at the transformation in his rugged features. Devilishly attractive. A dangerous distraction. He was the enemy. He'd bought Esherton, practically stolen her home, with no regard to how that would affect her family.

Don't be fooled by his wild good looks.

He shoved wet strands off his high forehead again.

Freddy crept closer, his button nose twitching.

Brooke brushed away a few of Freddy's hairs clinging to her skirt, unexpectedly ashamed of her outdated and worn gown. She hid her calloused hands in the folds of her gown. She would wager the Culpepper sapphires that women threw themselves at Lord Ravensdale.

Fashionable ladies dressed in silks and satins, with intricately coiffed hair, and smooth, creamy skin, who smelled perfectly wonderful all the time. Lord Ravensdale's women probably washed with perfumed soap. Expensive, scented bars from France. Pink or yellow, or maybe blue and shaped like flowers.

Brooke couldn't remember the last time she'd worn perfume or used anything other than the harsh gel-like soap that she and Mrs. Jennings made from beef tallow. Their precious candle supply came from the smelly lard too.

Why the notion rankled, Brooke refused to examine. Except, here she stood attired like a country bumpkin covered in dog and cat hair, with her curls tied in a haphazard knot and ink stains on her fingers. She couldn't even provide his lordship a decent repast or light a candle to guide him to the study, let alone produce a dram of whisky or brandy to warm his insides.

Nonetheless, they...*she* must win his favor.

She straightened her spine, determined to act the part of a gracious hostess if it killed her. "Sir, you should take off your coat. It's soaked through."

While his lordship busied himself removing his gloves, she studied him. He had sharp, exotic, almost foreign features. She shouldn't be surprised to learn a Moroccan or an Egyptian ancestor perched in his family tree somewhere. High cheekbones gave way to a molded jaw and a mouth much too perfect to belong to a man. A small scar marred the left side of his square chin. How had he come by it?

She could almost envision him, legs braced and grinning, on the rolling deck of a pirate ship, the furious waves pounding against the vessel as the wind whipped his hair.

Stop it.

Hand on his sword, he would throw his head back and laugh, the corded muscles in his neck bulging; a man in command against nature's wrath.

"The ride here turned most unpleasant."

Lord Ravensdale's melodic baritone sent her cavorting pirate plunging off the side of the fantasy ship and into the churning waves. Brooke clamped her teeth together. What ailed her? She'd never been prone to fanciful imaginations.

After tucking his wet gloves into his pocket, his lordship unbuttoned his tobacco-brown overcoat.

Almost the same color as his eyes.

"A tree fell as I passed by. I'm afraid it left rather a jumble on the drive." He flashed his white teeth again as he advanced farther into the entry.

Retreating, she allowed him room to shrug off the soggy garment. A pleasant, spicy scent wafted past her nose. Naturally, he smelled divine. She peered past him and to the lane. A tree and a tangle of branches lay sprawled on the road to the house. She stifled a groan. How were they to remove that disaster with one horse and a pair of axes?

Releasing a measured breath, she closed the heavy door.

Lord, I don't know how much more I can bear.

"If you'll permit it, my lord, I shall have my cousin take your coat to the kitchen to place beside the stove." She extended her hand. Not that it would dry completely in the few minutes he would be here, but perhaps he would appreciate the gesture.

He passed her the triple-caped greatcoat then removed a wilted handkerchief from his jacket pocket. A slight shudder shook him as he wiped his face. “I’m afraid the elements did rather get the best of me.”

As if he’d cued it, a blast of wind crashed into the house, rattling the door and windows. The corridor grew dim as the storm renewed her fury. The pewter sky visible through the windows paralleling the door suggested dusk had already fallen. Brooke furrowed her brow. His lordship didn’t dare delay at Esherton. His return journey to—wherever he’d come from—became more perilous by the moment.

And he couldn’t stay here.

They hadn’t an empty bedchamber to accommodate him other than Papa and Mama’s, and a stranger amongst five eligible women might give rise to gossip. Besides, expecting her to house him when he’d arrived to put them from their home was beyond the pale, accommodating hostess or not.

Playacting wasn’t her strong suit. Pretending to welcome the earl when she wanted to treat him like a plague-ridden thief strained her good manners and noble intentions. Had she been alive, Mama would’ve chastised Brooke for her unchristian behavior and thoughts.

“Blaire, please take his lordship’s coat to the kitchen and fetch one of Papa’s jackets for him.”

Papa’s coats had been too old to sell, and Brooke refused to make them into rags. It seemed disrespectful, almost disloyal, to treat his possessions with such little regard. She’d allowed Duffen and Mabry their pick. Therefore, the remaining coats were quite shabby. Still, a dry, moth-eaten jacket must be preferable to saturated finery.

“You and the others join us in the study as soon as the tea is ready.”

Brooke wanted the quartet present for the discussion. After all, the sale of the lands affected their lives too. Besides, the earl made her edgy. Perhaps because much was at stake, and there’d been no time to prepare an argument to let them continue as they had been.

Her cousin seized the soaked wool, and after a swift backward glance, marched to the rear of the house.

Lord Ravensdale inspected the stark entry once more. Rectangular shadows lined the faded walls where paintings had once hung. He ran his gaze over her, lingering at the noticeable discolored arc at her neckline where a lace collar used to adorn the gown. She hid her reddened hands behind her lest he notice the missing lace cuffs as well. They’d been sold last year for a pittance.

She hadn’t been self-conscious of her attire or the blatant sparseness of her home before, but somehow, he made their lack of prosperity glaring. Rather like a purebred Arabian thrust into the midst of donkeys.

Pretty donkeys, yes, but compared to a beautiful stepper, wholly lacking.

Freddy crept forward and dared to sniff around his lordship's feet. Then, to Brooke's horror, the dog proceeded to heist his leg on one glossy boot. Yellow pooled around the toe as she and Blythe gaped.

"Freddy, bad boy. Shame on you." Blythe scolded, bending to scoop the cowering dog into her arms. Her cheeks glowed cherry red. "I'll put him in the kitchen, Brooke."

Whispering chastisements, she scurried away, the dog happily wagging his tail as if forgiven.

Mortification burning her face, Brooke raised her gaze to meet Lord Ravensdale's humor-filled eyes.

"Perhaps I might trouble you for *two* towels?" He raised his dripping foot and grinned.

Brooke tried to stifle the giggle that rushed to her throat.

She really did.

A loud peal surged forth anyway. Partially brought on by relief that he wasn't angry, partially because in other circumstances, she might indulged in a flirtation with him, and partially to release nervous tension.

If she didn't laugh, she would burst into tears.

He smiled while pulling at his cuffs. A bit of dirt fell to the scarred floor. "So what's this nonsense about Gainsborough selling me Esherton? Your cousin lost the place to me in a card game and said you were months behind in rents."

6

In the event one is unwise enough to venture down wagering's treacherous pathway, decide beforehand the rules by which you'll play, the exact stakes, and at which point you intend to quit.
~Wisdom and Advice—The Genteel Lady's Guide to Practical Living

Heath clamped his jaw against a curse at the devastation that ravaged Miss Culpepper's. One moment she'd been glowing, mirth shimmering in her gaze and pinkening her face, and the next, her lovely indigo eyes pooled with tears. They seeped over the edges and trailed down her silky cheeks, though she didn't make a sound.

How often had she wept silently so others wouldn't hear? He'd done the same most of his childhood. He brushed his thumb over one damp cheek. What was it about this woman that plucked at his heart after a mere ten minutes acquaintance? He didn't know her at all, yet he felt as if something had connected between them from the onset.

Did she sense it too, or was it only him? Perhaps he'd caught a fever and delusions had set in.

She blinked at him, her eyes round and wounded. And accusing. "We're not behind in the rents. He's been paid on time each month. Except the month I broke my arm."

Shit, another lie. What have I gotten myself into?

Deep pain glimmered in the depths of her eyes, which were too old and wise for someone her age. This woman had clearly borne much in her short life.

And she hadn't known her home had been lost in a wager gone awry.

She'd thought Heath had bought the estate. Though what difference that would have made in her circumstances, he couldn't fathom. Gambled away or purchased, the consequence remained the same for the women. They'd be ousted from their home. At least he held a degree of concern for their wellbeing, unlike their callous cousin.

Surely they must have someone who could be of assistance to them.

What sort of a vile blackguard gave no thought to his kinsmen, especially five females without means? As apparent as the mud on his boots and sticking uncomfortably to his spine, they were poor as church mice. In all likelihood, the holy rodents fared better since they would eagerly accept crumbs. Gut instinct told him the Culpeppers might have little else, but they had their pride and wouldn't accept charity.

Miss Culpepper drew in a shuddering breath and averted her head. She wiped her eyes as her sister entered the corridor bearing a meager tea tray upon which rested a mismatched tea service, a napkin, a single teacup and three small biscuits.

A wave of compassion, liberally weighted with remorse, engulfed him. He'd never experienced poverty such as this, and yet, they offered him what little they had.

Damnation.

He didn't want a blasted dairy farm, even if angels did make it their home.

Composing herself, Miss Culpepper shifted toward a door farther along the hallway and offered her sister a wobbly smile.

Miss Brette—wasn't that her name?—peered between him and her sister, her nose crinkled in puzzlement. Her gaze lingered on her sister's damp cheeks.

Astute woman.

One of the twins trailed Miss Brette.

Heath had no idea what her name was, but she bore a large black jacket and a towel. He strained to distinguish the women's features in the shadowy corridor. Another violent surge of air battered the house, and the women's startled gazes flew to the entrance.

He feared the windows might shatter from the gale's force. A breeze wafted past, sending a chill creeping along his shoulders. The house radiated cold. This drafty old tomb must be impossible to keep heated, but not one of the Culpepper misses wore warm clothing.

"My lord, this way if you please." Miss Culpepper motioned to the doorway the girl dressed in green had disappeared into earlier. "We'll give you a moment of privacy to dry yourself and exchange your coat for Papa's. It's rather worn, I'm afraid, but it should be a mite more comfortable than wearing yours."

The trio filed through the entrance, slender as reeds, each of them. A natural physical tendency or brought on by insufficient food? Mayhap both.

Heath followed, guilt's sharp little teeth nipping at his heels. He glimpsed the tray as Miss Brette arranged it on a table before the fireplace. How they could be charitable, he didn't know, and, had their situations been reversed, honesty compelled him to admit, he mightn't have been as hospitable. Not much better than their snake of a cousin, was he? The notion left a sickening knot in his middle and a rancorous taste on his tongue.

Actually, the foul taste might have been a spot of mud he'd licked from his lip. Pray God the dried crumb was mud and not some other manner of filth.

"Let's give his lordship a moment, shall we?" With a wan smile, Miss Culpepper ushered her wards from the study.

Frenetic whispers sounded the moment they left his sight.

Heath made quick work of exchanging the jackets. The one he donned smelled slightly musty and a hint of tobacco lingered within the coarsely woven threads. Too big around, the garment skimmed his waist. The Culpeppers didn't get their height or svelteness from Mr. Culpepper's branch of the family. Heath tugged at a too-short sleeve, and his third finger sank into a moth hole.

What had brought this family to such destitution?

He'd lacked human companionship and love his entire childhood—and by choice, a great deal of his adulthood also—but never wanted for physical comfort or necessities. Their circumstances appeared the reverse of his. Company and affection they possessed aplenty, but scant little else. Nonetheless, they didn't act deprived or envious, at least not from what he'd observed in his short acquaintance with them.

The truth of that might prove different upon further association. In his experience, the facade women presented at first glance proved difficult to maintain, and before long, they revealed their true character. Rarely had the latter been an improvement upon his initial impression.

Standing before the roaring fire, he relished the heat as he toweled his hair and dried his neck and face again. Heath glanced around the room, taking in the extraordinarily ugly chairs and cracked leather sofa. He'd seen nothing of value or quality in the house. Everything of worth had likely been sold ages ago.

He scraped the cloth inside each ear and came away with a pebble-sized clump of muck from his left ear. Too bad he daren't untuck his shirt and rid himself of the irritating blob resting at the small of his spine like a cold horse turd. He eyed his boots. No, he wouldn't ruin the tattered scrap he held by wiping the filthy footwear. If it weren't wholly unacceptable, he'd have left the Hessians at the door, but padding around in one's stockinged feet wasn't done.

He rolled his eyes toward the ceiling. Much better to soil the floors and carpet instead.

No sooner had he set the cloth aside than a sharp rap sounded beside the open door. Miss Culpepper peeked inside. Her gorgeous violet gazed skimmed him appreciatively. "Better?"

"Much, thank you." Spreading his fingers, he warmed his palms before the blaze. How had he managed to get dirt beneath three nails? He glanced sideways at her. "I don't recall a storm quite this furious."

"Yes, it's the worst I can recollect as well." She glided into the room, perfectly poised. She might have been starched and prim on the exterior, that heinous dress doing nothing for her figure or coloring, but a woman's curiosity and awareness had shone in her eyes when she took his measure a moment ago.

The corgi peeked around the doorframe then made a dash for the sofa. His fat rear wriggling, he clambered onto the couch. Freddy stood gazing up at Heath, panting and wagging his tail, not a jot of remorse on his scruffy face.

So much for banishment to the kitchen.

The four other young women filed in behind Miss Culpepper, their demeanors a combination of anxiety and curiosity.

God above, Heath would relish the expressions on the faces of the *ton's* denizens if these five—properly attired, jeweled and coiffed, of course—ever graced the upper salons and assembly rooms. He had half a mind to take the task on himself, if only to witness *le beau monde's* reaction.

He smiled, intrigued by the notion. Might be damned fun.

There'd be hissing and sneering behind damsels' fans as the milksops, dandies, and peers tripped over one another to be first in line to greet the beauties. One incomparable proved difficult enough competition, but an entire brood of them? What splendid mayhem that would cause. One he could heartily enjoy for weeks...months perhaps.

Heath rubbed his nose to hide a grin.

Yes, the Culpepper misses would provide the best bloody entertainment in a decade.

Course, without dowries or lineage, the girls' respectable prospects ran drier than a fountain in the Sahara.

He firmed his jaw. Not his concern. Making arrangements to sell the farm and return to London posthaste was. And not with five beauties in tow, even if he could persuade them to toddle along.

His gaze riveted on the blondes, Heath perched on the edge of one of the chairs. It tottered, and he gripped the arm as he settled his weight on the uneven legs. What did one call this chair's color anyway? Vomit? He'd seen pond scum the exact shade outside Bristledale Court's boundary. Why in God's name would anyone choose this fabric for furniture?

After sinking gracefully onto the sofa, and nudging aside a sleeping cat in order to make room for two of the young women to sit beside her, Miss Culpepper poured his tea. "Milk or sugar?"

The girl in yellow sat in the other chair while the twin attired in green plopped onto a low stool and, chin resting on her hand, stared at him.

Never had Heath experienced such self-consciousness before. Five pairs of eyes observed his every move. What was their story? His task would've been much easier if they were lazy, contentious spendthrifts sporting warty noses and whiskery chins.

"My lord?" Tongs in hand, Miss Culpepper peered at him, one fair brow arched, almost as if she'd read his thoughts. "Milk or sugar?"

He flashed her his most charming smile—the one that never failed to earn a blush or seductive tilt of lips, depending on the lady's level of sexual experience.

Her eyebrow practically kissing her hair, Miss Culpepper regarded him blandly. The twins salvaged his bruised pride by turning pink and gawking as expected. The older two exchanged guarded glances, and he swore Miss Brette hid a smirk behind her hand.

Heat slithered up his face.

Poorly done, old man.

These weren't primping misses accustomed to dallying or playing the coquette. He doubted they knew how to flirt. Direct and unpretentious, all but the youngest pair had detected his ploy to charm them. Rather mortifying to be set down without a word of reproach by three inexperienced misses.

Miss Culpepper waved the tongs and flashed her sister a sideways glance, clearly indicating she thought him a cod-pated buffoon.

"Just sugar please. Two lumps." He ran his fingers inside his neckcloth. The cloying material itched miserably.

Heath relaxed against the chair, squashing a cat that had crawled in behind him. With a furious hiss, the portly beast wriggled free and tumbled to the floor. Whiskers twitching and citrine eyes glaring, the miffed feline arched her spine, and then, with a dismissive flick of her tail, marched regally to lie before the hearth.

"I'm afraid you've annoyed Pudding." Chuckling, a delicious musical tinkle, Miss Culpepper lifted the lid from the sugar bowl and dropped two lumps into his tea. Four remained on the bottom of the china. "She holds a grudge, so watch your calves. She'll take a swipe at you when you aren't looking."

She passed him the steaming cup then scooted the small chipped plate of biscuits in his direction. Her roughened hands that suggested she performed manual labor. The other cat, its plump cheeks the size of dinner rolls, raised its head and blinked at him sleepily. The animals, at least, didn't go hungry around here. Miss Culpepper's keen gaze remained on him as she settled further into the couch,

The other girls' attention shifted between him and her, as if they anticipated something. They obviously regarded her as their leader. A log shifted, and sparks sprayed the sooty screen.

Heath took a swallow of the tea, savoring its penetrating warmth and pleasant flavor. A most respectable cup of tea, though a dram of brandy tipped into the brew wouldn't have gone amiss.

A branch scraped the window. What he wouldn't give to stay put in this snug study, sipping tea and munching the best, buttery biscuits he'd ever tasted. But Leventhorpe expected him for dinner and had requested his cook prepare chicken fricassee, a particular favorite of Heath's. Still, the return ride, battling the hostile elements after darkness had blanketed the land, didn't appeal in the least.

"My lord, you—"

"Miss Culpepper, could—."

She smiled, and Heath chuckled when they spoke at the same time.

Biscuit in hand, he gestured for her to continue. "Please, go on."

"You said Cousin Sheridan lost Esherton Green's lands to you in a wager?" Smoothing her rough skirt, she crossed and uncrossed her ankles.

Was that a hole in the bottom of her boot? A quick, covert assessment revealed the other women's footwear fared little better.

Heath paused with the teacup to his lips. "Yes."

"Might I ask when?" Her gaze rested on his lips before sliding to the cup. A dash of color appeared on her high cheekbones, made more apparent by the hollows beneath them.

She'd experienced hunger and often.... Still did, given the thinness of her and the others. Compassion swept him. If he were their blasted cousin, they'd never want again. Except, a cousin didn't inspire in him the kind of interest Brooke did.

"You see, I only received his correspondence today and the letter had suffered substantial damage." She shrugged one slender shoulder while running her fingers through the sleeping corgi's stiff fur. "Truthfully, I couldn't decipher half of it, but I had the distinct impression he'd sold the lands, and we'd be permitted to remain in the house if we paid rent. I can prove payment in full through this month."

That's only a few more days.

Her words rang of hope and desperation.

And how would they pay future rent? Open a house of ill-repute?

His skimmed his gaze over the assembled beauties. They'd make a fortune, but a more repugnant notion he'd never entertained. Besides, the house had been wagered as well.

Hadn't it?

Hell, he hadn't read the vowel, but rather made a show of perusing the note. He preferred not to read anything in public, especially not surrounded by *le beau ton.* A hint that he struggled to read the simplest phrase and the elite would titter for months.

But the fact remained that he journeyed here to sell whatever he'd won. Except now, he didn't know precisely what had been wagered. He would have to return on the morrow, after he'd spent the evening studying the slip of paper in—

Blast. The marker lay tucked in his greatcoat.

In the kitchen.

The two women who'd hustled away with his dust coat wouldn't dare go through his pockets. Would they?

Miss Culpepper mistook his silence for encouragement. "You see, Mr. Mabry and I—and the girls as well as the other staff—have run the dairy ourselves for the past five years. Cousin Sheridan received half the proceeds each quarter for allowing us to remain here and operate the farm. We hoped the new owner would permit us the same arrangement."

She raised expectant blue eyes to his. Her hands fisted in her skirt and her toes tapping the floor belied her calm facade.

He swept the other girls another swift glance.

Their thin faces were pale, and worry and fear filled the eyes peering back at him.

A wave of black rage rose from Heath's boots to his chest. When he got his hands on Gainsborough, he'd thrash him soundly. Pretending absorption in chewing the rest of his biscuit, Heath forced his pulse and breathing to slow.

He relaxed into the chair and placed an ankle on one bent knee, smearing his trousers with mud. Hopelessly stained, they'd be sent to the church for the beggars. Drumming his fingers on the chair's threadbare arms, he scrutinized the women again.

Features taut, gazes wary, they held their breath in anticipation of his response.

A litany of vulgar oaths thrummed against his lips. Blast their cousin to hell and back for putting him in this despicable position.

Heath did not want a dairy farm. He did not want to care for or worry about these women more than their own flesh and blood did. He most certainly did not want to *ever* have to venture to this stinking, remote parcel of green hell again. And he didn't have it in him to put these women out of their homes.

"We would work hard, your lordship." The girl in rose—Blaire or Blaike? Maybe he ought to number the lot of them—gifted him a tremulous smile.

Heath rubbed his forehead where the beginnings of a headache pulsed. "I'm sure you would."

God rot you, Gainsborough.

Her twin nodded, a white curl slipping to flop at her nape. "Yes, besides the milk, we also sell vegetables, flowers, and herbs..."

Anything else?

"And eggs, mushrooms, pastries, and jams," Brette finished in a breathless rush.

What no sewing, weaving, or tatting?

She threw her sister a desperate glance. "And I sew and take in embroidery."

Ah, there it is.

"And Blythe..." She pointed to the girl wearing yellow.

Yes, what does Blythe do?

Heath's gaze lingered on the eldest Miss Culpepper.

Or Brooke? *Surely she has a skill to sell too.*

He uncrossed his leg then leaned forward, not liking the direction the conversation had taken, the distress in the girls' voices, or his cynical musings. "You're to be commended and sound most industrious—"

Blythe squared her shoulders, a challenge in her eyes. "I give music lessons, and Flora takes in laundry."

Who the blazes is Flora?

He straightened and cast an uneasy glance at the doorway.

Good God, please tell me not another sister or cousin?

"Brooke maintains the books and manages the production and sale of the milk and cattle." The first twin spoke again.

Devil it, impossible to tell the two apart except for their clothing. Identical, right down to the mole beside their left eyes.

The other twin piped up. "We all—"

Miss Culpepper raised a hand, silencing her. A long scratch ran from her small finger to her wrist. Her ivory face seemed carved of granite, the angles and lines rigid. She slowly stood, her bearing no less regal than a queen's, and the stony look she leveled him would've done Medusa proud.

God, she was impressive.

He pressed his knee with his chilled fingertips. Yes, warm flesh, not solid rock. *Yet*.

"Enough, girls." Resignation weighted her words. They echoed through the study like a death knell.

The four swung startled gazes to her. A rapid succession of emotions flitted across their lovely faces, each one convicting him and adding more weight to the uncomfortable burden he already bore.

Damn. Damn. Damn.

"You're wasting your breath, dears. His lordship made his decision before he arrived." Miss Culpepper angled her long neck, her harsh gaze stabbing straight to his guilty heart.

"Didn't you, Lord Ravensdale?"

7

A woman of discernment understands that a deck of playing cards is the devil's prayer book, and a gentleman possessing a pack is Satan's pawn.
~*Wisdom and Advice—The Genteel Lady's Guide to Practical Living*

Brooke waited for Lord Ravensdale to deny her accusation.

He ran his hand through his shiny hair and stared past her shoulder. A muscle jumped in his jaw.

Tic or ire?

She curled her nails into her palms against the anger and despair sluicing through her veins. If she had to look at his handsome face or listen to his half-hearted platitudes one more minute, she wouldn't be able to keep from whacking him atop the head.

Yes, blaming him seemed unfair, but this situation was too, made more so because she'd kept her end of the bargain these many years and that slug...worm...*maggot* of a cousin had gambled away their lives.

How dare Sheridan?

His lordship turned his attention to her. Did concern tinge in his eyes?

She briefly closed hers to hide the rage that must've been sparking within them, and also to block his lordship's troubled expression.

Don't you dare pretend to care, you opportunistic cawker.

Lord Ravensdale heaved a low sigh.

Her eyelids popped open.

Ought to be on stage so someone can appreciate his theatrics.

He rubbed his nape. "Miss Culpepper, ladies, I—"

Duffen shuffled into the study, scraping a hand atop his wild hair in an unsuccessful attempt to tame the unruly bush. "Miss Brooke, Mabry will come up as soon as he can. A calf's turned wrong. Said he couldn't leave just now."

Brooke simply nodded, not trusting herself to speak. Mabry wasn't needed, in any event.

"I rubbed your horse down, my lord, and saw him settled." Duffen rested his bleary gaze on Lord Ravensdale, his dislike tangible.

His lordship curved his perfect lips into a narrow smile before placing his hands on the chair's arms and shoving to his feet. The signet ring on his small finger caught the fire's glow. "Thank you for your trouble, but I'm set on leaving in a moment. I don't wish to travel after dark. I require a few more minutes of your mistress's time, and then I'll be on my way."

His intense stare heated the top of Brooke's head as surely as if he'd placed his fire-warmed palm there. Refusing to raise her attention from the hole in the carpet, she slid her foot atop it. Had he noticed? She drew in a long, controlled breath. Her composure hung by a fine strand of sheer will, and she'd be cursed if she would let him see her cry again. Or let the girls see, for that matter. She didn't cry in public.

Their faces when Brooke had exposed his lordship's purpose...the despair and hopelessness... God, to have been able to spare them that anguish. They didn't lack intelligence and understood perfectly what their circumstances had been reduced to in the course of these past two hours.

So blasted, bloody unfair. Men didn't have these worries, but women without means had few opportunities.

"Miss Culpepper?" Lord Ravensdale prompted.

Persistent isn't he?

Mud-spattered boots appeared in her line of vision. She followed the lean length of his lordship's leg, past muscular buckskin-covered thighs, narrow hips, and his hunter green and black waistcoat to the pathetic excuse of a neckcloth drooping round his neck. An emerald stick pin glinted from within the folds. She'd missed the jewel earlier.

Firming her lips, she stared pointedly at his faintly-stubbled chin. Must be one of those gentlemen who required a shave twice daily. Humphrey hadn't.

What would it feel like to trace her fingers across his jaw?

Brooke Theodora Penelope Culpepper, have you lost your wits? Cease this instant!

He had the audacity to tilt her chin upward, forcing her to meet his chocolaty gaze.

Why must he be the man to awaken her long dormant feelings? Feelings she thought she'd succeeded in burying. Tears flooded her eyes, and she attempted to avert her face.

He would have none of it, however. "I will call at eleven tomorrow, at which time we can continue this discussion."

"Why?" Brooke jerked her chin from his gentle grasp. She angrily swiped at her eyes and retreated a couple of paces. "Why bother returning? Just send a note round, and tell us when you've sold the lands and what your directives are. I won't have you coming here and upsetting my family or staff anymore."

Duffen angled closer, his eyes gone hard as flint. "Did I miss somethin'? I thought, Miss Brooke, you planned on askin' his lordship if we could carry on like afore."

Brette rose and wrapped an arm around Brooke's waist. She gave it a reassuring squeeze. "Unfortunately, the earl has other plans, Duffen."

"I didn't say that." Lord Ravensdale retreated and planted his hands on his hips. His ebony gaze roved each of them, perused the study, lit on Freddy and Dumpling still sleeping soundly on the couch, before finding its way to Brooke once more. He sent a glance heavenward as if asking for divine guidance. "I'm not sure what I shall do. Give me the evening to ponder and see if I can devise something that will benefit us all."

"I assure you, my lord, I'll not concede our home without a fierce fight and before I use every means at my disposal."

And you can wager with the devil on that.

His lips turned up in a wickedly seductive smile, and he caressed her with another leisurely glance. So sure of himself, the pompous twit. Used to taking what he wanted, consequences be hanged.

A wave of scorching rage swept her. The earl needed to leave. Now. Before Brooke lost what little control she held. She wasn't given to violence, but the urge to punch him in his perfect, straight nose overwhelmed her.

She patted Brette's hand. "Please retrieve his lordship's coat, and take the others with you. I wish to have a moment alone with him."

With a curt nod, Brette whisked from the study as their cousins scrambled to stand. After sending Lord Ravensdale glances ranging from accusatory to wounded, they scurried from the room.

Brooke squeezed her hands together to stop their trembling. She'd only eaten a piece of toast today, and hunger, along with the disastrous afternoon, made her head spin. "Duffen, please see to the earl's mount."

"Did that, an' now I have to go into Satan's playground again?" He stuffed his cap onto his head, and with a mutinous glower, buttoned his coat. "Should've waited by the entrance. I'd have been no wetter or colder."

Muttering, he stomped to the door. "Bet my breeches he'll get lost on the way home, he will. Pretentious cove, strutting about in his fine togs, lording it over the poor gels. Haven't they been through enough?"

Brooke made no effort to chastise him, since her sentiments closely echoed his. She followed him to the doorway. Presenting her back to Lord Ravensdale, she spoke softly for Duffen's ears alone. "Please tell Mabry he needn't bother coming to the house."

Duffen gave a sharp nod. "Why'd he bother to come at all? Upset the young misses, he did. Lord or not, the man hasn't the sense of a worm."

He slashed Lord Ravensdale a scowl that would've laid out a lesser man before disappearing into the dark corridor, still grumbling beneath his breath.

"Yes, why bother coming at all? Couldn't your man of business have seen to the sale? For surely that's what you intend." She crossed her arms and glared at Lord Ravensdale, unable to keep the scorn from her tone. "You don't look the sort to worry yourself about the running of an estate. You probably don't venture to your own holdings unless you make a token visit once every now and again. Probably more concerned with the tie of your cravat or the goings on at White's or Almack's."

I've become a harpy.

His lordship appraised her coolly while exchanging Papa's coat for his own.

No, definitely not padded. Those broad shoulders and chest are natural muscles, more's the pity.

It seemed most unfair that he should be gifted with wealth, looks, and a physique to rival a Greek god's. An attractive package on the exterior perhaps, but the trappings hid a blackguard's treacherous heart.

With a great deal of difficulty, he struggled into his coat, the wetness and tight fit presenting a humorous challenge. Swearing beneath his breath, he wriggled and twisted. Had her life not been shattered, she might've chuckled at his antics.

His elbow caught at an awkward angle near his ear, and he curled his lip in irritation. He glanced her way and opened his mouth.

She arched a brow.

Don't you dare ask for my assistance.

Freddy would fart feathers before she offered to help the earl.

He snapped his mouth shut and a closed expression settled on his features. "You know nothing of me, Miss Culpepper, and your blame is sorely misplaced."

"Indeed. And on whom shall I place the blame then?"

"If you must blame someone, blame your confounded cousin for being a self-centered sot. Blame your father for not providing for you." At last, he rammed his arm into the sleeve. He waved a hand in the air. "Blame The Almighty for making you a woman, and not a man capable of providing for himself and his family."

Too far!

Brooke gasped and narrowed her eyes. She fisted her hands and clamped her teeth together so hard, she feared they would crack.

Forget the blasted cane. She longed to run Lord Ravensdale through with the rusty sword hanging askew above the fireplace, the arrogant bastard. She *had* provided for her family, despite the odds against her, and despite being a woman.

God forgive her, but she hoped the earl did catch a nasty chill or get lost on his journey to wherever he stayed. Or, better yet, fall off his magnificent horse and suffocate on a pile of fresh cow manure. She doubted he'd experienced a moment's discomfort in his entire life, and he had the gall to amble into Esherton today—as if strolling Covent Garden or perusing the oddities at Bullock's Museum—and nonchalantly destroy their lives.

She might be able to forgive him for winning the wager. After all, the rich thought nothing of losing a few hundred pounds, a prized piece of horseflesh, or a millstone of an estate. Josephina assured her gambling was the rage in London's upper salons. But the earl's indifference to their dire circumstances? And then having the ballocks to lay the blame for her predicament on her sex?

How callous and coldhearted could he be?

As coldhearted as Sheridan, and he is your cousin, which makes him the greater fiend by far.

Seething, Brooke pointed to the door. "Take your—"

Brette returned with Lord Ravendale's greatcoat. Mouth pursed, she passed it to him then moved to stand and stare into the waning fire. Her slumped shoulders and bowed head spoke of her distress.

He'd done this to her gentle sister.

Brooke clenched her jaw to quiet her quaking and suppress the vulgar suggestion she longed to make regarding where he could shove his opinions. She continued to shake uncontrollably.

Rage? Cold? Fear? Hunger?

Yes, those had her quivering like the leaves on the tormented trees outside.

Hugging her shoulders, she gazed out the blurry window. The rain had ebbed. Dusk wasn't far off, the mantle of night hovered on the horizon though the afternoon hadn't seen its end. She swept the clock a glance. A jot beyond half-past two. He'd been here a mere half an hour? The disastrous change he unleashed upon their lives ought to have taken much longer. Unfair how one man could snuff what little joy had survived at Esherton in less than a blink of an eye.

After securing his jacket, his lordship donned his damp overcoat. He gave his right chest a light pat, and a slight smile skewed his lips.

Done with the niceties, Brooke faced him fully.

"See yourself to the door, and don't bother us with your presence again. The house and surrounding five acres are entailed. Sheridan had no legal right to use them as collateral. Do what you will with the rest of the property, but understand I intend to seek counsel regarding the ownership of the herd and the use of the outbuildings. They sit on entailed properties, and you won't be permitted use of them. I...*we* haven't labored like slaves for five years to have you destroy everything we've worked for."

Would he call her bluff?

She hadn't any right to make those claims. Only Sheridan did.

Would Lord Ravensdale know that? Would he make an arrangement with her cousin regarding occupation of the house? God, then what?

The two devils would deal well together, she had no doubt.

"Believe me when I say, my lord, I'll cause you no small amount of grief for the havoc you've wrought on my family." How, she had no idea, but when an uneasy look flashed across his features, she relished the small victory her false bravado provided.

Brooke presented her back. If she never laid sight on the man again, it would be too soon.

It infuriated her all the more that she had ever entertained the slightest interest in the fiend.

She closed her eyes and drew forth every ounce of faith she possessed. *We've been through hard times before*. God would see them through this too. *Wouldn't He*? He'd met their needs thus far. *Barely.* He wouldn't fail them now.

He already has.

She opened her eyes, blinking away another round of burning tears, further testament to her overwrought state. Since when did she snivel at the least little thing? Why, until today, she hadn't cried since Papa died.

See what the earl had reduced her to? A weeping ninny.

Freddy snorted and rolled onto his back, still sound asleep. His tail twitched and his paws wiggled. A low whimper escaped him. Likely dreaming of his younger days when he drove the cattle. He'd been quite the herder until old age relegated him to snoozing the day away.

Get up, Freddy, and pee—or worse—on his lordship's boot again.

Brette gathered Pudding from the hearth before settling into one of the wingback chairs. She obviously didn't intend to leave Brooke alone with the earl again. Propriety prohibited it, as did Brette's protective nature.

Thank you, Brette.

The cat curled into Brette's lap, her leery gaze on the earl. She'd not soon forgive him for crushing her into the cushions. Pudding was a pout.

After sending Lord Ravensdale an unreadable look, Brette petted the cat and stared into the fire's remaining embers. No sense adding another log when they'd vacate the room as soon as Lord Ravensdale took his leave.

Brooke whirled around at a light touch on her shoulder.

He stood mere inches away, close enough that she smelled his cologne once more. Such forwardness wouldn't be tolerated. She opened her mouth to say as much, but his chestnut eyes held no hostility, only warm empathy.

She swallowed, wanting to glance away, but her dratted eyes refused to obey. What was wrong with her today? Out of character for her to be mawkish over a man, weep like a child, or wallow in self-pity.

"I will go, for now, because this weather forces me to." Brows pulled into a vee, he looked to the window. "But be assured, I will return with a satisfactory solution, and I intend to communicate with your cousin regarding the matter of the house and grounds."

A bitter laugh escaped Brooke. "Unless your solution involves allowing us to run the dairy farm and remain in our home, I strongly doubt you will have any suggestion I would welcome."

"You will agree to what I propose, Brooke." He ran his forefinger along her jaw and smiled. "You haven't a choice, have you?"

Brooke tried to ignore the flash of sensation his touch caused. Why did this man have this power over her? "We'll see about that, my lord, and I haven't given you leave to use my given name."

He glanced at Brette.

Her eyes shut and head resting against the chair, she appeared to have dozed off. No wonder. She'd been up past midnight finishing a lace collar for Josephina.

Lord Ravensdale edged closer to Brooke and bent his neck, his mouth near her ear. “Oh, I intend to use much more than your name, Brooke.”

8

Always remember, gaming wastes two of man's
most precious things: time and treasure.
~*Wisdom and Advice—The Genteel Lady's Guide to Practical Living*

Heath grinned as he marched to the entrance.

Brooke smelled incredible. Not of perfume, but her natural scent. Womanly, warm, and sweet.

He'd wanted to gather her in his arms and bury his face in the hollow of her neck. After less than an hour's acquaintance, he already ached for her. Of course, three months of forced celibacy might have something to do with his randy state.

Cheeks glowing, Brooke had stared at him, dazed. However, a spark had glinted in the center of her eyes, and male instinct assured him the glimmer hadn't been entirely shock or ire. He'd piqued her interest and what's more, she'd responded to him physically.

His remark about using her had ruffled her feathers. True, he had been a mite crude, but she didn't seem the sort who'd appreciate flowery speeches or false flattery. She'd been honest and direct with him and deserved the same in return.

Brette, on the other hand, had scowled at him, not a hint of anything but hostility within her narrowed gaze. Tiny she might be, but Brooke's sister remained a force to be reckoned with and one he didn't want to cross. Much better to have the other four as allies in his newly formed quest to win Brooke over.

A notion had taken hold as they'd sat in the study, one that would provide for her and her family, and allow him to dispose of the albatross he'd won. The whole debacle seemed quite providential when he considered the situation, though he didn't believe in that sort of mythical nonsense. The facts remained: he required a new mistress, and Brooke was desperate for a means to provide for her family.

They complicated things a bit, but could work to his favor too, especially if his contract with Brooke included settling a monthly sum on her that would allow her to continue to care for the other four until the quartet married.

Several delightful ways she might express her gratitude crossed his mind, including a bottle of his finest champagne and a bath teeming with fragrant bubbles.

Why not marry her?

Heath faltered mid-step.

Where had that ludicrous thought come from? The bowels of Hades?

He wasn't ready to marry, didn't want to ever, truth to tell. But if he didn't, his reprobate of a cousin, Weston Kitteridge, would inherit and obliterate what scant remnant of honor and respect the Ravensdale legacy retained. Holding a title wasn't all pomp and privilege. The earldom required him to marry. A martyr for his title.

Eventually.

Heath resumed his progress through the hallway, his pace somewhat slower.

Brooke had intrigued him from the moment she appeared in the doorway. No woman had gotten his attention, snared him, so completely in such a short time. That he couldn't ignore. Not only a delectable morsel, she possessed a keen mind, evident in the years she'd operated the dairy. She had a practical head on her lovely shoulders—shoulders he itched to strip naked and trace with his lips—and she'd already proven she would willingly sacrifice herself for the wellbeing of others.

In all likelihood, she remained as chaste as the day she'd been born, but wisdom dictated an examination by his physician before Heath penned his signature to any agreement between them. He would be generous, of course. Provide her with an annual income and a comfortable cottage once he tired of her.

No doubt she'd prefer the farm, but instinct told him he wouldn't grow weary of her soon. He had no intention of nursing the dairy along in order for her to return to it in a few years, and resume the heavy responsibilities of operating the place. Besides, no woman should have to labor so hard to live in poverty.

He could give her that much at least—a comfortable existence for the rest of her days. Perchance she would even decide to marry after their association ended. Many women made respectable, even exceptional, matches, after being a kept woman.

Daphne's features sprang to mind.

And others didn't bother waiting until they'd been given their congé.

What had started as a miserable outing had proved advantageous after all. Not a direction he'd expected the day to take, but such an opportunity shouldn't be squandered. Some—not him, mind you—might call it a blessing in disguise.

Opening the entry door, he released a soft chuckle.

Taken aback, she'd gaped at him like a cod fish, her blue-violet eyes enormous and her pink lips opening and closing soundlessly. Heath had bent halfway to kiss them when her sister's exaggerated throat clearing had brought him up short. He'd forgotten Brette napped in the chair.

Rather touching, how protective the sisters were of one another. He hadn't experienced that sort of bond with another human. Not that it bothered him. One didn't miss what one had never had. Emotional balderdash and sentimental claptrap he could do without, thank you.

The esteem he held for his friends, Alexander Hawksworth and Leventhorpe, was the closest Heath had ever come to an emotional attachment with anyone, including his mistresses. Must be a family curse handed down from his glacial parents, and theirs before them. The Ravensdales weren't hailed for their warmth and geniality, but that didn't stop them from coupling like rabbits with any partner willing.

He had put a stop to that practice...almost.

Grateful the storm had abated somewhat, he ran down the stoop stairs. An occasional blast of cold air accompanied a thick drizzle. Far better than the monsoon that had blown him here, nonetheless.

Hunched within his baggy coat and oversized cap, Duffen waited at the bottom of the stairs.

Ebéné, however, was nowhere in sight.

Heath scanned the drive before casting a glance at the barns. "Where's my horse?"

"Hadn't the heart to make the poor beasty stand in the rain an' cold. I thought…" Staring at the ground, the servant stuffed his hands into his jacket pockets and shuffled his feet. He darted a quick look at Heath before returning his attention to the dirt. "Thought I might take you to your horse an' give him a few more minutes out of the weather."

He scuffed his boot uncertainly.

"Most considerate of you." Heath shook his head, curling his mouth at the corners. "Ebéné is already miffed at me for the journey here. I'm sure he won't welcome the return trip. Thank you for thinking of his comfort."

Duffen rolled his shoulders before angling toward the outbuildings. "Aint the horse's fault you got a hair up your arse an' set out in weather evil enough to bewitch the devil himself."

Heath scratched his upper lip to cover his smile.

Ought to reprimand him for his impudence.

After turning away, the servant lumbered down the path to the barn. Amusement outweighed propriety and Heath dutifully followed the disgruntled little elf of a man. The pathway forked, and instead of continuing on the trail to the stables, Duffen veered to the other branch.

Heath stopped and looked at the barns. "Isn't my mount stabled in one of those?" He pointed to the buildings. Light shone from the south end of the farthest one. The lowing of cattle echoed hollowly from within the two long structures.

Duffen looked over his shoulder and shook his head. He didn't stop plodding along.

"No, the herd's indoors 'cause of the storm. There's no room. Besides, several cows have newborn calves, and more are in labor or expected to birth their babes any day." He jerked his head toward a beehive-shaped stone building. "Puttin' your stallion in the carriage house seemed wiser. There are stalls in there, an' it's quieter."

That's a carriage house?

Heath would bet Ebéné a carriage hadn't graced the inside of the building for a good number of years. Lady Bustinza's monstrous bosoms drooped less, and the dame was six and eighty if she was a day. He shook his head, and with another brief glance at the stables, raised his collar and continued onward. He wouldn't make it to Leventhorpe's before darkness fell. Traveling at night—the only thing he hated worse than riding in the rain.

Other than a dagger in his boot, he bore no arms. Not that he expected trouble, but a wise man prepared for any eventuality. *Should've taken Leventhorpe's carriage.* He allowed himself a rueful smile. He'd grown soft, too used to the comforts of his privileged life.

Duffen faced forward again but waited for Heath to catch up.

Scrunching his eyes and pulling his earlobe, the servant gave him a sideways glance. Duffen opened his mouth then snapped it closed, glaring past Heath. "Don't s'pose you'd help an old man with somethin'."

Heath grinned. Despite himself, he liked the cantankerous fellow.

The poor man shouldn't have been working at all at his age. He could spare a minute or two more. "And what might that be?"

"We store the extra feed and grain in the dovecote 'cause it's harder for the vermin to get to it. The only way inside is through them holes on top and the door." He cackled and shoved his hat upward, exposing his wizened face. "The rats sure do try, though, let me tell you. Caught one gnawin' at the door the other day. Clever little beasts, they are."

"I'm sure." Heath took the servant at his word.

A crow perched on the dovecote's upper edge took to the sky, its croaking call stolen by a gust of wind whipping past. Heath shivered and secured the top button of his coat then dug around in his pocket and found his gloves. Damp leather didn't do much to stave off the chill permeating him, but he tugged them on, nonetheless.

Damn, but he'd never been this miserably cold.

"Dark omen that." Duffen pointed to the bird zig-zagging across the sky. "Bad luck to see a lone crow atop a house."

Heath eyed the dour man and swallowed a chuckle. Like anyone could see the moon tonight with clouds thick as porridge. Not the least superstitious, he didn't believe in fate either. "Well, I don't think a pigeon cote qualifies as a house, so there's nothing to worry about, is there?"

"You city coves don't know much, do you?" Disgust puckered Duffen's face. "It's a house for pigeons an' doves, aint it?"

Not in the last century.

Heath surveyed the ancient structure, and the spots of grass sprouting atop the roof.

Or two.

"Mark my words, my lord. You'll wish you never set foot on Esherton Green's lands afore the moon rises."

Almost sounds like a threat.

Where in God's name had Brooke unearthed the man? Was he the best she could find to employ? She probably couldn't afford to pay him much and no one of substance would work for the pittance she offered.

His patience running thin, Heath strode across the grass. "So what is it you need help with?"

"Can't get the door open. Think it's jammed." Duffen planted his hands on his hips and scowled at the barns. "Mabry an' the other hands don't think I pull my weight round here. I'll be damned—beg your pardon, my lord—before I ask 'em for help."

He begs my pardon now?

"Let's be about it then. I truly need to be on my way." The drizzle had turned into rain once more, though the wind hadn't returned in force.

"This way, your lordship."

Duffen trudged round the backside of the building, Heath in his wake.

Heath obligingly turned down the latch and, levering his legs and shoulders, gave the door a hefty shove. It sprang open with surprising ease. He tumbled to his knees on the circular floor, cracking the left one hard. Pain wrenched the joint.

Damnation.

Eyeing the hundreds of dung-encrusted nesting holes lining the sides, he brushed his palms on his coat. "It didn't seem all that stuck—"

Pain exploded at the base of his head.

9

A prudent woman holds this truth close to her heart:
gambling is the mother of all lies, and good luck, her fickle daughter.
~Wisdom and Advice—The Genteel Lady's Guide to Practical Living

After telling Brette she needed a few moments alone and to tell Mrs. Jennings to serve dinner early, Brooke puttered about the study. She banked the fire before closing the drapes and blowing out all but one candle. Brette had taken the cats when she left, and only Freddy remained curled on the couch, dozing. Every now and again, he opened his eyes to make sure she hadn't left him. She'd rescued him as a puppy from an abusive, slick-haired showman at a county fair, and Freddy seldom let Brooke out of his sight.

A flush suffused her for the dozenth time since Lord Ravensdale had left her gaping like a ninnyhammer.

He'd been about to kiss her.

She was positive.

Mesmerized by his beautiful eyes and mouth, she would have let him. *Let him*? Encouraged him.

With her sister sitting right there, watching.

What had come over her?

Brooke had experienced desire before. She'd nearly married Humphrey, though the mild pleasantness he'd stirred in her didn't compare to the wild tempest of sensations his lordship had rioting through her. Thrilling and frightening and certainly not the sensations a practical spinster should've been entertaining.

Must be because he was a practiced man of the world with a swashbuckler's bold good looks and comportment, and Humphrey had been a quiet, mild-mannered man. More of a reserved poet sort than a swaggering, cock-sure, womanizing—*remember that, Brooke...the earl's no doubt a womanizer*—pirate.

Brooke rubbed her fingers against the sofa's roughened backrest as the last embers of the fire faded. Did Lord Ravensdale think her circumstances so desperate, he could take liberties with her? Had she given the rogue cause in the few moments they'd been acquainted to think she'd be receptive to his advances?

Brow knitted, she stilled her fingers, replaying the few minutes he'd been here in her mind. No, she'd behaved with complete propriety, and absolutely nothing about her attire was remotely suggestive or alluring. A nun wore finer, more seductive clothing.

Did the man go about kissing women he'd just met on a regular basis? The notion, much like soured cream, curdled in her belly.

Enough ruminating.

She wanted to inventory the larder before dinner. While they'd waited for the calving to occur, their stores had declined severely. Could she make do for a little longer since she didn't know whether she could sell the calves now?

There's always the bull fund.

Brooke flexed her hands and firmed her lips. No. She wouldn't touch the hoarded reserve. If she did, then she admitted she'd lost Esherton Greens. Her heart wrenched. That she could not do. Not yet. Not until every last avenue had been explored. There must be a way.

Please, God. A miracle would be most welcome.

She pivoted to the door, and her gaze landed on the small package sitting where Blythe had set it earlier.

What a perfectly horrid birthday. Brooke wouldn't celebrate the day ever again. Not that there'd been any real festivities in the house since Mama died. There'd been little time or inclination, and even less money, for such frivolity.

Poverty and grief had denied the girls much.

Brooke lifted the forgotten gift. She turned it over and squeezed gently. Something soft. What had the sweethearts done?

She slid the ribbon from the package. Dangling the yellow strand from a finger, she unfolded the plain cloth—one of the girl's handkerchiefs—and a stocking slid to the floor.

Tears welled again as she bent to retrieve the white length. Where had the dears found the money to buy yarn to knit a pair of stockings? Hers had been repaired so many times, the patched and knobby things scarcely resembled the pair she now held to her face.

A sob escaped her, and she pressed the back of her hand to her mouth to stifle the others scratching up her throat. Tilting on the precipice of hysteria, she drew in a measured breath. Where was the logic Papa boasted of? The common sense Mama instilled in her?

Histrionics solved nothing. Her guide must be calm reason.

And cunning.

She would outmaneuver Ravensdale, the jackanape, one way or another.

Stupid, stupid Sheridan to wager her farm in a miserable card game. For Esherton *was* hers. Perhaps not legally, but in her heart, it had always been hers. She loved the drafty house—crumbling entry and shoddy condition and all—and often daydreamed about restoring the treasure to its former glory. As a child, she'd roamed the meadows and orchard, climbed the gnarled trees, and petted the newborn calves. Every night, the soft moos of the cattle lulled her to sleep, and most mornings a songbird's trill woke her.

Somehow, she must persuade Lord Ravensdale to allow them to stay.

But how?

She fiddled with a loose thread dangling from her cuff.

Stop before you unravel the whole edge.

Could she offer Lord Ravensdale more profit? Use the parure set as collateral? Was there another way to procure funds; anything else they could sell or barter?

She glanced around the office. Not in here, or the rest of the house, for that matter. Oh, to have a treasure buried somewhere on the estate. Alas, her family tree held no buccaneers, addlepated relations ranting of secret stashes of gold, or long-lost kin seeking to bestow a fortune on their surviving family members.

Brooke tapped her chin.

They'd already searched the attic, and hadn't unearthed anything of value. Still, some of her ancestors had traveled broadly, and perhaps an artifact or two that might be pawned or sold remained buried in a corner or trunk. She would send Blythe and Brette above stairs tomorrow to burrow around in the clutter a mite more.

When he'd first inherited, Brooke had asked Sheridan if she might buy the unentailed lands from him, using the parure set as a down payment. The grasping bugger had said no. He'd wanted the regular income and possession of the grounds too.

Would Lord Ravensdale be open to the suggestion?

That only partially solved the problem, though, since Sheridan retained the house and would continue to demand rents. She couldn't afford to make land payments and also send him money monthly. Not on the dismal profit the farm made.

Swiping a hand across her eyes, Brooke sighed, her shoulders slumping.

What a blasted muddle.

She would have to write Sheridan. Discover exactly what he proposed. Bile burned her throat. This helplessness, the lack of control over her fate and the others', nearly had her shrieking in frustration.

Damn the injustice.

She would send a note to Mr. Benbridge, seeking an appointment. He and his wife had been absolute dears after Papa died, despite Brooke breaking their son's heart. They'd assured her they understood her decision to decline Humphrey's proposal. An unpleasant suspicion had always lay tucked in a cranny of Brooke's mind; she hadn't been good enough, of a high enough station for their son. Her refusal had relieved them.

After Humphrey left, Josephina admitted her parents—landed gentry with deep, deep pockets—wanted their children to marry into a higher social class. Mr. Benbridge had refused no less than seven offers for Josephina's hand—none from gentlemen with a title greater than a viscountcy—and now at one and twenty, Josephina feared she'd end up like Brooke.

On the shelf. No offense intended.

However, Brooke hadn't anyone else to ask for advice. Mr. Benbridge would know what direction to point her, and Mrs. Benbridge claimed many connections in London. Her sister, the Viscountess Montclair, was an influential woman, or so Mrs. Benbridge often boasted. Brooke would ask her for a reference and to pen letters on her behalf, should, God forbid, they actually have to leave Esherton.

Brooke dropped the stockings and wrapping onto the desk. Shivering, she sank into Papa's chair. Had she known she would remain in the study longer, she'd not have let the fire die. She placed two pieces of foolscap before her then stared at the paper.

She shoved one aside. Not now. Impossible to write Sheridan today. Too much anger and hurt thrummed through her to pen a civil word to the cull.

She tapped the other piece of foolscap, not certain how to approach Mr. Benbridge about her delicate situation. Best not to say too much. Just send a missive along, ask if she could call in the next day or two, and also, if he might spare her a few moments to ask his advice.

Wiggling her toes against the chill permeating the room, Brooke wrote the brief note. She put the quill away then sprinkled sand on the ink. If the weather cooperated, she would send the letter round with one of the stable hands in the morning.

A short rap on the door preceded Duffen poking his head inside.

Freddy lifted his ears and thumped his tail once.

"Do you have need of me this evenin', Miss Brooke? My bones have ached somethin' fierce all day. This wicked weather is hard on old joints. Thought I'd ask Cook for her sleepin' tonic an' retire early."

Duffen shuffled so slowly, she expected his stiff joints to creak.

"Certainly," Brooke said and smiled. "Please forgive me for the necessity of sending you into the rain twice today."

Grimacing at the new ink stain on her forefinger, she stood. Why couldn't she manage a quill without getting ink on herself? Rubbing her fingers together, she came round the desk and, after gathering her new stockings in her unstained hand, collected the candlestick with her other.

She gave Duffen another warm tilt of her mouth. "Thank you for seeing our guest on his way. Let's hope he doesn't make an appearance again any time soon."

"Don't like the man." He frowned and rubbed his amulet. "Greedy, no good churl."

At his fierce tone, Brooke gave him a sharp look. "I understand you're angry with him. I am too, but we must get him to cooperate with us."

"I aint grovelin' for the likes of that cheatin' bugger," Duffen muttered. "Mebe he'll take you at your word an' not come back."

They exited the study into the unlit hallway, Freddy pattering behind.

"I think he'll return, but I plan on being better prepared the next go round." She raised the candle to look Duffen in the eye. "I promise you, as I told Lord Ravensdale, I shall do everything within my power to keep our home."

"What about...nicking him off?" Duffen averted his eyes and tugged on his earlobe.

Brooke stopped abruptly and stepped on Freddy's paw. "Pardon?"

The dog yelped and scampered away, giving her a wounded stare.

"I'm sorry, Freddy. Come here, let me see. Duffen, hold the candle please." She bent and examined the dog's paw. After assuring herself he hadn't sustained a serious injury, she straightened.

Arms crossed, she regarded Duffen. He did say the most peculiar things at times. What went on in that head of his? "Don't jest about something so appalling. Lord Ravensdale may be our adversary, but I do not wish the man dead."

"He'd let you and the other misses starve." Duffen jutted his chin out, his eyes suspiciously moist.

"That's harsh, Duffen, and I believe you know it. His lordship doesn't realize how dire our circumstances are."

"Beggin' your pardon, but he'd have to be blind not to see our sorry state." He scratched his scrawny chest, frustration glittering in his toast-brown eyes.

Brooke retrieved the candleholder, her heart aching for the old retainer, and they continued along the barren hallway. "He's only acting to better his interests, and it's a wise business move on his part."

"Why are you defending him?" Duffen snorted and gave her a look suggesting she'd gone daft.

Why am I defending him?

She entered the welcoming kitchen, Duffen at her side.

"You don't need to worry yourself, Miss Brooke. I promised your father I'd take care of his girls. I've done what needs be done."

10

One who desires peace and contentment, neither lays wagers nor lends.
~Wisdom and Advice—The Genteel Lady's Guide to Practical Living

Eyes closed, Heath rolled onto his back, and instantly regretted the movement as agony ricocheted inside his skull. He covered his face with an elbow and swallowed. Nausea toyed with his stomach and throat.

Holy Mother of God.

Not dead then. Death wouldn't be painful, would it? Unless this was hell. No, hell was hot. Dank and cold permeated this place. Where was he?

He forced his eyes open a slit.

Ah, the dovecote.

Duffen had clobbered him, the crusty old goat.

At Brooke's direction? What did she say to the servant before he stomped from the study?

Heath squinted at the faint light filtering into the top of the domed ceiling.

Early morning?

He'd been unconscious the entire night. Slowly, afraid any sudden movement might send his head rolling across the grain-smattered floor, he sought the entrance. Closed and likely locked tighter than a convent of giggling virgins.

He sucked in a long breath and wrinkled his nose at the stench. Pigeon *and* cow manure.

Splendid.

He flexed his stiff shoulders and spine. The stone floor didn't make for the most comfortable sleeping accommodations. In the weak light, he scrutinized the culvery. To his surprise, a flask and a lumpy cloth—perhaps a napkin—lay atop a pair of ratty blankets beside a bucket atop bulging grain sacks.

All the comforts of home.

Groaning, he struggled to a sitting position. He removed his gloves and waited for another dizzying wave to subside before exploring the source of pain. Heath brushed a tender fist-sized lump behind his left ear and, wincing, probed the area gently.

No blood.

His skull hadn't been split open, thank God, but he would boast a cracking good headache for a day or two. He coughed, flinching and holding his head as agony crashed through his brain again. Make that a whopping headache for a bloody week.

What had the puny whoremonger bashed him with? A boulder? No, more likely one of the several bricks scattered near the door.

Heath inhaled then released a holler. "Help, I'm locked in the dovecote."

His brain threatened to leave his head through his nose. Shouting like a madman would have to wait a few hours, until he could be certain the act wouldn't slay him.

Would Leventhorpe start searching for him immediately or assume he'd taken refuge at an inn along the way. In that event, his friend might delay until as late as tomorrow to sound the alarm. But sound it, his friend would.

Had he mentioned Esherton Green by name to Leventhorpe?

Heath couldn't remember, blast it.

He could scarcely string two thoughts together. He closed his eyes and sucked in an uneven breath to lessen the throbbing in his head and ease his churning stomach. Neither helped a whit.

He pressed two fingers to his forehead.

Think. What will Leventhorpe do?

Aware of Heath's reputation for fastidiousness, Leventhorpe would dismiss any notion of a woman waylaying him. Besides, when expected somewhere, Heath didn't cry off unless he sent a note round.

Leventhorpe had probably been in the saddle since before dawn. He possessed a dark temper, far worse than Heath's. Miss Culpepper had no idea the nest of hornets she would disturb if the Marquis of Leventhorpe became involved. The chap couldn't abide any form of lawlessness or breach of conduct.

Heath had underestimated Brooke's desperation. What did she think to accomplish by having her servant knock him in the head and confine him, both severe offenses against a peer?

My God, maybe she'd intended to kill him.

Disappointment like none he'd ever known squeezed his lungs. He didn't want to believe that of her.

He slid two fingers inside his right boot. His knife remained sheathed there. His gaze wandered to the supplies. Why bother with food and water if she planned on disposing of him? Perhaps she thought to blackmail him into giving her the lands. He'd have to rethink that mistress notion. Bedding a bloodthirsty wench didn't appeal.

If he hadn't felt so bloody wretched, he would've given vent to the fury heating his blood. No matter. There'd be plenty of time for anger later—after he'd escaped or been freed, for he hadn't a doubt his stay in this oversized birdhouse wouldn't be an extended one. Either she would come to her senses—because he wouldn't bend to coercion—or Leventhorpe would out her scheme.

She'd better hope it wasn't the latter.

Just you wait, Brooke Culpepper.

A crow's harsh call sounded.

Heath lifted his gaze to the ceiling and met the beady, ebony gaze of an inquisitive bird sitting on one of the upper beams. Hopping sideways, the crow eyed him then the supplies. The storm had passed, and jagged rays of sun formed a crisscross pattern within the structure. Nonetheless, the place held as much hominess and warmth as a tomb.

Terribly thirsty, he half-crawled, half-scooted to the flask. His skull objected by cruelly stabbing him with each lurching motion. After unscrewing the top, he took several satisfying gulps of rather tangy water. Better, but food might help settle his stomach more. He pulled the cloth away and revealed two hard rolls, a chunk of Cheshire cheese, and dried apples.

Not the most sumptuous of meals, but prisoners couldn't be persnickety.

Did the Culpeppers break their fast with this simple fare every morning? Probably, and inexpensive porridge too.

Despite the coolness, sweat beaded his brow and trickled into his temple hair. God, he feared he would cast up his accounts. Except he hadn't eaten since yesterday morning, and his stomach lay empty. He sought his handkerchief. Gainsborough's marker crackled inside his greatcoat. After patting his face and returning the hopelessly wrinkled cloth to his pocket, Heath withdrew the paper.

Time to find out exactly what he'd won in that confounded wager.

Sighing, he relaxed against the grain sacks and bent his knees. He unfolded the I.O.U then smoothed the paper atop his thighs. He stared at the writing. One short, sloppy paragraph with Gainsborough's—*damn his eyes*—and a witness's signature affixed to the bottom. His forehead scrunched in concentration, Heath nibbled a roll and squinted at the black scrawls.

Despite the best tutors and regular beatings meant to encourage him to pay attention to his lessons, he could barely read. Heath was known for his sharp wit and droll humor, and few people knew the truth. Those who did, he paid well, *very well*, to keep their silence on the matter.

He traced his forefinger over the top line. The letters on the page didn't always make sense. They appeared turned around, the words and sentences impossible to read. He long ago decided the issue a deficit in him, and the knowledge mortified him to his core. Toddlers scarcely out of diapers could read better than he.

The page blurred. His eyelids felt weighted with stones, too heavy to lift. He blinked drowsily, jerking his neck abruptly when he nearly dozed off. Pain seared him once more.

"Dammit to hell."

His shout startled the crow. The bird screamed in alarm and streaked to the exit atop the dovecote. An ebony feather spun slowly to the floor.

His movements sluggish, Heath crammed the unfolded paper into his pocket. Reading the marker would have to wait. Mouth dry, he licked his lips. He fumbled for the flask, intent on quenching his thirst before resuming his slumber. The cool liquid slid into his mouth, and bitterness assailed his tongue. He went rigid.

Drugged?

He spewed the water onto the floor and hurled the flask against the opposite wall.

Struggling to keep his eyes open, he tugged a horse blanket from the sack beside him. After draping the threadbare length across his chest and shoulders, he slumped against the bags.

Words slurred and chin resting on his chest, he mumbled, "Brooke Culpepper, you'll regret the day you crossed me."

Sleep claimed him a moment later.

Brooke rose before dawn, having lain awake most of the night. While drinking a cup of tea—more hot water than tea—she had pored over the farm's ledgers, searching for the slightest way to afford rent and make land payments at the same time. Even if Lord Ravensdale agreed to sell her the land, which she doubted, it was painfully clear she hadn't enough money to pay both.

Now, midmorning, she sat at Papa's desk, a throw Mama knitted draped over her shoulders. Freddy slept in his favorite corner of the sofa. No fire burned in the hearth or candles in the holders. Heavy shadows hovered in the corners the light from the windows couldn't penetrate.

Similar darkness haunted the recesses of her heart.

She had concocted every conceivable scenario she could imagine, and each resulted in losing Esherton and leaving the only home she'd ever known. Brooke tapped her fingertips together, pondering the pile of notes before her. The funds for a bull lay upon the scarred desktop. Sufficient to see her and the girls to London and settled in inexpensive lodgings, but scant more to live on and no provision for the servants at all.

The parure sat atop the desk too.

She lifted the blue velvet lid, worn thin on the edges from hundreds of fingertips touching the fragile fabric. The sapphire and diamonds winked at her from their secure nests. She lifted the tiara high and rotated the circlet so the stones glittered in the cheery ribbons of sunlight filtering through the window. This set had adorned Culpepper women for five generations, since her blond-haired blue-eyed Spanish grandmother wore it for her wedding. Tragically, she'd died before reaching her new home, but her legacy lived on through the jewels.

Selling the gems…a betrayal of Brooke's and the quartet's heritage. Who could she entrust the set to who knew how to barter and wouldn't cheat her? She must receive top price for the sapphires, and that would only occur in London.

Perhaps the Benbridges would know of someone.

She'd sent Rogers, a stable hand, round to their house with the missive over an hour ago. The girls had headed above stairs straightway upon her suggestion they search the attic one more time after breaking their fast this morning.

A stuffed pheasant missing an eye as well as part of a wing and foot propped the study door open part way. Its remaining eye reproached her for the indignity. Fingering the knobby wool atop her shoulders, Brooke half-listened for a knock at the house's entrance. If Rogers returned with an invitation for her to visit the Benbridges this afternoon, she'd need to change into her best gown and set out at once in the dog cart.

She also wanted to speak to Duffen this morning. His peculiar declaration last night before he trundled to bed still nagged. He assured her he'd only warned Lord Ravensdale to stay away from Esherton Green—not the servant's place at all, as she sternly reminded him—but doubt niggled, nonetheless. One more thing to compound her stress.

Duffen hadn't been happy at her reprimand, and for the first time, turned surly toward her. He'd stomped away, mumbling beneath his breath. Mayhap the time had finally arrived to relieve him of his duties—he had become more confused and difficult of late—but to set him aside would destroy the dear. Especially since he, too, had nowhere else to go.

She returned the tiara to its place on the once-white satin, now yellowed to ivory. Would Lord Ravensdale put in an appearance today as promised, despite Duffen's threat? If his lordship came round, she prayed she'd be at the Benbridges. Otherwise, she'd not be at home to callers.

Fewer than twenty-four hours didn't allow time enough to hatch a fool-proof plan.

Fool proof?

She didn't have a plan except to sell the jewels. Rather difficult to hatch a scheme when something nullified each idea she dreamed up. Elbows on the desk, Brooke closed her eyes, buried her face in her hands, and let the tears flow.

Papa, I vowed I'd take care of the girls, and I've failed you. And them. I don't know what to do. Our situation is impossible.

Raucous pounding at the entrance followed by raised voices in the hallway snared her attention. Brooke swiftly wiped her cheeks. She yanked the ratty throw from her shoulders, and after glancing around for a place to hide it, settled on stuffing the makeshift shawl into the desk's kneehole.

"Excuse me. What do you think you're doing?"

Blythe? She'd answered the door instead of Duffen? Where was he?

Brooke slid open the desk drawer then pushed the hidden latch to the secret compartment. One eye trained on the doorway, she rapidly gathered the money and jewelry case. After cramming them into the small cubicle, she clicked the latch, shoved the drawer closed, and locked it. She returned the key to its hiding place in a slot beneath the chair's seat.

Blythe, a strange inflection somewhere between irritation and awe in her tone, exclaimed, "You cannot push your way inside, you great looby."

Drat, Lord Ravensdale—more persistent and annoying than an itch one couldn't reach.

Still, Brooke's lip curved at Blythe's pluck. "Probably the first time the earl's been called a looby, eh, Freddy?"

Barking, the dog bounded to his feet and then ran up and down the length of the couch, pouncing and yapping.

"Hush, I cannot hear."

Freddy obediently plopped onto his bottom before snuffling his haunch in search of a flea.

Brooke leaped from the chair, smoothing a few wayward tresses into place. She'd been in rather a hurry when she'd piled the mass into a loose knot, mainly because she couldn't stand to see herself in the gown she wore—one of Josephina's cast-offs from several seasons ago. Brooke swept the front of the saffron muslin a critical glance and grimaced. The heinous color washed out her complexion, making her look sallow and sickly. However, her wardrobe consisted of four gowns, and she couldn't be picky. She pinched her cheeks and bit her lips to add a dab of color to her face.

Thankfully, no pet hair clung to this garment, and the cut and fit were acceptable. She stopped short of scrutinizing her reflection in the window to make sure her appearance met the mark. She'd tired of the thin, pale face staring at her from her dressing table mirror.

Why did she care how she looked anyway? She wasn't trying to impress Lord Ravensdale. The opinion of the flea Freddy scratched away at concerned her more than anything the earl might think.

Rubbish.

"I insist upon seeing your master or mistress," a cultured male voice—clearly irritated and condescending—demanded. "And you would do well to show your betters more respect."

Brooke cocked her head. Assuredly not Lord Ravensdale, but two visitors in the same number of days? Unheard of.

"My betters?" A dangerous inflection entered Blythe's voice. "And who might *you* be?"

A theatrical, masculine sigh carried into the study. "Lord Leventhorpe, if you insist on knowing. You really are the most impudent servant."

"And I believe you're the most pompous ars—donkey's rear I've ever had the misfortune of meeting," Blythe retorted.

This man clearly possessed the common sense of a potato, speaking to Blythe that way. She would verbally filet him—in the most ladylike manner possible, of course. Blessed with a quick wit and sharp tongue, Blythe did have a most…eloquent way with words.

Brooke strained to hear their conversation, more amused than she'd been in a long while.

"Again, I must insist on speaking with the proprietor of this… er…house," Lord Leventhorpe said.

"Well, your high-and-mightiness, you can insist all you want, but I already told you before you rudely shoved your way inside, no one is home to visitors today." Exasperation rang in Blythe's voice. "Leave your card, if you must, then take your odious self off."

"I shall do no such thing. I'll remain until I am received." Heavy footsteps tread along the corridor. "Where might I wait? In one of these rooms?"

Doors swished opened then clicked closed in rapid succession.

Snoopy bugger.

"Oh, for the love of God, are you completely dense? Do feathers occupy your skull, or is it altogether empty?" Slightly breathless, as if she'd had to scurry to keep up, Blythe said, "You cannot go poking about in people's homes."

"Then be a helpful chit, and tell me where I might await your mistress or master. A good friend of mine has gone missing, and Ravensdale intended to call here yesterday."

11

'Tis a simple truth that life depends on probabilities, and those who wager had best be prepared to pay the penalty for taunting fate.
~Wisdom and Advice—The Genteel Lady's Guide to Practical Living

Lord Ravensdale. Missing?

Brooke didn't need to see her reflection to know she'd grown pale as milk. She felt the blood rush to her feet, washing her in a wave of dizziness. She'd never fainted before, but feared she might swoon from alarm. Pressing a hand to her forehead, she tore to the study door.

"Duffen, what have you done?"

Rushing through the opening, she barely stopped short of plowing into a giant of a man with fiery auburn hair and a scowl fierce enough to set demons to trembling. She toed aside the pheasant and pulled the door closed behind her.

Freddy didn't need to anoint another lord's boots.

She craned her neck to meet the man's eyes.

And I thought the earl tall.

"I tried to stop him, Brooke." Blythe hurried to Brooke's side, delivering the gentleman a glower as hostile as the one he leveled at the women. "But the pig-headed oaf wouldn't listen."

So I heard.

"I'm aware. I heard him." Brooke met Lord Leventhorpe's cynical gaze, shadowed beneath thunderous brows. "I beg your pardon. I didn't mean you're a pig-headed oaf."

Though your decorum dictates otherwise.

"Yes, he is, and a boorish buffoon too." Blythe gave an insincerely sweet smile, ire radiating from her.

He quirked those hawkish eyebrows, his gaze swinging between Brooke and Blythe before settling, heavy and disapproving, on Brooke.

Judgmental, uppity prig.

"Am I to assume you are mistress here?"

She angled her head in affirmation.

He turned startling blue eyes to Blythe, and stared for a long, rude moment. The corners of his mouth tilted upward fractionally. "And I've blundered and called you a servant. However, you must admit," he flicked a black-gloved hand up and down, "your attire lends one to leap to that conclusion."

As did the cobwebs and dust clinging to her gown from rummaging about in the attic.

Blythe grunted, and thrust her chin out. "Fools jump to conclusions, *my lord*."

Brooke dipped into a reluctant curtsy. False deference peeved her, but Mama had drilled proper decorum into her, and rousing this irritated man further was foolishness.

"I am Brooke Culpepper, and this is my cousin, Miss Blythe Culpepper." Brooke canted her head toward Blythe, who grudgingly bobbed a shallow curtsy. "She and I, as well as our sisters, are the mistresses of Esherton Green."

"Tristan, Marquis of Leventhorpe. My estate is several miles east of here." His attention riveted on Blythe, he bent into the merest semblance of a bow—so short as to be almost insulting.

Seemed Lord Ravensdale chose friends as arrogant and pretentious as he, or did the marquis play a game with her cousin? *Tit for tat*? *Cat and mouse*?

Blythe narrowed her eyes and firmed her lips before averting her gaze. Wise on her part.

They hadn't time for verbal sparring. Duffen must be found at once.

His lordship canted his head in the open door's direction. "Are you aware there's a tree blocking the drive? Rather a mess to traverse."

"Yes, it fell yesterday, and I haven't set the servants to removing it yet." As if she had the manpower for such a task.

"Not bad enough to keep you from intruding." Blythe scratched her cheek, leaving a faint smudge. Attic grime.

His lordship's lips quivered again, and mutinous sparks spewed from Blythe's eyes.

Time to separate them.

"Blythe, we must find Duffen. He was the last to see Lord Ravensdale yesterday. Get the other girls to help you search." Brooke slid a sideways glance to the serious-faced man watching the exchange. "In fact, ask Mabry to have the stable hands look as well. As long as no cows are in labor, that is."

Lord Leventhorpe made a sharp gesture. "I think my friend's disappearance takes precedence over cattle."

The caustic dryness of his words could have set kindling afire.

Brooke folded her arms and returned his harsh perusal. "Not around here, it doesn't, my lord."

Worry crinkled Blythe's usually smooth forehead. She laid a hand on Brooke's forearm. "Do you think something is truly amiss?"

A grunt-like snort exploded from the marquis.

Brooke met his lordship's gaze square on.

Yes, I do, but I'll swallow snails before I admit it without more evidence.

She'd known Duffen three and twenty years and this irksome man three minutes. Her loyalty lay with the servant. For now.

His lordship coolly returned her scrutiny, his features granite hard. He didn't seem the merciful, forgiving sort. No, more like the eye-for-an-eye type of chap.

"Duffen is dotty and prone to muttering beneath his breath, but to suggest he would have anything to do with anyone's disappearance, most especially a lord's, is pure silliness." Blythe brushed at a cobweb on her skirt. "He's always been protective, almost grandfatherly, toward us girls."

"Rather like a decrepit, old rooster trying to rule young chicks and just as comical, I'd wager." His lordship offered this droll opinion, earning him frowns from the women.

"As you've never met him, I'm quite sure I don't know how you arrived at that assumption, my lord." Renewed ire tinted Blythe's cheeks. "Brooke, what are your thoughts?"

"I honestly don't know." If only she could reassure her cousin. She looked to the entrance, still gaping open. A gargantuan russet horse stood docilely out front, awaiting its owner. The sun streamed into the entry, and tiny dust particles danced in the bright warmth. Such a contrast to yesterday. "He did make a peculiar remark last night, and I haven't seen him today. Have you?"

Where were Duffen and Lord Ravensdale?

"No." Eyes wide, Blythe shook her head, setting the curls framing her face to bobbing. "He might be off napping. He's done that oft of late."

Dread knotted Brooke's stomach. She didn't dare contemplate what Duffen might have done. Perhaps the earl's disappearance was a horrid coincidence. *And the cows pooped green gold.*

"I'll notify the girls. Where do you want us to search first?" Blythe pointedly avoided looking at Lord Leventhorpe. Not intimidated easily, her cousin might have met her match in the daunting behemoth. "His usual haunts in the house and on the grounds?"

"Yes," Brooke said. "I'll be along to help as soon as I can."

As soon as she could escape the marquis's suspicious regard.

Blythe spun about then hurried down the corridor, his lordship's fractious gaze never leaving her.

Before turning the corner, she cast a swift glance over her shoulder.

Please let her find Duffen right away so we can sort this out.

God willing, Lord Ravensdale had taken shelter somewhere on the way to the marquis's. Or perhaps he'd been thrown from his horse and lay injured on the route. But wouldn't Lord Leventhorpe have come upon the earl then? Not that she truly wished Ravensdale harm, regardless of the mean-spirited thoughts she'd harbored about him yesterday. But after Duffen's menacing remarks last night...better the earl be lying hurt somewhere than the alarming alternative.

She swallowed a lump of revulsion and fear.

"So you admit Ravensdale called?"

His lordship's terse question wrenched Brooke's attention to the present unpleasantness.

"Certainly. I never implied otherwise. He arrived unannounced, soaked to the skin, I might add. After a small respite before the fire in the study, he went on his way. All in all, he didn't remain above three quarters of an hour." Brooke turned to enter the study. She looked behind her as she pressed the latch. "Would you prefer to wait in here or take part in the search?"

Freddy forced his stout body through the opening. He sniffed the air, and after taking one panicked look at Lord Leventhorpe, ducked his head and retreated into the study. He disappeared around the desk to skulk in the knee well.

His reaction to Lord Leventhorpe caused Brooke no small amount of discomfit. Freddy loved everybody...except the marquis, it seemed. Her unease heightened, she made a mental note of Freddy's reaction. Dogs were good judges of characters. A moist, black nose pressed against the small space beneath the desk's middle panel and sniffed loudly through the crack.

Lord Leventhorpe removed his hat and followed her into the room. "I'd like to ask you a few questions, starting with the peculiar remark this Duffen fellow made."

Shouts and clamoring roused Heath from a fitful slumber and an equally disturbing dream. A hobgoblin had knocked him on the noggin and locked him in a giant birdhouse, intending to feed him to an elephant-sized gray-plumed bird with violet-blue eyes and a shock of curly white feathers atop its head.

The commotion grew louder and closer.

"Lord Ravensdale?"

"Ravensdale!"

"Yer lordship, can you hear us?"

Heath bolted upright, pain and memories simultaneously assaulting him. He stumbled to his feet, his head throbbing with a crusader's vengeance.

"In here." A hoarse croak emerged. He swallowed. "I'm in here. Inside the pigeon cote."

More commotion echoed outside the building before the door jerked open.

Heath blinked at the outline of several people illumined in the archway. Unsteady on his feet, he waited until they stopped wavering before speaking. "Someone send for the magistrate. I've been attacked and abducted."

A small figure dashed away. Brette. No doubt to warn her sister she'd been found out. He couldn't wait to hear the elder Miss Culpepper's fabricated explanation for his treatment.

A fellow Heath didn't recognize stepped forward. "Your lordship, I'm Richard Mabry, Esherton's overseer. I'll send one of my lads to fetch the magistrate straightaway. Are you injured?"

Mouth dry as sand, head stuffed with wool and swollen three times its normal size, and tormented by an invisible hand that jabbed a jagged knife into his skull each time he spoke or moved, Heath barely contained a snarl. "If you consider being wacked on the head with a brick and then drugged senseless injured, then yes."

Shock registered on Mabry's craggy features before his gaze sank to the toppled bricks left of the entry. "Do you require a physician? Can you walk to the house, or do you need us to carry you?"

Hell of a lot of dignity in that, carted about like an invalid or a babe. Heath lifted an unsteady hand to his stinging face. A cut lay across his cheekbone. He hadn't noticed the scratch the first time he awoke. "No, yes, and no."

Mabry's beetle brows wiggled. "Sir?"

Heath forced his leaden feet to move forward. At least he thought he moved. A slug in molasses moved faster.

"No, I don't need a physician." *Might be a good idea to have one take a gander.* "Yes, I can walk. And no, I do not need to be carried." *You will if you keel over onto your face.*

Mabry gestured to a short, lanky man. "Run to the house, and let Miss Brooke know his lordship has been found."

As if she doesn't know where I've been all along.

The fellow bobbed his head before trotting away.

"I'd feel much better if you'd allow me the honor of assisting you, my lord. Miss Brooke will have my head if further harm comes to you." Mabry tentatively wrapped a burly arm around Heath's waist.

Heath choked on a scoffing laugh. "I doubt that, Mabry."

Nonetheless, Heath leaned into the man, grateful for the support. Lurching outside, he closed his eyes. The sun's glare proved excruciating and increased the ferocious thrumming inside his skull.

"I'll go on ahead and tell Brooke to prepare a chamber for his lordship. He shouldn't travel in his condition."

Heath turned his head in the direction of the voice and cracked one eye open. Blythe, the feisty oldest cousin.

"I would appreciate it." Pretenses be damned. He needed to sit down, before he toppled like a tap house drunkard. Devil it, how far away was the house?

Another sturdy arm wrapped around his other side.

"I see you've managed to make a muddle of things, Raven. Could have sworn you toddled here to sell the place, not take a snooze in a pigeon coop half-filled with shi—er...dung."

Leventhorpe?

Heath squinted at him, the sun's rays slicing straight to his brain. He'd have smiled but wasn't certain the motion wouldn't have split his skull like walnut. "About damned time you showed up."

"And that's the thanks I get for parting with my mattress before the sun awoke. I even missed breaking my fast and my customary cups of coffee." He gave Heath's ribs a gentle press. "You're welcome."

Several torturous minutes later—minutes which left Heath seriously considering asking someone to knock him unconscious again—Leventhorpe and Mabry hauled him up the steps.

Like blond-haloed angels of mercy, the Culpepper misses hovered at the entrance.

Leventhorpe's stride faltered, and he shot Heath a look of such incredulity, he would've laughed if he hadn't been afraid he'd disgrace himself on his friend's overly shiny boots. His reaction upon meeting the women yesterday had been much the same.

"Five bloody unbelievable beauties," Leventhorpe muttered beneath his breath. "My God, five. And not one a hopper-arsed or corny-faced."

Only one snagged Heath's attention. The one that had captivated him from the start, damn his eyes. *Damn her eyes.*

Her face somewhere between ashen and a sickly yellow, and wearing a dress uglier than the one she'd worn yesterday, Brooke met his gaze for an instant before squaring her shoulders and issuing orders. "Mr. Mabry, he needs a physician. Please ride to the village as soon as you've assisted his lordship upstairs."

"I'll notify the magistrate too, Miss Brooke."

Her eyes rounded, the irises growing enormous, and the slim column of her throat worked. "Yes, yes, quite so."

She blinked then blinked again, regaining her composure, but the unsteady hand she raised to tuck a silky curl behind her ear betrayed her true state.

"Blythe, have Flora bring the tea you brewed upstairs, and the hot water and towels too. Oh, and please have Mrs. Jennings heat the leftover stew from last night." She faced the twins. "Everything is prepared in Mama and Papa's room?"

They intended to put him in the master suite?

As one, the lookalikes nodded, but remained silent and exchanged an anxious glance. They turned reproachful gazes on him.

Their silent chastisement grated against his pride. Confound it, he was the victim here.

Not the only one, as you well know.

"Any sign of Duffen?" Brooke laid a hand on Brette's chill-reddened arm.

Why didn't they wear outer garments? He shivered within his greatcoat. Didn't they possess pelisses, or spencers, at least?

"Not yet, Brooke." Brette stepped aside to allow Mabry and Leventhorpe to guide Heath into the entry. "We wanted to get his lordship to the house as quickly as possible. We'll start looking again."

Heath wavered, and Brooke steadied him with a palm to his chest. The contact burned through his garments. She must have felt something too, because she snatched her hand away and rubbed it against her hip. Brow creased, she stared out the doorway.

He detected no mercy in the gaze Brette directed at him. So much for winning the cousins and sister to his cause. The task would be harder without their support. Did he still want Brooke for his mistress? Despite his suffering and the ghastly gown she wore, he couldn't pry his gaze from her pretty face.

Yes, confound it to hell and back again. He did. Why did he want her when any number of females would eagerly warm his bed? He'd address that particular after he determined her guilt. However, everything about her demeanor this moment screamed innocence.

"Where is the chamber you're putting him in?" Leventhorpe's grip tightened. "He's about to collapse."

Acting his overbearing self, as usual. Bossy as an old tabby.

"I am not." Heath took another swaying step.

Brooke whirled to stare at him. Sincere concern shimmered in her dark-lashed eyes, or else she was the best damned actress he'd seen in a long while. Better than that petite morsel he'd contemplated making his paramour. Compared to Brooke, the other woman seemed a tawdry tart.

"Do you need to be carried, my lord?" She wiggled her forefinger, beckoning the stable hands enter who'd followed them to the house.

"No. I am not going to collapse." Wouldn't do to have Brooke think him a weakling. That he cared an iota about her opinion of him gave testament to how hard he'd been whacked. Dashed the sense out of him.

"Stubble it, Ravensdale." Leventhorpe adjusted his support as he assisted Heath up the risers. "A ninety-year old, one-legged crone leans on her cane less than you're hanging on me."

Mabry grunted his agreement. "Not a light cove either."

"True, Mr. Mabry." Leventhorpe hoisted Heath higher. "You might consider a slimming regimen, Raven."

"Shut up, Trist," Heath all but growled, past caring what anyone thought of him. Flecks darted and danced before his eyes. He needed to lie down. At once.

Upstairs, Mabry took his leave, although Heath insisted he didn't need a physician.

"Nevertheless, my lord, I think it wise to have you examined." Brooke fluffed a pillow on the turned-down bed. Uncertainty clouded her indigo eyes. Her gaze flitted to Leventhorpe before she exchanged a telling glance with Blythe. Leventhorpe unnerved her. Good. She wasn't likely to try another stunt with Trist looming over her.

Her cap askew, a timid maid limped into the chamber. Arms twig thin and her gaze riveted on the floor, she bore a wooden tray laden with a teapot, cup, steaming bowl of something scrumptious smelling, two slices of bread, butter, and a spoon and napkin.

His stomach growled when he inhaled the heady aroma.

Brooke cast him a disconcerted glance then gave the servant a kind smile. "Thank you, Flora. Please set it on the table, there."

She pointed to a three-legged table near the toasty fire in the hearth.

Heath held his breath as Flora shuffled to the table, the tray wobbling with each awkward step. She had one leg shorter than the other. He inspected her shoes. A cobbler could build up the left sole, and she would walk much easier. Not a priority when money at Esherton appeared scarcer than frost in Hades.

"Need anythin' else, Miss Brooke?" Head cocked to the side, Flora peeped upward through stubby eyelashes and played with the stringy strand of hair that had escaped her cap.

Brooke offered another encouraging smile. "No. You may go. Make sure you eat luncheon today. You forgot again yesterday."

"I'll do it now." Flora hobbled out the door, leaving it open behind her.

Heath stared at Brooke's lips. What would they taste like? Sweet or fruity?

Why did she have him obsessing over every part of her anatomy? He could find no fault in her appearance, from her oval face, perfectly sculpted rose-pink lips, dove-white hair, surprisingly dark, winged brows, and thick lashes framing astonishing purple-blue eyes to her creamy skin, breasts he guaranteed would overflow his palms, and a backside that begged to be fondled and ridden.

Must be the injury to his head—had him waxing raunchy poppycock.

Leventhorpe propelled him toward the bed, and after urging Heath to sit, tugged off his boots and tossed them on the floor. Arms folded, Leventhorpe perched a hip on the arm of an overstuffed chair beside the bed.

Clearly exasperated, Blythe faced him, hands on her hips. "My lord, your presence isn't needed. Why don't you wait in the study?"

"Good idea." Brooke nodded her agreement as she dipped a cloth into a basin of water. "I shall come down and answer your questions when Lord Ravensdale's hunger is appeased and he is he resting comfortably."

Which hunger?

Heath must've made a noise—*Good God, did I say that aloud?*—for Brooke frowned, and Leventhorpe let loose a hearty guffaw.

"I'm staying." Leventhorpe looked down his superior nose, something he'd perfected over the years to put underlings in their place. One look usually sufficed to send the offender dashing for cover.

Blythe rolled her eyes heavenward, muttering, "Of course you are, obstinate bore."

"I heard that." Leventhorpe removed his gloves then his hat and tossed the lot on the chair's torn cushion.

Blythe offered a syrupy smile. "You were meant to."

He chuckled, and Heath speared him a sharp glance. A roguish grin lingered on Leventhorpe's face. Not a typical reaction from his reticent friend. As Brooke went about removing Heath's greatcoat and jacket, Leventhorpe looked on.

Every innocent brush of her hand or bump of her arm stoked Heath's awareness of her. She bent to her task, and her bodice gapped. He itched to touch the flesh his eyes caressed, but forced his focus away, all too aware they had an audience. Perusing the rather dusty chamber, he caught the sardonic curling of Leventhorpe's mouth.

Brooke tossed the overcoat to the foot of the bed and turned her attention to his jacket. She released the top button. Did her fingers tremble the merest bit?

"I can undress myself," he said, though the way the bedchamber weaved up and down, he wasn't at all certain he could.

Leventhorpe stopped scrutinizing the room—or was it Blythe that he studied?—to quirk a brow at Heath. "Of course you can, but let her fuss over you anyway."

Heath's neckcloth came next. He hated the confounded things. Always felt half-choked, but gentlemen of the *ton* didn't go about with their necks exposed.

"Lie back, my lord." Brooke passed the strip of cloth to her cousin.

At her prompting, Heath reclined against the pillows, and once he'd settled, she drew the bedcoverings to his waist. The pounding in his head lessened to a steady pulsing, and the chamber ceased to dip and sway like a ship on stormy seas.

Her lower lip clamped between her pink lips, she dabbed at the cut on his face.

He inhaled her fresh fragrance. A mole peeked at him from the right side of her neck, and he longed to kiss the small dot then explore the long swan-like column with his lips. The décolletage of her gown hinted at the lush swells of flesh it partially concealed. Would her nipples be pert and rosy or ripe and pink? Unbidden images of him laving her succulent tips with his tongue bombarded him.

His manhood jerked, momentarily stirring the bedcovers.

Busy spreading a pleasant-smelling salve on the scratch, Brooke didn't notice. He hoped. Irritated at his lack of control, and to keep from embarrassing himself, he turned a bland stare on Leventhorpe. The wicked twinkle in his friend's eye said plainly that *he* had noticed. "I don't need you mothering me, Trist. Go below and find someone to pester."

Leventhorpe yawned behind his hand and blinked drowsily. He looked done in. Likely he'd never sought his bed when Heath didn't return last night.

"I've no intention of mothering you, Raven. Removing your boots is the extent of my nurturing skills, I assure you." He inclined his head toward the women. "I'm making sure one of these sirens doesn't slide a knife between your ribs to finish the job."

Harsh gasps escaped the women.

Fury snapped in Blythe's eyes, but censure shimmered in Brooke's.

Bristling with indignation, Blythe whirled to Leventhorpe. Voice quivering, she stabbed a finger at him. "How dare you? We've been nothing but hospitable to Lord Ravensdale, and your ugly insinuations—"

Brooke touched Blythe's arm. "He has the right to worry about his friend."

Blythe pursed her lips and lowered her gaze. "But he doesn't have the right to accuse us of such evilness."

"I agree, but Duffen is in our employ." Brooke's gaze rested on Heath. "If he is responsible—"

Heath gave a derisive snort and paid the price as pain kicked its hind feet against his skull. "He is responsible. He deceived me into helping him then clobbered me with a brick when I turned my back."

"Then we must make things right." Her steady gaze met his. Nonetheless, he swore dread lingered in the depths of her unusual eyes. "It's the honorable thing to do."

My God, so convincing. She even had him believing her theatrics. He observed her through half-closed eyes. Unless this wasn't a performance. Perhaps he'd wronged her, and she hadn't been behind Duffen's actions. Difficult to believe, but perhaps the gnome truly had acted of his own volition.

Some of the tension eased from Heath.

Duffen, on the other hand, was in it up to his eyeballs. Did he understand the consequences of his misplaced bravado? Imprisonment or worse if Heath brought charges against him. And Leventhorpe would insist upon it.

Brette hustled into the chamber, the corgi on her heels.

Upon spotting Leventhorpe, the stout canine skidded to a halt. His nostrils flared and twitched before he crouched and skulked to hide beneath the draperies. Leventhorpe's mouth slanted downward, and he scratched his nose. He regarded the snout visible under the frayed window coverings.

Heath pressed his fingertips to the knot behind his head. Dogs usually adored Leventhorpe, but Freddy had clearly taken an aversion to him.

Breathless and pushing a damp lock off her forehead, Brette made straight for her sister. "We found Duffen. He's in a bad way."

Brooke paled and clutched the cloth she'd been tending Heath's scratch with.

"And, Brooke, Rogers has returned from the Benbridges." Panting, Brette tossed Heath an anxious glance.

Who's Rogers?

Brooke dropped the wet rag into the basin before reaching for a dry towel.

Heath breathed a mite easier, grateful for the reprieve. Her hovering over him, her breasts and lips mere inches away...pure torment.

"Rogers isn't alone," Brette added.

Blythe turned from the teapot, giving Brette a puzzled stare. "He's not? Did Mr. Benbridge accompany him?"

A nonplussed expression swept Brooke's face.

"Did Mrs. Benbridge and Josephina come to call? It isn't like them not to send a note round first." She shook her head and tossed the towel aside. "I cannot possibly receive them at the moment. We haven't any tea left, and with Lord Ravensdale and Duffen—"

"No, Brooke." Brette drew nearer and clasped her sister's hand. "Humphrey's here. In the drawing room."

12

Man is a gaming animal by nature,
which is why he'll make foolish wagers against
impossible odds and still remain convinced he'll come out ahead.
~Wisdom and Advice—The Genteel Lady's Guide to Practical Living

Grateful for the interruption in her ministrations to Lord Ravensdale, Brooke would've hugged Brette if her news hadn't been so horrendous.

Touching and smelling him, gazing into his gold-flecked irises scant inches away rattled her senses and strained her composure past endurance. His tense muscles had bunched and twitched while she undressed him, tantalizing her wickedly. The tautness of his jaw and erratic breathing suggested she had affected him as much. Yet he'd uttered not a sound apart from one gravelly groan—quickly silenced—when she'd brushed his torso while unbuttoning his coat.

A shiver of desire had rippled from her breasts to the juncture of her thighs at the guttural noise. What kind of woman lusted after an injured man, and one who sought to deprive her of her home? Perhaps she'd lost her faculties. Perhaps the strain of running the farm and caring for her sister and cousins had addled her at long last.

Add that to the tidings that Humphrey had returned from abroad, and at this moment waited below stairs, and she teetered on the verge of hysterical laughter or frenzied weeping.

Humphrey? For the love of God. Why now?

Could anything else possibly happen to make this day more calamitous?

Brooke took a steadying breath. First things first.

"Where did you find Duffen?"

"In the carriage house. The earl's horse is there too. He's fine, my lord," Brette assured Lord Ravensdale. She spared Lord Leventhorpe a brief glance. "Oh, and I had your mount taken there as well. The barns are full of cattle at present."

Both men murmured thank you, and Lord Ravensdale smoothed the bedding over his lap, as if uncomfortable or in pain.

Guilt prodded her.

"Most wise." Brooke searched her sister's pale face and stricken eyes. She wouldn't be this distraught if matters weren't grave. "What's wrong with Duffen? Does he need a physician as well?"

God's bones, how could she afford a physician's fee for two patients? Her remaining finances dwindled faster than ale in a hot tap room full of thirsty sailors.

On the cusp of tears, Brette nodded. "I think he's had an apoplexy. He cannot move or speak."

Voice breaking, she covered her face and wept.

Dear God.

The day just worsened considerably.

"Losing his home has been too much for him." Her back to the men, Brooke shut her eyes and pressed a palm against her forehead where a vicious beating had begun.

It's been too much for me too.

She sensed the lords' contemplative gazes trained on her and lowered her hand. Had they any notion of the havoc their presence wreaked on this household? Drawing on the last dregs of her composure and fortitude, she schooled her face. She mustn't show signs of feminine weakness, for Lord Ravensdale must be convinced of her ability to operate the farm.

Let it go, Brooke. That dream has died a drawn out, excruciating death.

If only she could turn the clock back to yesterday. Relive the past twenty-four horrific hours. Somehow, some way change the course of destiny.

"See to your man and your guest, Miss Culpepper. I'll stay here until the physician arrives." Lord Leventhorpe spoke to Brooke, yet his attention remained focused on Blythe pouring a cup of tea. He yawned again.

Perhaps a thimbleful of humanity warmed the marquis's blood after all.

"I'll even feed him," Leventhorpe offered with a sly twist of his lips.

"You bloody well will not." Lord Ravensdale levered himself more upright, his shirt rumpling at the neck and exposing a delicious expanse of hairy chest. "I can feed myself."

Brooke swallowed and tore her focus from the black, springy curls. What had she done to deserve such unholy torture? Shouldn't an adversary be reviled? Not in her case. She flitted around him like a moth to a flame. Stupid. Fatal.

"Go, stay with Duffen. Keep him calm and comfortable." Brooke gave Brette a swift hug. "Tell him I'll come as soon as I'm able. Doctor Wilton should be here within the hour."

Wiping her eyes and face, Brette gave a sharp inclination of her head and swept from the room.

Brooke gathered the bowl, napkin, and spoon. How could a man's muscled chest be so devilishly tempting? And why did she notice when disaster raged around them? *Stupid question.* He'd mesmerized her, that's why.

Brooke jerked her gaze to Blythe. "Please go with her. Duffen may need your herbal tea too."

"Of course, although if he's had an apoplexy, I don't want to give him anything until the doctor examines him." Blythe carried the teacup to Lord Ravensdale, seemingly oblivious to his lordship's physical charms. "Sip this slowly. It will ease your stomach. I'm sorry, but I cannot give you anything for your headache until you've seen Doctor Wilton. It's unwise if you have a concussion."

"Thank you." Lord Ravensdale sniffed the light brew. "May I ask what kind it is? It smells minty."

"It is. We grow three kinds of mint at Esherton. It's a favorite of the villagers." She flashed Lord Leventhorpe a mocking glance. "Should I taste it first, my lord? Aren't you worried I might try to poison Lord Ravensdale?"

Those two rubbed each other the wrong way—like flint and steel, sparks and all. Their immediate and intense dislike hadn't lessened a jot.

His lordship moved his hat and gloves to the floor then edged onto the chair's seat. Lines of exhaustion creased the corners of his eyes. He crossed his legs at the knee and, elbows resting on the chair's arms, tented his fingers together. "I regret my earlier accusation. I'm sure the brew is perfectly harmless."

Blythe paused at the threshold, her scrutiny shifting between the men. Her features strained, she searched Brooke's face. "Do you want me to stay with you until you've seen our unexpected guest?"

Bless her. Blythe understood how awkward the encounter with Humphrey would likely be. Brooke shook her head, though facing Humphrey alone after these many years had her palms damp and pulse skittering. "No. Duffen is more important."

"If you're certain." Misgiving resonated in Blythe's voice. Nevertheless, she took her leave after another scathing scowl at Lord Leventhorpe.

Brooke passed Lord Ravensdale the soup, deliberately keeping her attention on his forehead. Her traitorous eyeballs kept trying to sneak a peek lower. "Be careful, my lord. It's hot."

"I'm neither an invalid nor a lackwit, Miss Culpepper." He regarded the cup and bowl he held. "Am I to hold and consume the tea and soup at once?"

Heat singed her face. Ungrateful cur. She bit her tongue. *Be gracious.* No sense riling the ornery bear further.

"No, of course not." She accepted the teacup he extended and, after moving a lamp aside, set it upon the bedside table within his reach.

His rancor took Brooke aback and cooled her ardor as effectively as diving naked into a snow drift. He couldn't be too bad off if he was this disagreeable, could he? She fussed with the items on the nightstand. "I'll return as soon as I know Duffen's condition and see my guest on his way."

She rounded the end of the bed, but paused halfway to the door.

Except for his wan face and a pinched look about his mouth, Lord Ravensdale didn't appear too incapacitated. The pulse in his corded neck beat rhythmically as he regarded her, his countenance indecipherable. A healthy brute like him ought to recover quickly, oughtn't he?

"Please believe me, I honestly had no notion of Duffen's actions." She clasped her hands, when Ravensdale only blinked, his face an impassive mask. Didn't he believe her? More disconcertingly, what did he intend to do when the magistrate arrived? "I am horrified you've been harmed. I pray you recover swiftly."

He slanted his dark head but remained stone-faced and silent.

Hope shrank. Not quite ready to forgive and forget. Not that she blamed him, entirely. She'd be hard-pressed to muster a speck of compassion for a bounder who cracked her on the noggin.

"Who's Humphrey?" Lord Ravensdale's quiet question reverberated as explosive as a cannon in the silent room.

Nearly out the door, she halted and looked over her shoulder. He held her gaze captive as his, accusing and condemning, scraped over her. Leventhorpe appeared to have dozed off, but roused himself to crack an eye open and peer her way.

Busybody.

Her hand on the doorjamb, she whispered, "He's the man I almost married."

Brooke flew down the corridor, Lord Ravensdale's astounded expression etched in her brain. What? Didn't he think her capable of having a beau? Was she too old and unappealing in her cast-off gown that the notion stretched the extremes of his imagination?

The idea hurt more than it ought. Lord Ravensdale's opinion of her shouldn't matter a jot, but confound it all, it did. She sighed. Upstairs lay a man who fascinated her beyond common sense and shouldn't even cause her to bat an eyelash, and below waited a man she should be eager to see, but wasn't.

Humphrey.

Brooke descended the stairway, in no hurry to reach the drawing room. Shouldn't she be more excited at the prospect of seeing him again? She'd loved him beyond reason at one time. Now she felt nothing more than warm sentiment at seeing an old friend. Why had he come, anyway? Could he still harbor a morsel of affection for her?

Her heart fluttered.

Excitement or trepidation? It mattered not. Her circumstances remained much the same, except Papa no longer lived, and paupers claimed deeper pockets than she.

She couldn't wed Humphrey, not unless he could accept the whole bundle that came with her. Why didn't the idea of becoming his wife hold the thrill it once had? Hold up there. Putting the cart before the horse, wasn't she? His visit could be attributed to any number of reasons, and jumping to conclusions generally led to trouble.

What if he had married or was betrothed?

No, his sister would have mentioned it.

Unless either had occurred recently. Possible. Brooke hadn't seen Josephina in weeks. Almost...almost as if she'd been avoiding the Culpeppers.

Nonsense and rot. Goodness. See what fatigue and an overactive imagination wrought.

Unease slowing her steps, Brooke approached the open double doors. She could do this. Taking a bracing breath, she painted a bright smile on her face and silently entered the same room in which she'd told

Humphrey she couldn't marry him.

Unaware of her presence, he stared out the window's narrow leaded glass window. Sunlight played across his features, emphasizing his perfect profile. A crimson riding coat strained across his broad shoulders. Cream pantaloons, tucked into boots, hugged muscular thighs. He held his hat in his right hand and, every once in a while, tapped it against his leg.

"Hello, Humphrey."

He spun to face her.

The same, but different.

He'd filled out, become more striking in a mature man-of-the-world sort of way. His tawny blond hair and hazel eyes hadn't changed. Neither had the charming smile that brightened his suntanned face upon seeing her.

His appreciative gaze stroked her, and then he hurried across the room, his boots rapping a sharp staccato on the bare floor. He lifted her fingers to his warm lips and pressed a light kiss to the knuckles. Scandalous to touch his mouth to an unmarried woman's bare hand, but this man had kissed her lips, so pretending shock would be pointless.

The top of her head and his were almost level. She'd never noticed that before. Probably due to the recent acquaintance of the two towering Titans above stairs.

"Brooke. Even lovelier than I remembered." Humphrey clasped her hand, joy shimmering in his eyes. Her insides gave a strange quiver. "I've missed you, more than words can express. Please accept my belated condolences for the loss of your father."

"Thank you. I miss him still." Moisture glazed her eyes for a moment, not only for Papa's early death, but for what she and Humphrey had lost, and what could never be. She forced a cheerful smile. "So, what brings you to Esherton today? I must say, I was quite surprised to hear you had paid a call."

He offered a sheepish grin, reminding her of the shy, young man who'd courted her.

"I was with Father when your note arrived. I begged him to allow me the honor of responding in person. He and Mother request your company—and the others too, of course—for tea tomorrow at three o'clock." He passed her the invitation, a scented piece of fine stationery. "We'll send the carriage round for you."

He chuckled, the familiar melodic rumble warming her troubled heart. "When I left, Josephina had interrupted her preparations for

London to make a list of sweets she wanted Cook to prepare."

"London?" Bother it all. The London Season. The Benbridges usually departed after the calving ended. Brooke had contacted Mr. Benbridge just in time.

"Yes. My sister is determined to snare herself a husband this Season. My aunt has suggested that a certain marquis would be a brilliant match, poor chap." Humphrey peered behind her. "Where are the others? Josephina said you're all unmarried, as impossible as that is for me to believe. Given your uncommon beauty, I must wonder at the lack of intelligence of the eligible men in the area."

What men? Your arrival home brings the total to precisely one.

Shouldn't she feel a rush of pleasure at his compliment instead of this slight edginess?

He caressed her palm with his thumb. "I'm delighted you didn't find another to take my place in your heart."

There it is.

Her pulse gave a happy little skip, despite her misgivings. His glowing eyes and appreciative smile provided a much needed salve to her chafed womanly confidence. A pair of seductive, black-lashed eyes, a hint of cynicism flashing in their depths, rudely intruded upon the special occasion. She kicked them aside, much the same way she would a mouse attempting to scurry up her skirts. Lord Ravensdale would not rob her of this moment.

"I'm afraid we've had a pair of unfortunate events since I sent my letter round this morning. I'm awaiting the physician's arrival." Brooke gently withdrew her hand from his and then clasped hers together.

Humphrey frowned, genuine concern creasing his forehead. Such a kind man. "What's happened? Is it your sister, or one of your cousins?"

"No, they are fine, but Duffen—you remember him, don't you?"

"Indeed, I do." Humphrey nodded. "Who could forget that crusty devil?"

Brooke gave a half-smile. "Unfortunately, we think he's had an apoplexy. Brette and Blythe are tending him."

"Most unfortunate." He cupped her elbow. No rush of pleasure accompanied his touch.

"You said a pair of events. What else has happened to distress you?" Humphrey laid a finger on her cheek. "I see the anxiety in your eyes and in the stiff way you hold yourself when you're distraught."

He did know her so very well. Comfortable and safe. He'd always made her feel that way. Not disjointed and tumultuous and confused and...tingly, like the growly beast upstairs did.

"A visitor to Esherton has been injured. He's with his friend above stairs waiting for the doctor to examine him as well."

She couldn't tell Humphrey of Duffen's perfidy. Or that the most alarmingly attractive man she'd ever laid eyes upon now owned the farm, leaving them paupers. Or that two powerful peers occupied her parents' bedroom, and what they might do to her and Duffen turned her spit to dust and stopped the blood in her veins.

"Visitor? A beau?" Humphrey scratched his jaw, appearing a bit uneasy...or jealous?

Ridiculous. He'd been gone five years and hadn't once written to indicate he yet harbored feelings for her. And she wasn't naive enough to think he'd played the part of a monk during that time. Brooke waved her hand and gave a short shake of her head. "No, no, nothing of that nature. He's curious about the dairy operation, that's all."

Ravensdale did have an interest in Esherton's dairy, in a manner of speaking.

Humphrey darted a glance to the window. "You do have some of the finest cattle in the area."

Brooke suppressed a smile. She knew more about distilling whisky than he did about milk cows. He'd never possessed a desire to step into his father's and grandfather's shoes, even if they had become vulgarly wealthy producing the most coveted cheese in all of England.

"What's the nature of his injury?" His regard sank to the expanse of rounded flesh visible above her bodice, and Brooke stifled an urge to tug the neckline higher.

"I'm afraid," Lord Ravensdale said, "I suffered a rather nasty crack to the base of my skull."

Brooke gasped and whirled to face the entrance.

He stood in his stockings, buckskins, and gaping shirt, looking for all the world like the man of the house. Pain darkened his eyes to jet and ringed his mouth in a tense, white line.

The idiot. Brooke feared he'd plop onto his face at any moment. Serve him right, odious man, except he'd probably sustain another injury and blame her. My God, all she needed was for Ravensdale to injure himself further while in her home.

Surely that's what she felt, worry he'd further injure himself, nothing more.

Humphrey's eyes widened as he took in his lordship's dishabille. Gentlemen did not present themselves half-dressed and shoeless. He flashed Brooke a bewildered look. Nonetheless, good breeding and faultless manners prevailing, he bowed.

"Humphrey Benbridge, at your service."

Always the proper, irreproachable, *predictable* gentleman. Where had that unbidden thought sprouted?

Humphrey clasped her hand and raised it to his lips again, almost as if claiming her. Silly man. He needn't worry Lord Ravensdale contended for her affections. A flush heated her cheeks at the absurd notion.

"You must be the visitor Miss Culpepper spoke of. She and I are old, and very dear, friends." Humphrey gave her a jaunty smile and a conspiratorial wink. "And I hope to become much more in the near future."

What? Seriously? He just waltzed in here after five years and wanted to take up where they'd left off? *The gall.*

"Isn't that so, Brooke?" He attempted to draw her to his side, a possessive gleam in his eyes and a challenge firming his jaw. "Our time apart has been quite unbearable."

Yes, and that was why he'd corresponded regularly and hurried home at the first opportunity. Brooke nearly gnashed her teeth at his forwardness and posturing, but instead schooled her features into what she prayed resembled composure. "Mr. Benbridge, may I introduce you to Esherton Green's guest, Heath, Earl of Ravensdale?"

A suitable expression of awe skittered across Humphrey's boyish face. Like his parents, men of rank and prestige easily impressed him. Foolish. A title didn't automatically signify good character. This very moment, Esherton housed two examples attesting to that fact.

Humphrey bent into another fawning bow. "It's an honor, your lordship."

Such shallowness rubbed Brooke the wrong way, and the momentary happiness at seeing her old friend faded.

Lord Ravensdale inclined his head the merest bit, likely afraid further movement would part his head from his shoulders, the fool. Where was that dimwit Lord Leventhorpe? Why had he let the earl out of bed?

Ravensdale sauntered forward, his movements measured.

To the casual observer, he appeared confident and relaxed. Brooke, however, recognized someone struggling to disguise their pain with self-assured cockiness. The set of his jaw, taut shoulders, closed hands, and straight line of his brows all screeched pain. She wasn't catching him if he plunged to the floor. He deserved to be knocked halfway to senseless. Once again, she withdrew her hand from Humphrey's, her gaze trained on his lordship the whole while.

What was he about? Why torture himself by leaving his bed when he obviously suffered?

Lord Ravensdale folded his arms and rested an entirely-too-muscled shoulder against the fireplace. His ebony gaze slashed between her and Humphrey. The predatory glint smoldering in the depths of his eyes hitched her breath and raised the hair at her nape. The urge to flee the room overwhelmed her. Instead, she dug her toes into her boots and defied him with her gaze.

Lord Ravensdale placed a hand at the back of his head.

He's in pain.

His handsome mouth inched upward. "Well, this is rather awkward."

What was?

"How so?" Puzzlement replaced Humphrey's friendly smile. He shot her a questioning glance.

She raised her eyebrows and inched a shoulder upward then angled her head, scrutinizing the earl. She hadn't a clue what he blathered about.

His lordship's magnetic gaze held Brooke's in silent warning. "Brooke's my mistress. Aren't you, love?"

13

Wagers gone awry at the gaming table turn
friends into foes and lovers into enemies.
~Wisdom and Advice—The Genteel Lady's Guide to Practical Living

Four days later, wrapped once again in the tattered throw and wearing her gray gown, Brooke leaned against the barn and gazed into the far pasture. Blast, but she wished she could call Ravensdale, the rakehell, out for his scurrilous declaration.

Whirring wings and vibrant plumage announced a cock pheasant's taking wing. A refreshing breeze teased the loose curls framing Brooke's face and set the blushing pink cuckoo flowers bordering a marshy patch to swaying. The morning sun's rays caressed her upturned face.

She would freckle.

She didn't care. Let her fair skin turn bread crust-brown and wrinkled as a crone's.

A few minutes ago, Mabry had let the dappled black-and-white newborns into the paddock for the first time. They explored the thick green grass, never straying too far from their mothers' sides. Occasionally, a frisky calf approached another curious baby, and they'd frolic a few minutes, butting heads and kicking up their heels, before a soft, maternal moo had them skipping to the safety of their anxious parents.

Buford had sired fourteen calves, including a set of twins.

Fourteen, four, or forty, it mattered not.

Not anymore.

There would be no more calves bred at Esherton. At least not beneath her watch.

Most of her hard-earned notes lined Doctor Wilton's pocket, and the rest would soon follow as he returned daily to check his patients' progress. Despair unlike Brooke had ever experienced sank its ruthless talons into her fragile heart and her little remaining hope, tearing them into lifeless shreds.

Two evenings ago, after the magistrate had finally arrived and attempted to question him, Duffen suffered another seizure and lapsed into unconsciousness. Doctor Wilton didn't expect him to survive until nightfall, which meant she'd never know why the servant attacked the earl. Perhaps a misguided notion about protecting the women had coiled, serpent-like, around his fragile mind until the pressure meshed reality with delusion.

She shut her eyes against the disturbing image of him lying, frail and frightened, on his narrow cot. People would do all manner of reprehensible things when driven by desperation. To protect those they loved. She'd already forgiven Duffen for the harm he'd caused, but suspected hard-hearted Lord Ravensdale never would.

No, not hard-hearted. Distant and reserved more aptly described him. An impenetrable shell encompassed the earl. Except his keen eyes. Emotions glittered there, most of which stripped her bare, leaving her vulnerable and uncertain. Yet, she yearned to find a way through his hard exterior, to see if, as she suspected, the man within was warm and caring.

He'd suffered a serious concussion and wasn't permitted anything more strenuous than lifting a fork for a week. His alarmingly brief consultation with the magistrate had Brooke fretting about what they'd discussed. The doctor admitted he'd told Lord Ravensdale that, had his injury been any lower, his lordship would likely have died.

God. Brooke opened her eyes, blinking several times to focus in the glaring sun.

However, Doctor Wilton also reassured her that if the earl obeyed his orders, he would make a full recovery. After his preposterous declaration in the drawing room, he'd fainted dead way, and only Humphrey's quick reflexes had prevented the earl from splitting his head on the cracked tile hearth. He and Leventhorpe—who'd stumbled in half-crazed with worry upon awaking and finding Ravensdale missing—carried Ravensdale upstairs, where he still remained.

Humphrey made his escape shortly thereafter, promising to extend another invitation to tea when things returned to normal at Esherton.

That would be never.

He breathed not a word about Lord Ravensdale's ludicrous declaration, but his gaze, hurt and betrayed, accused her just the same.

Had there been a glimmer, an iota of a chance for reconciliation between her and Humphrey, the earl had successfully snuffed that light out and thrust her into bleak darkness once more.

Heaven help her if Humphrey believed the preposterous lie, bandied the falsehood about, told his parents and sister...

He would. Without a doubt.

Social status meant everything to the Benbridges. They'd want no further association with her. Any hope of help or advice from them had gone up in tiny cinders when she burned the unopened tea invitation.

No, when his lordship let loose the colossal lie.

Brooke shuddered and tugged the shawl tighter.

She cared not for her reputation—well, perhaps that wasn't entirely true, but naught could be done for that besmirched travesty at this point—but the quartet's characters could be tarnished by association with her. Rumors that she'd become a kept woman, factual or not, further damaged any hope of them making respectable matches.

Damn the earl. Damn him for winning Esherton and being so eager to sell the farm. Damn him for the wily game he played. And double damn the attraction she felt for him.

Had he given no consideration to the number of lives he ruined with his fabrication? Mistress indeed. As if she'd ever agree to such a sordid arrangement. What in blazes did he hope to gain by sullying her? She sighed and pursed her mouth. Perhaps her ruination had been his sole intent. A perfectly executed revenge for an offense he presumed her responsible for.

Furious beyond civility, she'd left his care to the others, refusing to see him, even when he requested her presence. Then demanded it.

She wasn't a servant he could order about at his whim. Yet, a part of her desperately longed to check on Ravensdale. To brush his hair from his forehead, touch his warm skin, make sure he fared well. Bah, she was hopeless.

When had her emotions become so fickle?

Since she paid his fee, the physician reported the earl's progress to her daily. Seemed his lordship possessed the constitution of a draft horse and the temperament of caged lion, and he'd be up and about—and hopefully, on his bloody way—in no time.

Leventhorpe had forcefully let it be known he had no intention of vacating the premises until his friend could travel. To his credit, the marquis had sent for food and clothing. Likely the sparse meal he dined on the first night, more watery stew, thinly-sliced bread, and a complete absence of spirits of any kind, had alerted him to the desperate condition of Esherton Green's barren larder.

Every able-bodied man had spent the next morning clearing the road to the house. By early afternoon, a path wide enough for a carriage to pass through had been opened and a wagon had arrived, stuffed with food and other supplies, accompanied by not one, but two coaches. A pair of haughty valets, three plump, giggling maids, a monstrous black groomsmen, two footmen—who appeared to be twins and set Blaike and Blaire atwitter—and a French chef, Leroux, had streamed from the conveyances.

For the first time in years, Esherton boasted a full staff and larder. Beside herself with glee, Mrs. Jennings hadn't stopped grinning, despite her missing front teeth.

At least everyone had plenty to fill their stomachs now, except that Brooke possessed no appetite. Worry tended to rob one of the desire to eat, even if the menu boasted the most elaborate meals the household had ever known.

The house overflowed with people, and no room had less than three occupants at any given time. Servants slept in the halls, for pity's sake, hence Brooke's sojourn to the stables for few a moments of much-needed solitude. She'd told no one of her destination, needing a place to grieve in peace.

Fragile as her tattered dignity, her facade of poise and self-control threatened to shatter with her next breath. She rested her head against the barn's splintery wood. In less than a week, her life had crumbled to dust. A fat tear crept down her cheek. Then another. And another.

They poured forth as wrenching sobs worked their way past her constricted throat. Awash in misery, Brooke pressed a length of the shawl to her mouth, shut her eyes, and tucked her chin to her chest, at last giving vent to her desolation.

"Here now, there's no cause for waterworks," Lord Ravensdale's baritone rasped as he enfolded her in his strong arms. He rested his chin upon her crown. "Hush, sweetheart. Things aren't entirely hopeless."

"Yes. They are. Completely and absolutely. You've ruined everything," she whispered against the wall of his chest. She should pull away. Curse him to Hades and hell. Plant him a facer or yank out his splendid hair by the roots.

Instead, she burrowed closer, wrapped her arms around his waist, and wept like an inconsolable infant. Strong and sensible had become wearisome, and she was exhausted from the burden she'd carried for years. So tired of worrying and scraping to make ends meet.

His scent wrapped around her senses, soothing and reassuring as he rubbed her spine and shoulders. Long moments passed, and calm enshrouded her at last. She released a shuddery sigh.

Lord Ravensdale placed a long finger beneath her chin and tilted her face upward. He kissed each tear-stained cheek then her nose, likely red as a pie cherry. Lowering his mouth until it hovered a mere inch above hers, he closed his eyes. He grazed her lips, his warm and firm, at first feather light then more insistent, demanding a response.

Her resistance fled. Moaning, she slanted her head and allowed him the entrance his probing tongue sought. Heaven surged through her, melting her bones, bathing her in a haze of sweet sensation. Humphrey's kisses hadn't been anything more than mildly pleasant, not this mind-wrenching, searing blast of desire.

A cow bawled, and Brooke tore her mouth from Heath's. Head lowered, she stepped from his embrace and dried her damp face on the wrap. She braved flashing him a glance.

Hatless, his black hair gleaming in the sunlight, he wore a sky blue jacket and white pantaloons. Brilliant colors to emphasize his olive skin. He lounged against the barn, ankles crossed and arms folded, looking the perfect picture of health. Perhaps a little wan about his wickedly dark eyes—definitely some foreign blood there somewhere—but otherwise, his handsome self. The scratch on his cheek had faded to a slender brownish ribbon. He observed her every move, those intense eyes of his missing nothing. Like his namesake, the raven.

Why must he be so blasted attractive?

Why did she react the way she did in his presence? To his kisses? She'd never dreamed a kiss could scatter her wits to the stars.

He gave a knowing smile, as if he'd read her thoughts. A man of his caliber and experience probably knew exactly what his kisses did to her.

Adjusting the shawl, Brooke swiveled to gaze at the calves again. Better than making a spectacle of herself. A few strands of hair had worked loose when she'd hugged his chest, and the breeze blew them into her face. She swept the tendrils behind her ear. She should say something, anything, to break the awkward, sensual silence between them.

"What are you doing out of bed? You're not supposed to be up for another three days."

She could have bitten her tongue in half for asking. It was nothing to her if he chose to ignore the physician's orders.

Liar.

"I couldn't stand one minute more confined to that room or Leventhorpe's incessant fussing. My God, who knew the man was such a nervous old biddy?" He chuckled, the low rumble sending delicious tingles along her flesh. "You'd think I'd nearly died."

She glanced over her shoulder then pushed the bothersome strands flitting across her face from her eyes. "You could have. Doctor Wilton said as much."

His lordship grinned, and her stomach lurched peculiarly. Ought to have broken her fast. Needed her wits to banter with the crafty likes of him. Why had he sought her here, anyway? To steal a kiss?

Theirs had been no stolen kiss but given freely.

He tapped his head as his long strides carried him to her side. "No, too stubborn and too hard-headed to cock up my toes. At least that's what my friends tell me."

"Hmph." She wasn't about to dispute his assertion. Add arrogant and indulged to the list too. Oh, and fabricator of enormous taradiddles designed to ruin innocent young women. She compressed her lips, her earlier feelings of magnanimity giving way to irritation.

"So, Brooke, what are we to do?"

"Pardon?" Holding her wayward hair in place, Brooke leveled him an inquisitive look.

Hands clasped behind him, he stared straight ahead. He could do whatever he pleased. She, on the other hand, had as many options as a condemned woman standing on the gallows with a noose tightened round her neck.

He levered away from the barn.

"I'm aware how dire your circumstances are." He flicked her an unreadable expression before boldly tucking a tress behind her ear.

Sensation spiraled outward at his soft touch.

He cupped her head, gently caressing the sensitive area below her ear.

She clenched her jaw against the sigh, or rather the purr, which had the impudence to try to leave her mouth.

He is your foe, Brooke.

She peered at him. "And...?"

"I have a suggestion, a proposition to make that would—"

She released such a loud, unladylike snort, two calves venturing near the fence scampered to their mothers. "Hmph, that mistress nonsense? You don't seriously think I'd consider becoming a kept woman? Especially of a man I met just days ago."

She tilted her head to look directly into his eyes. Damn his beautiful, thick-lashed eyes. They turned her knees to porridge and caused peculiar flickers elsewhere too.

Come now, Brooke. You're made of sterner stuff. Where's your backbone?

"Why would *you* want that, my lord? It makes no sense at all. Is this revenge for what Duffen did to you?" She narrowed her eyes and gestured between them. "Your way of punishing me? I told you, I had nothing to do with his idiotic decision to smack you on your hard head."

Lord Ravensdale bent nearer and trailed his fingers along her jaw. "No, I took a fancy to you immediately."

She gasped. Her legs nearly gave way, and her already frayed nerves burst with longing.

His pupils dilated, nearly covering the iris.

With desire? Had hers done the same? Just in case, she averted her gaze. He already held too much power over her. Had the nature of their acquaintance been different, she might have dared pursue the attraction between them. He stirred her like no other. But the lots had been cast and providence hadn't favored her.

"Immediately?" She rearranged her shawl. "Are you always so impetuous?"

"No, but I made the decision to offer you my protection while sitting in the study the day we met. I decided it was the least I could do to rescue you from your circumstances."

Her attention snapped to him. *He's serious.* Did he think she'd thank him for his chivalry?

"I'm quite fond of you already, though I'm sure you'll find that difficult to believe." He smiled tenderly and brushed his thumb across her lower lip. "You'd be well-cared for, and I'd treat you kindly. I would also provide for your family."

Brooke gawked at him, her befuddlement swiftly turning to blistering outrage.

I'll bet you would, you cawker.

"Just like that?" She snapped her fingers in his face.

Startled, he blinked. Did he think she'd leap at his offer? Throw herself at him and cover his face with grateful kisses? Toss up her skirts and let him have his way with her behind the stables?

"I've taken a fancy to her, so I'll make her my fancy piece?" she mocked in imitation of his deep voice. "How magnanimous of you."

He had the audacity to grin, one hand resting on her shoulder.

Blast his handsomeness.

Ooh, if only she were a man... She'd wipe that smug look off his face.

"Of all the brazen, buffleheaded, conceited things I've ever heard, that tips the scales as the most contemptible. Pray tell me what about me makes you think I'm a loose-moraled strumpet?" Tears stung behind her eyelids. Why did he alone make her cry?

"Quite the opposite, Brooke." His focus sank to her mouth. "It's your innocence and purity I find irresistible."

"If that's meant to be a compliment, I assure you, it fell far short of its mark, my lord." She whirled away from him. Her thoughts rattled around in her head like pebbles in a tin when he touched her. Of all the outlandish—

Her innocence and purity? Not after he finished with her.

What an infuriating, insulting man!

She'd wager he hadn't considered her desires...er, mayhap not her desires, but her wants. Drat, not wants either, her needs. Bother and blast, why did everything she think regarding him sound provocative and lust-filled?

Arms crossed, she spun to face him. She had a proposition for him too. Let's see how willing he was to gamble for what he wanted. She had nothing to lose at this juncture.

She'd risk it all, everything she owned.

Lord Ravensdale regarded her calmly. He possessed the upper hand, and the cur knew it.

She clenched her hands, itching to box his ears. "You won the lands in a wager, so you're obviously a gaming man, my lord. Give me the opportunity to win them back. We have nowhere else to go. This is our home, though I'm sure to you it's rather a hovel. But my sister and cousins, we have each other, and we're content with the little we've been granted."

Not precisely true. The girls wanted more, deserved more, as did the servants, but they'd done the best they were able with the pathetic lot God or providence had handed them. Grumbling and complaining only served to ferment bitterness. Mama had always preached thankfulness and contentment. Easier said than done, however.

"And what do you have to wager?" He arched a dubious brow. "I mean no disrespect, but the house and grounds are bereft of anything valuable."

"I have the Culpepper grand parure set. It's worth a sizable sum." Brooke savored the dash of victory his astounded look provided.

His intense gaze chafed her. "And you would wager the jewels, the only thing you have left?"

"I'd hoped to sell them to provide Brette and our cousins with small marriage settlements, but keeping our home is more important." She notched her chin higher. "Besides, I haven't anything else of worth to wager."

"I disagree."

Brooke frowned. "What? Look around you. You can see we've only cast-offs, worn-out and broken furnishings. I don't know if the cattle are mine to sell, and I own no other jewelry. Trust me when I tell you there are no stores of silver or fine art hidden in the attic."

He slowly swept his heated gaze over her then bent his lips into a lazy smile.

"You mean me?" She released a caustic laugh. "You want me to wager my virtue?"

14

Beware: wagers are war in the guise of sport,
and there can only be one winner.
~Wisdom and Advice—The Genteel Lady's Guide to Practical Living

That's precisely what Heath meant.

Granted, that made him a cur, a blackguard, and a rake of the worst sort. He hadn't come to Esherton Green intending to despoil an innocent, but once the idea formed, he'd pursued it. He'd been an unmitigated ass announcing Brooke was his mistress in front of Benbridge. Jealousy must have loosened his tongue and warped his common sense. He regretted the outburst, even if he couldn't remember a word of it.

He didn't even recall making his way below stairs or anything beyond Brooke leaving the chamber to speak to her former love. Nothing for the next twelve hours either. Leventhorpe took it upon himself to apprise Heath of the sordid details once he'd regained his senses.

Heath would rather have remained oblivious to his stupidity.

It didn't make a whit of sense, his fear of losing her. Still, he offered Brooke the one thing, short of marriage, he had available. From what he'd observed, mistresses generally fared better than wives, anyway. Besides, didn't she realize that tongues already flapped? He and Leventhorpe had been sleeping in her house for days, for God's sake.

Servants talked. Benbridge *had* talked. Tattle had already circulated back by way of Leventhorpe's staff.

Now Heath must see the act done.

Her position was worse than when he'd arrived, and most of the blame lay on his shoulders. If he gave her the money to restore the place, not only was it a horrid business move, people would still assume she'd traded her favors for the funds. The consequences would be the same; she and the girls would be shunned. He'd learned that, if nothing else, in his lifetime. People assumed the worst, almost as if they relished another's misfortune.

Yes, he was selfish. His conscience could raise a breeze and rail at him all it wanted, but he couldn't get Brooke out of his mind, and he intended to have her. And deserting her and her family, leaving them as paupers, her reputation in tatters with no recourse was not an option.

If she wanted a wager, fine by him. Let her believe she held a degree of power. It cost him little enough, and if it helped her salvage a remnant of pride, well, he'd make the concession. He owed her that and much more.

Taking a broken woman to his bed didn't appeal, but introducing this seething temptress to the pleasures of the flesh...that would be worth suffering a scratch or two. Her resourcefulness, her feistiness, even her mutinous violet eyes spewing darts at him this moment fascinated him. He'd enjoy teaching her to channel her spiritedness in the bedchamber. Oh, the wild romps they'd have. His groin contracted in a rush of pleasure.

She'd captured his admiration and his lust.

He had more than enough blunt to set up a house for her and another for her family. He'd allow her servants to tag along if they wanted. However, he had no intention of that brood being underfoot when he introduced Brooke to passion. Therefore, he would mandate separate residences.

Her eyes flashing ire, she pursed her prim little mouth, in all likelihood to keep from telling him to go bugger himself, something he had seriously considered, truth to tell.

Even with his head thrumming severely enough to turn his hair white and grind his teeth to powder, he'd battled arousal for four days straight. She'd consumed his thoughts and dreams. Hour upon hour of lying on the lumpy mattress, constantly thinking of her, imaging all the erotic things he'd like to do to and with her, had him marble hard. If he hadn't shared the chamber with Leventhorpe, Heath would've been tempted to relieve his randy state himself. A perpetual erection ached like the devil.

Why she consumed him, he hadn't the foggiest notion. He'd bedded beautiful women before, many exceedingly intelligent and witty too. But Brooke...something about her, something he couldn't quite name, mesmerized him, bewitched him until he'd become consumed with her.

Her sultry eyes and subtle shudders proved she wasn't immune to him. She'd kissed him freely and, given her heated responses, desire consumed her too. However, she didn't recognize her need for untapped passion, which hinted all the more of her innocence. He'd be glad to teach her to recognize what she felt, and more. Much more.

Warm heaviness weighted his loins. Too bad they didn't have a signed agreement already. Taking her against the barn or over the fence held a provincial sort of appeal. Well, perhaps not with chocolate-eyed calves looking on. He twisted his lip into a droll smile.

Hell, who did he think he fooled? He would take her anywhere, anytime, as many times as he wanted once she'd become his.

Her concern for her reputation was only natural. Women of her character and integrity didn't barter their bodies in exchange for protection on a regular basis. Nevertheless, he recalled a handful who'd been content as pampered Persians with their decision to accept a gentleman's protection.

Besides, Brooke had several people to think of other than herself. Had it been only her welfare at risk, the war Heath intended to wage to win her would've been much more difficult and complex. But instinct told him she'd accept the stakes he demanded for their wager to ensure the others' wellbeing if convinced she would be the victor.

She worried her lower lip and fingered the god-awful cover, which had slipped to her lower spine. Her work-worn hands revealed how hard she'd labored. Never again would she have to do so. He'd see to her comfort for the rest of her days.

He eyed her shabby clothes, the toes of her half-boots worn almost through. First order of business as her protector: hie her to a London modiste and order an entire wardrobe, right down to her unmentionables. Naturally, he'd be present for the fittings.

She heaved a gusty sigh, her full bosom straining against her gown's fabric.

Well, perhaps not the very first order of business. Slaking his desire topped the list.

"Let's be totally candid regarding the stakes, shall we?" She scooted her gaze around the area. Only docile cattle chewing cud peered at her.

Did she worry someone might overhear?

He sent a casual glance to the meadows and the curving path to the house. Alone. No one eavesdropped on their conversation, though a small rotund ball of fur scuttled their way. The corgi had escaped.

"I'll wager my—

Heath raised his hand. "I have one, rather personal question I require an answer to before we proceed."

A confused expression whisked across her face. "And that is...?"

Deucedly awkward this.

He cleared his throat. He had to know if she'd been intimate with Benbridge, damn his jealousy. "I am most selective in the women I take to my bed."

Her fair brows dove together, and a strangled sound, not quite a gasp, escaped her. A rosy glow tinted her cheeks. "I really don't care to hear about the women you've bedded, my lord, since I have no intention of *ever* becoming one of them."

"You've asked for a chance to win your farm. Do you want to hear my terms or not?" Irritation liberally dosed with pain raised its gnarly head. A punishing cadence had begun in one temple a few minutes ago, stealing his patience. Heath rubbed the side of his head in small, circular motions with two fingers.

Brooke glared at him then waved her hand in an arc. "By all means, my lord. Shout it from the rooftops for all I care."

"Are you a virgin?"

The air left her in a long hiss, and her eyes fairly spat indignation. "You mean to tell me you only take innocents as your mistresses? What kind of despot are you?"

"No, if you are, you'll be the first." He nonchalantly straightened a cuff. Damn, but the notion she hadn't slept with Benbridge exhilarated him. Silence reigned, and he lifted his gaze.

Emotions flitted across her features so quickly, he was hard-pressed to identify all of them. Her chest rose as she inhaled a large expanse of air, scorn sparking in her eyes.

"That's it, you cocksure toff. Take your confounded wager and...and stuff it up your stiff arse! I'll find another way to save my home." Brooke hoisted her skirts and spun on her heel toward the house. "Asking about my virginity. My God, who does that?"

She caught site of Freddy scampering their way and frowned.

"I'll take that as a yes." It pleased Heath beyond ridiculous. He would be her first. *And only.*

She whipped around. "You insufferable blackguard. Why, if I were a man—"

"I'm heartily grateful you're not." He winked and gave her an unabashedly wicked grin. "Calm down. I only meant to spare you a degree of embarrassment. I usually have my physician examine my mistresses for disease prior to signing our agreement and regularly thereafter."

She fisted her small hands, an expression of such incredulity on her face, he fought not to laugh aloud. His humor would rile her all the more.

"Please tell me you're not serious? Do you have any idea how utterly degrading and offensive that is?" She patted her thigh, silently calling the wheezing dog to her side.

Heath shrugged. "Nevertheless, I require it, but for you, given your innocence, I'll make an exception."

She rolled her eyes heavenward as she shook her head. "How benevolent of you. What if I'm not? Is our deal off?"

A flicker of jealousy stabbed Heath. Perhaps his earlier joy had been premature.

Freddy plopped to the ground beside her, tongue hanging out and panting as if he'd just competed in the English Triple Crown. How old was the pudgy beast, anyway?

"No, you'll endure an examination before a contract is signed." He didn't doubt she wished him to the devil at the moment. "So, I'll ask you again. Are you a virgin?"

She responded with a terse nod, and another shock of color flooded her cheeks.

He bit the inside of his mouth to keep from smiling.

Brooke folded her arms and cocked her head to the side. "What else?"

"I'll have my solicitor draw up a document which will include provision for you, your family, and the terms of our separation when the time comes. You will relocate to London, and I will sell the lands I won in the wager from your cousin."

Her eyes narrowed to slits, and she pressed her lips together but remained silent. Outrage and frustration oozed from her.

"Our initial contract will be for a year." He'd never kept a mistress longer. Brooke might be the first. "I'll provide a cancellation clause if we don't suit."

"I don't care about your contract poppycock. My word is my oath. But know this, I will not agree to the sale of Esherton Green. Forfeiture of my body and virtue are worth more than the lands."

She had him there.

Brooke planted her hands on her hips, and Freddy licked his chops and wagged his tail.

"Here are my terms, my lord, and they are not negotiable." She shut her eyes for a second before snapping them open. She launched her battle plan. "Should I lose, I will accompany you to London as your mistress, but you will allow everyone else to remain here, including the servants. You will bestow generous marriage settlements on the four girls, and arrange for sponsors for their come outs. You will also permit Esherton to retain the proceeds from the dairy and farm."

Heath folded his arms. Came up with that too damn quickly for his liking. "Is that all?"

"No." She scowled and pushed her wayward hair behind her ear again. "Mabry will carry on as overseer, and you will permit me to hire a respectable woman of quality to act as a companion to my sister and cousins, both here and when they are in London. An annual allowance to further the estate's recovery wouldn't be amiss either."

She paused, appearing deep in thought, her brows drawn together. "Oh, and I shall be permitted at least two extended visits to Esherton Green annually."

Heath should've suspected Brooke wouldn't acquiesce without a skirmish. He didn't half mind her terms, except the stipulation for keeping the blasted farm. But if he didn't have to manage the place, he would concede the point.

"And if you win?" He braced himself for her demands.

My ballocks fried to a crisp.

"If I win the wager, you sign over to me, free and clear, the lands you won from Sheridan."

That's all she wanted? No bulging purse, new wardrobe, household furnishings...or the hundred other things she and the others lacked?

She extended her hand. "Agreed?"

Heath clasped her roughened palm. It fit neatly within his grasp, as if it had been molded to nestle there. "Yes, the instant you win."

She wouldn't be allowed the victory. They had yet to decide on what game to play, but it mattered not. He might not be able to read worth a damn, but he remembered every playing card dealt and didn't lose at the tables.

Across the expanse of deep green, three figures separated from the house and moved toward the barns. Leventhorpe and two of the other Culpepper misses. At this distance, which two Heath couldn't discern. "What's your pleasure?"

"Excuse me?" Her back to the house, Brooke squinted up at him from where she squatted beside the dog, now lying with his feet in the air, eyes closed, enjoying a tummy rub.

"*My pleasure*?" She almost choked on the words. "Awfully confident you'll be the vanquisher, aren't you? Pride goeth before a fall, my lord."

He chuckled. Never short on pithy remarks, was she? "What game of cards do you prefer?"

Her chagrin transformed to cunningness. A shrewd smile bent her mouth. "I never agreed to a card game."

Alarm dug its sharp little talons on his already pulsing scalp. "Not cards?"

Devil it, what had he agreed to?

A horserace? Did she ride? He examined the barn. Did she own a horse? Surely not a drinking game. Visions of Brooke guzzling brandy or whiskey like a saloon tart churned his stomach. Blister it. What did women wager on besides cards? The color of silk best suited for an embroidered flower?

Men gambled on any number of outlandish things. White's betting book overflowed with one ludicrous wager after another, from what soup might be served at Lady Jersey's to how many pups a hound would birth and everything conceivable in between. Once there'd been a stake on the number of gentlemen a certain courtesan could service in one night.

Heath never participated in that sort of rubbish. Irresponsible and a waste of good coinage, especially when London's streets teemed with orphans and beggars. Even a small portion of money gambled away daily would improve the lives of the less fortunate.

He silently saluted Brooke for outwitting him this round. He ought to have realized she wouldn't choose the obvious. Hadn't he learned anything about her? Predictable she was not.

"Very well, what sort of challenge did you have in mind?" Good God, what if she chose a stitching or baking contest or some other such womanly nonsense? "It must be a competition we're equally capable of."

"Sounds as if you're worried, my lord." Her smile widened, and still crouched beside Freddy, she twisted to look at the milling cattle in the paddock.

Mabry exited the barn and made for the far side of the enclosure where a gate hung. The nervous cattle shifted away from him. Freddy wriggled to his feet then ran to the fence. He trotted up and down, snuffling and whining.

"Hold there, Mr. Mabry." Brooke straightened and waved at the servant.

He pivoted toward them and doffed his hat. "Miss Brooke, your lordship, I didn't know ye were out here."

Was that a Scottish brogue? Heath hadn't noticed it before. But then, he'd barely been able to stand.

"We've only been here a few minutes. I wanted to see the calves." She approached the fence. "They are healthy, it appears."

Heath trailed her, his uneasiness increasing. What was she plotting?

"Hearty lot, these calves be." Mabry gestured in the cattle's direction. "Each one sturdy and healthy. Even the twins there."

He pointed to a pair of spotted calves suckling, while their poor mother straddled them.

Freddy yipped, repeatedly looking at Brooke then the cattle, and then placed his front paws on the lowest fence rail. Mabry bent and scratched behind the dog's ears.

Heath winced as the servant stepped in a pile of warm cow dung.

Unperturbed, Mabry scuffed his boot in the dirt several times and laughed. "He wants to herd the beasties. In his blood, it be."

"And so he shall." Brooke turned triumphant eyes to Heath, her exquisite features alight with joy. "I wager Freddy can separate the calves from their mothers and herd them into the barn in under five minutes. Mabry will stand at the door to prevent the calves from reentering the paddock. You may keep the time." Her gaze slid to his torso, and his muscles bunched as if she'd touched him. "You do have a watch, don't you?"

Heath removed the silver time piece and flicked it open.

"Wager?" Mabry scratched his chest and glanced between them, leeriness scrunching his weathered face. "What sort of wager?"

Brooke inclined her fair head at the dog, caressing him with a doting glance. "Freddy is going to save Esherton for us. His lordship and I have agreed on the stakes. If I win, the lands his lordship won from Sheridan belong to us."

"And if you lose, Miss Brooke?" Mabry's penetrating gaze probed Heath's and disapproval laced his voice. Did he suspect the nature of the rest of their bet?

"Not to worry, Mr. Mabry." She smiled and hugged her wrap tighter. The loose hairs framing her face fluttered in the light breeze. She gave a small shudder. From cold or excitement? "Trust me. I'd never place a bet I wasn't confident I would win. I'm not a fool."

The overseer firmed his mouth and gave a sharp nod. "I do trust ye, lass." His expression sour, he shifted his focus to Heath, "You, sir, I do not."

Brooke laughed and the sound pelted Heath with another round of...what? What did she make him feel? He'd never experienced the taxing sensation before.

Panting, his fluffy tail wagging furiously, the squat corgi pranced before her, all but begging to take after the cattle.

Heath eyed the old dog then counted the calves. Fourteen. Almost three calves a minute, and Freddy had gasped as if dying from his jaunt from the house. Not bloody likely he could get the calves inside in five minutes.

"Are you sure he's up to it? He's not a young pup." Brooke would never forgive him if the dog dropped dead from exertion.

"I'm sure. And he is too." Her eyes sparkling with mirth, she broke into an excited grin before stooping again. She gathered the dog into her arms. "So, my friend, are you ready to have some fun, just like you used to?"

Freddy squirmed and licked her face.

Heath had never seen Brooke this happy, and unbidden warmth washed over him at her delight. If only he were the source of her joy, rather than her consternation.

Yes, women coerced into becoming mistresses are generally elated at the prospect and with the men who compel them, idiot. A wife on the other hand...

No. Wife.

She seemed most confident she'd win. What then? He didn't give a fig if she won the lands. He did care that she might escape his bed, and, even after their short acquaintance, the knowledge that he'd not see her again left him more disquieted than he would have believed possible.

Marry her.

Holy hell, why did the bothersome thought keep bludgeoning him? Marriage didn't loom on his horizon for many years yet to come. And it wasn't as if she'd have him now, in any event.

"You'll not win, your lordship." She smiled, a sad little twist of her plump lips. "You see, I have too much to lose, while you have nothing."

Heath rubbed his chin, and ignored the stab of guilt her words caused. "We shall see."

Brooke handed Freddy to Mabry. The little dog, a quivering bundle of concentration, kept his black-eyed gaze riveted on the uneasy bovines.

Freddy in his arms, Mabry moved to the barn's entrance. His stiff-legged gait and cinched mouth revealed he disliked Brooke's decision, but he respected her enough to allow her to carry on.

The cattle shifted and the cows sidled the humans nervous sideways glances. The calves sensed something afoot and huddled near their mothers. Easier or harder for the dog to work them? Heath knew damn little—all right, nothing—about the four-legged pooping machines except how a thick steak covered in onions and mushrooms tasted on his tongue.

Brooke stood on her toes, arms resting on the top rail. Yes, her shoe had a hole in the bottom. She slid Heath a glance then dropped her attention to his pocket watch. "Are you ready?"

Confidence oozed from her. Rather adorable. He, on the other hand, experienced unfamiliar apprehension. Most troubling.

"Once I say start, the clock doesn't stop for any reason. Agreed? There will be no multiple trials." Freddy didn't have more than one go round in his roly-poly little body in any event.

"Of course." She wrinkled her nose and swatted at a fly buzzing about her head. Hundreds of the pesky insects hovered near the animals and manure littered ground. "Why would we need to stop?"

"Just so, but I won't have you crying foul and demanding another go."

Do you hear yourself? You've already cornered her. Show a modicum of empathy, for God's sake.

Brooke's mouth formed a thin-lipped smile, though her gaze rebelled. "I would have the same assurance from you then, my lord."

"You have it."

"Are ye ready?" Mabry called.

She crooked a winged brow at Heath, and he gave a curt nod, his watch at the ready.

"Yes, Mr. Mabry. You may proceed." She scooted closer to the fence, tension radiating from her.

Mabry placed Freddy on the ground by his feet then dropped to one knee beside the trembling animal. Speaking softly, he stroked Freddy, and the dog lay down, his beady gaze fixed on the cows. The next instant, the overseer gave two shrill whistles.

Chunky body scraping the ground, Freddy tore to the cattle, scattering them every which way. With unbelievable finesse, the small dog worked the livestock, separating a calf from the rest. One, two, three—he swiftly isolated the calves and drove the bawling trio to the barn. Whipping about, the corgi headed into the fray of milling hooves once more.

He showed no signs of fatigue, devil a bit.

Sweat beaded Heath's brow.

Brooke chewed her lower lip, her hands clenched atop the rail.

He glanced at his watch when Freddy maneuvered four more calves through the open doors. Heath had assumed the dog would work the animals one at a time. Ignorance on his part. Brooke might very well have him on the gibbet, a rope about his neck.

Then what? He wouldn't let her go.

You'll have to marry her, old chap.

"Will you shut the bloody hell up?" he muttered beneath his breath. Damnable shrew, his conscience.

Brooke gave him a hurried, quizzical look. The clouds overhead reflected in her clear eyes. "I beg your pardon? Did you say something to me?"

"No, just having a bit of difficulty with the sun glaring on my watch."

She fidgeted with the travesty of a shawl across her bosom, her worry evident. "Did you start timing when Mabry whistled?"

Did she fret Heath would cheat? Well, he hadn't shown himself to be an honorable chap, to this point, now had he?

"Not to worry. I started at the whistle."

"What goes on here?" Waving his arm toward the paddock, Leventhorpe planted a booted foot on the bottom rail. The weathered wood shuddered and groaned.

At Leventhorpe's appearance, Brooke's eyes rounded, the irises shrinking to a miniscule ebony dots. She stiffened before her lips split into a welcoming smile for her sister and cousin.

God above, Heath adored her expressive eyes and ready smile.

Facing the now-dusty enclosure, the Misses Brette and Blythe sandwiched Brooke and spoke in quiet tones. Each sent him a glower of such blue-eyed antagonism, he'd no doubt Brooke had shared the terms of their wager. Thank God they weren't men, or he'd be called out at once. Deserved to be run through by all of them.

Heat slithered from his neck to his face.

Accustomed to women's admiration, he'd never experienced such feminine enmity and found the hostility most disturbing. However, he acknowledged he'd brought their censure upon himself. The oddest urge to check his head for horns and his bum for a twitching, pointed tail gripped him.

Contrition lanced sharp and burrowed deep, where, every now and again, it gave him a vicious jab, reminding him what a cur he'd become. He'd proved no better than the men who'd held his title before him. Self-seeking, arrogant bastards, the entire lot.

The stink from a fish lingered long, especially rotten ones. He, too, bore the familial stench prevalent in his lineage. He'd prided himself on being superior to his forefathers, yet today proved he'd become the worst sod of the bunch. Though his ethics, conscience, integrity—whatever the blasted thing was that kept hounding him to do right by Brooke—nagged worse than a fishwife, he couldn't let her go.

"What's the little terror doing to the cattle?" Leventhorpe peered at Heath before scanning the chaos on the other side of the fence.

Heath cleared his throat. "If Freddy manages to get the rest of the calves—" *Damn, only five left.* "—into the barn in the next," he checked his watch, "three minutes, Miss Culpepper takes ownership of the Esherton's lands I won in the wager."

Leventhorpe chuckled and slapped Heath on the shoulder. "You're letting that fat, ancient dog decide something of such importance?"

"So it seems." Heath kept his attention glued to the puffball darting about the pen, yipping and snapping at the bovines' feet.

Leaning over the top rail, Leventhorpe studied the dog's progress. He canted his head toward Freddy. "And if he doesn't get them all inside, what then?"

Heath angled his back to Brooke and murmured, "She becomes my mistress."

Leventhorpe's jaw slackened for an instant. He jerked upright, condemnation blistering in his gaze. "You are an absolute, reprehensible arse, Raven."

"I'm aware."

"I do believe I'm ashamed to call you friend. I should call you out." Shaking his head, Leventhorpe directed his attention to the paddock. "Ho, there, Freddy. Good boy."

Freddy almost had another pair of calves to the barn.

Leventhorpe hollered and clapped his hands. "There's a smart chap."

Scooting around a stubborn cow bent on protecting her calf, the dog stiffened. He skidded to a halt, his nose in the air then spun and faced the fence. One glimpse of Leventhorpe, and Freddy tucked his tail between his legs and bolted for the barn.

15

A sensible woman realizes that to achieve the
greatest advantage in gambling, one doesn't wager at all.
~Wisdom and Advice—The Genteel Lady's Guide to Practical Living

"Freddy, no." Brooke's distressed cry was echoed by her sister and cousin.

His craggy face mirroring the devastation that must surely ravage hers, Mabry trotted into the barn after the dog.

I lost. Oh my God, no. I lost.

Pressing close to her sides, Brette and Blythe each wrapped an arm about her shoulders and glared murderously at both men. Brooke was half convinced that, had her sister and cousin possessed a blade, they would have run the lords through. She might very well have cheered them on and helped dig the graves afterward.

Ruined.

Her head swam with dread and disappointment so pungent, she could taste it, bitter and metallic on her tongue.

"Brooke, your lip is bleeding." Brette plucked a handkerchief from her bodice.

Brooke hadn't noticed she'd bitten her lip. She dabbed at the cut as wave upon wave of panic surged ever higher, rising from her stomach, to her chest, and thrumming against her throat.

His mistress. I am...will be...a fallen woman.

She clutched her shawl and swung to glare at Lord Leventhorpe. "You did that on purpose."

His eyes darkened to cobalt. "Miss Culpepper, I had no notion of what went on here when I asked these ladies to point me in the direction my senseless friend had wandered."

The calves Freddy had directed to the barn trotted out and, amid much mooing and lowing, found their anxious mamas. Several set to nursing at once.

"You didn't have to call out to Freddy." Tears clogged her throat, but she refused to cry in front of these scapegraces or her family. "You know he's terrified of you."

"I but encouraged the dog. I assure you, there was no deliberate intent or subterfuge to cause you to lose."

"He did so do it deliberately." Blythe's voice dripped venom. "He and Ravensdale whispered back and forth when we arrived."

The marquis shook his burnished head. "Such a suspicious mind, Miss Blythe. Does it ever become wearisome?"

"Not where you're concerned." Blythe planted her free hand on her hip. "What did you say to him then?"

"I told him he was an absolute a—" Lord Leventhorpe cupped his nape. "Um, that is, a disreputable fellow, and promptly fell to cheering the dog along."

"Hmph. I'll just bet you did." Brette didn't believe his excuses either.

It didn't matter. What was done was done.

Brooke had given her word, and integrity compelled her to keep it. Ironic that. She would lose her virtue because of her honor. The devil must be dancing a jig in hell at her quandary. Had the situation been reversed, and she'd won by means less than laudable, would she have given the earl another chance to best her?

No. Too much depended on winning.

Lord Leventhorpe crossed his arms and addressed Lord Ravensdale. "You should be in bed instead of making silly wagers to ruin young innocents."

Blythe and Brette inhaled sharply.

Did the man have no filter on his mouth? Did every thought gush forth like a muddy river breeching its banks during a flood? However did these two featherheads manage in London amongst the *haut ton*?

Leventhorpe frowned, his keen gaze vacillating between Ravensdale and Brooke. "I, for one, cannot condone this ill-conceived wager."

"Leave off, Trist." Lord Ravensdale raised a hesitant gaze to Brooke. Instead of triumph and gloating, his eyes teemed with compassion and an unfamiliar glint. He snapped the watch closed then returned it to his waistcoat pocket.

Leventhorpe sent a vexed glance skyward. "Why the confounded theatrics? It's a simple enough fix. I'll leave and you can retrieve the mongrel—

"Freddy is not a mongrel, you red-headed baboon," Blythe snapped.

Blythe acted a constant shrew with Lord Leventhorpe. Why? Dear God, surely not for the same reason Lord Ravensdale flustered Brooke out of her polite decorum.

Brette jutted her chin upward a notch and nodded her head. "To us, he's family."

Leventhorpe sighed, a put upon expression on his face. Did he understand what had just transpired? Had Ravensdale explained the whole of it?

"You can start the affair again, and I give my word, I shall stay in the house, out of sight the entire time." Leventhorpe jerked his thumb in the manor's direction.

Brooke shook her head as she stepped away from her sister and cousin's protective embraces. "No, your lordship, we cannot start over. Lord Ravensdale and I agreed to a single challenge, one time only. That, too, was part of our bargain."

Mabry exited the barn, Freddy in his arms. He approached the fence, his gaze seething. "Cheap shot, that was. I've a mind to call ye out, uppity lord or not."

"You'll do no such thing." Brooke took Freddy from him. "I need you to carry on for me until this conundrum is fixed."

How could she sound composed? Inside, she tilted on the precipice of histrionics. Quaking, Freddy buried his head in her shoulder. Why did Lord Leventhorpe frighten him so? Freddy would've won her the wager if Lord Leventhorpe hadn't intruded. The knowledge she'd set this trap and snared herself...well, it grated her raw.

Ravensdale taking her to his bed didn't scare her. Or repulse her. Quite the opposite, truthfully. He'd unearthed feelings in her she hadn't realized existed. She would've been lying if she denied that his dark good looks and well-defined muscles enticed her.

Before his outlandish proposal, she'd given up on knowing a man intimately—although if mating proved anything like what she'd witnessed between Buford and the cows, the act seemed rather violent and favored the male of the species. The only benefit to the females, as near as she could discern, was the babes they'd soon bear.

Good God!

What if a child resulted from her union with his lordship? No, she'd insist measures be taken to prevent a pregnancy. Such things existed, didn't they? She'd ask Doctor Wilton on his next visit and pray he didn't expire from shock at such a scandalous question from an unmarried woman.

"Miss Culpepper, I would speak with you privately."

Brooke jerked her attention to Lord Ravensdale. Serious and somber, he gazed at her intently. Why the Friday face? He'd trounced her. Shouldn't he be grinning and celebrating? Instead, his eyes, the planes of his face, even his sculpted mouth suggested poignant reserve.

"We've serious matters to discuss." His expression grew grimmer.

Eager to get on with it, the boor. If he thought to bed her at Esherton, butterflies flitted about in his head. She wouldn't bring shame to the family home by lifting her skirts beneath Esherton's roof.

The morning breeze had ceased, and the chorus of innumerable flies within the paddock, in addition to the bees zipping from clover to flower in the fields, carried to her. The faint scent of sandalwood wafted by.

Which of the lords did it belong to?

Leventhorpe.

Raven's…Ravensdale's scent had been burned into her memory, and he didn't smell of sandalwood. Realization blindsided her. Freddie's first owner, the abusive charlatan, had reeked of the scent. No wonder the dog hied for the nearest hiding spot when he whiffed Lord Leventhorpe. If only she'd made the connection sooner. She nearly strangled, stifling her scream of frustration.

Odd that this perfect spring day should portend the onset of her tainted future. Yet, in the innermost recesses of her being, in a miniscule cleft she'd allow no one access to, a bud of relief formed. She'd secured the girls' futures, and the knowledge lifted a tremendous burden from her mind and heart.

A year wasn't so terribly long. And, in fact, she rather suspected she might enjoy her time as his lordship's kept woman. So be it. She'd make the best of this. Mama always said when the bread went stale, add some spices, egg, and cream, and make bread pudding.

"Please take him to the house and give him a treat, poor thing." Brooke passed Freddy to Blythe then kissed his snout. "You did your best, didn't you, my sweet boy?"

He thumped his tail once, his brown eyes apologetic.

Blythe hugged the quivering dog to her chest and murmured into his fur. He crawled up to snuggle against her neck.

Leventhorpe approached and, after a slight hesitation, scratched behind Freddy's ears.

Brooke held her breath as Freddy went rigid, his small eyes leery.

"No need to be afraid. I won't hurt you," his lordship said while petting the dog. At least Freddy hadn't bitten him.

A song thrush swooped to perch atop a post several lengths farther along the fence. The bird cocked its head before flitting to the ground and poking about for insects. Oh, to live the simple life of a bird.

"Brette, go with Blythe, please, and ask Cook to prepare two tea trays. Have one served in the parlor for Lord Leventhorpe and yourselves. Have the other delivered to the study." Brooke tucked her hand in the crook of Brette's elbow and guided her away from the paddock to where Blythe waited.

Brette patted Freddy when Lord Ravensdale moved aside. "Certainly. I believe we've fresh ginger biscuits, Shrewsbury cakes, and tarts baked just this morning."

How long it had been since they'd indulged in such lavishness? The quartet wouldn't go without again. The notion brought Brooke a measure of consolation.

Half-turned in Lord Ravensdale's direction, Brooke said, "I shall meet you in the study in twenty minutes, my lord. I must speak with my overseer. If you will excuse me, please?"

"Brooke. Blythe. Brette!"

Everyone turned to the frantic shouts coming from the house.

Blaire, skirts hoisted to her knees, hurtled through the grass, her white stockings flashing as she dashed to them. Her ragged sobs rent the air. "Duffen's gone. He's dead."

Esherton Green's Cemetery
Two Mornings Later

"Amen." Reverend Avery closed his Bible, the slight thump jarring Brooke to the disagreeable present.

Over already?

She'd been woolgathering, remembering happier times at Esherton with Duffen. Dry grittiness scraped her eyes when she blinked.

Hiring the reverend to preside over the funeral had consumed the last of her money. He'd been most reluctant to perform the ritual. Duffen had once called him an ignorant hypocrite more interested in lining his pockets than saving souls. Brooke rather agreed with Duffen's assessment, but as no other clerics resided within a day's ride, Reverend Avery it must be.

Would Duffen approve? Brooke didn't know, but she couldn't bury him without a ceremony, no matter how brief or coldly delivered by the officiator.

Shouldn't she be crying? Why couldn't she weep? Her heart ached, but no tears would come.

She scanned the huddled foursome's red-rimmed eyelids before shifting her attention to Mrs. Jennings and Flora, also sporting ruddy noses and cheeks. Not a one wore a coat, but instead had a blanket wrapped around their shoulders against the deceptively mild day's chilliness. Mabry's bloodshot gaze gave testament to his sorrow at the loss of his long-time comrade.

Was she alone incapable of grieving? No, she mourned Duffen's loss deeply, but she'd no more tears to shed, and she had the futures of many people to organize in a short amount of time. A niggling headache pinched behind her eyes from the constant strain. His lordship hadn't said when they would depart for London, but she doubted he'd twiddle his thumbs for a couple of weeks.

Perhaps later, when duty and responsibility didn't demand her attention, she could find a private spot to vent her heartache. At present, the manor overflowed with bodies. Why, just this morning, she'd made her way to the kitchen before first light, bent on a cup of the delicious new tea Leroux had brought. In the near dark, she'd stumbled upon a footman sprawled on a pallet and mashed his hand beneath her foot.

The starchy clergyman gestured to the rich mound of soil piled beside the yawning hole in the earth. Steam rose, a silvery-white mist, where the sun warmed the ground. "Miss Culpepper?"

Brooke drew in a fortifying breath. Since Duffen had no relatives, and as the senior woman of the house, the task of sprinkling Duffen's coffin with the same dirt he'd toiled in most of his life fell to her. She'd discarded protocol and allowed the girls to attend the graveside eulogy. Duffen deserved more than a pair of stable hands, Mabry, and herself to bid him farewell.

Lords Ravensdale and Leventhorpe—*would the man never leave?*—paid their respects as well. It rather astounded her and warmed her heart, despite her misgivings about the taciturn pair. Leventhorpe, however, repeatedly checked his watch and glanced to the drive, as if anxious to have the matter done with. Boorish of him, given he attended of his own volition.

Brooke loosened the glove from her hand, one finger at a time, reluctant to bring the simple service to an end and leave the dear little man who'd guarded her and the others fiercely for years. He'd been the grandfather they'd never had. A peculiar little bird of a grandfather, but loving all the same.

Lord Ravensdale waited a discreet distance away, determined to have their postponed conversation today. What did he seek anyway? She harbored no secrets. They had their agreement. Did he fear she'd renege on the bargain? Quite the couple they made, neither trusting the other, but they would share a bed and the most intimate of relationships. She firmed her lips against irony's cutting reproach.

The man had followed her about, much like a nervous puppy, the past pair of days. All solicitousness, almost as if he cared for her, he said little, but watched her every move with his unnerving gaze. His concern and attention warmed her, wooed her, further eroding the crumbling barrier she'd erected to keep him at bay.

Why of all men, flying in the face of everything logical and wise, had her disloyal heart picked him? A shuddery sigh escaped her. She couldn't deny the truth any longer; not even to herself.

She didn't like how vulnerable that made her.

"I'll take your glove, Brooke." Blaire held out her hand.

"Thank you."

Brooke passed the glove and unused handkerchief to her cousin. She crouched and stared at the humble casket. Sighing again, she scooped a handful of damp earth. A day past a week since Lord Ravensdale disrupted their lives.

And Sheridan, don't forget his dastardly part in this misfortune.

She swept the graveyard with her gaze, lingering a moment on the house and barns in the distance. The cattle, like giant dollops of cream, blotted the emerald meadows.

So much had changed in such a short amount of time.

"Kingdoms rise and kingdoms fall in a day," she whispered to herself.

"What was that, Miss Culpepper?" Reverend Avery peered down his nose at her.

"Nothing." After standing upright once more, she opened her fingers and allowed the dirt to drop. The clump hit the coffin, the sound harsh and final. Tears finally welled. Muffled weeping from the others filled the air as the small crowd turned and trekked down the lengthy, wending path to the house.

"Reverend, please join us for our midday meal." Lord Ravensdale extended the invitation. "I would beg a moment of your time afterward to discuss procuring a grave marker for Duffen."

"Yes, yes, of course. Shall I meet you at the house? I'm recovering from a bout of poor health and don't wish to linger outdoors any longer than I must." Prayer book tucked beneath his arm, the long-faced cleric eyed the house in the distance, a hungry glint in his eye. He swallowed, and his over-sized Adam's apple fought to escape the folds of turkey-like flesh drooping his collar.

"Certainly." Brooke brushed her hands together. "We'll be along in a moment or two, after I say my final farewells to Duffen. Have a drop of brandy in your tea. That should help stave off any ill effects of the out of doors."

She had forgotten the sumptuous spread Leroux had promised to have prepared for them after the funeral, at Leventhorpe's request. The marquis's attempts to get into the women's good graces were endearing, if somewhat audacious.

The same couldn't be said of Reverend Avery. She didn't want to suffer the stodgy cleric's depressing presence for a moment longer, but for Duffen, she would. She hadn't the funds for a headstone, and when pride attempted to rear its horned head and object to his lordship's generosity, she slapped the emotion aside like a fly atop a pastry. Duffen's loyalty warranted the honor. Besides, as her protector, Ravensdale was within his rights to make the decision and pay the fee.

Protector.

Despite her acceptance of her new station, and the startling realization she loved him, her stomach quavered. He'd made no demands on her, nor presented a contract either, as yet.

Brooke bent her forefinger and wiped beneath her lower eyelashes, touched by Heath's...Raven's—drat it all—Ravensdale's kindheartedness. How *did* mistresses address their protectors?

My lord? Master?

Not exactly something taught in the schoolroom.

"Here, allow me." His gaze tender, he patted the moisture from the edge of her lashes with the edge of his handkerchief. He did have the most mesmerizing eyes she'd ever seen in a man. After drying her face, he rubbed the dirt from her palm and then each finger in turn.

Such a simple act, but sensual too. Her irregular breathing and cavorting pulse gave testament to her awareness of him as a desirable man. She searched for similar discomfit in him but found unruffled composure.

"How am I to address you?" Heavens, she sounded wanton as a wagtail. Dry mouth, that was why. Brooke swallowed before running the tip of her tongue across her bottom lip. "Do you prefer Ravensdale, my lord... Raven... Heath?" *Good God, babies babble less.* "Please understand, I have no notion of how this mistress business works."

Except for the amorous congress part. One didn't breed cattle and not have a firm grasp of what coupling entailed. Rather undignified to be approached from behind, but under the cover of dark and with one's eyes—*and ears*—firmly squeezed shut, she ought to be able to manage well enough. She pursed her lips when he still didn't answer her.

"What *do* I call you?"

He kissed her forehead, his lips soft, yet firm, at the same time.

"How about husband?"

16

Understand this: once the die is cast,
everything you've gained can be lost.
~Wisdom and Advice—The Genteel Lady's Guide to Practical Living

The quandary ricocheting in Heath's mind burst forth like a cannonball scuttling a ship, blasting his defenses wide open and setting him adrift. Yet subjecting Brooke to the degradation he'd proposed gnawed and chafed him until his conscience and soul lay raw and bloody. Seemed he wasn't cut from the same stuff as bounders and scapegraces after all.

He would marry her, though every fiber of his being cringed in trepidation. Cold, unfeeling, heartless—the negative traits of his sire, and the Earls of Ravensdale before his father, haunted Heath, reproachful and condemning. Could he summon the modicum of deep regard or warm sentiment that created satisfied wives and contented children?

Would he endure contention and strife the remainder of his wedded life as his parents had? Their battles had been legendary. Or, God forbid, do to his offspring what they'd done to him?

No, Brooke possessed a loving nature and generous spirit, unlike his mother. The knowledge was a balm to his wounded soul. A soul he'd not recognized needed healing until Brooke forced him to tear open the protective cover, rip off the scars and scabs, and see the festered wound deep within. She would help heal the putrid mess, restore wholeness to him.

Her character and birth alone made Brooke entitled to more than the degrading position he'd offered her. Brooke was nothing like the wife he'd determined would suit him. He feared one day Brooke would break his once impenetrable heart. Exposed and vulnerable, he possessed no protection from the winsome witch. She'd charmed and enchanted, bewitched and beguiled, cast her spell to where he no longer governed his thoughts.

But to lose her…let her go…

No, his noble intentions didn't extend that far. He would give her a choice. The parson's mousetrap, or revert to their original agreement. He must have her one way or another.

What woman wouldn't choose countess before courtesan?

He wouldn't let himself examine his fascination with Brooke past his physical fascination. Too dangerous... terrifying. What did *he* know of love? Nothing. No, better not to scrutinize his feelings too closely.

A week's acquaintance made a feeble foundation for marital bliss, but a few brilliant matches had started with less. Peculiar how seven days ago, marriage constituted nothing more than a business arrangement, a mutually beneficial union of convenience the earldom required of him. Today, he had selected Brooke, for no other reason than he couldn't bear to leave her or face another day without her.

His life prior to this was shrouded in an ash-gray cloud; seeing, hearing, tasting, living life in part, unaware of how much more vibrant and intense each sense—everything, for that matter—might be experienced. Brooke had awoken him to this new brilliance, and he'd lay odds, he'd only had a glimpse of what was possible.

Hell, she'd practically emasculated him. And worse? He didn't mind. Besotted by a violet-eyed, fair-haired Aphrodite with a heart bigger than England's tax coffers.

"What say you, Brooke?" Heath cupped her jaw, and rubbed his thumb across her soft cheek.

"Beg pardon?"

Her pale face, incredulous gaze, and mouth rounded into a perfect O of surprise, suggested she believed him insane, or perhaps he'd sprouted another nose or two upon his face.

Heath glanced around. Alone. The others had trekked halfway to the house already. Good. No one needed to witness Brooke's bafflement or his ineptitude at proposing. Should have done it properly, with flowers or a piece of jewelry. Perhaps a sonnet or a poem.

Women liked that sort of thing.

"Husband? You?" Her strangled squeak echoed with the same finality as the rat he'd seen seized in the jaws of a wharf cat one day at the docks.

"Yes." He grinned when her eyes widened further. "I thought you might prefer becoming my wife rather than my mistress."

High-minded of you, ruddy bounder.

Brooke shook her head. "Wife. Me?"

Had he so dazed her she couldn't string more than two words together? He'd shocked himself, so her stupefied expression didn't surprise him.

She spun away and stomped a few feet before halting to peek over her shoulder as she spoke to herself. "Why would he marry me? I'm a nobody, and he's an earl. We don't know each other, let alone like one another."

He flinched inwardly. Thorny prick, that. Couldn't fault her for her bluntness or the truth as she perceived it. She'd no reason to think he felt anything other than lust. Worse than a stag in the rut, he'd been.

Like, lust, love, luck...all different sides of the same die.

"Perhaps his head injury has addled him?" Hand on her chin, she squinted at Heath for an extended moment. "How does one know, I wonder? Surely there are other signs."

"Am I supposed to respond?"

Emotions vacillated upon her face. She stared, scrunched her eyebrows, and twisted her lips one way then the other. She rubbed the side of her face, blinking several times, and then pressed her mouth into a single, hard line.

He could almost hear the pinging of the thoughts careening about in her head. He cocked his. Not the reaction he'd expected, but Brooke had yet to do anything predictable. Heath strode to her. Best lay it out bare as a baby's arse. He gathered her into his arms, pressing a kiss into the soft hair atop her crown.

She didn't resist, although she trembled like a newborn kitten.

"These past days I've realized there's no woman more worthy of the title of countess than you, Brooke. You are more generous, noble, and self-sacrificing than any female of my acquaintance." He shrugged a shoulder and tweaked her pert nose. "I have to marry, in any event."

"How gallant of you." Mockery dripped thick enough to scoop with a shovel.

"Brooke, are you coming?" The Culpeppers hesitated at the bottom of the sloping hill. They exchanged wary glances before grasping their skirts and clomping up the rutted track. Four damsels to the rescue. A flock of yellowhammers pelted to the sky, yellow smudges against the blue, when the women tramped by.

Deep in conversation, Mabry and the man of God continued on their way. Mrs. Jennings and Flora had made the drive already, anxious to get inside and see to the rest of the meal preparation.

Leventhorpe faced them and planted his fists on his hips. He sent a peeved glance heavenward and lifted his hands. In supplication? Irritation?

Heath chuckled, enjoying his friend's aggravation. The Culpeppers had Leventhorpe at sixes and sevens, and a mouse in a maze fared better than the poor sot.

"I must be mad." Brooke twisted her glove in her hands and darted the oncoming quartet a guarded look. "They'll think me dicked in the nob—my head in the wool pile."

Heath's heart skidded sideways. Would Brooke say yes? He hadn't been altogether sure. Still wasn't.

She wobbled her glove at the others, who'd paused in ascending the hill. "Go on. I'll be inside shortly."

"Are you sure?" Brette's intelligent gaze flicked to Heath then to her sister. "We can stay. It's no bother."

Plucky for someone so tiny.

"Yes, I'm sure. His lordship and I have some, um, business details to discuss."

Business?

Is that how she saw his proposal? Well, why wouldn't she? There hadn't been a hint of anything remotely romantic in the way he asked her. He'd not wooed her, offered any trinkets, or pretty speeches.

Become my wife or mistress? Which will it be?

She presented her sister a tight-lipped smile and gestured at the house. "Go along, and check if everything is in order for our meal. And see that the reverend has a warm toddy."

They turned and obediently trundled in the direction they'd come. Several times one of the blondes either glanced over her shoulder or turned halfway round to observe Brooke. The scowls they hurled at Heath condemned him to a fiery afterlife and eternal damnation. No easy task winning their favor. Or Brooke's, though only her approval mattered.

The women met Leventhorpe on his way up the hill, and he circled one hand above his head. "Oh, for God's sake, are we performing some heathen burial ritual designed to ruin my boots?"

"Yes, your lordship." Her face serious as a parson's, Blythe pointed to the cemetery. "March around each headstone two times, skip through the center of the graveyard, perform a somersault while reciting The Lord's Prayer, and kick your heels together before taking a hearty swig of pickle juice."

She winked. "That will assure Duffen turns over in his grave."

A chorus of giggles erupted, Blythe's the loudest.

Leventhorpe emitted a rude noise, somewhere between a snort and a growl.

Heath laughed outright.

Brooke couldn't prevent the smile twitching the corner of her mouth. "He's not been around women much, I'd guess. Has he sisters?"

"No, and his mother died when he was a toddler. The marchioness was a dotty dame. Ten years older than her husband, she didn't permit a single female house servant." Heath winked then waggled his brows. "The old marquis had a wandering eye and roving hands."

"Have *you* any sisters? If we marry, you're essentially inheriting four." She set her jaw, and a stubborn glint entered her eyes. "And the dairy farm too. I won't give it up."

Infernal farm and confounded cows. After the week he'd just spent, his favorite cheese could go to the devil with his blessings. He'd never be able to eat the stuff without remembering the dairy's stench.

"No, I haven't any sisters, but I rather like the chaos a gaggle of spirited women stirs up. I've been imaging the response the five of you would garner in London."

"Have you? Why?"

"Let's just say the *ton* has never experienced anything like the Culpeppers."

"Hmm, I suppose not."

They wandered to the cart track used to haul coffins to the graveyard. "I expected you would insist on the farm in your settlement negotiations. I'll make it a wedding gift to you."

Brooke stopped abruptly and stumbled over a root.

Heath grasped her arm to steady her. His fingers completely encircled her upper arm. Too thin. He'd see to it she'd not experience hunger again, darling girl.

"You will? Truly? To do with as I wish?" She clutched his arm, her eyes sparkling with excitement. "Would you allow me to build a simple house on the acreage so there's never an eviction worry again?"

A calf bawled, and a cow answered with a series of lowing grunts. Several more entered the fray, calling and mooing, their cries disturbing the peaceful morning.

Who would want a house nearer that racket?

Heath edged closer until his thigh brushed her skirts. He placed his hands on her shoulders, drawing her further into his embrace.

"Build a mansion, if you like. Anything to make you happy and keep a smile on your face." He touched her lips with his thumb. "Do you know, you rarely smile? Your lot in life hasn't been easy, has it?"

Brooke shook her head, the fair curls framing her face dancing. "I'm not complaining. It's been worth it." She contemplated the retreating women. If she retained regrets, she masked them behind the pride and love shining in her eyes. Her gaze brushed him, hovering an instant on his lips before flitting to a hawk circling overhead. She rolled a slender shoulder. "They needed me."

Simple as that. No excuses, pouting, or compunctions. She'd done what needed doing and did the job a far cry better than most men of his acquaintance would have. Any idiot decreeing women the weaker sex ought to be rapped upon the head with a cane.

"What of that Benbridge fellow? Do you love him?" Heath could have bitten his tongue off for blurting the question. He sounded like a jealous beau. What if she loved the young scamp? Jagged pain stabbed his middle.

Brooke's eyes rounded for a moment before she shook her head. "No, Humphrey is an old friend, but his parents would never permit a match between us. Besides, as I told you, we're a package deal. He had no interest in taking on such a large encumbrance." A forced smile bent her mouth the merest bit. "Truthfully, I cannot say I blame him. They've been a challenge."

"I promise, things will be better from now on. I'll do everything in my power to make your life easier and to make you happy." And by God, he meant it. Could Brooke hear the sincerity in his voice? He'd become a moon-eyed milksop. And liked it. A great deal, truth to tell. He, the reticent earl, known for his restraint and reason, issuing whimsical promises like a love-struck swain.

He almost touched his jaw to make sure it didn't hang slack at the epiphany that jostled his carefully structured life. In one week's time, Brooke had come to mean more to him than anything else: his title, his fortune, his friendships—few though they were—even Ebénè.

Nonsensical fairytales consisted of such fluff.

Stuff and nonsense.

Wonderful stuff and nonsense.

"I..." Her eyes misted, and she blinked as she stared at him, a mixture of awe and wonder on her face. She laughed and threw her arms around his neck in a fierce hug. "Thank you. Thank you. I feel like the weight of the world has been lifted from my shoulders."

He angled away to see her face. "May I take that as a yes?"

Gaze averted and pink tinging her cheeks, she nodded. "Yes, I'll marry you."

"Immediately?"

"Yes, as soon as the banns are read and arrangements can be made." Her flush deepened to rose and her gold-tipped lashes fanned her cheekbones. "But I still don't know how to address you."

"My friends call me Raven, but I like Heath best." He opened his hand, splaying his fingers over her smooth cheek and jaw.

Her focus slipped to his lips, and her voice acquired a husky edge. "When we first met, I would have said Raven suited you better."

"Coming from your lips, the name takes on an entirely different significance." He could almost imagine she'd whispered an endearment. Sap. Captivated, enamored sap. "By all means, call me Raven."

"No." Her eyes had grown sultry. "While it's true they are intelligent birds, they're also associated with dark omens."

"Then call me darling, or my love."

Her mouth formed another startled O, and she tucked her chin to her chest as color flooded her face.

He tipped her chin upward until their gazes met. A quick glance behind him assured Heath the others had almost made the orchard. "A kiss to seal our agreement?"

"All right." She shut her eyes and parted her lips in invitation.

No hesitation.

His soul leaped. How quickly could he secure a special license? Soon his week-long erection would finally be appeased.

The devil it will.

Not with Brooke as his wife. He'd have a perpetual rod jabbing his leg for the next fifty years. Long after his legs became too feeble to support his weight, his eyes too weak to see her delicate features, or his ears too dim to hear her delightful laugh, his penis would jump to attention whenever her scent teased his nostrils.

Her essence...addictive. An aphrodisiac of innocence and womanliness.

He feathered kisses atop her cheeks and chin, until at last he tasted her honeyed lips.

She sighed and opened her mouth, melting against him like wax above a flame.

Passion laced with a sweetness he couldn't identify engulfed him. A little moan escaped her when he cupped her buttocks and urged her against his hardness. She stood on her tiptoes, nestling her womanhood against the evidence of his arousal.

The jangle of harnesses followed by the creaking of coach springs, clomping of hooves, and snorts of winded horses yanked him from the ambrosia he'd been sampling.

One arm encircling Brooke at her waist—he doubted she could stand on her own, she leaned so heavily on him—he examined the road to the house. Two carriages drew up before the structure, one quite unpretentious and the other a crimson and black monstrosity he didn't recognize.

As Leventhorpe and the Culpepper misses approached the conveyances, the girls' heads dipped together and bobbed a bit. Probably pondering who the passengers were. Leventhorpe increased his pace and, in a few steps, led the small troupe.

"Who in the world?" Brooke shaded her eyes. She gasped and clutched Heath's arm too tightly, her nails biting into the flesh through his coat and shirt. "No, it cannot be."

He covered her hand with his. "What is it? Who is that?"

Pale as the fine blackthorn blossoms amidst the overgrown hedgerow surrounding the graveyard, Brooke turned her alarmed gaze to him. "I cannot be sure because I've never met him, but I think he," she pointed at the man peering from the carriage doorway, "might be our Cousin Sheridan."

17

Marrying without love is like gaming with an empty purse;
alas you have lost before you begin.
~*Wisdom and Advice—The Genteel Lady's Guide to Practical Living*

"You've met him." Brooke gripped her skirts, raised them ankle high, and matched Heath's stride as they hurried along the path. She sidestepped a muddy patch. Laden with bulging pink blossoms, wild cherry tree branches overhung the roadway, which was littered with the damp remnants of last evening's rain shower. Brooke neatly stepped over a dinner plate-sized puddle. "Is that my cousin?"

Please say no.

"Indeed." Tension firmed the contours of Heath's face into taut lines. "I'm curious why he's here on the heels of losing the wager to me and threatening you with eviction. You say you've never met him?"

He maneuvered around a deep puddle.

"No." What business had Sheridan here?

"Watch your footing. This path is a travesty of ruts and hollows." Heath dipped her a swift glance before regarding the new arrivals. "Gainsborough hasn't visited prior to this?"

Brooke shook her head. "Never. He left the farm's operation and the girls' care to me."

Sheridan yawned then frowned as he examined the house and courtyard. Displeasure contorted his features and curled his upper lip into a sneer. What did he expect? An opulent mansion with manicured grounds on the pittance he allowed them? Upon spotting the girls, he stopped scowling, and a disturbing smile skewed his mouth.

She leaped over a larger puddle. No man should regard his cousins with such speculation, like a commodity to market and sell to the highest bidder. Hound's teeth, she'd been afraid of this. Why did men regard her sister and cousins like delectable fruit, free for the picking and sampling?

"Heath, I don't trust Sheridan. Do you see the way he's leering at the girls?" She hitched her skirts in order to quicken her pace. "He's guardian to them. I cannot help but think his presence here doesn't bode well."

Heath gave a curt nod and quickened his stride. She possessed long legs but had to trot to keep up. They were practically upon the group, although no one appeared to have noticed them.

"That's deucedly unfortunate. How old are they? How old are you?" He regarded Brooke, running his gaze from the worn toes of her half boots, to the dated bonnet atop her head. "Ought to know if I'm leg-shackling myself to a chit long on the shelf."

Brooke's heart skipped an uncomfortable beat. Did he tease, or did he think her too old?

His strong mouth edged upward on one side, and he winked.

Brooke chuckled. "I'm afraid I'm ancient. Three and twenty."

"Tsk, tsk. You'll need a cane and spectacles before the year ends, as will I. I'm eight and twenty. What are the ages of the others?"

Brooke hastily told him.

"Immediately upon reaching London, I'll petition for guardianship." He gave her hand a light squeeze. "My connections reach much farther and higher than Gainsborough's. Your cousin's reputation isn't, shall we say, pristine. Leventhorpe's distantly related to the Lord Chief Justice, and I won't hesitate to request his help. I have little doubt my request will be granted."

"But what happens in the meanwhile?" She sucked in an unsteady breath. "He...he cannot take my sister and cousins, can he?"

Heath slipped an arm around her waist and gave her side a quick caress. "Over my dead body."

Relief flooded her. It had been so long since anyone else had helped bear the burden of the quartet's wellbeing. They reached level ground at the same time the foursome and Lord Leventhorpe gained the horseshoe-shaped courtyard.

Sheridan waited for them, appraising her sister and cousins much the same way a perspective buyer for one of the cows or calves did. She wouldn't have been surprised if he lined the quartet up on the auction block, peered in their mouths, and took a gander at their legs to see if they would bring a high enough price.

Another man, attired entirely in black, climbed from the second carriage.

Four visitors in a week? All male? Had Esherton Green become a favorite destination for men who wished to wreak havoc on the quiet, respectable lives of the Misses Culpepper? They had better not plan on staying in the house. Unless she crammed one on a larder shelf and stuffed the other in the drawing room window seat, no sleeping quarters remained.

The sun glinted on the newcomer's honey-colored head as he too peered around before stretching. Her sister and cousins resumed their covert whispers, taking his measure as assuredly as Sheridan took theirs. The golden man broke into a wide grin and lifted a hand in greeting as Leventhorpe marched to him. They knew each other?

"Blast me, what's Hawksworth doing here?" Heath's question harnessed Brooke's musings.

Winded from her near run—surely that caused her breathless voice and not his lordship's hand curled at her waist—she regarded the Adonis. Josephina had shown her a book portraying Greek gods and goddesses. This man with his curling hair and hewn features very well might have stepped from the pages of the volume. "You're acquainted with him?"

"Yes, he's Alexander Hawksworth. A good friend of Leventhorpe's and mine. He's the rector of a large parish outside London."

A man resembling a mythical god preached about the Christian deity? She'd wager his church's pews didn't sit empty Sunday mornings.

"Perhaps he should marry us." Heath grinned, amusement crinkling the corners of his eyes, but then the humor slipped from his face faster than a hot iron erased wrinkles. "No, never mind. I wouldn't hear the end of it from either of those buffleheads."

At the precise moment Sheridan and Reverend Hawksworth swiveled in her direction, Brooke lost her footing on a slick spot. She clutched Heath's coat and scrambled to regain her balance. One moment she skidded along, legs spread wide, the next, she lay on her back, Heath half atop her. She opened her eyes, and ceased to breath. From knee to shoulder, his sinewy form mashed into her, and she welcomed his weight. The blistering heat in his eyes sent a pang burning from her breast to her nether regions before suffusing her entire body in prickly warmth.

The sensation wasn't unpleasant. Not at all.

"I say, remove yourself from my cousin's person at once." Sheridan charged in their direction, his mouth puckered tighter than an old maid expecting her first kiss. "Get off her, this instant."

Heath whispered in her ear. "Let me handle this, please."

Oh, I don't think so.

She hadn't time to respond before Sheridan descended upon them. He glared at Heath then turned a vapid gaze on her as she sprawled beneath him. "Which one are you?"

Heath rolled off her, and after standing, extended his hand to Brooke.

"I'll assist her, Ravensdale." Sheridan thrust his square hand at her. "She's my ward, after all."

"Hardly, since I'm of age. Besides, I've never set eyes on you before in my life." Brooke ignored Sheridan's assistance and accepted Heath's. Her cousin would get no quarter from her. If he thought he could troop into Esherton and take over now, he was in for a most unpleasant surprise.

When Heath didn't promptly release her hand, Sheridan's crafty gaze narrowed, but he bent at the waist, nonetheless. "Sheridan Gainsborough, your cousin, come to survey my estate before taking you and your sisters to—"

"Three are my cousins, which you ought to know since my father appointed you their guardian five years ago." God's bones, fury whipped her temper. Who did the lickspittle think he was, showing up unannounced and having the ballocks to dictate to her? "And you only own the house and five acres. Or did you forget you wagered away the rest to Lord Ravensdale here?"

She jabbed her thumb at Heath's chest.

Brooke extracted her hand from his loose hold and glanced behind her at her skirt. Mud-streaked from hem to bum. She skimmed Heath's tight buttocks and long legs. Him too. Nevertheless, she quirked an eyebrow at Sheridan.

Well, she silently challenged him. *Deny it, you cur.*

"Er, yes, quite right." He puffed out his chest and attempted to look down his bulbous nose at her, reminding her of an outraged bantam rooster. All bluster and no might.

Considering she boasted four inches on him, his pretense proved ridiculous.

Heath's lips quivered, and amusement glinted in his eyes. Or mayhap approval lit his gaze.

"Brooke, are you all right?" Brette, wide-eyed with worry, reached her first. The twins and Blythe came next with Leventhorpe and

Hawksworth bringing up the rear.

"I'm perfectly fine." Aside from wanting to lay Sheridan out.

Blaike edged around Sheridan, her eyes averted. Astute girl. She perceived a lecher when she encountered one. She examined Brooke's gown. "I'm afraid the material might be permanently stained. Best we get you into the house and have it laundered at once."

"That rag is hardly worth salvaging." Sheridan scrutinized her sister and cousins. "Every one of you looks like you stepped from the poorhouse. What have you been doing? Gallivanting in the woods? It's a good thing I arrived, cousin. From what I've observed, you have no notion whatsoever of how to run a profitable estate or supervise young ladies of quality."

The hawk screeched. At least Brooke thought the bird had made the harsh cry. It may have been one of the girl's irate shrieks. Or hers.

Jackanape.

Brooke's breath left her on a drawn-out hiss as slurs romped about in her head, begging to be hurled at the oaf. She clenched her teeth and fists to keep from spewing the vulgar filth—a proper lady didn't know such foul oaths—in front of those assembled and to keep from popping Sheridan in his globular nose. Her betrothed didn't need to see or hear her acting the part of a termagant.

"I'd watch my tongue if I were you, Gainsborough. You haven't a pickle's knowledge about the commendable efforts these women," Heath swept his hand in an arc to include all the Culpeppers, "have made to keep this farm operating, no thanks to you."

"And I suppose you do?" Sheridan speared Heath a dark look. "By the by, why are you here?"

"I might ask you the same thing." The devil inhabited the stare Heath stabbed at Sheridan.

Sheridan's bravado wilted. "If you insist on knowing—

"Oh, I do." Silky, but dangerous.

A flush further reddened Sheridan's blotchy cheeks. "I decided to take a break from the London scene and acquaint myself with my cousins."

"Chased out of town by debt collectors or threatened with debtor's prison, I'd bet." Leventhorpe took a position beside Heath. "Have I the right of it?"

A ruddy hue turned Sheridan's ears purple. He shuffled his feet and pulled at his neckcloth. "Um, nothing of the sort."

Ah, the marquis had hit the target, spot on.

The reverend made a leg. “Lovely ladies, please allow me to introduce myself, as neither of my ill-mannered friends has done so. Reverend Alexander Hawksworth, but please call me Hawksworth. I look round for my esteemed uncle when I hear anyone say reverend outside my parish.”

Brooke and the foursome curtsied, but Sheridan smirked and made no move of deference.

Heath made the necessary introductions.

“Didn’t your uncle skip off with the baker’s daughter?” Leventhorpe scratched the back of his neck. “Or was it the tailor’s? I cannot quite remember, but the gossip columns buzzed for weeks.”

“Neither, you dolt.” Hawksworth smiled, a flash of white teeth, and his green eyes crinkled. “Aunt Elspeth was a nun. Terrible scandal. Anglican priest hieing off to Gretna Green with a Catholic nun. But He,” he pointed heavenward, “had other plans for her. She had six children at last count. Happy as grigs, they are.”

“*Reverend*?” Blaike wiggled her brows at Blaire. “I must say, I didn’t see that coming. I thought he commanded the stage or opera. Something much more...colorful, with those looks.”

Blaire nudged Brette. “Told you he wasn’t Sheridan’s valet.”

Hawksworth pressed his hands to his chest in mock offense. “Valet, dear me. Really?” He glanced at his somber garb. “It’s the togs, isn’t it? But the church frowns on me wearing anything flamboyant or ornate. I really rather adore bright colors, particularly blue.”

He looked pointedly at her blue gown.

“Enough of this drivel. Might we make our way into the house?” Sheridan swept the structure a disdainful glance while fussing with his waistcoat.

Brooke bristled. He had no right to criticize the staid old manor. Through prosperity and poverty, the building had been a pleasant home and for generations had witnessed the births, lives, and deaths of Culpeppers.

The breeze shifted direction, filling the air with the barn’s aroma. Sheridan’s bug-eyes bulged and, frantic, he groped around in his jacket. Gasping, he yanked a handkerchief free. He slapped the cloth over his nose. “My God, what is that unholy stench?”

“I said the same thing when I first arrived.” Heath gave a hearty laugh. “You’ll get used to it.”

“Not as long as I draw a breath.” Sheridan shook his head. His face pressed into the fabric muffled his words. “Gentlemen, I really must discuss my plans with my cousins."

He notched his nose higher, daring to put on a superior facade. Didn't he realize he ranked the lowest of the men present? Pretentious toady, and with his face mashed into the handkerchief, Brooke found it impossible to take him seriously.

He drew the cloth away and took a tentative sniff, scrunching his nose at once. Considering the size of the appendage, it rather resembled a pleated dinner roll. Not an attractive sight. "I am famished, and I must change from these travel-soiled clothes."

"Not too terribly road-stained as London is less than an hour's coach ride away," Leventhorpe muttered.

Touché.

Sheridan curled his lip but kept silent.

Leventhorpe might not be such a bad sort, after all, once you got past his prickly exterior.

"Indulge me a moment, Gainsborough." Reverend Hawksworth flicked his hand as if Sheridan were a bothersome insect before turning a brilliant smile on Brooke. Each service, his church probably burst with parishioners, and mostly of the female persuasion, or she wasn't a Culpepper.

Sheridan rolled his eyes skyward and huffed his displeasure. Crossing his arms, he tapped one foot impatiently and scowled like a lad denied a bonbon.

Worse than a petulant child.

Reverend Hawksworth lifted her hand, although his mouth remained a respectable distance above it. Good thing, too, since she hadn't donned her glove again. "May I tell you how honored I am to meet the future Countess of Ravensdale?"

How in the world did he know about Heath's proposal?

"Countess?" A chorus of voices echoed, including Sheridan's, which ended on a hoarse squeak. Fury radiated from his rodent gaze.

The quartet swung their confused gazes between Brooke and Heath, before, one by one, they rested their attention on her. Their expressions fairly screamed the questions they didn't voice.

Better his wife than his mistress, righto?

She flashed Heath a sideways glance, distrust and betrayal squeezing her ribs between their vice-like claws. Had he feigned ignorance regarding the timing of Hawkworth's arrival? Possibly. Yet to this point, Heath hadn't been dishonest. That she knew of, in any event.

She scrunched her toes in her boots. Face it. Theirs hadn't been the sunniest of acquaintances from the onset. And she did say yes to his proposal despite that. Had her good sense flown in the face of desperation?

Lovely way to start a marriage.

Forced marriage, Brooke.

No, not forced. Convenient.

Everything about the union smacked of convenience on both their parts. Except, her heart had become engaged somewhere over the course. When, she couldn't quite say. When he'd fallen in the drawing room? Kissed her outside the stables? Followed her around like a trusting puppy after Duffen's death?

Fear kept her from acknowledging in her mind what her heart had insisted for days. Laughable if the situation weren't so pathetic and clichéd. The whole matter screamed of a Drury Lane drama.

The reverend released her hand. "I hope you'll permit me the honor of performing the ceremony."

The claws dug deeper, drawing her soul's blood.

"You knew of Lord Ravensdale's plans to marry me?" How? She'd only learned of them a few minutes ago.

"Indeed." Hawksworth patted his chest. "I have the special license right here."

Brooke whipped round and confronted Heath.

"You pretended to know nothing about his arrival, yet he has a license?" Brooke poked him in the chest. Hard. "You deceiving bounder. What else have you lied about?"

18

He who mistakenly believes gambling a
harmless amusement has never looked into the ravaged
faces of those made victims by another's wasteful pastime.
~Wisdom and Advice—The Genteel Lady's Guide to Practical Living

Heath rubbed the back of his head as Brooke and her angel-haired entourage flounced inside the manor. Brilliant. An infuriated, distrustful bride.

Sheridan trailed them like an unwelcome stray, his mangy tail tucked between his legs.

"Am I mistaken, or is all not as it should be between you and your lady, Raven?" A deep furrow creased the bridge of Hawkworth's nose. When the last woman disappeared through the entrance, he turned an expectant gaze on him.

Heath brushed mud from his elbow as he made his way to the house. "How the blazes did you know we'd become betrothed?"

Falling in step beside him, Hawksworth pointed at Leventhorpe. "He sent a message two days ago. Said to get a special license and be here today, ready to perform your nuptials."

Hawksworth cast a practiced gaze to the graveyard. "And a funeral? The same day? Not precisely tasteful. I ran a bit behind schedule in London obtaining the license, hence my tardiness. I did wonder why Leventhorpe, and not you, made the request though, Raven."

"Because he's a bloody, interfering arse." Heath marched to the house, just short of a run. He needed to talk to Brooke, explain the situation to her, convince her he'd known nothing of Hawksworth's arrival until the moment he exited the carriage in all his celestial glory.

What if she changed her mind?

No, with Sheridan's unexpected arrival, she had more reason than ever to marry him.

He hoped.

He'd seen the fear she'd tried to hide. Her cousin frightened her, or perhaps the power he'd been granted over her sister and cousins caused her trepidation. But that didn't mean she wasn't livid with Heath.

"Explain yourself, Trist, and be quick about it." Heath gave Leventhorpe a sideways glare.

Leventhorpe shrugged as the trio climbed the steps, their boots clinking on the stones. "You talk in your sleep, Raven."

Heath snorted. "I do not."

"Trust me, you do, and you snore like a bloody lion in the process of choking on haunch of water buffalo. Your bride has my condolences in that regard. I really ought to warn her, but she might change her mind, and you'd be an even more unbearable sot." Leventhorpe gave a theatric yawn behind his hand. "It's a wonder I'm able to function at all, I've become so deprived of sleep."

Hawksworth chuckled and gestured between Heath and Leventhorpe. "The two of you share a room? That ought to be interesting."

"Yes, and he's been muttering on in his sleep about marrying Miss Culpepper for days now...or, rather, for nights."

"I have not." Had he? Damn.

"Yes, you have. Incessantly. Enough to force me to bury my head beneath my pillow to muffle your nattering and become desperate enough to send for Hawk."

They handed their hats and gloves to the waiting footman. He promptly trotted down the hallway, no doubt to assist in serving the meal.

"I thought I'd give you a nudge, Raven, since your conscience had already made the decision for you. And until last evening, we didn't know if Avery would officiate at the funeral." Leventhorpe inhaled deeply, peering in the dining room's direction. "Hmm, something smells delicious."

"Damned presumptuous of you." Heath scraped his hand through his hair. "Now she's furious with me. Thinks I manipulated her again."

"Again?" Hawksworth peered at him, his gaze teeming with amusement and curiosity.

"Yes, that respectable miss lost a wager to Raven and agreed to become his mistress." Leventhorpe gave Heath a brusque nod. "His terms, by the way."

Shit.

The comment pealed loud and reproachful in the entry.

"You intended to make that young woman your paramour?" Disapproval sharpened Hawksworth voice and features. "Far below par, and you well know it."

"Yes, I bloody well know it, which is why, after the funeral, I asked her to marry me."

Hawksworth grunted and folded his arms, looking very much an avenging angel. "Is there a single romantic bone in your body? Anywhere? I realize you're not a sentimental chap, but proposing on the heels of a funeral service... Damned crass, that."

"Exceedingly gauche." Leventhorpe nodded his agreement, his attention straying down the corridor again. "But when one is desperate..."

"Why marry someone you've only known..." Hawksworth glanced to Leventhorpe for help.

"A week."

"Eight days." Heath promptly regretted the correction when his friends exchanged mocking glances.

"Yes, the extra day makes *all* the difference." Leventhorpe drawled the word, earning him another murderous scowl from Heath.

"I should think a longer acquaintance would be beneficial to both of you." Hawksworth narrowed his eyes, his astute gaze probing. "Intelligent people do not decide to marry after a week unless they fall in love at first sight. Which I find beyond belief in your case. No offense intended."

I'm not supposed to be offended when one of my closest chums insults the hell out of me?

Leventhorpe's shout of laughter muffled Heath's rude noise.

"Raven? Love at first sight? Oh, that's rich." Leventhorpe's shoulders continued to shake. "Lust, yes. But love? Not him. Never him."

He hooted again.

Fine friend, boorish knave.

"Well, I cannot stay here, and I won't leave without her."

Where was Brooke? Heath craned his neck, gawking first along the passageway and then up the stairway. Had she retreated to her chamber to avoid him?

"Neither will I take her with me unless she's my wife. It would spell her ruination."

He peeked in the study. Nope, not there.

"I promised her and her family a better life than they've had, and I mean to keep my word."

Maybe she'd escaped to the barn again.

"And that rat bastard of a cousin will dance naked in court, scrawny ballocks bared for the royals, before a single Culpepper accompanies the sod anywhere."

"Sounds like love to me." Hawksworth lifted a hand and raised his fingers one at a time. "Putting her needs before yours. Unwilling to be apart from her. Wanting to provide and care for her...and her family."

He wiggled his four fingers and waggled his eyebrows like an inebriated court jester.

"Oh, and the desire to protect her." Up sprang his thumb.

"Don't preach to me, Hawk, when you know nothing of love." Was she in the kitchen?

Leventhorpe regarded Heath, a speculative spark in his eye. "Hmm, as impossible as it is for me to believe, Hawk's made some valid points. And you did mumble something that sounded like love in your sleep, though your speech was so garbled—rather like a drunk chewing a mouthful of marbles—I might have been mistaken."

"Don't be an imbecile, Trist." As much as Heath wanted to deny everything Hawk had said, a measure of truth resonated in his friend's words. He'd be hung if he'd admit it to his two smirking cohorts.

Do I love Brooke?

The theory explained much.

Hawksworth shook his head so hard, a shock of hair tumbled onto his brow. "It's either love, or the knock on your head Leventhorpe wrote me about has deprived you of your reason, in which case, I cannot in good conscience perform the ceremony."

"My thoughts exactly." Thumping echoed above, much like a toddler kicking their heels during a fit of temper. Leventhorpe raised his gaze to the vibrating ceiling. "What's going on up there?"

Heath rolled a shoulder and raked his hand through his hair again.

A calculating gleam entered Leventhorpe's gaze. "Did she say yes when you proposed?"

"I did." Brooke stood just inside the drawing room.

A small sigh of relief escaped Heath. He detected no trace of anger. Wasn't she still upset? He ran an appreciative gaze over her. She'd changed into a simple cream gown, with puff sleeves and a wide emerald ribbon below the bust. Pink and green embroidered flowers edged the hemline. An odd combination of vulnerability and determination shadowed her hollow cheeks and wary eyes.

His heart welled with emotion. *Love.* He loved her. Damn, but this pleasure-pain wasn't what he'd expected. It was more, so much more, and it scared the hell out of him.

Had she heard their entire exchange? Her gaze skimmed Leventhorpe and Hawksworth before landing on Heath. Her soul stretched across the room and touched his.

Yes. She had.

A loud crash reverberated overhead, followed by hollering and violent banging. She flinched, her face draining of color.

"What the devil is happening above stairs?" Heath pointed upward.

Anxiousness replaced Brooke's composure. She clasped her hands before her.

"It's Sheridan." After a hurried glance behind her into the drawing room, she glided farther into the entry and lowered her voice. "I'd like us to exchange vows at once."

"You're not still upset that Leventhorpe arranged for Hawksworth to be here? That he has a license?" Heath extended a hand in entreaty. "Please believe me, I didn't know until the moment you did."

Her shoulders slumped, and she sighed. "It's of no consequence. You'd already asked me to marry you, and I agreed. I've explained the situation to my sister and cousins. Although they are not happy with the circumstances, we are in agreement that the urgency of the situation requires an immediate wedding."

The caterwauling and crashing overhead increased in fervor.

Her gaze searched his. "If you are willing, my lord."

"Of course, I am. Nothing would please me more." He spoke the truth. Marrying her had become his greatest desire, more so than bedding her. Heath glanced at his dirty pantaloons. "You don't want me to change first?"

"No." She cast a troubled glance toward the stairs. "Sheridan's determined to keep me from marrying you and forcing us all to return to London with him. He's threatened to raise an objection during the ceremony on the preposterous, and untrue, grounds that I'm betrothed to another. He thinks to delay the wedding long enough to take custody of my sister and cousins, and I haven't a doubt in the world that his intentions aren't honorable."

"Rotten bounder." Murder glittered in Leventhorpe's eyes. "I'd like to see him try."

She thrust her adorable chin upward and squared her thin shoulders.

"We've locked him in the twin's bedroom. That's what the commotion above stairs is."

"Well done, Miss Culpepper. A little isolation usually calms the soul." The reverend raised a speculative glance to the ceiling as bits of dust and plaster sifted down. "However, in this case, given the ruckus above, I'm inclined to believe demonic forces might have been released instead."

He stepped forward. "May I ask how old you are? I cannot legally marry you in England unless you are of age."

"I'm three and twenty. I have proof in the study."

"Good by me." He gestured to the drawing room entrance. "Shall we?"

"Um, what of the vicar?" Had everyone but Heath forgotten about the other man of the cloth?

Brooke's lips curved into a closed-mouth smile.

"He's feasting in the dining room. I explained a dear friend of the groom's had arrived and desired to perform the nuptials. I don't know which peeved him more: missing the promised meal or the ceremony fee." She fidgeted with her skirt, her gaze cast to the floor. "I'm afraid I assured him he'd be paid anyway, and I...I don't have the funds."

A ferocious hammering and several unsavory curses sounded from above.

"I'll pay the fee, but I think it's best we get on with the vows, posthaste." Heath took her elbow and guided her into the drawing room. Petal soft skin met his fingertips. Was the rest of her as silky? He would know tonight.

And he'd worship her with his heart and body.

Her family sat primly on the sofa and ugly chairs, Freddy perched on Miss Blythe's lap. Wariness cloaking them, they stood when Brooke and the men filed into the room. The dog eyed Leventhorpe but remained on the sofa where Blythe had placed him. He wagged his tail once.

Progress.

"Hawk, is there an expedited ritual?" Heath gave Brooke's arm a reassuring squeeze.

The sound of wood cracking and more cursing rent the air.

Everyone's attention raised to the ceiling. To the Culpepper misses' credit, all remained composed aside from disconcerted expressions.

"Sheridan's destroying the house," Brooke whispered. "He's a madman."

"Hawk?" Urgency prodding him, Heath bit out the name harsher than he'd intended. "The ceremony?"

"Short and sweet it is." Hawksworth glanced round to everyone assembled. "I'll assume no one here objects to the union?"

Leventhorpe and the Culpepper misses gave negative shakes of their heads.

"Excellent. Ravensdale and Miss Culpepper, join hands."

Heath clasped Brooke's hands.

She raised her gaze to his, her eyes bright and clear, before she flushed and her lashes swept her cheeks. He almost convinced himself something more powerful than desperation and fear warmed her eyes.

Hawksworth faced Heath and Brooke. "Miss Culpepper...what's your full name?"

"Brooke Theodora Penelope Culpepper." Did her voice tremble the merest bit?

Hawksworth cleared his throat. "Why, Ravensdale, I don't know your full name. Three and ten years acquainted and I just now realized that."

"Oh, for the love of God." Leventhorpe stomped to lean against the closed doors. "Do get on with it before that lunatic," he jabbed his forefinger straight up, "interrupts."

"It's Heath Adrian Lionel Sylvester Kitteridge, Earl of Ravensdale." Heath clasped Brooke's cold, damp hands tighter. Yes, she quivered like a newborn lamb.

Hawksworth scratched his chin. "Hmm, five names? Most impressive."

One of the twins tittered, but a stern glance from Brooke hushed her.

"Wise to leave off the preliminary parts, I think." Hawksworth pointed above them. "Wilt thou have this woman to be thy wedded wife, to live together after God's ordinance in the—"

"I will. I take Brooke to be my wedded wife, for richer, for poorer, in sickness and in health, to love and to cherish, till death us do part." Heath bent his head toward Brooke. "Her turn. Hurry."

"Wilt you have this man to be thy wedded husband—"

Footsteps pounded above along the corridor leading to the stairway.

Bloody maggoty hell.

Heath shook his head. "Skip that part."

Hawksworth shot a knowing glance overhead. "Yes, quite. Forget the formal mumbo jumbo too. Brooke, will you take Heath to be your husband?"

She tilted her head and met Heath's gaze head on. "I will."

Thumping on the stairs caused the quartet to gasp and clutch one another's hands, except for Blythe, who bolted to the desk.

Heath slid his signet ring off his little finger. "I'm sorry, it's much too big. I'll purchase you a wedding ring when we reach London. Maybe amethyst to match your eyes."

Leventhorpe snickered but turned the laugh into a hearty cough at Heath's scowl.

Heath slipped the heavy gold onto Brooke's slender finger.

She covered the band with her other hand before shooting the doors a distressed look.

Hawksworth inhaled in a huge lungful of air and raced through the last few lines. "Forasmuch as Heath and Brooke have consented together in holy wedlock, and have witnessed the same before God and this company, and thereto have given and pledged their troth either to other, and have declared the same by the giving and receiving of a ring, and the joining of hands; I pronounce that they be man and wife together. In the Name of the Father, and of the Son, and of the Holy Ghost. Amen."

Hawksworth grinned and wiped his perspiring forehead. "Just barely legal in God's eyes. You may kiss your bride."

"No. Later." Blythe held a quill at the ready. "Hurry, you must sign the license."

Footsteps thundered in the entry.

Hawksworth, Heath, and Brooke dashed to the desk.

Heath snatched the quill as Hawksworth spread the license atop the desk.

He couldn't read the damn thing. No time for pride. "Where do I sign?"

"Just there." Hawk pointed.

Heath scribbled his signature then passed the quill to Brooke.

"And Lady Ravensdale, you sign here." Hawksworth indicated another place on the parchment.

She neatly affixed her signature.

"Let me in. I forbid Brooke to marry that cur." The drawing room door handles rattled violently before the panels shuddered as Gainsborough smashed something against them.

"I don't believe I care for our cousin, Brooke." Brette frowned at the door.

The others murmured their assent.

"Dammit, I say. Let me in."

"If you insist." Leventhorpe yanked the door open then dodged aside.

Red-faced and sweating, a blob of spittle hanging from the corner of his mouth, Gainsborough plowed into the room. He skidded to a stop and tottered when the carpet wrinkled underfoot.

Growling deep in his throat and hackles raised, Freddy leaped to his feet.

Gainsborough swung his furious gaze from Brooke, to Heath, to Hawksworth then fixed his attention on Brooke. A jeer contorted his features. "I'll never permit the marriage to be consummated. I'll have it annulled."

A small gasp escaped Brooke. She grasped Heath's hand. "I'm of age. He cannot do that, can he?"

"No, he cannot..." Leventhorpe followed Gainsborough into the room's center.

Gainsborough spun to face the other man. "I most certainly—"

"...if he's incapacitated and locked up." Leventhorpe planted Gainsborough a solid facer.

Bone crunched, and Blaire buried her face in her twin's shoulder. Gainsborough teetered, his eyes rolling back into his head, before he crashed to the floor, blood seeping from his nose.

Blythe grinned and clapped. "Well done, my lord."

He swept her a courtly bow.

"I believe this gentleman, and I do use the term with extreme disdain, has a reservation in a dovecote for the next, oh, say three days?" He flexed his fingers then rubbed his knuckles. "Is that sufficient time, Raven?"

"Indeed." He lifted Brooke's hand and kissed the back of her hand. "This time tomorrow, we'll be in London, and I'll be seeking guardianship."

She gifted him with a brilliant smile.

Hawksworth leaned forward and examined Gainsborough's prone figure. "I believe you broke his nose, Leventhorpe."

"Which can only improve the hideous appendage," Brooke said. "Looked rather like a bull elephant seal I saw in a book once."

After moment of astounded silence, laughter filled the room.

"Ladies, would you care to show me to the dining room?" Hawksworth extended both elbows. "The wonderful smells have tempted me beyond resistance this half hour past."

Blaire and Blaike swooped in like bees to a flower.

Typical reaction to Hawksworth—women making a cake of themselves. Surely The Almighty had a delightful sense of humor, permitting a man with Hawk's extreme good looks to be a man of God. Not that the vocation had been Hawk's first choice, but a parish proved a more desirable workplace if one must earn one's living than the battlefield or the deck of a rolling ship.

"By the by, Raven, I'm grateful you and your lovely bride came to an accord on your own. I asked Hawk to bring a license because I wouldn't have permitted you to besmirch her by making her your mistress. I fully intended to see you marry her, even if it meant I held a gun to you during the ceremony." After winking at Brooke and giving Heath a mocking salute, Leventhorpe offered his bent elbows to Blythe and Brette. Wearing bemused expressions, they, too, departed the room.

A grin etched on his face—Leventhorpe had flummoxed him, by God—Heath directed the footmen to remove Gainsborough to the dovecote and see him secured there.

Brooke stared out the window, her profile illumed by the filtered rays bathing the window. She appeared almost ethereal, her hair a shiny halo in the golden light. Twisting the ring on her finger, she turned soulful violet eyes to him. "Could we wait until we get to London to consummate the marriage?"

19

Some claim fortune favors the bold. However,
believing such rationality applies to love and happiness
is as ridiculous as wagering against the sun rising each morn.
~Wisdom and Advice—The Genteel Lady's Guide to Practical Living

Brooke ran the brush through her hair, the long strokes soothing her rattled nerves. She'd passed the remainder of the day in a haze except for Heath's response to her question. That she remembered clear as crystal.

"*No. We cannot.*"

His scorching gaze had threatened to singe the ends of her hair and turned her insides quivery and warm. Disturbing, yet tantalizing too. What that man did to her with a simple look...

She trembled head to toe.

"Of course he wouldn't want to wait."

She didn't really want to either, but fear of the unknown made her hesitant.

Brooke glanced at her bed covered in a handmade quilt Mama had sewed many years ago. The small bed had suited her well all these years. With Freddy tucked at her side, dozens of books had been read snuggled beneath the comforting bedclothes. And buckets of tears had dampened the pillows too.

Her gaze swept the tiny chamber meant for use as servants' quarters and scarcely bigger than the kitchen larder. Its ceiling sloped to the eaves on one side. Heath had better watch his head, or he'd be cracking his noggin on a beam. The girls shared the other two larger bedchambers, the twins' now affixed with a temporary door thanks to Sheridan's earlier violence. Brooke didn't mind. She liked her private sanctuary, the one place she could go and be alone. No expectations or demands in this cranny of the house.

Until Heath came to claim his husbandly rights tonight. Thank goodness her chamber was situated on the uppermost floor and the opposite side of the house from the quartet's. Nonetheless, everyone beneath the roof would know what she and Heath were about. Heat consumed her, and she lifted the heavy mass of hair from her neck, allowing the air to cool her nape.

Brooke pondered the bed again. Would his feet stick over the end? "Hardly big enough for me, let alone two people."

An image of them toppling onto the floor amidst the marriage act leaped to mind.

Good God. Every thump and bump would be heard below. She pressed cool hands to her hot cheeks.

Someone, likely Brette or Blythe, had put fresh sheets on the bed and set a vase of flowers on her dressing table. Extra candles had also been placed throughout the room. A wine bottle and two glasses sat upon a tray. Leventhorpe's doing, likely. Brooke jumped to her feet, her nerves threatening to erupt from her skin. She rubbed her hands up and down her bare arms, not to warm her flesh, but to lessen her tension.

Poor Freddy had been banished to the twins' room for the night. He'd slept with her every night of his life. Would Heath forbid it in the future? Maybe he would be one of those husbands who only entered her chamber to conduct his conjugal visits and then returned to his room to sleep. The notion didn't cheer her. Mama and Papa had always shared a bedroom.

Brooke sighed, hugging her arms snugger around her shoulders.

Married to a practical stranger. Yet far preferable to becoming Heath's mistress. She wouldn't lie to herself and pretend she didn't find him deucedly attractive—his raven hair, intelligent eyes, sharp-hewn face, and sinewy muscles... She secretly thrilled that he'd chosen to wed her. And bed her.

Brooke smoothed a wrinkle from the bottom sheet before fluffing the pillows. No palatial chamber here. She straightened the primrose and sage coverlet. Fingering the silky border, she smiled.

How could she love Heath? Ridiculous. Impractical. Unwise.

Affection took time to develop. Didn't one need to know everything about someone to become enamored and fall in love?

No. She'd known Humphrey for years and had intimate knowledge of his likes, dislikes, preferences, and habits. The mild, comfortable affection she'd harbored for him resembled a skiff ride on a calm lake. Only an occasional fish jumping to catch an insect interrupted the serenity.

Heath, on the other hand...what she felt for him: wild, intense, unpredictable sentiments that left her muddled and excited and...yearning. A journey on rolling waves to an undetermined destination, but one she'd gladly travel with him by her side.

A soft *click* as the door closed announced his arrival.

Brooke whirled to face her husband. Her breath left her in a whoosh.

Attired in a black banyan, he held a pink rose. Where had he gotten a rose? The black hairs exposed by the vee of his robe tantalized. Were all women so obsessed with chest hair?

She wiped damp palms on her nightdress. White, unadorned, and nearly sheer from frequent laundering, the garment wasn't in the least alluring, yet his eyes darkened and the lines of his face tautened as he examined her leisurely.

A seductive grin skewed his lips, and he extended the rose, advancing farther into the room. "For you."

"Thank you." Brooke reached for the blossom.

Rather than releasing his hold, he wrapped his other palm around her hand and drew her near. Heath trailed the silky petals over her cheek then lower to her neck and finally brushed the flower across the flesh exposed above her modest neckline.

Brooke parted her lips on a silent gasp, her nipples going rigid. How could such a simple gesture make her want to crawl atop him and kiss him until she couldn't breathe? He couldn't breathe?

"When I touched your arm today, I wondered if the rest of your skin would feel as petal soft." He ran two fingers over her collar bone before dipping one into the valley between her breasts. "It does."

Brooke shivered and closed her eyes lest he see the lust he stirred in her. She'd never considered herself a sensual woman, but Heath wrought cravings and sensations impossible to ignore.

A moment later, his firm lips replaced his exploring fingers. He feathered little kisses and nips behind her ear, the length of her jaw and neck, and then nuzzled the juncture of her throat. A pleasant, aching heaviness weighted her breasts and filled her abdomen and between her legs.

She shifted, restless for something. Drawing away, Brooke smiled at him and laid her palm in the crisp mat on his chest. She rubbed her hand back and forth, enjoying the friction of the curls and the ecstasy on his face. Wanton power sluiced her. She had caused his response.

He groaned and gripped her buttocks, lifting her against his turgid length.

Brooke kissed his chest, pushing aside the silk covering his molded shoulders. She couldn't get close enough to him, couldn't taste enough of his salty-sweet skin. She darted her tongue out, tracing it over one of the chocolate-colored circles on his chest. His nipples were much darker than her pink-tinted ones, though hers were larger by far.

Another gravelly moan escaped him, and Heath tossed aside the rose before scooping her into his arms.

"I feared you'd be reluctant tonight." He traced his tongue across her parted lips. "I see I needn't have been worried." His fingers clenching her ribs and thigh, he sucked her lower lip into his mouth. "Tell me you want me too, Brooke."

He swept his tongue into her mouth, sparring with hers for a moment.

Heady dizziness encompassed her. If his kisses did this to her, what would making love with him do? She would never be the same. Didn't want to be. Heath brought an awareness she hadn't known existed. Hadn't known she'd lacked.

"I want to feel you against me. Your legs entwined with mine." Brooke wrapped her arms around his neck, pressing her breasts against his chest. "I want you inside me—"

He pulled his head back, his expression gone stern. "And just how do you know about that, pray tell me?"

Laying her fingertips across his mouth, she grinned. "I raise cattle. Did you forget?"

"Hmph." His disgruntled expression softened as he carried her to the bed. "Not the same at all."

"At all?" Brooke smiled, twirling her fingers in the long hair at his nape. "How is it different?"

"Animals mate out of instinct, a primitive drive to reproduce and appease lust-born urges. Some humans—most, actually—are little better." Heath's knees bumped the mattress, yet he didn't lower her. His gaze unfathomable, he stared at her, an intensity she'd never seen in his eyes before. "But humans, the few fortunate ones, find love. The act is an expression of their adoration."

His embrace tightened when he said the last words.

Brooke went completely still. Falling in love in a week's time was improbable and irrational. Could Heath—this proud, enigmatic, wonderful man—feel the same for her as she felt for him?

"Brooke... I..."

She laid her hand on his cheek and summoned every ounce of bravado she possessed. "Are you saying you love me?"

What if he says no?

"Yes, although I don't understand how or why it came to be." Happiness sparked in his eyes, and he turned his head to place a kiss in her palm. "I only know I couldn't leave you and return to London alone. Ripping my heart from my chest would be less painful."

His eyes grew misty and his voice hoarse. "And I was such an unmitigated, unforgiveable arse, suggesting you..." His gaze caressed her face before he bent and kissed her mouth reverently. "Suggesting you become my mistress."

He rested his forehead against hers. "Dare I hope, in time, you might come to forgive me and perhaps feel tenderness for me?"

Brooke blinked away the tears pooling in her eyes.

"I already have, and I already do." Unaccustomed bashfulness seized her, and she nestled her face in the crook of his neck. His pulse beat—strong and steady, like him—beneath her cheek.

"Oh, God, I love you." A shudder rippled through Heath, and he crushed her closer. "I didn't believe in love, dismissed it as foolish nonsense, didn't believe it ever possible for the likes of me."

She nodded against his chest. "I know. I'm as stunned as you."

He laid her on the bed then fanned her hair over the pillow.

"You have the most beautiful hair I've ever seen." His hands at his waist, he paused in untying the belt. "I know I said we couldn't wait to consummate the marriage because of the risk your cousin poses, but if you're afraid, we could delay a day or two."

Heath loved her. She had wanted him for days. Brooke lifted her arms to him. "I don't want to wait."

"Thank God." A wicked smile curved his mouth as he bent and tugged her night-rail over her head. He inhaled sharply, and his nostrils flared as his ravenous gaze feasted on her breasts in the muted candlelight.

She yanked the covers over her chest, not ready to wantonly display her womanly assets to him. Perhaps in time.

He shrugged from the ebony silk and the garment slid to the floor. As if he sensed her need to become acquainted with his body, he stood like a Greek statue, allowing her to look her fill. She couldn't detect an ounce of fat on his powerful form. A well-muscled chest and torso, covered in curly raven hair, tapered into a narrow waist and hips. The dense thatch at his groin arrested her attention. From the patch sprang an impressive phallus.

Bloody gorgeous and arousing beyond belief.

His member twitched, bobbing up and down, and grew even larger.

Her mouth went dry. Just how enormous did the thing get, and more on point, could she accommodate something that size?

Heath edged onto the bed and slid beneath the covers. He gathered her into his arms, tucking her to his side and laying one muscled thigh across her legs. His penis, greedy beast, flexed against her hip.

"Aren't you going to snuff the candles first?" Brooke cast an anxious glance at the flickering tapers. They bathed the room in a soft light a more experienced woman might consider romantic.

"No, love. I want to see and worship every inch of you. I want to cherish the expression on your face when I enter you and bring you to completion." He splayed his fingers atop her abdomen. "And I want you to see what you do to me. The power you hold over me."

He reached between them and laid his manhood on her thigh.

"You do this to me." Pressing her hand atop the velvety length, he spread hot, fervent kisses over her breasts. He traced one nipple with his tongue before pulling the tip into his mouth and sucking.

Brooke gasped. Sparks streaked from her breasts to her toes, igniting every pore along the way. "Dear God..."

She arched into his mouth and let her legs fall open to his exploring hand. Heat spiraled higher and hotter, threatening to consume her with each lave of his tongue and flick of his experienced fingers. The warm stiffness of his penis pulsed against her palm. She grasped the flesh and squeezed gently. "It's so soft, yet hard too."

Heath moaned against her neck. "You're killing me."

Brooke stopped fondling him instantly, biting her lip as he slipped his long fingers into her. She instinctively clamped her muscles around him, squeezing tighter as aching pleasure surged to her womb. A throaty cry tore from her.

"No, don't stop." He groaned and ground his pelvis against her hand.

The urge to rotate her hips overtook her with such ferocity, Brooke had no resistance. She bucked and pumped, aware of the hungry, whimpering noises she made, but not caring.

"That's it, sweetheart. You're nice and wet, almost ready for me."

Wet? That was a good thing?

He moved his fingers faster, deeper.

Oh God, yes, wet is good. Very good.

She spread her legs wider.

"Good girl," Heath breathed in her ear.

He positioned himself over her, the tip of his penis bidding entrance. Cupping her face between both palms, he kissed her with such tender reverence, if he hadn't already told her of his love, his kiss would have exposed the secret.

"Look at me, Brooke."

She forced her eyes open, drowning in overwhelming sensation and need.

"Heath? I need..." A throaty groan escaped her. "I want..."

He smiled, the corners of his eyes crinkling. "I know."

Slowly, he entered her, refusing to relinquish her gaze.

Brooke sighed at the rightness of it. *This* was what she wanted. Needed. Yet, it wasn't enough. More. There must be something more. Clutching his back, she wriggled her hips. Almost frantic with yearning, she rubbed her breasts against his chest.

He stopped his gentle invasion into her womanhood and wrapped one strong arm around her shoulders and one beneath her hips. "Now, love. Now."

Brooke surged upward as Heath plunged. A gasp tore from her as stinging pain seared her center. She trained her gaze on him, trusting him as the most marvelous of feelings radiated from where he joined with her.

"It feels wonderful," she whispered, testing the sensations by rocking her hips.

"It gets better, darling." He arched his spine, his corded neck muscles rigid. "Let me take you to heaven, where angels like you belong."

His breathing harsh and heavy, he began a rhythmic thrusting.

Brooke caught his tempo as he ground into her. She wrapped her legs round his waist and let him carry her heavenward. The world ceased to exist around her. Only she and Heath and this moment of incredible bliss mattered. And just when she thought she could bear no more, when her soft whimpers become small cries of desperation, she fractured and screamed his name, convulsing over and over as indescribable ecstasy ravaged her.

A moment later, he roared his fulfillment.

She welcomed each pounding thrust, knowing he enjoyed the same rush of pleasure she just had. Breathing heavily, he flopped onto his back, pulling Brooke atop his sweat-slicked chest. Several moments passed before her ragged breathing and thrumming heartbeat returned to normal. Delicious drowsiness surrounded her. No wonder Buford had rutted until the moment he'd keeled over. Not a bad way to die at all.

"Never, in all my days, have I ever experienced anything that...that incredible." Heath hugged her fiercely, his lips pressed to the top of her head.

Brooke snuggled into his side and yawned. Head on his shoulder, she ran her fingers through his chest hair. "Can we do it again? I should like to try making love the way the cows do, with you from behind."

Heath grinned and tweaked her nose. "In a bit. I need awhile to recover."

The candles had burned to nubs when Brooke finally roused enough to pull the coverlet atop her and Heath. She gazed at his sleeping form. Her husband. She smiled and shook her head then lay down, her head nestled on his shoulder again.

"What are you smiling about?"

She tilted her head to look at him. Exotic eyes regarded her. She really did need to ask him about his heritage. "I thought you were asleep."

"Hardly, with a tantalizing siren beside me. I shall be in a constant state of arousal until the day I die." The bedding shifted above his pelvis.

She peeked beneath the blankets and giggled. "Poor man. That has to be uncomfortable."

He caressed her shoulder and arm. "Why were you smiling when you thought I was asleep?"

"I imagined what I'd tell our children when they asked how we met." She scratched her nose where his hair tickled her. "I'm not sure I want them to know a wager brought us together and we wed after a mere week. Not a very good example, I shouldn't think."

"Ah, but imagine what a romantic tale we've created. It will serve as an inspiration for our children, to believe true love really does exist." Heath chuckled and palmed her breast, gently pinching the peak.

A jolt of pleasure speared her. "It does, doesn't it?"

The wisest of gamblers have this in common:
They quit while they are ahead.
~*Wisdom and Advice—The Genteel Lady's Guide to Practical Living*

London, England
Late May 1822

Brooke drew in a steadying breath and smoothed the satin of her lavender ball gown for the umpteenth time as the carriage lurched to a stop before an ostentatious manor. Nervous didn't begin to describe her state, not only for herself, but her sister and cousins. A horde of insects rioted inside her stomach, making complete nuisances of themselves, horrid little pests.

Beside her, Brette fidgeted with the silk tassels of her reticule, and on the opposite seat, Blythe, Blaire, and Blaike's features suggested they were about to be offered up as human sacrifices. Not too far off the mark, truth to tell.

In their evening finery, hair intricately coiffed, and jeweled to the hilt, thanks to Heath's generosity, the Culpepper misses and her, the new Lady Ravensdale—blast, but it was proving difficult to remember to answer to her new title—were about to attend their first formal ball. Brooke would rather have stood on her head naked in Hyde Park. But as soon as the Season ended, they would return to Culpepper Park, the name they'd dubbed the lands Brooke now owned, to check on the new house's progress.

Sheridan had signed an agreement and greedily accepted a sizable sum to disappear from their lives forever. Hopefully, they were rid of him for good.

Heath squeezed the fingers of her gloved hand and grinned like a Captain Sharp with a winning hand at cards. “Trust me, dear. None of you has anything to fear.”

“Easy for you to say. You’re accustomed to the predators and vipers in there.” She pointed at the house, every window ablaze with light. A good dozen people paused to stare at their coach.

The carriage door swung open, and a black liveried footman placed a low step beside the carriage. His eyes widened to the size of moons when he glanced inside. A delighted smile stretched across his handsome face. He turned and motioned to another footman.

The second footman hurried to their conveyance. Upon spotting the women, he tripped, nearly planting his face on the coach floor.

Heath slid Brooke a smug glance that said, *See, I told you.*

Yes, but gullible footmen were a far cry from the denizens of High Society, who were wont to devour young ladies with the swiftness of piranhas.

As they assembled on the pavement, Brooke took the girls’ measure. Heath had suggested the jeweled tones for their gowns. Amethyst for her, light blue sapphire for Brette, jonquil beryl for Blythe, emerald green for Blaike, and pink ruby for Blaire. Superb choices, and with the matching gemstones each wore, truly regal.

A hush settled upon the guests lined up like docile cattle on the pavement and steps to enter the manor. Every eye turned to look at the new arrivals, and the crowd parted to allow them entrance. Heath and Brooke led, Brette and Blythe followed, and the twins brought up the rear.

Brooke’s jaw almost bounced off the floor upon entering the glittering mansion. Never had she seen such opulence. Two eight-foot chandeliers blinded her with at least one hundred candles each. She couldn’t decide which offended worse: the garish rose marble floor or the abundant gold gilding plastered on practically everything not moving. Even the hostess wore copious layers of gold.

Brooke sent a reassuring smile over her shoulder. The quartet’s stunned faces no doubt mirrored her own.

“Steady on, ladies. Chins up and eyes forward. Incomparable, every last one of you." Heath led them to a gaping butler, his jaw sagging so widely, a pigeon might've nested in the cavity.

"Pretty much the reaction I had, too, upon seeing them for the first time, Withers."

Withers drew himself up, his prickly black eyebrows wiggling like caterpillars in the throes of mating...or dying. "Indeed, my lord. A most astounding collection of young ladies, if I may say so."

The majordomo bowed so low, his nose threatened to scrape the floor. Several dandies also made exaggerated bows, while the *haut ton* ladies' fans snapped to attention and waved furiously. Their tongues probably flapped just as fast.

Heath murmured their names into the butler's ear.

"Ah, may I offer my most sincere solicitations, my lord?"

Heath inclined his head. "Thank you."

Withers cast a languid gaze over the crowd then notched his nose skyward. "Lord and Lady Ravensdale, and the Misses Culpepper."

A low buzz built in volume as more people pushed and shoved their way into the entry and peeked from the ballroom, including the flummoxed Benbridges.

Blythe waved her fingers at their neighbors who continued to gawk.

A tall, auburn-haired man elbowed his way through the gawkers. A blond god followed, a merry twinkle in his eyes. Thank goodness. Brooke had never thought the day would come that she'd welcome Lord Leventhorpe's intimidating presence.

"We thought you might need a hand." Leventhorpe grinned and winked.

Reverend Hawksworth chuckled. "I do believe a near insurrection is at hand."

The gentlemen extended their elbows and, with a Culpepper on each arm, led the way into the ballroom. Elbowing and shoving one another in a most ungallant fashion, a score of gentlemen trotted after them. Miffed ladies did too, but for entirely different reasons—to snatch wayward beaus and husbands back to their sides.

Heath placed Brooke's hand on his arm and whispered in her ear. "My love, the Culpepper misses have tumbled the stuffy *ton* tits over arse."

Brooke burst out laughing. “Come, husband. I’ve a feeling we’ll have our hands full with those four. I did warn you before we married and you became their guardian, however.”

“I wouldn’t have it any other way.” He tilted her chin up, and in full view of the scandalized onlookers, kissed Brooke full on the mouth.

If you've enjoyed reading **The Earl and the Spinster**, *The Blue Rose Regency Romances: The Culpepper Misses Book 1*, then perhaps you'd enjoy the rest of the books in the series:

The Marquis and the Vixen
The Lord and the Wallflower
The Buccaneer and the Bluestocking
The Lieutenant and the Lady

Triumph and Treasure

HIGHLAND HEATHER ROMANCING A SCOT, BOOK 1

1

Boston, Massachusetts
Late March 1818

Angelina Ellsworth—no, she was Mrs. Moreau now—cast her husband of six hours a look of adoration as he escorted her across the marble floor of the luxurious Plaza Hotel. She resisted the urge to dance a giddy jig.

She was married.

She tried not to gawk at the immense glittering eight-foot crystal chandeliers, marble pillars, and life-size, almost nude—*er, make that entirely nude*—statues of mythical gods and goddesses. Cherubs, their chubby feet and legs immersed in the water, edged a towering fountain burbling cheerily in the lobby's center.

"Rather dazzling, *chérie, non*?"

Meeting Charles's amused expression, heat tingled her cheeks. She'd been craning her neck, staring at the *trompe l'oiel* ceiling depicting gods and other immortals—also bare as Norfolk dumplings.

Papa would've been utterly scandalized.

Nudity, mythical gods, vulgar displays of wealth. Blasphemous.

And utterly splendid.

She released a happy sigh.

If Papa had been alive, he'd never have consented to Charles courting her. Papa had been determined she marry a gentleman of his ilk: a staid, devout, *dull* fellow. Better yet, a man of the cloth. And with dowries the size of thimbles, Angelina and her sisters had few suitors, let alone debonair young men such as Charles.

Thank goodness, Mama entertained her ideas, and after his passing, had voiced and implemented them with complete disregard as to what her late husband would've preferred.

A romantic at heart, once Mama realized Angelina loved Charles, she readily consented to the match.

Angelina shook off her dreary thoughts.

This was her wedding day. A rush of excitement caused her breath to quicken. In two days, she and Charles would sail to the Continent for a lengthy honeymoon in Italy by way of France.

Prior to meeting him, she'd only dared hope that, perhaps, someday, she might visit her aunt and uncle, the Duke and Duchess of Waterford, in England. She'd never met them. Aunt Camille was her mother's twin, and they exchanged correspondences on occasion.

"Here's your room key, sir."

The skeleton key clinking onto the countertop reined in Angelina's ruminations.

"Thank you." Charles slipped the key into his coat pocket before taking her arm. "Is the room prepared?"

"Yes, sir. Everything is as you requested." The clerk's lips bent into a knowing smile. "May I offer my congratulations, Mr. and Mrs. Moreau?"

"Thank you." Angelina and Charles spoke simultaneously.

He patted her arm, giving her a crooked grin.

Her stomach wobbled with that peculiar flip-flop it did whenever her new husband smiled at her. She cast him a sidelong peek as he guided her toward the curved staircase. A mere three months ago, this splendid man had entered her life.

If it hadn't been for Mama's insistence that Angelina attend the Dennison's Yuletide ball, she might never have met him. She hadn't wanted to attend, aware her father's cohort—horrid yellow-toothed Abraham Stockton—would be there. The paunchy man always stank of garlic and sweat. And he was five and forty if he was a day.

Despite Mama's adamant refusal to allow him to call upon Angelina, he'd been trying to court her the three years since she turned seventeen. Mama claimed the man was dicked in the nob if he thought to marry Angelina.

For her part, Angelina suspected, had he lived, Papa would've arranged a match between her and Mr. Stockton. She shuddered at the notion. In fact, she'd been hiding from him in a curtained alcove at the Dennison's when a man darted into the enclosure.

Unaware she huddled on a sofa tucked in the corner, he peeked between the heavy velvet panels, muttering, "A more persistent match-making *maman* I've never encountered. And *zut*, four plainer, pudgier mademoiselles—"

Angelina had erupted into laughter. "Mrs. Twiggels and the quartet, I'd wager."

Charles had spun around, peering into the shadowy nook. He'd chuckled, a pleasant low vibration deep in his chest. "*Non,* Twiggels? Please tell me you jest."

Yes, indeed, God had smiled on her that evening, for Charles had arrived in Massachusetts that very day, brought to Salem on business. His presence at the ball had been pure chance. His associate had received an invitation and insisted Charles join him for the festivities.

Angelina swept Charles another love-filled gaze.

His lips skewed into a devilishly wicked smile, and the glint smoldering within his tawny eyes caused her heart to patter in anticipation.

With his black hair and high cheekbones, he cut a dashing figure. The navy blue of his coat enhanced his unusual brandy-colored eyes and emphasized the breadth of his shoulders. Shoulders, she itched to feel beneath her fingers.

Despite her gloves, her palms dampened. She brushed her hands against her champagne-colored silk gauze gown, allowing herself to imagine Charles's hands caressing her.

Soon they would be.

They'd shared several fervent kisses during their short courtship, and once betrothed, he suggested they become more intimate. Raised by her zealot father, Angelina couldn't bring herself to sin *that* way. Not that she wasn't anticipating the marriage bed.

She most definitely was.

Followed by four porters carrying their luggage, she and Charles climbed the arched risers. Their trunks had already been sent to the ship.

As they ascended the stairs, Charles's caressed her spine.

A delicious tremor spiraled outward from where his palm lingered. She suppressed a slight gasp. Something more than curiosity stirred, making her impatient for his touches and kisses.

And he was a *most* skilled kisser.

A widower, forced at the tender age of twenty to marry a much older woman to save his family's estate, in the seven years since, he'd made a fortune in commerce.

Angelina held no doubts his handsomeness availed him of many a willing bed partner, though she wasn't supposed to know of such things. If the Dennison's ball was any indication, women threw themselves at him in droves.

However, much to her astonishment and delight, he'd chosen to make her his wife.

Charles vowed he'd never loved another and that Angelina would be his until the day he died. She had no misgivings about his affection. A man couldn't pretend the warmth in his amber eyes or the husky timbre of his voice when he spoke of his adoration.

She pressed her fingers against the ruby and diamond ring encircling her finger.

Yes, this is real.

"Happy, *mon ange?*" He gave her waist a slight squeeze.

His angel?

Smiling, she nodded, releasing a contented sigh. "Yes, blessedly and deliriously happy."

How could she not be? She'd found love. Something her parents' marriage had always lacked. Until meeting Charles, she hadn't been altogether certain love existed outside her novels.

"Here we are." Charles's rested his hand on the curve of her ribs, his thumb rubbing against her gown. It tickled.

To stifle her giggle, she bit her lower lip.

He waited for the attendant to unlock their suite, a glint of anticipation in his eyes. The door swung open, revealing a room resplendent with roses of every imaginable shade.

Stepping inside, she spun in a slow circle, her skirts swishing about her ankles. The heady perfume of a hundred fragrant blossoms permeated the air. She sniffed in appreciation. Surveying the chamber, she spied more flowers in the adjoining bedchamber and dashed to the parted door.

After peering within, she sent a glance over her shoulder. "What in heaven's name?"

Still speaking to the porters, Charles didn't hear her.

Untying the ribbons at her chin, Angelina breathed in the heady aroma before removing her bonnet. Her spencer followed. She placed the items on the table beside the bedchamber door, adding her reticule atop the pile.

She studied the bed dominating the room. A monstrous thing with carvings on the bedposts and along the canopy, from which hung scarlet bed curtains, it was a blessed wonder the frame supported the oversized mattress.

She stepped closer, inspecting the engraved posts.

Oh, my.

Nude forms entwined in various acts of intimacy coiled around the wood.

Good heavens.

Heat burned her cheeks.

Similar images of Greek and Roman gods adorned the walls and ceilings. Wicked as Sodom and Gomorrah. For the first time since entering the dazzling hotel, she experienced a tinge of discomfit. Though very luxurious, the chamber's blatant carnality embarrassed her.

She wandered to the bedchamber's entrance.

Charles finished speaking to the remaining attendant and passed the young man a coin.

"Of course, sir. Right away." The porter smiled widely and stepped into the corridor. He hesitated, staring at the luggage piled about the entrance. "Do you wish me to have a maid sent up to unpack your bags?"

Charles shook his head, a strand of midnight hair falling across his forehead. "*Non*, we're only staying two nights. We sail the day after tomorrow. I'm confident my wife and I can manage."

He turned to wink at Angelina.

She grinned in return. *Incorrigible rogue.* But he was *her* rogue.

He closed the door before crossing to her in several elongated strides. Sweeping her into his arms, he nuzzled her neck.

She adored how she fit beneath his chin. At five feet eight inches, she stood taller than most women of her acquaintance. Yet, within Charles's embrace, she felt dainty and feminine.

Angelina laughed huskily. "My goodness, why all the roses?"

"For you *mon ange* rose. I wasn't able to fill the room with angels, but roses? That I could arrange. I've imagined you naked, lying on a bed scattered with rose petals for weeks."

Should she be shocked? For the life of her, she couldn't summon a jot of chagrin.

My, I've become scandalous since meeting Charles.

He stepped away and unbuttoned his cutaway coat. The gleam in his eye caused her pulse to do all manner of odd things. Good Lord, he didn't intend to—

She glanced at the window, searching the sky. Enshrouded in a smoky violet-gray, dusk had scarcely fallen. Making love was most improper during the daytime. Wasn't it?

Charles wound his arms around her once more, reining in her

wayward thoughts. He kissed her like a man long-starved.

Looping her arms behind his neck, Angelina returned the kiss.

He nudged his hips against her belly, his desire evident. "I must have you now, *mon amour*. I cannot wait."

She hadn't expected he would be quite so eager to bed her—and before dinner, it would seem. The knowledge both thrilled and disconcerted her.

"Help me with the hooks, will you?" She made to turn her back, needing his assistance to unfasten the gown.

"*Non*, that will take too long."

Before she knew precisely what he intended, he scooped her into his arms. In two strides, he reached the bed then laid her upon the lush counterpane. Charles shoved her skirts to her thighs, and after fumbling with the falls of his trousers, parted her legs.

Apprehension swept her.

"Charles, I'm not…This is so sudden. I don't—" She gasped on a choked cry.

"Mon Dieu," he groaned against her neck.

Blinking back tears and biting her lip against the stinging pain, Angelina stared at a lurid picture on the wall. Was the act supposed to hurt this much?

Charles stiffened, giving a final moan before collapsing atop her.

That's it?

All the whispered fuss was about *that*? Awash in disappointment and miffed at his callousness, she barely took note when he rose from the bed and fastened his trousers.

He chuckled, trailing a finger across her lips. "You resemble a *femme légère.* A wanton, lying there with your breasts revealed and your legs spread."

Shame and humiliation surged through her. She turned her face away, shoving the gown to her knees with one hand and tugging the bodice over her breasts with the other. She swallowed against the tears burning at the back of her throat.

How could he say that?

"*Chérie*?" Charles touched her cheek, turning her face and forcing her to meet his eyes. "Forgive me, *mon amour*. I'm a selfish oaf. I promise I'll take my time next go-round. You will see how wonderful making love can be."

He bent and kissed her.

Someone knocked on the outer door. Another rap immediately

followed this time with more insistence.

"Ah, that must be our food." He gave her a boyish grin as he fastened his jacket. "I hope you don't mind. I requested an intimate dinner in our rooms rather than the noisy restaurant below."

After helping her off the bed, he placed another tender kiss on her lips. "I love you, *amoureux*."

The outer door rattled once more. Someone was most impatient.

"I'll answer the door while you repair your appearance." Whistling, he left the chamber, closing the door behind him.

Repair her appearance?

She'd much rather take a hot, lengthy bath liberally dosed with scented oil. She'd been anticipating becoming a woman for weeks, and truth to tell, the unpleasant experience didn't measure up to her naïve expectations.

Something wet trickled down her thighs, and she rushed to the bathing chamber. After dampening a cloth from the washstand pitcher, she made quick work of cleansing herself, grimacing at the blood on the linen. After washing away the evidence of her virginity and Charles's virility, she smoothed her chemise and dress, shaking the fabric until the folds fell into place.

The pearl pendant above her breasts, a wedding gift from Charles, hung askew. She straightened the necklace, and then adjusted her bodice, wincing slightly. He had certainly been exuberant in his attentions.

Mama had explained what to expect, nonetheless…

As she tidied her hair, Angelina examined her face in the looking glass. Several curly tendrils had escaped the Grecian knot atop her head. Other than rosy lips and cheeks, she didn't appear different from the woman who had entered the chamber a few minutes ago.

Except, I am no longer an untried maid.

She trusted the next time would be more satisfying.

As she made her way through the bedchamber, men's angry voices clashed in the other room. She hesitated, listening.

"Up to your old tricks, Pierre?" an unfamiliar, slightly French-accented voice accused.

Pierre?

Angelina opened the door but stopped short at the threshold.

The man before Charles was no servant. Sporting a thin mustache, the stranger stood attired in the latest fashion. From his gleaming Hessians and cream-colored pantaloons to his jade green coat and knotted neckcloth—from which a jeweled stickpin glistened—he exuded quality.

He was profoundly handsome. And extremely angry.

Another man stood by the entrance. Much less refined, he grasped the handle of a gun tucked into his waistband.

She slapped a hand to her mouth in an effort to stifle the gasp that tore from her.

Thieves?

As one, the men's gazes came to rest on her: Charles's worried and angry, the rough fellow's, aloof, and the handsome man's curious *and compassionate*?

"Whatever is going on, Charles?" To calm her tumultuous stomach, Angelina wrapped her arms about her waist.

Her husband's face had taken on a distinct greenish hue, and she feared he might cast up his accounts. He opened his mouth to speak, but no sound emerged.

The mustached man shook his head contemptuously. "*Charles?* How unoriginal."

He turned his attention to Angelina and into a formal bow. "Mademoiselle Ellsworth, allow me to introduce myself. I'm Jacques, Baron Devaux-Rousset."

Angelina didn't extend her hand. Instead, she tightened the grip around her middle.

Pale, his lips pressed into a thin line, Charles glowered at the Frenchman.

This man was no friend.

"My lord, did Charles not inform you? I'm Mrs. Moreau. We were married this morning. Please excuse my forwardness, but how are you acquainted with my husband? And who, pray tell, is Pierre? Him?" She pointed at the surly giant who continued to toy with his weapon.

The brute smiled, a humorless twisting of his thick lips.

Lord Devaux-Rousset speared Charles with an indiscernible glance before answering. "I'm his stepson. Though, paradoxically, we are the same age."

Oh, the older woman Charles married.

He hadn't mentioned she'd been a baroness or that she had children. Whyever was her son here? Boston was too far from France for Angelina to believe this was a chance encounter. Something was too smoky by far.

She sent Charles a sidelong glance.

Why didn't he say something?

He stood seething with silent fury and glared daggers at the baron.

Angelina angled her head in deference. "Charles told me of his marriage to your mother. Please accept my sincere condolences for your loss."

For a moment, the baron's composure wavered. He gaped at her before turning a steely glower on Charles. "*Vous avez dit que sa mère était morte*?"

Drat, she didn't speak French, but the baron had mentioned something about his mother's death. That much she'd gleaned. Perhaps, she shouldn't have offered her sympathies. The mourning period had ended months ago. At least she thought that was what Charles had told her.

Or, mayhap, it hadn't been that long, which explained the baron's annoyance at the news of Charles's nuptials.

"Charles, are you not out of mourning?"

"*Merd*e." Charles stared at the floor and fisted his hands.

"There is a lady present, *imbécile*," the baron snapped. "Hold your foul tongue."

He turned his attention to Angelina, and his expression softened. With a wave of his manicured hand, he indicated the ivory and gold striped sofa beside her.

"Mademoiselle, perhaps you should have a seat, and I'll explain."

"Thank you, no. I'd rather stand, my lord."

Why did he insist on calling her mademoiselle? Rather boorish of him. No, pointedly rude, truth to tell.

The baron regarded her for an extended moment. He gave a slight shrug. "As you wish."

He turned to the brute blocking the door. "Please wait in the corridor and deter any staff. I don't wish to be disturbed."

After perusing Charles contemptuously one final time, the baron's henchman gave a curt nod and exited the chamber.

Lord Devaux-Rousset sighed and slapped his beaver hat against his thigh. His gaze skimmed Angelina from her hair to her shoes, taking her measure. "You are lovely. I understand Pierre's fascination. Thank God, I arrived before he compromised you."

Angelina frowned, utterly confused. Was the man daft?

"Pierre? *Who* is Pierre? And how, in God's precious name, can my husband *possibly* compromise me?"

His voice very soft, and equally as gentle, Lord Devaux-Rousset murmured, "I sincerely regret having to tell you, but the man you call husband is the well-known slave-trader, Pierre Renault."

"What?" She blinked rapidly, certain she'd heard incorrectly. Charles couldn't be slave-trader. He wouldn't be a party to something so abhorrent.

Rousset leveled Charles a blistering glare. "And, I assure you, his wife, my *mère*, was very much alive when I left France."

2

This is not happening.

Clutching her stomach, Angelina struggled to breathe. Shock and disbelief had rendered her speechless.

The baron and his man escorted a protesting Charles from the suite, leaving his luggage behind. He didn't even attempt to say farewell.

I'm not married.

Charles deceived me.

I am despoiled.

She shook her head against the onslaught raging in her mind. The lengths to which Charles had gone—to win her hand, her affections—and he wasn't free to marry anyone.

He claimed he loved me. How could I have been so wrong? So gullible and stupid?

Tears streamed from her eyes. She crossed her arms, hugging her shoulders tight. Bent double and moaning, she stumbled to the sofa. Collapsing in a heap, she buried her face in a silken pillow. She sobbed until the reservoir of sorrow yielded no more tears.

Her eyes gritty and swollen, she sighed and flopped onto her back. She stared at the myriad of roses dotting the room, hating them.

Hating *him.*

What was she going to do?

Good God, a slave-trader. The vilest of professions.

How could she have been that mistaken about Charles? She closed her eyes against the monologue echoing in her head, a tormenting refrain in her benumbed mind.

Charles vowed he loved me. He's married. What am I to do?

A few scant hours ago, she'd been rejoicing and thanking God for answering her prayers. And now? The foundation of her faith had crumbled. Tears threatened once more, and she threw her forearm across her eyes.

A soft tapping at the door stirred her from her misery. Opening her eyes, she inched into a sitting position, her movements that of an old woman. Bloody wonder her bones didn't creak in protest. She'd aged a century this day.

Except for a single thin moonbeam valiantly cutting through the shadows, darkness inhabited the chamber.

"Who—?" A raspy croak emerged. She cleared her throat. "Who is it?"

"It's Andrew, one of the porters, Mrs. Moreau. I've brought your dinner and a missive from Mr. Moreau."

Charles dared yet call himself her husband?

Angelina supposed she should be grateful lest the staff learn of her humiliation and her reputation be further tarnished. Wiping her face with the palms of her hands, she stood and, on leaden legs, plodded to the door. Lord, she felt ancient.

She opened the panel a crack, scarcely wide enough for the paper to be passed through.

"I don't care for dinner, thank you. I'm not feeling well." She spoke the truth. She was sick to her soul. How did one recover from a blow like this? The scars wouldn't soon heal—if ever.

After shutting and locking the door, Angelina sagged, boneless against its welcoming support until the clanking and clattering of the dinner cart faded. Sighing, she forced herself upright and then set about lighting a few candles.

Kicking her satin slippers off, she turned the note over. She recognized Charles's neat handwriting. He'd written her a score of poems professing his love with those precise, slanted strokes.

Meaningless words. All lies.

Plopping on the plush sofa once more, she broke the letter's wax seal before tucking her feet beneath her. A brochure fluttered to the cushion. Retrieving the scrap of paper, she gaped in infuriated disbelief.

"The post chaise schedule. What audacity."

A disquieting mixture of curiosity and dread prompted her to read the letter. She unfolded the crisp paper.

Chérie Mon Amor,

Return to Salem and wait for me. You must believe me, I love you, Chérie. You are mine. I promise I'll come for you as soon as I have rectified this misfortune.

Misfortune?

As if his being married was an unfortunate accident or a stroke of bad luck. Scanning the rest of the page, she muttered, "How very generous, you lying blackguard."

She crumpled the paper into a tightwad and hurled the ball across the room. The letter bounced off a vase, jarring loose a handful of buttered-colored petals.

Charles, or rather Pierre, had paid for the suite until the end of the week. He'd also made arrangements for her trunks to be delivered to the Plaza. She was to use a pouch of coins hidden within his luggage to secure a ticket to Salem.

Oh, and would she be so kind as to have his bags sent to the lobby? The baron's man would retrieve them.

No, to his bags.

No, to being his.

And no, by God and all of the divine powers, to waiting for him.

Nor would she return to the only home she'd ever known. She possessed more mettle than that.

Jumping to her feet, determination in her steps, Angelina marched to the secretary. After removing a piece of foolscap, she dipped the quill in ink and swiftly penned a letter to her mother and told her of Charles's duplicity.

The time had arrived to pay Uncle Ambrose and Aunt Camille a visit.

As Angelina suspected and prayed she would, her mother arrived two days later. Encased in Mama's arms, her familiar gardenia perfume a cocoon of comfort, she gave vent to her tears and humiliation.

Once her sorrow was spent, Mama handed her a lacy handkerchief.

"Come, dry your eyes, and have a seat." She guided Angelina to the sofa. "You're right about not returning to Salem, Lina. The gossip would be your undoing and the twins,' too. I've written a letter to my sister explaining the delicacy of the situation."

"What will you tell Lily and Iris?"

Mama hesitated, then sighed, her shoulders sagging. "The truth, I think. They know I hurried here at your behest."

She tenderly tucked a wisp of hair behind Angelina's ear. "You'll go to England for a lengthy visit. No one else will ever know your marriage was a farce."

I know. Charles knows. The baron knows.

"Oh, my angel. I am sorry." Though her eyes glistened, her mother attempted a brave smile. "I should've been more diligent, but you were so happy. True love, if you're blessed enough to find it, is a treasure. I felt like that once. A very long time ago."

A far-off look shadowed Mama's expression, and she dashed at the tear slipping from the corner of an eye. "Mine was not meant to be, however."

She schooled her features. "I've purchased a ticket for you on the next packet to London, Lina. Praise God, Stapleton Shipping has a ship sailing at high tide tomorrow. I managed to secure the services of a gentle-bred Englishwoman. A Mrs. Pettigrove, who has agreed to act as your chaperone. She assured me she frequently travels between Boston and London, and she would be most grateful for a genteel companion on the voyage."

Patting Angelina's cheek, her mother gave a wobbly smile. "You'll arrive in England in early May, stay a few months—mayhap a year—and then, *tragically*, you'll be widowed, and you can come home."

She must've spent the two days of travel contriving a believable story.

A teasing glint entered her eyes. "Or, perhaps, you'll meet a charming young man or a rich, handsome lord."

"Mama, please stop." Angelina shook her head with such fervor, several strands of hair worked loose of their pins. "I don't want to meet anyone. I'll never be able to trust a man again."

She slumped against the sofa, cradling a pillow against her chest. "Mama, we…" Her cheeks flamed. "He…"

"Oh, dear." Mama paled, and her blue eyes widened in comprehension. Concern etched her face. "I thought the baron arrived before …"

Angelina pressed her palms to her burning cheeks. "It was only once and rather quick at that."

And uncomfortable.

Did that make a difference? Surely it must take many times to conceive. Otherwise, married women would be with child continually.

"It's not likely you're with child, my dear. It seldom happens the first time." Mama's voice wavered. She closed her eyes and raised a hand to her forehead as if in pain.

Fiddling with the pillow's silk tassels, Angelina whispered, "I'm sorry to bring this shame on you."

"Nonsense. You loved and trusted Charles. There is no disgrace in that." Mama squeezed her hand. "You've done nothing to be ashamed of, dear."

Nevertheless, Angelina drowned in shame and humiliation. And gut-wrenching fury toward Charles. Actually, all men at the moment, the rotten hypocrites.

"Unfortunately, as you've learned, men, in general, cannot be trusted." Mama's voice developed a strident edge Angelina hadn't heard before.

Yes, that she'd learned too well, bitter lesson though it was. God would judge Charles's deception and harshly, too, she prayed.

Judge not, that you be not judged and forgive others their trespasses.

Two of Papa's favorite scriptures sprang to mind. Two principals her father broke daily.

Hypocrisy, again. Apparently, a common male trait.

Angelina firmed her lips together lest she twist them into an unladylike sneer. Overflowing with pain, sorrow, and anger at her naiveté, her battered soul lacked room for forgiveness at present.

Gads, she'd been a cork-brained ninny. Utterly trusting and gullible.

Where were the honorable males? The men of integrity?

Did nothing more than charlatans and frauds populate the world?

How did one know the difference?

Not by listening to pretty compliments or tender words. Or by allowing herself to be beguiled by devilish smiles and faces-too-handsome-for-words.

Charles Moreau, Pierre Renault, whoever the blasted fiend was, better hope he never encountered her again. He wouldn't find a gullible moon-eyed miss next time. Narrowing her eyes and resolutely squaring her shoulders, Angelina made a rule.

Never again trust a man or allow my emotions to make me a victim.

3

London, England
Early May 1818

Champagne flute in hand, Flynn, Earl of Luxmoore scanned Lord and Lady Wimpleton's overflowing ballroom.

Where was she?

Dozens of bejeweled and elegantly gowned ladies swirled by, but none were the charming damsel he sought. He'd met the delectable Miss Lydia Farnsworth three weeks ago and had made a point to appear at every function she was rumored to attend from that evening onward.

Avoiding the eager hawk-like gazes of plotting mamas and the hungry expressions of their husband-hunting daughters, he sent a questioning look to the Duke of Harcourt lounging against the ballroom's entrance.

Sporting a cocky grin, Harcourt shrugged and raised his champagne flute in a mock salute.

Blast the man.

He'd sworn the Scotswoman, a distant relative of Harcourt's, would be in attendance tonight. Should Flynn make his excuses and try to find Miss Farnsworth at another gathering?

Which one?

He'd received at least a dozen *haut ton* invitations for this evening.

Flynn feared he'd fast become a besotted fool. He took a swallow of champagne and grinned. He rather liked the idea. In fact, he intended to call on Harcourt tomorrow and state his intentions regarding Miss Farnsworth.

How long should Flynn wait to propose to the refreshingly intelligent and witty young lady?

Confident she returned his admiration and would accept his offer, he wouldn't delay. He'd propose to Lydia tomorrow after he'd spoken to Harcourt.

Was he authorized to speak on behalf of her family? Wasn't her father still alive in Scotland?

It didn't matter. Flynn would still ask for her hand.

Yes, when next he ventured into the social fray, he would be betrothed.

A melodic feminine laugh echoed behind him.

Turning slowly—it wouldn't do to appear too eager—he spied the raven-haired beauty in a stunning pink and white gown. As usual, a bevy of calf-eyed beaux surrounded her. Little did they know by this time tomorrow, she'd be unavailable to the drooling milksops.

He took a leisurely sip of champagne, trying to decide on the best strategy to steal Miss Farnsworth away for the next waltz. And the supper dance, of course. Perhaps, she'd agree to stroll the gardens with him, and he could finally sample her sweet lips.

In his mind, he'd already claimed her as his countess.

Catching his appraisal, she sent him a dazzling smile, mischief sparkling in her hazel eyes. After murmuring something to the smitten swains, who promptly frowned and glowered at Flynn, she glided toward him.

Oh, yes. Miss Farnsworth would accept Flynn's offer. Of that, he'd no doubt. Allowing himself a triumphant smile, he handed his half-full glass to a passing servant.

"My lord." Miss Farnsworth's lilting voice vaguely hinted of her Scottish heritage. She dipped into a deep curtsey, giving him a most delectable glimpse of her generous bosom.

Flynn indulged in an unhurried perusal before bending over her gloved hand. He boldly skimmed the material with his lips. Her perfume teased his nose. Fresh, light, seductive. The roses entwined amongst her glossy curls were the exact shade of pink as her lips.

"Miss Farnsworth, finding you in attendance this evening is such a lovely, yet most welcome, surprise."

A loud snort announced Harcourt's presence. "*Wholly* unexpected surprise, I'm sure."

"Forgive me, dear cuz." He'd sidled near Flynn, and bowed to his cousin. "Luxmoore, boor that he is, pestered me incessantly at White's today until I told him where you'd be tonight."

Her lips curved, and she blushed prettily. "Is that the truth of it, my lord?" A hint of flirtation laced her question.

Harcourt veered his attention to the trio approaching on his right. "Ah, Sethwick and Faulkenhurst, you were at White's with Yancy. Wasn't Luxmoore making a nuisance of himself? And didn't he leave the moment I divulged my cousin's intentions for the evening?"

"Lord and Lady Sethwick, Mr. Faulkenhurst, it's wonderful to see you again." Miss Farnsworth executed another graceful curtsy

"Miss Farnsworth." Yvette, Viscountess Sethwick, smiled at Lydia before leveling Flynn with a knowing look. Lady Sethwick's sapphire eyes twinkled, and her lips twitched with suppressed mirth.

"Indeed, he seemed determined to know your whereabouts tonight." Chancey Faulkenhurst half-bowed, keeping his left hand partially tucked inside his coat. Recently returned from India, he'd lost two fingers and the partial use of his arm in the Third Anglo-Maratha War.

Sethwick winked conspiratorially at Harcourt. "It's true. Luxmoore was most persistent, and he did beat a hasty retreat. As a matter of fact," Sethwick shifted toward Flynn, "you left before your father arrived. As I climbed into my curricle, I glimpsed the marquis stepping from his carriage. Were you aware he was in London?"

At the mention of his father, a stab of unease gripped Flynn. Nevertheless, he chuckled good-naturedly, not at all abashed by their teasing. Despite their needling, Sethwick and Harcourt, two of his closest cohorts, had expressed their pleasure at his interest in Miss Farnsworth.

"Guilty, as accused. I simply had to know whose home the fair Miss Farnsworth would grace this evening. And I'm delighted Father is in Town, though I didn't know of his arrival until now."

What business had Father in London?

Had Mother traveled with him?

Why hadn't he sought Flynn upon his arrival?

Mayhap, he had.

Flynn had given his butler leave to visit his ailing, elderly mother. No doubt, an inexperienced footman or parlor maid answered the door when Father called and forgot to inform Flynn upon his return to the house this afternoon.

He glanced at Miss Farnsworth to find her raptly staring at him. He smiled and let his gaze linger on her lips a trifle longer than acceptable.

A charming flush once again pinkened her cheeks.

Still, Father's visit to White's disconcerted him. His father had sworn off drinking, gambling, and the London Season seventeen years ago—after the accident that crippled Francesca, Flynn's younger sister.

The marquis hadn't ventured to Town in as long either. Although a good distance from London, he and Mother were content at Lambridge Manse.

The Duke of Waterford owned a country estate adjacent to Lambridge. To Flynn's knowledge, the cantankerous duke never called upon Mother or Father. Not since the accident, in any event. The last he'd heard, Waterford contemplated selling Wingfield Court. He might've already done so by now.

Worry niggled, but Flynn quashed it. Nothing could be done tonight. He'd call on Father tomorrow, and if Mother was in London as well, ask her to host an intimate dinner party.

This presented the perfect opportunity to introduce Miss Farnsworth to his parents. With scant few weeks left in the Season, he'd best move quickly if he wanted a wedding date set before she returned to Scotland. If he had his way, she wouldn't be returning at all, except to visit. Instead, they'd be enjoying an extended honeymoon on the continent.

Perhaps, fate had orchestrated Father's return to London on the cusp of Flynn deciding Miss Farnsworth would make an exquisite countess. He turned his attention to the delectable woman before him. "I'd be honored to introduce you to my parents."

"I'd wager you would." Harcourt waggled his eyebrows and boldly elbowed Faulkenhurst in the ribs.

Miss Farnsworth blushed enchantingly, giving Flynn another, somewhat shyer smile. "It is I who would be honored, my lord."

"Gentlemen, for shame." Lady Sethwick waved her closed fan at them. "The poor dear's coloring under your infantile banter."

The Viscountess linked her elbow with Miss Farnsworth's and began to lead her away. "Were you aware Flynn and my husband are distant cousins?"

"No, Lord Luxmoore hasn't mentioned it." Miss Farnsworth swept a sideways glance toward Flynn. "Does he have Scots blood in his veins too?"

If the sparkle in her eyes was any indication, the notion delighted her.

"Yes, I believe the connection is on his mother's side." Lady Sethwick gave her husband a warm, promise-filled smile.

"I'm quite parched. Let's make our way to those chairs along the wall." She motioned at the row of chairs neatly lined against a jonquil papered wall. "I'm sure we can persuade one of the gentlemen to signal a footman for us. Some ratafia would be just the thing, don't you think?"

"Hold there, Lady Sethwick." Flynn disregarded Harcourt's raised brow and Sethwick's good-natured grin. "I intended to ask Miss Farnsworth for the next waltz."

"Oh, and he must," Miss Farnsworth blurted. Nibbling her lower lip, she slanted a nervous glance around the room. "I've been rather ill-behaved, I'm ashamed to admit."

She subtly gestured at the young bloods clustered like disgruntled Bantam roosters where she'd left them. Holding her open fan before her face, she whispered, "I made my excuses to the other gentlemen, telling them Lord Luxmoore had claimed my hand for the next dance. A complete taradiddle, I confess, but if he doesn't dance with me, my reputation—"

"We cannot have the lady's reputation tainted, can we?" Flynn advanced and deftly placed Miss Farnsworth's dainty hand on his arm. "A true gentleman would never permit such a thing to occur. He does everything within his power to preserve her good standing."

Lady Sethwick raised winged brows in amusement at his inane drivel.

He winked at Miss Farnsworth before issuing Harcourt a mocking challenge. "Does he not, Your Grace?"

"Indeed," Harcourt drawled, sardonic-humor crinkling the edges of his eyes. "Doing it up brown, isn't he, Falcon?"

Chuckling, Faulkenhurst nodded. "Thick enough to shovel, I'd say."

Flynn smiled at Miss Farnsworth, noting the green flecks in her irises and her softly parted lips, begging for his kiss.

"There's nothing for it. Honor demands it. We must share this dance." He escorted her onto the dance floor as the first violin strains announced the start of the waltz. The floor filled with other couples, and Flynn grasped Miss Farnsworth's hand, placing his palm upon her slender waist.

Her head scarcely reached his shoulder.

What a petite darling.

"That was forward of me, wasn't it?" She smiled, a trifle anxious. Her troubled gaze dipped to his neckcloth, and a faint hint of pink grazed her ivory cheeks. "And terribly rude, as well."

She did color rather a lot. No doubt due to her youth and inexperience. How old was she? He would ask Harcourt tomorrow, not that Flynn considered himself too advanced for her. He hadn't yet seen his eight and twentieth birthday.

Miss Farnsworth timidly met his eyes once more. "I don't know what possessed me."

She swept the ballroom a tentative glance, as if expecting a vexed peeress to swoop down upon her at any moment.

Flynn bent his head near her ear. Her perfume flooded his sense, and he breathed in her essence, whispering, "I shan't tell, if you don't."

"Oh," She trembled and missed a step.

He dared to draw her the minutest degree closer, but she didn't protest. The music ended, and he reluctantly turned her toward the chairs edging one side of the ballroom.

He came to a sudden stop upon spying a grim-faced Yancy, the Earl of Ramsbury, striding purposefully across the sanded floor. Sethwick, Faulkenhurst, and Harcourt— equally severe expressions on their countenances—accompanied him. All headed in Flynn's direction.

A concert of curious gazes, accompanied by murmurs and whispers, followed the quartet approaching him.

This didn't bode well.

Lady Sethwick whooshed in from behind him. Tears shimmering in her blue eyes, she hustled Miss Farnsworth from his side. "Come, my dear. Lord Luxmoore needs a moment."

Miss Farnsworth peeked over her shoulder, her forehead furrowed in worry as Lady Sethwick maneuvered her through the throng.

Flynn curved his mouth into a reassuring smile. He'd find her in a few minutes.

She half-smiled, cocking her head to listen to something Lady Sethwick said as the viscountess guided her away by the elbow.

"Luxmoore, I need to speak with you," Yancy said, his voice low and hoarse. "Wimpleton has made his study available if you'd be so good as to accompany us."

Flynn searched the strained faces of his friends. An alarm ticked along his nerves, and his gut wrenched sickeningly. He inclined his head and headed toward the ballroom's entrance.

Premonition, reminiscent of the day Franny had been crippled, engulfed him.

4

Flynn stared blindly at the crackling fire blazing in Wimpleton's study.

How had he come to be here? His mind was a muddled mess. Thoughts spiraled around and around, bouncing off his skull. His head throbbed, and he rubbed his forehead, trying to curb the pounding in order to gather a coherent thought.

Father is dead.

Sethwick sank into the chair beside Flynn's. The viscount stretched his legs before him and raised a half-full glass of whisky to his mouth. The flames reflected off the crystal, covering Sethwick's fingers with miniature rainbows.

"Brandy or something stiffer, Luxmoore?" Yancy waited beside the liquor cabinet, holding a glass in one hand and a carafe of umber-colored liquid in the other.

Harcourt, like Sethwick, already nursed a drink. He stood to one side of the mantel, staring morosely at the cavorting flames. Every now and again, he shot Flynn a worried glance.

Faulkenhurst sat silently in the shadows near an overflowing bookcase beside the fireplace. His dark gaze, brimming with concern, never left Flynn.

"Luxmoore, a dram might do you good," Faulkenhurst softly prompted.

A dram? Hardly. Flynn wanted an entire damn bottle, perhaps two, of hardy, aged Scots whisky. He could drink himself into oblivion and stop imagining the horror of his father's final moments.

The last time Flynn had seen him, Father had, once again, teased him good-naturedly about grandchildren.

"I'm not getting any younger, my boy." He had slapped Flynn on the shoulder. "I'd like to live long enough to take my grandsons hunting and fishing and spoil my granddaughters with baubles and trinkets."

Yes, Flynn wanted a bloody stiff drink. Instead, he shook his head. "No, not now."

Not later, either.

He needed a clear mind. Attempting to absorb the shocking news imparted moments before had befuddled him enough.

Drink was something he refused to use as an escape. Too many years of watching his sire and grandfather take that route effectively squelched any tendencies Flynn might have to engage in overindulgence. When he did imbibe in anything stronger than ale, he limited himself to one glass.

No exceptions.

For the past three generations, the Marquises of Bretheridge had reputations as sots. Tipplers. Drunkards. *That* notoriety ended with him.

Yancy replaced the tumbler but brought the carafe to the sofa situated opposite the leather wingback chairs Flynn and Sethwick occupied. Once he'd placed the crystal bottle on the table between the men, the earl eased onto the couch. The leather creaked in soft protest as Yancy crossed his legs and slung one arm atop the sofa's low back.

Flynn closed his eyes, resting his head against the chair's padding. "I wish I knew whether Mother is in Town."

"She's not," Yancy said.

Flynn opened one eye. "How do you know?"

Yancy tossed his drink back. His gaze flashed to Sethwick's for a brief moment.

"I made inquiries after…" He paused, and a pained expression flitted across his face, tightening his mouth. He rubbed between his eyes with two fingertips.

Flynn swallowed and permitted his eyelids to drift closed, hiding the moisture pooling behind them. "Thank you," he managed through the emotion, closing his throat.

Should he leave for Lambridge tonight? Or would the morrow be better? It would give Mother, Grandmamma, and Franny another day without heartache. Father's solicitor must be consulted as well.

Before or after Flynn traveled to Lambridge?

Before, since he wouldn't leave his family after breaking the ghastly news to them. Not that he intended to tell the women the truth of it.

No doubt, an inquiry of some sort would be required.

Where was Father's body?

Lord, he felt as if his head would explode from all the thoughts ricocheting inside.

He pinched the bridge of his nose. Managing the gossip would be a colossal undertaking. The scandalmongers would have fodder enough to last them until next Season and beyond if the truth leaked out.

"Why? Why did Father come to London? Why did he go to White's after all this time? Blister it! What the hell happened?" Flynn slumped forward, his elbows on his knees. "Yancy, you were there. Did you see or hear anything?"

Harcourt shifted his steely stare to Yancy.

Sethwick, too, settled his troubled gaze upon the earl.

Flynn turned to observe Faulkehurst.

His brows were drawn into a sharp vee.

What did they know?

"Well?" Flynn drummed his fingertips together.

Yancy poured a generous dram of whisky into his glass. After taking a healthy quaff, he slowly nodded his head.

"Luxmoore…Flynn?" His face grim, Yancy sighed, his chest deflating. He set his glass aside, and mouth pulled into a severe line, raked a hand through his hair.

What was it he feared saying?

Father was dead. *Dead.* How much worse could things become?

"Your father went to White's searching for you. He encountered Waterford there, and the duke persuaded the marquis to join him for a meal and a drink. 'For old time's sake,' his grace claimed. At first, Bretheridge declined, saying he had pressing news for you."

Yancy hesitated. "He appeared done in, Luxmoore."

"Aye, he did," Harcourt concurred. "I barely glimpsed him as Faulkenhurst, and I left, but the marquis looked exhausted. Or ill."

Ill? Flynn scowled at the cheerful flames. Had his father been ailing? He'd had no word of failing health from either parent.

"What's this about Waterford? Father hasn't spoken to him in seventeen years." Realization slammed into him with the intensity of a frenzied bull. Flynn's attention leaped to Yancy. "*A drink?* My God, Father wouldn't have been that stupid. He hasn't touched a drop of alcohol since—"

"I'm afraid it grows worse." Yancy hung his head for a moment then raised his gaze to meet Flynn's.

The remorse there took Flynn aback. He narrowed his eyes and through tight lips said, "I presume you're going to explain how?"

Father shot himself. It couldn't possibly become worse.

Flynn wanted to smash something, and at this moment, the urge to plant Yancy a facer overwhelmed. He knew Father's history with Waterford—his long-time drinking chum. *Damn the duke to the seventh layer of hell*. Yancy also knew why Franny would never walk again.

Waterford and Father had spent an afternoon practically drinking themselves under the table at White's. On his way home, Father had come upon Nurse taking the air with Franny. She was six at the time and had begged their father to take her on the saddle before him. Despite Nurse's vehement protests, Father had hauled Franny onto his lap.

True, it wasn't his sire's fault three dogs had come tearing along the path, chasing a terrified cat, at that precise moment. Nevertheless, had he not been ape-drunk, Caesar wouldn't have bolted when the yowling cat ran beneath him. Father would've remained in his saddle, sparing Franny the tumble that broke her back.

"Waterford plied the marquis with drink." Yancy's tired voice yanked Flynn to the present.

"He challenged your father to a game of piquet. I joined them, hoping to talk some sense into the marquis," Yancy explained. "He'd been dipping rather deep and was far in his cups by then. A sizable sum was at stake, and Bretheridge was well into it."

Flynn's mind raced. Most of his monies were invested in his Caribbean sugar plantations, though he did have several thousand pounds on deposit in Ringwood and Hampshire's Bank. "Sizeable? How much?"

Yancy hesitated, looking rather sick himself. "In excess of one hundred thousand pounds."

Harcourt whistled, and Sethwick slapped his hand on his thigh with a muttered, "*Merde*."

"Holy hell, and you were a part of that?" Flynn glared daggers at Yancy. Yes, he absolutely did want to pummel the earl. And Waterford. And anyone else who'd been present, yet made no effort to intervene. How many more men's lives would be destroyed after being seduced into wagering away their very existence?

By God, he could count seven in the past year alone.

Now eight.

"No." Yancy raked a hand through his hair. "I didn't play. You know piquet is between two players. I did insist the marquis was foxed. I told Waterford it appeared your father was also ill, and that it was beyond the pale for the duke to continue to play."

Waterford would seize such an advantage, the scurrilous blackguard.

Yancy took a short swallow of whisky. "Though, at that point, your father was ahead."

Flynn scrubbed a hand across his gritty eyes. "I don't understand."

"Your father refused to toss in his cards, Luxmoore. He thought winning might help temper the news he had for you. He was positive he'd beaten the duke." Yancy heaved a gusty sigh. "In fact, I was certain he had too. But Waterford, the devil take it, suddenly began scoring points. A lot of them too. Almost as if he held enchanted cards."

"And you watched this transpire?" Flynn pressed two fingers to his thrumming forehead. "And did nothing? *Nothing*?"

"What was *I* supposed to do?" Yancy lurched to his feet and jerked his hand toward the door. "Grab Bretheridge by the ear and haul him from the place like a lad in short pants instead of a grown man? For God's sake, Luxmoore, be reasonable!"

"Precisely, how much did he lose?" Flynn clenched his hands until his nails cut into his palms. He could sell the horseflesh and prize cattle, and if he must, some of the unentailed properties. There was a small fortune in silver, art, and jewels, too.

"It's not only how much, Luxmoore, but what." Yancy swung a desperate, pleading glance at Sethwick and Harcourt.

Dual scowls marred their foreheads.

What had Yancy told them that he'd yet to reveal to Flynn? An odd foreboding filled him, yet he remained curiously calm.

Something had been set in motion tonight. Something he'd no control over, but nevertheless, would thrust him, tumbling and churning like wintertime rapids, along an unknown, predestined path. All he could do was hold on and pray he would emerge, if not unscathed, at least, somewhat intact.

Flynn stood, unable to sit an instant longer. He crossed to stare out the French windows facing the street. The guests were leaving.

Had Miss Farnsworth departed already?

The delectable Miss Lydia Farnsworth. The woman he wanted to make his wife.

He quirked mouth at the irony. He wouldn't be entering into a betrothal anytime soon now. He was in mourning.

"Well? What else did he wager?" he tossed over his shoulder, flinching at the bitterness in his voice.

"Everything not entailed, Luxmoore. *Everything.* Including the spittoons and chamber pots." Yancy flopped onto the sofa and buried his face in his hands. He was silent for several painful moments.

His eyes brimmed with sorrow when he lifted his head and drew in a ragged breath. "When your father, at last, comprehended what he'd done, he called for his carriage then signed the vowel. Despite his drunken state, he courteously bid Waterford a good evening and after bowing, took his leave. I confronted the duke and insisted he cancel the wager."

With his fingertips, Flynn brushed the smooth velvet of the deep charcoal-colored drapes festooning the window. "Which, naturally, he refused to do."

Waterford would, the greedy sod.

Yancy slammed his fist on the sofa's arm. "The bloody cur tucked the vowel into his pocket. He had the unmitigated gall to say, 'You know Bretheridge's honor won't permit me to. A man has nothing if he doesn't have his honor.'"

"What a load of fustian rubbish, coming from his ilk," Sethwick rasped, his voice scarcely more than a growl.

Fustain rubbish? It was bullshit.

Harcourt had wandered to stand before the study's double doors as if guarding against unwelcome intruders.

Yancy pressed his fingers to his eyes. "The shot sounded moments after your father left White's. He was inside his carriage."

Father never traveled unarmed.

Flynn stared blankly at Yancy. What did one say after that?

Fury like none Flynn had ever known before surged through his veins, heating his blood, scorching his mind.

Blistering rage, that's what this feeling is.

It was illogical and unfair and unlike him, but he did blame Yancy. Yes, the earl should've hauled Father out by his ear, accursed wagers be hanged.

Sethwick unfolded his tall frame from his chair. The thick Turkish carpet muffled his steps as he approached. Compassion and regret in his eyes, he stood before Flynn. He touched Flynn's forearm.

"Luxmoore." Sethwick cast a glance toward Yancy, staring glumly at the fire's dying embers. "Your father came to London to tell you that your mother suffered apoplexy."

5

Cheshire, England
Late June 1818

Huddled over a porcelain chamber pot, Angelina pushed a damp curl off her forehead and waited for the wave of nausea to pass. She held her breath in hopeful anticipation. Her stomach seemed to be settling. Finally.

Another strand of hair slid forward, dangling near her nose. Bothersome hair. Why couldn't she have Mama or the twins' smooth tresses?

Murphy, the maid Aunt Camille assigned to Angelina, clucked and fussed, no condemnation in her round, brown eyes. Steadying her, Murphy pressed a cool, damp cloth into Angelina's hand.

"Here, Mrs. Thorne, wipe your face. You'll feel much better."

Mrs. Thorne?

Angelina still hadn't become accustomed to the name Uncle Ambrose had invented.

"Thank you," she managed, swallowing against the bile burning her throat. How many more weeks did she have to endure this? Shouldn't her morning malaise be finished by now?

She didn't have the wherewithal to be embarrassed any longer. The entire household realized she was increasing, although they thought her newly widowed. Their constant pitying glances and efforts to ease her discomfort, while endearing, were wholly discomfiting.

Angelina lived a colossal lie. The truth would out in a matter of time.

Unmarried and with child. Just the one time and...

The pain of betrayal lanced sharply, almost doubling her over. She squeezed her eyes shut and gritted her teeth against the onslaught.

Curse you, Charles—Pierre.

He asked her to wait for him and said he'd come for her. What, and bring his wife along for companionship? He should be horsewhipped. But she bore guilt too. Guilt for being too blasted trusting.

Stupid, green girl.

"Please sit before you swoon," Murphy urged, leading her to an armchair. "You're white as me da's prize sow."

Angelina's lips twitched as she smoothed her palms over her nearly flat stomach. She would be the size of a sow in a few short months. At present, only the slightest bump hinted at her condition. The mound wasn't noticeable beneath her nightdress or her black empire gowns.

Once she'd gratefully sank into the overstuffed chair, she tucked her bare feet beneath her bottom. The balcony door stood open, allowing the fresh morning air to cool the chamber. It wouldn't stay cool for long.

A curious pigeon stood beyond the threshold, cocking its dappled head back and forth. The bird peered into the chamber with black button eyes. Every now and again, it cooed softly. The breeze ruffling the lace panels shading the beveled windows carried the scents of honeysuckle and jasmine into the chamber.

If today proved anything like the past two weeks, this afternoon would be sweltering. Nature seemed to be making up for last year's complete lack of summer with unusual warmth this year.

After hearing Aunt Camille's complaints about the trials of a late summer delivery, Angelina thanked God her babe wouldn't make an appearance until sometime near Christmastide.

The same time of year I met—

No, she wouldn't think of *him*. That was another rule to add to her list.

No wasting thoughts on worthless deceivers.

She purposefully redirected her attention to a more pleasing subject. She enjoyed becoming acquainted with her cousins: Pembrose, two months her junior, and Felicia, a charming minx of eleven. Aunt Camille had relinquished hope of having more children and doted on Felicia.

Closing her eyes, Angelina propped her head against the back of the chair. She found the English countryside to be utterly delightful and yearned to walk the shady path visible from the balcony. It led to a stream burbling beside an unkempt orchard. The water begged her to come and wade in its refreshing depths.

She and her sisters had often walked in the shallow creek meandering through Endicott Hall's five acres. She could be found barefoot inside the house most of the time, too, except when visitors came to call. She didn't like shoes much. It drove Mama to near distraction, particularly since Angelina was forever misplacing her slippers.

However, Aunt Camille didn't want Angelina engaging in such vigorous physical activity in her delicate condition, so the stream and path were forbidden.

Pshaw. What twaddle.

Opening her eyes, Angelina surveyed the well-appointed room. The bedchamber, in pale shades of blue and green with a hint of peach, was the epitome of femininity. Several canvases and painted plates adorned the walls. Each porcelain portrayed kittens engaged in some form of mischief or other.

Aunt Camille had a distinct penchant for cats. She owned three immensely pampered, flat-faced, oversized white beasts. The trio spent their days lounging in the sun or draped upon whatever piece of furniture had taken their current fancy.

They occasionally visited her, making themselves comfortable in her favorite spot as well; a corner holding a cozy niche. She spent hours nestled in the window seat there, stitching and embroidering garments and blankets for the babe.

Oh, how she hoped—*prayed*—she carried a girl.

Not that she wouldn't adore a son. But for a boy to be raised without a father's influence seemed unjust. And having had no brothers, or a father interested in anything but his books and prayers, she wasn't altogether certain what a boy required outside of a decent education and a mother's love.

But a daughter, God willing, she could do well by even if the infant's father was an unconscionable pig.

"Drink this, Mrs. Thorne. It will ease your queasiness." Murphy offered a steaming cup of tea. "Would you care for some dry toast?"

Angelina shook her head. "Just tea, thank you."

She raised the cup and sniffed the fragrant mint brew. "Murphy, I do wish it were acceptable for you to call me Angelina or Lina. I cannot bear being called Mrs. Thorne."

That was true enough. Each time she heard the false name, it grated along her already fragile nerves, taunting her with the lie she portrayed.

"Oh, no, I couldn't possibly." Murphy ducked her head. Alarm written on her plain face, she plucked at her starched apron. "His grace is most strict about such things. I'd lose my position for certain."

"Good heavens. Truly?" Relaxing against the chair, Angelina took a sip of tea. "I'm sorry I mentioned it then. We assuredly cannot have that."

This wasn't the first time she noticed the servants feared her uncle. What manner of man was the duke? Mama never talked much about him—come to think of it, at all. Her rare conversations about her relatives in England focused on her twin.

Except for the color of their hair, her mother and Aunt Camille were as different in appearance as roses and daisies. Aunt Camille boasted several inches on Mama, was more voluptuous, had brown eyes, and wavy hair. Mama's hair was straight, and she was petite with blue eyes.

Better add that business about foul-tempered men to her list of rules.

A man who causes fear should be avoided as a husband.

Not that she would ever find a husband now. Nor, truth to tell, did she want one, except for the baby's sake. Men were untrustworthy toads.

Once Angelina's condition had been discovered—and although only the first part of May and several weeks remained in the Season—Uncle Ambrose had hustled the family off to his country estate, Wingfield Court.

At her uncle's insistence, she promptly began wearing black. He remained in Town attending to business for a few more weeks and had joined the family a mere four days ago.

She felt certain he'd chosen to summer at his country house farthest from London because of her. Aunt Camille confessed Uncle Ambrose was exceedingly conscious of social standing and appearances. It wouldn't do to have the *ton* speculating about the recent arrival of a pregnant and husbandless niece. The gossipmongers might jump to all manner of conclusions.

Or hit upon the truth.

Angelina's face heated. Would she ever become accustomed to the shame? She must. Soon her condition would be apparent to others. The widow facade offered a degree of protection for her child, even if the ploy was a mammoth taradiddle.

At least here, unlike in Salem, she had some anonymity. The story Uncle had concocted explaining her missing spouse was quite believable, if somewhat simplistic.

Spencer Thorne, her husband of two weeks, died in a hunting accident. Overwrought and grieving, she departed Massachusetts and the tormenting memories America held for her.

That last portion was true enough, except Mrs. Pettigrove, the abrasive and intrusive chinwag Mama hired as Angelina's chaperone on the ship, knew she wasn't married.

Worse, Mrs. Pettigrove's sister was none other than Lady Clutterbuck, a notorious gossip, according to Aunt Camille. And unfortunately, one that traveled in the same social circles as the duke and duchess. Hence, the expedited departure from London less than a week after Angelina's arrival.

It wouldn't take long for the two windbags to put the pieces together, and when they did… *God, help me*. Her stomach churned once more, but the babe wasn't the cause this time.

Unfortunately, on the ship, she hadn't thought to lie when answering Mrs. Pettigrove's dozens of prying questions. Gads, the woman never stopped prattling or prying.

Yes, Angelina was related to nobility. Her grandfather had been the Scottish Earl of Tinsdale, and she journeyed to England for an extended visit with her aunt and uncle, the Duke and Duchess of Waterford.

No, she'd never been to England before, nor did she speak French. Yes, she played the harpsichord, not the harp, and was fond of treacle scones. No, she didn't think pickled eggs or herring were delicious.

No, she'd never been married.

No. She most certainly was not in the market for a husband.

Those last snippets would be Angelina's undoing should they become known. She took another sip of the tea, welcoming the soothing warmth that calmed her roiling stomach.

She should've told the intrusive fussock she was married to an Arabian sheik and shared a harem with fifteen other wives and three dozen concubines. Oh, and when Jazib had guests, she danced half-naked, wearing nothing other than a *bedlah* for their entertainment.

It would've been worth the scandal to see the expression on Mrs. Pettigrove's face. Possibly, it would've silenced her for a blessed moment or two as well.

Thank God they hadn't shared a cabin, or else Angelina would've been hard-pressed not to shove the woman overboard. Though, given the matron's girth, it would've been a substantial feat. She probably would've bobbed alongside the ship the entire Atlantic crossing, caterwauling and complaining about the unsatisfactory, damp accommodations.

The weather grew rougher as strong winds pushed the vessel onward ahead of schedule. Nausea had plagued Angelina, but other passengers were confined to their cabins suffering the same malady. Having never sailed before, she assumed she suffered from seasickness. She was almost grateful. Her infirmity meant she avoided Mrs. Pettigrove's tiresome company.

Until Angelina arrived at her aunt and uncle's and continued to be wretchedly ill, she didn't suspect something more was afoot. A discreet examination by the Waterford's personal physician confirmed her pregnancy.

She had no more tears to weep when dear Aunt Camille, smelling of lilies, rather than gardenias like Mama, took Angelina in her arms.

Her aunt patted her shoulders, and in her soft, almost undetectable brogue, said, "None of this is your fault. Love blinds us until it's too late, and we cannot remedy the choices we've made. There's naught to do but press on, chin raised, and shoulders squared, and make the best of it, my dear."

A wistful tone had leeched into her voice as she attempted to console Angelina. Nonetheless, she wasn't the least bit reassured.

She couldn't remain with her aunt and uncle indefinitely. She refused to hang on someone else's sleeve and be supported as a poor relation. Neither could she return home with the tale of a deceased husband. Heavens, Charles might very well be gallivanting around Salem or Boston even now.

If he'd returned to Salem as he'd vowed he would, her mother and the twins would be disgraced. It wasn't fair that they should suffer for her ill-conceived choices and Charles's treachery.

A myriad of women before her had borne a child outside of wedlock and still made something of their lives. She could too. But how?

There weren't many alternatives for unmarried women without means. The respectable options included milliner, modiste, companion, or governess. The others: mistress, demimonde, or courtesan—whatever one wished to call them—all equated selling oneself.

That, she would never do.

She could eliminate employment as a companion or governess, because no one would hire her with a newborn babe. A trade of some sort, then. Except, she possessed no real talent except sewing and tatting.

Eyes narrowed in consideration, she tapped her chin.

Perhaps, she could find a position as a seamstress or a lace-maker with a reputable modiste. Or better yet, open a cozy establishment herself.

Another thought intruded, and she grimaced. Uncle Ambrose and Aunt Camille would object. They'd already protested that gently-bred women didn't smell of the shop.

Setting the teacup aside, Angelina yawned before unfolding her legs from beneath her. Ah, that eased the tightness clenching her belly a trifle. She smoothed a hand over her stomach. When would she feel her precious child move within her?

She wasn't quite done up. She did have the modest inheritance from Grandmother Tinsdale and the bag of coins Charles had left behind. Her wedding gift from him—the pearl pendant, bracelet, and drop earrings—in addition to her wedding ring, would each bring a tidy sum. She twisted the ring that Uncle Ambrose insisted she still wear.

She was a fraud.

Angelina bore no qualms about selling the bitter reminder of Charles's perfidy. Especially if it meant supporting the babe he'd implanted in her. She could claim a rather good eye for fashion, and for pleasure, had designed several of Mama's and the twins' dresses.

Sighing, she placed a hand atop her stomach again, rubbing away the familiar pressure that plagued her several times a day.

What's to become of us, little one?

6

Sitting behind his father's desk in Lambridge Manse's study, Flynn suppressed a sigh. He shifted his attention from the ledger he'd been studying with his steward, Preston Fleming, since half-past seven this morning.

"You're sure there's nothing more?"

Flynn had no choice but to confide in Fleming and explain why everything of value must be inventoried. After his initial dismay, the steward tackled the task with his usual efficiency.

Fleming shook his head, sliding his spectacles to the bridge of his nose.

"No, my lord, nothing. I've listed the whole of it here at Lambridge." He pointed a spindly finger at the open ledger. "And the other properties as well. Right down to the salt and pepper shakers."

He waved at the stack of leather books piled on the desk. "Unless there's a buried treasure somewhere, we don't know about, that's everything."

And it wasn't enough.

That knowledge, like a millstone around Flynn's neck, weighed heavily on him.

"Thank you, Fleming. You've done exceptionally well, and I appreciate it. You may go."

The sympathy in his steward's eyes nearly undid him.

"I'll have your letter of reference penned by this afternoon. It is with deepest regret I must release you and cannot keep the other staff on past August."

Humiliation didn't cause the lump in Flynn's throat. Letting the servants go was akin to turning family out onto the street.

"My lord, the missus has been prattling at me to take down my shingle, as it were, for the last five years. So, I respectfully decline your offer, and instead, tender my resignation." Fleming withdrew a folded paper from his coat pocket and slid it across the desk. "And since I'm a man of leisure now, and my time is mine to do with as I wish, I'll carry on as before. With your permission, of course."

The steward's devotion rendered Flynn speechless. He swallowed against the sentiment clogging his throat. "Thank you, Fleming. I'm most grateful."

Fleming began buttoning his coat. He smiled wryly as he secured the last button. "We may want to keep this conversation to ourselves, my lord. I fear Mrs. Fleming mightn't understand."

Asleep on the sofa, Moll and Lasses, Flynn's King Charles spaniels, stirred. Moll raised her head and yawned. She rested her head on her paws, watching him with her soulful brown eyes. Lasses cracked a sleepy eye open, then snuggled into her sister's warm side and resumed her slumber.

Fleming gathered his hat and gloves. "Is there any other way I can assist you?"

Worry creased the aged steward's face. Trusted and loyal, Fleming had been Lambridge Manse's overseer for more than thirty years—three years longer than Flynn had been alive.

"No, you've been most thorough, and I appreciate your diligence." He stood and extended his hand.

Fleming hesitated a moment before gripping Flynn's palm in a firm handshake.

After releasing the steward's hand, Flynn gripped the back of his neck and rubbed tension-knotted muscles, trying to ease the tautness. "I suppose you could start by making inquiries about selling the assets."

"Very good, sir." Uncharacteristically anxious, Fleming shuffled his feet, fiddling with the brim of his hat. "My lord, if I may be so bold as to inquire, how does the marchioness fare?"

Flynn pulled his attention from the figure printed boldly at the bottom of the ledger's column. He smiled in genuine pleasure. "Mother is recovering remarkably well. Her speech is much improved."

A welcome shred of light to illuminate Flynn's otherwise gloomy existence. Ye gods, his life had fast become the makings of a bloody stage melodrama. What travesty would befall the Bretheridges next?

"Ah, that is good to hear. Mrs. Fleming will be well pleased. We've kept her ladyship in our prayers."

If only Fleming and his wife would join Flynn in praying for the miraculous means to meet the gaming debt owed to Waterford. "Thank you. Your prayers are most welcome, and I'll be sure to tell Mother you asked after her health."

After Fleming took his leave, Flynn settled into his father's chair. Unease enshrouded him as if he intruded in Father's private domain. How long would it take for the feeling to dissipate? Would it ever entirely?

The study exuded Father's presence from the lingering aroma of his fragrant pipe tobacco to the scent of the beeswax candles he preferred.

Flynn blinked and crimped his mouth against the momentary grief seizing him. The stag he shot as a boy of twelve peered from sightless eyes above the glass cabinet containing a valuable collection of snuff boxes.

Those, too, must be sold.

He shifted his attention to the packed gun cabinet. Most of them as well. And the carved ivory and jade collections displayed upon the shelves. The family heirlooms. Everything.

Moll jumped to the floor, and after a long stretch with her rump in the air, she pattered to Flynn. Rising onto her haunches, she rested her chin on his knee. Not to be outdone, Lasses trotted to him and did the same. Dogs had an uncanny way of knowing when something was amiss with their masters.

He scratched behind their ears. "What's to become of us, little ones?"

Glancing at the door, he half-expected Father to be standing there, the familiar merry twinkle in his eyes. Flynn swallowed the lump of emotion rising to his throat again.

He'd left for Lambridge at the break of dawn two mornings after the Wimpleton's ball. It took that long to meet with Father's man-of-affairs, speak to the authorities, close the house, and make the arrangements for the transference of his father's body.

He feared the worst when Sethwick told him of Mother's apoplexy. The entire journey to Lambridge, he'd been petrified he'd arrive and find she'd already passed.

Although impaired on her right side, Doctor Dawes was optimistic about her recovery.

"I don't expect the marchioness to ever return to her previous physical condition." Doctor Dawes scraped a beefy hand along his square jaw. "That's unrealistic given the severity of her illness. But with the appropriate therapy and around the clock care, she should improve in time."

He'd slapped Flynn on the shoulder. "I've heard of a successful new procedure in France—costly and lengthy, but highly effective. Let me write to my associate in London. He's referred several patients for the treatment. I'll bring you the details when I acquire them."

Evidently, Doctor Dawes hadn't heard of the financial setback—no, ruin—befalling the Bretheridges.

The truth would out soon enough.

Until then, Flynn would do everything he could to keep the calamitous news from his womenfolk.

If Mother and Franny didn't need him here, Flynn would be aboard the first available sailing ship to Trinidad and Tobago to sell his sugar plantations. At present, he didn't dare risk spending the funds on hiring an agent to make the trip and make the negotiations on his behalf.

Waterford could—*would*—call the wager due any day. Flynn had yet to speak with the duke. At least the boor had allowed Flynn that small reprieve—to deal with Father's death first.

He hadn't an iota of doubt the duke would demand payment. The debt wasn't enforceable under the law, but Flynn's honor mandated the obligation be paid. To fail to do so would lead to social ruin and shunning.

Elbows on the glossy desktop, Flynn buried his face in his hands.

He must find a way to keep his family in residence at Lambridge. And just as crucial, he must, at all costs, prevent them from discovering the truth regarding Father's death and his gaming away the lifestyle they'd always known.

"Flynn, dearest?"

Grandmamma.

He raised his head and offered a crooked smile as she puttered into the study.

Moll and Lasses rushed to sniff her skirts.

Stooped-shouldered, she scuffed across the floor, leaning on her cane, her black bombazine skirts crackling with her labored movements. Already petite, she had shriveled even more since burying her only son.

At once, Flynn rose and hurried to take her arm and assist her to a chair, neatly stepping around the excited dogs scurrying around their feet.

"Grandmamma, you've risen early today." He kissed her papery cheek.

She smelled of roses and lemon—had done so for as long as he could remember. She'd encouraged his love of botany and often made intelligent and useful suggestions regarding the new species of roses he created in the conservatory.

A senseless luxury. He couldn't justify spending time or funds on rose-breeding any longer.

After patting each dog on the head, and receiving welcoming licks in return, Grandmamma leaned back with a hearty sigh. The chair engulfed her fragile frame.

"I'm sorry, my dear boy, and I don't mean to intrude. But I couldn't help overhear your conversation with Mr. Fleming."

She shifted more firmly into the cushion. Her small feet didn't reach the floor.

Funny, Flynn had never noticed that before.

"I came to ask if Eunice might come for a few weeks," Grandmamma touched the mourning brooch at her throat. It held a lock of Father's hair. "She wrote and asked for an invitation. Your father's death has been difficult for her."

And you too, dear one.

Although she braved a smile, anguish glistened in her eyes.

Overcome, she'd collapsed when he told her of Father's death. Thank God, she'd only swooned. Given her delicate constitution and advanced age, Flynn had feared it more at the time.

He nodded, shooing the dogs away. "Of course, Aunt Eunice may come. Do extend an invitation and ask her to stay as long as she wishes."

Once his aged aunt settled in, Flynn would wager she'd stay on. Widowed and childless, Father's elder sister had hinted she'd like to reside at Lambridge Manse for quite some time.

"You're troubled." A statement of fact, not a question. Grandmamma peered at him expectantly. "And did I hear mention of selling assets?"

Her eyesight might be fading, her pretty blue-gray eyes slightly cloudy and unfocused, but his grandmother's hearing and her mind remained as sharp as ever. She wasn't going to let the issue with Fleming go.

Flynn fixed his focus on the carpet and crossed his Hessian-clad feet, rubbing his nape again. Egads, had rocks taken up residence there?

He'd never been able to lie to his grandmother. She detected his deceit and had taught him as a child to come clean and confess the truth rather than weave a web of lies.

You will be a marquis someday, Flynn, and you must sow honor. Put away falsehoods, and always speak the truth, my boy.

Flynn sighed and rested his hip upon the edge of his desk. "I'm obligated to sell some properties to meet an unexpected debt that has arisen."

"Ah, I see."

She cocked her silver-haired head to the side and studied him with intelligent eyes. She reminded him of an inquisitive mouse. Her gnarled hands gripped the engraved cane's top, and she leaned forward a jot.

What did she actually see?

The lines of fatigue and worry lining his face? The despair and concern that no doubt showed in his eyes? Or that he kept something from her? She had enough on her frail shoulders without fretting about him.

He forced his lips into a semblance of a smile. "All will be well, Grandmamma, I promise you." He bent and lifted a blue-veined hand. Kissing the back of it, he gave her fingers a gentle squeeze. "We have each other: you, Mother, Franny, and me. And soon, Aunt Eunice will join us. That's what matters at present."

Her eyes misted. "Yes, I take great comfort in knowing that."

Although, if he didn't find a way to extricate himself from the yoke he'd been pressed into, their circumstances would dive south faster than a bird after an insect. They might find themselves stacked atop one another like biscuits in a tin, living in his decrepit hunting cottage a stone's toss on the other side of Scotland's border.

How could he deign to move a woman two and eighty, an invalid, and a cripple to a four-room hovel?

7

Moll and Lasses pushed their snouts between his hand and Grandmamma's.

She chuckled, rubbing their silky heads. "The girls feel ignored, don't you, darlings? Naturally, he meant to include you."

"I beg your pardon, my lord." Chatterton entered the study holding a silver salver. A white calling card stood out starkly upon it. "His Grace, the Duke of Waterford, wishes to know if you are at home."

Flynn's gut plummeted to his booted feet. The time for reckoning was at hand.

It's too damn soon. I need more time.

And a plan. He needed a bloody plan.

Clamping his teeth together until a muscle jumped in his jaw, he prayed for strength. There was nothing for it. He must receive the duke. Flynn couldn't very well say he wasn't at home with Grandmamma eyeing him.

"How nice." She turned toward the door. "I've not seen Waterford in a good number of years. I've missed his eloquent company."

By deliberate design, Grandmamma. Trust me, dear lady. He is far from eloquent these days.

"Chatterton, please show him to the study." Flynn would be hung before he'd order tea or refreshments for the sot.

Calling this early was outside the bounds. He didn't want Waterford feeling welcome or lingering a second longer than necessary. Had Grandmamma not been present and sure to ask questions he wasn't prepared to answer, he would've asked Chatterton to claim Flynn wasn't receiving visitors.

And never would be when that vulture came calling.

"At once, my lord." Dipping his head, Chatterton slipped from the room as silently as he arrived.

"Grandmamma, the duke and I have business to discuss, which I'm sure you'd find tiresome." Flynn reached for her hand.

She chuckled again.

"Trying to be rid of me, are you, my boy?" Placing her hand in his, she struggled to stand. "Very well. I'll greet him on my way out."

Flynn reached to grasp her elbow and help her from the room.

She waved his hand away. "Go on with you. When you have a moment, your mother and sister want a word."

He arched a brow. His mother and sister were awake this early as well?

"Don't look at me like that." Humor danced in her eyes. "Like you, we have much on our minds. Now, give me a kiss." She pointed to her cheek. "And I'll be on my way."

After placing a dutiful peck on her wrinkled face, he sought the chair behind the mammoth desk. Better to put something between the duke and him. Flynn wasn't certain he could keep from popping Waterford on the nose.

Or calling the duke out.

A notion he'd seriously entertained until common sense prevailed—more like planted him a facer. He couldn't risk an injury. Not with so many others dependent on him.

Waterford was a dab hand at pistols, although Flynn's sword skills exceeded the duke's. That the duke had never handled a blade well was common enough knowledge. However, Flynn didn't doubt Waterford's weapon of choice would be pistols.

As unconscionable as the churl was, he wouldn't hesitate to call in the gaming debt if Flynn was wounded or killed.

Where would that leave his family?

Destitute.

No, better to keep a tight rein on his temper and tongue. Something he'd found deucedly thorny to do of late. Truth be known, something he struggled with for the first time in his life. His anger lashed against good sense at present.

He didn't possess a foul temper, finding life more enjoyable as a pleasant, amiable chap. Those days were forever behind him—*curse Waterford's black heart*.

And blast Father for choosing the coward's way.

Moments after Grandmamma scuffed from the room, Flynn heard her offer the duke a congenial greeting. If she knew the truth, she would soundly whack the bounder on his nob with her cane. And then kick him in the bum when he hit the floor.

The image brought a faint arc to his mouth.

"Your Grace." Chatterton indicated the duke should enter. "Shall I request a tray from Mrs. Plum?"

Flynn closed Lambridge's ledger then with precise movements, stacked the record atop the others. "No, his grace won't be staying long."

"Very good, my lord." With what could only be described as a glower of contempt directed at the back of Waterford's head, Chatterton backed out, not quite closing the double doors behind him.

Ah, so the staff was aware of the change in Flynn's circumstances.

No surprise there. It would've been easier to drain the River Thames than hide the truth from the servants. Almost as protective of the women as he, his loyal retainers wouldn't breathe a word to Mother or the others. He could wager on it, and that would be a bet he'd win.

Since coming into his majority and becoming a regular attendee at *haut ton* assemblies, Flynn couldn't recall speaking more than a handful of words to the duke. The man's unmatched arrogance and condescending mien were off-putting. Flynn shifted his attention to Waterford and took his measure.

Thinning auburn hair topped the duke's head, and he'd developed a distinct paunch. Excess drink tended to do that. Bags cradled his watery, bloodshot eyes, and fine red veins laced his bulbous nose. It proved difficult to identify him as the handsome man once Father's closest friend.

Had his father ever told Waterford why he severed his friendship? The duke must have an inkling. News of Franny's tragedy had circulated amongst the upper salons.

Confidence in his step, Waterford strode into the study. The cocksure set of his head and shoulders suggested he thought he had Flynn at a disadvantage.

And he bloody well did. God rot the pompous cull.

Moll and Lasses, their hackles raised, circled the duke, sniffing the air and growling low in their throats.

Waterford froze and eyed the spaniels, his dislike tangible. He raised his foot as if to deliver a kick. "Call off your dogs."

"If you value your legs, I wouldn't do that." Flynn flicked a wrist to the study entrance, where a good-sized Dalmatian stood issuing a throaty growl.

Waterford uttered a filthy oath. "Call them off!"

"Lie down." Flynn pointed to the sofa.

Tails between their legs, Moll and Lasses skulked to the couch. Their distrustful scrutiny never left Waterford, and intermittent rumbles echoed in their chests.

Smart creatures.

He would love to let them have a go at the duke, but Waterford proved so foul, they'd likely collapse and die after the first nip.

Having waited to rise until the duke stood directly before the desk, Flynn strode to the entrance and nudged Sir Freckleton—Franny's choice of a name for the Dalmatian—out the door.

"A mite early for a social call, Waterford."

"We both know it's nothing of the sort."

The duke settled himself into a chair. Crossing his legs at the knee, he drummed a beringed hand on the time-worn arm. "Aren't you going to offer me a drink, Luxmoore? I could do with a dram or two of that fine Scotch your father always kept on hand."

"I'm the Marquis of Bretheridge now, as you well know, and I don't condone spirits before noon." Flynn resumed his seat and folded his fingers atop the desk, lest he wrap them around the duke's neck. "Besides, other than for medicinal purposes, there is no alcohol in the house."

"Pity." Waterford reached inside his moss-green coat and withdrew a piece of neatly folded paper. He placed it on the desk, edging the vowel toward Flynn. "I'm sure you know what this is."

Flynn flicked a disinterested glance at the marker. "Indeed."

"I've come to discuss the terms of collection." The duke tensely eyed the dogs. "Could you have those beasts removed?"

They lifted their heads and growled in unison.

On pain of death.

If the spaniels' presence gave Flynn the slightest advantage against the smug pissant lounging across from him, he'd seize it. "I'm in a position to pay a portion of the debt. I shall need additional time to acquire—"

"Don't waste your breath. I know you cannot possibly pay the blunt." The duke waved his hand dismissively, and a triumphant glint entered his eyes. "Besides, that's the least of it. There are properties and other assets to discuss."

With his greedy green-eyed stare and bloated belly, he reminded Flynn of a giant, gloating toad.

"My father's been dead mere weeks. It has taken that long to determine his effects as well as what's entailed."

The dogs growled again. Seldom had the pair showed this degree of hostility.

Taking a calming breath, Flynn narrowed his eyes and brushed his fingers along a ledger's edge. "You may not be aware, but Mother's recovering from apoplexy. I've kept the details of Father's wager and his death from her. I'll not have her, my grandmother, or my sister further traumatized."

The wrath thrumming through his blood made maintaining his composure a monumental feat. He now understood why some men were driven to murder.

The duke's lips pursed. "I suppose you contrived some drivel about a robbery or something equally unimaginative to explain his death."

In fact, Flynn had. He pressed into his chair, the urge to hurdle the desk and pummel Waterford so intense, it staggered him. He'd never considered himself a violent man. That had changed when Father put a pistol to his head and pulled the trigger.

Nevertheless, he forced a calm facade. "You were my father's closest confidant for two decades. Though it may come as a surprise, he continued to hold you in high regard, as does Mother, still."

That took the wind out of his ducal self's sails. He visibly sagged, his jaw falling open. After an awkward moment, Waterford snapped his mouth shut with an audible click. His features hardened, and his haughtiness returned full on. "Be that as it may, there's the matter at hand."

He stabbed the vowel with a gnarled finger.

Flynn focused on the paper before meeting the duke's cold eyes.

"I need more time." He clenched and unclenched his hands beneath the desk's kneehole. God help him. He was on the verge of losing control. "Mother won't survive another attack. It would kill her if she learned the truth. Surely there must be a smattering of compassion buried beneath the man you've become."

Flynn doubted the truthfulness of his statement. The duke had acquired his reputation because of his ruthlessness, not tenderheartedness. He'd earned his notoriety as a merciless fiend.

"Indeed. I have a most—ah—magnanimous solution." Waterford smiled widely and relaxed against the chair. He uncrossed his legs, then recrossed them, his other knobby knee now on top.

"I'm hoping you'll be amenable to the proposition I have for you." He pointed to the vowel again. "If you agree, I'll cancel the entire debt.

Burn it as you watch."

Despite some foreboding, Flynn straightened at once, his interest piqued.

"Thought that'd catch your attention." The duke chuckled snidely.

"What could you possibly propose that would be worth forgiving a debt of such magnitude?" Flynn's mind raced. Perhaps, God had heard his prayers after all. Was there a way he could save everything?

"It's quite simple." A smug grin contorted Waterford's face. "All you have to do is marry my niece."

Flynn gaped.

Was the man addled? Had too much drink pickled his brain? Had a disease rendered the duke unhinged?

"You're not serious." Flynn found his tongue, at last, his voice a harsh rasp.

Moll and Lasses perked up. They stood on the sofa, swinging their wary gazes from him to Waterford.

The duke didn't respond, just tilted his head arrogantly, his smile deepening.

The mantel clocked ticked a steady rhythm.

Flynn's pulse didn't. For a moment, he couldn't breathe.

"I'm in mourning, for God's sake. Even if I wanted to become leg-shackled to some chit I've never met—which I most assuredly don't—I cannot. Propriety prohibits it."

Lydia's pretty hazel eyes sprang to mind.

He couldn't even marry the woman who'd enchanted him last spring. Lydia had returned to Scotland, and no doubt, some glib-tongued, unfettered, *wealthy* Highlander in a kilt with great, hairy legs and no drawers courted her now.

Waterford slapped his palms on the chair's arms and uncrossed his legs. "Of course you can. I have everything arranged."

I'll bet you do, you manipulating bugger.

The duke scrutinized the dogs, still watching him suspiciously. As he angled to his feet, both spaniels jumped off the sofa and stood at the ready.

"I'll expect you at Wingfield at four today for tea. It will give you a chance to become acquainted with my niece before dinner, which of course, you'll stay for."

He strode to the door. Gripping the handle, Waterford turned and offered his first genuine smile. "She really is quite lovely."

8

Angelina cast a quick peek at the house as she rushed along the path, without the benefit of a bonnet or gloves. Raising her black parasol to see Wingfield better, she breathed a sigh of relief.

Good. No one in the family had noticed her departure.

The creek wasn't forbidden to her, but she didn't want to explain her destination. And she very much needed time alone. Not to brood. That was a useless waste of energy and emotion.

No, she wanted to think further on how she might support herself after the babe came. The modiste idea merited further consideration, as did the lace making. She did have a talent for tatting.

Right after a light luncheon, which Angelina declined to eat, Aunt Camille withdrew to her chamber for her afternoon lie down.

Her aunt had unknowingly provided Angelina the opportunity she needed to escape the house. She hadn't meant to be rude by skipping the meal, but the forced cabbage, cold meats, including headcheese, along with tongue and pickled eggs, had sent her stomach cartwheeling once more.

She'd made do with a piece of dark, dry bread which nourished without nauseating.

According to Murphy, Uncle left well before breakfast this morning. He'd yet to return. Felicia played with a litter of month-old kittens, and Pembrose had ridden off with a couple of chums to do whatever it was young men his age did.

Eyes raised to the cloudless sky, Angelina grimaced. As she'd predicted, the day was indeed warming to an unpleasant temperature.

An old, craggy stone structure, the ground floor of Wingfield Court stayed quite comfortable. However, after a hot day, the third story sleeping chambers became unbearably warm.

She ought not to sneak out, yet Brooke Tweadle tempted beyond resistance. Wading for a short while sounded so refreshing. Afterward, Angelina would return to the house to rest in the cool parlor before teatime.

In Salem, they'd never fussed with afternoon tea unless a rout or ball portended for the evening, which meant supper wasn't served until midnight. Most silly to have a light repast when one just ate and would dine again in another few hours.

How many times did a person need to eat in a day? She already grew round with child. She didn't need chubby cheeks and thighs, as well.

Such a ridiculous practice, too. Drinking a warm beverage on a hot day. Now a cool, refreshing lemonade. Oh, that would be most welcome. Or better yet, one of those delicious fruit ices she'd tasted once when visiting Boston with her parents.

The grass brushed her skirts, making a soft rustling sound as she hurried along the overgrown path. Even through her parasol, the sun's rays beat down upon her.

Beyond the orchard lay a fenced meadow where a sizable herd of strange black cattle milled beneath the shade of a single massive oak. A chorus of bees buzzed among the bright wildflower dotting the grounds. Nary a hint of a breeze stirred the leaves or meadow grasses.

As Angelina approached the grove of oaks lining the stream bed, a startled rabbit bounded from the underbrush, and she yelped in surprise.

Another panic-stricken rabbit darted after the first.

Laughing softly as its white tail disappeared, she folded her parasol and turned to the burbling stream. The brook proved every bit as charming as she'd hoped. This was going to be simply marvelous.

The shallow water gurgled over and between time-worn rocks. A pair of brilliant turquoise dragonflies flitted above the stream, and an unfamiliar songbird's warble filled the air. She scanned the treetops seeking the bird. Ah, there it was. A tiny yellow-green chested warbler hopped on a branch.

Angelina considered the magnificent oaks. They must be at least two hundred years old. Many of their sprawling branches, too weighty to reach heavenward any longer, grew atop the ground, forming a giant gnarled web.

If she weren't increasing, she would indulge in the temptation and climb one of the twisted monstrosities. Resting her parasol against a smallish boulder, she sat upon the stone and untied her half-boots. After pulling them off and setting the footwear aside, she scanned the banks.

Yes, she was alone.

Shoving her skirts knee-high, she reached beneath the hem. Once she removed her garters, she unrolled her stockings then draped them carefully on the stone beside her before standing.

Flexing her toes around the pebble-sized river rock blanketing the shore, she released a happy sigh. How wonderful to be shoeless. Lifting her gown, she gingerly picked her way to the water. It wouldn't do to fall.

She already cherished the child nestled in her womb. She might be angry at Charles's deception and the gross unfairness of her circumstances, but she wanted the babe she carried. Children were a gift from God, and she would do everything within her power to be a good mother.

Tiptoeing into the water, she sucked in a startled breath.

My, it's so cold.

She hoisted her hem above her knees and waded deeper until the water swished around her calves. Farther downstream, a log straddled the banks. Another giant oak angled from the embankment, providing a shady nook and a perfect place to sit and swing her feet in the water.

Balancing on the log, she gently kicked her legs and enjoyed the sensation of the water swishing between her toes and lapping around her ankles.

Irate chattering overhead caught her attention. A pair of red squirrels scampered atop a branch. A wave of nostalgia swept her, and she blew out a sigh. Even the birds, rabbits, and squirrels had mates.

She wasn't likely to ever have one now.

Her heart twinged at the painful truth. Women in her position were hard-pressed to find husbands. Even more so if the ruse of her widowhood became known. She would be labeled as immoral and fast.

See what love cost me.

Before meeting Charles, she'd never understood why anyone would wed for convenience or consent to an arranged marriage. Hopeless romantic that she'd been, her heart had yearned for a love match. And where had that landed her?

In the family way without a husband.

She gave an angry kick, and water splashed her gown. Perchance, those choosing convenience rather than love had the right of it. At least they understood precisely where they stood. Weren't all the sordid details in the marriage settlement?

Yes, pen the terms and seal it with a cold, impersonal signature.

No expectations. No disappointment. No heartbreak.

A nice tidy, emotionless package. Safe and secure. With an aching void inside the couple never to be fulfilled.

Angelina pressed her hand to her stomach and shifted her position on the log, cautious not to catch her gown on the coarse bark.

She hadn't written Mama about the babe. She begged Uncle Ambrose and Aunt Camille not to as well. They reluctantly agreed. Angelina would tell her mother, in time. Just not quite yet. A grandchild resulting from her eldest daughter's ruination would shatter Mama.

Uncle Ambrose, in particular, seemed obsessed with Angelina's increasing. More than once since he'd arrived at Wingfield Court, usually when deep in his cups, he had patted her shoulder in passing and muttered, "I'll see that you're taken care of."

She didn't wish to be unkind or judgmental, but he appeared half-foxed more often than not.

Lips pressed together in censure, Aunt Camille observed him, worry and something else in her eyes.

Trepidation?

How absurd.

Lately, Angelina's imagination flourished too much. She'd never heard Uncle Ambrose as much as raise his voice to Aunt Camille or the children.

Glimpsing the house through the tree trunks, she sighed. She ought to return. It wouldn't do for her aunt to awaken from her nap and finding her missing.

Always anxious and fearing the worst, the dear woman possessed an overprotective, suffocating nature. In that way, she was wholly different than Mama. Wisdom and cautiousness were one thing, but Aunt Camille's obsession with dark thoughts was something else entirely.

Edging off the log, Angelina made her way to where she'd entered the stream. A loud snort caused her to whirl toward the sound, and she slipped. To keep her balance, she dropped her skirts.

A cow, her eyes huge and suspicious, stood between the trees eyeing Angelina.

The pasture fence must be broken somewhere nearby. The animal lazily swished her tail, chasing away a hoard of flies while chewing her cud. She didn't appear hostile, but Angelina was no expert on the behavior of cattle, and her pulse quickened all the same.

She'd never been this close to a cow. And this one was like no other she'd ever seen. Covered with thick, long hair, the poor thing must be sweltering. No wonder she sought the creek.

One eye trained on the animal, Angelina slogged as rapidly as she was able the remaining few feet to her belongings. Her skirts, soaked to above her knees, hindered her movements. So much for sneaking into the house unnoticed. She would have to confess her excursion.

She retrieved her parasol and stockings. She'd put some distance between herself and the cow before donning them. As she bent to grab her boots, more snorts and thudding hooves echoed on the other side of the embankment.

Hounds' teeth. She jerked upright, her breath catching.

Five more cows—four accompanied by chocolate-eyed calves—lumbered to the stream. She froze upon spying the bull leading them and tossing his mammoth head back and forth.

In warning?

The first cow mooed a soft greeting.

Good Lord. What was one supposed to do when faced with a beast like him?

Angelina edged away. She could hear the blood whooshing in her ears. She'd always thought that depiction was an exaggeration by cowardly ninnies.

It was real. Very real.

The bull advanced a step, pawing the ground.

Gads. That couldn't be good.

The irascible beast glared at her. She was positive.

He lowered his shaggy head and growled.

Good God above!

A screech of terror ripped from Angelina's throat. Flinging her possessions aside, she sprinted for the nearest tree. Heart in her throat, she jumped onto a branch hugging the ground. She darted up its thick length then jumped into the vee of an adjoining branch.

The bull, the devil dancing in his black eyes, bellowed and stamped beneath her. Bits of dirt and bark flew from his mashing hooves.

She crawled farther up the limb, grateful the old tree sported nice, wide branches she could easily scale. Craning her neck as she gripped the stout oak, she awkwardly twisted to peer over her shoulder. *Bother.* The manor loomed a good distance away. It hadn't seemed nearly as far when walking here.

Sweat trickled the length of her spine and between her breasts as well as soaked the fabric of her gown beneath each arm.

Charging up the tree, she'd caught her hair on a thin branch. The twig had yanked the ribbon loose entwined in the neat knot atop her head. A few curls teased her face while the rest of her hair hung in a blob at her nape.

Her cheek stung mightily, too.

Angelina touched the area, unsurprised when her fingers came away smeared with a trace of blood. Even without a mirror, she knew she was a sight to behold, thanks to the cantankerous beast snorting and stomping below.

"This is a fine kettle of fish you've found yourself in." Closing her eyes, she pressed her head against the scratchy trunk.

More pounding hooves and low moos announced additional uninvited guests.

God's toenails.

The cattle tromped into the stream, muddying the water in their quest for a cool drink. What fool hadn't maintained his fences? Likely it was Uncle Ambrose's negligence.

How long would the creatures loiter until they returned home? Before she finished the thought, six cows and two calves folded to their knees and lay down.

Well, that was just perfect. Now, what was she to do?

Objecting to Angelina's crouched position, her stomach cramped. After shifting to alleviate the tightness, she peered through the leaves.

If she waved an arm, could anyone at the house see her? It would be helpful to have something colorful to flap. At this distance, the black of her dress probably blended into the tree's dark trunk and rendered her undetectable.

She rose a bit, snagging her big toe on a rough piece of bark. Tears sprang to her eyes.

Blast and blister it.

Maintaining her grip on a nearby limb, Angelina examined her throbbing toe. Scarlet droplets trickled off the side. Why had she ever defied Aunt Camille and ventured to the stream alone? She might be trapped here for hours.

The splashing, soft moos, and rustling of the cattle milling about below rose to her ears. Mayhap, if she called out someone might hear her, although, with the ruckus the animals were making, that was doubtful.

Still, she drew a deep breath and released a most unladylike shout. "Help. I'm stuck in a tree. Help, someone, please."

"Are you in need of assistance?" A man's voice—a deep, smooth baritone—floated up to her.

Angelina started and swung her head to gawk at the much-too attractive gentleman atop a light dun gelding squinting up at her. Why couldn't a groom or a tenant have found her?

"I'd think that was obvious. That foul-tempered brute chased me up here." She pointed to the bull, now affecting a completely docile demeanor as he rubbed his head against a contented cow.

The gentleman stared at her, an odd glint in his eye. His rugged good looks made Charles seem almost effeminate.

Heavens, where did that come from?

"You're American."

The way the man spoke bordered on accusatory. Did he have something against Americans? Perhaps. The war hadn't ended so very long ago.

She shook her head, never releasing her death grip on the branch beside her. "Not exactly. I was born in Scotland. My parents, both Scottish, settled in Salem when I was an infant. I recently arrived—um—for a holiday and to visit my family."

"In Scotland?" He appeared a trifle confused.

"No, in England. My uncle is English."

She surveyed the area. From whence had he come?

As if he heard her unspoken question, he pointed to the meadow. "A gate has fallen on the other side, and a length of fencing requires attention."

He surveyed the cattle. "These are mine. I'll send word for some of my stable hands to retrieve them and make the repair."

"What kind are they?" Angelina leaned over a fraction. "I've never seen cattle with such long hair. They're enormous."

"Indeed. They are Galloways, a Scottish breed. Very hale and hearty." Though polite, his tone held a distinct coolness.

She angled her head, fully observing him for the first time—quality for certain. His seat was excellent, and his attire first-rate from his black coat to his gleaming boots. Not more than thirty, he possessed an angular, rather chiseled face, and his nose sported a distinct bump.

A most handsome man. Truth to tell, sinfully handsome, and young and virile as well.

A tremor of awareness skittered across her skin.

Cease this instance.

She'd yielded to that temptation once before, and the outcome had been wretched.

An aura of sorrow lingered about the gentleman, evident in the set of his finely molded mouth, the shadows beneath dark jade eyes, and the haunted glint in their depths.

She'd wager this man had known recent suffering, and her heart lurched in sympathy.

No.

She'd no business taking note of any gentleman's appearance, especially his mouth. And what in heaven's blessed name was she doing sitting in a tree, talking with him as if they were making polite conversation over tea in a drawing room? She didn't even know his name, for pity's sake.

"Can you climb down yourself?" He dismounted in one agile movement. After removing his gloves and hat, he placed them on the same boulder she'd used for her stockings. He spied her discarded belongings, his gaze pausing on a stocking dangling from a bush. A purely masculine smile bowed his mouth.

Mortification swept her.

He held his riding crop as he purposefully made his way to the tree. He placed a booted foot atop the branch resting on the ground. "Here, I'll come up."

"No, I can manage perfectly on my own. You just assure that devil keeps his distance."

Sure-footed, Angelina edged along, gripping the limb with her bare feet. Her injured toe protested, but the pain was inconsequential. She must make haste. It wouldn't do to be discovered with a man without a chaperone present.

The stranger released a hearty chuckle and raised the crop. "That's what this is for. One or two sound smacks on his muzzle usually does the trick nicely."

Usually?

"And what happens if it doesn't do the trick?" She maneuvered the last few inches to the fork in the tree.

The gentlemen pointed the crop at the tree. "We run for it. He's not named Deamhan for nothing."

She sniffed. "Deamhan? Is that Scots?"

"Yes, Gaelic, for demon."

"A most fitting name. Only Satan would be more appropriate."

Shoving her hair off her face, she stepped onto the lowest limb and hesitated a moment before taking his outstretched hand. She nearly jerked hers away when a jolt of sensation vibrated clear to her shoulder.

Once safely on the ground, she disengaged her hand. “Thank you.”

“I’d bow before I introduce myself, but I don’t trust him.” Waving toward the dozing bull, the man flashed a smile.

He would have perfect teeth. Just like Charles. And what a bounder he’d turned out to be.

New rule.

Don’t trust men with nice teeth.

She met the gentleman’s curious perusal.

Or beautiful eyes with sinfully thick lashes.

“I’m Flynn, Ear—” A grimace shadowed his face. “Marquis of Bretheridge. My estate, Lambridge Manse, borders these lands.”

Should she curtsy? A little late for conventions. Better to be on her way as soon as possible. Not trusting the behemoth resting a stone’s throw away, Angelina warily gathered her belongings.

The marquis’s focus sank to her bare feet. Muddy toes, one bloody, peeked from beneath her soaked and soiled skirt.

She swore his mouth quivered in amusement. The first English peer she’d met besides her uncle, and she resembled a street urchin. Aunt Camille would have apoplexy if she found out. And Uncle Ambrose?

Gads. Angelina didn’t want to imagine his reaction. His response would be unpleasant, to be sure. “Thank you again.”

Lord Bretheridge regarded her expectantly. “Aren’t you going to tell me who you are?”

In another time and another place, she might’ve—before she learned not to trust.

“No. I shouldn’t even be speaking to you. We’ve not been properly introduced.”

She spun on her heel and ran barefoot to the house.

9

A wry half-smiled bent Flynn's mouth as the black-clad young woman rushed along the path until she reached the house's terrace. Would she turn around?

Pausing, she flicked a swift peek behind her before disappearing through an open door.

The niece?

He'd wager Lambridge she was.

Waterford couldn't possibly think Flynn would marry a woman he never met. Well, they had just met, although he still didn't know her name. Come to think of it, why would the duke subject his niece to an arranged marriage?

The woman was an enigma.

She refused to give her name because they hadn't been introduced, yet offered no apologies for her bare feet and unkempt appearance.

He didn't know many women who could scale a tree the way she had either. That accomplishment suggested she'd a great deal of practice.

Why he found the notion intriguing, he couldn't say. Perchance her rustic, American charm stimulated his interest. She reminded him of his free-spirited Scottish cousins. The mystery woman claimed to be part Scots. Mayhap that explained his fascination.

A dim image of a Scottish lass possessing midnight locks and hazel eyes surged to his memory. Another vision replaced the memory almost immediately. One of a pixyish, scratched face, peach lips, and wild reddish hair.

The duke hadn't lied. The niece, for surely that was who the nymph had been, was lovely. Indeed, beautiful. Her rumpled state couldn't disguise the intelligence in her arresting eyes framed by dark auburn lashes.

He'd been close enough to see the deep emerald ringing her unusual ocean green irises, flecked with shards of blue. And her hair, a shade somewhere between copper and honey, was magnificent. How long was the tangled mass of flopping curls?

Her attire suggested that she, too, was in mourning. Orphaned, perhaps? It made sense and explained why she resided at Wingfield Court.

Still, Flynn sensed something more nefarious was afoot. Given the duke's dubious history and sullied repute, he doubted he would like whatever Waterford connived. A tenant for life with an absolute stranger didn't appeal to Flynn any more than being blackmailed did.

Driven by curiosity, if for no other reason, he'd put in a teatime appearance. The afternoon might prove an amusing distraction from the worries plaguing him.

Fortunately for the young lady, he'd needed some air and had decided to take a leisurely ride to Wingfield for the mandated appearance. Time in the saddle helped clear his thoughts. Besides, he wanted to personally inspect the exceptional herd of cattle before he sold them. His father had been so proud of the Galloways.

Father couldn't boast an ounce of Scottish blood, though Mother's grandmother had been Scots. He'd not only fallen in love with Mother but all things Scottish.

Particularly the whisky.

Flynn had long suspected if it hadn't been for his title, Father would've hied off to Scotland with Mother and lived the remainder of his days in some drafty old castle. Mayhap wearing a baggy kilt and tooting a bagpipe.

Imagining the sight, he cracked a smile.

If his parents had spirited off to the Highlands, then Lord help the poor soul who might've been subjected to Father's long shanks and knobby knees. Or hear the man attempt anything remotely musical. Tone-deaf, as a stone, was his father. Mother used to say he couldn't carry a tune if it was strapped to his back.

Using the shortcut his father often took through the meadow, Flynn had come upon the broken gate. Spying the fresh cow manure trail—some of the piles yet steaming— he accurately deduced the situation.

Devil it. How long had it been since Father or the duke inspected the fences?

Crossing onto Waterford's estate and finding a young, attractive, *barefoot*, treasure crouched in a craggy oak had been wholly unexpected. At first, he'd thought his eyes deceived him when he spied the sprite's hair gleaming between the leaves.

He'd glimpsed trim calves and well-turned ankles as she descended the massive oak. From her appearance and lack of shoes, he'd guess she'd been wading in the stream. Other than his Ferguson cousins, he didn't know another woman who would dare such indecorous behavior.

She hadn't begged his pardon for her disheveled appearance. But then, he hadn't apologized for his unrepentant ogling of her shapely limbs either.

Grinning, he shook his head.

Deamhan and his harem wouldn't have left the shade or the stream on their own. The lazy brute couldn't be bothered to wander the quarter-mile to where Brook Tweadle crossed Flynn's lands. No, the obstinate bull tromped his way to the duke's property.

Had Flynn not come along, the chit likely would've perched in the tree for a long while. Conceivably, the entire night.

He waved his hand at a persistent fly hovering about his face. One eye trained on the bull, he withdrew his pocket watch and flicked open the engraved gold cover. *Quarter-past three*. If he made quick work of it, he had time to muster his stable hands and set them to gathering the cattle and repairing the fence before he called at Wingfield Court.

So much the better if he arrived a trifle late. Waterford, the old bulldog, would soon learn Flynn wasn't dancing attendance on anyone.

He placed his hat atop his head once more. As he bent to grasp his gloves, a black hair ribbon caught his eye. After retrieving the silky strip, he lifted it to his nose. A subtle mixture of flowers met his nostrils.

Unexpectedly, his manhood twitched. *Interesting.* He hadn't felt an iota of arousal in weeks. He folded the ebony length before stashing it in his pocket.

Surveying the contented cattle, he swung into the saddle with practiced ease. He reined the dun toward the broken fence. The animals would stay put for a while longer. Most lay serenely chewing their cud and enjoying the shade.

Perusing Wingfield Court, he patted the four-year-old gelding's neck. "Come, Kane. We've tea to attend and a proposed bride to meet."

Precisely forty-eight minutes later—Flynn checked his timepiece for the fourth time since galloping from the stream—he cantered along the sloping flagstone drive to Wingfield Court.

A footman garbed in ebony and garnet red dashed from the manor. "I'll see your horse to the stable, my lord."

Flynn started to demur but changed his mind. He'd no intention of staying for dinner, but tea would assuredly take more than fifteen minutes, and Kane would be cooler in the stables. The temperature had peaked this afternoon, enough to wilt Flynn's starched neckcloth.

"Thank you. If it wouldn't be too much trouble, make sure a groom waters him and rubs him down. He's been galloping off and on for the better part of an hour." He passed the reins to the footman.

The footman nodded, beads of perspiration popping out on his forehead and upper lip. "No trouble at all, sir. He's a beautiful stepper, he is."

Fondly rubbing Kane's muzzle, Flynn agreed. "Indeed, he is. Smart too. Make sure to draw the bolt home on his stall door. Otherwise, he'll open it and start snooping about."

Now, if he could only survive this preposterous farce of a tea without telling the duke to bugger off. In this hot weather, he wasn't sure he would be able to choke down the steaming brew. He wasn't fond of the beverage in the dead of winter, let alone midsummer.

Removing his handkerchief from his pocket, he daubed his upper lip and forehead. Hopefully, the interior of the house offered respite from the temperature. A movement from a ground floor window revealed someone covertly watched him.

His lips twitched in a combination of amusement and curiosity. The niece, perhaps? It would be interesting to take in her appearance once she was primped and polished to snare a husband. He rather preferred the ragamuffin dangling in the oak sporting a bloody toe.

As the servant led Kane away, Flynn scanned the structure before him. Well over one hundred years old, the stones—mellowed by age and the elements—held an appealing provincial attraction.

Vague memories of visits as a young lad flitted into his mind. There'd been a pony. A stout, plodding Shetland, he'd been permitted to ride around the glistening greens. And sweets. He particularly remembered Shrewsbury cakes, still his favorite confection.

He considered the area. The immediate grounds, garden beds, circular driveway—even the shutters—showed signs of neglect, although, not longstanding.

Tilting his head, Flynn squinted.

Was that a nest atop one of the chimneys?

Dangerous, that. He'd best advise Waterford. Why hadn't the staff taken notice? And, why hadn't the duke seen to the repairs and upkeep before coming for the summer? The man not only enjoyed everything in tip-top shape, he demanded it.

Perchance, he planned on inventorying everything that needed attention before putting the place on the market. The lands, prime for cattle grazing, also boasted decent stables and superb hunting.

If Flynn's pockets weren't windmill dwindled to a nutshell, he'd make an offer himself. The duke's properties and Lambridge's marched parallel to one another for a good fifty acres.

Flynn's common sense and gut instinct shrieked for him to turn tail and dash, neck or nothing, for home. Pure folly, venturing into the viper's pit.

What about my family?

He sighed. Best to get to it and see what gammon Waterford pitched him. No one forgave a debt as colossal as Father's with something as simple as an arranged marriage.

Well, not when there was a bride as young and attractive as the niece. The scales tipped grossly uneven unless the duke had something else to reveal. Or mayhap, the confounded lout made a May game of him and sought to see how malleable he was to being manipulated.

Constantly reminding himself, he had his family's wellbeing to consider kept him from planting a fist on Waterford's red-veined nose.

The drape fluttered again.

Flynn suppressed the urge to wave or cut a cocky salute. As he climbed the steps, he firmed his jaw and inhaled a deep breath. Instead of giving in to the impulse to let loose a stream of profanity that would cause Hades to blush, he forced a pleasant expression to his face.

He nodded to the austere-appearing butler standing at the entrance before stepping across the threshold, greatly relieved to find the temperature within the house much cooler.

The butler gave the briefest of bows. So brief as to be insulting. "Good afternoon, Lord Bretheridge."

Upon straightening, he peered down his reedy nose.

Considering the top of the fellow's head didn't meet Flynn's nose, the effect was rather comical. He was sorely tempted to stand taller to see if the man would tilt his head further. Except, he worried the majordomo might tumble tail over top backward if he did.

He almost grinned at the image. "Good afternoon to you as well.

And your name?"

"Saunders, sir." The butler exhaled an exaggerated sigh. "I suppose you wish to be relieved of your hat and gloves?"

No, I intend to take tea with them.

Flynn hadn't imagined the annoyance in Saunders's voice. Where in God's name had Waterford found the surly chap? And why hadn't he sacked him long before this?

"Sir, your hat?"

"Yes, please." Flynn passed the items to the butler's outstretched hand.

Saunders placed them on a table before closing the thick, arched door. Nose in the air once more, he marched past Flynn, sparing him nary a glance. "Their graces and Mrs. Thorne await you in the drawing room. Tea has already been served."

What the blazes? Mrs. Thorne?

The niece was married—no, had been married? Ah, thus the black garb.

The plot thickened.

Why so desperate to marry off a widowed niece? Something didn't add up. A huge piece of the puzzle was missing. No doubt during tea today, that tidbit would be served up, whole and raw, and he'd be expected to swallow the distasteful thing without complaint.

"Sir, are you coming?" Impatience laced Saunders's voice.

"Yes, forgive me, I was distracted by…" Flynn swiftly skimmed the entry for a logical excuse. "Distracted by *that*."

He pointed to a moth-eaten five-point red stag with a dangling ear and missing a glass eye. The stuffed animal hung askew above the entrance, dusty cobwebs lacing its antlers. "What a spectacular trophy." He nearly choked on a suppressed chuckle. "Did the duke shoot the buck on the estate?"

Saunders elevated a haughty brow, no doubt thinking Flynn was a cork-brained ninnyhammer. "No. He did not." The majordomo continued marching along the corridor.

No, the duke didn't shoot it, or no, it hadn't been shot on the estate?

Saunders stopped outside a partially opened door. The low murmur of conversation floated through the crack. He rapped once before sweeping the door open and announcing, "The Marquis of Bretheridge."

Prepared to do battle, Flynn entered the cozily appointed room. He stopped when a teacup clattered to the floor. As he'd expected, the intriguing woman from the stream sat upon a settee.

"Oh, dear, see what I've done." She gathered the pieces of broken china strewn on the floor. Not once did she lift her attention from the carpet. As she leaned forward to retrieve a saucer shard, her dress gaped, affording him a tantalizing glimpse of a plump bosom.

"Forgive me, Aunt Camille. I'll replace the cup, naturally. I'm not usually this clumsy." Her gaze swept upward for a fraction then lowered just as swiftly. "I wasn't aware we expected a guest for tea."

Curious. She hadn't been informed he'd been invited. What else wasn't she privy to? The proposed nuptials?

Flynn eyed Waterford. What was he about?

"It's quite all right, Angelina." From her seat opposite the settee, the duchess gestured to Saunders, who'd poked his head into the drawing room at the sound of breaking porcelain.

He sent Flynn an accusatory glower and pursed his lips.

Flynn narrowed his eyes. He'd had enough of the pompous butler. Someone needed to put the servant in his place.

"Saunders, please send William at once," the duchess directed with casual aplomb. "Mrs. Thorne has dropped her teacup. Oh, and we shall need another cup, as well."

Her grace made no effort to assist her niece, frantically blotting the spreading puddle of tea. Nor did the duchess seem the least concerned that a costly china cup had been destroyed. The latter raised his opinion of her a trifle.

"Angelina-Rose, do cease at once." The Duke of Waterford's strident voice rang with unconcealed censure. "We've servants for that sort of thing. Gentle-bred ladies don't wallow about on their knees, cleaning up muck."

Mrs. Thorne jerked her head toward her uncle. Her eyes rounded in humiliated astonishment before she dropped her focus to the floor. "Of course, Uncle Ambrose."

Waterford truly is a monumental arse.

A rosy flush tinting her ivory cheeks, she placed her sopped serviette on the tea tray as she gracefully climbed to her feet. She'd yet to meet Flynn's eyes.

"Really, my dear." Waterford's voice grew even sterner. "Lord Bretheridge will think you've been raised by those red-skinned savages in America we hear so much about."

No, I'll think you're a mean-spirited churl who enjoys humiliating others.

Mrs. Thorne's generous breasts rose as she took a deep breath. Her color high and her features schooled into a polite mask, she finally turned her attention to him. A tight smile on her face, a hint of moisture glinted in her eyes.

She's mortified.

The duke didn't bother rising to make the introductions. His slurred speech hinted as to why. He flapped a hand in Flynn's direction. "Angelina, may I present Flynn, Marquis of Bretheridge. Bretheridge, my niece, Mrs. Ells—er, that is, Thorne."

At the slip of a tongue, Flynn cocked an eyebrow.

Waterford released a hiccupping belch. He patted his distended belly and licked his lips. "Beg pardon."

Egads, the man was half-soused.

Her grace appeared unaware. Or else, chose to ignore her pickled spouse deliberately. Focused on sipping her tea and nibbling biscuits, she avoided gazing at her husband altogether.

Not that Flynn blamed her.

Waterford's resemblance to a drowsy lizard lounging atop a rock was uncanny. If the duke's tongue flicked out and caught the annoying fly buzzing about the ginger biscuits, he wouldn't have been altogether shocked.

Chagrin coloring her cheeks, Mrs. Thorne scooted around the table. "I'm honored to make your acquaintance, my lord." She sank into an elegant curtsy.

The woman before Flynn bore scant resemblance to the sprite he met earlier. Other than several curls framing her oval face, her hair was neatly coiffed. The black of the muslin gown she wore emphasized her unusual greenish eyes and trim figure. Only the faint mark on her flushed cheek hinted she'd been splashing about in the stream and climbing trees.

He bent over her hand. The jolt he experienced earlier when helping her from the tree shot through him again. "Forgive me, Mrs. Thorne. Have we met before? You seem quite familiar."

Most wicked of him to tease her.

She inhaled sharply, tossing her uncle an uneasy glance.

So, she didn't want the duke to know about her little adventure. Why?

"No, I don't believe we have, my lord. I'm newly arrived in England, you see."

"I was so sure," Flynn murmured. He positioned his back to their graces and stared pointedly at Mrs. Thorne's slipper-clad feet. Grinning, he snared her gaze then winked.

Her amazing eyes widened, the pupils growing huge with hilarity, and her pretty mouth trembled.

He swore she bit the side of her cheek to keep from laughing. What an utter, unexpected delight, she was.

Saunders entered the drawing room, teacup in hand. A footman toting a basket and linens followed on his heels. The butler placed the cup on the tea tray and swept a bland eye over the duke before addressing the duchess. "Have you need of anything else, Your Grace?"

"No, that will be all." The Duchess of Waterford arranged the new cup to her satisfaction. She expertly poured tea for Mrs. Thorne and Flynn, still avoiding looking upon her reptilian spouse. Sugar tongs in hand, she glanced upward. "Cream or sugar, my lord?"

"Both and three lumps, please." And that barely made the stuff tolerable. He must be one of a handful of his countrymen who didn't enjoy the beverage. Traitorous for an Englishman.

He followed Mrs. Thorne to the settee and waited until she sank onto the cushion before claiming a seat for himself, mindful of maintaining an acceptable distance between them.

Waterford rudely gawked, a speculative glint in his rheumy eyes.

Flynn quirked his mouth and raised his brows in a silent challenge. No doubt the cur plotted when he'd introduce his despicable scheme.

Smiling and murmuring her thanks, his niece accepted another cup of tea from her aunt. Could Mrs. Thorne actually be unaware of her uncle's conniving?

"A moment, Saunders." Her grace turned to the butler who had gained the door. "Please speak with Miss Simpleton, and inquire if Felicia's been found yet. I wish to be informed the moment she has."

Flynn bent toward Mrs. Thorne. "Is Felicia a pet?"

Mouth curving slightly, Mrs. Thorne shook her pretty head. "No. She's my much younger, mischievous cousin. She finds it amusing to hide from her governess. Felicia's quite cunning, but poor Miss Simpleton doesn't find her clever in the least."

Flynn nearly snorted into his teacup, biting his tongue to suppress a bark of laughter. *Miss Simpleton, the governess?* That was outside of enough. As for the missing child, she must be the window peeper. "You might search the room directly to the left of the entry."

"Indeed?" Eyebrows arched to his hairline, Saunders thinned his lips.

Flynn took a sip of his tea and suppressed a grimace. "Someone peeked at me through the draperies when I arrived."

That caught the duchess's attention. She paused, teacup halfway to her mouth. "Didn't you search the music room already, Saunders?"

After sending Flynn a withering glare, the butler turned to her grace. "I did. Twice. I am *quite* sure," he slid Flynn a haughty sidelong glower, "something as obvious as a child would not have escaped my notice." Saunders managed to pull his spine even straighter.

Neither of their graces chastised his insolence.

After Flynn examined the surly butler from toe to top, his smile deepened. Voice smooth as silk, he murmured, "Saunders, perhaps something as obvious as a child mightn't have escaped your notice, but fastening the top button on one side of your falls did."

Every eye in the room speared to the butler's groin.

The duchess gasped. William sniggered. Mrs. Thorne made a peculiar coughing sound that Flynn was convinced concealed laughter. And the duke snapped, "Good God, man, fasten yourself up!"

Without a word, the majordomo stamped from the room, his ears bright red.

Poorly done. I humiliated the man.

Though, truthfully, Saunders brought his mortification on himself.

Waterford's attention followed the butler, and he rubbed his chin. "Ought to dismiss him without reference this very instant."

Flynn stared in disbelief. Not a word of chastisement for Saunders's rude and impertinent behavior to a guest, but a missed button and the duke threatened to dismiss the servant?

He forced his tongue to form the insincere words. "Don't be hasty, Waterford. A competent majordomo is a prize worth keeping."

If he hadn't directed everyone's attention to Saunders's unfortunate state of undress, Waterford likely wouldn't have noticed. Such vindictiveness wasn't typical of Flynn, and his behavior gave him pause. He'd been acting out of character the entire day.

"Yes, yes, well. Possibly so." The duke hid a broad yawn behind his hand.

William finished cleaning the tea mess, collected the basket, then turned to the duchess expectantly.

"Thank you. You may go." Her grace selected a piece of shortbread. "Please ask Saunders to prepare more tea and to send the fresh brew in at once. This pot grows cool."

"Yes, Your Grace." William bowed.

"William?" Laying a hand on his arm, Mrs. Thorne stopped the footman. She smiled kindly. "Thank you for cleaning my spill. I'm sorry to have put you to any trouble."

The man broke into a toothy smile. "It wasn't any trouble."

He bowed again before leaving. No sooner did he exit, than a flustered middle-aged woman escorted a beautiful, doll-like child into the room.

"Ah, I see you've found my darling." Her grace patted the cushion beside her. "Come my pet, kiss Mama. Miss Simpleton, you may have your tea now. I'll ring when you're needed."

"Thank you, Your Grace." Relief and gratitude swept the governess's haggard face. Dipping a hasty curtsy, she bolted for the door, no doubt eager to escape before the duchess changed her mind.

Felicia dutifully pecked her mother's cheek. An exquisite child, she would someday be a stunning woman. Given her penchant for mischief, she'd lead some poor sot a merry chase, Flynn would wager.

She turned her curious forget-me-not blue eyes on Flynn. "Who are you?"

Already having risen when the governess entered the room, he bowed. "I'm the Marquis of Bretheridge. I believe I detected you peeping at me from the front window."

Grinning, Felicia jumped to her feet, clapping her hands. Excitement danced in her sparkling eyes. "Oh, splendid. You're the man marrying Lina."

10

For the second time in a quarter-hour, a teacup slipped from Angelina's fingers.

This time, thank goodness, Lord Bretheridge deftly caught the cup and saucer before they met the same fate as the first. Other than a paltry amount of tea sloshing into the saucer, he averted another disaster.

Her heart beating an irregular staccato, Angelina gaped at Felicia before scanning the faces of the others assembled. She'd heard wrong. Hadn't she?

Aunt Camille, pale as the lace rimming her bodice, sat dumbfounded, a half-eaten ginger biscuit partway to her slack mouth.

Felicia, beaming with excitement, bounced on her toes, while Uncle Ambrose, his face an unreadable mask, thrummed his spindly fingers on his rotund belly and considered the marquis.

Lord Bretheridge's dark eyebrows swooped into form a harsh crease above the bridge of his strong nose. He pressed his lips into a stern line, a muscle flexing in his granite-like jaw.

Oh, he wasn't amused in the least by Felicia's silliness.

Once his lordship placed the cup on the table, he shifted his position to regard Uncle Ambrose squarely. Unconcealed hostility glittered in the marquis's eyes.

Angelina fidgeted with her serviette. Why didn't anyone say anything?

At the very least, deny Felicia's giddy outburst? Whatever had given the child such a preposterous notion?

Pinching her fingers together, Angelina drew in a labored breath. Striving for calm when a swarm of bees hummed in her belly, she attempted a smile. "Felicia, my love, what a wonderful imagination you have."

She dashed Lord Bretheridge a peek from beneath her lashes.

He regarded her, anger and pain evident in his eyes.

She steeled her features as another flush scorched her face, and she directed her attention to her cousin. "I'm sorry to disappoint you, darling, but the marquis and I just met. We certainly are not affianced."

A pout formed on Felicia's pert mouth as a scowl settled upon her features. Hands on her hips, she shook her head, her flaxen curls pirouetting about her shoulders.

"You are, too. I heard Papa say so." She whirled to face her father. "Tell them, Papa."

"My darling, how could you have heard such a thing?" Aunt Camille set her biscuit aside. Brushing crumbs from her lap, she studied her daughter. "Papa has never discussed anything of this nature with *me*. I assure you, I'd be the first to know of such an arrangement."

Did she truly believe that? Angelina mightn't know her uncle well, but she did know he was a man who did what he wanted when he wanted without regard to others.

Her aunt turned her attention to Uncle Ambrose. Eyes mere slits, she spoke between stiff lips. "Lina is *my* niece, and as she's underage, her mother would need to consent to a match."

Not underage for much longer, dear aunt.

Aunt Camille's modulated voice held a distinct trace of accusation. After folding her serviette, she set the linen beside the tray. Did her hand tremble the merest bit? She made a pretense of straightening the tea service.

"In her last letter, my pet, Aunt Lucille made no mention of any such thing." She bathed Felicia with a doting smile. "That's not something she would likely overlook, now is it, kitten?"

Indignation simmered in the outraged glare Aunt Camille leveled her husband.

He kept his scrutiny fixed on Angelina and Lord Bretheridge. A peculiar predatory glint sparked in Uncle Ambrose's blurry eyes.

A chill crawled from Angelina's waist to her shoulders. She didn't know this man who was her uncle at all.

Tension radiated from the marquis, evident in his taut shoulders, fisted hands, and flexed jaw. Yet he remained disconcertingly silent. His unyielding stare challenged Uncle Ambrose, and their hostile gazes clashed.

Angelina swung her attention between them. A silent battle raged, one green-eyed gaze dueling with the other. But why?

Her mouth gone dry, she wet her lips. "Felicia, I don't think—"

"I'm not lying." Felicia's eyes misted, and her lower lip trembled. She stomped her foot and fisted her hands at her sides. "I'm not!"

"Of course you're not, darling." Angelina offered a reassuring smile. She'd never known her cousin to spin falsehoods. An incorrigible imp given to practical jokes, she wasn't dishonest. "Perhaps, you misunderstood Uncle?"

"No, I didn't," Felicia denied vehemently, shaking her head and causing her curls to bounce wildly. A mutinous glower descended upon her face. "I heard him quite clearly. I was hiding from Miss Simpleton behind the draperies in Papa's London study when a man came to call. His name was Mr. Did—Diddles—"

Her forehead furrowed in concentration and mouth taut, she rubbed the side of her nose. "He had a silly name."

"Diddlethwaite?" Aunt Camille managed, though her hand clutched her throat, and she croaked as if she'd swallowed a good-sized dill pickle. Whole. "Your man-of-affairs, Waterford?"

From the grayish tint and strained expression on the duchess's face, Angelina feared her aunt was about to faint dead away. She swayed, and Angelina surged to her feet.

Grinning, Felicia nodded her head. "Yes, Mama, that was his name. Papa said," she lowered her voice in imitation of her father, "'You have the documents?'"

She checked to make sure Lord Bretheridge listened. Satisfied that she had his full attention, she carried on. "The other man said," Felicia changed her voice to a high nasally twang, "'Yes, my lord, everything is in order.'"

Angelina bit her cheek to stifle her chuckles. This wasn't a humorous situation, but gracious, Felicia was quite the consummate actress.

"Then Papa said," Felicia dropped her tone again, rubbing her belly in imitation of her father, "'Good, good. My niece shall be the Marchioness of Bretheridge before the summer ends.'"

Proud of her cleverness, Felicia smiled brightly. "So, you see, I do have the right of it. Lina is to marry his lordship before summer ends."

She sighed and clasped her hands together. "I do so adore weddings."

Good Lord. Does she have the right of it?

What in heaven's name was Uncle Ambrose plotting?

Angelina sent an anxious glance to Lord Bretheridge and discovered, to her chagrin, he observed her, his eyes hooded and unreadable. For certain, he realized she wasn't part of this…this preposterous scheme.

A spasm tightened her stomach uncomfortably. She needed to stand and move. Her nerves and muscles were as taut as a bowstring. Struggling to control her indignation, Angelina swung her focus to her uncle.

"Uncle, what is the meaning of this?"

Tugging his ear, he stared at Felicia. A slight frown marred his face, his irritation obvious, yet controlled. "You ought not to have been eavesdropping, Felicia. That was most improper."

"I'm sorry, Papa. I know I should've revealed myself." Felicia averted her eyes and fidgeted with the wide blue ribbon around her middle. "I was afraid you'd be angry with me and—"

Uncle Ambrose stood abruptly.

Felicia took a reflexive step backward, and Aunt Camille rose as well, wariness in her stance.

Uncle reached to pat Felicia atop the head.

Startled, she gasped and shrank away.

He tossed a quashing glare at his wife. Pointing his forefinger, he admonished Felicia sternly. "Young lady, I'll visit your room later to discuss your punishment for spying on me."

She paled, sidling closer to her mother.

Aunt Camille wrapped a protective arm about Felicia's shoulders and tucked her near her side.

This was the first Angelina had seen of this sort of discordant familial interaction. The conflict set her nerves on edge all the more.

Uncle Ambrose straightened his rumpled waistcoat before crossly considering his wife. "Your Grace, please return Felicia to Miss Simpleton's care. You and I shall address this matter later."

His tone brooked no argument. Gone was the slurred speech of minutes earlier. Evidently, anger sobered him with great alacrity.

Aunt Camille angled her head, studying him. For a moment, their gazes wrestled, and it appeared she might defy him.

He returned her regard, his bearing uncompromising and overbearing.

Something momentarily sparked in her eyes, but the glint faded as rapidly as it had appeared. She sighed before shifting her attention away, her shoulders slouching the merest bit.

She marshaled her composure and smiled at Felicia. "Come, lamb. I wish to hear your progress on the harpsichord before dinner."

Aunt Camille skirted the chair she'd been sitting in and sailed to the entrance, Felicia, in tow. Her aunt opened the door, murmuring to her daughter. "You go on, dear, and find Miss Simpleton. I'll be but a moment."

"Yes, Mama." Felicia turned to Lord Bretheridge. "It was a pleasure to make your acquaintance, your lordship." Eyes lowered, she dipped a pretty curtsy. "Lina." Felicia darted a hesitant glance to her father. "Will you read with me tonight, as we usually do?"

Angelina gave her a reassuring smile. "I'd like to very much. I'll do my best to pop into say goodnight. Perchance, we can squeeze in a chapter or two."

Aunt Camille stared intently at his lordship. "Lord Bretheridge?"

"Yes, Your Grace?" The marquis's lips slid into a kind smile.

She tucked her quivering chin to her chest. "Please let me assure you. I knew nothing of this *arrangement*. I'm mortified that given the recent tragic events in your life, you've been subjected to more consternation by this *family*."

By Uncle Ambrose, you mean.

From the corner of her eye, Angelina considered the marquis. What else had Uncle done to Lord Bretheridge?

"That's enough." Uncle Ambrose sternly warned Aunt Camille, his voice harsh.

He reminded Angelina of the bad-tempered bull she encountered earlier today. The same dangerous gleam shimmered in his ruthless eyes.

"Angelina, your uncle is not your legal guardian." Her aunt speared him a defiant glare before rushing on. "He cannot force you into anything, no matter his reasoning."

A furious expression on his face, Uncle Ambrose strode to the door. He seized Aunt Camille's arm none too gently. "Come with me."

"Uncle Ambrose—"

"Waterford—"

The Marquis appeared at Angelina's side in a blink, his mouth set in severe lines once more. Surprised, yet thankful, she advanced with him toward her aunt and uncle.

Aunt Camille stayed them with a flip of her hand. "Really, Waterford, you cannot leave Angelina unchaperoned with Lord Bretheridge."

"Yes, Uncle. It would be most improper." Angelina sent Lord Bretheridge a conspiratory smile. "I'm newly acquainted with his lordship. What would the servants say?"

Not that it would make a difference in my case.

"Indeed," Lord Bretheridge drawled. "Consider the gossip such negligence would cause. You wouldn't want that *on dit* attached to *your* name or title, now would you?"

Angelina regarded him closely. Did mockery color his voice?

"Don't feed me that drivel and rot." Uncle Ambrose urged his wife from the room. "If the door is open and a footman stands outside, it's perfectly acceptable."

Aunt Camille halted at the threshold. She turned her head, searching both ways in the corridor, then tapped her husband on the arm. "Yes, but there is no footman present, is there?"

With an irritated huff, Uncle Ambrose conceded. "Very well, I'll let the issue go for the present. This is not finished, however. I'll speak with you about the matter later, rest assured."

"Excellent. I've meant to have a conversation with you regarding a pressing concern. A serious concern I've let go far too long." She met her husband's perturbed glower head-on.

"What pressing concern?" Uncle tossed Lord Bretheridge a cautious glance, noticeably uncomfortable with the direction the conversation had taken.

Aunt Camille lowered her voice. "You've a loose tongue when you're well into your cups, Waterford."

With those clipped words, she swept past him and out of sight.

Angelina stifled a groan. Even in America, one didn't speak of personal difficulties before servants or guests. And one assuredly didn't express differences of opinions in their presence either. What could her aunt and uncle be thinking? Mama never hinted at discord between them, yet something was definitely amiss.

Facing Lord Bretheridge, Angelina forced herself to smile and meet his eyes. "I'm terribly sorry, my lord. Please excuse—"

"Don't make excuses for your aunt and me, Angelina."

Uncle Ambrose stomped to the bell-pull. Impatience written on his face, he gave it a vicious yank.

She cast Lord Bretheridge another apologetic smile, which he returned, understanding in his kind eyes. What must he think? Drat, her uncle and his untenable behavior.

A properly buttoned Saunders appeared at once, almost as if he'd been lurking outside the door. Had he been waiting for a summons? Why hadn't Aunt Camille seen him? Unless he'd been skulking around a corner or in the library opposite the study.

She wouldn't put that behavior past him.

"Sir, you rang?" Spine ramrod stiff, the butler avoided facing Lord Bretheridge.

"Yes," Uncle Ambrose acknowledged with one sharp nod. "Show Bretheridge to the guest room prepared for him so he may rest and freshen himself before we dine."

"That won't be necessary." His lordship straightened a sleeve. "I shan't be staying for dinner."

Angelina didn't blame him in the least. If she were the marquis, she'd also make her excuses and beat a hasty retreat.

Egads. Invited to tea only to have a child declare he was to marry a perfect stranger. Then subjected to his hosts' quibbling. Not to mention, Saunders's insufferable impertinence.

And the British accused Americans of being uncultured.

Hands on his hips, his mouth bent into an ugly sneer, Uncle's bleary-eyed gaze rested on Lord Bretheridge. "I believe I made it perfectly clear that my invitation extended to dinner as well, Bretheridge." Deceptive softness and civility tempered his words.

Another prickle of unease washed over Angelina.

Saunders turned his attention to the marquis but trained his focus at some point beyond Lord Bretheridge's shoulder. A distinct smirk skewed the butler's mouth.

Why hadn't she noticed Saunders' insolence before today?

"Yes, you did." Lord Bretheridge clasped his hands behind him and rocked back on his heels, not a whisper of unease in his form. He tilted his dark head. "However, I've been away from Lambridge too long as it is."

He did have a striking jawline. Nothing like Uncle's weak, sagging chin, which nearly vanished into the folds of his neckcloth and caused his head to resemble a turtle poking halfway out of its shell.

The marquis's handsome mouth curved into a smile. "As I informed you earlier, Mother recently suffered an apoplexy. I don't wish to be away from her for lengthy periods. Since Father's death, she becomes easily worried."

"How awful, your lordship. Naturally, you must go at once." Angelina couldn't believe her daring. She linked her arm with his and began leading him to the door, ignoring the peculiar fluttering where her heart should be.

He grinned, mirth dancing in his green eyes. "Are you so very eager to be rid of me, Mrs. Thorne?"

Angelina stumbled to a stop, the heat of a blush racing to her hairline. "No, no. Of course not." She dared a peek at her scowling uncle. "I'm extremely close to my mother. I know I'd be worried silly if she had an apoplexy, and I wasn't nearby to care for her."

"I was teasing." Lord Bretheridge patted her hand atop his arm as he propelled them forward.

They reached the room's entrance, and he bowed. Lifting her hand, he brushed his lips across her skin. "It was a pleasure to have made your acquaintance."

Gracious, the wee babe must be spinning somersaults. A conglomeration of peculiar sensations ricocheted around in her innards, making it difficult to concentrate.

"Yes, it was."

He grinned.

"I mean, I enjoyed yours as well, my lord."

His cocky grin widened.

"That is, it was a pleasure to meet you, too." *Bother*. The stream she waded in earlier babbled less than she did.

Angelina ducked her head as unfamiliar reticence gripped her. If only she'd made his acquaintance before her life had taken its ill-fated turn. Now, she was set upon a path that destined the marquis, and she must go their separate ways.

She couldn't say why, but he fascinated her. Not in the overwhelming, irresistible way Charles had with his glib tongue and smooth manners.

There were two more rules for the taboo list.

Disregard flattering lips and charming comportment. Both are meaningless.

No, she suspected the marquis could claim a depth of character Charles lacked. She could see it in Lord Bretheridge's kind eyes. Perhaps, that was what snared her interest. Who, precisely, was the man behind the title?

It mattered naught. She wasn't in a position to become better acquainted with any man, nor would her bruised heart or distrustful soul permit her to do so. She'd been duped once and could lay part of the blame at Charles's feet. To allow herself to be fooled twice would be solely her fault.

Time to bid Lord Bretheridge farewell and have a serious, doubtless, unpleasant discussion with her uncle.

Angelina gave Saunders her brightest smile. Her mama had always advised that one attracted more ants with molasses than mud. "I'd be happy to see Lord Bretheridge to the door."

"Very good, Mrs. Thorne." The butler gave a stiff bow. He spun on his polished heel and marched from the drawing room, his back stiffer than a ramrod.

Evidently, Saunders wasn't the forgiving sort.

Lord Bretheridge regarded Uncle Ambrose standing silent and fuming beside the door. Ire reddened her uncle's already mottled nose and cheeks.

The marquis dipped his head. "Your Grace, this afternoon has been most, shall we say, *entertaining*."

"I'll say." Angelina chuckled, pushing a wisp of hair off her forehead. "I don't know what came over my cousin. Thank you for being so understanding about her storytelling."

"She wasn't telling a story." Uncle Ambrose skewered them with his shrewd gaze.

Angelina's eyes meshed with Lord Bretheridge's for a brief moment. Did hers reflect the same shock as his?

"Felicia heard correctly." Uncle stomped to stand before them. He pointed at Angelina then the marquis. "Neither of you is in a position to object. As I see it, you're at *point non-plus*."

"Whatever do you mean?" Utterly bewildered, she tried to make sense of his odd declaration.

He folded his arms and swung his smug gaze between them, a self-satisfied smile on his mouth. "You've no choice except to wed."

11

God curse the bugger!

Flynn bit his tongue, swallowing the vulgar oath he ached to launch at Waterford's retreating form. Only Mrs. Thorne's presence prevented him from doing so. He eyed a bronze bust that he felt certain would lay the cur out. He ached to heave the figurine at the duke, too.

No, he itched to flatten Waterford with his fists. God forgive him, but he truly hated the man. He could hear the cocky weasel's boots clacking the length of the entry as he left his niece without a proper chaperone.

Flynn turned his attention to Mrs. Thorne.

Eyes closed, her dark reddish-brown lashes fanned her cheeks. Pale as the snowdrops lining the drive to Lambridge each February, she drew in a trembling breath. Her hands cradling her middle, she swayed, and he feared she might swoon.

"Are you well? Here, have a seat." He grasped her elbow and tried steering her toward the settee.

At his touch, her eyelids flew open, the twin pools of emerald wounded and glistening with tears.

"No, no, thank you." She raised her chin a notch. "I'm not some ninny who swoons at the drop of a teacup."

He scratched his nose. "Or when a mean-tempered bull chases you into a tree?"

"Indeed." She offered a wobbly half-smile.

Angst on her lovely face, she stared at the empty doorway. With the inborn diplomacy of a true lady, Mrs. Thorne collected herself and sought to reassure Flynn. "Please forgive my uncle. I'm mortified that he dared threaten you."

Threats and coercion. That was how vermin like Waterford operated.

In a vexed whisper, she added, "And rest assured, I entertain no ideas of marriage. To *anyone*." Her cheeks glowed rosy, and she pressed a trembling hand to her forehead as if unwell.

To be so opposed to the notion of marriage, she must still grieve her husband deeply. How long had she been widowed? Quite recently, he'd guess, given her tender age. She couldn't be more than one and twenty. How tragic someone so young had already endured a loss of such magnitude.

What could her uncle be thinking, trying to pressure her into an unwanted match when she was still in mourning? Did the bounder hold something over her as well? Unless…

Perhaps, she wasn't as opposed to the match as she so adamantly claimed.

Rubbing the back of his neck, he tried to ease some of the tension yet snarled there. "You needn't be embarrassed, nor should you apologize for your uncle."

"I dare say, you will never accept another invitation for tea again," she allowed. Her lips quivered, though whether from amusement or dismay, he wasn't sure.

Despite the gravity of the moment, he couldn't contain his delighted chuckled. "I suppose it would depend on who was in attendance."

Dealt as severe a blow as he just now, Mrs. Thorne hadn't once objected on her behalf. Her concern had been for him. She possessed a generous, caring nature. Either that or she'd mastered a consummate actress's skill.

He studied her closely again. No, she wasn't acting. The tightness around her mouth and chagrin in her eyes held no hint of deceit.

"I confess I'm not fond of the drink." He gestured toward the abandoned tea service before his gaze lit on the mantel clock. Surely it was later than half-past four.

"I prefer coffee myself. It's absurd serving a hot beverage in this heat." She fanned herself with her hand. "We're already warm as fleas in fleece."

What a delightful wit. Despite the somberness of the past few minutes, he laughed.

"Do let me see you to the door." Motioning to the entrance, she drifted in that direction.

"A moment, Mrs. Thorne, if you please."

She sent him a questioning glance. "Of course, my lord."

Though tall, and not a diamond of the first water by Polite Society's standards, she was indisputably a treasure. He canted his head, considering her.

Dewy pink-tinted lips, petal-soft skin, and golden hair with fiery highlights, combined with those arresting green eyes, she was more of a prize flower than a jewel. Yes, an exquisite bloom.

Hadn't her uncle called her Angelina-Rose?

A rose. Perfect.

Quick-witted, gracious, and possessed of a compassionate nature, she would make an acceptable wife. Mayhap, not his first choice, but as Waterford gloated, Flynn didn't have many alternatives.

Actually, not a one at present.

He'd come to Wingfield Court anticipating an introduction to a long-toothed harridan, ages past her prime. Possibly cross-eyed, rotund, and given to snorting when she laughed. Instead, he'd been presented the delectable Mrs. Thorne. A future with her wouldn't be dreadfully objectionable. Given time, it might even develop into a companionable arrangement.

Prior to meeting Lydia, Flynn had never contemplated marrying for love. Thus, an arranged match wasn't abhorrent to him. Being forced into one by Waterford was repugnant as maggots on a corpse, however. Of greater concern was Mrs. Thorne's role in this scheme. Innocent pawn or devious siren?

Lydia's smiling face edged to the forefront of Flynn's mind. He doggedly shoved the vision aside, finding it easier to do than he'd expected.

He had responsibilities. Duties. Others' entire existence depended on him.

Their wellbeing must take precedence over the desires of his heart. As things stood, he didn't have the means to provide for his family. If he didn't agree to marry Mrs. Thorne, he might have a week—two at most—before Waterford demanded his winnings.

"Lord Bretheridge?" Mrs. Thorne's slightly husky voice interrupted his musings. "You wished to say something?"

"Would you mind terribly if we moved farther away from the entrance?" He darted a guarded glance toward the drawing room's open door and lowered his voice. "I've no wish for eavesdropping servants, or anyone else, to be a party to our conversation."

She scrutinized the doorway, her brow puckered. Did she worry about an interruption or her reputation? Her demeanor hesitant, she consented. "Near the terrace windows would suffice, I suppose."

"Thank you." He forced his lips to tilt reassuringly.

Once they'd crossed the room, he faced her. "I think it only honorable to tell you. Your uncle called on me this morning."

Other than the slight raising of her finely arched brows, she didn't respond.

Ah, so she wasn't the sort who pried or jumped to conclusions. He rather liked that. Unless, of course, his revelation came as no surprise. The notion didn't sit well at all. That meant she was a fraud—as much a charlatan as Waterford.

More than one woman of his acquaintance concealed a treacherous heart behind her beauty. Those women used their allure to manipulate and deceive.

He searched her green eyes, peering beyond the composure and leeriness lurking there.

She met his gaze unflinchingly.

"He told me he wanted us to marry." An edict better described the duke's request, but she needn't know that.

Mrs. Thorne gasped and retreated a step from him. "Pardon?"

Confusion, rapidly followed by alarm, flitted across her face. She threw a panic-filled glance at the entry. "You conspired with him and then pretended ignorance when Felicia mentioned what she overheard?"

His gut coiled at the patent betrayal in her voice. The fear in her eyes pierced him as sharply as a blade. Why did *he* feel guilty? It wasn't as if he'd plotted with Waterford.

Had she?

"No, not at all. His suggestion staggered me too." Flynn shoved a hand through his hair.

Pulling her eyebrows together in consternation, she folded her arms. "I think you had better start at the beginning. You're not making sense."

At least she'd allow him to speak his peace instead of flouncing from the room in a fit of temper.

"Yes, perhaps, I should. Let's have a seat, shall we?" He pointed to wine-colored wingback chairs arranged before the west-facing mullioned windows.

The manor cast elongated shadows the length of the terrace at the rear of the house and wrapped it in welcome coolness. Lilac bushes framed either side of the window, their blossoms now only a memory.

Sinking gracefully onto the cushions, Mrs. Thorne adjusted her crisp skirts. She folded her hands neatly in her lap and settled her gaze on him, calm wariness in its verdant depths. Nevertheless, a strained pinch remained about her full lips.

Flynn sat opposite her.

Where to start?

With the worst.

Still uncomfortable with the signet ring around his finger, he twisted the band and took in a fortifying breath. "My father died in May. He… he took his own life—"

"Lord, no!" Mrs. Thorne clasped a hand to her mouth. Moisture edged the rims of her eyes. She blinked, obviously struggling against tears. "I'm so very sorry."

"As am I." He closed his eyes briefly. "You and only a handful of others are aware of the truth, and I beg you, please keep my confidence. The knowledge would cause immeasurable grief to the women of my family."

"I shan't breathe a word." She wiped a tear leaking from the corner of one eye with her knuckle. "I promise."

Flynn gripped the chair's arms and struggled to control the grief and rage suffusing him. The emptiness gnawing at him every waking moment and haunting his restless dreams squeezed the air from his lungs.

"Plied with drink, he gamed away everything he owned. Outside of entailed properties, nothing else remains." Flynn examined the scenery beyond the window, unable to bear the desolation simmering in her beautiful eyes.

"How utterly awful," Mrs. Thorne whispered tightly.

"Your uncle won the wager." Flynn kept his voice deliberately devoid of emotion. He'd no idea what the nature of her relationship was with Waterford.

"I… I…" Her soft weeping drew Flynn's attention indoors. She swiped at the tears, covering her cheeks.

He withdrew his handkerchief from his pocket. "Here."

Giving him a grateful nod, she took the linen and dabbed at her tears. "I don't know what to say, other than I'm profoundly horrified and ashamed. And remorseful beyond words."

Her sorrow seemed genuine.

"It's no fault of yours," he observed.

"True, but we carry the sins of our families, don't we?" She plucked at the fine material of her overskirt. "Please explain how these atrocious events led Uncle to suggest we marry. I'm afraid I don't see the connection. I'd think he would steer far clear of you after what he's done."

"He offered to cancel the entire debt if I took you to wife." Flynn relaxed farther into the chair. Was she also a puppet in this game Waterford played? Or, did she participate willingly?

"Oh."

Oh?

Flynn had just revealed her uncle's plot to pressure him into marrying her. Surely she could muster a stronger response than, 'Oh.'

Mrs. Thorne stared at the carpet, seemingly obsessed with the floral pattern. Or perchance, her slippered foot fascinated her. She kept brushing the toe back and forth on the floor.

He leaned forward, his elbows on his knees. "Why is that, do you think?"

"I cannot marry you." She raised her tormented gaze to his.

"Why?"

A disconcerted expression whisked across her face.

The question surprised him as well.

She stared at him, her eyes huge and round. And *guilty*?

Interesting.

His title alone made him a prime catch on the Marriage Mart. It wasn't as if there were an abundant number of marquises searching for eligible women to take to wife. If Waterford canceled the vowel, Father's holdings and monies would be restored. That, combined with Flynn's personal wealth, gave him very deep pockets.

If he accepted the duke's proposal, he'd be considered a brilliant match once more. Unfortunately, Flynn would have but one choice for a bride.

Her.

A fact, mayhap, she knew well.

Mrs. Thorne regained her composure. Not quite meeting his eyes, she fidgeted with her wedding band. "Surely you're not serious? There must be dozens of women more suitable for you to take to wife than me."

He remained silent, noting her nervousness in the pulse fluttering at the base of her slender throat.

She tucked a loose curl behind her ear. "Besides, we have just met and know nothing about one another."

"I cannot argue the truth of that." He idly rubbed the velvety arm of the chair.

Mayhap her marriage hadn't been a love match, and she was

distrustful of wedding again. On the other hand, conceivably it had been, and still broken-hearted, she needed more time to mourn.

So, why Waterford's push for an immediate union?

Flynn scanned her left hand. A rather garish ruby and diamond ring encircled her third finger. "You were widowed quite recently?"

"Er, yes, though I was married for a very short time." Anger tinged her strangely constricted voice. "However, as you know, when one loses a spouse or a parent, a lengthy period of mourning must be observed."

Flynn stretched his legs before him. God's teeth, he was weary. The emotional stress of the past weeks had taken a toll on him physically. He'd risen before dawn every day since Father's death—the few nights he sought sleep at all.

His head pounded from lack of slumber, too much sun, and now this conundrum. He felt half-foxed as if he fished his thoughts from a deep, murky pool.

He pressed two fingers to the bridge of his nose. "Typically, yes. Your uncle is aware we're both in the early months of our mourning period, yet he insists we marry. And soon. I'm given to wonder why a man who strictly adheres to social conformity would toss off mourning protocol."

She didn't respond, only wadded his handkerchief into a tighter ball. His laundress would never rid the cloth of the wrinkles.

"It would be to my advantage to wed you." Flynn tapped the fingers of one hand on his thigh. "If I refuse to make good on Father's wager, my honor won't be worth the muck in a pigsty. It would spell social ruination for me and everyone I hold dear."

She remained silent. Deafeningly so.

He crossed an ankle over a knee. "However, should the gaming debt be canceled, I'd have the means to care for my family—"

"Excuse me." Mrs. Thorne's expression tightened with concern. "You have family other than your mother?"

"I have a sister, Francesca—we call her Franny—who's confined to an invalid chair, the result of a riding accident many years ago. My aging grandmother resides at Lambridge Manse, and soon my aunt will as well."

He quirked the corners of his mouth, minutely, and waved his hand in a circular motion in the air. "I'm surrounded by women. They're all quite extraordinary. I think you'd like them."

"It would be a pleasure to meet them someday," she replied politely.

"As I mentioned earlier, my mother's convalescing from apoplexy."

Flynn fought a wave of ire.

He never imagined he'd be in this position. Dependent on the benevolence of a man he loathed in order to care for his loved ones. It went against every grain of decency in him. The blow to his pride stung sharp as a rapier's tip.

Mother's recovery and her treatments added more reasons why speedy nuptials benefited him. Yet, what did Mrs. Thorne have to gain, if anything, from wedding him? Did she have family members with a need as well, and marrying a wealthy, titled lord would enable her to help them?

The marquisship alone is incentive enough for many position-hungry women.

"Have you family other than the Waterfords, Mrs. Thorne?"

"Yes, my mother and two younger sisters, Patience and Prudence. They're twins also. Mama is Aunt Camille's twin." She settled further into the cushion as if she sought the protection of the chair's high back and sides.

He arched an eyebrow. "Twins run in your family? How extraordinary."

An expression of utter devastation ravaged Mrs. Thorne's face for a fraction of a moment before she recovered. She gave a stiff nod. "Every generation for as far back as anyone can recall, there has been at least one set."

Her eyelids fluttered closed, and she rested her head against the chair. Pale as cream, she seemed completely done in.

"Mrs. Thorne?"

Her eyelids inched open. She stared at him silently, despair shadowing her face.

What haunted her? What secrets did she hide?

Now wasn't the time to press for answers. He made a swift decision. "May I call upon you tomorrow?"

"I don't think that would be wise, my lord." Her attention dropped to her hands, entwined atop her lap.

"Wise?" Flynn rubbed his jaw. He needed a shave. "I suspect you're in need of assistance as much as I am."

This curious need to reassure—and yes, to comfort her—though he didn't, couldn't, trust her, intrigued him. She was kin to Waterford, after all. That ought to make her his enemy from the onset.

"I'd like to help you. If you'll allow me," he said with gentle candor.

"You cannot." Despondency obvious in her hunched shoulders, Mrs. Thorne sighed and faced the window. "No one can. My situation is impossible."

He persisted, needing to understand for some perverse reason. "Surely, your circumstances are not as hopeless as that?"

Unless…Was she ill? Dying? Did she have some ghastly sickness? Mayhap cancer? Why marry her off then? It didn't make sense. True, she was drawn and pale, and quite slender, but she didn't appear deathly ill.

"Are you unwell?" *Ye gods*. Couldn't he control his blasted tongue? He tried again. "Are you declining to enter a union with me because you're sickly? Ailing?"

Confound it.

Flynn's tongue formed the questions of its own accord, his sleep-deprived brain plainly too sluggish to stop the unruly appendage. He bit down. Hard.

No more questions.

Mrs. Thorne threw him an incredulous, infuriated glare. She vaulted from her seat, her beautiful eyes flashing green fire. "First, *my lord*, I don't recall hearing a proposal from you."

She held up two slender fingers. "Second, I'd have to be addled to entertain the idea of marrying an absolute stranger. And third." Up shot another finger. "I'm not sick. Not unless you consider being in the family way an illness."

12

God above!

Angelina clamped her teeth together until they ached.

Why had she blurted *that* to Lord Bretheridge? Was she insane? Did pregnancy cause one's tongue to flap like laundry in the wind? If only she could stuff the words back into her mouth. Then stitch her loose lips shut.

Stupid, stupid ninny.

His lordship sat there, legs crossed, his forearms resting casually on the chair, speculation in his flinty eyes. Eyes narrowed the merest bit, he leisurely took her measure.

The knowledge rankled. The silence in the room grew thicker and more uncomfortable by the second. Why didn't he say something?

She checked the French Empire mantle clock—scarcely past four-thirty. If his lordship would leave, she could retreat to her room and rest before dinner. Her head and stomach swirled sickeningly.

A bird pecked the window behind her, and Angelina jumped. Head cocked in confusion, a spotted woodpecker perched on a branch. It struck the window again.

"Not too terribly bright, is it?" Lord Bretheridge flicked his long fingers toward the bird hopping along the branch. "It thinks its reflection is another woodpecker, and our winged friend is protecting his territory."

Why was he blathering on about birds, of all things?

She'd just blurted she was with child. She expected him to sprint from the room as fast as his long, entirely too-muscled legs could carry him.

The marquis's scrutiny sank to her abdomen. "You're not very far along."

Now he wanted to discuss her increasing? Such things were not mentioned in mixed company, and never, *ever* with a male acquaintance.

And Dear God, what if I carry twins?

The thought had never occurred to her before today. She wanted to wallop Lord Bretheridge for planting that worrisome seed in her mind. One child was worry enough, but two? *Good God and all the divine powers.* How could she possibly care for twins?

Why hadn't Uncle Ambrose banished her to some remote corner of Scotland until the babe arrived? And his preposterous plan to force Lord Bretheridge to marry her?

His lordship probably thought her a willing accomplice in her uncle's underhanded calculating.

She swallowed against a fresh wave of nausea. If only the floor would open right this second and swallow her, obliterating her existence.

God, what did I do to deserve this? I loved a man. Was that so wrong?

Lord Bretheridge unfolded his tall frame, rising from the chair and yawning behind his hand. "Pardon me. I've not enjoyed much sleep of late."

He boldly eyed her belly again.

Boorish lout.

Her gown's draping hid the evidence of her increasing. Did he try to determine if she really carried a child? She covered her stomach with both hands in a protective gesture. "The baby is due in December."

Brilliant. Volunteer the sordid details, why don't you?

Angelina could see him calculating in his mind. Chagrin heated her from bosom to hairline. Likely, she glowed pink as the roses on the fireplace mantel. She pivoted to stare out the window. She would become used to this kind of censure, wouldn't she?

Never.

"When did you say you arrived in England?" Though gently asked, the question wasn't idle.

Turning her head, she scrunched her eyebrows together. "The first part of May. May the second, I believe. Why?"

"You don't think it's rather convenient you arrive in England, *enceinte*, and my father is ruined by a wager he lost to your uncle a mere two weeks later?" A stony glint entered the marquis's eyes, deepening their color to dark green agate. He raked his fingers through his sable hair again.

"Which begs the question, why is Waterford blackmailing me into marrying you?"

Did he accuse her of something nefarious?

Angelina faced him fully, gripping the chair for support. She darted a hesitant glance to the door. Saunders might be listening. Likely *was* listening, and the boor would report every word to Uncle Ambrose.

Aiming for nonchalance, she shrugged but kept her voice lowered. "How could it be anything except coincidence?"

His lordship stalked to her chair, his stormy eyes narrowed. His nostrils flared as he towered above her, waves of fury pouring off him. "What aren't you telling me, Mrs. Thorne?"

Yes, accusation most definitely rang in his tone. And blatant hostility. She'd become the adversary.

The self-righteous prig.

Lifting her chin a notch, Angelina met his infuriated regard. "Lord Bretheridge, you need to leave."

She wouldn't let this man, to whom she owed nothing and to whom she had no obligation, accuse her of wrongdoing. She'd had quite enough of men running roughshod over her. First Papa, then the vermin she thought she married, and now Uncle Ambrose, whose saneness she seriously questioned.

This brazen oaf could take his infernal allegations and...and choke on them. Enraged and trembling, Angelina pointed to the door. "Leave. Now!"

He could see himself out.

She would never make it that far without her composure crumbling or her knees failing her. Swallowing, she raised a hand to her forehead, forcing her eyes to focus on the infuriated man before her.

She needed to lie down.

"Will you please leave?" she managed with a degree of civility she didn't feel.

His lordship shook his head forcefully, several strands of chestnut hair falling onto his high forehead. Glaring at her, he made a rude sound in his throat. "No. Not until you tell me *everything*. What are you hiding?"

"Of all the unmitigated gall. Are you making demands of me in my uncle's home? Who do you think you are?" Angelina balled her fists. She itched to slap him. If she were a man, she'd call him out.

His insulting perusal traveled the length of her person once more, hovering an instant too long on her bosom. "Precisely, what is your role in Waterford's extortion plot?"

"I knew nothing of my uncle's deviousness until," she sliced a glance to the clock once more, "ten minutes ago."

An unpleasant jeer contorted the marquis's handsome mouth. He planted his hands on his lean hips. "What a fine arrangement for you. An American carrying someone else's child foisted off on an English marquis. Quite the merry widow you'd be, wouldn't you?"

"No, you're wrong." Angelina stared at him, this vengeful, hateful man. Where had the kind stranger at the stream gone? Or even the considerate lord who had come for tea? "I'm not American, and I—"

Lord Bretheridge stared at her stomach again, and she protectively covered the slight mound with her hands.

His eyes widened with sudden comprehension.

Her instincts screamed he'd stumbled upon the truth.

His gaze careened to hers. "You've never been married, have you?" He laughed harshly. "Now it makes sense. Why you've come to England and are sequestered here."

She closed her eyes, the bitter accusation lancing her soul. This judgment and condemnation were what she could expect, what she had expected.

May God curse you, Charles.

"You know nothing of my circumstances." Tucking her chin to her chest, Angelina fought the scalding tears demanding release.

"By all that's holy," Lord Bretheridge muttered as if speaking to himself. "Waterford's trying to shackle me with someone else's by-blow."

She winced. He might as well have struck her. Fury, dark and blinding, enveloped her. "You unconscionable lout. Despicable cur. Contemptible blackguard—"

"Don't forget cuckolded intended," he drawled, mockery dripping from his voice.

Angelina slapped him, the sound echoing ominously in the room. Tears streamed from her eyes. She jerked her hand back to strike him again. "Bloody bastard."

Lord Bretheridge caught her wrist in a gentle, yet unyielding grip. "You don't get a second time. And, I don't think you should be calling anyone a bastard—considering."

Angelina flinched and gasped, feeling the color drain from her face. Her head spinning dizzyingly, she drew a deep, measured breath. Her chest ached, where his words had impaled her heart, slicing a gaping wound to her soul.

"As I said before, you know nothing of what has happened to me. You've no right to pass judgment." Forcing the words through stiff lips, she wrenched her wrist. "Let me go."

I must get away from him.

Another few seconds and she feared she'd topple over. A grayish haze blurred her vision, and her blood whooshed loudly in her ears.

"Were you… assaulted?" Doubt colored the marquis's question.

Directed at her or himself, she couldn't say. Of course, he'd rather believe her an immoral tart. Once more, she tugged against his strong grasp.

He released her.

Angelina slowly swiveled toward the door. Swaying, she squinted and blinked several times, trying to focus.

Too far.

The settee, then.

For the babe's sake, she must gain the couch before blackness claimed her. She took three stumbling steps. Her vision narrowed to a tiny pinprick. Extending her arms, she edged forward a couple of unstable paces. Surely the settee must be near.

"Mrs. Thorne?" Lord Bretheridge's voice echoed, muffled and distant.

Good. The bugger has finally decided to leave.

She never wanted to lay eyes on the fiend again. Dizziness spiraled around her. Faltering, Angelina swayed for a moment before crumpling. She cried out weakly and attempted to shield her stomach. "No. My baby—"

Strong arms caught her as utter darkness descended.

Someone patted one of Angelina's cheeks, then the other.

Go away. I want to sleep.

"Mrs. Thorne, wake up." The deep voice sounded vaguely familiar.

Fabric rustled, and the scent of lilies wafted past her nostrils. "Good heavens! What has happened?"

Ah, dear Aunt Camille.

"Saunders, fetch my smelling salts at once," her aunt ordered.

No, not smelling salts. I'll surely gag. Better stir myself.

"Yes, Your Grace."

Angelina cracked an eye open.

The butler hustled to the entrance.

"What did you do to the gel, Bretheridge?" Uncle Ambrose's grating voice set her teeth on edge.

Wait. Bretheridge? The toad remained?

She groaned, as memory and full awareness flowed through her. Perchance, she should pretend to faint again in hopes he'd be gone when she roused. A more disagreeable man she'd never met.

"There, there, dear." Aunt Camille patted Angelina's hand.

Daring to open her eyes for a brief moment, she glimpsed the half-circle of concerned faces hovering above her. She struggled to sit upright, her limbs leaden, and her head wooly as dirty fleece.

"No, don't try to sit yet, Lina." Aunt Camille bent near, supporting her. "You swooned."

"I don't swoon."

A soft, deliciously deep chuckle rippled throughout the room. "Call it what you will, Mrs. Thorne. You were insensate for a good five minutes."

Ah, the oaf. Go away.

Despite her aunt's protest, Angelina angled herself into a sitting position, sagging ungracefully against the settee's corner. "I've never had a fit of the vapors in my life."

No one voiced the obvious reason for her fainting spell. Her aunt and uncle had no idea Lord Bretheridge was aware of her condition, and his lordship didn't dare reveal she'd told him.

"It must've been the heat," she said, cursing inwardly at the feeble excuse. Couldn't she have fabricated something a scant more believable?

"Indeed. It can be most draining." Lord Bretheridge stood at the end of the settee, his expression one of cool politeness.

Angelina didn't believe his perfect gentlemanly pretense. She'd seen otherwise. Despising the shame he caused her to feel, she averted her gaze. Would the man never take his leave? "I'm perfectly fine. Truly. Perchance, I'm only hungry."

Aunt Camille pursed her lips. "Yes, that might cause a spell of lightheadedness. I imagine you're famished. You didn't eat anything substantial at luncheon, and Murphy told me you consumed nothing other than mint tea to break your fast this morning."

Aunt Camille, do hush.

Lord Bretheridge coughed and turned aside.

Angelina narrowed her eyes until they were thin slits. Was he laughing? Best add that to the list of conditions.

Peculiar senses of humor are to be avoided in males.

Holding her gown in place, Angelina swung her legs off the couch. Other than a trifling weakness, she did feel better. She would be happy as the birds gorging themselves in her uncle's cherry trees the moment the marquis left.

"Here, Lina." Her aunt thrust a chocolate biscuit at her. "Eat this. It will help you regain your strength."

Aunt Camille's cure for everything involved food.

"Your Graces, Mrs. Thorne." The marquis, his jungle eyes trained on Angelina, edged closer. "I'd be honored if you'd join me for tea at Lambridge Manse tomorrow."

Angelina's gaze careened to him. Had he taken complete leave of his senses? What game did he play? She would sooner embrace an asp or drink arsenic.

Meeting his eyes, Angelina glowered and mouthed an emphatic, "No!"

He couldn't mean to pursue this farce of a match between them. Why the sudden change in tactics? *Pity?* He could take his misguided nobleness and gag on it. She hadn't been interested before he spewed those hateful things. But now? She wouldn't have him if the Prince Regent himself requested the union.

Lord Bretheridge flashed his white teeth and turned to Aunt Camille. "Your Grace?"

Startled, she pressed a plump hand to her even plumper bosom and sent an apprehensive peek to Uncle Ambrose.

Nodding, he beamed his approval.

He would, the traitor.

"Why, that would be lovely, my lord." Her aunt tittered nervously. "As long as Angelina has recovered and feels capable of an excursion."

Bless you, Aunt Camille.

Her aunt cleverly provided the excuse Angelina needed. Indeed, she had. She would be indisposed indefinitely—right up until the time she gave birth.

His lordship dipped his head in deference. "Excellent. I'm sure Mrs. Thorne will be in finest form by tomorrow afternoon. She expressed an eagerness to meet my family."

Eagerness? What utter balderdash.

"I'll inform my staff and shall expect you at three o'clock." After a smart bow, Lord Bretheridge strode from the room.

Angelina scowled at the empty doorway.

So, his lordship wanted to play that game, did he? He had best be prepared. She was about to lead one pompous, overbearing marquis on a very merry chase.

13

At precisely five minutes past three the next afternoon, Flynn examined his pocket watch for the fourth time in ten minutes. He paced before the drawing room's unlit fireplace as Grandmamma and Franny silently observed him.

Next to his grandmother, Franny knew him better than any living soul.

Where are they?

After Mrs. Thorne's revelation yesterday, he'd every intention of telling Waterford to bugger himself. Flynn intended to refuse to pay the wager and accept the social disgrace accompanying such ignominy.

He had a hunch the duke had cheated during the game with Father, though it would be deucedly thorny to prove. He needed a witness or the cards themselves.

Yancy had sat at the same table and hadn't noticed anything amiss. And he possessed a keen ear and sharp eye. His position as War Secretary made those skills essential.

Nonetheless, Flynn remained convinced the sequence of events leading to Waterford's magnanimous offer stank of subterfuge and was altogether too convenient for the situation to be happenstance.

He wanted to feel nothing except antipathy for Mrs. Thorne, but his conscience railed against him. The god-awful wounded expression in her eyes pricked something deep within. One didn't pretend that kind of suffering. His tortured soul recognized another tormented spirit, and her anguish called to him on a level he didn't fully understand.

Remorse plagued him for his harsh treatment yesterday. His ugly accusations kept him awake until dawn's timid glow ventured into his chamber. For reasons he didn't want to examine, he needed to know the truth about her and her pregnancy.

She didn't seem the duplicitous sort, nor did she appear

promiscuous. It churned his stomach to think she'd been set upon unwillingly. How had she found herself in this most difficult of situations?

That enigma had compelled him to invite the Waterfords and her to tea, when fifteen minutes prior, he'd never wanted to lay eyes on her uncle again.

Given the lethal glowers she speared Flynn after awakening from her faint, he'd wager his cattle she regarded him just as unfavorably. It further convinced him she had no part in her uncle's plotting. Her outrage and fury toward Flynn hadn't been feigned

He resisted the urge to peek at his timepiece's hands again. Instead, he slid a glance to the mahogany longcase clock ticking beside the door.

Blister it.

He'd no hope of winning Mrs. Thorne's favor if she refused to be in the same room with him. Their mutual adversary made her a kindred spirit, not just an easy solution for Father's gambling debt. What other reason could there be for the unexplainable connection he sensed with her?

"Flynn, do stop pacing. You're giving my neck a crick." Franny touched her chin and gave him a wide-eyed stare. "One might think you nervous—"

"Her Grace, Camille, the Duchess of Waterford, and Mrs. Angelina Thorne," Chatterton announced in his most imperious tone.

"I told you they'd come." Grandmamma's eyes contained a mischievous twinkle as well as approval. "Wise move that, leaving the duke at home."

A trifling reprieve, for which Flynn admitted eternal gratitude.

Unable to think of a plausible explanation for the Waterfords coming to call after years without contact, Flynn had confided in Grandmamma. The duke's desire for a match between Mrs. Thorne and him earned a raised silver eyebrow but no more. If Grandmamma suspected he withheld the entire truth about their visit, she kept her thoughts to herself.

"Do forgive us, our tardiness." Breathless, the duchess bustled into the drawing room. "Angelina couldn't find a shoe."

She sent her niece an affectionate gaze.

A reluctant, albeit exquisite, Mrs. Thorne trailed her aunt into the room. Her ebony gown emphasized the reddish highlights in her golden hair. More color shone in her face today, and her delicate jaw contained a determined set that hadn't been there yesterday.

She wasn't happy to be here. Not at all. How had her aunt coaxed her to come?

"Waterford sends his regrets, my lord. Something unexpected arose." The Duchess of Waterford's artificial smile revealed what she couldn't.

Likely, he's foxed.

Far more probable, their lateness could be attributed to the duke than a misplaced shoe.

Flynn ceased pacing and snapped his pocket watch closed. Tucking the fob into his waistcoat, he skirted the sofa. He waited until both women were well into the room before he bowed. "Good afternoon. Thank you for coming, ladies."

"My lord." Mrs. Thorne curtsied without meeting his eyes. In fact, she gazed everywhere except at him—rather discomfiting.

He took the duchess's arm and guided her farther into the drawing room. "Your Grace, you're acquainted with my grandmother, the Dowager Marchioness Bretheridge, and my sister, Lady Francesca."

"Indeed, though it's been many years." The duchess didn't hesitate to buss the other women's cheeks. "It's such a pleasure to see you again. Lady Francesca, you've grown into a comely young woman."

"Thank you, Your Grace." Franny inclined her head.

The duchess sat on the settee opposite Grandmamma and eagerly eyed the assortment of delicate pastries and dainties displayed.

"It's lovely to see you as well." Grandmamma extended a steaming cup of tea to the duchess.

Flynn indicated Mrs. Thorne with a wave of his hand. "Grandmamma, Francesca, may I introduce Mrs. Angelina Thorne to you?"

Mrs. Thorne's pretty mouth curved as she took a seat beside her aunt. "Lord Bretheridge has spoken of you."

Barely.

"It's wonderful to make your acquaintance." Grandmamma's eyes sparkled warmly before she turned her attention to pouring more tea.

"Delighted, Mrs. Thorne." Francesca caught Flynn's eye and winked while Mrs. Thorne arranged her skirts.

Once settled, she sent another friendly smile to his grandmother and sister.

And ignored him entirely.

He might've been a picture on the wall or a flower on the carpet for all of the attention she paid him. Clearly, the floor held more interest than he did, for her gaze remained focused there.

Flynn sat on the settee, positioning himself directly opposite her. *Now let her avoid me.* "Mother is recuperating and won't be joining us. I'm confident you understand."

"But of course." The duchess selected a pastry and glanced about the room. "How is your mother's health?"

"She's improving daily, for which we're very grateful." Flynn accepted the cup his grandmother extended. "Thank you."

"My lord, are these some of your blossoms?" Her grace waved at the vases of flowers scattered throughout the room. "I've heard of your successful venture into breeding these beauties."

That caught Mrs. Thorne's attention. Her jewel-green eyes swept the roses. A line formed between her brows, and she mashed her lips together, lowering her gaze to her cup. She took a dainty sip of tea.

Didn't she care for roses? Or, possibly, the tea displeased her. *Dolt.* He ought to have had coffee served as well since she preferred the beverage.

"Oh, indeed, they are." Pride rang in Grandmamma's voice. "See those stunning blooms on the mantle? Have you ever seen roses that particular shade of pink? Why, they appear almost lavender. Makes me think of fresh highland heather on the Scottish moors. And Flynn raises a rose that is almost black in hue."

"Mrs. Thorne, don't you like roses?" Franny also noticed Mrs. Thorne's expression.

The Duchess chuckled indulgently. "With a name like Angelina-Rose, of course, she does. Tell them of your gardens in Salem. Your mother wrote of your fascination with the flower."

A becoming flush pinkened Mrs. Thorne's high cheekbones. So, she entertained a penchant for roses, after all. Precisely the excuse he needed to invite her to tour his conservatories and spirit her away from the watchful eye of the duchess. Franny could accompany them and act as a chaperone.

Flynn controlled the satisfied grin threatening to twist his lips. "Did you know the great bard, Shakespeare, claimed a fondness for them? He said, 'Of all the flowers, methinks the rose is best.'"

Mrs. Thorne nodded, her interest fixed on a vase reposed on a side table. "I'm partial to them myself, though I cannot claim to such a complicated endeavor as breeding them. I simply tended a few humble plants in our gardens. I don't believe they numbered more than ten in all."

"Flynn." Franny leaned forward in her chair. "You must take Mrs. Thorne to see your blooms. Would that be acceptable, Grandmamma?"

Franny's intense perusal switched from their grandmother to the duchess. "Your Grace? I don't wish to seem rude."

"What a splendid idea." Grandmamma, a scheming gleam in her eyes, shifted her pale gaze to the duchess.

"What say you, Your Grace? We can have a nice coze. I'd so like to hear the latest *on dit* from London." She fluttered a hand toward Flynn and Franny "And these young people can enjoy the outdoors. The conservatories and rose gardens smell heavenly this time of day after the sun has heated the blossoms, and they release their perfume."

The duchess set her cup in its saucer. "I don't mind in the least. I would, however, beg a bouquet to take home."

"I'd be delighted." Flynn stood. "Mrs. Thorne?"

From the daggers she sent him from beneath her lashes, she realized she was good and snared. She turned to her aunt. "Aunt Camille, are you certain you don't mind? I'm loath to abandon you."

"Not at all, my dear. Go along and enjoy yourself." She patted Mrs. Thorne's hand and gave Flynn a lengthy, candid stare. "See that my niece enjoys herself, won't you, your lordship?"

Her meaning was clear as ice on a pond.

Watch your step.

"Of course. I should like nothing more." He bowed his head and gripped the handles of Franny's invalid carriage. "Franny, do you wish me to push you, or should we ring for Penny?"

"Penny, please, Flynn." She gazed up at him, her lips twitching. "I don't tolerate the heat well. I'll likely take only one turn about the closest garden. I shouldn't want to cut short Mrs. Thorne's enjoyment, however."

Just like Franny to worry about others.

Her eyes sparkled, and she grinned. "They are spectacular, Mrs. Thorne. He has hundreds and hundreds of bushes."

Franny's enthusiasm seemed contagious, for Mrs. Thorne grinned in return. "Well then, lead on, oh-mistress-of-the-gardens."

Franny chuckled and winked at him. "I like her, Flynn."

He bent and kissed the crown of her head. "I do too."

"We can *all* hear you." Grandmamma's eyes glittered with mirth.

Helping herself to a Naples biscuit, her grace chuckled. "I do believe that's the idea."

Did approval glimmer in her eyes?

Flynn shifted to find Mrs. Thorne staring at him, a perplexed expression on her face. Far better than anger. He'd see what he could do in the next hour to turn her puzzlement into a betrothal agreement.

Careful to keep her parasol between her face and the sun, Angelina bent to sniff an enormous blood-red bloom. Lady Francesca hadn't exaggerated. The gardens were outstanding. Row upon row of flowers, as well as arbors, trellises, and raised beds boasted roses of every conceivable size and color.

What a glorious, fragrant rainbow anchored to the earth by roots and soil.

"That one doesn't have much scent. Smell this flower instead." Lady Francesca indicated a delicate yellow and orange rose beside her.

Angelina obediently lowered her head to inhale. "Lovely. The size of the blossom doesn't indicate the strength of its perfume, does it?" She traced the petals with her forefinger. "I adore these multi-colored blossoms."

Two spaniels and a Dalmatian darted amongst the manicured rows for several minutes before trotting over to sit panting at his lordship's feet. Tongues lolling and tails thumping, they gaped at him, adoration in their round, coffee-colored eyes.

"Mrs. Thorne, I've several other specimens in the conservatories. A favorite of mine is a deep pink and white rose." Standing a few feet away, Lord Bretheridge waved toward a pair of buildings on the other side of the green. "Would you like to see them?"

Did she dare? No doubt, she would come to regret it. She searched his face for a brief moment. Nothing except kindness showed in his eyes today.

Why not?

She swept her lips upward. "Yes, that would be wonderful."

Angelina had always loved flowers. In the past few minutes, she'd discovered several shades of roses she hadn't know existed. What harm could there be in seeing the other blossoms? A few minutes more, and she would return to the house and claim a headache.

It wouldn't be a lie. Pain had niggled behind her eyes since speaking with Uncle Ambrose this morning.

A headache signaled Aunt Camille that she wanted to leave. Her uncle might be determined to shackle her to the marquis, but her aunt was just as adamant she wouldn't be forced into marriage.

Thank goodness for her sweet aunt.

Aunt Camille had displayed much more gumption over the matter than Angelina had previously credited her aunt with having. Though not outwardly contentious, her aunt exhibited the same firm resolve Mama did. Behind closed doors, her aunt wasn't as biddable as she appeared in public.

Although the day was warm, Angelina shivered, remembering the exceedingly unpleasant conversation with Uncle Ambrose this morning. He'd flatly disregarded her refusal to marry Lord Bretheridge.

He'd dared to seize her arms and shake her while snarling he'd send her back to Salem if she didn't comply. Afterward, he'd stormed into his study where Aunt Camille found him, hours later, in a drunken stupor.

His actions confirmed Angelina's growing suspicion that her uncle wasn't above physical violence. She now bore bruises proving his brutality. *Good Lord.* Imagine what her aunt and the children had suffered at his hands. And the servants too, she ventured to guess.

Thank God, he wasn't her guardian. No telling what he'd do if he were.

In a matter of days, she'd be of age, and she intended to sell her jewelry and make arrangements to live somewhere else as soon as possible. If she became desperate, the distant relatives in Scotland remained a possibility. A remote possibility.

Uncle Ambrose's obsession with her unfortunate situation perplexed Angelina. For pity's sake, she wasn't his daughter. She breathed out a silent sigh. As to that, she had best write Mama and tell her she would soon be a grandmother.

A bittersweet announcement, to be sure.

"Franny, will you join us?"

Lord Bretheridge's question reined in Angelina's unpleasant musings. Of course, Lady Francesca must. For Angelina to venture into the conservatory alone with him would be most unwise.

"No." Lady Francesca gave him an innocent look. "I'll wait beneath the magnolia for a spell. Take your time. Should I become too warm or tired, I'll have Penny take me indoors."

Angelina already adored the young woman. A beauty, greatly resembling Lord Bretheridge, from her emerald eyes to her dark chestnut hair, she owned a ready smile and a quick wit.

What most impressed Angelina, however, was Lady Francesca's

sweet spirit and the complete lack of self-pity the young woman exhibited for her thorny situation. She'd graciously accepted her limitation. Where others might've become depressed or bitter, Lady Francesca exuded peace and professed a charm like that which Angelina first believed his lordship possessed.

"Are you positive you don't want to come along, Lady Francesca?" Angelina fingered a velvety petal.

Lady Francesca grinned impishly. "As I'm sure we'll become great friends, please call me Franny, but no." She sent her brother a sideways peek. "I know my brother wants a few moments alone with you."

Angelina pretended absorption in the rose she admired. She most definitely didn't want to be alone with the marquis. Had he mentioned something to his family about her? *Them*? She swore she detected a speculative gleam in his sister's eyes.

That would not do.

"Mrs. Thorne? The conservatory, if you please?" His lordship waited patiently, hands clasped behind his back, and a tolerant turn to his lovely mouth. When he spoke, the dogs' tails renewed their swishing.

A man's mouth shouldn't be beautiful. Was that on her list already?

Drat. If he were ugly as a toad, he'd be much easier to dismiss. *Remember his behavior yesterday.*

Adjusting her parasol, Angelina smiled at her. "We'll only be a few minutes. I promise." Hesitation in her step, she made her way to Lord Bretheridge's side. She did wish to see more of his roses. Along with peonies, they were her favorite flowers.

The dogs turned eager faces in her direction as she approached, yet their haunches remained planted on the ground.

"What are their names?" She bent and patted each dog on its silky head, earning wags of approval.

He gave her a boyish grin. "The gentleman is Sir Freckleton, and the spaniels are Moll and Lasses. Franny named the girls when I brought them home after a trip to my sugar plantations in Trinidad and Tobago."

"Moll and Lasses? for molasses?" Despite her vow to remain unaffected by him, her lips twitched in amusement.

"Exactly so." He regarded his sister affectionately. "She named my horse Kane."

"She did not." Angelina grinned unabashedly. "Truly?"

"Indeed." He winked. "As I'm sure you've deduced, for sugar cane."

"Have you other pets?" She made a pretense of perusing the grounds intently. "A cat named Sugar or Sweetie, perhaps?" Angelina petted Sir Freckleton's mottled head. "I'm surprised he's not named Sir Bonbon."

The marquis pressed a palm to his broad chest in mock offense. "Mrs. Thorne, are you poking fun at my pets' most noble names?"

"Most assuredly, my lord," she quipped.

Oh, this gaiety was not prudent. Not at all. He might develop the wrong impression regarding her interest in him. Not that she was interested. Because she wasn't. However, if ever, she became fascinated with a man again— *For pity's sake, Angelina. Do stop your mental prattling.*

They'd dawdled long enough. Point in fact, she wasn't altogether comfortable with this light-hearted bantering. The cordiality seemed too personal, too intimate. And after what Charles had put her through, she never wanted to be intimate physically, or emotionally, with a man again.

She purposely changed the subject to something benign. "Now, about those roses?"

Lord Bretheridge didn't offer her his arm as they headed for the conservatory. Gratitude suffused her. She'd no desire for her traitorous body to respond to his touch. For surely, she would, despite her determination otherwise.

Feasibly, some ailment afflicted her. That was why she found herself attracted to handsome men who turned her to quivering plum pudding whenever they touched her. Well, two men had, at least. Although, everything beyond Charles's kisses had proved wholly disappointing.

New rule.

Avoid attractive men. And those causing curious quivers in unmentionable places.

She felt cheated as if she'd missed out on something wonderful. Now, she'd never experience that mystical phenomenon between a man and a woman. Suppressing a sigh, she followed the marquis into the conservatory.

One step into the structure and Angelina pulled up short. "Oh, my," she breathed, reverently. She gawped awestruck.

Her rooms at the Plaza Hotel didn't compare to this loveliness. After folding her parasol, she propped the accessory beside the door. Sending Lord Bretheridge a delighted little laugh, she advanced farther into the building.

"This," she made a sweeping gesture, "is beyond breathtaking." Thousands of blossoms perfumed the air, and closing her eyes, she greedily filled her lungs.

"Wonderful," she whispered, afraid to disturb the tranquility of the magical place.

"I'm glad you like it."

At the provocative timbre of his voice, her eyelids popped open. The gleam in his eyes mesmerized her. Lord help her, but she could drown in those smoldering depths.

Her breathing unsteady, she tore her gaze away and hurried to a rose brushed in shades of peach. "Would you look at these colors? They don't appear real. It's almost as if they've been painted with a fine brush."

"Yes, by the hand of God." He chuckled and wandered to her side. "No human is capable of creating such beauty."

"Quite so. Please tell me, my lord, how does one manage something of this magnitude?" She waved her hand about, indicating the vast array of blooms.

"I don't tend them myself. It's impossible, given the time I spend away. I have a professional staff of gardeners, and they follow my directives unerringly."

Angelina peered around as she sauntered from plant to plant, tenderly touching a silky petal now and again. "I'm duly impressed."

She threw him a peek over her shoulder.

A contemplative expression on his face, he observed her. His unnerving scrutiny focused on her hair for an extended moment before roaming the conservatory. A satisfied grin tilting his mouth, he strode past her and plucked a bloom from a bush. He sniffed the rose before extending the flower. "It reminds me of you. Your hair."

Pale yellow and sporting light coppery-red edges, the rose was exquisite.

Angelina took the bloom, her fingers accidentally brushing his. She ignored the jolt of awareness touching him produced and pressed the fragrant petals to her nose.

"Do you know that every shade of rose has a meaning?" Lord Bretheridge leaned against a wooden table, his ankles and arms crossed.

"I only know a few." She bowed her neck to inspect a white tea rose. She pointed to the pale bloom. "White means purity, I believe. Red is love and passion, of course. And yellow means joy or jealousy. Odd that it represents such conflicting emotions, don't you think?"

"I suppose," he murmured a trifle distractedly.

Stroking the smooth rose, she closed her eyes for a blink. "And pink means thankfulness?"

He nodded, the same inscrutable glimmer in his eyes. "Dark pink does. Light pink means admiration."

"What about this one?" Angelina studied the rose between her fingertips. "I don't know the meanings of roses containing more than one color."

He straightened from his relaxed stance, his movements almost predatory, and closed the distance between them. Encasing her hand in his, he raised the full blossom to his nose then touched it to his lips.

She couldn't tear her attention away, though her sensible self shrieked for her to turn on her heel and bolt from the building.

"This rose has a *very* special meaning." His provocative murmur sent her heart to skipping.

Rule number…ah…rule…whatever.

No skipping heart. No quickening pulse. No... No… anything!

"What…?" She swallowed before wetting her lips. "What does it mean?"

"Friendship." His eyes darkened, and the hand encircling hers tightened the tiniest amount as his mouth arched seductively. "And—falling in love."

His gaze dipped to her mouth a mere moment before he brushed her lips with his.

A feather's touch. No more.

14

Angelina sprang away from the marquis with such alacrity, she nearly fell in her haste.

He steadied her with one hand, which caused another frisson of desire to sluice through her arm.

She pressed her trembling fingers to her burning lips.

He chuckled and rubbed the back of his neck. "Not the reaction I'd hoped for."

"You overstep the mark, my lord!"

His tender kiss undid her. Sent her self-control and convictions spiraling crazily.

Though hardly more than a whisper, the soft pressure of his lips sent sparks from the tips of her toes to the top of her head. Was her hair standing on end? Every hair on her arms seemed to be. Heavens, what would a passionate kiss from him do to her?

Melt her like wax near a flame.

Goose!

A stallion amidst a herd of mares in season had more self-control than she did. One wee barely-could-pass-for-a-kiss touch on the lips and her rules might as well be dry as dust kindling.

Self-castigation liberally dosed with distrust sparked another desire; to put as much distance between her and his lordship as she could before she humiliated herself further. She swirled toward the door, her head pounding full on now.

Her intuition had warned her not to come in here with him. But did she listen to reason and caution? *Oh, no.* She'd been swept up by romance and sensation before. And look where that had landed her. *Never again, by God.*

You are a fool, Angelina, her conscience scolded. *An utter and complete fool.*

She stomped across the straw-scattered floor. Had common sense completely abandoned her?

Another rule.

Don't accept roses from men. Ever.

"Wait, Mrs. Thorne, please."

Lord Bretheridge's boots crunched an even rhythm atop the straw as he followed her.

The need to escape the conservatory, and him, overwhelming her, Angelina didn't slow her pace. She didn't trust herself. Couldn't trust herself. She already proved she couldn't claim a whit of intelligence when it came to men. An internal alarm shrieked a warning that his lordship was far more dangerous than Charles had ever been.

The marquis's strong hand gently grasped her elbow, forcing her to stop. "Please, Angelina, I beg a few moments. Let me have my say, and then, if you still wish to, I'll let you leave without another word."

Using her anger as a shield, she bristled and twisted from his grasp. "Pray, tell me why I should listen to a single word you have to say? Yesterday, you judged me and found me wanting without knowing anything about me or my situation."

Breathing hard, she planted her hands on her hips. "You insulted me, insinuating I'm after your title and position—which I don't give a rat's whisker about, by the way. And what's worse, you accused me of conspiring with my uncle to entrap you into marriage."

She poked his solid-as-marble chest. "You lure me here—" she flung a hand in the air "—on the pretext of showing me your bloody flowers, and you dare to kiss me."

Thrusting her chin skyward, she glared at him, daring him to refute her. Yes, ire proved much safer. This frenzied pounding in her chest was driven by anger, not desire.

Isn't it?

"Everything you've said is true, Mrs. Thorne."

Lord Bretheridge met her eyes, his verdant gaze steady and calm, though she detected a measure of remorse. His avid attention sank to her mouth and lingered there.

And God help her for being a dolt, feminine awareness coursed through her.

Angelina pressed her lips together to prevent licking them. She wanted him to kiss her again—only harder this time. Much harder.

She was wicked—a wanton, pure and simple.

Father had called her a spawn of Satan. With her red hair, green eyes, and apparently a Jezebel spirit, too, perchance, his words held a morsel of truth, after all.

What other explanation could there be for her reaction to the marquis when her womb cradled another man's child? A cur who, a few short months ago, she'd been convinced would hold her capricious heart for eternity. Now thinking of Charles made her want to cast up her accounts.

Becoming enamored ever again was unthinkable. She wouldn't survive another betrayal.

Lowering his chin, Lord Bretheridge cupped his nape. "The honest truth is I believe I've greatly misjudged you and must beg you to accept my apology."

Cocking his head, he gave her a boyish grin.

She hadn't expected him to apologize. Her indignation evaporated, replaced by overwhelming sadness. "I'm sure you won't be the last. I suppose ridicule is something I must become accustomed to."

"Perhaps, not." Confidence weighted his words.

Fighting tears, she peeked at him through trembling eyelashes. "No?"

"Why don't you tell me what brought you to England?" He flashed his charming smile again. "Only what you're comfortable sharing, naturally. Afterward, I'll tell you the solution I arrived at last night. Which, I hope, might provide what we both most need at present."

What she most needed was not to be pregnant and to have never met Charles.

She couldn't fathom God reversing time and permitting her to relive the fateful day she'd bumped into the conniving lickspittle she'd married. With the knowledge she had now, she'd shriek like a banshee the instant he plunged into the alcove at the Dennison's ball.

Doubt prodding her common sense, Angelina crossed her arms and considered Lord Bretheridge. What could he possibly suggest that would remedy their situations? She knew nothing about him other than he owned a neighboring estate, and contention existed between him and Uncle Ambrose regarding a gambling wager.

And he kissed divinely.

Stop it.

Her lower spine and abdomen twinged. She longed to rub her hips and back but didn't dare draw attention to her condition. She shrugged and turned away. "I really don't see—"

"Please. Give me this one chance." He laid his hand upon hers. Fine dark brown hairs feathered his knuckles, and he had a heart-shaped mole on his index finger. “Please.”

The entreaty in his voice undid her.

Her shoulders drooped in resignation. “Very well. Five minutes, my lord.” She perused the conservatory. “And I should like to sit.”

Needed to sit before she plopped onto the ground in an undignified heap.

Transparent relief softened his expression. “Of course. There’s a bench underneath the magnolia tree.”

Taking Angelina by the elbow, he guided her to the door. At the entrance, he stopped to collect her parasol. He swept the blooms with one last, approving glance, much like a proud papa. Satisfaction glimmered in his eyes as he passed the parasol to her.

“Thank you. What of your sister?” Not so much as a whisper would pass her lips in the presence of anyone else.

Releasing her arm, the marquis stepped aside. “See for yourself.”

No one sat beneath the umbrella-like tree. The dogs had vanished as well. *Botheration.* She promised Lady Francesca she’d only be a few minutes. Now the girl probably thought her a feckless fribble enamored with the marquis.

“I’m sorry to have missed your sister. She’s truly delightful. I suppose she tired of waiting.”

Angelina popped open the parasol, resisting the urge to rub her palm against her elbow to settle the perturbing prickles lingering from his lordship’s touch. The cool shade below the flowering tree beckoned. Even with both end doors wide open, the hothouse had been overly warm and muggy.

“Franny usually reads to Mother for an hour in the afternoon.” The marquis fell into pace beside her. “My sister doesn’t tolerate the heat. I think her chair is partially to blame. The contraption is rather confining, and the material doesn’t allow much air circulation. She prefers an armchair or her window seat in the solar.”

“How long has she been confined to an invalid chair?”

“Since she was six.”

A hardness edged the marquis’s tone, and Angelina pressed no more. She settled herself on the marble bench, practically sighing in pleasure at the wonderful coolness of the stone. If Lord Bretheridge hadn’t been present, she’d have laid her cheek against the cold surface.

His lordship sat beside her, his leg brushing her skirt. He shifted as far away as the bench would permit—a full six inches.

He sat much too close for her peace of mind. His subtle cologne wafted past her nostrils, the heat of his body beckoned enticingly, and his even breathing soothed. It shouldn't soothe. She covertly stared at his muscled thighs. Her muddled thoughts confused her as if she'd woken from a deep, dreamless slumber.

She stared at him, blankly.

What were they supposed to discuss?

"We'd best not dither." The marquis snapped his fingers. "Five minutes will fly by in less time than it takes to return to the house."

Humor leeched into his voice.

No doubt, the knave knew exactly what thoughts churned about in her head. Irritation welled within her chest, and she rolled a shoulder. "I'm not sure what it is you wish to hear, my lord."

"Why are you here?"

"Why? Because you invited us to tea," Angelina retorted.

She didn't want to have this awkward discussion about something so painful and humiliating. And none of his affair, truth to tell. Except, the ugly business had become the marquis's affair when Uncle tried to foist her off on him. Like a scraggly, flea-infested kitten.

"*Touché*." His lordship offered a mocking salute. "Let me rephrase my question. Why did you journey from America to live with the duke and duchess?"

Angelina fidgeted with the edge of her glove. She hated this.

"It's an age-old story. Sordid and scandalous. As you already know, I'm expecting." Pausing, she drew in a calming breath, her gaze focused on her lap. "Though in my defense, I believed I'd wed the babe's father."

She risked raising her eyes to Lord Bretheridge's. No condemnation sparked there today, just warm patience. She shifted her attention to the rose beds. Two birds hopped about beneath the bushes, occasionally pecking the ground as they hunted for a meal.

"I met Charles Moreau last December. I later learned that it wasn't his real name. I was smitten from the moment I laid eyes on him, as I believed he was with me."

Charles's husky professions of love still rang in her ears.

Why did remembering sting so?

Wounded pride.

She definitely retained no tender feelings for him, which proved all the more she didn't understand the first thing about love—only that affection shouldn't be so short-lived.

"We enjoyed a whirlwind courtship and married three months later." Angelina shifted her weight, trying to alleviate the persistent throb in her back. She sighed. How many of the unpleasant details did she want to share with this stranger?

She plucked at her skirt, her attention on the horizon.

"Charles is French. Did I mention that?"

"No." His lordship's gaze probed hers. "What is his real name?"

"Pierre Renault."

Lord Bretheridge stiffened, sucking in a ragged breath.

Stomach clenching, she regarded him. "Do you know him?"

How utterly discomfiting, if so.

His lordship pressed his lips together in a small grimace. "No. We've never been introduced. I've heard of him in passing. His *profession* is somewhat…questionable."

Staring at her hands, she nodded, regretting the movement instantly as it worsened the unpleasant pulsing in her skull. "Yes, I know. He's a slave-trader. I learned that moments after I discovered Charles—I still cannot think of him as Pierre—was already married. I'm a bigamist."

"The devil, you say!" Lord Bretheridge struck his palm with his fist.

His vehemence startled her, and Angelina turned to him. The oddest expression shadowed his face, a combination of compassion, disbelief, pity, and fury. And, he was livid.

At Charles? On my behalf?

Gratitude engulfed her, and she swallowed a sob. He'd taken her at her word.

"Go on." His expression remained grim, a pinched look about his eyes and mouth.

"We arrived at the hotel and…" She couldn't share *that*. Heat flooded her face. No doubt, her cheeks glowed crimson as cherries. "A short while later, there came a knock at the door. It was Lord Devaux-Rousset, Charles's stepson."

"Stepson?" A perplexed frown knitted Lord Bretheridge's brow.

She focused her concentration on the gardens once more. "When Charles was quite young, he married a French woman several years his senior. The baron, though the same age as Charles, is his stepson. He'd been searching for Charles for some time. Evidently, the man I thought I married has a history of reprehensible behavior."

She closed her eyes as a fresh wave of humiliation and anguish encompassed her. How could she have been so naïve? There must've been signs. Hints. Something to alert her to Charles's duplicity.

"Words cannot express the measure of my regret." His lordship covered her clenched hands with his palm, giving her an encouraging squeeze. "How is it you came to be in England?"

"I couldn't very well toddle back to Salem." She gave a watery laugh. "Everyone believed me married. Mama and I decided a trip to Aunt and Uncle's would be just the thing. No one would know I'd been an utter fool."

Angelina relaxed her spine against the tree. "During the voyage, I suffered from *mal de mer* and continued to experience malaise once I reached England. A physician was consulted and my pregnancy confirmed."

Removing his hand from hers, the marquis finished for her. "And that's when your uncle concocted the widow tale and hied you off to Wingfield Court."

"Yes." She inhaled a steadying breath. "So there, you have the whole ugly tale in a nutshell."

"Mrs. Thorne—"

"Please, don't address me as such. I loathe living that lie." Angelina touched his arm. The firm flesh rippled beneath her hand. "When we're alone, might you not call me something else? I know it's improper."

As is clasping his arm.

"And I suppose forward, too. Except every time I hear that *wretched* name—" She tucked her hand beneath her leg to alleviate the burning on her palm.

The marquis slanted his head, reminding her of a contemplative owl. After a protracted moment, he smiled. "What about Rose?"

Angelina chuckled, darting him a glance before continuing to observe the birds searching for insects. "I prefer Lina. Although Rose is quite appropriate."

"How so?" He, too, leaned against the trunk, his long legs stretched before him and crossed at the ankles. "Oh, because I raise roses?"

Must he wear his trousers so formfitting? She found the sight most distracting.

"No, although that is rather ironic." A twig dropped onto her skirt. Thankful for a diversion, she brushed the stick from her dress. She examined the branches above her head, seeking the culprit.

"Our father named my sisters and me, and he's the only one who ever addressed us by our first names." She glanced at him, careful to keep her interest on his face and off the bulge prominently displayed in his loins at the moment.

She had his full attention.

"As you know, mine is Temperance, and I told you before, my sisters are Patience and Prudence. Mama's of a more romantic bend than Papa was. She gave us our middle names." Angelina pointed to herself. "I'm Angelina-Rose, and my sisters are Angelisa-Lily and Angelica-Iris."

Hilarity danced in his eyes, and Lord Bretheridge appeared to fight the amusement tugging at his lips valiantly.

Angelina giggled. "Go ahead and laugh. It's really quite awful. I've always wondered what in the world she would've named a son. Angelo?"

"Whatever possessed her?" He chuckled, a low and pleasant rumble.

She shrugged. "I've no idea. Mama calls us her three angels. With their pale hair and cornflower-blue eyes, Lily and Iris do, indeed, resemble angels. I, on the other hand, have green eyes." Angelina wrinkled her nose and motioned toward her head. "And distinct coppery streaks in my hair. Papa thought I looked anything but saintly."

A stab of familiar pain gripped her.

Many Godly men believe red hair is stolen hell-fire, Temperance. And with your green eyes...

Papa would shake his balding head in disapproval and mutter some nonsense about witches and curses before taking himself off to pray for her soul.

"I think you have the most magnificent hair I've ever seen. The color is unique." Lord Bretheridge touched a curl near her ear.

"Thank you." A delicious warmness bathed her, replacing the pain of her father's rejection with a sense of happiness. Angelina ducked her head, breaking the contact. She needed to change the subject. *Now.* "In any event, the twins are called Lily and Iris. I've always been Lina."

"Not Rose?"

"No, though, I never questioned why. Mayhap, because I was the firstborn, and Mama thought it would be too confusing to call my sisters Lisa and Lica." She crinkled her forehead. "Lica does sound rather odd. I expect, that's why."

The marquis snorted. "Your uncle couldn't fabricate anything better than *Thorne* for a fictional name for you?"

Angelina Rose Thorne.

"I suppose he imagined himself clever." A grimace touched her lips, and she shifted to stand. "I'm positive more than five minutes have passed. We shouldn't remain here alone any longer."

He touched her shoulder, staying her.

"I beg you. Please do indulge me further and grant me a few more moments." Lord Bretheridge straightened and motioned toward the house. "Besides, the drawing room window faces directly this way. I'm sure Grandmamma and the duchess have their avid gazes trained on our every move."

Angelina swung her gaze between his lordship and the house. Through the sun glaring on the beveled glass, the indistinct outlines of two women were visible. Whether they directed their attention toward her and the marquis was difficult to determine at this distance. However, their presence, though separated by a large expanse of lawn and French windows, did add a level of respectability.

She acquiesced with a sideways nod. "All right. What is it you wish to say?"

"I've put a great deal of thought into this—your uncle's unusual proposal." Lord Bretheridge gave her an apologetic smile. "I'll be perfectly honest. I don't have the means to pay my father's gambling debt. To not do so would mean absolute ruin of a different sort. The sum is an astronomical amount. But, Waterford's willing to cancel the obligation if we marry."

Angelina puckered her forehead. "I've already told you, I cannot—*won't*—marry you."

"Please, hear me out." Such earnestness and humility gleamed in his eyes.

Why wouldn't he listen? His tenacity drove her to distraction. She sighed and started to shake her head.

The marquis shifted to face her. "I'll do anything to protect and care for my family. And yes, I'm willing to agree to Waterford's insane scheme—especially after hearing the truth of your situation."

Now he believed her?

"How do you know it's the truth?" Angelina arched an eyebrow. "I could be lying."

His gaze roved her face. "You're not. Some people are consummate liars—"

"Such as Charles." She scowled, recalling the lies which so easily poured from his mouth. Like grains of sugar spilled from a spoon; sweet and too numerous to count.

"Yes, such as him, but others, like you…" Lord Bretheridge hesitated, gazing deep into her eyes. "Your eyes reveal everything. I don't have a single doubt you've told me the truth."

"Come now, my eyes?" She peered at him, trying to read his. "Surely you cannot be persuaded simply by gazing into my eyes. Yesterday you believed me a party to this whole sordid affair."

Reading my eyes. How ridiculous.

"Oh, but I can." He pushed his hair off his forehead. "When you're happy, your eyes are a bright, ocean green, and the blue flecks within them shimmer. When you're upset or worried, they darken to a mossy jade. And when you're angry, they become a fiery emerald with gold shards."

Dash it all. Now he waxed poetic.

How could she resist such romantic discourse? Her lips curved of their own accord but thinned into a disapproving line almost at once. Charles also possessed a knack for prose, and a more deceitful tongue she'd never encountered.

Rule number—*how many have I now*? It mattered not.

New rule.

Men who spout poetry are to be shunned like the plague.

"I expected green sparks to shoot from them and incinerate me in your uncle's drawing room yesterday afternoon." The line' of his lordship's face creased in merriment.

Angelina squirmed beneath his penetrating stare. Was she truly so transparent?

"I concede that I can appreciate how our marriage might be of some benefit to you. But frankly, my lord, why would you saddle yourself with a woman who is expecting? No one who can count will believe the child is yours, and the stigma will be profound." She fanned her fingers over her stomach.

His attention fixed on the house, he nodded. "True. For the babe's sake, we'll have to continue the widow charade."

"No." She gasped and firmed her hands atop her belly.

"Let me explain." He lifted one of her hands. Cradling it in his, he ran his thumb back and forth across her palm. "Please?"

Through the material of her glove, delicious frissons erupted under his touch. She should tell Lord Bretheridge to stop. Instead, she stiffly inclined her head. This was ridiculous. Sheer lunacy to even listen. A marriage between them would never work.

"Once the debt is canceled, I'll be extremely wealthy again." He stilled his thumb's movement as if he suddenly realized what he did. "I'm certain there's nothing in the contract Waterford has had drawn which stipulates a period we have to remain together. It's not done."

Angelina stared at their joined hands. "I'm sorry. I don't follow you."

What did he imply?

"We marry, my fortune is restored, and I can care for my family. If you don't want to remain wed, after a year, we can attempt to have the marriage annulled. I'll settle a substantial amount on you. You and the child will live comfortably for the rest of your days."

Had he lost his bloody mind?

Mayhap, the strain had addled him. Perchance, madness was a family tendency. His father had taken his own life, after all.

"After I've given birth?" She choked on a scoffing laugh. "Surely you jest. No one will believe the marriage wasn't consummated."

Lord Bretheridge shrugged. "Well then, I'll petition for divorce. If that's what you want."

"*If* a divorce is granted, and we both know that's an almost insurmountable *if*, you'll be ruined."

Why couldn't he let the marriage idea go? Desperate with no other recourse available, wouldn't she do the same? The women of his family did present quite a burden.

He released her hand before crossing his arms.

"You face more ruin than I. I understand how abhorrent marriage must be to you right now. I'm only asking for a year. Who knows?" He winked, mischief lurking in his eyes. "We might find we're compatible."

As compatible as a fox and a hen.

Yet, the ludicrous idea did have merit, especially since she didn't care a whit about the scandal. "What grounds will you give for the divorce? You cannot claim you were cuckolded."

He didn't answer her. Instead, he stared at her a lengthy moment before his beautiful eyes shifted slightly lower.

"You could agree to stay with me until you provide me with an heir. Afterward, we're both free to go our individual ways."

An heir? Good heavens. It mustn't come to that.

She'd never be able to walk away from a child she'd born. Ever.

Her mind awhirl, Angelina surveyed the gardens and greens. A lovely estate, Lambridge Manse, would be an ideal place for her babe to begin its life. Lord Bretheridge's family losing their home, and those sweet women forced to live in poverty, didn't bear contemplating. Agreeing to wed the marquis could prevent that very thing.

Lord Bretheridge would likely be gone to London and his other holdings a great deal of the time. She harbored no serious notion of remaining with him. What would it hurt to agree to a year? He could have his annulment or divorce, or if both proved unachievable, she would leave. They wouldn't be the first husband and wife to live apart.

He did need an heir, however. That particular, they'd have to discuss further.

She angled to face him. "My lord, may I ask you something?"

"Of course. Anything." He flashed his ever-ready smile.

"I, at least, have experienced what I believed was love. What of you?" She gestured toward him, searching his face. "In all likelihood, if we marry, you're relinquishing your only chance to love someone and be loved in turn."

15

Angelina tried to read Lord Bretheridge's emotions.

"Are you quite certain that is what you wish to do? There is no going back, reversing our decision, once the deed is done." She glanced away for a moment before leveling him with a carefully bland stare. "It's only fair to tell you. I don't believe myself capable of loving again."

His face settled into a somber expression, his eyes guarded. "I met someone last Season. She's Scots. I thought to court her intending to ask for her hand."

The knowledge stung sharper than it ought to.

Could she marry a man who loved someone else?

He was willing to wed her although she carried another's child. And she thought she'd loved Charles before he brutally annihilated her affection.

"Do you love her?" Her tongue formed the words of their own accord.

"I found her fascinating and most enchanting, yes. But I don't think I can claim to have come to love her." The marquis directed his contemplation overhead. "Mayhap, the true test of my affection lies in whether I'd be willing to sacrifice my family and honor for her."

He veered a sideways glance toward her before returning his attention to the cloudless sky. "And I can unequivocally say the answer to that question is *no*. I imagine true love—if the sentiment actually exists—would tempt me to do so."

Smoothing her skirts, Angelina made her decision. If he meant what he said, he'd agree to her terms. If not, well, she would be no worse off than she was now. Except Uncle Ambrose would be even more intolerable until she escaped his household.

"I'll want a contract in advance, stating each specific condition.

Including the monetary amount, you'll settle on me as well as the precise stipulations about an heir. I'll require a house too, nothing elaborate, but adequate to raise my child. And I'd like the child's education paid for."

Mortifying heat flooded her as she voiced her demands. She'd become calculating and mercenary, not so very different than a mistress listing her conditions. Her scruples lay in tatters. The knowledge rankled as well as humiliated.

She took a bracing breath and avoided meeting his eyes. This was for *her* child. "I'll concede to live with you for a year, after which time I'll leave, and you agree to seek an annulment or divorce."

"And if neither is attainable?" He studied her, his mien impossible to decipher.

Folding her hands, she squeezed her fingers together until she couldn't feel the tips. She must be fair. "If, after two years, you've been unsuccessful in obtaining either, I'll acquiesce to your request to provide you with an heir."

A wave of bitter bile threatened to choke her. Negotiating for a child as if their offspring held no more value than a new landau or a team to put before it. Did she dare stipulate that any issue resulting from their joining would reside with her, and she'd permit his lordship visitations?

"Only one?" Humor crinkled the corners of his eyes. "No spare?"

Angelina lanced him with a stern glare. Nothing about this could be construed as amusing. "Yes. Only one."

"I'll expect you to keep your affections from becoming otherwise engaged during the entire duration." His tone grated low and insistent.

She couldn't mistake his meaning. She almost asked if he intended to impose the same restriction on himself. Understanding the carnal nature of men, she needn't bother. What was that old saying, *Do as I say, not as I do*?

Giving a stiff nod, she managed to mutter, "Of course."

As if I'd allow a suitor to sniff about my skirts as a married woman.

Pondering what else she might need, she fiddled with the lace at her wrist. Planning the details in such a rush, particularly when her traitorous mind kept returning to that alarming business about an heir, proved most difficult.

She'd require a carriage and a team. "I'd like a conveyance too, something simple, as well as a suitable team and modest furnishings for the house."

"Is that all? Perhaps, you should make a list. Don't forget to include stipulations in the event you give birth to twins."

Irritation reared its head, prepared to strike sharp and lethal. Teeth clenched, Angelina sucked in air until her lungs could hold no more, then exhaled with deliberate control. She quelled her exasperation, willing the terse response on the tip of her tongue to subside.

The pinpricks of fear that assailed her at his mention of twins proved harder to dispel. Nonetheless, her emotions had been worthless guides up to this point. Logic and reasoning made better rudders even if they were somewhat difficult to procure, given her vacillating moods of late.

Lord Bretheridge quirked a sable brow, a hint of cynicism in his eyes.

"Don't look at me like that, my lord. You're benefiting greatly from this arrangement—for the sake of your family. Why shouldn't I do the same for my child? The babe I carry is as innocent as the people in that house." She pointed to the mansion. "Whom you love dearly."

Presenting her with his profile, he regarded the manor. "There's nothing I'd not do to keep my loved ones from suffering. Nothing."

A jay swooped to the ground a few feet from where they sat. Peering at them, it took a couple of cautious hops. His lordship shifted to face her once more. Releasing a raucous cry, the startled bird took to the air.

She followed its swerving flight before meeting Lord Bretheridge's gaze straight on. "You know, another argument wouldn't have won me over. Your concern for your family made me decide in your favor."

"And when you were about to swoon, your distress for the child you carry convinced me of your intrinsic goodness." Something beguiling flickered deep in his eyes.

A flush of pleasure suffused her, and she cleared her throat. Best to get right to it. "When did you want to wed? Are we to go through the farce of reading the banns when we're both in mourning?"

"I think not. We could wed by special license." Lord Bretheridge rubbed his chin contemplatively. "That would raise brows and questions, too. Ones I'm sure you, as well as I, would prefer not to answer."

A good deal of truth in that.

He slapped his thighs with his palms. "I suggest we go to Scotland. It's a long day's journey from here. I have family I'd like to visit while we're there as well."

He *had* thought this through.

Weren't divorces permissible in Scotland? Did one have to reside there to obtain one?

For how long?

Would Mama know?

Angelina needed to pursue that notion at once.

Rising, she firmed her resolve before facing him, preferring to have her back to the house for this discomfiting part of their conversation. No telling how closely Aunt Camille and the Dowager Marchioness watched.

"There is one more matter we need to discuss, my lord."

Lord Bretheridge considered her affably, apparently not the least concerned. "And that is?"

"I don't intend to consummate the marriage."

His jaw slackened even as his dark brows ascended to his hairline.

Scorching heat swept her cheeks at his expression of disbelief. Nonetheless, she forged onward. "Not even after the baby is born. Unless, of course, an annulment or divorce cannot be obtained. I think it best if you send me to live somewhere else immediately after the wedding. No one can question—"

He raised his hand. "I understand the logic of your reasoning, but I'm afraid I cannot agree."

She fidgeted with a curl. "Whyever not?"

"It would upset my mother, as well as Grandmamma and Franny. I shan't do anything to jeopardize Mother's recovery." He rose as well and straightened his waistcoat and jacket before facing Angelina.

For a moment, she thought he would take her hands in his. Anticipation deluged her. She wanted him to.

Instead, he let his fall to his sides.

"Lina, you've not met her yet, but Mother's the most amazing woman. Her illness, compounded by Father's death, almost killed her. If I wed and send my bride away post-haste, she'll know something's afoot." His voice rang with admiration and devotion.

She couldn't help but respect his dedication.

The marquis's well-formed lips curved at the corners. "Mother's not one to let things go. She wouldn't rest until she uncovered the truth. If she ever learns Father was foxed to the gills and gambled away his very identity before shooting himself—"

His throat worked for a moment as he pulled at one cuff. "I have no doubt it would destroy her," he softly murmured.

Angelina laid a hand on his arm. "I understand. Rightly so, she mustn't ever know. I only thought to lessen the gossip. Vile rumors will swirl thick and ugly when I do leave and might prove trying for them as well."

"Let's worry about that when the time comes, shall we?" Lord Bretheridge covered her hand with his much larger palm.

"How soon can you have the contract drawn up?" she asked, venturing a new-found boldness.

Without each provision in writing, she refused to move forward with their plan. And, the contract between her and Lord Bretheridge must remain a secret. If Uncle Ambrose caught so much as a whiff, he might attempt to add stipulations to the marriage agreement.

She couldn't take that risk.

"I'll leave for London tomorrow, after speaking to your uncle. I'll claim I want my man-of-affairs to review the agreement. Waterford shouldn't suspect anything untoward."

"Yes, I think that's wise." She paused, torn between loyalty to her family and this man who would soon be her husband. "My lord?"

"Since we're about to wed," he said, a drop of irony tinting his tone, "I think it's acceptable for you to call me Flynn or Bretheridge."

Angelina disregarded the warmth sweeping her. The weather was to blame, not any misplaced fascination with him. "Yes, well, that will take some getting used to since I've known you scarcely more than a day."

Gads. She'd agreed to marry a man she met yesterday afternoon. Was *she* addled? And why did she sense she could trust him? More than her uncle or Charles?

"You were saying?" His lordship gently prompted.

"I don't believe my uncle should be trusted. At all."

Flynn's hearty chuckle took her aback. What, pray tell, could he find the least bit amusing about this appalling situation?

"I agree whole-heartedly." He crossed his hands over his heart. "I promise I'll be on my most diligent guard."

He dared mock her?

Eyes narrowed, she snapped, "I'm relieved you find this entertaining."

That sobered him considerably. "No, you misunderstand. Please don't take umbrage. What I find humorous is your adorable need to protect me by advising me not to trust Waterford. Rest assured, he's the last man I'd put my faith in."

Wise on his part.

Flynn grasped her hand and raised it to his lips. "I apologize for offending you. It was not my intent."

"I…" *Good, Lord, when he touches me—* A movement caught her attention, and she angled away, peering past his shoulder.

Chatterton stiffly marched across the lawn. From the disgruntled set of his mouth, he appeared none-too-pleased.

"Your butler approaches."

Flynn tucked her hand into the crook of his elbow and turned them in the direction of the house. "Yes, Chatterton?"

"The Duke of Waterford has arrived, and he's—ah—*not* at his best." Censure riddled the majordomo's voice as he sent Angelina a shielded glance.

Flynn clenched his jaw and stifled the oath pressing against the back of his teeth. Difficult enough to reason with sober, in his cups, Waterford was a consummate ass.

Unless…

This might work to Flynn's advantage, after all. He allowed a small, gratified quirk of his lips. *Catch the duke unaware by announcing the betrothal today.* Yes, that would do quite nicely.

Once he collected his copy of the contract at Wingfield Court tomorrow morning, he'd depart for London. Mother's recovery progressed remarkably well. He needn't be as concerned about leaving her as he'd been even a day ago.

The legality of the contract Angelina insisted upon presented the greatest challenge. He'd bet his bread the agreement wouldn't be enforceable in court. She need never know that, however. Flynn intended to honor their bargain to the letter *after* he had an heir.

"I assisted the duke to the drawing room, my lord," Chatterton said. "But the Dowager Marchioness is most anxious for your return."

"That cannot bode well." Angelina bit her lower lip, her gaze riveted on the drawing room windows. She trembled slightly, as if nervous. *Or…afraid?*

"Thank you, Chatterton," Flynn said. "We'll be along directly,"

"Yes, my lord." After a subservient nod, the butler returned to the house.

Angelina furrowed her brow and clamped her lower lip between her teeth.

Flynn patted her arm. "What say you to announcing our betrothal now?"

"*Now?*" Eyes enormous, she cleared her throat, uncertainty skating across her features. "Do you think that best? Uncle Ambrose is… It's possible he is not… He mightn't be as sharp—."

"Exactly so." Flynn bent his head nearer, savoring her scent. "Waterford won't be as sharp-witted, and I hope he won't object to us departing for Scotland immediately. He may wonder at our eagerness to wed, however."

He gave her a naughty wink, enjoying the becoming hint of color bathing her face. The dozens of freckles smattering her nose stood out, impishly reminding him of the pixie in the tree yesterday.

"I suppose now is as good a time as any." She sighed, and her shoulders drooped.

Slowing his steps, he drew her to a halt behind a shrub bordering the terrace. "I know this is sudden, and you haven't been allowed time to grow accustomed to the idea. However, I do believe it's to both our benefits to move swiftly."

Did Angelina already have second thoughts? She'd be daft not to.

He had plenty himself. Yet hours of ruminating and devising possible alternatives inevitably led to the same conclusion. A match between them appeared the least of the evils available. The heir issue seemed the biggest rub. Only God knew what might happen in a year.

Flynn wasn't opposed to bedding Angelina. No, not opposed, at all. In fact, he quite anticipated winning her to his bed.

Emotions played in concert upon her lovely face. Though drawn, her fair skin glowed smooth as ivory. Was she that pale everywhere? The intoxicating notion earned a twinge in his groin.

He touched her cheek. *Soft as silk*. "Are you in agreement?"

"Yes, given my condition, expediency is prudent." The severe line molding her pretty mouth revealed her wariness.

In the conservatory, her lips had been warm and soft, tasting slightly of lemon. She tilted them weakly. "Can I trouble you to post a letter to my mother when you're in London? I need to inform her of our marriage and where she may reach me in the future."

"It's no trouble at all." Flynn gave her hand a tiny squeeze as they continued to the entry. "Ready? Chin up and steady on. Your uncle cannot be worse than Deamhan."

"If you'll recall, my lord, that devil-of-a-bull treed me."

Her demeanor cynical, they stepped onto the paving stones.

"Ah, but I rescued you from *that* beast." He waggled his eyebrows at her. And by heaven, Flynn would see that Waterford bullied her no more. "I'll protect you from your uncle, too. Trust me."

The surprised look she sliced him, offended and gratified at once. Had no one ever championed her?

The terrace doors sprang open, and the Duke and Duchess of Waterford sailed forth. Well, more aptly, the duke lurched out the doorway, tottering unsteadily, followed by Grandmamma leaning upon her cane.

Severe displeasure lined her aged face.

Flynn tucked Angelina closer to his side. "I'm delighted to inform you all, Mrs. Thorne has agreed to become my wife."

"Good thing." His grace leveled bloodshot eyes on his niece. "And the shooner, the better," he slurred.

God's bones. The bounder was ape-drunk.

Had the man no care for his wife's tender sensibilities? Her strained expression hinted she would very much like to throttle her husband.

Grandmamma eyed the duke with thinly veiled distaste. Her hand flexed around her silver-topped cane as if she'd like to thwack him with it.

The duke slid Flynn a sly peek before attempting to focus on Angelina again.

"A letter from your mother arrived thish afternoon, girl. From some Frenchie chap named Morneau. Or was it Mourant?" Weaving slightly, Waterford scratched his head. "Doesn't matter," he mumbled, squinting at her belly. "He's trying to find you. He's in England."

16

Angelina sank her fingers into Lord Bretheridge's arm and stiffened against a surge of panic.

Aunt Camille blenched and gasped. She clutched her throat, staring at her husband as if he'd sprouted another head.

What of Charles's wife?

He'd lost his mind if he thought Angelina would take up with him again. Her future mightn't be altogether bright at present, but life would be far better without that blackguard. She tried to draw enough breath to calm her jangled nerves, but the constriction in her lungs only permitted shallow breathing.

Poking around inside his wrinkled coat, Uncle Ambrose withdrew a crumpled paper. "Here. Your mother sent one for you, too."

He thrust the missive at her.

"Let's leave Mrs. Thorne to her letter, shall we?" The Dowager Marchioness of Bretheridge deftly guided her guests into the drawing room.

Angelina's stomach dived straight to her shoes and flopped there a bit. What must the dowager think?

Lord Bretheridge stood a mere step beyond the glass doors, obviously reluctant to follow the others.

Once inside, his grandmother stopped and swung her cane to prevent the marquis from entering. "Flynn dear, why don't you show Mrs. Thorne to the blue salon? She can read her letter without interruption there."

"Excellent idea, Grandmamma." He kissed her papery cheek. "Will you give our excuses to their graces, please?"

"Well, of course, I shall, foolish boy." She patted his face. "Might also order some strong coffee." She gave the duke a reproachful glare. "*Very* strong coffee."

The moment Angelina entered the salon, she dropped her parasol on the divan. She removed her gloves, and after tossing them on a marble-topped table beside a stuffed male peacock, she cracked open the letter's seal.

Dated June first, after the perfunctory greeting, Mama wasted no time getting to the purpose of the letter.

My Darling Daughter,

That despicable man came to call. You can imagine my surprise and anger at his effrontery. He claimed his wife had died, and he was now free to truly marry you.

Can you believe his audacity? Well, I tell you, I cannot!

He demanded to know where you were.

Naturally, I didn't tell him. He became quite belligerent, cursing and shouting. He threatened your sisters and me if we didn't reveal your whereabouts. He's a cunning one, though. He recalled your desire to visit your aunt and uncle.

I had him forcibly removed from the premises. I even notified the local authorities, he frightened me so.

Dearest, I don't think he's right in the head. He's determined to find you in England. He blathered on about you belonging to him; that he owned you. I'm so very worried...

Charles had kept his macabre vow to come for Angelina.

A jolt of dread speared her. Strange. She'd never been frightened of him prior to this. However, that was before she'd become aware of the depths of his deviousness.

Refolding the once-crisp sheets—she would read the rest later when the pounding in her head didn't threaten to cross her eyes—she placed the letter on the table before wandering to the window and staring blindly through the glass.

Oh, Mama, things are far worse than you know.

Angelina turned to face Lord Bretheridge. "How soon can we be married?"

"May I ask what the communication contained?" He pointed to the letter.

"It seems Charles—er, Pierre—is in England, searching for me. According to Mama, his wife died, and he thinks to marry me. *Again*." She couldn't keep the derision from her voice, though the Lord knew, she prayed that she wouldn't become embittered daily.

The marquis's keen green eyes bore into hers. "And you don't want to, even though you carry his child? Wouldn't that solve your problems?"

She could detect no condemnation, only sincere concern in his voice. Her heart gave a tiny flip. Was he truly so unselfish? For if she married Charles and not Lord Bretheridge, his lordship, as well as his family, faced certain devastation.

Angelina spun to the window, pressing her forehead against the cool glass. The throbbing in her temples mirrored the pulsing in her ears.

"If you'll have me, I'd rather marry you. In one day, you've shown me a depth of decency Charles could never hope to achieve."

And Charles would have to leave her and the babe alone if she were wed to another. Perhaps, more importantly, she could guard her fractured heart. Marriage to Lord Bretheridge constituted a business arrangement beneficial to them both. She'd no misguided illusions about love or devotion, and therefore, she'd be spared more heartache.

What about when our contract term is over? What if Charles still pursues me?

Unlikely.

She would climb that hill when she came to it.

Uncle Ambrose would prefer her to marry the marquis, though she carried Charles's child. Since the Napoleonic Wars, the duke despised all things French.

"Do you love him?" Lord Bretheridge probed, his deep baritone oddly soothing.

Ironic that he asked the same question she posed not more than a quarter of an hour ago. They made quite a pathetic pair.

Shrugging, she toyed with the navy silk tassel holding the drapery open. "I thought I did. I swore undying love for him the day we exchanged our vows. These past few months have taught me much."

Love most assuredly is not a giddy, warm feeling fueled by attraction and desire.

Releasing a beleaguered sigh, she rested her shoulder against the window frame. "No," she shook her head, "I don't believe I do—at least not anymore—if I ever truly did."

She certainly sounded fickle. Angelina rubbed her lower back, past caring what his lordship thought. She needed to relieve the muscle cramps.

Scanning the barely discernible bump below her waist, he frowned. "You don't sound very convincing, I must say."

Hands braced on her hips, she arched her spine and released a soft groan.

He shifted his attention to her breasts, the merest hint of desire in his eyes.

Her nipples tingled and hardened. She stifled a gasp. Her pregnancy made them more sensitive, not his visual caress reaching across the room.

Liar.

Arms folded to hide the tips of her traitorous breasts, she searched his face. "My lord, I'm a woman of my word. I promised I'd marry you, and in doing so, my uncle will cancel the gaming debt. Your reputation will remain intact, and your fortune will be restored."

Angelina crossed to him, standing beside the table where her gloves and letter lay. Peering into the marquis's eyes, she placed a hand on his arm and suppressed the shiver of awareness touching him caused.

"Most importantly, the women you love will be provided for, as shall my child. That's a far better thing for me to do than marry a lying cur who had no thought or care for me when he deceived me into matrimony."

Removing her hand from his lordship's muscular forearm—she couldn't think straight while touching him—she clasped her hands before her. "I cannot help but think my child shall be the better for having you in its life, if only temporarily, than having that bounder's influence for years on end."

Lord Bretheridge broke into a dazzling smile, pleasure lighting his eyes. Some ancient unspoken communication passed between them.

Angelina blinked several times.

Why did he affect her like this?

Curling her toes in her shoes, she forcibly lowered her focus to his neckcloth. Much safer and more dignified than gawking into his stunning eyes with her mouth hanging open.

"I could *never* marry a slave-trader in any event," she said.

She couldn't keep the venom from leaking into her tone. To expose her child to such an abomination was unthinkable. She'd expressed her abhorrence of the practice with a great deal of vehemence more than once. No wonder Charles had kept that vile detail from her. He'd known she'd never accept his address if she'd been aware.

Yes, he'd treated her despicably, but how could he sell humans and profit from the contemptible practice? Surely devils such as he had a special place reserved in Hades.

The marquis placed a finger beneath her chin, tilting her head until she reluctantly met his eyes once more. He grazed his thumb across her lower lip, taking her breath away.

"I'd be honored to make you my marchioness as soon as possible."

Tears blurred Angelina's eyes and burned her throat.

Why couldn't she have met this decent man before Charles? When she didn't fear love? When her heart beat whole and healthy, without wounds or scars? Or, when the ability to ever completely trust another man hadn't been ripped from her?

Nevertheless, dread choked her. Did she trade one unpleasant kettle of fish for another? She swiped at the corner of an eye, dashing away a tear. "Thank you, my lord."

"Here now, none of that." Lord Bretheridge caught another droplet with his bent forefinger. He brushed her cheek softly with the back of his hand. "Won't you call me Flynn?"

Uncharacteristic shyness swept her. Closing her eyes, she tucked her chin to her chest, lest he see the blush on her cheeks and the pathetic gratitude that assuredly simmered in her gaze.

Or the tears determinedly seeping from between her lashes. Angelina also blamed the weepiness on her pregnancy. Though unaccustomed to such reverent tenderness from the males in her life, she didn't need to act a sniveling fool.

Perchance, she should make that a rule.

Compassion in a male is to be desired, but keep your distance from men who make you cry.

"Come here." Flynn gathered her in his strong, comforting embrace, one large hand cuddling her head against his broad chest. "You've every right to a good cry."

That did it.

She lost the tenuous grip on her self-control. The walls she'd erected against her pain and humiliation crumbled like week-old biscuits.

Wrapping her arms around his trim waist, she pressed her face to his jacket and bawled like an infant. And she wasn't a dainty weeper either. Great gasping sobs, wrenched from the bowels of her anguish, spewed forth, harsh and loud, as her tears saturated the front of his coat.

"That's it. Let it all out, darling." He made soothing noises in his throat and whispered calming words into her hair as he gently caressed her back and shoulders. Several times, he pressed soft kisses onto the crown of her head. "There's a dear, poor thing."

Long moments passed, until at last, peace settled upon Angelina. The cadence of Flynn's steady heartbeat beneath her ear calmed her. Her tears spent, she drew in several ragged breaths.

Where was her handkerchief? *Drat.* In her reticule—sitting primly beside the tea service atop the table in the drawing room.

Head bent, she stepped out of his arms. "May I trouble you for your handker—"

He pressed the cloth into her shaking hand.

"Thank you." She dabbed at her eyes and dried her cheeks, before turning away from him and blowing her nose in a most unladylike fashion.

No doubt, her eyes and nose were red and swollen, and patchy blotches covered her cheeks. Several strands of hair dangled loose from the once-neat knot atop her head, and tendrils hung in waves about her face and ears. How did some women manage to weep and appear as fresh as a peony afterward, and she resembled a mashed strawberry?

"I'm sure I look a fright." She gave a shaky laugh, fisting the soaked cloth. It smelled of him, a musky yet clean, manly scent. She'd have it laundered and then return the handkerchief.

"You could never be anything other than lovely." He tucked several wisps of hair behind her left ear.

Another watery chuckle tumbled forth. "You, sir, are a bold-faced liar. But a gallant one. I've seen my face after a cry." She scrunched her nose. "Not, I fear, the stuff of which fairytales are made."

My, how relieved one felt after a good cry.

Except for the thickness in her skull, as if a bale of cotton resided where her brain had once been. And for her stuffy nose, which made her sound as if she was recovering from a nasty cold. Yes, exactly how one wanted to appear when discussing wedding plans with one's betrothed.

The stuffed bird atop the table boasted better looks than she did. *Poor thing.* She brushed the peacock's bright feathers with her fingertips, momentarily distracted.

At least her headache had disappeared, although the ache in her abdomen persisted, as did the one in her heart.

Flynn gathered her gloves, the letter, and the forgotten parasol. He passed her the two former items, keeping the latter. He wedged the sunshade beneath his arm. "Given the urgency of your situation, I think we ought to move the marriage forward. We should make for Scotland immediately."

"Immediately?" Angelina jerked in surprise. She faltered in donning her second glove. "As in *today*?"

Flynn tapped her nose. "In that much of a hurry to become my wife, are you?"

"No—yes—that is, I—"

She stared at him, certain a myriad of emotions flitted across her face. Averting her attention, she folded the letter into a small, tidy rectangle before inserting it into the palm of her right glove.

"I think tomorrow morning should suffice." Chuckling, he tucked her left hand into the crook of his elbow and ushered her toward the door.

She pulled him to a sudden stop, her eyes mere slits. "What of *our* contract?"

Flynn tried to quash his amusement. "Do you know suspicion is fairly shooting from your eyes?"

"It is not." She gave a perturbed huff but dropped her gaze just the same. "You and your nonsense about reading my eyes. Balderdash."

"Steady on, and fear not." He again raised her chin with his forefinger. "My steward practiced law before Father lured him away from his London office, promising a heavy purse and relaxed existence. I'm confident Fleming can draft an acceptable settlement by tomorrow."

"But what of Uncle Ambrose's agreement?" She crinkled her adorable nose and eyed Flynn hesitantly. "I thought you had to take the document to your man-of-affairs in London."

Ah, she'd remembered that detail, had she? Angelina possessed a sharp mind. It would be interesting to discover just how intelligent she was.

He nodded. "I thought too. We shall have to make do with Fleming's perusal. As long as the contract language is standard, I don't foresee any complications. Once I've signed the copies and Fleming acts as witness, we can proceed with our private bargain."

A tinge of guilt speared him.

He ought to tell her there wasn't a court in England that would enforce every term she'd specified of their secret agreement. He doubted she'd marry him then, and if she didn't, she'd be at Renault's mercy.

What Flynn wouldn't give for fifteen minutes in the ring with the bugger. He'd thrash him soundly for what the wretch had done to

Angelina. He'd also ask Yancy to use his significant influence and have Renault deported to France and charged with bigamy.

Flynn stepped forward again. She fell in beside him, the soft swooshing of their feet on the thick Oriental carpet the only sound for a few moments.

"And when shall I sign our contract? Not in the carriage?" Angelina peeped at him from beneath her lashes.

He didn't blame her for being suspicious. The men in her life had given her good reason to be guarded. In time, he hoped she'd come to trust him.

God's blood. A marriage without trust?

As bad or worse, than one lacking mutual respect. Affection didn't measure into the equation for a successful union. However, respect was essential.

"I'll request a meeting with Waterford for this evening and leave you a copy of our proposed agreement. That should give you time to note changes you wish to have made." He glanced at her pert profile. "Will that suffice?"

She eyed him cautiously, her nose yet a bit rosy from her cry. "I suppose so."

Anxious to see his niece wed, Flynn didn't expect genuine resistance from the duke. With any luck, the lush would agree to an appointment tonight. "I'll also arrange to collect you and your maid. You do have a lady's maid, don't you?"

Flynn surveyed the corridor from one end to the other. *Empty.* With a staff of nine, one could never be certain where or when a servant might pop up. He didn't need more tales carried to those below stairs until he'd a chance to address the domestics himself.

"Yes, Aunt Camille assigned me one."

He returned his attention to Angelina, guiding her into the passageway. "You'll want to choose your own, of course. For now, however, she'll suffice as a chaperone. As I was saying, I'll have my carriage at Wingfield at first light tomorrow. We can stop in Barrington. The township boasts a cozy pub, The Fox's Lair, where Fleming can meet us to witness our signatures."

"What shall I tell Murphy? She'll be suspicious when we stop so soon." Angelina swept a stray lock of hair off her cheek.

Was her hair as silky as it appeared? He longed to see those fiery tresses down, run his hands through their softness, and bury his nose in the sweet fragrance.

A clock chimed, reminding Flynn he'd best hurry if he hoped to accomplish everything that he needed to tonight.

Should he try to introduce Angelina to Mother today? No, he'd speak with his mother this evening. Although improving, she wasn't up to receiving guests.

The news that Renault hunted Angelina set Flynn's teeth on edge. Whispers of the slave-trader's grim activities had reached his ears more than once. The tales had been grisly. She mightn't believe it, but Angelina was well-rid of the scapegrace.

"My maid, my lord?" Her soft question reined in his unpleasant musings.

"It's Flynn." He smiled into her upturned face. "And your concern is valid. Mayhap, you could suggest you want to break your fast since you left Wingfield Court before eating?"

"Yes, that should do it." She chewed her lip before plowing onward. "I don't think Murphy ought to be present when I sign. She's been an absolute dear to me. However, Uncle pays her wages. I'm not sure where her loyalty lies. I don't want him to know of our *arrangement*."

He pressed her hand. "Once the contract is signed, she can warble it from the rooftops, and Waterford won't be able to change as much as a pen-stroke."

She flinched and flattened the palm of her other hand to her stomach. Did a woman typically suffer discomfort early in her pregnancy?

He made a mental note to ask Dr. Dawes when next he saw him. When was the last time she'd seen a physician?

"Are you positive you can travel?" Flynn scrutinized her pale face. He hadn't considered that difficulty. If forced to marry in England, he'd have to procure a special license.

She nodded. "I believe so. If I don't overexert myself, I foresee no problems. How lengthy is the journey?"

"It's an extended day's drive. We could break it into two, stopping for the night at an inn along the way." He escorted her through the doorway and turned her into a long corridor lined with landscape paintings. "My coach is quite comfortable, although I think for the child's welfare, that choice the wisest."

She graced him with a beatific smile. "Thank you. That relieves me greatly. I confess I do worry for my babe."

He admired her all the more for loving her unborn child. While some women would've resented the child, Angelina cherished hers.

Despite the despicable situation, she found herself in. He traced his fingers along her arm, noticing the momentary hitching of her breath.

Passion simmered beneath her surface.

"If you don't mind, I'd like to stop at my cousin's castle, Craiglocky Keep, on the return trip." Flynn snapped his fingers. "Why didn't I think of this before? We'll travel straight there instead of Gretna Green. It's a shorter journey by several hours, and there's bound to be a cleric in Craigcutty—the nearby village—if not at the keep itself."

"Won't they think it odd, you marrying so...*abruptly*?" Uncertainty flickered in her eyes.

He detected the merest tremor buried in her last word. *Hell, yes, they'll think it peculiar.*

Sethwick and Yvette knew he'd intended to propose to Lydia. But they'd keep their questions to themselves. At least within earshot of Angelina, and he'd only disclose enough to ease their confusion, no more. "They'll be curious. I've no doubt. They won't pry, though. There's no need to be concerned."

"And your family won't mind us arriving unannounced?" Her hand on his arm trembled. Head tilted to the side, Angelina idly toyed with a curl dangling near her shoulder as they walked.

"Not in the least." He sent her an amused expression. "The keep is usually overflowing with kin and kith."

"Overflowing?" She paled and bit her lip.

Flynn released a soft laugh. "My cousin, Viscount Sethwick, is Craiglocky's laird. He resides there with his wife and son, as well as his mother, stepfather, four siblings, a slew of cousins and an aunt and uncle or two. We'll be most welcome."

"Oh. If you're confident of our reception, Craiglocky does sound preferable." She gave him a contrite half-smile.

"I'm not particularly fond of carriage travel, even when I'm not—" Her gaze sank to her abdomen. "I don't care for the jostling. My stomach takes exception to the bumping along."

As they approached the drawing room, every now and again, a low, grating sound interrupted the women's muted murmuring.

Snoring? By God. Had Waterford fallen asleep?

She faltered to a stop and giggled, a winsome, musical tinkle. "I'm sorry. It's terrible of me, I know."

As another sonorous noise resonated from within the room, she clutched her stomach with one hand and clapped the other over her mouth.

"Dear me." Grandmamma's voice quaked, either with humor or disgust. "Are you *quite* sure he's not ailing? That sounds most unhealthy."

"Oh, to be sure. He's perfectly fine, although I fear the china is at risk of shattering with the racket he's making," the duchess quipped.

Grandmamma chuckled, a contagious, merry cackle.

Angelina convulsed with another round of laughter. "Shatter china?"

Transfixed, Flynn stared. She was exquisite, given over to mirth, her eyes sparkling, cheeks flushed, and joy rippling from her.

"Come now," she managed between giggles, "Surely you—"

He pressed his lips to hers in a swift, hard kiss.

Gasping, she clutched his arms reflexively.

Instantly aroused, he slid his tongue into her sweet mouth. Lips petal-soft, she tasted of strawberries and mint. She made no effort to break the kiss or push him away.

Emboldened, he wrapped an arm around her shoulders and pressed her flush to his chest, deepening their contact. Desire raked him in fierce waves, and he groaned low in his throat.

She tore her mouth from his, panting slightly as she stared, her eyes a blend of passion and confusion. She touched unsteady fingers to her lips. "Why did you kiss me?"

Because you're delectable, and I couldn't eschew the opportunity.

Another great, rumbling snort followed by an unmistakable, grotesque noise floated from the drawing room.

"Good Lord! Waterford, wake up." Annoyance and chagrin colored the duchess's voice. "Waterford. Ambrose. *Wake. Up.*"

Flynn clamped his lips shut, stifling the guffaw surging to his throat. What an uncouth churl. The poor duchess. He was chagrined for her. Not giving Angelina time to inquire again why he'd kissed her, he led her directly into the room.

The Duchess of Waterford bent near her slouching husband, prodding him insistently in the chest with her brisé fan.

Grandmamma had her nose buried in a serviette, either to hide her mirth or to block the aftermath of the duke's ill-timed bodily function.

"What's that?" The duke pawed at his face and shoved himself into a semi-erect position. Heavy-lidded and muddled, he peered at the four of them, before yawning widely. "Must've dozed off. Late night and all that."

"Waterford, I should like to sign the marriage settlement tonight."

Flynn crossed to the bell-pull. He gave the gold and sapphire cord a firm yank.

"*Tonight*?" The duke jerked upright, his keen perusal shifting between Flynn and Angelina. He rubbed his hands together. *Greedy bugger.* "Yes. Yes. Of course." He nodded eagerly, what little chin he possessed, disappearing into his cravat's rumpled folds. "Splendid idea."

Chatterton entered. "My lord?"

"Please send for Mr. Fleming. Have him wait for me in Father's office."

The butler regarded the duke warily. "Yes, sir. At once."

Flynn guided Angelina to the settee. Apprehension lingered in her lovely eyes. Because she had agreed to wed him? Because Renault pursued her? Because she feared Waterford would somehow roust their plan and put a stop to their private agreement?

Or had their kiss caused her anxiousness?

Likely, a combination of everything.

He yearned to take her into his arms and assure her she could trust him; that he would protect her as fiercely as he would the other women in his life. However, it was far too soon for protestations of that nature.

Settling beside her aunt, Angelina folded her hands primly in her lap as if she waited for Flynn to explain what transpired between them.

Rather than sitting, he strode to the fireplace. Hands clasped behind him, he faced the others. "Given the Frenchman may have already learned of Mrs. Thorne's whereabouts, she has agreed we should journey to Scotland tomorrow and wed with due haste."

He sent Grandmamma a silent message.

She signaled her understanding with a barely perceptible nod. She would wait to learn the particulars. Thank God, his grandmother wasn't given to meddling or histrionics.

"You're certain of this?" Her grace laid plump fingers on Angelina's hand. "This is what *you want* to do?"

Her gaze trained on him, Angelina inhaled deeply. As she released her breath, her shoulders drooped the merest bit. She nodded once. "I think it the most prudent course of action."

"If you're convinced, my dear." Mouth pursed, the duchess tilted her coiffed head regally and stared hard at Flynn, an unusual intensity in her gaze. After a disquieting moment, the line of her lips softened. Moisture glinted suspiciously in her eyes. "She's a priceless treasure, my lord. Treat her as such."

Flynn acquiesced by bowing his head.

A blush tinted Angelina's high cheekbones, and she kept her attention focused on her hands.

The duke's face flushed cherry-red as he beamed with satisfaction, barely this side of gloating. He rose clumsily and, tottering, grabbed at his chair back to steady himself. A pained expression strained his face but disappeared with the next blink.

"Why don't you accompany Angelina and the duchess to Wingfield, Bretheridge? Waterford asked. "You can join us for dinner."

Angelina tossed Flynn a panicked glance before lowering her lashes, no doubt to conceal her alarm. Her stiff shoulders and the taut line of her mouth revealed her discomfiture to anyone who cared to notice.

Only Grandmamma did. She quirked a gray brow at him, her gaze moving pointedly between Angelina and him.

"I regret, Your Grace, I must decline." He tempered his refusal with a jaundiced half-smile and a pacifying platitude. "Though I do appreciate your generous offer. I'll call after supping. I must inform my mother and sister of the nuptials, and I prefer to ride. It will save your driver a round trip as well."

Waterford's countenance grew perturbed. "Come in your carriage then, and plan to stay the night. You can depart directly from Wingfield in the morning."

Why was the sod so insistent?

Did he fear Flynn would change his mind?

Good. Let the bugger stew a bit.

Flynn spared a glance at the longcase clock as he shook his head. "I'm sorry, Waterford. I require time to pack and to give my man-of-affairs my instructions."

Angelina concerned him. She'd been observing the exchange with poised anxiety, and obviously worried about their private agreement. There'd be no wedding without it, and a sudden change of mind on her part would be deuced difficult to explain.

"I assure you, Mrs. Thorne and I have come to an agreeable arrangement, and we both recognize the prudence and benefits of a prompt wedding."

"Glad to see you finally scrounged up a dash of common sense." His movements sluggish, Waterford shuffled toward the door, effectively ending the visit.

Grandmamma *hmphed* her displeasure but remained blessedly silent. Nevertheless, her faded blue eyes shot daggers at the duke's back.

Through half-closed eyes, Flynn considered Waterford. Did he ail? The man didn't appear well. He gave a mental shrug. Or, possibly, the duke but experienced the aftermath of excessive indulgence.

The duchess gained her feet and scrutinized her husband. The tension creasing her face revealed her concern. With admirable aplomb, she painted a composed expression upon her features. "Come, Angelina. We've much to do if you're to depart tomorrow."

"Mrs. Thorne, I'm delighted you're going to be a part of our family." Warm acceptance wreathing her face, Grandmamma reached across the table and patted Angelina's hand.

Her countenance brightened, and a pleased smile bent her mouth as she gathered her reticule before rising. "Thank you, my lady."

"Pshaw, enough of that '*my lady'* nonsense. I must insist you call me Grandmamma. I'll refuse to answer to anything else." For emphasis, Grandmamma thumped her cane soundly on the floor, rattling the china on the table before her.

Not the least intimidated, Angelina released a light laugh. "Then you must call me Lina."

Flynn bowed over the duchess's fingers. "It's been a pleasure, Your Grace."

"I trust you'll make my niece happy, Bretheridge." A subtle warning lay buried beneath her polite words.

"I promise I'll endeavor to do so." Straightening, he released her hand. He faced Angelina and lifted her fingers as well. Brushing his lips across the fabric of her glove, he boldly caressed her wrist with his fingertips. "Until this evening."

"I shall look forward to it, my lord." Her eyes cast down, a faint tremor shook her.

Did she feel the sensual spark between them, too?

He stroked the sensitive spot inside her wrist again.

Her nostrils flared the merest bit, and when she brought her startled gaze to his, her eyes—the pupils enormous—deepened to emerald. Ah, unmistakable signs of sexual arousal. *Excellent, indeed.*

His manhood responded eagerly, but he tamped down his desire. He didn't need a raging erection with the duchess and Grandmama but feet away.

Mrs. Thorne possessed a strong, sensual nature. She responded every time he touched her. Did she recognize her passion? Given her high color and sudden obsession with the beadwork on her reticule, he'd bet his prize roses she did.

Precisely how much experience did she have? He anticipated finding out.

Flynn forced his attention to Waterford, hovering by the doorway. "I'll call at seven o'clock. Please, have the paperwork ready."

"You're both much too amendable to this marriage, of a sudden." His mouth skewed into a jeer, Waterford squinted at Flynn. "Yesterday, you squawked like a couple of old hens on the chopping block."

The duke's shrewd, watery eyes shifted between Flynn and Angelina. His beetled brows wriggled in consternation. "You two are up to something." His red-veined nose twitched. "I smell it."

"Hush, Waterford. The only thing anyone smells is the unpleasant, lingering aftermath of your digestive disruptions." The duchess joined her surly spouse beside the door.

Brava, Your Grace. Flynn's esteem of the duchess raised another notch.

"There will be no devilry or changing your minds!" The duke's eyes snapped his displeasure. "You've made a verbal commitment before witnesses. I'll petition Prinny to see the contract enforced—"

"You'll do no such thing, Uncle Ambrose." Fire in her eyes, Angelina faced him. "His lordship and I've agreed to wed. All that's required of you is for you to honor *your* part of the bargain."

Grandmamma perked up upon hearing that, and she gave Flynn a severe stare.

No doubt, he'd be explaining himself later.

"*Your* part? What bargain?" The duchess wore a stunned expression. She gripped the duke's arm and hissed between tight lips, "What have you done *now*?"

"Only after I have proof of your marriage shall I make good on my pledge." Waterford glowered at his wife before jerking his arm free. He lifted his nose, his saggy chin wobbling. "I'll accompany you to Scotland."

Angelina blanched and clutched her throat.

Flynn feared she'd topple if someone so much as sneezed. The desperate plea in her eyes knotted his gut.

"By God, you shall not." The duchess's strident tone ripped through the tension as she pinned her husband with a lethal glare. "I shan't have it."

And neither would he.

In less than a half dozen strides, he stood before the duke. Taller by several inches, he forced the annoyed man to peer up at him. "You will not intrude upon our wedding. You've meddled quite enough already. I'll provide a letter from the officiating cleric that includes the signatures of at least three witnesses."

Wan and wilted, Angelina slumped onto the settee again.

"You're hardly in a position to stop me," Waterford sneered, daring to poke Flynn in the chest.

"Oh, but *I* am." Fury crackled in her grace's eyes as she grasped her husband's arm and fairly dragged him, loudly protesting, from the room. "Have *you* forgotten, Waterford, who holds the winning cards *this* time?"

What the devil?

17

"I do," Angelina softly murmured.

She stood before the ornate alter in Craiglocky's quaint chapel. Bright morning sun shining through the brilliant stained-glass windows offered the only light. The beams blanketed her and Flynn in jeweled tones as they bowed their heads for the cleric's blessing.

Within her, the final flicker of a girlhood dream withered. She'd done it—married for convenience rather than love. The irony didn't escape her. Her second marriage in less than four months. Only this time, uncertainty and wariness filled her.

And a keen, hope-crushing sense of loss and loneliness.

Unable to meet her new husband's eyes, she stared at the emerald and garnet cluster ring he'd slipped on her finger moments before.

"It belonged to my grandmother. She insisted I give it to you. She is genuinely happy you are part of our family now."

What a dear lady.

The rest of the ceremony passed in a blur, except for when the clergyman said, "I now pronounce you husband and wife."

The declaration rudely yanked Angelina's attention back to the present.

"May I steal a kiss from my bride?" Flynn's seductive voice caressed her.

Oh, Lord.

Her gaze raced from the floor, past his thighs encased in form-fitting cream trousers and an equally snug black tailcoat emphasizing his much-too-broad shoulders, before coming to rest on his strong mouth.

He wouldn't dare kiss her in front of everyone.

Would he?

She'd hoped only the reverend and the witnesses Uncle Ambrose required would be present for the exchanging of vows. That wasn't to be.

Flynn's family at Craiglocky Keep, at least a dozen, insisted on attending the simple ceremony. She'd stopped short upon entering the chapel and seeing everyone already assembled.

"They only wish to show their support," he'd reassured her.

Her stomach fluttered. Or did the babe move within her? Would Flynn kiss her as he had in the corridor at Lambridge Manse?

Heavens. She prayed not.

Angelina wouldn't be able to stand without assistance if he dared to. Her lips, not to mention other parts, had tingled for an hour afterward. She wouldn't have believed such a thing possible if she hadn't experienced the phenomenon herself.

For pity's sake. She wasn't an innocent miss ignorant of the marriage bed. She'd lain with a man. By her measure, the act was highly overrated, and the pleasure exaggerated. Why must people make such a fuss of something so awkward and messy?

Still, the way Flynn made her feel—

That certainly hadn't been in any of the romance novels she'd read. And there'd been no powerful, sensual cravings with Charles. *Ever*.

"Lina, look at me." Flynn tenderly slanted her chin until her eyes reluctantly met his.

She flushed at the heated expression in his gaze. Why must he be so devilishly handsome? His eyes so beautiful and thick-lashed?

He bent his neck, his lips grazing her ear.

She inhaled his heady aroma, and at once went soft in the knees.

Another rule.

Stay clear of men who smell extraordinary and make one's legs turn to jelly.

Except, all of her foolish rules had been for naught. She'd violated the majority when she married Flynn. No doubt, she would suffer more heartache as a result.

"Lina." His mouth touched her again, his warm breath tickling her ear.

Drat. Pinpricks shot along her nerves once more. Her traitorous body's responsiveness mortified her.

"I was teasing about the kiss. Please try not to appear so frightened."

"I'm not afraid. It's just that your kisses cause all sorts of—"

The clergyman gave an exaggerated cough.

Her new husband grinned like a hound with a cornered fox. He *did* mean to kiss her. Cupping her cheek, he caressed it with his thumb.

Angelina permitted her eyelids to flutter closed. She parted her lips in anticipation and clutched his shoulders to remain upright.

Flynn didn't disappoint. He pressed a soft, sensual kiss upon her lips. Though far too brief, it held a delicious promise she yearned to have fulfilled.

Impossible.

The very terms she dictated in their contract specified no intimate relations for at least two years, and only if the union couldn't be dissolved.

The thought promptly cooled her wayward ardor.

How crass, contemplating a termination of the marriage mere minutes after speaking her vows.

She opened her eyes and stepped away, conscious of the speculative onlookers.

More than one male sported a wide grin. Oh, Flynn's relations were curious, all right. However, not an unkind or prying word had passed their lips. At least, not within earshot of her.

"See, that wasn't so bad, was it?" He squeezed her waist. He bent his handsome mouth into a lopsided grin, and a satisfied gleam shone in his eyes as he perused those assembled.

No, it was wonderful.

Momentary regret swept her. Neither his closest family members nor hers were here to witness their union. Just as well, she supposed, since the occasion was hardly celebratory.

She pasted a pleasant expression on her face. There was no sense giving anyone cause for additional speculation as to why they'd arrived unannounced last evening and married before breaking their fast this morning.

"Yer lordship, I have the letter ye requested." Reverend Wallace patted his coat pocket. "The witnesses need only pen their signatures."

Flynn nodded. "Can we wait until after we've eaten?"

"Aye, of course." The reverend winked. "I heard there's an entire roasted hog."

That sounded positively horrid. Her stomach agitated, Angelina fought a wave of nausea. She'd be lucky to keep a dry roll down.

"Come, I'm famished, and I know Aunt Giselle and Yvette rose at dawn to oversee the wedding breakfast." Flynn grasped her elbow and guided her the length of the short aisle.

Her mind raced as she attempted to match faces with names. *Aunt*

Giselle. That was Lady Ferguson. Her mammoth Scots husband was Sir Hugh, and Yvette was the Viscountess Sethwick. Though here, her husband Ewan, usually went by his Scots title, Laird McTavish.

Gads, this is so confusing.

In America, there hadn't been as great a need to know how to address the nobility and gentry properly. Her head spun from trying to recall their names and how they were related to Flynn.

Well, her head might be spinning because she felt wretched this morning.

Miss Isobel, Lord Sethwick's sister, was easy to remember. The most exquisite woman Angelina had ever laid eyes on, she possessed Laird McTavish's turquoise eyes. And the younger brother, Dugall, was the male equivalent of his sister's goddess-like beauty. So many stunning people in one family could hardly be considered fair. One had to wonder if God did indeed play favorites.

Another huge Scot winked at Angelina. She passed by the pew he and his brother sat in, along with a handsome couple in their middle years.

She grinned, liking him at once.

"Flynn, who are those two large, blond Scots again, and how are you related to them?"

"That would be Gregor and Alasdair McTavish. They're Sethwick's cousins on his father's side. I'm not related to them. That's their parents, Duncan and Kitta, sitting beside Gregor in the pew. Duncan is Sethwick's uncle. Kitta is Norse, which is why the sons are fair *and enormous*," Flynn added with a wry chuckle.

"I'll never keep them straight." Angelina sighed and blinked as they emerged from the chapel's dim interior into the brighter corridor of the castle.

He gave a husky chuckle again.

How she enjoyed his good humor. Such a far cry from her grouchy father and cantankerous uncle.

"It may take you a while, but eventually, you will," he assured her. "This isn't all of Sethwick's kin, either. He has two more sisters. Seonaid is in France visiting an aunt, though she's due to return any day. Adaira lives in England with her husband, the Earl of Clarendon. Then there are the clan members."

Shaking her head, Angelina groaned and covered her face with her hands. "No more."

He kissed the top of her head. "Did I tell you how stunning you are in that gown? The color matches your eyes almost perfectly."

She peeked at him between her fingers. Feeling silly, she lowered them, ridiculously pleased with the compliment. "Thank you."

"I prefer you always dress in something other than widow's weeds." His eyes darkened as he stared at her. He flicked the ruffle of one of her sleeves, though his attention seemed trained on the low neckline of her gown.

Her full breasts pushed against the fabric. They'd grown larger in recent weeks and threatened to spill from what once had been a modest neckline. She hadn't thought to include her hand-made fichu when she'd rushed about, gathering items to pack for their trip.

Angelina refused to wear black for their wedding. She'd had enough of the widow farce. Gratified the garment still fit, she donned one of her favorite gowns, a Pomona green with a gold lace overskirt embroidered with tiny leaves and a thin gold braid beneath the bosom.

Murphy had twisted her hair into an intricate Grecian knot, entwining green ribbons and a gold beaded circlet into Angelina's curls.

Green satin slippers embroidered with gold rosettes cocooned her feet. Other than the slightly loose wedding ring, she wore no jewelry. She wasn't about to wear the gems Charles had given her, and she didn't own any other gems.

Flynn's gift of his grandmother's ring meant a great deal to her. Perchance, he held her in some small regard after all.

"Thank you for the ring. It's exquisite."

"You're welcome," He responded somewhat perfunctorily.

Fingering the band, she mused. She far preferred this ring to the one Charles had chosen. Curious, even after their short acquaintance, Flynn already knew her taste better than Charles had.

Had he told his family she was a widow? Or that she expected another man's child? *God above.* She prayed not. Shame pricked her, humiliation's ruthless claws scratching away at her confidence. She didn't know these people, yet she loathed for them to think poorly of her.

Waiting for them to approach, the distinguished butler stood in attendance beside the entrance to the hall. With a sweep of his arm, he indicated they should enter. "My lord. My lady. If you please."

My lady? I'm a lady now.

"Thank you, Fairchild." Flynn guided Angelina into the great hall, his palm pressed to the small of her back.

Such a natural, intimate gesture. In fact, whenever he touched her, she sensed a completeness she didn't understand. When her mind wasn't running amuck, imagining him doing all kinds of unmentionable things to her with his hands and mouth, that was.

Overwhelmed by fatigue and nervousness, she hadn't paid much attention to the keep last night. Today, was another matter, and she tried not to gawk like a bumkin. She'd never seen anything so rustic—practically medieval—yet splendid in its antiquity.

The great hall, dominated by an enormous trestle table situated at the other end of the room, was huge. Easily seating fifty or more, it abutted a dais reserved for the laird, and others, holding positions of honor.

Towering bronze candelabras perched atop the heavy table. Dozens of unlit sconces lined the twenty-foot walls, except where a minstrel's gallery balanced. Several shields boasting the McTavish crest, as well as various pieces of ancient weaponry, streaming pennants, and intricately woven tapestries, adorned the aged stones.

Encased in elaborate frames suspended from silken burgundy cords, at least two dozen fierce Scots stared at their decedents below. Angelina could only imagine the triumphs and tragedies those ancestors had witnessed through the decades.

The keep was centuries old, yet oddly enough, the great hall exuded a friendly, welcoming atmosphere. She suspected the ambiance was due to the occupants rather than the structure.

Three gigantic, charcoal-colored dogs wrapped together in a comfortable tangle slept before the hearth.

Boarhounds?

She'd never seen one before. The size of small ponies and reputed to be gentle, devoted beasts, they appeared impervious to the chaos around them. Two more dogs, these speckled, black spaniels, lay sprawled in the vibrant rays of sun pouring in the mullioned windows.

Last night, after the briefest of introductions, she'd been hustled to a cozy chamber for a hot bath. A tray of steaming venison stew, oat rolls, something sinfully delicious called clootie dumpling, and strong, aromatic tea arrived soon after. The tea might very well have contained a draught of whisky.

Less than an hour after arriving, she'd crawled into cool, heather scented sheets and drifted to sleep without seeing Flynn again.

She worked her gaze over her new husband.

He waited near the dais while a footman pulled a chair out for her. "I thought you'd be uncomfortable sitting on the platform, on display for all. I asked Sethwick if we might sit here."

He already knew that about her as well?

Never before had a man considered her needs or treated her as thoughtfully. A sweet warmness spread around her guarded heart. "Thank you. I don't care to be the center of attention."

"Neither does Yvette. That's why Sethwick happily honored my request."

"Flynn, why do you address the laird as Sethwick, even here?" she asked. "Answering to different titles must be confusing."

She found the whole title business rather baffling, truth to tell. She worried she'd commit some social *faux pas* and address someone incorrectly.

"It's a habit, I suppose." He took the seat the footman indicated beside her. "I see far more of Sethwick in England than I do in Scotland. There, he's only addressed by his English title."

Flynn scooted his chair in a fraction, his thigh brushing her skirt.

One of those wonderful little tremors careened along Angelina's senses. She unfolded her serviette. Placing it in her lap, she eyed the entrance through lowered lashes. The chapel crowd had swollen in number and now included a small army of clan members.

"What did you tell them? About us?" She bobbed her head toward the jovial throng billowing into the hall. Did her voice reveal her anxiety? No, to her ears, she sounded quite serene. She was anything but calm. "I woke in the middle of the night and realized I had no idea what to expect this morning."

He offered a contrite smile. "I apologize. I meant to check on you before you retired. Once I realized the late hour, you were already abed."

If he had come to her chamber, he'd have found her sound asleep.

He cast a swift gaze about as if to make sure no one eavesdropped. "In any event, I told them I'd met a magnificent woman who fate decreed I marry at once. I let them make assumptions as to what that meant."

Placing his hand atop hers, he gave it a comforting squeeze.

Another sensual jolt stabbed her.

Did he feel it, too? His face held a rather strained expression.

Isobel took the seat opposite her.

One of the burly blond Scots—*Gregor*?—nudged his handsome brother aside to sit beside Isobel. She giggled, impishness glimmering in her spectacular eyes.

"Behave, you two." She admonished them as only someone on intimate terms would do.

The brother shrugged his massive shoulders and winked at Angelina before tromping a few feet farther along the table and finding a seat.

Evidently, the Scots didn't stand on protocol when it came to dining. Or, perhaps, the casualness could be attributed to the intimacy of the group gathered. At least two-thirds of the seats surrounding the table remained empty.

"Have ye tried the smoked salmon, my lady?" Gregor pointed to the fish, a grin arching his mouth. "I caught it myself."

It took her a moment to realize he spoke to her. That *my lady* business would take time to accustom to.

"No, not yet. There's so much food," she said.

Normally, she would've indulged. Smoked salmon was a particular favorite of hers. However, as could be expected of late, her stomach objected. Fish most definitely wasn't on the menu for her today. Neither was the hog displayed on a side table where a footman carved great slabs of meat from the wretched beast.

Suppressing a shudder, she clenched her balled serviette, waiting for a wave of nausea and a spasm in her lower spine to pass. Her back had been a deuced nuisance almost from the moment they'd left The Fox's Lair. Flynn's comfortable carriage boasted thick squabs and fine springs. The journey hadn't been overly strenuous, either. Yet the dull ache persisted.

He speared a mouthful of the flakey copper-colored fish with his fork. "Superb as usual. There's nothing quite like fresh salmon."

"Aye, that's true." The Scot called Gregor dove into his meal with gusto.

More than once, Angelina caught Flynn surveying the hall. His gaze briefly met several men's, including the laird's penetrating stare, as if in silent communication.

She felt all the more an outsider. She should've been relieved at the vague excuse Flynn gave his family for their hasty marriage. Worry teased her, nonetheless.

He seemed distracted. There was a tension—an edginess—about him she'd not noticed before. Not even at Lambridge when he'd worried, she might change her mind about marrying him, or when Uncle Ambrose had insisted, he should attend the nuptials.

Thank God, that hadn't come to pass.

Flynn had told her Uncle Ambrose had signed the contract at

Wingfield Court without incident. Later, after requesting she accompany him for a walk about the gardens, Flynn had smuggled her a copy of their private agreement.

At the inn, Murphy hustled straight to the kitchen to brew mint tea and oversee a light repast for Angelina. By the time the maid returned to the common room, the document lay signed and neatly tucked away in Mr. Fleming's pocket.

Flynn had included every stipulation Angelina requested and bestowed a generous monetary settlement on her as well. Still, her unease lingered.

Nibbling a piece of dark bread, she observed him through her lashes.

His lips edged up occasionally, but restraint shadowed his eyes. His attention repeatedly shifted to the hall's entrance. As the meal progressed, his eating slowed, and he spoke less and less.

The slightest crease marred Isobel's brow as if something troubled her. And numerous times, she caught one of the Scots staring at her. They'd dip their head or smile, and then their gaze would shift away, often toward the entrance as well.

Something wasn't right.

Well, of course, it's not, ninny. Everything about this isn't right.

She and Flynn had both agreed to the joining. Nevertheless, she remained convinced something else was afoot. Even the dogs sensed it, raising their heads and looking expectantly at the double doors framing the entry.

"Flynn, what's wrong?"

"*Wrong*?" Fork midway to his mouth, he paused. His eyes were shielded green shards. "What makes you think something is amiss?"

"I may have only known you for a couple of days, but I recognize uneasiness when I see it." Leaning nearer, she turned her head and dropped her voice, cautious about making sure no one else could overhear. She laid her hand on his arm. "Cannot you tell me what bothers you?"

Face reserved, his gaze flitted to the other diners.

"Ah, it's us. Of course. This must be awkward for you." Of a sudden uncertain, Angelina lowered her hand to her lap and wadded her serviette. She lifted her gaze, perusing the table. "And them too. I'm sorry, I don't know what—"

What could she say?

"No, never think it. That's not the cause." Sighing, he patted his mouth with his napkin. After taking a lengthy drink of ale, he put the tankard aside.

"There's unrest between some of the northern clans. I learned of the discontent last night." He drummed his fingertips on the tabletop as if to alleviate the tension he suppressed. "In recent years, such incidences are rare and typically occur amongst the remoter tribes."

His fingers stilled, and he toyed with his fork instead. "Unfortunately, we've arrived at such a time. Sethwick has invited important members of another tribe to stay here until matters are settled, and it's safe for them to return home."

"I take it they're expected at any moment?" Angelina skipped a glance at the entry.

Nodding, Flynn took a bite of grouse. "Sethwick has sent several men to act as an escort. A messenger arrived late last night. The party is expected here this morning."

"Is there a need for concern? From the rival clan, I mean." She frowned slightly. "Forgive me. Although I'm Scots by birth, I have no real knowledge of their ways."

Flynn shook his head. "No. Sethwick seems to think this matter will subside quickly." He turned to examine her more fully. "You're pale. Would you care to take a turn about the bailey or stables? Sethwick boasts some of the finest horseflesh in the country.'"

Fresh air would be welcome.

He searched her face. "Or would you rather rest when we're finished—"

A commotion in the outer hall proclaimed the arrival of the anticipated guests. The butler stepped through the doorway and opened his mouth. But before he could utter a syllable, like a swollen river breaching its banks, the newcomers flooded into the chamber.

Several Scots boasting McTavish plaids trooped in, followed by a tall, serious gentleman and a lovely brunette wearing a violet traveling ensemble.

Her eyes locked on Flynn, and joy swept her face. Stopping abruptly, she mouthed his name. Behind her, five Scots wearing a different patterned tartan, plowed into one another, muttering low curses.

It's her.

The woman Flynn had wanted to court before his father's death. The woman he'd wished to wed.

Angelina knew it beyond a doubt.

Barely visible behind the wall of Highlanders, forming a semi-circle around the young lady and her companion, stood two more men and an older female. Even from across the room, Angelina recognized the adoration shining in the young woman's eyes.

She'd regarded Charles like that. A lifetime ago.

The poor thing stared at Flynn, her heart on her sleeve for everyone to see. She'd be crushed and humiliated when she learned he'd spoken his vows less than an hour before.

Angelina forced herself to face him. She couldn't read his shuttered expression.

Jaw clenched with suppressed strain; he flexed his fingers around the tankard.

She'd never seen him this way—like a tightly coiled spring or an adder ready to strike.

A fresh blow of betrayal slammed into her.

He'd known.

Oh, God. He'd *known.*

And hadn't told her. Warned her. Prepared her.

Her gaze raced around the room, from person to person. His family must've been informed as well. Married to one woman, and the woman he loved and had planned on wedding arriving a short while later. *Too late.* Too late to change her mind. Too late for him to wed his true love. Too, damn late.

A dizzying rush of shame suffused her.

Now would be another good time for the floor to open and swallow me, God.

Gripping the table, Angelina stood, shoving her chair away as she did. She urgently sought another exit.

"I… I need…" She couldn't finish, fearing she was about to vomit. Her back pained her something fierce.

Flynn whipped his head in her direction. His eyes darkened to jade with worry. "Angelina?"

"No." It came out a strangled croak.

No. No. No. Tightening her hold on the table, she refused to look at him. "Not now. Not here," she managed, her voice scarcely more than a whispered rasp.

You should've told me, she screamed silently, swallowing convulsively as what little she'd eaten threatened to reappear.

Dear God, don't let me be sick in front of everyone.

She couldn't bear more humiliation.

Eerie silence hung thickly in the room. Their faces constrained, even the newcomers seemed to sense something amiss.

Her attention fell on a narrow door.

The kitchen. Yes. If I can make the kitchen.

Angelina headed for the nondescript door on the opposite side of the hall she'd seen the servants using this morning. She kept one eye on the young woman the whole while.

Confusion and uncertainty marred the girl's refined features as she stumbled toward Flynn. One of the other men pushed his way to the front of the crowd gathered at the hall's entrance.

Desperate to flee, Angelina trained her entire focus on her means of escape.

Put one foot in front of the other.

Keep your head up. Breathe.

Keep going. Ignore the pain.

"Mademoiselle Ellsworth, it's imperative I speak with you at once."

She went rigid, halting in mid-stride and swaying.

Dear God, it cannot be.

"Ellsworth?" someone whispered.

"I thought her name was Mrs. Thorne."

So, Flynn *had* spread the widow falsehood.

She closed her eyes, the bile rising in a searing flood against the back of her throat. Agony lanced her middle, spreading in a crushing wave to her spine and pelvis. That she still stood upright could be attributed to her sheer stubbornness and pride.

This horror replicated another ghastly wedding day.

What else, in God's blessed name, could possibly go wrong?

Well, Charles could pop in for a chat.

She stifled a hysterical giggle.

Slowly, her legs and heart leaden, she rotated to the center of the room. Fisting her hands in her skirt, Angelina strove for a poised comportment. She feared the tenuous grasp on her emotions would dissolve like a lone snowflake on a blazing hearth.

"I must say, you do have an unfortunate habit of appearing at the most inopportune times, Lord Devaux-Rousset."

18

Flynn tossed his monogrammed serviette on his almost full plate and lurched to his feet.

As if things aren't bloody complicated enough, Renault's stepson happens to totter in on Lydia's heels.

His presence could only mean one thing.

Given the stricken expression on Angelina's face, she'd guessed the truth.

The slave-trader must know her whereabouts, too. It mattered not; she was Lady Bretheridge now. The scurrilous bigamist she'd first married would find it most difficult to approach her. Flynn flexed his fingers. God, for the opportunity to have a go at Renault. To teach the bastard a long-overdue lesson.

Flynn sensed more than thirty pairs of eyes boring into him as he skirted the table, his boots clicking unnaturally loud on the stone floor. The meal and conversations forgotten, everyone's attention fixated on him and Angelina.

Aunt Giselle and Uncle Hugh traded worried glances.

Yvette laid her hand on her husband's arm and whispered urgently into his ear.

Lydia took a couple more steps in his direction before coming to a faltering stop. Her fine eyebrows furrowed, she considered him and Angelina appearing totally bewildered. "Lord Bretheridge?"

Flynn would've spared her this hurt and humiliation. He'd asked to be informed the moment she arrived in order to speak to her privately.

Tricky business, that. Excusing oneself from one's wedding breakfast to tell another woman you couldn't pursue her any longer.

Fate possessed a cruel streak.

Mayhap, Sethwick had overlooked advising Fairchild of Flynn's request. Or more likely, the majordomo hadn't been able to insert a word in edgewise when the exuberant party descended upon the keep.

Fairchild had been Yvette's butler in America before she married Sethwick. The poor man still hadn't become accustomed to the forwardness of some Scots. *Most* Scots.

Angelina raised eyes laden with eviscerating pain and cutting indictment to Flynn's.

Guilt coiled sharp and intense in his gut, and he feared, in that moment, he'd lost her forever.

Without another word and blinking unnaturally slow, she turned away and, once again, headed toward the other side of the great hall. Her pace stiff and controlled, she moved as if each step cost her monumental effort.

She'd been through too much already. This was cruel. Bloody, damned cruel.

He should've told her Lydia was expected. It would've been the decent thing to do. She deserved that courtesy, but he'd acted a coward.

In truth, he hadn't been altogether certain of his feelings until this very moment. Of the two women nursing wounded pride that he owed explanations to, Angelina mattered more. That astounded him. How had she burrowed beneath his skin—no, wormed her way into his heart—in such a short time?

Conceivably, because she needed him the most. Needed his name. Needed his protection. Needed a man she could depend upon and trust unequivocally.

He'd made a merry mess of that last bit. Hell, she might never trust him again. And rightly so.

The baron strode toward Angelina, purpose in each step. "Mademoiselle…"

By God, the man was persistent as flies on manure. And brazen as hell.

Gregor and Alasdair rose from their seats, no doubt prepared to intervene.

Sethwick descended the dais in two quick steps.

Flynn halted them with a raised hand. "Lord Devaux-Rousset, as I'm sure you can see, Angelina isn't feeling quite up to scratch."

Devaux-Rousset stopped but narrowed his black eyes at Flynn.

Flynn spared Angelina a hurried glance. *Blister it.* Wan and visibly swaying on her feet, pain pinched her mouth and the corners of her eyes. She appeared about to cock up her toes. "I'd be happy to discuss whatever it is you find so pressing. First, however, I must tend to my wife."

"Your wife?" The baron arched a brow in incredulity as he eyed her. "Since when?"

"Your *wife*?" Lydia echoed, her rasping gasp ricocheting about the hall.

Flynn set his jaw, meeting her stricken eyes. "Yes, this," he gestured at the table, "is our wedding breakfast."

Her face crumpled, and she clapped a gloved hand to her mouth. She spun on her heel and tore from the hall. Not before he saw her cheeks awash with tears.

The tall man accompanying her glowered at Flynn and Angelina before rushing after Lydia. Another man and a stout woman parted from the rear of the crowd and trailed behind them.

Flynn stepped forward, intending to follow Lydia, to explain the situation. Common sense pulled him up short. He couldn't clarify *anything to* her. Not without betraying his wife's confidence.

"Ah. Accept my congratulations." The baron smoothed his mustache. "I certainly can wait to have an audience with you and your new *bride*."

He wandered to peer out one of the windows facing the bailey.

The bugger seemed far too pleased by the news. How had he found Angelina anyway? That bore investigating. Until Flynn extracted some credible answers from the baron, he wouldn't trust Devaux-Rousset a quid more than Renault.

Flynn flicked a pointed glance to Sethwick, and then once more to the Frenchman.

Sethwick gave an almost indiscernible inclination of his head.

Good. He understood. The baron wouldn't be able to scratch his well-turned-out bum without his actions being reported to Flynn.

"Lady Bretheridge?" Alarm sharpened Yvette's voice.

Flynn wrenched his attention to his wife.

She'd halted a few yards from the kitchen door. Ashen as the snow at dawn, she stood hunched, her eyes squeezed shut, clutching her stomach.

My God. The babe.

Yvette and Gregor rushed to her.

The Scot swept her into his arms and, without hesitation, marched through the gawking onlookers.

Yvette hiked her skirts to her calves. "Ewan, send for Midwife Gilchrist and Doctor Paterson at once."

Isobel's and Aunt Giselle's eyes meshed in horrified unison before the two dashed from the hall, Flynn scarcely a hair's breadth behind them.

God, be merciful, he prayed, taking the stairs two at a time, knowing even as he sent up the silent plea, his prayer was far too late already.

No, no. God, no!

"No," Angelina sobbed into the soggy pillow, pounding the sodden lump with her fist again. "It's so unfair."

She'd lost her baby.

A boy. A precious, darling boy.

Doctor Paterson concluded the pitiable thing had been much too small and poorly developed to ever have survived. Losing the baby had been inevitable.

Guilt gnawed at her, nevertheless.

Had she caused the miscarriage? Had her body rejected her son, because she'd been furious and resentful when she first learned of her pregnancy? Had her hatred of Charles adversely affected the child growing in her womb? Or had the wee babe sensed she feared raising a son alone?

She asked the midwife those same questions, refusing to spare herself any discomfort.

Compassion brimmed in Midwife Gilchrist's warm brown eyes. She'd taken Angelina's hand, patting it soothingly.

"Lass, ye had nothin' to do with the loss of the bairn. Sometimes the Good Laird, for reasons we'll never know or understand, sees fit to take the wee one to heaven before it's ever born. Such was the case with yer laddie."

"But I was shamefully bitter and angry in the beginning. Perhaps—"

Doctor Paterson shook his shaggy head. "Dinna torture yerself with such thoughts, lass. Ye are a healthy young woman with a strong constitution. There was naught ye could've done to prevent this. Frankly, I'm surprised ye carried the bairn as long as ye did."

That had been hours ago.

Angelina didn't care everyone in the keep likely knew she'd been expecting when she married Flynn. Didn't care they no doubt speculated whether he fathered the child, given he'd been enamored of Miss Farnsworth mere weeks ago.

Lady Ferguson offered a glass half-full of a cloudy liquid. "Drink this, dear. It will help you sleep."

Eyes red-rimmed from crying, and her arms piled with soiled linens, Murphy had been sent below to have a bite of soup and a cup of restorative tea. Her weeping only added to Angelina's despair.

"I don't want it." She turned her face away and stared at the wall. She didn't deserve to sleep, to forget her little one.

Fate was Satan's black-hearted mistress. To take the baby a scant hour after Angelina had shackled herself to a stranger. A man in love with someone else.

A soft knock jarred the chamber door.

"Please, I don't wish to see anyone," Angelina whispered raggedly against the bedding.

Most especially not Flynn. What would she say to him?

By-the-by, I don't need your name or protection anymore. Feel free to take up with your former love.

He'd fulfilled Uncle Ambrose's demand. The wager would be canceled. No need remained for them to stay married.

Angelina vaguely recalled Gregor carrying her above stairs and Flynn hovering near her bed. He'd held her hand and whispered encouragement, his handsome face etched with worry and something else. He hadn't left until the doctor and midwife hustled in and shooed everyone, except Murphy and Lady Ferguson, from the room.

"Let me see who it is, *chérie*."

Angelina found Lady Ferguson's soft, French accent oddly comforting.

Her ladyship patted Angelina's shoulder. "Flynn's been beside himself, pacing the corridor this whole while."

Not sequestered in a nook somewhere, professing his love while comforting the distraught Miss Farnsworth?

Angelina had learned her name. She pitied the young woman whose humiliation must be only marginally less than hers. Chagrin poked her as well. Flynn possessed a good heart and didn't deserve her snide speculations.

The door vibrated again.

"*Oui*, just a moment." The swishing of skirts as Lady Ferguson glided to the door revealed she intended to answer the summons. The heavy door whisked open, accompanied by a low creak. "I'm sorry, Flynn."

Flynn.

Angelina didn't want to see him.

Lady Ferguson tried gently to dissuade him. "She's not feeling quite up to visitors yet. I'm sure you understand. Possibly, later this evening?"

"I *must* see her. She shouldn't be alone in her suffering, and she knows no one else here. Please." Gruff emotion reduced his voice to a hoarse rasp.

From the desperation in his voice, she could almost believe he felt something for her. At this moment, she so needed someone who did. The tiny rudder guiding her choices and decisions for the past weeks no longer existed, and she was utterly, absolutely lost.

Fresh tears seeped from beneath Angelina's lashes, and her shoulders shook with renewed grief. She pressed her swollen face in the pillows to stifle her heartbroken sobs.

Tomorrow, or the next day, or the next, she would worry about her future.

At present, all she wanted to do was yield to the grief laying siege to her heart and mourn her nameless son. The injustice of his loss tormented her. She almost welcomed the bitterness that taunted her soul.

A firm, yet quiet *click* announced the door shutting. The mattress dipped a moment later as Lady Ferguson sat on the other side of the bed. Such a kindhearted, nonjudgmental woman. She smoothed the bedding around Angelina's shoulders, brushing the moist curls from her cheek with calloused fingers.

Calloused fingers?

Angelina's breath caught.

Flynn.

She breathed in his familiar musky, slightly spicy scent.

"Go away. Please, go away." Hunching her back, she buried her face in the once-crisp linen. The scent of heather teased her nose.

Instead of leaving, he stretched his length behind her and wrapped one powerful arm around her waist, wedging the other beneath the pillow cradling her head. A moment later, his warm breath heated her nape. His lips touched her neck in a comforting whisper of a kiss.

"I'm so sorry, Lina." The low timbre of his voice trembled with sorrow. "Is there anything I can do?"

She could only shake her head as weeping wracked her once more. He held her against his solid length, his body a haven, a wonderful cocoon of protection as she vented her heartbreak.

At long last, her store of tears exhausted itself. She opened gritty, swollen eyes. The chamber, now dimmed by purplish evening shadows, sat silent except for Flynn's even breathing.

Did he sleep?

Drawing in a shaky breath, Angelina wiped her face with the sheet, having long since lost track of the handkerchief Lady Ferguson had provided.

He shifted until he lay on his back, then turned her toward him and tucked her into his side, her head resting on his broad shoulder. He nuzzled her hair.

"Would you like to have a service for the baby? Reverend Wallace offered to officiate, and Sethwick's carpenter made a tiny coffin. Isobel and Kitta padded the interior, lining it with a piece of McTavish plaid."

Emotion threatened to overwhelm Angelina again. Unable to respond, she scrunched her eyes closed, biting her lower lip. The coppery taste of blood bore witness to her effort to contain her sorrow.

When she didn't answer, Flynn ran one hand along her arm and shoulder in a soothing caress. "There's a lovely view of Loch Arkaig from Craiglocky's cemetery. Aunt Giselle has a white tea rose she'd like to transplant to beside the baby's grave."

"White for innocence," Angelina whispered through dry lips.

"Yes. Also, honor and reverence as well as remembrance. A white rose is symbolic of heavenliness, too." He uncrossed his ankles, stretching his muscles for a brief moment. He breathed out a long, gruff sigh.

What was he thinking? Why wasn't he consoling his Miss Farnsworth instead of her?

"Why are they so kind to me?" Angelina mumbled against his shoulder. "Surely, they have deduced my circumstances and realize I was well along with child when we exchanged our vows."

"Shh, Lina." He placed a long finger on her lips and lifted his head to peer into her eyes. "That was no fault of yours."

Tenderness radiated from his sympathetic jade gaze, unlike anything she'd ever experienced from a man. Or mayhap, the deepening shadows caused her imagination to seek that which didn't exist.

He relaxed against the pillows again. "They are kindhearted people and feel for you. That you grieve for your child makes your tragic loss much more devastating. They only seek to ease your pain and, thereby, their own, in some small measure."

Could she leave her baby here, only visiting his grave at irregular intervals? In time, likely never returning anymore, forgetting the precious darling might ever have been? After she and Flynn separated, returning to Craiglocky to visit her son's resting place would be awkward for everyone.

As if reading her mind, Flynn nestled his nose in her hair again. "Unless you'd prefer to have the babe buried at Lambridge Manse, in the family cemetery. I could arrange for him to be transported there tomorrow, though Doctor Paterson advised it will be at least a week before you're capable of traveling. You'd miss the infant's burial, but we could have a service once we returned."

That sealed it for Angelina. She refused to have her son's tiny body laid in the cold, uncaring earth without his mother there to wish him a loving farewell.

She stared at Flynn's jaw, lightly shadowed with stubble. She didn't deserve anyone's compassion. If she hadn't been heaven-bent on marrying Charles so quickly, she might've learned his true nature. Might've discovered he was already married. And she might've been spared the agony of losing a child and the loneliness of a marriage of convenience.

Where would that have left Flynn? He'd needed this marriage every bit, if not more than she had. The knowledge brought little comfort.

"I should like to name my baby and, perhaps, have a stone carved for a grave marker." She dared to meet his eyes for a moment before focusing on his strong jaw once more. "Possibly, one with an angel or a cherub?"

"I think that a splendid idea. Do you have a name in mind?" He tenderly kissed her forehead, hugging her to his chest.

She shook her head. "Do you know one that means cherished or dearly loved?"

He was silent for a few moments. "Davy means beloved in Scots, and its Hebrew meaning is cherished. Many a mighty Scottish king has proudly born the name." He hesitated. "Davy was also my favorite uncle's name."

Beloved. Her son had been beloved.

"Davy." Angelina tested the name. She sighed as peace finally embraced her. "Perfect for a tiny innocent. Not too austere or pompous. Yes, that will do."

Something seemed perfectly right about lying in Flynn's arms, even though the reason for being there was tragic. Shutting her eyes, she savored the momentary tranquility. She'd been married twice, yet this was the first time she'd fall asleep encompassed in a man's arms.

God, let me sleep for a time and rest in blessed forgetfulness.

As she drifted into slumber, Flynn pressed his lips to her hair. "I've already spoken with Reverend Wallace. Once you're better, we can move forward with the annulment."

19

Flynn's thoughts clanged around in his head as he paced Reverend Wallace's small office. "So, is an annulment even feasible?"

"Are ye certain an annulment's what ye be wantin', yer lordship?" The reverend scratched his nose, his keen gaze peering deep into Flynn's soul. "Seems to me, ye are mighty attached to that lovely lass. Even if the bairn wasna yers."

There'd been no way to keep that particular a secret. Not with Devaux-Rousset in residence. Flynn used discretion with whom he shared the truth. As for those he hadn't taken into his confidence, well, he didn't give a blacksmith's double damn what they thought.

He slapped his hat against his thigh. "It's her happiness I'm concerned with."

Angelina's happiness, above all else.

He paced the short distance from the cleric's well-used desk to the door of the holy man's office.

"We wed so my father's gaming debt would be canceled, saving my family and me from social and financial ruin. And, also so that Angelina wouldn't have to endure the shame of bearing a child outside of wedlock."

Reverend Wallace balanced his rickety chair onto the two back legs, folding his hands atop his ample girth. The chair groaned and creaked its protest.

Flynn worried the hefty man of God might topple backward at any moment.

"I'd say that was most unselfish of ye both," Reverend Wallace said.

"Hardly," Flynn scoffed, planting his hands on his hips. "At *point non-plus,* we selected the best solution to two wholly undesirable situations. We knew precisely what we agreed to, and I assure you, selflessness didn't figure into the equation. Ours is a business arrangement—a matter of convenience."

That wasn't altogether true. Protecting his family had motivated him. Angelina had acted to safeguard her baby. He supposed some might call that noble. He unquestionably hadn't planned on developing an attachment to her this early on. Perchance, after a few months, but a dab beyond a week?

Preposterous.

Yet, he had. And considerably more than a simple attachment.

Implausibly. Inconceivably. He'd fallen in love with her.

In any event, it mattered not. He relaxed a shoulder against the diminutive window overlooking the church's graveyard. Three chickens scratched and pecked at the weeds amongst the dirt.

"She thought she was married to the child's father," he said, mindful to keep the fury from his voice.

Why had he offered up that sordid morsel?

He knew perfectly well why. He didn't want the rector to think poorly of Angelina.

"Ah, I see." The cleric resumed his calm regard. His silence hung heavy and reproachful in the minute office.

Flynn quirked the corner of his mouth as a scruffy kitten crept up on one of the unsuspecting hens.

"You advised yourself, Reverend, our best hope of acquiring an annulment is now when there are witnesses who can swear that the marriage hasn't been consummated." He turned from the window and considered the clergyman for an extended moment.

"True. The longer ye wait to begin proceedin's, the harder it will be to attain one." Reverend Wallace seemed intent on scraping a bit of something from beneath a thumbnail before studiously examining his other fingers.

"Have ye considered where Lady Bretheridge will live in the meantime?" He tugged his earlobe. "She canna very well reside with ye. If she stays here, and ye return to England, I can attest to separate residences. In fact, that would strengthen her plea for an annulment, if ye *abandon* her."

Leaning his elbows on the desk, he clasped his hands together, almost challenging Flynn.

Abandon? Bloody hell.

Flynn returned his attention to the chickens poking about the dirt. The kitten pounced and missed. The intended target squawked her outrage, and neck out-stretched, charged after the diminutive ball of fluff.

"I thought I'd let her decide…" He shrugged a shoulder, afraid he'd give himself away in tone or expression.

Angelina deserved a modicum of joy.

Waterford would protest, no doubt. Given the babe's death, the lout had as much leverage as a strand of wet straw in manure.

In the days since Angelina had lost her son, Flynn had written Fleming, sending along the letter bearing the witnesses' signatures Waterford had mandated. The duke had promptly signed the settlement contract. He'd given it to Fleming, who trotted off to Flynn's man-of-affairs in London. Afterward, Fleming sent Flynn a succinct missive. The agreement was ironclad. The duke couldn't renege on as much as a farthing.

The cleric slapped his palm on his desk, the sound startling Flynn from his reverie.

"That's exactly what I was going to recommend, lad." He stood and ushered Flynn to the door. "Ask the lass what she wants. I believe ye'll be mighty surprised."

Before he realized what Reverend Wallace was about, Flynn had been nudged through the doorway and found himself staring at the closed wooden expanse an inch from his nose.

A week later, Flynn sat at Sethwick's desk, a composed and somber Angelina sitting across from him. Skin creamy, lips pink and dewy, and her wide green-eyed gaze unfathomable, she regarded him.

"Just to clarify, you don't want an annulment?" He forced the words from his dry mouth. Seizing the quill atop the desk, he tapped the tip sharply on the surface, desperate to release some of the tension flooding him.

Blast, what a deuced, complicated mess.

An annulment was possible *if* Angelina remained in Scotland. The marriage hadn't been consummated, and more than a dozen witnesses could testify to that fact. If not an annulment, a divorce was certainly feasible, wasn't it?

He hadn't discussed that option with the reverend.

The wise thing to do would've been to investigate the Church of

Scotland's marriage laws more thoroughly *before* toddling off across the border for a hasty wedding.

Idiot.

The knowledge that Renault had been snooping about trying to find Angelina added danger to the already simmering situation. To keep her safe, Flynn must make haste.

He caressed her with his gaze.

Lord, she was beautiful.

How could he let her go? Yet he would, to allow her the happiness she'd been denied.

If she were, in fact, bound to him for life, she would be beside herself. Her terms had been quite specific. He'd never be able to convince her he hadn't deliberately deceived her.

But now she indicated she mightn't want an annulment after all.

Shifting his attention, he scrutinized the rather austere study. He doubted Sethwick spent much time in the dismal room. Dark and drafty, even in the summer, the chamber was tomb-like with its drab stone walls and high, narrow windows.

The library was considerably brighter and more welcoming. Besides, Yvette's desk was located there. She and Sethwick were as inseparable as a turtle and its shell.

Flynn hadn't dared hope for something as wonderful. Still, he hadn't expected to pursue a means to terminate his marriage after a mere week, either.

Earlier, he'd learned Angelina intended to leave her chamber today. He'd asked her to join him in the study at her convenience. Except to attend a short funeral for her son, she'd not ventured from her chamber.

He was convinced her self-imposed isolation was as much to avoid the keep's other curious residents as it was to mourn her loss. Lydia and her entourage were in residence indefinitely, and it appeared Devaux-Rousset had settled in for an extended visit as well.

Bloody damned awkward for all.

Upon learning the baron's mother had been a girlhood friend, Aunt Giselle had insisted he remain for as long as he desired.

God rot good manners.

There'd be no getting rid of the man until he had his discussion with Angelina. And since she wasn't receiving visitors, the Frenchman would be loitering about the place and poking his nose into Flynn's private affairs.

Namely, his marriage.

Reverend Wallace believed—given the events of the wedding day—an annulment would likely be granted, and possibly quite speedily. The Church of Scotland was considerably laxer than England's regarding such matters. His and Angelina's wasn't the typical annulment situation that required several months' residency in Scotland.

So now, here, Flynn sat in this gloomy crypt-of-a-study, trying to decide the best course of action. Words didn't usually fail him, but he still hadn't formulated what he intended to say to her. Mayhap, because nothing had ever mattered this much before.

Asking Angelina what she wanted to do was the hardest thing he'd ever done. Truth to tell, he didn't want an annulment, but he dared not let hope spring up. Not yet.

Contemplating her walking out of his life when he'd only begun to know her, left him feeling destitute. Beyond any shadow of a doubt, he'd never treasure again in his heart what he felt for her.

Pretending absorption in the quill, he observed her through half-closed eyes. He ran a finger the length of the feather, ruffling its stiff edge.

She had yet to answer his question about the annulment. Her gaze roved the study, avoiding him. Was she nervous? It reminded him of her first—her only—visit to Lambridge. She'd avoided looking at him that day, too.

Angelina finally regarded him full-on, cocking her head and studying him with her usual honest appraisal. A reddish-gold curl dangled against her neck. A wave of envy swept him. He ached to take the strand's place and touch her silken, ivory skin.

Despite bluish shadows beneath her eyes, which only served to make them appear a more remarkable shade of sea-green, she was radiant. She wore a simple morning gown of russet and peach, the colors highlighting the burnished hues in her hair. Even after losing the babe, she'd not returned to mourning garb.

Though many would frown at her breach of protocol, he was glad.

A treasure, she deserved to wear finery, enhancing her loveliness. Once again, she wore no jewels.

He'd have to see about that.

The marquisship owned a yellow topaz and emerald necklace with matching drop earrings. His mother had worn the set several times. The gems were perfect for Angelina's coloring.

Fiend seize it. He still mentally concocted plans as if she would remain his marchioness. *If only...* Flynn balanced the pen between two fingers. Trying to sound nonchalant, he repeated, "You don't want an annulment now?"

"I never said that." She traced the armchair's satin piped edge with her fingertips. "I simply want to clarify. Are you assuming I expect an immediate annulment because my reason for marrying you—*the poor, dead babe*—no longer exists?"

Other than a slight catch when she spoke the last words, her voice remained strong. She fiddled with her wedding band, twisting it round and round. It slid with ease, attesting to the weight she'd lost in recent days.

"I do understand if you wish to pursue other—ah—ventures, and that's why you wish to seek a prompt end to our marriage," she murmured, the epitome of poise.

Flynn strained to hear her last words.

After replacing the quill, he stood. Raking a hand through his hair, he stared at her.

Angelina regarded him serenely, yet he detected a hint of apprehension in her expression. What was she thinking? Did she, or did she not, want to terminate their union?

No longer encumbered with a child, she could move on. He well knew the babe had been the only reason she'd agreed to their union. She'd made that abundantly clear in England, and he'd even admired her sacrifice for her child's sake.

He'd see her well-settled. She'd want for nothing until she married again, for he had every confidence she would.

Strikingly beautiful, as well as witty and intelligent, some lucky sot would snatch Angelina up the moment she ventured into the Marriage Mart.

An almost feral growl of possession tried to form deep in his throat.

Mine. Mine. Mine. His heart and soul silently cried. *Mine to love. To cherish. To adore.*

Flynn hadn't the faintest notion what he'd tell his family about the dissolution of their marriage. He'd concoct some believable balderdash. Perchance, even share the truth. It was as farfetched and implausible as any tale he'd ever heard spun.

Except for Father's death, of course.

They mustn't ever know the whole of that ugliness.

"Angelina? What if I don't want to pursue other *ventures*? What if I would prefer to remain wed to you?" He laid it out quite plainly. As obvious as a wig on a pig, as Grandmamma would say.

Here was her chance—no mincing words or beating around the bush.

Angelina's gaze flashed to his, examining his features. Her astute attention shifted from one of his eyes to the other. The vulnerability in hers twisted his heart and hitched his breath.

"I thought…that is…" She clamped her lower lip between her white teeth, her eyes huge. *And hopeful?*

His heart gave an excited start. Did *he* dare hope?

"Do you not intend to wed Miss Farnsworth?" she quietly asked.

Flynn drew Angelina to her feet, his fingers enfolding her small hands as if they'd been sculpted to fit neatly within his palms. "I thought I did. Until I met you."

Delighted surprise illuminated her face.

He kissed her knuckles. "But, you snared me the moment I spied you perched in that old oak tree."

"I did?" Her wondering eyes searched his. "Barefoot and a disheveled mess?"

"And completely charming with dirt smudged on the tip of your nose."

He could see the turmoil churning in the depths of her eyes and could almost read her mind.

She doesn't know if she dares trust me and doesn't know if I'm telling her the truth or wrapping her in another web of deceit.

Her hesitancy was tangible. How hard it must be for her to put her faith in a man again. Everyone that had touched her life so far had betrayed her.

"We could go on as we intended." Her gaze sank to his mouth, and her pink tongue peeked out to wet her lips. "Stay together the designated year and see what might develop between us." A rosy hue brightened her high cheeks, but she valiantly met his gaze. "That is if you're quite certain…"

Hesitation mingled with hope, tinged her words.

At that moment, it struck him. Gaining her complete trust would be a monumental undertaking. Not only didn't she trust men, even more significantly, she didn't trust herself.

Renault had done that to her. Had the blackguard been present, Flynn would've rearranged his face. After pounding an apology from him.

Stepping nearer, he drew her ever closer until his thighs and chest brushed hers. "I'd like nothing better. I assure you."

She darted her tongue out to dampen her lips once more.

With a strangled groan, he claimed her sweet mouth, crushing her against him.

She responded timidly at first, almost as if afraid to relinquish control.

"Open to me," he whispered against her soft lips. He teased the seam of her mouth with his tongue.

Her lips parted on a sigh.

Flynn plunged his tongue into her honeyed depths.

Angelina leaned into him, draping her arms about his shoulders and angling her head to give him deeper access to her mouth.

Desire, at first a glowing ember, burst forth into a consuming conflagration of want and passion. He tenderly ravaged her mouth, reaching behind her to grasp her lush derrière and lift it, pressing her insistently against his hardness.

She squirmed, tightening her arms around his neck and trying to edge closer, her kisses every bit as voracious as his own.

Yet, even in her hunger, an innocence prevailed he couldn't ignore.

How knowledgeable was she about these matters?

He trailed his mouth along her jaw and, feathering tiny nipping kisses the entire way, ventured to the juncture of her neck and shoulder. He'd yearned to kiss the silky flesh since seeing her in that gorgeous green gown on their wedding day.

Clutching his shoulders, Angelina moaned and sagged against him. The plump pillows of her breasts surged above her bodice, begging to be kissed. Her perfumed skin taunted him unmercifully.

Flynn sank his face between the velvety mounds, almost overcome. He inhaled deeply, her subtle scent intoxicating him.

God's blood. If she'd not recently been through the trauma of losing a child, he'd be hard-pressed not to lift her skirts and take her against the desk. Unbearable pressure surged in his loins, threatening to explode in blissful release.

Returning his attention to her mouth, he nibbled and sucked while battling to control his rampant lust. His rigid cock-stand could shatter bricks.

Three bold raps upon the door interrupted the moment.

Breathing heavily, he stepped away from Angelina. Eyes closed, her lips parted and ruby-red, she bore a bemused expression. He ran a finger along the edge of her bodice, before adjusting the fabric to cover her once more completely.

Her eyes opened languidly, a nascent smile of sensual delight, framing her mouth.

Two firm knocks rang again, this time more insistent.

Flynn brushed one, last tender kiss across her lips. "Methinks someone without is quite desperate to disturb us."

"Yes, except they don't know what they're interrupting, do they?" Her voice husky, she peered pointedly at the swell in his trousers.

Ye gods. Who is this sultry siren?

His manhood flexed in response. He closed his eyes and groaned.

Minx.

A seductive chuckle rippled from her. "Shall I answer while you seek privacy behind the desk?"

He forced his eyes open.

Angelina had already taken half a dozen steps in the door's direction.

He gulped and hastily strode to the desk. Once seated, he checked to make sure she faced away before adjusting himself. Attempting to woo her to his bed would wreak havoc on the unhappy comrade in his trousers. Mayhap, he'd take to bathing in the frigid loch. That ought to cool his overheated libido.

She grinned coyly before opening the door and revealing the baron. A startled look skittered across her face, promptly replaced by leeriness. "My lord?"

"Please pardon my intrusion." Lord Devaux-Rousset bowed. "As I explained when I arrived, it's imperative I speak with you, my lady. I've dallied in Scotland too long, and there are pressing matters I must attend to in England as well as at home."

Flynn stood, and waved the man in. Best to let him have his say and pray he'd been on his way in short order.

Angelina dipped her head and stepped aside, allowing the baron to enter.

Devaux-Rousset's mustached mouth tilted a fraction. "*Merci*."

"Would you care for a glass of wine or brandy, or do you prefer whisky? Sethwick boasts a fine Scotch." Flynn gestured to the liquor cabinet, reluctant to cross the room in his still-aroused state. Instead, he regained his chair.

"*Non*, I'd rather come to the point of my visit."

"Of course. Please, have a seat." Flynn indicated one of the comfortable chairs before the desk.

Angelina remained poised beside the closed door, indecision in her stance. Almost as if contemplating fleeing.

Flynn extended an arm, inviting her to stand beside his chair. "My lady?"

Her lips curved in gratitude, and she hastened to his side.

At once, he took her hand in his.

Ice-cold and faintly damp, her trembling fingers clutched his. Angelina fairly quaked in terror.

He gave her a reassuring smile.

"So, Baron, what matter could possibly be of such urgency, you'd venture to Scotland to speak with my wife?" Flynn relaxed against the worn leather chair. "Actually, I'd very much like to know how you located her in the first place."

She shivered slightly, and he squeezed her hand.

Devaux-Rousset inclined his head. "A reasonable question. I have a skilled network of associates adept at locating persons I seek."

Network? Spies, Flynn would vow.

The baron cut a speculative glance toward Angelina. "As your wife may have told you. I've had the unfortunate task of finding my mother's wayward husband more than once using such measures."

His voice and eyes grew hard and cold. The steely glint glimmering in his dark gaze gave no hint of the amiable man entering the study moments before.

Trepidation radiating from her, Angelina made an inarticulate sound and swayed.

Swallowing a sailor's foul curse, Flynn stood. He wrapped a bracing arm about her shoulders and led her to the chair beside the baron. "Sit, please, my dear."

She sank onto the cushion, murmuring, "He tracked Charles and me to the Plaza Hotel in Boston."

"Actually, I'd lost Pierre's trail," the baron admitted. "I didn't learn of your sham marriage until I traced him to the hotel, an hour after you arrived." Devaux-Rousset swept her with a compassionate gaze. "I sincerely regret I didn't arrive earlier."

Her face flamed crimson, and she averted her eyes.

Devil it. Devaux-Rousset needn't have brought up that unpleasantness.

"Rather an odd sort of occupation, clandestinely pursuing people." Flynn retreated until his hips rested against the desk's edge. He folded his arms, waiting for the baron to explain.

"*Non*, not really, and please, call me Devaux. My complete name is rather a mouthful." He shrugged, adding, "Surely you have men whom you trust to procure information for you, *non*? It's the same for me."

"And you came here because—?" Flynn's patience had worn bloody damn thin.

Angelina perched in her seat as taut as a bowstring. Clearly, her last encounter with the baron hadn't been pleasant.

"My lord?" She folded her hands neatly in her lap, more composed. "If you've come to inform me of your mother's death, I'm already aware. Mama wrote and told me. Charles, that is, Pierre called upon her in Salem and revealed that unfortunate news."

Anger stirred again that the bounder had ballocks enough to return to Salem.

Sympathy shadowed her eyes. "Please accept my condolences."

"Mine as well, Devaux," Flynn offered, recalling how close he'd come to losing his mother.

Surprise flitted across the baron's features before they hardened into sharp angles once more. "*Merci*. Her loss has been most difficult, made more tragic as her death was suspicious. A maid found my mother drowned in her bath."

Eyes round with shock, Angelina gasped. Horrorstruck, she shook her head. "No."

"Damn." Flynn dared voice his suspicion. "Renault?"

The baron replied with a curt nod. "I've no proof. Only the word of a hysterical servant. But water puddled the floor outside the bathing tub, and a towel covered *Mere's* face."

If a man was capable of selling humans and committing bigamy, murder wasn't that much of a leap.

His dark gaze sank to his boots for a protracted moment as he struggled with his anger and grief. Firming his mouth, he smoothed his mustache and raised his eyes.

"But that isn't the only reason I seek to warn you. France declared slave-trading illegal last March. That hasn't stopped Pierre. He, and others like him, have simply become more covert in their endeavors. However, if the *on dit* is accurate, he's become involved in another despicable, yet extremely profitable trade."

He paused, seeming done in. "Bretheridge, might I trouble you for a dram of whisky after all?"

"But of course." Flynn straightened then strode swiftly to the liquor cabinet. He poured Devaux a generous two fingers' worth and one for himself as well. Replacing the stopper, he tipped a scant amount of brandy into a glass for Angelina. He'd swear she was about to swoon.

How much more would the Good Lord ask that poor woman to endure?

Balancing the three glasses, Flynn returned to the armchairs. Delivering the drinks, he urged her to try hers. "It'll fortify you, my dear."

Wrinkling her nose, she took a timid sip. "It's awful."

Lord Devaux chuckled. "Many of my countrymen, as well as yours, would heartily disagree."

"Well, they're welcome to it." Grimacing, she eyed the amber liquid dubiously. With a slight shudder, she passed the glass to Flynn

Tipping his head, he swallowed his whisky in one gulp, welcoming the fiery spirit burning a path to his stomach. "The other matter?"

He set both glasses on the desk.

The baron tossed back a portion of his drink. "Rumor has it, Pierre has resorted to abducting women of European descent, particularly innocents and those of quality. They bring a higher price."

"Price?" Angelina pulled her eyebrows together, her confusion evident.

"Yes, my lady. He sells them to buyers in the Middle East and Asia." The baron took another swallow of his whisky. "It's a very, *very* lucrative business."

"What has this to do with me?" Her troubled gaze traveled between Flynn and the baron.

"If Pierre cannot marry you, he's mad enough to abduct you." Urgency deepening his voice and thickening his accent, Devaux leaned forward. "Or your lovely sisters. They've just arrived in England."

20

Angelina swore her heart stopped as fear surged to her throat, threatening to choke her. She clenched the chair arms so hard that her fingers grew numb.

"Pardon?" Surely she'd heard wrong. She had to have done. Charles couldn't be that evil. Could he?

"Bloody damn hell." Flynn lurched to attention, standing erect and tense. "Beg your pardon, Lina."

She waved him silent. "What do you mean, my sisters are in England? How do you know? When did they arrive? Where are they? Is my mother with them?"

Her mind vied for an explanation, discarding the logical possibilities one after the other with alacrity.

"We must go to them straightaway." Trembling, she jumped from her chair. She spun toward the door, only to whirl back to face Flynn. "Something awful has happened. I know it."

"Calm yourself, my lady." Devaux spoke soothingly, as one would to a skittish mare. "Your mother is safe with your sisters. Though I'm reluctant to reveal, she was unwell when I left."

"Unwell? How so?" Fear caused Angelina's knees to weaken, and she sank into the cushions of the overstuffed chair once more. She rubbed her bare arms brusquely against the sudden chill permeating her.

"She has acquired a foul cough that seems to have settled in her lungs." He smiled at Angelina encouragingly. "She assured me, however, that she was much improved having left the stale bowels of the ship."

Angelina pressed a hand to her brow, though it did nothing to quiet the jumbled thoughts crashing about in her head like waves on a rocky shore. "I don't understand. Why did they leave Salem without telling me?"

"They came at my urging. There wasn't time to notify you." The baron crossed his legs, settling further into his chair.

For the first time, Angelina noticed the lines of fatigue and tension edging his mouth and eyes. Devaux was a handsome man when not irritated. Had they met under different circumstances, they might've been friends. Not once, but twice, he'd made a valiant effort to protect her, a total stranger.

And now, he tried to protect her sisters.

How could some men be intrinsically decent and others purely wicked? A vision of a plaque on Papa's office wall came to mind.

The good person out of his good treasure brings forth good, and the evil person out of his evil treasure brings forth evil.

Perfectly apt, and strangely comforting in its simplicity.

Too bad Papa hadn't modeled *his* behavior after the verse.

"Given Pierre's threats, I persuaded your mother that remaining in Salem was dangerous." Lord Devaux closed his eyes for a long moment. He truly appeared exhausted. Opening his eyelids, he said, "She was reluctant to leave, I assure you. I offered her my protection and that of my men for the voyage. And I left two of my finest, most-trusted employees guarding your family while I journeyed here."

Not trusting herself to speak, Angelina compressed her lips and stared at a huge sword mounted on the wall behind the desk. Charles posed a very real threat, or the baron wouldn't have gone to such lengths, would he?

His intense regard shifted between Angelina and Flynn. "In France, more than one gentle-bred woman of Pierre's acquaintance has gone missing."

Angelina gasped, her gaze leaping to collide with Flynn's.

"I've heard rumors he's in England, though I suspect he knows I'm on to him. For the time being, he seems to have vanished." The baron rubbed his forehead.

Her voice trembled as another chill scraped its jagged nails along her spine. "But why would you insist Mama and my sisters travel to England if you knew Pierre's location?"

"My lady, at least in England, I can offer them a degree of protection." Devaux flicked his hand. "They had none whatsoever in America. He threatened your mother and your sisters when they refused to reveal where you'd gone. If he is indeed here, he's newly arrived, as are we."

That was little comfort.

One side of Lord Devaux's mouth quirked. "I had your family travel in disguise, under false names."

Flynn made his way behind the desk. Once seated, he opened one drawer and then another, until he found what he sought. After removing a sheet of crisp foolscap, he slid the drawer shut and retrieved the pen he'd set aside earlier.

"You think he'd truly try to abduct them?" He met the baron's intense gaze.

Devaux pondered for a moment, then sighed. "I think he's capable of anything, and therefore, isn't to be trusted. He is, how would you say… *Fou*? Mad. Unhinged."

"How could I have been so deceived?"

She hadn't realized she'd spoken out loud until both men turned their sympathetic expressions on her. She stiffened her spine. This wasn't the time for self-recriminations. "You know him better than we do, my lord. What do you advise?"

"What she says is true. I, for one, would appreciate any insight you might have to help me protect my wife and her family." Flynn returned to scratching away on the paper.

Angelina whisked him an astonished glance. He'd not bargained for this when he took her to wife. Gratitude bloomed in her heart. Some women might not appreciate having a man care for their wellbeing. She, however, found his concern comforting and welcomed it. She needed his strength, for hers was sorely strained.

That didn't in any way mean she wasn't strong. It simply meant she appreciated his support.

"I think you should be prepared for anything. I'd be happy to leave some of my men to act as guards. I'm sure McTavish could spare a few of his clan as well." Lord Devaux tapped the fingers of his left hand on his bent knee. His signet ring gleamed bright against the black of his trousers.

Pausing, Flynn stared at the baron for a protracted moment. His mouth curved into a half-smile. "I appreciate your generous offer, and I gratefully accept."

Another wave of gratitude for the baron's generosity swept her.

Returning his attention to the letter, Flynn sprinkled sand on the ink. He folded his hands atop the desk, waiting for the letter to dry. "I suggest we leave for—" He hesitated. "Do you know where the Ellsworths are staying?"

"*Oui.* I rented rooms for them and their maid at a reputable boardinghouse operated by an acquaintance of mine. I used fictitious names again, of course." Lord Devaux finished his whisky.

Did Uncle Ambrose and Aunt Camille know?

Naturally, they must. Mama would've notified them. "Perhaps, they've journeyed to Wingfield Court by now."

"*Non*. As a matter of fact, I'm quite certain they remained in London." Lord Devaux stood, pulling his timepiece from his waistcoat. After a quick glimpse, he snapped the gold case closed. "Mrs. Ellsworth's health wouldn't permit her to travel as yet, and she adamantly refused to impose upon the duke and duchess."

"Impose? She hasn't seen her sister in twenty years. I hardly think Aunt Camille would think it an imposition." How ludicrous. Why in the world would Mama insist on staying in London this time of year? Unless her health was poorer than she let on.

Angelina worried her lower lip.

How much money did her mother have?

Enough for expenditures and to secure the services of a physician? They'd never enjoyed deep pockets but had lived in modest comfort and lacked for nothing of import. Perchance, Mama didn't have the coach fare to travel to Wingfield and was too proud to say so.

Surely Uncle would cover the cost, wouldn't he?

Standing, Angelina smoothed her skirts, more from the need for something to do with her hands than anything else. Outwardly calm, a nagging unease within demanded she act at once. "I'd like to leave for London as soon as your carriage is readied, Flynn."

"I agree." He brushed the sand from the paper, then folded the letter. Once sealed, he lifted the note. "This is for Fleming, giving him my directives."

He skirted the desk and wrapped an arm about Angelina's shoulders. "Can you be ready within the hour?"

"Yes, of course." She released a drawn-out breath. She was leaving her baby already. But Davy was gone, and there was naught she could do for his little soul. The same couldn't be said for Mama and the twins.

Flynn gently pressed her arm as he swiveled to face the baron. "May I impose upon your men to accompany us? I must speak to Sethwick at once and learn how many clansmen he can spare. I'll need enough to provide guards at my country house as well as men to travel to London with us."

The baron's features softened. "Consider it done."

The three of them continued to the exit, Angelina making a mental list of what she needed to do.

Flynn opened the door and stepped aside, permitting Lord Devaux and her to go before him. Advancing into the hall, they paused. Exuberant voices rang throughout an adjacent corridor.

"I'm glad you're home, Seonaid. I've missed you terribly." Isobel and a sable-haired young woman turned the corner, arm-in-arm.

Ah, the other sister.

She possessed Lady Ferguson's darker coloring. Her chestnut brown eyes, however, she'd clearly inherited from Sir Hugh. She appeared young too, not more than seventeen or, possibly, eighteen. She possessed a curious aura of peace about her.

Isobel glanced behind them.

"Lord Ramsbury, I believe Flynn is in Ewan's study. I *cannot* imagine he'll be pleased to see *you*." Isobel's words became clipped, and her tone frosty as she addressed his lordship.

A striking man followed the women, the hunter green of his coat a perfect match for his eyes. He wore a smirk upon his mouth, and Angelina swore his attention had been trained on Isobel's swaying bottom until she turned her head toward him.

As if sensing the perusal of those standing like sentinels outside the study, the Ferguson sisters and Lord Ramsbury faltered to a stop.

Seonaid's mouth dropped open then snapped shut. Her entire body suddenly rigid, she pointed a shaking finger at Baron Devaux. "What is *he* doing here?"

Isobel sent her sister an astonished glance. "Lord Devaux? You're acquainted with the baron?"

"Oh, I know him, all right." Seonaid squared her shoulders and jutted out her small chin. Shards of russet fire spewed from her irate eyes. She folded her arms, fury radiating from her petite form. Her voice dripping sarcasm, she seared him with a scathing glare. "Shall I tell them *how* we became acquainted, *my lord*?"

The baron took a step forward, but he stopped short, clenching his hands at his sides. Face flushed, he regarded her with a warrior's wariness. "Trust me, mademoiselle, I had *no* idea this was *your* home."

"You'll forgive me if I don't believe you," she retorted before spinning on her slippered feet and marching away.

What in the world?

Angelina sent Flynn an inquisitive glance.

He lifted one shoulder in answer.

Evidently, he had no idea what that spectacle was about either, and given the confused expression on Isobel's pretty face, she was at a loss, too.

"She's the other unmarried sister. The one who was in France?" Angelina whispered from the side of her mouth.

"Yes, and a sorry day for *la bon France* it was when she arrived," the baron muttered, obviously overhearing her. "If you'll excuse me, I'll speak to my men. They'll be ready to depart when you are." Glancing around the corridor one last time, he strode away, as angry as the young woman who left a moment ago.

Angelina would give up coffee for a year to know how they'd become acquainted and why they were so incensed with each other.

Flynn furrowed his forehead in puzzlement. "Seonaid is usually mild-tempered and amiable. She does have the gift of second sight, though. Mayhap, something occurred."

Something most definitely had occurred between them.

"There you are, Bretheridge." Lord Ramsbury continued toward the study, giving Isobel a cocky salute and rakish grin as he passed.

She scowled blackly. Muttering something about boorish louts beneath her breath, Isobel took her leave as well.

Good heavens. Why was everyone so peevish this morning?

"Yancy, what are you doing here?" A guarded expression settled on Flynn's face, and wariness echoed in his voice, yet he stepped forward to shake Lord Ramsbury's hand.

His lordship surveyed Angelina curiously. His mouth quirked at the corners revealing strong, white teeth. "Ah, you must be the lovely new Lady Bretheridge."

She angled her head. "I am."

"Please allow me to introduce myself since this clod seems incapable of doing so." He swept her an exaggerated bow. "Bartholomew, Earl of Ramsbury." He bent over her hand, placing a kiss on her knuckles and gave her a decidedly wicked wink. "Or, Yancy to my *closest* friends."

"That's enough, *Ramsbury*." Flynn glowered pointedly at her hand yet encased in the earl's.

The earl chuckled, clearly enjoying himself. "I've known this chap since he was barely out of a skeleton suit. Never took him for the jealous sort before."

"*Ahem.*" Flynn fairly growled in annoyance.

Was he jealous? Why, what an amusing notion. And thrilling, too.

Angelina couldn't contain her giggle as she lifted her hand from the earl's. She liked this charming rogue.

He raised his eyebrows and gave her another lopsided smirk. "Your bride is a good judge of character, Bretheridge. Indeed, she is."

"Thank you, my lord." She curtsied. Rising, she glanced down the passageway. "Please excuse me. If we're to leave as planned, Flynn, I must find Murphy."

Much to her surprise, he placed his hands on her shoulders and kissed her forehead. "Go along. It's early yet. If we should happen to leave later than intended, it's of no consequence. My team is sturdy, and they travel well. We'll make good time."

Yes, except she fretted about her mother and sisters. Even the smallest delay seemed unbearable. And knowing it would take at least three days to reach London—

"It was a pleasure to meet you, my lord." After another hasty curtsy, she hurried toward what, she hoped, was the great hall. Shaking her head, she chuckled upon hearing, "Come, give over, old chap. Wherever did you find *that* delectable treasure?"

"Yancy, I'm not fool enough to believe you traveled here to meet my bride." Flynn reentered the study, the earl at his side. He'd not spoken to Yancy since the night Father passed. Unreasonable though he might be, he harbored resentment toward his long-time friend.

If Yancy sensed it, he hid it well.

"In fact, how did you know I was here?" Flynn froze, spearing the earl with a hard glare. "Did you stop at Lambridge? You didn't reveal anything to my family, did you?"

"Of course not. I'm not an imbecile." Yancy made straight for the liquor cabinet. He held up a glass. "Care for a dram?"

Flynn shook his head. "I am preparing to leave—within the hour, actually."

"Was that Miss Farnsworth I observed riding when I arrived?" The earl leveled him a contemplative look. "If so, I'd wager things have been rather interesting around here."

Flynn quickly explained his hurried nuptials, Angelina's marriage to Renault, the baroness's mysterious death, and the peril Angelina and her sisters faced due to the Frenchman.

Yancy released a low whistle. "I've heard of the man. Nasty, contemptible blackguard. That beauty has you into it up to your elbows, I'd say." He took a swig of his brandy.

"Indeed," Flynn agreed dryly.

Lifting his glass, Yancy swirled the burnished contents. "You know, I could spare some agents from the Home Office to keep watch while you're in London. Could be deemed an international concern, I'm thinking. I could also put the word out and have my agents keep an eye open for Renault."

"That relieves my mind greatly. I might very well take you up on that offer, Yancy." The Diplomatic Corps boasted men proficient in subterfuge. Sethwick had worked as an operative for years before marrying Yvette.

Yancy shook his head in apparent disgust. "You ought to contact the Bow Street runners as well, Bretheridge. Especially given that slavery bit."

Flynn paused in straightening the items atop the desk. "You've not told me why you're here, although I suspect you have a distinct interest in Isobel."

"That obvious is it?"

As a two-headed goose.

Yancy kicked the rug's fringe with the toe of his Hessian. He resembled a schoolboy caught cheating at his sums.

Flynn quirked a brow.

The earl sighed and finished his drink. "She has an aversion to me. Though for the life of me, I vow I don't know the reason. I've no idea why I keep torturing myself, coming here on whatever flimsy excuse I can devise so that I can see her."

"Egads, man, you do have it bad." Flynn shook his head, offering a sympathetic expression. "Anything I can do to help?"

"Not unless you can convince Lady Isobel to let me address her." Yancy set aside his glass. "Or discover why she's put off by me."

As Flynn was leaving within the hour, he could do neither.

Shaking off his doldrums, Yancy gave a careless shrug. "I do have a legitimate reason for putting in an appearance this time, however."

"Indeed?" Flynn's attention sliced to the antiquated mantle clock. He really must be off.

"I've come to redeem myself." Wandering to the wall behind the desk, Yancy scrutinized an ancient scarred claymore. He tossed a satisfied glance in Flynn's direction. "I believe I've found the evidence you need to prove Waterford cheated your father."

21

Today was Angelina's birthday. She'd forgotten until this moment. Mama had always made a scrumptious trifle and presented her with a lovely trinket of some sort. This year, the best gift would be to arrive at the boardinghouse and find her and the girls safe and well.

Peering out the window into the dusky sunset, Angelina marveled at the beauty of the clouds glowing against a backdrop of pinkish-orange, magenta, and violet—the colorful remnants of the sun, now spent for the day.

She guessed they approached London's outskirts. More and more houses popped up across the countryside and appeared closer to the road. In the distant sky, an amber glow indicated they drew near the city.

Toying with the tassels hanging from her reticule's corded handle, she crossed and uncrossed her ankles. Nervous energy had her practically bouncing on the thick squabs. The trip had taken four unbearably long days to reach London, traveling dawn to dusk. As each mile passed, anxiety for her mother and sisters increased as did the soreness in her aching bum.

A wheel hit a hole in the road, and she cracked her arm and side against the carriage. "Ouch."

Pain shot from her shoulder to her elbow.

That's what comes of perching on the edge of one's seat.

One of the Scots escorts cantered his horse to the front of their procession. A total of six men—four of Lord Sethwick's, including his cousin and two of the baron's—made up their party.

"Gregor's knowledge of healing herbs and plants might be helpful to your mother," Flynn explained when the mammoth man had trotted his horse to the carriage the day of their departure.

Another four Scots traveled to Lambridge Manse. Murphy had returned to Wingfield Court with them. Thankfully, nothing remotely untoward had occurred on the journey to Town.

Rubbing her sore arm, Angelina studied Flynn.

He seemed absorbed in what scant vestiges of the passing scenery could yet be seen. He'd kept her company within the coach the entire time. She didn't doubt he would've preferred to ride.

His valet, Kimball, as well as their meager luggage, followed behind them in a second coach. They would require the additional vehicle to transport her family as well as their belongings.

Her focus sank to the wood panel behind Flynn's polished boots. He'd hidden a pair of pistols in the cabinet below his seat. From her position near the gatehouse the day they left Craiglocky, she'd observed him stashing the guns in the compartment. They might be dueling pistols, but she couldn't be certain. Her knowledge of guns would fit in a thimble with room left over.

No doubt, Flynn had borrowed the firearms from Lord Sethwick.

Were the guns loaded? Likely, given the precarious situation with Pierre.

"Are you anxious?" Flynn's intoxicating baritone interrupted her musings.

The expanding dusk made it difficult to see his expression. He must've sensed her unease.

"Yes, I don't know what to expect." She resumed fiddling with her reticule. "The fear of the unknown is somehow more intimidating. My imagination, always a bit fanciful, is running amuck, I'm afraid."

He scooted across the carriage and lowered himself beside her. Lifting her hand, he gave it a gentle squeeze before entwining their fingers and settling them on his solid thigh.

Was there a soft part anywhere on the man? Every time she touched him, she encountered hard planes and sinewy, lean muscles.

Except his lips. Now those were deliciously soft.

"I'm confident we'll find everything well." He relaxed against the seat, stretching his legs before him. The lengthy hours of carriage confinement must've been as taxing for him as they'd been for her. Probably more so, given his much larger frame.

Her muscles screamed to be stretched and exercised.

He stifled a yawn. "From all accounts, your mother is a wise woman, and remember, Devaux left armed guards."

But did Mama have sufficient funds to see to their needs? However, had she managed the fee for four passages? And coal, medicine, food? Though worried, Angelina wouldn't burden him. Naught could be done at this juncture, anyway.

Settling further into his warm side, she relished the peace touching him brought her. "True, but Mama has never had a robust constitution. This bout of ill health worries me as much as any threat from Pierre."

Forcing herself to think of Pierre by his real name had become a necessity. She found it easier to associate his villainous behavior with that identity than the man who had wooed and wed her.

Every time she dwelled on how easily he'd duped her, Angelina fell into doldrums. She hadn't, as yet, been able to forgive herself for her stupidity. Perhaps, in time, she could, enabling her to move on.

She snuggled the tiniest bit closer to Flynn, needing his comfort.

He wrapped an arm around her shoulders, nestling her securely against him. As was his habit, he dropped an absent kiss atop her bonneted head, only to promptly sneeze. No doubt, a feather adorning her hat had tickled his nose again.

"Another feather?" she asked

"I think I'll have to forbid you to wear anything upon your head that has the remotest chance of tickling me or making me sneeze." His gravelly chuckle accompanied the slow stroke of his fingers across her shoulder and upper arm.

The shivers of desire she'd come to expect at his touch made themselves known. Did she even remotely affect him as he did her? Dozens of times during their trip, especially at night when she lay alone in an inn's borrowed bed, her mind conjured up images of them lying naked together, picturing Flynn doing to her what Pierre had done.

Only with Flynn, she could envisage ever so much more. She did have a most vivid imagination. Warmth skimmed her face. Fortunately, the dim interior of the vehicle hid her blushes. *Goodness,* but she'd become wicked.

If she'd continued to keep her catalog of attributes that should be sought or avoided in a man, she would certainly have to add, *One who sets a lady's mind and body ablaze with desire,* to the top of both lists.

Wonderful and dangerous.

However, her silly inventory no longer mattered.

Neither does my reason for marrying in the first place. Davy... A wave of nostalgia caused tears to prick behind her eyelids.

She dare not contemplate the possibility of bearing Flynn's child. Not yet, anyway. Far too soon to wander down that mental path. Did they even have a future together? They barely knew each other. She wasn't prepared to let him see how vulnerable she'd become to his charm.

Your heart recognized its mate the moment you saw him.

Pshaw. Her fickle heart had led her astray before. Could she trust it this time? Did she dare?

If only God would give her a sign. Nothing miraculous. Something simple would do. Perchance, a pair of doves perched on a hedge or a triple rainbow after a shower.

She smothered a snort.

Were doves even native to England? She'd not seen one since arriving. And the chance of even a single rainbow in July was dismal at best. A triple one would be a phenomenon—a miracle from on high.

The *clip-clop* of the horses' hooves echoing on pavement revealed how far they'd traveled while she reminisced. Angelina leaned forward to peer into the darkness and tried to guess their location. London was much vaster than Salem.

"Are we close?" She settled back into the seat. "I've a terrible sense of direction. I cannot tell you the number of times I've become lost at a social function by taking the wrong passage or garden path."

Flynn gave her shoulder a slight nudge, his chest reverberating with silent laughter. "I wondered how you ended up in Craiglocky's kitchen rather than your chamber the day we departed."

"I spent half an hour trying to find the way to my room." Angelina sniffed in mock annoyance. "Those old stone corridors all resemble each other, and they go on forever. So, I followed my nose. I assumed someone in the kitchen could help me."

"I became lost myself the first several times I visited. Craiglocky is a medieval monstrosity. If I recall correctly, Sethwick once told me the keep has more than one hundred seventy rooms, though many aren't in use any longer. Lambridge Manse boasts but seventy-four."

Only seventy-four?

"Endicott Hall, my childhood home, is modest in comparison." Mama had made the sixteen-room house into a warm, inviting home, despite Papa's miserly ways and preference for austerity.

"Is it much farther?" A toddler possessed more patience than she. Angelina shifted, seeking a better view through the dusty window.

"Not too terribly. I've given Hodges the address Devaux provided."

The sound of flint being struck drew her attention. A flame sparked, and Flynn lit the carriage lamp. "Much better."

Extinguishing the char cloth, he smiled. "I'd like to move your family to my residence in Mayfair at once. When your mother is well enough to travel, we'll relocate to Lambridge. The country air will do her good and is much preferred to the coal-laden vapor that often hangs heavily in Town."

"That seems wise." Her attention remained fixed on the row of lamps glimmering the length of the street.

A misty fog swirled eerily around the lights as if seeking to warm itself. The temperature had dropped considerably in the past few hours. Her fingers, cold despite her gloves, she shivered and gripped the front of her buttoned linen spencer. She couldn't be altogether confident the weather had caused her chill or if the coldness portended something else.

A harsh and indifferent mood hovered about London. Angelina didn't much care for the city, preferring the freshness of the countryside.

The coach turned onto an unlit road. Its rumbling wheels gradually slowed until, amidst creaks and a last lurch of protest, the vehicle came to rest. The outriders clattered to a stop, and the low timbre of the men's voices carried into the vehicle.

Flynn didn't wait for the driver to climb down. After opening the door himself, he stepped onto the cobblestones. He spoke a few words to riders waiting beside the door. They answered softly before venturing farther along the foggy lane.

He turned and extended a hand, his gaze kind and encouraging. "I've asked the men to disperse and keep their eyes sharp, except for those two there."

He indicated a pair of Frenchmen. "I had them go in search of Devaux's other men and alert them to our arrival. It wouldn't do to have the others act rashly when we approach."

"That seems prudent, thank you." Angelina peered beyond him. Though outwardly collected, her stomach roiled as if a herd of goats leaped about inside.

"Your family is in that building." He pointed to a modest, three-story house. He extended his hand. "Are you ready?"

"Yes." She pulled in a bracing breath and allowed him to assist her from the coach. Anxious to see her mother and sisters, she also feared what she might find within the humble structure.

She lifted her hand and covered her nose, wrinkling it against the unpleasant odors assailing her nostrils. "Does it always smell this dreadful?"

"Unfortunately, yes. Except it's more bearable in the winter." Flynn indicated the direction they'd come. "The River Thames is scarcely better than a cesspool. Summer's temperatures intensify the stench."

He cast a practiced gaze the length of the lane. "Hodges, wait for us. I don't expect it will take us long to pack what they'll need for tonight. We'll send for the rest of their things tomorrow." He considered the carriage rounding the corner. "Tell the other driver for me, will you, please?"

"Yes, sir." The gangly driver made his way to the coach, clamoring to a stop behind theirs.

"Let's see you indoors, my dear. It's rather cool, and it won't do for you to take a chill." Flynn grasped Angelina's elbow and guided her toward the humble building. He looked up at the boardinghouse. "Devaux told me their rooms are on the second floor. More difficult for someone trying to sneak in to reach them."

She eyed the windows. There didn't appear any easy way to gain the upper level. The baron was rather shrewd. He'd promised to call when he returned to London and update her on news of Pierre.

Flynn clapped the knocker twice.

A weary, white-capped maid, wearing a less than pristine apron, ushered them inside. Mrs. Laroche, the proprietress, reeking of perfume and attired in a blood-red and black gown several seasons past the height of fashion, eyed them suspiciously. The immense red plume poking from her gray hair tilted forward a fraction more each time she spoke.

Angelina tried not to stare. The heart-shaped mouche above the left corner of Mrs. Laroche's mouth had come loose and wiggled like an oversized fly in the throes of death.

Flynn flashed the woman his irresistible smile and spoke to her in fluid French. "*La mère et les soeurs de ma femme sont ici. Seigneur Devaux a fait les arrangements.*"

The woman's cool demeanor evaporated as fast as droplets of water on a hot iron. Her keen gaze raked Angelina. "*Oui, je vois la resemblance. Elle est une beauté, non*?"

"I'll have to take your word about the familial resemblance. I've never met the others." Flynn drew her a step closer. He had the audacity to wink at Mrs. Laroche boldly. "But, I do know it takes a beauty to recognize one."

The woman swatted his arm in what could only be interpreted as a flirtatious manner. She made a moue with her mouth and batted her stubby eyelashes.

Angelina feigned a cough into her gloved hand to disguise a giggle. *Gracious*. The woman was sixty and ten if she was a day.

Mrs. Laroche pointed up the dimly lit stairwell. "Zah second door on zah right."

Angelina found herself hurrying up the stairs, Flynn one step behind her. Taking a deep breath, she tapped on the door.

No one answered.

"Are you positive this is the correct room?" She stepped back and checked either side of the faded yellow door before her. "She did say the second door, didn't she?"

He nodded. "I'm sure they're merely being cautious. Perhaps, we should've requested one of Devaux's men accompany us so they'd know there's nothing to fear."

He stepped closer and gave a firm knock.

A bit of scurrying could be heard on the opposite side before silence commenced once more.

She pressed an ear to the door. Giving a trio of rhythmic raps, she raised her voice. "Martha, Lily, Iris, it's me, Angelina. Please, open the door."

The door flew open so swiftly that it banged against the wall. Angelina grasped the frame to keep from pitching headfirst into the room. Amidst exclamations of surprise and delight, she was enveloped in exuberant hugs and kisses.

"Lina! We've been dreadfully worried about you," Lily gushed, diving in for another hearty squeeze.

Iris angled away and dashed at the tears trickling from her eyes. "Yes, it's been simply awful, not knowing if you were safe and with Mama being ill."

Angelina grinned at her sisters. "You missed me so much you came to England to see me?" she teased to lighten the mood.

Her sisters' once vivid blue eyes held a haunted glint. Dark shadows lurked beneath their lower lashes, and a haggard look lingered about their mouths. They'd lost weight, too. No doubt the result of being hunted by Pierre in addition to worrying about Mama.

She embraced them each again. Oh, how she'd missed her sisters. A swift scan of the shabby chamber showed no sign of her mother. Unease whispered rude speculation. Was she too sick to leave her bed?

"It's glad I am to see you, Miss Lina." Martha had been with the family since shortly after Angelina's birth. The servant stood beaming near a door on the other side of the cramped sitting room.

Fresh tears stung her eyes. She didn't care if it was proper or not; she dashed into her old nursemaid's arms. "Oh, Martha, I've missed you so."

Martha hugged her in return. "I've missed you too, pet."

Suddenly aware she'd left Flynn stranded at the doorway, Angelina waved for him to enter. "Please, Flynn, come in."

He'd waited on the threshold, hat in hand, patiently watching the emotional reunion with her sisters.

"I want to introduce you." She attempted a watery smile, digging in her reticule for her handkerchief.

He appeared beneath her nose while she rummaged in her reticule. How did he continually manage to have a clean linen square on him when she could seldom find hers?

"Thank you." She dried her tears and wiped her nose.

Three curious gazes swung between her and Flynn. Wadding his handkerchief into a tight ball, Angelina stuffed the cloth into her reticule and took a fortifying breath.

Gads, how awkward. Introducing a new husband, when the last time she'd seen everyone had been at her wedding—to another man. Nothing for it. Best to dive right into the chaos, like rats in a rubbish bin. "I'd like to introduce you to my husband—"

"Husband?" the twins gasped in unison. Their stunned blue gazes meshed in confusion.

"Yes, we married almost a fortnight ago," Angelina said.

Lily and Iris burst forth with a slew of questions.

"Where did you meet him?"

"How did you meet?"

"Was it at a ball?"

"Was it love at first sight?"

"Shush, girls. Let your sister finish." Martha gave Angelina an encouraging flick of her hand. "Go on, dear."

Angelina grasped Flynn's hand, needing his strength. Thank goodness the twins had been sensible enough not to mention Pierre. Mayhap, this ordeal had matured them a degree.

"This is my husband, Lord Bretheridge. Flynn, these are my sisters Angelisa-Lily and Angelica-Iris." She gestured to the servant. "And this is a longtime family friend, Martha Gibson."

After a stunned pause, the three women dipped into deep curtsies.

"A lord? Does that mean you're a *lady*, Lina?" Excitement glittered in Lily's eyes. She'd always been enamored of anything to do with royalty or nobility. She gaped at Flynn. "What is he? A viscount? Earl? Duke?"

"Lily, do hush. You're being rude and impertinent." Iris elbowed her sister none too gently in the ribs. And Iris had always been overly concerned with appearances.

His lips twitched as he bent into an exaggerated bow. "Flynn, Marquis of Bretheridge, at your service."

"*A marquis*," Lily breathed, awestruck.

Even Iris seemed suitably impressed, gawking at Flynn, her eyes rounded in wonderment.

"It's a pleasure to meet you, your lordship." Martha bowed her head respectfully.

"Martha? Girls?" Mama called weakly from behind the closed door. "Do I hear visitors? You know what the baron advised—"

A fit of coughing erupted from the other room.

Angelina grabbed the wobbly handle and swung the warped door open. "Mama, it's me. I've come to take you home."

Her mother, ashen as the linens she reclined upon, lay on a narrow cot. Pillows at her back and a worn quilt folded at her feet, only a single candle lit the meager room.

She tried to push to her elbows. "Angelina?"

"Yes, Mama. I came as soon as Lord Devaux told us you were in London." Sinking to her knees beside the bed, Angelina clutched her mother's hand. "Oh, Mama." She kissed the cool, papery skin as tears flooded her eyes once more. "I've missed you."

"And I you, child." Another round of coughing wracked her mother's thin frame. "Why, what day is it? The seventeenth of July?"

"Yes, Mama, it is."

"*Canty* birthday, my dear." Mama touched Angelina's cheek. "One and twenty." She sighed with a far-off expression in her eyes. "My, how swiftly the time has passed."

"I prayed you'd be well by the time we arrived." Angelina perused the sparse room again. The air hung thick and cloying, smelling slightly of cabbage and onions. No doubt from someone cooking on the lower level. "Have you seen a physician?" She brushed a tendril of graying hair off Mama's cheek. "You sound awful."

Her mother gave a feeble nod. "One paid a call last week. He left an elixir, and Lily has her herbs."

Mama waved weakly toward the rickety table, nestled beneath the lone window. A hat-sized basket and a pestle in a mortar sat atop its scratched surface. "She's been steeping them for tea and poultices. I think they're helping more than that foul stuff the doctor ordered me to take."

She patted Angelina's hand and formed the faintest smile, as though the effort cost her a great deal.

"Who's that you have with you?" Her mother peered at Flynn outlined in the doorway. "Please come in and introduce yourself. The doctor assures me I'm not contagious and that I'm well onto the road to recovery."

She chuckled, a rattling cackle deep in her chest. "That featherbrain also thought a swallow of whisky every hour would help my condition. Given his slapdash appearance, I'd guess he abides by the practice himself. Except, he likely indulges in a nip every quarter-hour."

Flynn strode to the side of the bed and made a half bow. "I'm Flynn, the Marquis of Bretheridge." He helped Angelina to her feet. "Angelina is my wife."

Surprise flashed across Mama's features, even as her pale lips curved. "So, Lina. You took my advice, after all, and found yourself a handsome, young lord."

22

"It's been a week, Yancy." Flynn tossed the playing card onto his desk.

He'd waited an entire week after moving the Ellsworth women to his house in Berkeley Square for Yancy to finally appear with the promised evidence. Propping one booted foot on his knee, Flynn relaxed against the plush chair and drummed his fingers on the arms.

"Yes, well, I was a trifle delayed in leaving Craiglocky." Yancy twisted his mouth into a mocking grin. Not a jot of repentance registered in his expression.

"No doubt a turquoise-eyed, tawny-haired beauty distracted you," Flynn muttered, irritated. He stared at his friend before turning his focus to the playing card lying atop his desk. "It's marked, yes. How do you know it's the duke's?"

"A footman found it wedged beneath the cushion of the chair Waterford sat in." Yancy scratched his chin. He leaned forward and flipped the card over, tapping the illustration. "And it's hand-painted. Notice the fine, red diagonal line on our friend, the king, here?"

He ran a manicured nail along the narrow, crimson strip.

Flynn bent closer then rolled a shoulder. "So? Custom cards always differ somewhat."

A satisfied grin split Yancy's face. "Ah, but how many have family crests boasting a red banner? Waterford couldn't resist having that detail added, the pompous arse."

"You're familiar with his crest?" Flynn picked up the card again. His father had no doubt touched this very one, unaware it was marked—or that he would be compelled to take his life as a result of the duke's cheating.

The marking was clever. An insignificant scratch, really. Unless one knew what to search for.

Flynn and Yancy did.

"Waterford's such a pretentious old bugger. He uses every occasion to flaunt his position and wealth." Yancy laughed harshly. A ruthless glint entered his eye. "I'll wager I can locate the artist who painted it. Perchance, even the deck missing this card. You could squash Waterford like an ant beneath your toe with either of those. *If* you wanted to."

He casually reclined in the leather wingback and took a sip of brandy, waiting for Flynn's reply.

Do I want to?

Fingering the card, Flynn directed his attention to the window beside his desk. Above the hedge paralleling the house, he spied Lily and Iris. Arms linked and heads close together beneath a single parasol, they circled the compact side garden, enjoying the late afternoon sun.

An iron fence, nearly hidden behind the tall hawthorn hedge, led to the street. On the opposite side of the garden, a scrolled cast iron arbor covered in jasmine and honeysuckle, under which sat a marble bench, provided a fragrant boudoir for those hoping to escape the sun.

Rained had pelted London for the last five days. A few tenacious clouds lingered overhead, threatening more showers. In the distance, ominous black billows gathered—likely a thunderstorm.

Standing in the lone patch of grass, Gregor guarded the women. Arms folded, he yawned, boredom evident on his face. He was not a man accustomed to idleness.

The giant Scot's knowledge of healing plants caused friction between him and Lily. He insisted Mrs. Ellsworth drink a tea of licorice root, ginger, and horehound for her cough and ailing lungs. Lily wouldn't permit the brew, arguing mallow and slippery elm were far better for treating such symptoms.

And Doctor Tuttle, the incompetent cod's head, wanted to bleed Mrs. Ellsworth and prescribe laudanum for her *putrid sore throat*.

An irate Gregor and Lily practically chased the man from the house. They eventually came to a grudging agreement concerning Mrs. Ellsworth's treatment. Nevertheless, neither seemed inclined to trust the other wholly.

Why hadn't Gregor ever continued his studies and become a physician or alchemist? He certainly entertained a fascination for treating the ill, and his healing skills were noteworthy.

Flynn chuckled as Gregor heaved a sigh, rolling his eyes skyward. Yawning and stretching his massive arms overhead, the Scot followed the twins indoors.

Flynn supposed Angelina's absence in the garden meant she tended her mother. Mrs. Ellsworth hadn't rebounded as swiftly as they'd hoped she would. Her condition didn't worsen, yet neither did it improve.

Angelina had written the duchess and told her aunt of Mrs. Ellsworth's arrival and her weakened state of health. A reply couldn't be expected yet. It struck him rather odd that the duchess and her sister hadn't seen each other in two decades.

Concern for his mother niggled as well.

Torn between staying in London to make sure his wife and her family remained safe and taking a short visit to Lambridge to look in on his family, he'd opted to wait. In another few days, and if Mrs. Ellsworth hadn't improved enough to travel, he would send someone to check on Mother's wellbeing.

In fact, he would do that anyway. No sense in delaying.

But he couldn't—*wouldn't*—leave Angelina, his wife.

His attempts to woo her were paying off by paltry degrees. At least, he believed he made headway. The sweet smiles she gave him made progress difficult to ascertain.

He'd never been this unsure of a woman before. Prior to meeting his wife, the ladies had always thrown themselves at him. He had chosen the one he favored at the moment.

Zeus, I sound like a shallow churl.

The evening they'd arrived at the Mayfair house, and after everyone had settled into their respective rooms, Angelina had come upon him nursing a brandy in his study.

Hands clasped and her nervous gaze cavorting about the room, she blurted, "I want you to know that Mama misspoke when she suggested I had taken her advice. Before I sailed for England, she jested about me someday finding another husband."

Angelina inhaled a long breath and rushed on. "I told her I wasn't interested in marrying again. Please believe me, when I tell you that I never—"

"I believe you, Lina."

"Oh. You do?" Her gaze sank to the floor. She seemed at a complete loss as to how to respond.

Flynn rose and set aside his glass. Taking a few steps, he stood before her and took her hands in his. He kissed the knuckles of each. "I know you didn't scheme to marry me."

Believing her proved easy. After all, he knew firsthand her reluctance to wed him. That seemed to be changing, however. He prayed it was. This past week, Angelina had been preoccupied with caring for her mother. The distraction gratified him. Her business helped to take her mind off Davy.

Had she told her family about her son?

He didn't think so.

She was too considerate to add to their burdens, and carried her afflictions alone, without complaint. That was too much for anyone to bear by themselves. He hoped in time, she'd learn to trust once more and share everything with him.

Such as, why she picked the particular scent she did for her perfume. The fragrance lingered in the room long after she'd left and drove him near to distraction with want every time he caught a whiff.

Or why did she sing when she bathed? Or would she like him to teach her French? Did she like champagne or peaches? Did she enjoy riding or the theater?

Could she be happy with me—for the rest of her life?

"A penny for your thoughts," Yancy prompted kindly, rather than in his usual bantering fashion.

Absorbed in his musings about his wife, Flynn had forgotten his friend waited for an answer.

"It's of no consequence now. I'm good and bound to Angelina. Had I this in my possession," Flynn lifted the card and waved it, "beforehand, I'd have pursued the issue and seen Waterford destroyed. The cheat may not have pulled the trigger, but nonetheless, I hold him solely responsible for Father's death."

He quelled the fresh wave of black rage that seized him, knotting his gut. "But the point is moot. I have a wife I deeply care for now. In fact, I suppose I owe that old bear a debt of gratitude for introducing us, though it galls me to the soles of my feet to admit it. She's worth far more to me than my fortune or reputation. Even my pride."

He tossed the card aside.

Yancy leveled him an extended contemplative stare. He raised his glass in a mock toast. "For where your treasure is, there your heart shall also be."

"Exactly so." Flynn smiled widely, truly optimistic about his marriage for the first time.

What irony. The reasons compelling Angelina and him to marry no longer existed. Convinced they'd never have met otherwise, he wouldn't regret his lack of choice in the beginning. Now, he couldn't imagine his life without her.

In a few short weeks, she'd become an integral part of his existence. How she managed to do so, he couldn't say, and it really didn't matter. He wasn't one to question his good fortune or a blessing once disguised as a curse.

Her belated birthday present tucked within, he patted his coat pocket. He was certain she wouldn't mind his tardiness. Before they dined tonight, he'd give her his gift.

He turned his attention to his friend. "Will you stay and sup with us?"

Shaking his head, the earl stood. "No, I promised Harcourt and Faulkenhurst I'd venture to a few gaming hells with them this evening."

"They're also in Town?" Flynn advanced to the door, holding it open as Yancy passed through. "I'll never understand why you three loiter in London's stench when you have comfortable country estates far more pleasant this time of year."

"There are still some amusements to be had for an unshackled chap, my friend." A scowl of distaste passed over his face. "Besides, my dear stepmother is in residence at Bronwedon Towers, which means Matilda—"

"Is there too," Flynn finished. "I take it, Cecily and Matilda are bent on making the chit the next Countess of Ramsbury?"

Poor Yancy. Since he unexpectedly came into his title four years ago, his stepmother plagued him incessantly about a match between him and Matilda.

"How old is Matilda now, anyway?" Flynn squinted at Yancy.

"Old enough to try and corner me in the solarium the last time I ventured to Bronwedon. And I don't believe for an instant it's the first time she's engaged in such behavior." Yancy grimaced. "That was no inexperienced miss, I tell you. I feared for *my* virtue."

He gave a dramatic shudder before slapping Flynn on the shoulder. "Don't bother calling for Jeffers. I can see my way out." He pointed and waggled his finger up and down. "It's there. That garishly painted pinkish door."

"It's not pink—it's puce. Mother picked the color."

"You, my friend, are color blind," Yancy said after snorting loudly. "*That* most assuredly is pink."

Despite Yancy's needling, Flynn followed him from the study, their boots clicking in unison on the parquet floor. "I'll walk you to the door. I wouldn't mind a breath of fresh air." He scraped a hand through his hair. "By God, I'm glad the rain has stopped. Typical of London: fog or rain, when the rest of the country enjoys the sunshine."

Yancy retrieved his hat and cane from the table beside the entrance.

Flynn had just grasped the latch when someone knocked briskly.

"Were you expecting somebody else?" Raising a brow, the earl donned his beaver hat.

Jeffers hurried to the entrance, tugging on his white gloves as he went. He slowed to a stop, uncertainty etched on his austere features upon spying Flynn already at the door.

He waved the butler away. "I'll answer, Jeffers, since I'm seeing Lord Ramsbury out."

"I think I'll linger and discover why someone's calling right before dinner, no doubt expecting an invitation to dine," Yancy said with a sardonic smirk. "That's what comes of having such an accomplished chef."

It was Flynn's turn to snort as he drew the door open. "Don't judge everyone by your boorish behavior, Yancy."

A rather chipper, Lord Devaux, greeted Flynn. Behind the baron loitered a handful of his men, some near a carriage and others holding their horses' reins.

"Are you in the habit of answering the door yourself, my lord?" The baron arched an eyebrow.

Chuckling, Flynn shook his head. "No, hardly ever. I was bidding Ramsbury farewell. I believe you met in passing at Craiglocky."

"Is that what you call that disaster?" Yancy pushed his way ahead of Flynn.

The earl and baron grinned in apparent mutual understanding. They'd each been on the receiving end of the Ferguson misses' less than cordial hospitality.

Introductions were made in short order. Yancy took his leave, whistling a jaunty tune as he strode along the sidewalk, swinging his cane. His residence wasn't more than a half-mile away, which at times could prove annoying.

Flynn never knew when the chap would pop in for a dram of brandy or dawdle about and irritate him with nonsensical twaddle.

Jeffers hovered nervously in the corridor, pretending to straighten the already perfect-as-a-painting bouquet of roses displayed on a narrow table.

"Do come in, Devaux, before my majordomo thinks I don't need his services any longer." Flynn scanned the men lingering on the street. "Would they care to visit the servants' quarters for some refreshment?"

"*Non*, there's no need. I'll only be a moment." Devaux stepped neatly across the threshold and dutifully moved aside so Jeffers could close the door.

"Your hat and gloves, sir?" The butler waited expectantly beside Lord Devaux.

"Sorry, Jeffers. The baron won't be staying." Flynn bit back a guffaw at the affronted pout the majordomo's mouth formed.

With a hurt sniff, Jeffers staidly marched to the end of the hall. With a last disapproving glower, he jutted his chin upward, looking rather like an oversized turtle, and vanished into the dining room.

"I'd say he's peeved at you." A distinct hint of humor edged the Frenchman's voice.

"He usually is." Flynn pulled a face. "If you please, my study is this way."

He headed to the room he'd occupied a short while ago.

Devaux's footsteps echoed behind him. "Bretheridge, I wanted to make you aware. Pierre's ship, *Ange de la Mer,* sailed with this morning's tide."

Halfway to the study, Flynn spun around to face Devaux. He narrowed his eyes, fresh wrath whipping his fury. "His ship is named *Angel of the Sea*?"

His lips clamped in a thin strip, the baron nodded. "A coincidence I cannot deny. I swear to you. She was named thus before he met your wife. Rather ironic when you consider his cargo."

"Indeed." Flynn rested his hands on his hips. "And Renault sailed? You know this for certain?"

"*Oui.*" Devaux strode farther into the entry. He rubbed his fingers along the brim of his hat. "I checked with the port officer myself. Pierre was seen boarding the vessel last night and standing at the bow when she sailed at dawn."

Heady relief surged through Flynn.

Angelina is safe.

"I showed the official a miniature to make sure. The man was positive. Pierre walked up the gangplank." The baron reached into his coat pocket.

Flynn could no more deny himself a perusal of Angelina's tormentor than he could ignore his growing feelings for her. The man gazing out from the miniature portrait was irrefutably handsome, except for the aloofness in his eyes and a cynical curl to his lips.

With a sharp nod, Flynn indicated he'd finished studying the image.

"Where's the ship bound?"

"She's to pick up goods in France. Nantes, to be precise. Which is a hub for the slave trade." Devaux slid the miniature into his pocket. "She'll sail to Gibraltar and from there, Bombay."

Flynn briefly scanned the entry and corridors, assuring himself they were alone. This conversation would be better served in the privacy of his study. No telling how Angelina or the twins would react should they come upon him conversing with Devaux.

"Are you certain you won't join me in my study?" Flynn gestured toward the open door.

"*Non*, I wish to be on the next ship to France, and I've much to do before I sail with this evening's tide." He put on his hat. "That *bâtard* doesn't bear discomfort well. A voyage of that length is beyond him. I'd swear upon my *mere's* grave. He'll disembark in France."

His eyes hardened, not a hint of mercy in their flinty depths. "I intend to seize him in our homeland where I aim to have charges brought against him for her murder, and if I can prove it, abducting women."

"Add bigamy to that list, will you?" Flynn asked, not a little discomfited by the coiled hatred in his gut toward a man he'd never met.

Devaux turned toward the door. He paused, shifting to face him once more. "If you've no further use of my men, I'll take them with me. You still have the Scots here?"

"Yes, by all means, take them." Flynn couldn't wait to tell Angelina. Her relief would be profound, as would her family's. "With Renault gone, we have no further need for guards. I'll send the Scots home tomorrow, as well."

"Come in." Angelina balanced on one foot, a hand on her dressing table for stability. She bent to tug on a beaded slipper. She would be late for dinner, again if she didn't hurry. A rumble of thunder announced the arrival of the storm that portended all afternoon.

Giving a firm tug, she slid the shoe onto her heel. Three times this week, she dashed to the dining room to see the others seated there ahead of her. Flynn always gave her a patient smile. She checked on Mama each evening before dining, and sometimes it took longer to escape than she'd anticipated.

She straightened and released a startled yelp when she bumped into a solid male body. She twisted to peer behind her.

"Flynn, I thought you were one of the girls." She laughed at the absurdity of the statement. The body pressing into hers was anything but feminine. She tried to turn around, but he stilled her by putting his hands on her bare shoulders.

A rush of desire nearly had her bones melting against him. As thunder rocked the house again, he dropped a kiss onto her nape. She jumped. Dear God, she was going to dissolve at his feet, like Devonshire cream on a warm tart.

He touched the sleeve of her turquoise gown. "I'm very glad you're wearing this color tonight. I have something for you."

"You do?" She craned her neck to peer behind her.

He slipped a long black velvet box from inside his coat.

She wriggled in an attempt to push him away so she could turn around. He didn't budge but remained pressed firmly to her backside. A very naughty image shoved its way into her mind.

Surely, *that* wasn't possible. *Or is it?*

For the first time, she noticed he wasn't wearing black. He'd donned a smoky blue tailcoat. The color made his eyes a rich, divinely sensual sea-green.

"Bend your neck," he whispered, his warm breath caressing her.

Her breath caught. *Lord, help me*. She dipped her chin to her chest, as much to oblige him as to hide the flush coloring her cheeks.

Flynn draped a necklace onto her bosom, gradually drawing the exquisite pendant up until the cool stones rested an inch above her cleavage.

"Happy birthday, Lina." His knuckles caressed her nape. "I'm sorry I'm late."

"Oh, Flynn, I didn't expect anything." She touched the smooth gem with her fingertips. "Is it an emerald?"

"It is indeed. A rare blue gem. Though you can see a hint of green within its depths, too." He secured the clasp, and the pendant sank lower. So did his hands until they rested on the curve of her ribs, a hairsbreadth from her breasts.

If she sagged the slightest amount…

A strand of the finest, perfectly matched, pearls she'd ever seen rested against her bosom. A triangular gold inlay lined with diamonds attached a tear-shaped emerald as big as her thumb to the pearls.

"It's absolutely brilliant. Thank you." She touched the beads at her neck. "I'll treasure it always."

"There are also earbobs." He released her. Opening her hand, he dropped a pair of teardrop pearl and emerald earrings onto her palm.

She placed them on her ears, adjusted a few dangling curls, then surveyed the result in the looking glass. She fingered the vibrant stone at her breast again. "I've never seen anything half as lovely."

"I have." He stared at her reflection, possessive pride darkening his eyes. His smile was both seductive and triumphant. "It's the same color your eyes are after I kiss you."

She swallowed an unladylike gulp. "It is?"

Bother. Was she incapable of acting the least bit sophisticated? Her voice sounded like a frog croaking, for pity's sake. A half-dead frog, at that.

"It is indeed." He trailed a finger from her neck, across a shoulder, and then to the treasure nestled between her breasts. "I confess, I'm curious."

Oh, dear God. She stifled a moan. "Curious?" she managed, sounding almost normal. *If breathy and sultry and utterly wanton are normal, that is.*

He turned her in his arms. His dark head inched lower until his lips hovered above hers. "Yes. I wonder what color your eyes will be while I make love to you. And afterward, when I've brought you to completion."

The scent of his subtle, spicy cologne wafted past her nose. She clasped his lapels to stay standing. Her dratted knees were of no use at all, ridiculous weak things.

Then his lips met hers. All sensible thought flew in the face of her passion. Time ceased as he explored the depths of her mouth. She caressed his tongue with hers, matching his gentle jousts. It was difficult to tell whose harsh breathing echoed louder in the chamber.

The man certainly knew how to seduce. Every nerve in her body sang. He played her senses like a maestro's bow upon a violin's strings.

Angelina was ready to toss up her skirts and let him have his way. At the unbidden thought, another day and another similar memory jarred her rudely into lucidity once more.

No, this is Flynn. He isn't anything like Charles.

Her door whipped open with a resounding thud. They sprang apart guiltily.

Iris, her face ghastly pale, stood in panting the entrance. "Lina. Come quickly. Something's wrong with Mama."

23

Angelina tore from her room. Her skirts hoisted knee-high. Flynn's thumping footsteps echoed behind her.

Fear hissed horrid conjecture in her ears as she dashed up the flight of steps. Careening around the corner, she spied Martha, tense and distraught at the foot of the bed.

Lily wept into her hands, Martha's arm about her shoulders.

Holding a steaming bowl, Gregor bent near Angelina's mother. "Mrs. Ellsworth, ye need to calm yourself. Inhale this. It'll relax ye, so ye can breathe."

Tears streamed from her eyes. She struggled to draw in the tiniest breath, only managing short, wheezing gasps.

Iris scooted past Angelina and rushed to her twin.

"What's happening? Why can't she breathe?" Angelina ran to her mother.

Gregor's attention remained trained on Mama. "She's havin' an asthma attack. Combined with her respiratory ailment, she canna draw air into her lungs." He swung his calm gaze to the frantic women at the end of the bed. "Miss Iris, I need a towel, please." He pointed to a table. "And that tonic I made yesterday.

"Mrs. Gibson, fetch more hot water and a larger basin, please. Miss Lily, we need air in here. This room is stifling. Open the drapes and window."

The women scrambled to do his bidding.

"What can I do?" Angelina took her mother's hand. Her stomach flipped at the terror on her mother's face. "You're going to be fine, Mama. You must do as Gregor asks. Try to breathe in the medicine." She gently urged her mother nearer the bowl. "Come now, that's it."

Gregor took the tonic and pointed to the towel Iris grasped. "Drape it about yer mother's shoulders."

Iris promptly complied.

"Bretheridge, I require my plants and herbs." He looked to Flynn. "Can ye fetch them for me?"

"At once." Giving Angelina a quick, reassuring smile, he strode from the room.

The distinct tramp of him breaking into a run shook the corridor. Warmth spread through her again, immediately erased by the damp air wafting into the room.

Lily scuttled from the yawning window to Iris's side. The twins grabbed hands.

Martha huffed into the room, appearing as if she'd run the entire way to the kitchen and back. She carried a kettle in one hand, its handle wrapped in a towel. Hurrying to the table, she cast Mama a worried glance before setting the pot upon another folded towel. She dashed to snatch the basin on the washstand.

Flynn pounded into the chamber, carrying two oddly-shaped leather bags.

"My lady, may I ask ye to hold this for me?" Gregor passed the bowl to Angelina.

One arm supporting her mother's shoulders, Angelina sat beside her on the bed. "Deep breaths. I know it's hard, Mama. Try to relax. Why, I believe you sound better already."

A few minutes later, Gregor removed the towel and offered a half-full eggshell thin teacup. "Can ye drink this, Mrs. Ellsworth? It is a tonic for asthma."

Mama nodded weakly, but she didn't try to speak.

Angelina held the cup to her mother's lips.

Her breathing, though ragged, had ceased to whistle. A speck of color had returned to her cheeks.

Angelina helped her mother relax onto the pillows, assuring she sat upright.

Lily drifted to the table, silently studying the assortment of plants Gregor had arranged. She picked up a dried sprig. "Can you teach me about them?"

The Scots' mouth dropped open, but his eyes lit up. "Aye, I'd be happy to teach ye." He seemed almost shy as he scooted nearer and began explaining the different herbs to Lily.

Angelina exchanged a telling glance with Flynn. Did his lips twitch? How old was Gregor, anyway? Apparently not *too* old, from the enamored way Lily looked at him.

Egads, wouldn't that be something?

"Li—?" Mama cleared her throat and tried again. "Lina?"

She leaned in to better hear. "Yes, Mama?"

"I need to speak with you." Her voice scarcely a whisper, her mother's eyes remained closed. "Privately."

Everyone turned to stare.

"Of course." Angelina patted her mother's hand and gazed around the room. "Please allow us a moment."

Gregor and Lily promptly tucked his medicines away, while Iris and Martha collected the other items scattered about the chamber.

Flynn gathered the towel from the bed. Fisting the linen in one hand, he bathed Angelina with a tender gaze. "I'll meet you below. I'll have Cook hold dinner."

He stared pointedly at the pendant, before raising his eyes to meet hers. With a wink, he quit the room, along with Gregor and the twins.

He'd done that on purpose—reminded her of their enticing conversation. Despite the blush heating her face once more, her heart fluttered happily. Charming scoundrel. *And he's mine.*

Where had that come from? She didn't mind the notion in the least. Perhaps, just perhaps, she *could* trust him not to break her heart.

"Lucille, I'll come and sit with you when you're done speaking with Lina." Martha hesitated at the door. Her gaze skimmed Angelina, and her hazel eyes crinkled with affection. "I'll bring some of that chicken soup Cook has simmering on the stove. There's fresh bread, too. It smells divine."

"Thank you, my dear friend." Her mother gave her a wan smile as Martha softly closed the door.

Angelina shifted into a comfortable position beside her. "What is it you wanted to say?"

Her mother pushed herself more erect then pointed to the wardrobe. "There's a valise in there. At the bottom—beneath some clothing and other things—is a small, locked chest. Will you fetch it for me, dear?"

"Are you positive you're up to this?" Angelina touched her mother's hand. "Cannot whatever's in the chest wait?"

Mere minutes ago, her mother labored to breathe, and Angelina feared she might die.

"No. I've put this off far too long." Mama reached into the neckline of her nightgown and withdrew a chain. A key dangled from the end. She rubbed it between her thumb and forefinger, a melancholy expression shadowing her face. "Go on. Fetch me the box."

Suppressing a sigh, Angelina slid off the bed.

When she set her mind to something, Mama could be most stubborn.

After a bit of rummaging about in the wardrobe, Angelina found the valise. She removed several items from inside and placed them on the floor. At last, she uncovered the wooden box. A charming old thing adorned with fine floral etchings.

She carried the container to her mother. "Here you are."

Did her mother need privacy?

"Do you wish me to remain?"

Mama sent her a surprised look. "Why, yes, dear. This is about you, after all." Placing the chest on her lap, she searched the table across the room and frowned. "Where's that brew Gregor told me to drink?"

"Right here." Angelina scooped the cup off the bedside table.

Her mother took a long swallow. "I wish I'd had this concoction all along. My breathing has eased a great deal already."

Lily must never know. She'd feel awful and blame herself for Mama's lack of recovery.

"Sit, Lina. You make me nervous hovering about. You're worse than a mama cat with newborn kittens, for pity's sake." Her mother took another sip. Sighing contentedly, she returned the cup to the table.

Angelina drew a chair up beside the bed. She sank thankfully into the padding. Mama's incident had taken a toll on her nerves.

Trying to insert the key into the lock, Mama fumbled for a moment. She laughed self-consciously. "I've not opened it in some time, and my eyes aren't what they used to be."

At last, the lock gave way with a soft click. Her expression solemn, Mama stared at the case. She ran a thumb along its scalloped edge. "I thought I was going to die tonight." She lifted tear-filled eyes to Angelina's. A haunted glint hovered in their depths. "And I realized I couldn't go to my grave without you knowing the truth."

"Don't speak of dying. You're going to recover. You just said you're feeling improved already." Angelina scrunched her forehead while patting her mother's arm. "I'm sure there's nothing in there that's of such importance, you cannot wait until you've recovered to show me."

She warily eyed the box. Some inner voice told her she didn't want to know what the unpretentious chest held. Sometimes secrets were better left undisclosed.

Davy.

She hadn't been able to tell her mother about her son yet. "Why don't we wait until tomorrow?" she suggested.

"No, I've been selfish and let fear keep me silent these many years. You deserve to know the truth. What you do with it," Mama raised a frail shoulder, "well, I suppose that's up to you.

"Mama, please—"

"I cannot carry this burden alone, Lina. I'm not strong enough. Not anymore." Tears welled in her mother's eyes again.

Angelina squeezed her mother's frail hand. "It's all right. You can tell me. We can be strong together." Though, how she would garner more strength, she didn't know. Her reservoir was tapped. Empty. Depleted.

Flynn's face floated into her mind, bringing a poignant sense of peace. Strong and powerful, he'd lend her strength. No, she'd asked too much of him already.

Mama inched the lid open. She cautiously withdrew a thin stack of letters tied together by a faded, crimson ribbon.

"These are from your father. I met him when I was almost eighteen. He came to Ayrshire to hunt with friends one weekend." Her mother brushed her fingers across the yellowed papers. "I was recuperating at my grandparents'. My family had gone to London to prepare for Camille's Come Out, although she'd already accepted a marriage offer."

"Recuperating?" Angelina kicked off her slippers." You'd been ill?".

"No. I'd been thrown from my horse and struck my head on a fence. I nearly died. The doctor ordered me to take to my bed for six weeks." Mama untied the frayed ribbon.

"Nothing more strenuous than a sedate fifteen-minute walk was permitted after my extended bed rest. That restriction lasted for several weeks, so traveling was out of the question." Her mother touched the side of her head. "That's why I suffer from those dreadful headaches sometimes."

"Oh, Mama, how awful." She couldn't suppress her gasp. Why hadn't she been told this before? There didn't seem any need for secrecy about the matter. She toyed with the gem hanging from her neck. "Aunt Camille was betrothed before her first Season?"

An expression of pain etched her mother's haggard face. "Yes, it had been arranged between the families when they were young children. You know, fathers." She released a despondent sigh. "Manipulating their offspring for their own benefit."

Yes, that sounded like Angelina's father, as well. He would've bound her to his repulsive chum, Mr. Stockton, without a second thought. "I think it rather boorish of your family to toddle off to London and leave you behind."

Her mother didn't respond.

Shifting on her seat, Angelina waved her hand. "Surely, Aunt Camille's Come Out might've waited. Especially if she was affianced already. It should've been your first Season as well."

"I didn't mind. The idea of a Season terrified me. In any event, I fell madly in love with your father the moment I saw him by the loch." Mama relaxed against the pillows, her fatigue obvious. She fingered the chain at her throat. "I was no promiscuous miss, I tell you. I insisted we marry before we—"

A pink hue swept her mother's face, hinting at the young, vulnerable girl she'd once been.

Although Angelina found the revelations rather perplexing, she attempted to digest what her mother shared. This was the first she'd heard of Papa ever hunting.

Fiddling with her wedding ring, she searched her mind. She couldn't recall a single instance of him handling a firearm. And, she didn't mean to be unkind, but she couldn't imagine Mama *ever* having been *madly* in love with him.

Angelina had long been aware her parents' marriage lacked something. Though always impeccably polite, no fire or passion simmered between them.

No arguments.

No stolen embraces.

Nothing.

Although she never voiced a disrespectful word against him, her mother hadn't been brokenhearted when Papa died.

Relieved better described her reaction.

Mama closed her eyes, her momentary embarrassment seemingly behind her. "We married right away. It's easy to do in Scotland. Your father insisted we keep the marriage a secret until my parents returned so that we could announce our joyous news together."

Her lips bent into a tremulous smile, and her lids flickered open. Sadness and resignation resided there.

"See, it's not as bad as all that. Everything worked out," Angelina said.

Did her mother care so very much that she married secretly?

Heavens, it wasn't a sin and by no means a novelty. Then or now—especially in Scotland.

"No dear, you misunderstand." That distant glint crept into her eyes again as she sagged into the pillows. "Richard—was not your father," she whispered, frail and exhausted. "I knew the man who fathered you simply as Edward Pennington. I didn't learn his full name until later."

Wasn't papa my real father?

Tears slipped from beneath her mother's lashes. "Ambrose..." *Ambrose?* "James Simon Edward—"

"No, not..." Angelina bounded from the bed, one hand at her throat. "Good God. Not Uncle Ambrose!"

24

Where was Angelina?

Flynn flicked his pocket watch open for the—*confound it*. He'd lost track of how many times he'd checked the timepiece.

She hadn't come below stairs. After waiting a full half-hour, he ordered dinner served. Another three-quarters of an hour passed, and her chair remained vacant.

The clanking of utensils as those seated around the table dined was only interrupted by the respectful queries of the footmen when a new dish arrived, or one needed clearing away.

Gregor and the twins seemed as disinclined to talk as he. Their worried gazes kept straying to the dining room entrance at regular intervals.

Angelina wasn't coming.

Flynn drained his wine glass. Standing, he set his serviette aside. "Please excuse me."

He didn't wait to hear their murmured consents. Intent on seeking his wife, he strode from the room. What had transpired between her and her mother that kept Angelina from joining them?

Taking the stairs two at a time, he hurried the length of the corridor to her chamber. He stood outside the door, uncertainty gripping him. Was she within, or still in her mother's chamber? He knocked softly and tried the latch. The door drifted open, revealing a dark interior.

He reached to close the door, but muffled sniffling caught his ear.

"Lina?"

He edged into the room and attempted to locate her in the gloom.

Angelina sat huddled in an armchair before the hearth. The golden highlights in her hair gave her away. The drapes remained open, and a few feeble moonbeams bravely shone between the cloud-covering. One of them touched her head in a celestial caress.

"Why are you sitting in the dark, love?"

After grabbing a candle from the corridor, he located a lamp on a table. He lit the taper then, after closing the door, approached her.

She wept like a chastised child, curled into the chair with her knees tucked to her chest.

He squatted and touched her shoulder. "What is it? What has happened?"

Shaking her head, she covered her face with a hand and continued softly weeping.

What in God's holy name had her mother said to cause this distress?

He rose and scooped Angelina into his arms. He turned in a half-circle before carrying her to the bed.

She didn't protest.

He sat on the edge of the mattress and cradled her in his arms, her face pressed to his chest. As he touched his lips to her perfumed hair, brighter than a copper penny, his mind raced.

She was as distraught as she'd been after losing her baby. With each of her shuddering sobs, his heart wrenched.

"Tell me, Lina. Please tell me so that I can help you." He kissed her crown again, desperate to comfort her.

"I'm illegitimate," she whispered brokenly.

Temporary shock caused him to stiffen. "Pardon?"

"Richard Ellsworth wasn't my father. A man named Pennington was…is."

She wasn't making sense. Her father was alive?

Flynn tilted her chin up, forcing her to meet his eyes. Misery and grief haunted the green pools.

"I'm sorry. I don't understand." He touched her damp cheek, wiping away her tears. "Please, explain everything to me."

Her face crumpled as fresh tears cascaded from her eyes.

Tilting her away from his chest, he withdrew his handkerchief from his coat. She never seemed to have one about when required. He'd have her order a dozen. No, two dozen. Better yet, a hundred of the confounded things, and see them stashed in every room—and the carriages as well.

Eyes closed and slightly scrunched as if in pain, she let her head fall against his shoulder.

He unfolded the handkerchief and tenderly wiped her face. "What happened? Why do you say you're illegitimate?" He dabbed a lingering tear from the corner of her eye and tightened his arm about her. "Tell me."

Her lashes, spiky from tears, lay like dark ribbons against her pale cheeks. She opened her eyes.

The agony glistening in their depths stabbed him to his core.

"Mama met a man before Papa."

"This Pennington fellow?"

"Yes." She half-nodded against his shoulder. "She fell in love with him, and they secretly married in Scotland."

He murmured against her ear, "That hardly makes you a by blow, my love."

"But I am. Pennington was already betrothed. The rotter merely sought to use Mama for…" She sucked in an uneven breath. "Well, you know. The way Pierre used me."

My God, this brings Renault's betrayal and treachery to the forefront of her mind once more, causing her to relive the pain.

"But if he married your mother, the betrothal wasn't valid."

"That's what I said." Angelina met his eyes for an instant before hers dropped to his neckcloth. "After he deserted Mama, she sought the clergyman who married them, hoping he knew how to contact my father. She discovered a church cleric hadn't performed the ceremony. Merely a duplicitous fellow and his cronies, acting as witnesses. All eager for a few crowns."

"What a despicable—" Flynn clamped his mouth shut. What he burned to say wasn't meant for a woman's ears.

"And that devil, he persuaded his intended to marry him immediately by way of a special license. They trotted off, happy as grigs, for a three-month honeymoon on the continent." Her voice shook with fury.

She swiped at a tear and offered him a wobbly smile. "I'll wager you'll never believe I'm not given to waterworks."

He dropped a kiss on her nose. "You've had much to cause tears of late."

"Indeed." She drew in a shuddering breath, then released it, bit by rasping bit. "In any event, the wedding wasn't supposed to take place for another several months. You see, the bride's sister recovered in Scotland from a near-fatal riding accident."

An eerie premonition skittered along Flynn's senses.

His legs growing numb from the odd angle he held her, he eased her onto the mattress. "And where was your mother in all of this? Surely she had something to say."

"My mother was the sister convalescing." Angelina turned her face away and stared at the candle on the bedside table. She sighed and pressed a hand to her forehead. "The Duke of Waterford fathered me."

A low whistle escaped Flynn's clenched teeth. "Does he know?"

Her throat bobbed as she swallowed twice.

This must be excruciating for her.

"Yes. Mama wrote and told him. He sent money now and again. To keep her quiet, I'm sure."

Or because he was compelled by guilt. *God curse the whoremonger.*

Angelina glanced his way. "Aunt Camille isn't aware, of course."

"That's understandable." Although Flynn guessed the woman knew far more than she let on. Taking Angelina's hand in his, he traced a circle in her palm. "I'm curious, and I hope you'll indulge me. Why didn't your mother recognize Waterford, or at least, know his name?"

Pushing a strand of hair off her face, she frowned. "Mama never laid eyes on the duke until they accidentally met. She'd only heard him referred to by his courtesy title, the Earl of Percy."

Flynn searched his memory. "I'm no authority on Scottish marriage laws, but I'm positive a clergyman doesn't need to perform the ceremony as long as the participants are willing, and there are witnesses."

She didn't respond. Had she heard him? Her eyes huge in her wan face, she stared blankly at the canopy. What was she thinking?

"Angelina, do you understand what this means?" He touched her arm. "Waterford is the last of his legitimate line. You're his legal heir."

25

Angelina swung her startled gaze to Flynn. "But wouldn't Mama know that?"

"Perhaps." He lay on his side next to her and propped his head in his hand. His gentle smile encouraged her to continue.

"By the time my mother heard about their wedding, she discovered she carried me." Touching her stomach, she remembered her precious babe. She would have done anything to protect him. Facing Flynn, she blinked several times against the tears pooling in her eyes.

"Mama nearly lost her mind from worry. She couldn't wait for them to return from their honeymoon. She'd be too far along, and Aunt Camille might be with child by that time, too." She shot a glance at the door. Worried someone eavesdropped, she lowered her voice. "She was, you know. Pembrose is only two months younger than me."

"So, to provide you with a father, and protect her sister from a heinous scandal, your mother married Ellsworth." He rubbed his chin, a speculative gleam in his eyes. "Even though she must've known their marriage wasn't valid."

"Yes." She pressed her lips together and dug her fingers into the counterpane to control the rage singing in her blood. Waterford deserved a flogging.

Lord, had Papa known, too?

He had. Of course, he had.

And that was why he and Mama had abruptly left Scotland and moved to Salem.

Angelina knew it in the center of her soul. She'd always sensed his rejection of her, and attributed it to what he called her *unholy* features. But it had been more than that. Much more. He couldn't bear to look upon her. Not because he disapproved of her appearance, he'd known she wasn't his flesh and blood.

That's why the twins look so different than me.

Why had Papa—*Richard*—kept silent for two decades?

The answer plowed into her mind as unwelcome as pox sores.

Money.

If she dug deep enough, she was confident she'd find evidence Papa had blackmailed the duke.

"Holy God above," Flynn said, reverence in his tone. "What an uncommon sacrifice your mother made."

Her admiration of her mother escalated even further. Mama could've been a duchess—in fact, legally held the title. Her life with Richard Ellsworth hadn't been easy either. Yet, to protect Angelina, she'd married a man she didn't love. Didn't much like, truth to tell.

"What will you do now that you know the truth?" Flynn trailed a long finger from her shoulder to her elbow.

What *would* she do?

Only one conceivable answer presented itself. A sudden peace encompassed her, and she turned onto her side. Peering deeply into Flynn's eyes, she whispered, "Nothing."

"*Nothing*?" He raised an eyebrow. A hint of approval teased the corner of his mouth as if he'd expected that very answer from her.

"I could never be that malicious. Imagine how eviscerating the gossip and disgrace would be if I revealed the truth." Did her expression show the horror she felt at the prospect? "My sisters and cousins would be dubbed by-blows. And Aunt Camille…"

It would kill her.

Angelina shook her head. "The scandal would destroy her. She's as much a victim as Mama."

"There's a good deal of truth in that." Flynn still trailed his finger along her arm. Only now, he'd extended the journey to include her neck and the sensitive flesh above her bodice.

Her nipples contracted, and her breathlessness couldn't be solely attributed to her bout of crying. Those disturbing little quivers she experienced at his touch made a deuced nuisance of themselves. She cleared her throat. "I couldn't even be that cruel to the duke, though he deserves it."

Flynn's face hardened to granite for a moment. "Indeed, *he* does."

"It's rather ironic, don't you think?" She brushed a strand of hair tickling her cheek away.

A puzzled frown marred his face. "What is?"

"Mama and I both marrying bigamists."

Something dark flashed in his eyes before the familiar twinkle returned. "Yes, to be sure."

That explained why Uncle—no, she couldn't think of him like that now—why Waterford desperately wanted her married. And why Mama never called her Rose.

Rose and Ambrose were too similar.

Nonetheless, her mother must've loved the duke to name her after him.

"You don't wish to inherit a dukedom?" Flynn's playful question drew her attention to him.

"Do you take me for a greedy wench, sir? I'm already a marchioness." She giggled, the weight of the past couple of hours gone, leaving her more content and happier than she'd been in a very long while. "Besides, I cannot inherit."

His gentle fingers continued to work their magic over her exposed flesh.

This was rather nice, lying beside him. She snuggled a mite closer.

"Well, there is precedent," he murmured huskily. "The Duke of Marlborough had his letter of patent amended to allow his daughters to inherit. Even without an amendment, legally, everything that is not entailed under the dukedom is yours by birthright." Flynn dipped his forefinger into the cleft between her breasts.

She bit her lip to suppress a groan. His wandering fingers caused her to imagine all sorts of wicked things.

"No." She managed to shake her head. "It would ruin too many lives." A breathless wanton sounded no less seductive.

"That it would." The timbre of his voice dropped to a sensual rumble as his exploring fingers inched further into her bodice.

Her gaze roamed over Flynn's face. My, but he was a sinfully handsome man. She lowered her attention to his lips. She wanted him to kiss her again. What would he do if she kissed him?

Would he be shocked? Repulsed? Excited?

His attention rested on her lips, too. Could he read her mind?

"Your mother and sisters are welcome to live with us at Lambridge. There's plenty of room. I'd like to settle dowries on the twins, and your mother is entitled to the life that was stolen from her."

He scooted closer until his thighs touched hers. His face was a handbreadth away as he laid one large palm across her waist.

"Oh, Flynn, thank you." She touched his chest, relishing the little jolt of pleasure doing so caused. "I'd like nothing better than for them to live with us. Your dowry offer is most generous, too. I'm afraid our marriage portions are rather miserable."

She really, *really* did want to kiss him. One tiny peck on that delicious mouth of his to show her gratitude for his benevolence. Nothing more. One minuscule taste would suffice.

What a colossal taradiddle.

"I think your mother would march along famously with mine. And I can already hear Franny's squeals of excitement at having young ladies her age in the house." His arm snaked behind Angelina, edging her closer.

If she leaned in two inches, her lips would touch his. Perhaps, she could make it appear accidental. She could slip forward—

His hand cupped her nape, and she was undone.

She surged toward him, her lips meeting his at last. She sensed his primal satisfaction even as her thoughts scattered on the four winds.

He turned her, pressing her into the plush bedding. His hands and lips were everywhere, awakening sensations she'd not known existed.

Arms entwined around his strong neck, she kissed him, conveying with her body what she didn't dare voice yet.

"I want to make love to you, Lina." Flynn nibbled his way from her earlobe to the hollow of her neck, then lower until he met the swell of her breasts. He spread hot kisses along the edge of her bodice.

Silently begging him to explore lower, she moaned and arched into him.

Did he sense her hunger? Was it the same for him? The gnawing, unfulfilled need?

He levered one hand beneath her shoulders and lifted her to meet his eager mouth. His firm groin nudged against her center, yet he didn't seem in a hurry to relieve his passion. Rather, he appeared intent on giving her pleasure.

He angled away and gazed into her eyes. "We won't do this if you don't want to. If you need more time. I'll wait as long as you need to be ready, Lina, because once we make love, our marriage is sealed."

Yes. Yes.

He placed a tender kiss on her lips. "You'll be mine, forever, to treasure the rest of my days."

"You want to stay married to me?" Angelina searched his eyes, finding desire, yes, but something infinitely more important as well. She touched his hard jaw, awed, and enthralled. "Forever?"

"Do you doubt it, jewel of my heart?" He traced her lips with a fingertip. "I love you."

He did.

She could see that truth in the depths of his soul, for it reflected the love that must be shining in her eyes as well. Could her overflowing heart hold any more joy?

"Yes, Flynn." She pressed a hot kiss to his mouth. "I want this, more than I've ever wanted anything before in my life."

It was true.

This man had become her reason for living. His very breath, echoing the rhythm of her once-broken heart. "Make me forget everything hurtful that came before you. Take my love, and make it yours."

A smile of triumph tempered with love lit his face. Helping her from the bed, he efficiently divested her of her clothing. Except for fuller breasts, her body showed no sign of her recent pregnancy. She reached to unclasp the pendant.

He placed a palm over the stone, halting her. "No, leave it on. But take your hair down."

Unsure whether her voice would work, she nodded and did as he asked. As she removed the pins from her hair, he undressed until he stood before her wearing nothing except his trousers.

Fine dark hair covered his chest and abdomen, gradually narrowing until it disappeared into his unfastened waistband. The trousers hung low and provocative on his narrow hips.

Her gaze roamed his godlike form. What a splendid male specimen. Although she'd seen him shirtless before, she'd forgotten the broadness of his sculpted chest.

He stepped to her and combed his fingers through her tresses, fanning them across her shoulders and breasts. "I've wanted to do that since the day I first met you." He lifted a handful of hair and buried his face in the mass of curls. "I've never before seen such glorious hair."

Angelina closed her eyes as a shudder rippled through her. Completely nude, she ought to be embarrassed. She wasn't. This seemed right. Natural. Destined.

She heard the rustling of clothing as Flynn shed his trousers and dared open her eyes.

He stood naked and magnificent.

Her mouth went dry, but other intimate parts dampened. Swallowing, she peeked at him from between her lashes. She'd never seen *it* before. Her uncertainty must've shown on her face.

Concern darkened his eyes to agate. Reverent and tender, he brushed her cheek with a bent finger. “I promise. I’ll be gentle.”

Angelina willed her rioting nerves to behave. “I’ve been with a man once, Flynn. I know what to expect. We were dressed, not naked like you and me, but I do know the gist of the act.” She tried to reassure him. Truthfully, she was a little hesitant about the pain again but not afraid. Never afraid of Flynn.

He made an odd choking noise.

Her gaze leaped to his. She’d said something wrong. What?

Jaw slack, he stared at her in amazement. “Once? Only once, and you were both still clothed?”

“Yes,” she said uncertainly.

A slow seductive smile spread across his molded mouth. “My lady, let me assure you, you’ve no idea what to expect. Rest assured, I’ll be delighted to teach you.”

He winked at her wickedly.

Angelina gaped, confused. What was he blathering on about? Of course, she knew what to expect. He would put his immense length inside her, bounce around a bit while making a great deal of noise, and in a minute or two, it would be over. The pain would cease then as well.

What else could there be?

Once he’d locked the door and pulled back the bedcovers, he scooped her into his arms. Reverently, his expression so tender, it brought tears to her eyes, he deposited her on the bed.

She resisted the instinct to cover herself.

Instead of immediately climbing between the sheets, he stared, his gaze caressing. “I cannot believe you’re mine. That you want to stay with me.”

“I do, Flynn, with my whole heart. I do.” Tears filled her eyes. She lifted her arms to him.

“Well, then it’s time for lesson one.” He skimmed his hands across her ribs before cupping her breasts and taking her mouth in a searing kiss.

The past weeks had primed Angelina’s passion. Every pore in her body craved his touch. She might shatter if he didn’t take her at once, yet the tiniest bit of unease lingered.

“Flynn?”

Staring into her eyes, he feathered a path to the juncture of her thighs, then brushed his palm between her legs. Gently cupping her curls, he glided his fingers along her damp, sensitive folds.

A spark of heaven ignited. She groaned and let her thighs drop open.

He slowly slid a finger, then two, inside her.

A jolt of pure bliss surged to her center. She bucked her hips, seeking more.

Face taut, and nostrils flared, Flynn traced her lower lip with his tongue. "You're more than ready. By God, I suspected you'd be passionate, but not this responsive."

"You did?" she whispered between gasps of pleasure.

"Aye." His fingers continued their magical play.

Angelina groaned, her nerves and muscles responding in ways she never dreamed possible. The sensations overwhelmed her. She could scarcely think or speak. Biting her bottom lip, she swallowed a moan of bliss. *Good Lord,* she was going to ignite. She hadn't anticipated this incredible yearning—the desperation.

"How…," she licked her lips. "How do you know I'm ready?" She clutched his shoulders. They bunched and trembled beneath her fingers. God help her, but the man knew his way around a woman's body.

"You're wet and slick." He moved between her knees, spreading her legs wider. Reaching beneath her, he angled her buttocks upward. The tip of his manhood hovered at her entrance.

He lifted his eyes to hers and went completely still. "Well, I'll be."

What? Is something wrong? Did she have some peculiar growth, or was she abnormal in some way? She gulped against the sudden anxiousness assailing her.

"You'll be what?" she bravely whispered.

"Your eyes. They're the color of the ocean after a spring storm. An absolutely brilliant turquoise." As he spoke, he sank into her, inch by inch, until his full length was buried within her.

"Flynn, you're so big. I…" She pressed her face to his shoulder. He stretched her almost beyond her capability to accommodate him.

"Shh, darling. Try to relax. You'll become accustomed to me inside you." Tracing soothing circles over her hips and thighs, he trailed little nipping kisses along her neck and shoulder. His breathing resonated deep and uneven as if he struggled for control. "I love you, Lina."

He loved her?

Flynn rocked his hips in one long thrust.

All her discomfort faded away as sweet sensation spiraled from where he touched her core.

"Wrap your legs around my waist," he said, his voice low and ragged.

Angelina curved her arms around his back and clung to him as if her life depended on this pleasure.

They mated, a wild, untamed symphony of thrusts and plunges, gasps, and moans, culminating in a crescendo of rapture.

She stiffened and cried out as a wave crashed over her, hurling her into ecstasy.

Flynn's arms tightened. He threw back his head, the lines of his face harsh with passion. He surged into her one final time, a primitive growl escaping through his clamped jaw.

Breathless, dazed, and utterly satiated, she hugged him, relishing the roughness of his chest hair brushing against her turgid nipples.

Heavens, she adored him.

Somehow, by some wholly unanticipated miracle, she'd won Flynn's love. Joy and triumph encompassed her. The wonder of that gift, and what they'd just shared, exceeded anything she'd ever fantasized.

He rolled onto his back, taking her with him.

Laying her head on his chest, she grazed her hand over the crisp hair. His sinewy muscles jumped beneath her fingers.

She'd never have her fill of touching him. Never.

He circled the sensitive spot behind her ear with his fingers. Then caressed a path from her shoulder to her derrière before giving her bottom a light squeeze.

She cupped his face between her hands and kissed him with all the love and happiness flowing through her. "Thank you."

"For what? For loving you?" He dipped his head and licked her nipple, then sucked it into his mouth.

She clutched his head, moaning. "Yes."

"For this?" He rolled her beneath him, then sank his delicious length into her once more. He pulled almost all the way out and plunged again.

She tilted her hips and grasped his buttocks, urging him on. "Oh, yes."

"And this," he grated between stacked teeth, surging against her, lifting her higher with every powerful stroke.

She spun out of control. "Yes. Oh, God, yes. Yes."

"How about this?" Reaching between their thrashing bodies, he rubbed her woman's bud.

"Yes!" she screamed, toppling over the blissful abyss once more.

26

"Good morning, darling." Flynn winked as Angelina took her chair at the breakfast table. He glanced at the Bracket clock ticking atop the mantel. Almost ten. "I trust you slept well?"

She hadn't drifted off until dawn; after he made love to her for the third time. By God, she proved an uninhibited temptress between the sheets. She colored prettily, dropping her gaze shyly. "Yes, thank you. And you?"

"Never better." And he hadn't. Not in years.

"Just toast, fruit, and hot chocolate for me, please, Collins." She smiled at the besotted footman.

Angelina was a vision in pink and yellow this morning. The pink enhanced her ivory skin and the rosy glow on her cheeks, while the yellow set off the gold tones in her hair.

He would never tire of gazing at her. His exquisite wife. Not in a lifetime. Not in ten lifetimes. Meeting her eyes, he deliberately lowered his gaze to her bosom, lingering on her right breast for a moment.

Another blush tinted her cheeks. Like him, she no doubt remembered the love bite he left there a few short hours ago.

His groin jumped to attention, contracting eagerly.

Down, lad. You'll have to wait a bit.

They broke their fast alone, which suited Flynn perfectly.

Her sisters didn't rise until after noon, and the Scots, save Gregor, had left for Craiglocky shortly after dawn. Flynn had asked Gregor to stay and continue to treat Mrs. Ellsworth.

"I almost forgot to tell you, Lina. Lord Devaux paid a call. Renault sailed for France at dawn yesterday. You're free of him."

Cup half raised to her mouth, she paused, hope shining in her eyes. "Truly? He's gone?"

"Truly, love."

The radiant smile she bestowed upon him had him rethinking his morning plans.

Jeffers entered the room carrying a salver. "The post is early today, my lord."

"Thank you." Flynn accepted the neat bundle. He quickly perused the pile and set aside three letters. The rest he passed to the butler. "Will you put those in the study, please?"

"*Naturally*, my lord." Jeffers raised his chin, seemingly offended he dare make such a request. Such a touchy fellow, wholly unlike Chatterton.

"Lina?" Flynn tapped the letters. "These are from the Duchess of Waterford. One for you. Another for your mother. The last is for me."

Angelina raised an eyebrow. "My, she felt chatty, didn't she?" She patted her mouth with her serviette before rising. "Forgive me. I know Mama has been anxious to hear from Aunt Camille. May I take the letter to her directly?"

"Certainly." He extended the missives. When she reached for the letters, he drew them away.

Obviously bewildered, she puckered her forehead. "Flynn?"

"I think they're worth a kiss, don't you?" he silkily suggested.

She tossed an uneasy glance about the room. Collins appeared absorbed in some task at the sideboard.

"No, Flynn," she whispered, her color high.

"Not even a peck? You're going to make me wait until—"

"Oh, all right," she huffed. "If it will make you hush." She closed her eyes and pursed her lips. After a moment, she opened one eye.

"You will have to do better than that, my love," he drawled.

"Flynn!" Her vexation palpable, her lovely eyes sparked with green fire.

Grinning wickedly, he shrugged.

"Fine." She grabbed his face between her hands and gave him a full-on kiss, even tracing her tongue along the seam of his lips. *The provocative minx.*

He instinctively reached for her, wanting to explore her mouth fully.

An exaggerated throat clearing broke the silence.

Angelina reared away, her face flaming. Giving Flynn a reproachful glare, she snatched the letters and fairly flew from the room.

Silver pot in hand, Collins made a valiant effort to maintain a straight face. And failed miserably. "Do you want more coffee, my lord?"

Coffee wasn't what Flynn wanted at all. He wanted to bed his delectable wife, but that would have to wait. Ignoring the knowing glint in the footman's gaze, he nodded. "Yes, please, and another slice of ham."

He broke the wax seal on the duchess's letter. Scanning the first page of dainty script, he permitted an uncharitable smirk to curve his lips.

Waterford, the old bugger, had finally been dealt a hand he deserved. Likely ape-drunk, he'd taken a *tumble* from his horse and knocked himself halfway to cork-brained and back. He now recovered from a broken leg, a dislocated shoulder, and a cracked skull.

Reading on, Flynn suddenly went rigid in his chair, muttering, "Well, I'll be damned. Will wonders never cease?"

It grieves me immensely to inform you that some weeks ago, I inadvertently discovered a pack of playing cards in my husband's possession.

I believe them to be marked, although I cannot be certain, as I'm not well-acquainted with what to look for. I sincerely regret I didn't make you aware sooner. I permitted fear to rule my decisions rather than decency.

I beg your forgiveness. They are at your disposal, should you require them.

The duchess offered the evidence Flynn needed to prove Waterford had cheated. She was a courageous woman, and her integrity spoke highly of her character. If he accepted her offer and exposed the duke's perfidy, she and her husband faced certain ostracization.

After folding the letter, he tucked the paper inside his coat. He'd made his decision yesterday. If Angelina could ignore the offenses committed against her and her mother, Flynn could find forgiveness in his heart as well.

The scandal would cause the duchess, as well as her children, immeasurable disgrace if he revealed the truth. They didn't deserve to suffer from Waterford's duplicity. Although Flynn wasn't beyond advising the duke, he knew Angelina's parentage. He might even suggest Waterford set aside funds for her.

Knowing her, she'd likely refuse the monies. Perchance, she could be persuaded to donate them to a charitable cause. Say, for instance, a home for unwed mothers.

He checked his timepiece. He had best hop to it. He had an appointment with Yancy, Harcourt, and Faulkenhurst at White's in thirty minutes.

Hiring an agent to sail to the Caribbean and sell his sugar plantations topped Flynn's list of priorities. He wasn't about to leave Angelina alone for weeks on end. No, with a wife as delectable as her, a wise husband stayed close to home.

In the foyer, he accepted his hat, gloves, and cane from Jeffers. "The carriage is readied?" Flynn asked.

"Assuredly, my lord." Long-suffering patience tinged the butler's words, and his expression bore the fortitude of a persecuted saint. "Shall I inform her ladyship when you're expected to return?"

"I don't imagine I'll be home before tea time."

After his jaunt to White's, he had several errands to run. He masked a grin as Jeffers opened the door, standing as stiff as the overly-starched neckcloth encircling his skinny neck.

Running down the stairs, Flynn glanced behind him. "I believe you have a spot of jam on your waistcoat, Jeffers."

The majordomo's gaze snapped to his stomach, and his mouth sagged in dismay. He brushed furiously at the offensive ruby spot, which only served to stain his white glove as well.

Flynn ducked his head to hide his laughter. Turning around, he careened full-on into a passerby. "I beg your pardon."

The fellow snarled a foul oath, and after yanking his cap into place, hurried on his way.

"Oh my, isn't that lovely?" Awestruck, Lily pointed behind the arbor where Angelina and Iris sat.

Unable to see what held Lily's attention from beneath the perfumed bower, Angelina set her embroidery on the marble bench and stood. Stepping from under the arbor, she backed up several paces and searched the sky.

Could it truly be?

"Look there. A triple rainbow," Iris exclaimed as she joined her. "I didn't know such a thing was possible."

"I didn't either." Tears of joy sprang to Angelina's eyes.

Had God heard her silly request? And only last night, she confessed her love to Flynn. Her arms about her sisters' waists, she stared at the brilliant arcs in wonder.

"Such an ugly storm yesterday, but see what the morning brings?" Ever the romantic, Lily sighed dramatically.

"It's hardly morning any longer, dear." Angelina couldn't keep the dryness from her tone. "You didn't come below stairs until almost noon."

Iris shook her head. "Hmph. Not everyone rises with the birds like you, Lina."

"*Bonjour,* mademoiselles." An unwelcome male voice shattered the moment.

Good Lord, no. No.

Angelina and her sisters whirled around.

Pierre stood before them. And he wasn't alone.

The twins cried out and clutched each other.

Angelina fought against debilitating fear. She must keep her wits about her. She shot a sideways glance at her terrified sisters. They were in shock and pale as death. There'd be no help from that quarter.

Pierre casually parted his soiled coat, revealing a pistol stuffed in his waistband. His meaning was clear, and her stomach and heart dove to her feet.

Two armed henchmen shifted from foot to foot, barely a yard inside the gate. That was no accident. The hedge concealed them from the house's view, as had no doubt been their intent. Their rodent-like gazes nervously darted around the garden.

An agonized "No," whispered out between her stiff lips. She shook her head in disbelief, still unable to fathom the object of her nightmares stood but a few feet away. "You cannot be here. You sailed yesterday. Lord Devaux told Flynn—"

"Idiots," Pierre jeered. "I knew Devaux had me watched, so I boarded the ship. But during the night, I was sneaked off in a barrel. I paid a man to wear my clothing and stand at the bow when the *Ange de la Mer* sailed. It was so easy to deceive the *des imbéciles*."

One hand encircling the gun's grip, he stalked forward, his lips warped into a cruel sneer. Madness glimmered brightly in his bloodshot eyes.

Fear and revulsion vied for dominance as a shiver rippled from her shoulder to her waist. How had she ever thought him handsome?

"My ship waits at Caldey Island for me to rendezvous with her. I had additional *cargo* to collect besides you three." His lewd gaze raked over them, lingering on the swell of Angelina's breasts.

Dread turned her blood cold. She didn't doubt she'd be subjected to Pierre's vile attentions. The twins, however, were more valuable as virgins. But once they reached the foreign markets—

A violent shudder rippled over her. *Dear God.* The vile thought didn't bear contemplating.

Stall him.

Yes, I must stall him.

"Cargo? Surely you're not serious." She grasped Lily's hand and edged her sisters toward the house. "What could you possibly mean to do with three women?"

She knew perfectly well what the bloody blackguard intended.

Pierre and his companions sniggered, lewd and nasty. "You'll make the last I need for a full dozen," he said. "*Mon Dieu*, do you have any idea how much European women bring on a Middle Eastern auction block?"

27

"God in heaven," Iris breathed. "He's Satan incarnate."

Lily whimpered, "Nooo."

Angelina scooted them another couple of inches closer to the door.

"*Zut!* Don't move another step." Pierre growled, his face contorted with rage. "I told you, Angelina, that you were mine." He sauntered a few paces nearer, fingering the pistol's brass trigger. "I returned for you, and what did I find? You weren't in Salem waiting for me as I asked."

"Waiting for you? Are you addled?" Yes, he was. Outraged whipped her fury anew, and she stabbed a finger toward his chest. "You were already married. I couldn't return to Salem. I was disgraced. Ruined. I'd have brought disaster upon my family had I returned."

"Despicable monster," Iris muttered beneath her breath.

Angelina scrutinized his weapon. Could the twins reach the house if she distracted him?

A befuddled expression flitted across Pierre's face, giving him an almost childlike appearance. "But, *chérie,* I came for you immediately after I—ah—*eliminated* that inconvenience. *Mon Dieu*, I vowed that I loved you. Didn't you believe me, *mon amour*?" A plaintive, deranged tone tinged his last words.

Her heart skipped painfully, and the hairs on her nape stood straight up at his confession.

Pierre *had* killed his wife so he could marry her. He *was* utterly mad.

She slowly shook her head. "You've no notion of what real love is."

Sacrificial, unselfish, patient, generous, and considerate. Everything Flynn was, and Pierre was not. Had never been.

"Oh, and I suppose your *new* husband does, *non*?" Pierre glared at her, venom spewing from his narrowed eyes. "*Oui*, it didn't take you long to replace me, *putain.*"

A hailstorm of wrath ripped through Angelina, scattering her common sense like a windstorm across a desert. "You dare accuse *me,* Pierre? You bloody bigamist. You were already married when you walked me down the aisle. And you had the sheer gall to demand I wait for you. While you were dragged off to your *real wife* in France, leaving me with child?"

"Lina!" Lily and Iris cried in unison.

Their gazes, along with Pierre's, hurtled to her stomach.

Damn, damn, damn. Would she never learn to control her tongue when angry? "I lost the baby in my fourth month." Angelina tilted her chin in defiance.

Giving a callous shrug, he pulled his ear. "Good. An *enceinte* woman is worth far less."

How could he be so heartless about a child he'd fathered? God forgive her, but she absolutely loathed him at that moment.

Smirking, he pulled the pistol from his waistband and waved it menacingly at her and her sisters. "Now move."

Hatred like none she'd ever known sliced through Angelina. Thank God she'd been spared a lifetime with this despicable villain.

Pierre jerked his head in the gate's direction.

His two grimy comrades advanced, their lips bent into lecherous smirks.

Lily and Iris shrank together, their sky-blue eyes wide as incoherent, panic-filled noises escaped them.

"We're not going with you. Not without a fight." Angelina frantically searched around the enclosure, seeking a weapon or a means of escape. Only a pile of twine near the arbor, a pair of forgotten gloves, and a bamboo rake were visible.

She had nothing to protect them except her sewing scissors. And they were too far away to be of help.

Where were the servants? Gregor? For certain, someone must occasionally glance out a window.

Was it possible that Pierre had only been here a few minutes? The seconds crept by, dread stretching them out as she desperately strove to find a way to escape this perilous situation.

"My lady, yer mother asked—" Gregor halted halfway out the door and immediately assumed a defensive stance. He met Angelina's speaking gaze as she tried to silently convey to him what went on. His keen attention shifted to Pierre. "Renault?" he mouthed.

Angelina dared to incline her head a fraction.

Murder in his eyes, Gregor edged further onto the stoop.

"*Imbéciles*. You assured me the Scots left this morning." Pierre flung a rage-filled glower at one of his henchmen. "Tie him up. Let's be away from here."

Pistols trained on Gregor, the two miscreants warily edged toward the mammoth Highlander.

"Stop your dawdling." Pierre nervously licked his lips. "You're armed. He isn't."

"How are we supposed to tie him?" The larger brute sullenly asked, eyeing Gregor.

Twice their size, he didn't seem the least intimidated by the intruders.

"Use…" Pierre's anxious regard roamed the enclosure. "There." He gestured to the twine. "That will do."

Not for long. Gregor would snap the twine in no time.

Pierre aimed his gun at the twins. "To the gate. *Rapidement*."

"Don't move." Angelina stayed them with her raised hand. "What's he going to do? Shoot us all? In broad daylight? With a houseful of servants as witnesses?"

"That's precisely what I'd like to know." Flynn's ire-laden words jerked her attention to him as he passed Gregor a flintlock.

Relief and panic beset her. The twins were safe, but Pierre now pointed his pistol at Flynn's chest.

Jeffers, Lord Ramsbury, and two men she didn't recognize stepped through the doorway, each bearing firearms and wielding dangerous-looking blades.

A pair of armed footmen entered the open gate behind the abductors.

"Flynn!" Angelina dashed toward him.

"*Non*!" Pierre roared, firing his pistol.

Searing pain slammed into her.

The impact threw her backward into her shrieking sisters. A peculiar golden-white aura spiraled before her eyes. The glow grew narrower and narrower as she sank beneath layers of thick, cottony clouds.

Another shot sounded.

Flynn. My love.

"Angelina!" Flynn's guttural cry was the last thing she heard before icy blackness claimed her.

Angelina moaned, moving her head back and forth, regretting it instantly when razor-hot pain stabbed her chest. To ease the agony, she inhaled shallow breaths.

What was all the sobbing about?

Who, by all the saints, was shouting?

God Almighty. Had a carriage hit her? Or was an elephant sitting on her chest? Something warm and sticky trickled onto her neck. Why was she lying on the ground? Her dress would be good for nothing except for the rubbish bin after this. And it had been one of her favorites, too, dash it all.

"Lina, stay with me. Lina, my love, please."

Is that Flynn? Heavens, he sounds dreadful.

"Flynn, ye must let go, and allow me to see to her."

Gregor. Such a kind man.

"Is she going to die?"

Lily, sobbing. Must she always be so dramatic?

"There's so much blood."

Ah, and Iris. Always one for stating the obvious.

Wait. Blood? Whose blood?

Angelina forced her eyes open. Four faces loomed above hers and beyond them, several more.

Don't they know it's rude to stare at a woman indisposed?

"Lina? We've sent for the surgeon. We'll carry you into the house in a few minutes. Hang on, love." Flynn tenderly touched her cheek. Were those tears in his eyes?

Goodness. Did he think she was dying?

Am I dying?

Her eyelids weighed a stone, and her freezing limbs felt leaden. She closed her eyes, the effort to keep them open too difficult. Her upper right chest and shoulder hurt something awful. Bloody excruciatingly, actually. Wouldn't dying be less painful?

I suppose I'll have to sit up and convince them all I'm not going to expire with my next breath.

Deuced nuisance, being fretted over. Couldn't they let her lay here and recover her bearings? It did rather rattle one to be shot. Wasn't that what had happened?

"Will you please stop your fussing?" Her tone shriller than she intended, Angelina opened her eyes. She almost laughed at their stunned expressions, except it would hurt like the devil if she did.

"I don't believe I'm at imminent risk of cocking up my toes." She met Gregor's concerned gaze. "Am I, Gregor?"

He lifted the cloth pressed to her shoulder. "I canna be certain of the nature of yer wound, my lady, without undressin' ye."

Flynn growled.

Angelina sent him a quelling stare and fisted her hands against the agony lancing her every time she spoke. "Do hush, Flynn, or you'll have to leave while I consult with Gregor."

She tried to glimpse her chest, but she couldn't bend her neck enough to see the wound. "I've been shot?"

"Yes. I think it's only a flesh wound." Gregor considered her shoulder. He clearly wanted to examine her closer but feared Flynn's reaction.

"Enough of this nonsense." Angelina struggled to a sitting position, biting her lip against the pain. *Holy heaven, it hurts*! She might well vomit.

"Lina." Flynn was as white as the cravat neatly tied about his neck. "Please, be careful. You shouldn't be moving."

The poor man sounded quite desperate. Like a man in love. With her.

If she didn't feel so god-awful, she'd be thrilled.

"Gregor, you had better carry me." She eyed Flynn. "My husband appears about to topple over. Jeffers, please be a dear, and assist his lordship into the house."

"Of course, your ladyship." Jeffers sprang forward and put an arm about Flynn's shoulders.

"Stop that, this instant." Flynn shoved at the butler's hand. "If you value your position, Jeffers, remove your arm from my person at once!"

"I'm sorry, my lord." The butler clamped his jaw and tightened his hold. "I cannot ignore her ladyship's request."

"Confound it, man, unhand me." Flynn twisted loose.

"I did try, my lady." Jeffers straightened his shoulders and adjusted his waistcoat, all wounded dignity. "I'll await the surgeon's arrival inside." Sniffing disdainfully, he pivoted on his heel and strode into the house.

Flynn was in a state, poor man. Angelina swore she heard chuckling. Ah, the earl and those other handsome fellows, no doubt. Rather droll friends, her husband had. Wasn't Lord Ramsbury a government official?

"Lord Ramsbury?"

The earl's handsome face appeared in her line of vision. "Yes, my lady?"

"There's a ship waiting at Caldey Island with nine women held captive aboard." Even speaking hurt. She blinked, trying to dislodge the dots whirling before her eyes. "They're meant to be sold as sex slaves in the Middle East. Please, can you do something to help them?"

"Hound's teeth," the blond man said.

Lord Ramsbury's lips thinned. "I'll be away at once." He touched her hand. "Well done, my lady."

Gregor edged closer. "It will hurt when I lift ye."

"I expected as much." She tried to summon a smile, but it was difficult to do when clamping ones' teeth against agonizing pain.

"You'll see to my treatment, Gregor, won't you?" She attempted to blink away the fuzziness blurring her vision. "Don't let the surgeon or a physician do anything you don't approve of, please?"

"I give ye my word." He nodded somberly.

"Thank you." Yes, she'd encourage his interest in Lily. She would quite like having this man as a brother-in-law. "Gregor?"

"Yes?" Concern creased his brow as he gazed at her.

What a remarkable grayish-blue his eyes are.

"I fear I'm going to…." She couldn't finish. A wave of dizziness crashed over her. Her pulse pounded in her ears. Blackness danced before her eyes.

Two days later, Flynn sat beside Angelina in the drawing room.

She relaxed on a divan, covered by a plaid Yvette had given them for a wedding present.

The footmen had moved the piece of furniture so Angelina could see the garden from the open French windows. Every trace of blood had been eliminated from the area.

This morning, she'd been told Jeffers had killed Pierre. The other two trespassers surrendered without a fight. Of equal import, Yancy had promptly dispatched two naval vessels to Caldey Island. The *Ange de la Mer* relinquished the women without a fight, and her crew had been taken into custody.

Flynn would never ridicule the fussy butler again.

Without hesitation, he'd flattened Renault the instant the Frenchman pointed his gun at Angelina. Jeffers's swift reaction had caused Pierre's mark to hit high, rather than her heart, and thereby saved her life.

The bullet had lodged in her shoulder, requiring surgical removal. Forbidden to lift so much as a hairpin lest she rip her stitches, the surgeon had ordered her to rest.

Flynn never wanted to feel that kind of heart-stopping dread again. To hear her passionately moan his name while they made love and less than twelve hours later, fear she'd never speak to him again. No, his heart couldn't bear it.

He raised her hand and kissed the back of the fragrant skin.

Angelina turned her head and brushed a lock of hair off his forehead. "You look tired. That's what comes of sleeping in a chair."

"I couldn't leave you." He reverently pressed her palm to his face.

"I know, my love." She caressed his cheek with her thumb. "I knew you were there. I cannot explain it. Even when I slept, I sensed your presence beside me."

She turned her attention to the window again. A smattering of snowy clouds floated in the brilliant blue sky, and the gladiolas had finally bloomed. They stood upright, bunches of colorful sentinels, basking in the morning sun.

"I never asked you how you discovered Pierre was here." Angelina continued to gaze at the garden.

"I bumped into a man on the walkway when I was leaving the house that morning. I didn't realize it was him until I arrived at White's." Flynn wrapped an arm around her shoulders, mindful not to jostle the bandage bulging from beneath her nightdress. "Of a sudden, I remembered where I'd seen his face before. I dashed inside, snatched the others, and alacrity we rushed here neck or nothing."

She rested her head against his shoulder. "But I thought you'd never seen Pierre. How did you know it was him?"

"Devaux showed me a miniature portrait." Flynn kissed her head, running a hand through the curls draped about her shoulders. He adored her hair.

With a sharp indrawn breath, Angelina leaned forward, the tartan sliding to the floor.

He reached to steady her. "Careful, Lina, your shoulder."

"Flynn." She pointed to the hedge. A pair of birds cuddled close, preening and billing one another. "What kind are they?"

He bent to see where she stared. "Turtledoves. They mate for life. If one dies, the other remains alone until it, too, dies. Rather sweet, isn't it?" He traced her jaw with a finger.

She gasped, then covered her face, weeping softly.

What in blazes had he said to make her cry? Or mayhap, she was in pain.

"What's wrong? Is your shoulder hurting?" Flynn turned her face to his. He couldn't bear to see her tears. "Shall I call for Gregor? Do you need more of the pain tonic he's been giving you?"

"No." She pressed a swift kiss to his lips. "I was terrified to trust you. So, I asked God for a sign. To show me, I could let myself love you."

Understanding dawned. His gaze veered to the doves once more. One rested its head against the other's neck. "The doves? Was that the sign you asked for?"

She gave him a trembling smile before she sought the birds again. "I asked for something simple—like a triple rainbow or doves sitting on a hedge."

"Ah, well. He gave you half of what you asked for. I'd say that's not bad at all. A triple rainbow would be rather hard to come by." Flynn chuckled, wiping away a tear on her cheek with his thumb.

She shook her head. "No, He did both. There was a triple rainbow the day Pierre shot me."

"You actually saw a triple rainbow?" He caressed her ear and grinned.

"Yes, and now the doves." She met his eyes, hers shimmering with unshed tears. "Do you think we were meant to meet?"

Gently, so as not to disturb her wound, Flynn gathered Angelina into his arms. "I've never been more convinced of anything in my life."

Brooke Tweadle
May 1820

"Oh, Flynn, do be careful. I nearly tripped." Angelina pointed to a gnarled, moss-covered root.

His attention dropped to her rounded belly. "Don't worry about me. Just make sure you don't fall."

She laughed. "I'm fine." As fine as a walrus waddling to a creek bed could be.

Flynn held Paisley in one arm and Peyton in the other as Nurse trundled behind, her arms full of necessaries for the twins.

They'd chosen to name the girls' old Scottish names in honor of the Scots heritage on both sides of their families. The toddlers, a scant two months past their first birthday, fussed at not being allowed to run to the creek.

Angelina neatly stepped over another root. "Are you sure you don't want me to carry one of them?"

"No, the blanket and basket are enough for you." Flynn walked the last few feet to the embankment.

After spreading the plaid, she laid out their food. This had become her favorite pastime. She and Flynn had begun these excursions right after they married, and he'd purchased Wingfield Court.

Nurse busied herself, arranging the babies' items, though she eyed the cattle warily now and again.

"I'm glad you bought Wingfield from Waterford. Mama's been

happy there. And now, we can come here as often as we like." Angelina settled herself on the ground then gathered Paisley close.

Her independent daughter promptly wiggled from her arms and began tottering around on pudgy legs.

"So long as Deamhan doesn't break through the fence again," Flynn drawled.

The disgruntled bull eyed them from between the slats of the newly built structure. Giving a low moo, he turned away and trudged across the field. His faithful harem and offspring trailed him.

Flynn lowered Peyton to the ground before sitting himself. She stood wobbling for a moment then followed her sister. Such was usually the case. Paisley led, and Peyton toddled after.

"I'll mind the darlings." Nurse scurried after the twins.

Angelina chuckled. "They're so much like Lily and Iris."

In temperament only.

They possessed Flynn's chestnut hair, Angelina's curls, and their eyes were vivid green. How could they not be with both parents possessing green eyes?

"Are you sure you don't regret not going to London for the Season? Most of both our families are there." He removed his coat before laying his head in her lap.

She ran her fingers through the soft, burnished strands. "Not at all." Patting her stomach, she said, "I'm as big as a walrus and about as graceful. Besides, we saw everyone for the girls' birthday celebration in March."

He caught her hand and kissed it then pressed his lips to her distended belly. "Who'd have thought Isobel and Seonaid would both be married and happy as grigs. And Harcourt, too?"

"True. The girls certainly gave Yancy and Jacques fits." Angelina giggled. "Though, the duke had the worst of it, poor man."

Flynn turned onto his side and relaxed onto one elbow. "Do you remember the day I found you in that tree?" He angled his head in the direction of the stately oak.

Smiling, she nodded. "Of course. I'll never forget it."

"I think I fell in love with you before you even clambered to the ground." He reached and grasped a curl, gently tugging the strands until she lay beside him.

Angelina giggled when his practiced fingers grazed her ribs. "You didn't."

"No, I did. One glimpse into your eyes, and I was lost."

He pressed his lips to hers, and as always, she melted into his arms.

If you've enjoyed reading **Triumph and Treasure**, *Highland Heather Romancing a Scot Book 1*, then perhaps you'd enjoy the rest of the books in the series:

Virtue and Valor
Heartbreak and Honor
Scandal's Splendor
Passion and Plunder
Seductive Surrender
A Yuletide Highlander

About the Author

USA Today Bestselling, award-winning author COLLETTE CAMERON® scribbles Scottish and Regency historicals featuring dashing rogues and scoundrels and the intrepid damsels who reform them. Blessed with an overactive and witty muse that won't stop whispering new romantic romps in her ear, she's lived in Oregon her entire life, though she dreams of living in Scotland part-time. A self-confessed Cadbury chocoholic, you'll always find a dash of inspiration and a pinch of humor in her sweet-to-spicy timeless romances®.

Explore **Collette's worlds** at
www.collettecameron.com!

Join her **VIP Reader Club** and **FREE newsletter**. Giggles guaranteed!

FREE BOOK: Join Collette's The Regency Rose® VIP Reader Club to get updates on book releases, cover reveals, contests and giveaways she reserves exclusively for email and newsletter followers. Also, any deals, sales, or special promotions are offered to club members first. She will not share your name or email, nor will she spam you.

http://bit.ly/TheRegencyRoseGift

Dearest Reader,

Thank you for reading LORDS IN LOVE.

One day, it occurred to me that a great way to introduce my readers to all of my series would be to bundle the first book in each series. I hope you enjoyed each romance enough to want to check out the other books as well.

You can see my entire back list on my website. I've also have a reading order list you can print there as well.

Please consider telling other readers why you enjoyed this book by reviewing it. I also truly adore hearing from my readers.

Here's wishing you many happy hours of reading, more happily-ever-afters than you can possibly enjoy in a lifetime, and abundant blessings to you and your loved ones.

Collette Cameron

CPSIA information can be obtained
at www.ICGtesting.com
Printed in the USA
LVHW081041271220
674889LV00026B/854